# NUCLEAR HORNET

A Story of Modern War

*By Greg Hodgson*

Nuclear Hornet

1st print edition
Published by Gregory Hodgson / Sander Enterprises
through CreateSpace Independent Publishing Platform

ISBN-13: 978-0615688718
(Gregory Hodgson / Sander Enterprises)

ISBN-10: 0615688713

*For those who serve and sacrifice for freedom...*

# TABLE OF CONTENTS

# PERSONNEL ROSTER

**THE CABAL:**
"Rannovich" – Former Soviet Army officer, now a Russian Mafia don. He is believed to be organizing a cabal of Russian and Chinese organized crime lords, renegade military commanders and oil interests and taking over Iran from within. Though his motives are unclear, his methods involve terrorism, corporate manipulation, and the theft of thousands of tons of military hardware.

Mahmoud Ahmadinejad – Iran's political leader and willing ally of Rannovich.

Mr. Sun – Chairman of New Patriotic Enterprises, Rannovich's main financial backer.

General Mikhail – Rannovich's chief of staff.

Colonel Victor "The Black Cobra" Lenonov – Former Soviet Air Force ace, later a Russian Mafia agent, now commander of a mercenary air force employed by Rannovich.

**THE CIA:**
Carter "Deke" Grayson – Director of Central Intelligence. As boss of the CIA, he is concerned more with the politics of intelligence and leaves the tasks of gathering intelligence and acting upon it in the hands of his deputies.

Jarrod E. Casey – Deputy Director of Operations. Oversees all of the CIA's covert operations. A former agent who operated undercover in Soviet military intelligence during the cold war.

Robert Cannon (aka Kahlil aka Kalinov aka "Mr. C" aka "Agent Caspian") – The CIA's top field agent in the Middle East, operates under many different aliases and code names. Early in his career he operated in Russia, undercover with the *Mafya,* connected with Rannovich and Lenonov. Now he is racing against time to uncover Rannovich's plot in Iran. Cannon has a special interest in the career of Karl Roche.

Evan Decker (aka Ivan Dyakir) – A former operative, now the head of the CIA's Russian Desk.

"Ellirat" and "Elessar" – the codenames used by two brothers who are former agents of the Mukhabarat – the Iraqi General Intelligence Directive under Saddam Hussein. In the free Iraq, they are freelance assets of the CIA, recruited by Mr. C.

Kujetski (aka Kujet) – an international arms dealer with an enormous network of underworld contacts, used routinely by the CIA to finance and organize resistance fighters or to infiltrate and sting terrorist groups. Works closely with Mr. C.

Mr. Samadad (aka "Sam") – a financial wizard who works in the upper echelons of the Central Bank of Iran, directing the funding of the CIA's operations in Iran as well as anchoring a courier chain between Tehran and Langley.

Razi and Nima Samadad – Mr. Samadad's sons, employed by the Central Bank of Iran (and occasionally by the CIA) as armed couriers.

Albie – a twenty-year-old Indian Muslim hacker who works for Kujetski.

## THE WHITE HOUSE:

Brett McNeil – the new President of the United States. A Vietnam Special Forces vet, former senator from the Southwest, served on senate armed forces and intelligence committees. His middle-of-the-road politics earned him support from the voting public and scorn from both sides of the congressional aisles. His detractors call him a man of Machiavellian ruthlessness. His admirers, especially from the military and intelligence community, call him a Reagan-esque leader combining character and experience.

Hal Bowman – Vice President of the United States. A former White House staffer for Reagan and Bush Sr.; he is privy to many dark secrets of the latter years of the Cold War.

Janice Rand – Secretary of State. Former under-secretary under Powell and Rice; fellow of the Council on Foreign Relations.

Mike McLeary – Secretary of Defense. Former Under-Secretary of Defense under Reagan and Bush Sr., and a military-industrial complex insider. Was once kidnapped in Russia by the mafia and rescued by a rogue CIA agent. In his many years working in the dark rooms of the Pentagon he has acquired a head full of national secrets.

Rick Harmon – National Security Advisor. An academic gifted with infinite skepticism.

Lane Bender – President McNeil's longsuffering chief of staff.

Evan Schwab – White House Press Secretary.

## THE UNITED STATES NAVY:
**TOPGUN:**

Captain Adam O'Wools – Commandant of the US Navy Fighter Weapons School.

Capt. Joshua "Deuce" Thompson – Navy aviator, Gulf War Ace, and widely considered to be the best fighter pilot in the world, now senior instructor at TOPGUN. There's an offer on the table for him to move back to the front lines as the Commander of the Air Group for Air Wing 13 on the USS *Ronald Reagan*. A man hardened by his experience, he is developing grudging respect and even affection for a student who shows him up.

Commander Sam "Blitz" Willard – an instructor at TOPGUN.

Lieutenant Commander Karl "Sharkey" Roche (aka "Polar Bear") – Navy aviator, former Navy SEAL decorated for meritorious service in Iraq. He bears physical and emotional scars from his brief but violent and heroic tour of duty. His combat injuries ended his Special Forces career but he was given an opportunity to apply his deadly skills to the controls of an F/A-18 Super Hornet strike fighter. At TOPGUN he has the chance to show off his talents, quickly getting the attention of the instructor staff. Upon graduating he will have a choice of assignments – the most enticing is the job of Executive Officer of a new composite squadron in the *Reagan*'s air wing.

Lieutenant Nick "Toymaker" Santos – a TOPGUN classmate of Roche's, and a genius with electronics in general and particularly the defensive systems of a modern combat aircraft. After graduating he hopes to be assigned to fly in the new EA-18g Growler.

## USS *Ronald Reagan:*

Rear Admiral Wally Krause – Flag officer of the USS *Ronald Reagan* battle group. Formerly the deputy director of the National Security Agency.

Capt. Brian "Nuke" Young – skipper of the *Reagan*.

Capt. Marcus DeTomaso – *Reagan*'s Battle Group Operations Officer.

Lt. Cmdr. Dr. Herbert Tobias – the *Reagan*'s chief medical officer.

Ensign Hammil – *Reagan* comm. officer.

## Air Wing 13:

Cmdr. William "Hannibal" Burke – CO of VFC-233 *Stingrays*. Burke is a born leader and a skilled aviator, and is being groomed for higher command.

Lt. Cmdr. Danny "Hardcase" Wilkes – a veteran strike-fighter pilot, and also a mixed martial arts expert. He was passed over for the assignment of the *Stingrays'* XO.

Lt. Cmdr. Jules "Hunter" Hidelmann – a Gulf War A-6 pilot who was injured in combat. Now returning to active duty as Roche's Weapon Systems Officer.

Lt. Jack "Blackjack" Masterson – a division leader in the *Stingrays*. Exuberant and affable, Blackjack strikes up a quick friendship with Roche, who moves in next door in the base housing of NAS North Island.

Lt. Hank "Hacksaw" Miller – veteran aviator and one-time Blue Angels tryout assigned to be Roche's new wingman.

Lt. Dennis "Hawk" Collins – a law student and naval reserve officer double-rated as a pilot and WSO, returned to active duty with the *Stingrays*.

Lt. Amber "Blaze" Worthy – widely regarded as the best female aviator (and the best one-night-stand) in the Pacific Fleet. Transferred to the *Stingrays* from Japan.

Lt. John Henry "Doc" Holliday – swaggering Top Gunner with a Wild West persona, but inexperienced in actual combat, and his antics don't lend themselves well toward a leadership role. Besides Roche he is the only TOPGUN graduate in the *Stingrays*.

Lt. Darren "Rooster" McCoy – despite his carefully cultivated backwater image, the Knoxville native is a highly intelligent electrical engineer and also an excellent pilot. He actually has the highest IQ among any member of the *Stingrays*.

Lt. Joe "Hitman" Armani – longtime friend and wingman of "Hardcase" Wilkes. Known for making difficult missile kills.

Lt. Eugene "Bulldog" Harris – although chronically overweight, he always manages to pass his physical, probably because everyone knows how good of a pilot he is.

Lt. Sherman "Shredder" Ferraby – Hannibal's pick as wingman. Shredder is a crack shot with the Vulcan cannon and is eventually bound for TOPGUN.

Lt. junior grade Maggie "Mystique" Banning – a quiet and withdrawn young officer. Her practice of Zen Buddhism makes her an excellent WSO and she was specifically requested by Cmdr. Burke to be assigned to the *Stingrays*.

Lt. jg. Jake "Gator" Palmer – prone to taking long midday naps, but highly regarded for his weapons skills. Rooster selected him as a wingman.

Lt. jg. Bobby "Buzz" Edwards – the youngest member of the *Stingrays*, an electronics genius and a highly talented weapon systems officer.

Lt. jg. Mike "Ronin" Shinano and Lt. jg. Kevin "Creep" MacGregor – childhood friends from Seattle, they stuck close until their first flight assignment with the *Stingrays*.

Lt. Reginald "Beowulf" Stamper and Sub-Lt. Ian "Claymore" Bruce – British Royal Navy pilots seconded into the US Navy as part of a cooperative joint forces training program and assigned to the *Stingrays*.

Chief Petty Officer Terry Newman – Chief squadron mechanic for the *Stingrays*.

Petty Officer 1$^{st}$ class Hector "Ming" Domingo – squadron mechanic for the *Stingrays*.

Cmdr. Darren "Worm" Bellbrook – Roche began his aviation career as Worm's wingman in a squadron based in Washington. Worm now commands VFA-97 *Warhawks*, another squad of Super Hornets assigned to *Reagan*'s Air Wing 13.

Lt. "Money" Emanuel – Worm's wingman.

Lt. Nelson "Bonzer" McGee – Australian-born division leader in the *Warhawks* squadron.

Cmdr. Scott "Palerider" Tachini – half-Navajo CO of the EA-18g Growler electronic warfare squadron VAQ-139 *Yellow Jackets*

Lt. Darius "Crush" Crenshaw – Palerider's Growler pilot.

Lt. Dane "Fozzy Bear" Foster – Electronic Warfare Officer in the *Yellow Jackets* squadron.

Lt. jg. Seth "Scooter" Jones – Fozzy Bear's Growler pilot.

Cmdr. Sean "Pain God" Mullen – CO of VF-24 *Renegades*, the *Reagan*'s Tomcat squadron.

Lt. Sergei "Deadeye" Unther – arrogant, tough-talking aviator in *Reagan*'s VFA-25 *Fists of the Fleet*, and defending champion of the *Reagan*'s pistol marksman competition.

Lt. Elroy "Chef" Jameson – aviator in the *Fists of the Fleet*.

PO1 Weller – Air Wing 13's rigging officer.

**SEALs:**

Lt. Cmdr. Arnold Ames – CO of 2$^{nd}$ Battalion, SEAL Team Three, ca. 2003.

Lt. Lance Nathan – Navy SEAL platoon commander, Grinder classmate of Karl Roche.

Commander Clark – Nathan's battalion commander.

Master CPO Matt Bowers – SEALs jumpmaster. (Formerly under command of Karl Roche)

CPO Travis Williams – SEAL platoon sniper under Nathan's command in 2$^{nd}$ Battalion, SEAL Team Three. (Formerly under Roche's command)

PO1 Louie Morris – explosives expert on Nathan's SEAL platoon. (Formerly under Roche's command)

SEAL 1$^{st}$ class Bernie "Cabbage" Coles – skilled member of Roche's original SEAL platoon.

SEAL 1$^{st}$ class Mike Ramirez – member of Roche's SEAL platoon.

SEAL 2$^{nd}$ class Jason Carter – rookie SEAL under Nathan's command.

SEAL 2$^{nd}$ class Charlie Yao – rookie member of Roche's platoon.

SEAL 3$^{rd}$ class Patrick Sherman – Grinder classmate of Roche's and member of his platoon.

**Other USN Personnel:**

Admiral Terrance Marsh – Chief of Naval Operations, direct commander of the entire US Navy and a member of the Joint Chiefs of Staff.

Vice Adm. Patrick Caldwell – C-in-C of the Pacific Fleet.

Cmdr. Parsons – CO of the attack submarine USS *Tucson*.

PO1 O'Brian – sonar officer on the *Tucson*.

Cmdr. Jim Edmunds – Skipper of the destroyer USS *Fitzgerald*.

## THE UNITED STATES MARINE CORPS:

General Albert Schilling – Commandant of the Marines.

Lt. Anderson – pilot of a Marine MV-22 Osprey.

## THE UNITED STATES AIR FORCE:

General Joshua Caleb – Chief of Staff of the Air Force.

Lt. Gen. Ryan Rovelli – Commander of USAF Strategic Command

Maj. Gen. Paul Rainier – Air Force weapons expert.

Lt. Colonel Gene Wheeler – commander of NORAD Satellite Tracking Operations.

Maj. Dave "Screwball" Duvall – leader of F-22 Raptor squadron "Orion Flight."

Lt. Dave Richards – Air Force E-3 Sentry AWACS radar officer.

LCol. Patrick Mundy, Maj. Will Escher – crew of B-2 bomber "Overlord Three."

Maj. Jesse Bermudez, Lt. Presley – crew of B-52 "Warhammer One."

Maj. Curtis, Capt. Wright and Lt. Martin – Crew of a USAF Aurora hypersonic spy plane.

## THE UNITED STATES ARMY:

General Paul Chappelle – Chief of Staff of the Army and Chairman of the Joint Chiefs of Staff. A veteran infantryman, having served in every major conflict since Vietnam.

Captain Rayford Pondsmith – US Army M1A2 Abrams tank company commander.

Capt. Johnny Mendez – National Reconnaissance Office image intelligence analyst.

## THE ISLAMIC REVOLUTIONARY GUARD:

Major Anju Duhamad – Iranian tank battalion commander.

Lt. Beiruz – commander of a Quds Force (Iranian commandos) unit sent on a strike deep in Chinese territory.

Sergeant Mauressh Ballid – young member of the Quds Force

## THE CHINESE:

Ambassador Chaung Li – Chinese consul in Washington DC.

Colonel Vong Cho – Naval Attaché to the Chinese consulate.

Admiral Laido – Flag Officer of the renegade Chinese carrier battle group.

Colonel Shin – CO of the Chinese carrier *Zheng He*.

## THE RUSSIANS:

Ambassador Pavel Dubovski – Russian consul in Washington DC.

Captain Alexei Myasnikov – Naval Attaché to the Russian consulate in Washington DC.

Mr. Lysenko – chief of security at the Russian consulate in Tehran.

Mr. Antonov – Russian civil engineer who built Rannonvich's command bunker.

## THE CIVILIANS:

**Boeing:**

Marty Silverman – chief support engineer for the Boeing Super Hornet program, working aboard the *Reagan*.

Greg Sander – Silverman's intern. An Air Force ROTC cadet and an aerospace engineering prodigy. Roche quickly befriends him.

**Family and Friends:**

Tracy Davis – Karl Roche meets Tracy when he sees her get in a car accident on the freeway. After he helps her off the road, Tracy takes him out to dinner. They begin an increasingly serious dating relationship destined to be cut short by Roche's deployment.

Loraine Thompson – Deuce Thompson's wife.

Larry and Sharon Roche – Karl Roche's parents. Larry is a former Navy doctor and is now a cardiovascular surgeon at Childrens Hospital of Orange County. Sharon is the daughter of a Royal Navy Admiral and was raised on Washington DC's Embassy Row.

Jeff Allison and Rick Jordan – Karl Roche's two best friends growing up. Allison now owns a custom 4x4 shop. Jordan is an ESPN football analyst and program producer.

# PROLOGUE: THE FORGOTTEN PAPERS

## BURDICK AIR FORCE BASE, NORTH DAKOTA
## JUNE 7<sup>TH</sup> 1985

The Air Force Base had been closed for seven years. The abandoned site was left to the weeds and prairie grasses; the weapons were left to wait out the Cold War unless the politicians changed their minds. The SALT II missile reduction treaty that Jimmy Carter had signed in 1978 condemned certain types of missiles in both the Russian and US arsenals. One such missile was the Atlas ICBM. And that was fine by the US Air Force. The Atlas was a dinosaur – a ninety-foot-tall relic. In the event of a war, it would take five hours to fill the rocket's liquid-fuel tanks and launch it. The missiles were expensive to maintain, and every fuel drill cost about half a million dollars per rocket. The new solid-fuel Minuteman III missiles were much cheaper, smaller and faster. Abandoning Atlas freed up the budget for the new weapons.

The Atlas missiles at Burdick were second-strike weapons. They sat deep underground in hardened concrete silos, intended to wait out the opening salvos of nuclear war. Then, once the Americans and Soviets had reduced each other's cities and military bases to radioactive slag, thousands of Atlases would launch, detonating their three-megaton warheads in a coverage pattern over Russia, and ensure that nothing at all would ever inhabit that country again. If there was no one left alive to fire the missiles, then the so-called "doomsday tapes" in a computer center under the missile complex would automatically unleash the weapons

The silos themselves were designed to survive a direct hit from a megaton-range bomb. They were spread out across the prairie – no silo was less than twelve miles from another. One-hundred-and-twenty-foot-thick lead-lined reinforced concrete blast doors sealed each of the holes. No bomb, conventional or nuclear, was supposed to be able to penetrate it. The computers and operating stations that controlled the missile launch systems were housed in bunkers buried even further underground.

The Russians, of course, had similar systems protecting their own missiles. In the arms race of nuclear deterrence, one goal for each side was to find a way to neutralize the enemy's missiles. If the other side had their missiles protected, a way must be found to defeat that protection.

A team of civilian and military experts from the Pentagon spent their entire lives drawing up such contingencies. Their holy grail was a weapon or attack plan that would wipe out the Soviet nuclear missiles before they could be launched. This was called a "zero strike option" meaning that it would end a nuclear war before it could really begin. In May of 1985, they believed that their prize had been found. They organized a test for their new plan, bringing in President Reagan and the Joint Chiefs to get authorization.

On the seventh day of June, a single aircraft took off from a tiny, mostly secret Naval Air Weapons Station in the middle of Southern California's Mojave Desert. The F/A-18b fighter could carry almost nine tons of ordnance, but for this sortie it carried only external fuel tanks, and one large bomb slung under the fuselage. The Hornet flew high across the desert and over the Rocky Mountains, on a straight course for Burdick AFB site 9. As the plane entered the restricted airspace above the base, it dropped the empty external tanks and dove toward the earth. The pilot's display showed a super-imposed hexagon pattern over the terrain below, representing the seven missile silos of site 9. The pilot guided his powerful jet over the center target and angled straight down. He accelerated to 1400 miles per hour, closing with the surface in under twenty seconds. When the fighter was only two thousand feet above the ground, the weapons officer in the back seat released the bomb. At the same moment, the pilot yanked back hard on the control stick, deployed his airbrakes, and pulled out of the terminal dive. The Hornet skidded into a horizontal angle of attack, and the pilot accelerated again, trying to gain as much distance as possible from site 9. Behind him, the earth erupted.

When it was released from the Hornet, traveling at twice the speed of sound, straight down, the bomb armed itself and primed the tiny nuclear device inside. The needle-sharp titanium-oxide nose sliced into the concrete like it was paper, ripping through all hundred and twenty feet of hard shielding in an instant. The bomb crashed through the casing of the huge missile deep below, and finally came to rest wedged tight in the empty fuel tank of the booster rocket. The precision-made, motion-sensitive gyroscope in the bomb tilted back to its natural position, which tripped an electrical circuit that detonated a cluster of high explosive charges surrounding a plutonium core.

10

A shaft of brilliant white light beamed out of the silo, followed by cloud of fire, dust, ionized metal and radioactive particles. The Hornet was three miles away and felt nothing. The Geiger counter in the cockpit read only a slight rise in radiation level. The fallout from the little nuke drifted back over the abandoned base, dispersed over a wide area and resulted in only 2% net increase in the existing contamination level. But even on an abandoned missile base a hundred miles from civilization, it was impossible for the nuclear blast to go completely unnoticed. But there was a plan for that as well. The Air Force said that an electrical fire had cooked off the fuel stores under the missile silo.

Two weeks later, the Pentagon team published a document detailing a zero-strike contingency plan, which called for naval strike-fighters to launch from the Sea of Japan and the Mediterranean, penetrate Soviet air defenses and supersonically dive-bomb Soviet missile silos deep inland. The Navy reviewed the papers and recommended against the plan, reasoning that the strength of the defenses would make such a strike too dangerous, and that the fighters would have to destroy thousands of missile sites in order to completely eliminate the Soviet ICBMs.

President Reagan also rejected the plan as a viable zero-strike option, but he thought of a different use for the report. He gave the papers to the CIA and ordered them to leak a slightly embellished version to the Soviet Intelligence. When the revised article reached Soviet Premier Mikhail Gorbachev, he was reported to be highly upset by the thought of supersonic Navy stealth fighters swarming the country and slamming tactical nukes down the throats of Russia's own missile silos. This, as much as the "Star Wars" Strategic Defense Initiative, convinced Gorbachev that his missiles would soon be useless and pushed him to meet with Reagan the next year to seriously discuss eliminating nuclear weapons. In a sense, the papers did actually help to prevent a global nuclear war.

However, the original Nuclear Hornet papers were locked in the most secure vaults at Langley and the Pentagon, and forgotten for the next twenty-five years.

# CHAPTER 1: TAG

## ABOVE THE DESERT, NEAR FALLON, NEVADA
## 1400PST MAR 29<sup>TH</sup>

The enchanting natural serenity of the Nevada Desert was shattered by the most unnatural of sounds. A total of four high-output turbofan jet engines drove a pair of sleek fighter planes, and the hundred-decibel roar of the jets echoed eerily across the canyons and crags of the lifeless lands miles below. One of the big fighters was chasing the other; the hunter was polished silver and painted with wide black stripes, the other was flat gray with white stripes. The gray jet spun and twisted wildly to stay out of the silver plane's line of fire. It would dip, pull up, bank to the right, dive steeply toward the ground, level off and roll to the left, and climb in an upward spiral while the black-striped fighter struggled to keep up. These were high-performance machines, and their pilots were forcing them beyond their design limits.

The pilot of the black-striped fighter glared at the other plane as it rolled away from his firing range. "C'mon you little punk," Captain Joshua "Deuce" Thompson muttered at his radar screen. Deuce was a great pilot, but he was facing the best opponent he'd ever seen. The white-striped plane was simply not going to present itself as a target; he would have to make an opportunity happen. The other fighter crossed in front of and below him, just out of range of his Sidewinder short-range heat-seeking missiles. Deuce pushed the throttles forward, and accelerated to 600 knots. He closed the range just as the gray-and-white plane dropped below and out of his sight. He slowed down and cranked into a hard turn, and just for instant, his heat-seekers had a target. With reflexes honed by over twenty years spent in a fighter cockpit, he fired the missile on his left wingtip at the very instant it acquired the lock. The tiny rocket motor launched the 190lb missile to Mach 3.5, and the accurate infrared guidance system steered it toward the target. "Gotcha!"

"Oh, please. You got no chance." Lieutenant Commander Karl "Polar Bear" Roche looked back over his shoulder at the missile streaking toward his gray-and-white Super Hornet. The missile was three miles behind him. Roche could outrun it if he wanted to, but that would only give the other pilot an opening to shoot at him with his long-range weapons. Instead Roche turned *toward* the missile, head-on, and closed the distance toward it. It was the last thing Thompson expected, and he was caught out of position to fire a second missile. The Sidewinder already in the air needed a steady lock on Roche's engines and exhaust, but with Roche approaching nose-first that lock was distorted. So when Roche rolled away at the last instant the missile didn't know where to turn to follow him. The missile was lost.

"Nice move, but now I'm right behind you." Thompson had turned around, and when Roche made his escape move Deuce was able to anticipate the turn and line up another shot. Roche didn't leave himself open very long. Deuce had his missile lock for only a split-second. But he was a lot closer time. "Now, I've really got you."

It was too close for Roche to turn in to the missile, and too close for him to run away. Didn't matter. Roche had another trick up the sleeve of his US Navy flight suit. He pulled up on the stick, and pointed the Hornet toward the sky. The missile fell in line right behind him. Roche rolled the plane and pitched forward, fooling the missile into following him into the sun. Then he twisted away with a hard rudder turn and a hard pull on the stick, forcing the Hornet into an impossibly tight maneuver that would stall any other plane. The missile's sensors were overwhelmed by infrared radiation from ninety-three million miles away and couldn't track their actual target. It continued to chase the sun while Roche was off in a completely different direction. And that direction was nowhere near Deuce Thompson's line of fire.

"No! Fuck, no!" Deuce yelled through the air on the open radio channel.

"Sorry, Deuce," the Polar Bear answered. "Was that your last Sidewinder?"

Now Deuce only had two radar-guided AMRAAM missiles and his cannon. He would need plenty of space and a good radar lock to use the AMRAAMs, or he would need Roche to line up at close range right in front of his nose to hit him with the cannon. Neither of those options would be easy to get.

Roche now had a tactical advantage and he knew it. He started looking for an opening to turn and get behind the aggressor, to become the predator instead of the prey. He'd launched his own long-range missiles at maximum range at the beginning of the engagement, as soon as he got Deuce on his radar. Thompson had dodged those easily. So Roche would be limited to close-quarters combat, but he wasn't planning on getting too far away from Thompson anyway.

As the pilots tested each other, Thompson recognized the one glaring weakness of his opponent: he didn't seem to use his throttle at all. A good fighter pilot thinks four-dimensionally, along the four lines of control: pitch, yaw, roll, and thrust. Roche was only maneuvering along the first three. So Thompson waited for the white-striped plane to make a broad turn, and as soon as it did, he pulled back his throttle to 200 knots. With the reduction in airspeed he was able to turn his fighter more sharply, and so he could turn inside the gray and white Super Hornet's curve. The Polar Bear saw the danger he was in immediately, and rolled his jet out of the turn and dove toward the ground. Deuce followed, watching his radar display. His missiles tried to track Roche's plane but the computer refused to give him the steady tone that would indicate a hard weapon lock. He swore and dove after the escaping Super Hornet.

Roche leveled at five hundred feet, and Thompson followed closely. "Let's change this up a little," Roche said, and then he unexpectedly pushed his throttles forward to the stops, and ran toward the wide canyons in the foothills of the Sierra Nevada Mountains.

Thompson laughed. He was an expert at terrain-following aerial combat – dogfights at low altitude. He had made his name in the canyons and wadis of Iraq, killing Saddam Hussein's MiGs. "There is no way you can lose me in there," he said.

But Roche led a hair-raising chase, using his throttle to its fullest extent now, blasting through long valleys at full thrust, cutting back to near stall speed to slide in to sharp turns, wrapping around mountains with only feet to spare, hugging the canyon floor and suddenly springing over rocky outcroppings with heart-stopping speed. Thompson was terrified; he had not anticipated this kind of ability from his opponent and he had to fly by the seat of his pants to keep up with the other fighter. Ahead he saw the white-striped jet hop over a long, high ridge. He knew there was a broad valley on the other side that offered no cover, so he climbed up to a thousand feet to catch the other plane in the open. He sailed over the ridge ready to catch the exposed Super Hornet and slam two missiles into him. There was no escape this time.

The entire battle to this point had been a farce; these two pilots were not actually trying to kill each other. They were playing more of an expensive game of laser tag. The missiles carried no lethal warheads, only small shaped charges that would detonate the missile harmlessly before it hit its target. The 20mm Vulcan rotary cannons were safe-locked and unloaded; only a small infrared laser beam fired from over the center barrel instead to mark simulated gun "hits." Both fighters were early production model F/A-18e Super Hornets – a highly advanced and versatile naval strike fighter. The US Navy runs such training exercises continuously, to maintain their aviators' status as the best in the world. These two pilots then, were the best of the best. Only aviators of their caliber were sent to TOPGUN.

TOPGUN, as it is known to the public, is the Navy Fighter Weapons School. Although made famous in the 1984 Tom Cruise movie, the real TOPGUN is actually a highly secretive institution. The movie depicted the school as being based in San Diego, as it was at the time, but in the late nineties it was moved from Miramar Marine Corps Air Station in San Diego to Fallon Naval Air Station, in the empty desert of northern Nevada. This gave the school the privacy it demanded and plenty of wide open space to run the sort of highly dangerous exercises its top pilots required to be in top shape.

Captain "Deuce" Thompson was TOPGUN's senior instructor; a veteran Hornet and Tomcat pilot who fought in the first Gulf War, Bosnia, and Yugoslavia, racking up six combat kills in as many years of frontline service. For a long time he was America's only "ace" fighter pilot – having killed at least five enemy aircraft in air-to-air combat. He earned his callsign in Desert Storm when he destroyed two MiG-23s with a single missile. Late in 2005 he was offered an assignment to be Commander of Air Group for the air wing aboard the new supercarrier USS *Ronald Reagan*. Thompson turned down the recommendation – even though the post would have been the last step before carrier captain and then Admiral – and became a teacher instead. Mostly because he wanted to fly the new Super Hornets as much as he could before he grew too old to fly at all. He had made TOPGUN his school for four and a half years, and now he was almost ready to opt back in to the CAG post, which would soon be open again.

The apprentice pilot of the white-striped jet, Lt. Commander Karl Roche, was an extraordinary warrior. His call-sign "Polar Bear" was a tribute to his legendary tolerance of extreme cold, as well as his white-bleached hair, enormous strength, icy intellect, and fierce fighting ability. He was a former Navy SEAL, but a combat injury forced him to seek a new career track, and he found flying fighter jets quite to his liking. His unique skills transferred readily from Special Forces combat to dogfighting. The Polar Bear was sent to TOPGUN after his first five carrier deployments – the earliest allowed by the Navy. So far he'd won every training dogfight, even against the instructors, which is almost unheard of at the Fighter Weapons School. His two previous fights with Deuce were the only exceptions. Those had ended in draws.

Roche had dived over the ridge at 520 knots, or nearly 600mph. As soon as he knew Deuce couldn't see him, he chopped his throttles down to a fast idle, opened his airbrakes and, as his speed dropped, yanked back hard on the stick. This made the 21-ton jet do a tailslide – the tail of the plane skidded forward while the nose snapped up sharply – and the plane assumed a vertical angle of attack while continuing to move in its initial forward direction. This burned his momentum into enormous G forces, and slowed the jet from over 500kts to only 50 in about two and a half seconds. The fighter hung nearly in suspended animation, pointing dead straight up, its engines on the edge of a stall. Roche looked straight out his windscreen, up into the sky, and watched Captain Thompson fly straight over him. Roche fired his cannon at the other Hornet's belly, only four hundred yards away. He followed Deuce with his crosshairs and fired three bursts of simulated 20mm shells into his teacher. The laser marked his accuracy, and Roche smiled with satisfaction as tiny red dots flashed across his target's fuselage. He was now beginning to drift downward; the stall had begun, and he would lose his engine pressure and crash if he didn't start moving forward again. So he pitched forward, throttled his engines back to the max and rocketed out of the gully behind his beaten instructor.

Just when Deuce realized something was wrong – that he should be able to see Roche but couldn't – system failure and fire alarms went off all across his control panels. The fly-by-wire force-feedback sidestick controller went limp in his right hand, as did the throttle stick in his left and the rudder pedals at his feet. He yelled "Ejecting!" for the benefit of the mission recorders, but he was too late. Had Roche been firing live ammo instead of a harmless laser beam, Deuce would be dying in a massive fireball. The autopilot took over and turned back toward Fallon at cruising speed; Deuce sighed, and sagged in his padded seat.

Roche pulled alongside in close formation and snapped a salute. Deuce gave the finger. Then his radio crackled. "Thank you for following your textbook examples, professor. You set yourself up perfectly."

"Enlighten me, Commander: how the hell did you get that far behind me?"

"Rapid vector change, sir; something the Rhino is inherently good at." Roche explained used the unofficial nickname for the Super Hornet.

"Dammit, man, you were far enough behind me for a cannon shot, that means you burned half a mile in three seconds. You had to have stopped in mid air, maybe even flown backwards. You couldn't have possibly decelerated that fast."

"There is a way to do it. It isn't particularly difficult," Roche humbly offered.

"Obviously; I'm dying for you to explain it to me in excruciating detail all the while passing it off as a trivial matter like you always do. But you will make me wait it out until the debriefing, playing coy like the self-assured cocky little punk you are... How fast were you going through that canyon, anyway?"

"Between one-twenty and six hundred."

"I've never seen you vary your speed like that. In fact, I don't think I've seen you use your throttle in a fight at all, until today. Why?"

"Until now, it wasn't necessary."

"Could you have beaten before, if you'd used your throttle, you think?"

"I don't think so, sir."

"Roche, stop screwing around with me. You weren't showing all of your abilities. What else can you do?"

"You will have to wait until I need to show you, sir."

"Brilliant move, Polar Bear. Whatever you did, it was brilliant."

They landed back at Fallon thirty minutes later.

United States Naval Air Station Fallon is located about sixty miles northeast of Carson City, the capital of Nevada, and about the same distance due east of Reno, the second-largest city in the state. The vast, empty desert of the Great Basin between the Sierra Nevada and Rocky Mountains makes for an ideal playground for warplanes, which is why the infamous Air Force test site "Area 51" is located near Tonopah, some 150 miles southeast of Fallon. Other less-known but equally mysterious facilities are scattered throughout the state. Fallon, NV, population 8000, is relatively accessible, as it is only twenty miles off the interstate. TOPGUN shares the base with a testing facility; its own logistics consist of two square miles of tarmac, several large fuel tanks, and a few dozen small hangers full of F/A-18c/d Hornets and -e/f Super Hornets, as well as F-14 Tomcats, F-5e Tigers and F-16n Sea Falcons. A cluster of corrugated steel Quonset huts, modular portable buildings, utilitarian two-story concrete multipurpose structures and small warehouses hide the most advanced flight training campus in the world.

Deuce and Polar Bear taxied their jets off the runways and followed green-vested crewmen to their assigned parking spaces. As usual, Roche started shutting down systems right after he landed. All that remained online when he stopped rolling were the engines, auxiliary computer and rudder controls. He shut those down along with main battery power and jumped out, ignoring both the ladder tucked ingeniously into the port wing strake and the crewman waiting to help him down. Deuce took his time shutting down his fighter. He double-checked the procedure list for every action even though he had been doing basically the same thing on a near-daily basis for twenty years. Deuce used the time to review the dogfight in his mind. He was still stumped when he tried to imagine how exactly Roche had beaten him. Finally, he reached the bottom of the list. He raised the canopy, turned the master power switch to off and exited the plane.

Deuce walked slowly to the main building, which looked just like three other structures but housed all the offices and classrooms of the Fighter Weapons School. Roche was waiting for him, standing at attention at the door of briefing room two. The room was unoccupied except by the School Commandant, Captain Adam O'Wools, who was ready to debrief them. Deuce marched past Roche and saluted as he took a chair to the captain's right. Roche entered the room and saluted as well, but stood at ease behind a chair to O'Wools' left.

Captain O'Wools looked up at Thompson. "You died," he said. He turned to the younger officer. "Good shooting, Commander. Please, sit down."

"Thank you, sir." Roche sat down.

"Did he really kill me?" Deuce frowned, as he leaned on the table. "I thought I called 'Eject' in time."

"At that speed and altitude you probably wouldn't survive anyway, but yes, he got you in the shorts." O'Wools displayed on a big computer screen a schematic drawing of the underside of a Super Hornet, splashed with red crosses. "You would have a little more than three pounds of high explosive incendiary ammunition going off in

18

your engines, fuel tanks, ammo bin, and right under your ass. You took thirteen hits, Josh. How many shots did you fire, son?" he asked, now looking at Roche.

"I fired three five-round bursts, sir, just like we're trained for maximum probability of hits on a maneuvering target."

"That's some good shooting. I just can't believe these groupings. His first burst tore three holes into your engines…"

"I fired a bit late," Roche explained.

Captain O'Wools raised his eyebrows at that and continued, "Then as he pitched forward he got a tidy little string of ten rounds from the center fuselage – where minor systems like fuel tanks and computers and hydraulic pumps are kept – right up to your cockpit. And then you said 'Eject.' So, yes, Josh, you were blown to little pieces a full one point six seconds before you thought about ejecting."

"Okay. How'd he get behind me?"

"I don't know. I'll get to that. The fight was by the book for the first few minutes." The computer screen now split into four displays; one showing forward camera views from inside each cockpit, another presenting a map plot tracking the flight, the fourth displaying flight data from both planes. "Right off the bat, Roche launches his AMRAAMs at you firing beyond maximum range – same way he killed Blitz last week. But you're able to dodge and then you come after him. He gets shifty, you can't get a radar lock, you get closer, take snap shots with the Sidewinders, almost catch him, but he just rolls around you. He charges one missile head-on, flies another into the sun… Here, right, here – this is the best dodge I've ever seen." The screen displayed Roche's fighter pulling up and away from the second AIM-9x Sidewinder, breaking its infrared lock, and rolling past Deuce's field of vision. The Hornet seemed to pirouette around the screen, going straight up and then suddenly straight down, making one of the most accurate missiles in the world miss by fifty yards. "So now, Deuce, you almost catch Roche inside his turn and give yourself some space for an AMRAAM shot. And then Roche does something we teach but don't exactly encourage. He hits the dirt moving fast, and your radar loses him in the grass. You chase through a canyon – both of you are moving way too fast for this, by the way – and the Bear is going through these turns like he's riding on a set of invisible rails. Now he goes over a ridge, and then… somehow he literally kicks your ass. I still don't understand exactly what you did right there, Commander." O'Wools and Thompson looked at Roche expectantly.

"Captains, I performed a maneuver known as a 'cobra.' That's when I pull a full vertical tailslide and use my wing area as an enormous airbrake. My forward momentum is chopped, and I hang on the edge of a stall. Then Deuce flies right past and I shoot."

"A 'cobra?' You mean that Russian air show stunt?" O'Wools asked. "That's only ever been done by Sukhoi Flankers. I've never heard of anyone here doing that. Did you guys ever simulate that?"

Both pilots answered "no" simultaneously. Deuce was trying to imagine how Roche could have learned or practiced such a difficult maneuver.

"So you pulled an untried maneuver – not just something you yourself have never tried but something no American pilot has ever done and certainly not in this aircraft – you pull that at high speed and low altitude and embarrass my best instructor?"

"More or less," Roche acknowledged.

"I am curious – and I am sure Josh is too – to learn the source of your audacity. Why did you think you could do this? You aren't exactly cautious, Roche, but you aren't stupid either, and this seems kind of stupid. You had no margin for error here. This is really out of character for you, Roche. Normally you never give yourself the chance to make a mistake. How did you decide this would work without practicing?"

"I was trained as an aerospace engineer, so I know a lot about airframe loads and vector calculus. I did some math this morning and decided it would work."

"You killed me with math?" Deuce appeared to be getting even more upset.

"The wing structure loads are the main thing – I had to make sure I wouldn't tear my wings off. By my calculations, I'm safe under five hundred knots. The Flanker can only do it up to three-ninety. The other factor was my momentum curve. It's an inverse decay – it starts to drop fast, but the curve shallows off before it reaches zero. So I have a two-point-five second window once I reach my angle of attack before I stall. The math itself is really elementary. I just had to find the formulas in some Russian manuals."

"You know Russian?" Thompson asked.

"I picked it up from my grandmother. I can't read in Cyrillic too well, but calculus is calculus."

O'Wools stared at him. "Where did you find those manuals?"

"Uh, online somewhere."

"You had Lieutenant Santos hack into Sukhoi's design database, didn't you?"

"Nnnmmaybe," Roche replied, sounding guilty but not looking like he felt it.

"That's illegal."

Roche shrugged. "Only if we get caught."

"I caught you."

"You don't care, sir, and neither does Captain Thompson."

"You're right again, Commander," O'Wools said with a hint of a smile. "We here at TOPGUN encourage outside-the-box thinking; pushing the envelope, whatever other clichés you like, it's all true. Our dictum is to fly on the edge of out-of-control. We do not, however, encourage our pilots to endanger themselves or their machines, and certainly not to perform dangerous stunts in dangerous conditions without a bit of practice. But since it obviously worked, you may consider yourself vindicated. The letter of reprimand I was going to send you is going into the shredder. But please, next time you are tempted to do something like this, clear it with me, okay?"

"Will do, sir."

"Captain, Commander, that is all. The official record will reflect the outcome of today's exercise; no further notes are needed."

The two pilots proceeded to the locker room to change out of their grimy flightsuits and shower. Aerial combat tends to make the human endocrine system kick into overdrive, and one symptom is prodigious amounts of sweat. Deuce stripped off his suit and rammed it deep into his locker, under a pile of other dirty garments. He then noticed his trademark playing card taped to his locker. It was a two of spades, which he had adopted as his logo. Some joker had beaten him to the locker room with a hole punch and put thirteen holes through it. Navy flyers are notorious for their practical jokes. Lockers are a common target for vandal attacks. Deuce had long ago bought a novelty deck of cards containing only the two of spades. He had used up almost the whole pack in the last several years replacing the card on his locker.

Roche's locker banged open down the row, and Deuce looked up as the younger pilot unzipped his flightsuit and pulled off his dirty t-shirt. Deuce tried not to stare at the scars on the commander's left arm and side – testament to the injury that forced his retirement from the SEALs. *Too bad for him,* he thought. *He'd be a good-looking kid, otherwise.* Deuce quickly shook that thought from his mind and turned back to his own gear, and stared blankly at his towel. He was beginning to accept that he had been beaten by a student, but he was still sure that he didn't like it.

"He beat you good, I hear." Deuce looked back and saw that Commander Sam "Blitz" Willard – another instructor – had found him. "You're supposed to be dead."

Thompson shrugged. "It took him a while longer than when he killed you."

"Ha. That just was a weapon lock exercise. And he actually fired first and locked on later. I coulda dodged the AMRAAMs for real."

"Ironic though; you, the master of the quick kill, downed by a student in only twelve seconds."

"And you, sir, the Canyon King, hit from behind when you hop a ridge."

"He broke the rules. He pulled an untried maneuver that I didn't even know a Hornet could do."

"Hey, that's combat, my friend. 'You can't ever expect your opponent to do what you expect.'"

"That doesn't even make sense."

"It's in one of the textbooks you wrote."

"It is? Damn. I'll have to fix that. It sounds real stupid, now that I hear someone else say it."

"So," Blitz pulled up a folding chair, "he's beaten all of us now. Humiliated us. What do we do with him?"

"I say we have him whacked," Deuce said, deadpan.

"I think the old man is gonna pass him, first in the class."

"I know. And he's right. Roche is the best pilot I have ever seen."

"But you're used to being the best. You don't want that to change."

Deuce gave Blitz a funny look. "What are you, a shrink?"

"Well, I was a psychology major in college…"

"Are you kidding me? What do you charge? Where's your couch? Where's your sarcastic receptionist? Come back when you know what you're talking about."

"I do know what I'm talking about. I can see it. You need to beat that kid or you think you're a wash-up."

Thompson shook his head. "Okay, so you got me. I'll have to beat him before we let him out of here. And I will do it in front of everyone."

22

"You mean the Alpha-Strike next week? That'll probably be Roche's last exercise, even if you do beat him. If he gets more than twenty points on his report – and that's just a safe take-off and landing – he'll be the top-scoring Top Gunner of all time and off to whatever plum squadron Executive Officer post he wants."

"Right. He'll get to lead the offense team. I'm sure I can get him then." Deuce looked back at Roche as he walked toward the showers. He decided not to follow him. He could clean up at home. He pulled his semi-dirty street clothes out of the locker and changed into them, and pulled a Macanudo from a box on the top shelf.

"How much are you smoking now?" Blitz asked as his friend cut and lit the cigar.

"Couple a week. Why?"

"That's a fresh one. You cut another one yesterday morning."

"Okay, maybe by 'couple' I mean four or five. What's it to you – you gonna be my medical practitioner, as well as my psychiatrist?"

"Can't a guy show a little concern? I know you've been seeing a cardiologist, and you've got a little tube of pills on you at all times. Maybe you oughta cut back on the stogies, Deuce, that's all."

"Thanks doc. You wanna check my prostate while you're already up there?"

Blitz grinned and shook his head. "I wish I had more time for you, but I've got an appointment with my girlfriend. I'll see you tomorrow, Deuce."

Roche toweled off his five-foot-eleven-inch, one-hundred-eighty-five pound body as he stepped out of the shower. He jelled and spiked his white-blonde hair, which drew a lot of derogatory comparisons to '80s rocker Billy Idol, but it was one of his trademarks. He'd worn his hair the same way ever since high school, and the girls seemed to like it. But Karl did not like what he saw when he looked at himself in the mirror. *You're a real mess, Karl,* he thought. He wasn't thinking of the scars that marred the left side of his body. Looking within, he saw something different, something he could not identify; something that deeply disturbed him.

Physically, he had changed little since he was a freshman at UCLA, and named starting fullback for the Bruins football team. He had elected to play fullback in high school, specifically because it wasn't a prestige position. He had always hated being at the center of attention. But that didn't stop him from setting school records for all-purpose yards as well as leading Esperanza High to two consecutive state championships. Roche could see holes form in the defensive line before they appeared, and he could almost read the minds of the opposing linebackers. Roche became the go-to guy on any third- or fourth-down conversion. He had the strong hands and instant acceleration of a wide receiver, the speed and agility of a running back, the strength of a blocker, and the read and awareness of a quarterback. He would have excelled in any position, and as a fullback he was Esperanza High's secret weapon. Roche was happy to let the glory go to the quarterback and the receivers, and he just played game after game making plays happen and pushing drives and letting his teammates make the touchdowns.

Roche didn't fool his coaches, or the scouts and recruiters from every top college in the country. They could see that Roche was more than just an exceptional player. He was the organizer – the de facto leader of the offense. The quarterback and even the coach deferred to him on play calls, because he was always right. Roche always made key blocks, knocking down blitzing pass rushers and escorting the tailback through the gauntlet of tacklers. In the blur of action, fans only saw the pass find a suddenly wide-open receiver or the running back emerge from the tangled line of scrimmage for a breakout play. Few saw Roche, in the middle of the game, engineering the plays, opening holes, making impossible blocks, and extolling his teammates to play like the fate of the world depended on it. During his four years, very few plays in which he was on the field resulted in negative yardage. The school was 39-2 in games Roche started in.

The college recruiters noticed. Especially when Roche's academic performance matched his athletics. Roche earned a 1480 SAT score out of 1600, with a near-perfect 780 on the math sections. He graduated from Esperanza with a 4.1 GPA. With his pick of any top football college in the country, Roche chose to pursue the University of California at Los Angeles, which offered to basically pay him to go to school there, between the football and academic achievement scholarships. Roche earned every penny freshman year. He earned the team's respect in his first game against no. 10 Arizona State. Roche started on special teams; UCLA received the opening kickoff. The sophomore returner fumbled at the twenty-eight yard line near the sideline. Roche was nearby, and he dove for the ball, knocking a 260-pound linebacker off the field. Roche scooped up the ball and carried it through ASU's formation straight into the end zone. For the rest of the game, Roche worked his magic from the fullback position. The Bruins scored on all but two of their drives. Every time Roche touched the ball, it seemed like an automatic first down.

The rest of the season, the legend of the Polar Bear grew. UCLA finished with a 10 and 3 record, 18th in the country, ranked for the first time in ten seasons. The offense was number two. They seemed impossible to frustrate. The Heismann-nominated quarterback had the fewest sacks in the NCAA, and the highest passer rating in the PAC-10 conference. The tailback also led the conference in yards per carry. Karl Roche made it happen on every play. Roche's freshman year culminated memorably at the conference championship game against Cal, when he scored two touchdowns, ran for sixty yards and received for over a hundred more. Next season, UCLA finished eighth, with one loss.

Roche's future was changed three days after the loss in the Rose Bowl game his freshman year. Upon his return to the UCLA campus, student services informed him that he needed to add another humanities course to his schedule. All that was open was a modern art appreciation workshop and a Navy ROTC session. Roche audited the ROTC lecture on military involvement in current affairs, and that was how he slipped sideways into an armed services career. After his sophomore football season, Roche had to choose whether to focus on his academic future or a football career. Then, one of his teammates suffered a concussion in practice, due to a faulty helmet. That was the incident which made Roche realize that a football career had no stability. Weighing his options and after long discussions with friends, family, faculty and coaches, Roche withdrew from the football program and applied for a Navy ROTC scholarship. Roche had found a new calling in the Navy.

He graduated in 2002, and four months later, on September 11th, 2002, he applied for the Navy SEALs, motivated by the terrorist attacks of the year before. He finished the Basic Underwater Demolition / Swimmer course first in his class, was promoted to Lieutenant, junior grade and given command of a platoon of SEALs, which was deployed to Iraq in March of 2003 in support of the invasion. He was there for less than a month before suffering a life-threatening injury in circumstances above and beyond the call of duty. He had jumped on a hand grenade in order to save his men from certain death.

His shoulder would never rotate properly again, limiting his effectiveness as a swimmer and therefore making it impossible for him to rejoin the SEALs. But his other injuries healed quickly and he was soon eager to return to active duty. The SEALs offered him a training post, even though he was really much too young for that. Instead he pursued what he had intended to do when he was in college – Naval Aviation. Switching careers from combat SEAL to carrier fighter pilot is highly unusual, but the Navy figured they owed him one. Also the Admirals that ran SPECWARCOM and the Flight School were personal friends of his father, a former Navy doctor. So Karl was admitted to the Naval Flight School as soon as the shoulder had healed.

Roche arrived at NAS Pensacola in August 2003 and immediately decided that he hated Florida. The humidity only got worse as summer stretched on, and the course inconveniently lasted fifteen weeks. Despite his discomfort with the climate, Roche proved to be an excellent fighter pilot. His skills with combat at all ranges, lethally honed by the SEALs, transferred easily to his new weapon. He aced all the engineering courses, which mostly repeated his last three semesters at UCLA, and mastered the T-45 Goshawk trainer as though he'd learned to fly it when he was learning to drive. He moved on to the combat-ready F/A-18d Hornet, was soon scaring the instructors with difficult maneuvers that he made look easy.

He graduated with highest honors in mid-November and was deployed with the USS *Abraham Lincoln,* which operated out of Puget Sound. Over the course of five tours in as many years, he ran over a hundred successful combat missions supporting operations in Afghanistan and Iraq. His downtime was spent training relentlessly and improving his skills far beyond the normal range for a mere aviator. And so finally, after embarrassing every instructor he'd ever had, Karl was sent to TOPGUN.

Roche went to the aviators' lounge – an air conditioned Quonset hut with couches, tables and TVs. He sneaked in to avoid having to recount his fight twenty times to twenty different aviators. He looked for a TV screen that was not showing replays of his dogfight, and found CNN. Wolf Blitzer was interviewing the US ambassador to Iraq.

*"So, Mr. Ambassador, what implications would this trade strategy have for the world oil market?"*

*"That's a good question. Few people realize the potential Iran has to impact the oil supply. They could, effectively, lock up the Arabian and Caspian supplies if they wanted to, using their military. They won't, of course, for fear of instant and massive reprisal, but they could. Further, they have their own supplies which are enormous, and while the most accessible wells have been tapped out, there's much more to be found by anyone willing to invest the time, money and*

*diplomacy. They have access to the great Arabian oil reserve, and the worlds third largest, which is under the Caspian Sea. Now, their deals with China, Russia and France allow those nations to explore and develop those reserves, and jointly refine and export the product. The Chinese have been using much of this oil themselves, and the Russians have been stockpiling. Before long, they will begin to export, and this will create a glut in the market."*

*"Do they want to create an actual glut? That seems to be the opposite of OPEC's strategy lately, doesn't it?"*

*"Well, that's what makes this situation so interesting. China is not a part of OPEC, and they are providing most of the financial backing for the project. They aren't interested in profits so much as a steady supply of cheap fuel. Analysts are saying that in twelve years the Chinese will require one quarter of the world's refined petroleum. Some economists say they will need half of it by the year 2050. Exploitation of the Iranian reserves will accomplish two goals for them: providing a secure source of oil well under market prices, and opportunities to expand their influence with trade and industry in the Middle East. Chinese pipelines, refineries and tankers providing a steady supply of much needed and inexpensive Iranian crude oil. That is the Chinese dream."*

*"What about Russia and France?"*

*"France is working along the same lines as the Chinese, on a much smaller scale. The Russians are strictly in this for profit. In fact, they've been making a fortune in the last few years pumping cheap crude out of Siberia and the Caspian, storing it, and selling it at the inflated market prices. By expanding their operations in Iran, they can potentially double their revenues and keep this racket up well into the future, even after the supply dries up. Nobody knows exactly how much oil the Russians have stockpiled, but they could conceivably be holding on to more oil than the rest of the world would use in twenty years."*

*"Is there any possibility that the US or UK could make a move into this process?"*

*"Not highly likely. President Clinton effectively neutralized the best chance our country had to get in on the ground floor of Iran's oil industry when he blocked an exploration and exportation deal Iran was making with Conoco back in 1995. Since then BP and Exxon-Mobil have both tried but without support of either our government or the Brits they couldn't get anywhere. Then by the time America had a President who was friendlier to the oil business, the Iranians had tilted*

back to the extremist side, and we simply couldn't do business with them."

"Has that changed in the last eight years?"

"I'm afraid it's gotten worse. It's a real shame too, because as we've seen with countries on the Arabian peninsula, nothing brings wealth, stability and pro-western attitudes to a country like a thriving oil trade."

"And now Iran's going to be getting richer, and more stable, and we'll be left out of the benefits."

"Richer, yes, but not likely any more stable or friendly. The Russians and Chinese simply don't have our good intentions. They as likely as not are going to encourage Iran's noisy and rude behavior, because any noise they make tends to make oil prices jump, and that's good for whoever's selling the crude they pump out of Iran."

"And when will we see that oil affect the market?"

"That's the interesting thing. A major construction effort has been underway in northern Iran for nine years. They've made enormous investments in infrastructure, and they've been producing far more oil than anyone's aware of. However, they haven't starting using their capacity to affect the oil market yet. But they will, and the consequences will be far-reaching and-"

Roche reached forward to change the channel, trying to remember where ESPN was in the cable listing in relation to CNN. Then one of the other pilots noticed him, and everyone wanted to talk to him. Roche had always been uncomfortable with that kind of attention. Usually he tried to downplay his skills, but beating the senior TOPGUN instructor was difficult to spin. They didn't believe him when he said he just got lucky.

## NAS FALLON – APRIL 2<sup>ND</sup>

The Alpha-Strike Team Exercise is the most complicated and expensive lesson TOPGUN teaches. In the team exercise a pilot will use all of his skills, but especially formation combat. The exercise's greatest value is how closely it simulates real-world missions. Usually the "offense" team is student-led, and in addition to defeating the other team in realistic combat they have an objective like a bombing target or a transport aircraft to shoot. The defending team is instructor-led. But there are instructors and students in both groups, to better measure both the individual abilities of the students and the leadership skills of the offense team leader. Also, the offense team has a 3-2 advantage of numbers; the defense would always win with even odds.

Roche began planning his mission the night before the exercise, before he even knew who would be in his team or what their objective would be. He knew for sure that Deuce would be leading the defense, and that he would set the engagement on his terms. Deuce would be setting the rules for both sides, which meant he would basically be able to see Roche's cards. What Roche needed was an ace in the hole. Actually it was more like a wild card. The Super Hornet uses a sophisticated active countermeasure suite called the ALQ-214, which can throw off most missiles, but not the best American weapons. There is an even more advanced defensive system to do that, called the mk77.

Requisitioning a dozen mk77 ECM pods was no easy task – Roche had to pick them up from a base warehouse himself and bribe a petty officer to get them out. Programming each pod was even more difficult, because the device was not preset to recognize and jam emissions from American-made systems. Roche had to break in to the TOPGUN munitions locker at 1 AM and remove the entire guidance system from an AIM-54g Phoenix missile.

The next step needed a little outside help. Roche's friend Lt. Nick Santos could hack or hotwire just about anything. Using an interface device he acquired from a gray-market Swiss supplier, he linked his computer with the internal computers on the ECM pods and the guidance computer from the Phoenix. Basically he taught the ECM pods to recognize and jam the radar from one of the most lethal missiles in the world. Roche counted on one thing: that Deuce would bank on the Phoenix.

Deuce was indeed banking on the Phoenix. He had given Roche's team the assignment of bombing a cluster of plywood buildings out on the range. Deuce would attack when Roche was most vulnerable: making a bombing run. Having a numerical advantage, Roche would surely take the option of splitting his forces and guard his group from such an attack. That's where the Phoenix came in. The AIM-54 is a long-range weapon, effective at nearly 100 miles from its target. It is only carried by the F-14 Tomcat – it is specifically designed to work in tandem with the Tomcat's Hughes APG-71 radar system. The APG-71 can track twenty-four targets and engage six simultaneously. That works out well because the Tomcat can carry six Phoenixes. The F-14's primary mission is fleet defense interceptor. As such, the combined might of the APG-71 and the AIM-54 makes the Tomcat an incredible weapon. Captain Thompson planned his opening move for two Tomcats to engage and attack the other team from maximum range. This was the "longbow" principle that had shaped fighter strategy for the last thirty-five years: first look, first shot, and first kill. He expected confidently to tag out at least half of Roche's Super Hornets before they could shoot back.

The exercise parameters were given to Roche at 0600, right before breakfast. Deuce's parameters called for a simple low-level bombing run. Roche expected he would be attacked once he committed to his bomb run, so he planned his defense and counterattack around that event. His plan took shape in his head at breakfast, and he spent two hours briefing his incredulous team.

The "defense" team took off fifteen minutes ahead of the "offense." Deuce's Tomcats, designated Firebird-1 and -2, flew to the edge of the exercise area and took cover in high clouds. The six Super Hornets were designated Sunburn-1 through -6; Deuce of course was Sunburn-1. Sunburn flight took station about thirty-six to forty miles away from bomb site. Sunburn flew with radar off at low altitude, relying on telemetry from the far-off Tomcats to track the other team. From a range of a hundred and sixty miles and an altitude of 40,000 feet, the Tomcats watched Roche's team lift off from the airbase and head directly for the bomb site.

"Terrier Flight, call in," Roche ordered.
The four Hornets he had designated as the bomber group checked in as op-ready.
"Doberman and Shepherd, call in." These eight were pure fighters, carrying only three Sidewinders, four AMRAAMs and an ECM pod. Roche was Shepherd-1. Satisfied that his mixed squadron of Hornets was ready for action, he focused on his ECM equipment that would alert him to radar traces. "Santa Claus, what do you think? Do we have company yet?"
In addition to being a world-class computer wiz, Lt. Nick "Santa Claus" Santos was the best Weapon Systems Officer in the class. He was in the back seat of a two-seat Hornet-F flown by Blitz. "No Hornets out there, that's for sure. Tomcats... maybe. There's a little spike in that band. Not enough for them to shoot us, but they're probably tracking us. Lemme see if I can sort this out." Santos adjusted his electronic warfare system to filter out the background clutter and concentrate on the spike. "Oh yeah, that's two Tomcats right there."

30

Roche checked his screen. "Yeah, I see that. I'm only seeing one spike."

"No, it's two. They're synchronized, but the spike is too wide to be one source."

"Okay, they think they're ready for us. Four minutes to target; let's all try to look real busy."

"Sunburn, this is Firebird One," the lead Tomcat pilot called. "They're all going right for the target; make it four-eight-zero knots."

"Firebird, Sunburn One," Deuce responded. "You sure you got all twelve?"

"Well, they're stayin' low and all bunched together so it's kinda fuzzy. But I don't have any other contacts on scope so…"

"Pulse them and be sure. I need to account for all twelve, ok?"

Roche saw the radar signal abruptly change on his screen, as the APG-71 radar transmitters used synchronized high-energy pulses to get a high-resolution picture of Roche's group. "They're scanning us, be ready, people. Where are they, Doby One?"

"Triangulating," Santa said. The Super Hornet Onboard Computer was taking input from the threat radar receivers on five other Hornets to geometrically calculate where the Tomcats were staked out. "Gottem. On our eight o'clock, seventy-six miles."

"Sunburn, Firebird; I make twelve Big Bugs. Time to target, one-fifty seconds."

"Good. So he *is* going for the rush. Sunburn flight: take position for daylight." Deuce's Hornets left their hold pattern and settled into a pursuit vector forty-five miles behind Roche's squadron.

"Sunburn, Firebird; they're rolling on."

Deuce gave the attack order. "Sunrise. Repeat, sunrise."

The Tomcats fired all twelve Phoenix missiles, each locked on to one of Roche's jets. The APG-71s were cranked up now, blasting the target area with multifrequency phased-pulse Doppler radar. Twelve Hornets were caught in the beam like trespassers caught by a floodlight. Between the AIM-54's own radar and the all-seeing Hughes monsters, the Hornets were pinned. Briefly.

As soon as the missiles passed Deuce's Sunburn flight, he signaled for his Hornets to power up their own radar and join the engagement. "Daylight. Repeat, daylight." His timing had been flawless. The Phoenixes would tear into Roche's bombers and force them to ignore the bombing run. Then in the panic Sunburn flight would bury the survivors.

"Sunburn, Firebird!"

Deuce thought the first missiles must have caught the Hornets. "Gimme good news, Fi-"

"There's something wrong with the 'Nicks, Deuce. Telemetry's screwy – I think they're bein' jammed!"

"Jammed by what?! How is that possible?"

"Oh, shit, you're in trouble."

Deuce watched his radar screen incredulously as eight contacts stopped moving, then reversed direction, coming back toward him. Then smaller contacts broke away and raced down the middle of his radar screen. It took him a second to realize that Roche's fighters had survived and just answered with a massive barrage of AMRAAMs. "Hooooly screaming Moses."

"They're BMR, sir; do we fight or fly?"

The other team's missiles were launched from beyond maximum range, but since Sunburn Flight was flying right toward them they would be locked on in about two seconds. Deuce had that long to decide whether to fight through the storm or get away. He wasn't fast enough. "We fight, I guess..." he said as two AMRAAMs picked him up. "...Aw, hell. We're toast."

The jammers worked perfectly, sending confusing signals on the same frequency as the Phoenix's radar. Terrier flight continued the bombing run unmolested, while Doberman and Shepherd turned around sharply and fired two AMRAAMs per fighter without even looking. AMRAAMs can be fired blind and pointed to a target while in mid-flight. Roche took full advantage of this feature, depending more on surprise than accuracy. His radar was calibrated for the range, speed and altitude he expected Deuce would be at, and as Roche's nose poked into that corner of sky, six Hornets appeared in sharp detail. This moment had been choreographed perfectly. The tables weren't just turned, they were thrown across the room pinning Deuce to a wall. "HOUNDS AWAY!!" Roche hit the afterburner and closed in on Sunburn Flight, followed by his other seven fighters. He singled out the foremost Sunburn and directed his in-air AMRAAMs to it, hoping it would be Deuce.

Sunburn Flight was gone. The targets they had picked out were rushing at them too fast to lock down, and no less then sixteen missiles were about to rip apart the formation. Deuce and Sunburn-5 fired AMRAAMs at unsteady targets, but the rest just turned and ran. Sunburns-2, 4, 5 and 6 all died within a few seconds; Sunburn-5 took Roche's missiles head-on, but the others were buried from behind by the wave of weaponry. Sunburn-3 dove for the ground as soon as the pilot realized what was happening, and was thus able to survive the counterattack. Deuce himself somehow broke three locks and rolled out of the line of fire. Then he made a broad sweeping curve, trying to position himself behind and below Roche's fighters. He'd lost the exercise, but if he could help it he wasn't going to lose another duel.

"We got 'em, guys. Split up: Shepherd Three and Four, go get those Tomcats; Doby Three and Four, find that other Hornet. The rest of you, hang close. I'm going to set up Deuce. Where is he, anyway?"

Deuce closed in without using his radar. From this angle, below and behind Roche's Hornets, he was completely invisible. He wanted to visually identify Roche. He picked up the white-striped markings from four miles away. He turned his radar back on, and locked on to him.

"Something's got me," Roche said, as the threat radar warning sounded. "I guess that's our man. You all know how to play this now." Roche pulled back to a sixty degree angle and dropped chaff as he jumped to full afterburner. Deuce's radar lock broke just as he fired his last AMRAAM. Deuce climbed after the Polar Bear, trying to close within Sidewinder range. Roche made that impossible by keeping his speed up and avoiding long turns that Deuce could cut inside.

Thompson's annoyance grew with every move the student made. Afterburner was only eating up fuel. Roche used his in pulses to stay ahead, and he had more fuel to spare then the instructor did, so there was no point for Deuce to be using afterburner at all. Deuce realized too late that he couldn't win. Roche would have to make a very serious mistake to let the Captain close within Sidewinder range. What was more, he wasn't trying to turn and get a shot on Deuce, which could only mean...

"Doby One has lock," Blitz announced on open channel, as he fired a pair of Sidewinders. "Fox-two, fox-two, range one mile. Thank you for making that so easy, Captain Thompson."

"What took you so long?" Roche asked.

"I wanted to see if he could catch you first, but it turns out he couldn't. Congrats, homeboy. You're through."

Deuce slumped in his seat, and let the autopilot steer. This was only the second time in the last twenty years that he'd experienced being "shot down." As soon as he landed, he ran over to where Roche parked, but he wasn't there yet. The Polar Bear and Blitz buzzed the airbase, making a pass at 500 feet at full afterburner. The resulting sonic boom left Deuce momentarily deaf. Roche landed at just slightly above safe speed, and taxied to his parking space a bit faster than allowed, but Roche always handled his machine at the edge of safety regardless of whether it was in the air or on the ground. Deuce's hearing was still fuzzy as Roche jumped out of the cockpit. "Okay, kid. How in God's name did you fool my Tomcats? They had you locked up and somehow you made yourself invisible to missiles. What did you do?"

Roche took of his helmet and pointed under his wing. Deuce looked, and started yelling more. "Is this a joke?"

"No sir, it's a Mark 77."

"Since when are we flying Growlers? You can't work a jammer pod on a single seat... I mean you can't fly and use this at the same time, can you?"

"No, I can't. You're absolutely right. It couldn't work."

"I told you before not to screw around with me. Obviously it worked. How?"

"Santos and I just told the pods only to look for and jam the radar signature of a Phoenix."

"You guys aren't supposed to know how to do that kind of stuff."

"Well, we didn't, but that's why God made user manuals. We programmed them all last night."

"How?"

"Well, I'd rather not say, because I'm afraid it might be cheating."

Deuce shook his head. "Don't worry about that. At this point, you could get away with anything."

After the debriefing, Deuce found Karl again. "I gotta hand it to you, that was the best mission plan I've ever seen, and you executed perfectly."

"Thank you, sir."

"Listen," Thompson said, sitting down next to him. "I yell at you a lot because you are making me look ridiculous, but I want you to know I really am darn proud of you. I'm proud to be able to say I taught you everything I know. But that's obviously not everything you know."

Roche smiled at that and nodded. "You're a good teacher, and it's been a great honor learning from the best."

"I don't think I'm the best anymore," Deuce replied. "You're on your own level, kid. Your problem now is going to be figuring out how you fit there."

## THE NEXT MORNING

"When were you going to tell me?" O'Wools asked sharply as Thompson entered the commandant's office.

"Tell you what?"

O'Wools said nothing; instead he pushed an open folder across the desk.

Thompson looked at the spilled contents. He recognized an EKG readout that had his name on it. "I didn't know you could get that. I thought there was doctor-patient privilege or something."

"You've been in the service long enough; you should know there's no such thing in the Navy. Now, when were you going to tell me you have an enlarged and weakened heart muscle, and shouldn't have been flying for the last month?"

"Today."

"I don't believe you."

Thompson said nothing; instead he opened the folder he had carried in with him, placed it on top of the one already open on the desk, and pushed them back across to Captain O'Wools.

"*Due to a recently diagnosed condition of cardiomyopathy and the associated health concerns,*" O'Wools read the cover letter aloud, "*I have been medically restricted from flight activity in combat or simulated combat until such a time as a Navy physician determines that my condition has sufficiently improved to allow a reinstatement of combat-ready status.*

"*Consequently, I an unable to continue my duties as senior flight instructor of the Fighter Weapons School, and must therefore request either an indefinite sabbatical or a transfer to a position that does not conflict with my medical restriction.*

"*Preferring the latter option, I have attached transfer papers which – pending your authorization – confirm my reassignment to*

*Carrier Air Wing Thirteen as Commander, Air Group. It has been my pleasure and honor to work with you at TOPGUN, and wish only that I could have completed my tour here and departed under better circumstances.*

"With respect, Captain Joshua 'Deuce' Thompson.

"Okay," O'Wools said, putting down the letter. "I believe you."

"Air Wing Thirteen is assigned to the *Reagan*, which is going out on a non-combat tour in a couple of months. The Flight Doctor is Lieutenant Commander Herbert Tobias – we've known each other a long time and he's agreed to clear me for duty as a CAG, so long as I don't participate in any exercises. In the meantime I'll have a couple months to relax in San Diego."

"You've had this CAG job lined up for a couple of years now," O'Wools noted. "You turned it down to take your first tour as my senior instructor."

"Yes, I did."

"Well, given the circumstances I can hardly refuse you." O'Wools signed the papers. "I hope you'll stick around for a few days until your last class graduates."

"There's no way I'd miss that," Deuce Thompson replied. "If I had a heart attack tomorrow, I'd still come back here on Friday to see them off."

# CHAPTER 2: WHAT LURKS

## SIDON, LEBANON – 1710 LOCAL, MARCH 30TH

A man stood patiently in front of a ten-story office building, apparently oblivious to the Imam's call to prayer being broadcast over the rooftops of the city. He was a white man with white hair, of medium height and build with an ugly, pockmarked face, almost looking like Gary Busey crossed with Edward James Olmos. He stood there, gathering stares as the Muslims finished their evening prayer and went on their way. Finally the limousine he was waiting for pulled up to the curb. He waited for another moment, expecting the driver to open the door for him. But the driver did not get out, and he was obligated to open the door himself. He sat down in the back seat and stared at the only other passenger, sitting in the front of the passenger cabin, watching him.

"Close the door," the other man ordered, speaking Russian. The white-haired man obeyed. The other man was shrouded in shadow once the door was shut.

The white-haired man looked around his surroundings. The windows of the limousine were tinted nearly opaque. His boss had an aversion to sunlight. He leaned forward to the well-stocked mini-bar, reaching for a bottle of vodka. "Mind if I have drink?" he asked his boss.

"Be my guest," the boss said. He turned slightly and ordered the driver "Airport, Beirut." He turned back to the white-haired man. "So, Lenonov, tell me how negotiations went with the French."

"Negotiations? They were hardly necessary," replied Colonel Victor Lenonov, formerly of the Russian Air Force. He replaced the bottle of Smirnoff Triple Premium after pouring himself a generous measure. "After all I've done for Dassault, setting up their factory here without the French government knowing, and designing the avionics package and integrating the control systems for the Defiant fighter, they were only too happy to discuss the sale of one hundred and twenty first-production aircraft at a steeply discounted price."

"Hmm. I'm sure they'll still make a considerable profit margin, now that they don't need to pay their government any export taxes. Imagine; they taxed sixty percent of the revenues on that deal selling Rafales to the Brazilians. Communism – absolute communism." The

Russian capitalist shook his head in dismay. "But the aircraft you ordered – how soon will they be ready for delivery?"

"Half the order is ready to be shipped right now. The rest will be shipped as they roll off the line, and I've been assured the order will be filled by the end of the month of May. They will be sent by railroad, partially disassembled, along with expert mechanics and assembly line workers to fit the engines and reattach the wings upon arrival at their destination, wherever that is."

"I will inform you of the specific destination and required time of arrival tomorrow. But all Dassault needs to know is that their mechanics are going to Iran."

"Of course, sir."

"How much time will you need to train the Iranian pilots on the new aircraft?"

"Well, that depends on how proficient you want them to be, Mr. Rannovich."

"I require them to be good enough to defeat an American F-22 Raptor in a close-range dogfight."

"From what I've seen of the test reports on the F-22, that shouldn't be too difficult for a stealthy, nimble little fighter like the Defiant. Eight weeks at the most."

"Excellent. Then I shall begin the operation in eight weeks."

In all the years Lenonov had worked for Rannovich, the boss had never adapted his schedule to fit someone else's timetable. The Defiant fighter must have been essential to the crime lord's plan.

Rannovich's satellite phone beeped twice. He answered it. "Yes? Both submarines have departed? And how long do you estimate it will take for the navy to realize they are missing? Splendid. Inform me once they surface for refueling."

"What about my Super Flankers?" Lenonov asked once the boss terminated the call. "Have they all been brought into the country?"

"Nearly. The Iranians are still digging camouflaged hangars in the southern part of the country. They will be done in time. I am keeping one squadron near my command bunker in the north. The rest of your aircraft will be divided into groups of four, distributed across the southern desert."

"How long are the runways?"

"Between eight hundred and one thousand meters, which I believe is adequate for the Su-37."

"More than adequate, thank you sir."

"Don't thank me yet. You have no idea what I shall be asking of you in the coming months."

"Taking on the American Navy and Air Force. Believe me, I look forward to it."

The Russian Mafia don known only as Rannovich smiled, unseen by Lenonov. "So do I."

## POLYARNYJ INLET, RUSSIA
## 0500 MOSCOW TIME, MAR 31<sup>ST</sup>

Two submarines moved slowly across the surface of the cold White Sea. The winter had stayed late, and the air was still fiercely cold. Salt spray froze to the sails of the steel warships. Somewhere ahead of them, under the surface, was a larger, nuclear-powered submarine; an *Akula*-class type 890 hunter-killer. The two on the surface were diesel-electric *Kilo*-class boats. The Kilo is slow and vulnerable in the deep ocean, but in shallow waters inshore, it can be an extremely lethal force. It is very difficult to find, because at speeds of fewer than five knots it makes absolutely no noise. The Kilo is a defensive submarine, not a tool of offense like the big, fast Akula. The Kilo is intended to sneak through shallow waters and lie in wait for the enemy. It is a weapon of ambush.

These three ships represented the largest submarine exercise the Russian Northern Fleet had put to sea in eight and a half years. The navy simply did not have enough money to keep their personnel or vessels in top form. This exercise was a rather simple one. For the Akula, it was a matter of acquisition. For the Kilos, the task was evasion. The Akula was to patrol a point about two hundred miles east of the port of Archangel on the Kola Peninsula. The Kilos would proceed one hundred miles further on the surface, conducting seamanship drills for the young, inexperienced crew, and then they would radio their position, dive, and try to creep back past the Akula and home to Polyarnyj.

The Kilo is an extremely quiet submarine, so the captain of the Akula was not too surprised initially that he had difficulty acquiring his targets. But after two days of searching nearly ten thousand square miles of ocean, it became obvious to the captain that the Kilos had given him the slip. So he zigzagged back to Polyarnyj, confident that he would come across the submarines and catch them from behind. No such luck. He came in to the dock behind schedule and very angry, but not as angry as the admirals were. The exercise had not gone according to plan for the Kilos, either. They never arrived back at any Russian port. The Akula was sent straight back out to assist in a massive search and rescue operation that turned up absolutely nothing.

The Russians assumed the two submarines had somehow smashed into each other as they began their return journey and the crewmen began to maneuver their ships underwater for the first time. The engineers decided that if the subs had a head-on collision at a closing speed of fifteen miles per hour, the impact would be sufficient to sink both boats without a trace. This was accepted as the solution for the mystery of the missing Kilos. The event stirred a little interest outside of Russia, but once it was announced that subs had no nuclear materials onboard the press forgot all about it. A fatal error in navigation was added to the textbooks for aspiring submariners; an example of a deadly mistake. But this was not what had happened.

The captains of the subs and some dockyard officials had been quietly bribed, and a few additional men were allowed to board. All of these men had Special Forces training, and most knew a thing or two about underwater navigation and other essentials of operating a diesel-electric submarine. They came from many distant places: some were Russians, others Chinese, some were from England, and about half were Middle Eastern. They had different beliefs: some were radical Muslim fundamentalists, others hardline communists. They spoke different languages belonging to their various homelands. They shared a common goal, however. They were to deliver these two submarines to the sovereign Islamic Republic of Iran.

The two submarines were taken over as soon as they cleared their docks. The captains had been bought at a substantial price – two million American dollars each – more than either could hope to make in their lifetimes in any sort of honest work in Russia. Chump change though, for a man known as Rannovich, who made at least twice that amount every day in a very dishonest line of work. The original crew did as their captain told. A few officers and warrants questioned and they were shot out the torpedo tubes with weights on their ankles.

Getting the submarines to Iran was a complicated process. It was actually impossible for the boats to do by themselves; they had a range of only 3,600 miles if they operated at maximum fuel efficiency. The Iranian seaport of Bandar Abbas is, by sea, 9,500 miles away from Polyarnyj. So the subs had to make two refueling stops, which would also be impossible because their new masters wished them to be kept secret. The boats had to be refueled at sea, and they were, in secret.

First stop was off the northern coast of Spain. A Very Large Crude Carrier (VLCC) – a 300,000-ton supertanker – was en route to Rotterdam. It stopped for a few hours to siphon some diesel fuel out of its own oversized and redundant tanks and into a pair of small submarines that surfaced in the middle of the night. No one watching thought anything of the VLCC parking in the middle of the ocean for six hours. These are crowded seas, and traffic was heavy. None of the men on the tanker was aware of the transfer except the captain and several new members of the crew. The second stop was in the stormy waters of the Cape of Good Hope, where no one would expect or watch a surface-to-subsurface fuel transfer. This was extremely dangerous. Eight Russian sailors were lost during the stormy night.

But the submarines finished the journey to the Persian Gulf without further mishap. Iran now had two new Kilo-class submarines. Keeping them required some juggling. Iran already owned three Kilos, bought legitimately from Russia. One was in decent shape; the other two were in complete disrepair and mostly used for parts. Three days before the stolen boats arrived, Iran's one good Kilo went out, supposedly on patrol. One of the new Kilos took its berth, and then left again after four days. Then the second new Kilo moved in, and then vanished. To outside observers, like the American intelligence community, it seemed like the one sub was operating on a short patrol routine. Then one of the two unused Kilos suddenly came to life. One had been completely stripped to refurbish the other. To American eyes, the Iranian Navy now had two submarines on active patrol, which Iran had never done before. Of course, there were actually four submarines, but even based on the assumption that there only two subs active, the sudden activity was a cause for concern.

Iran had been threatening for over a decade to use submarines to blockade or even mine tanker routes in the Gulf. So far, the Ayatollahs (the near-supreme religious leaders who act as de facto heads of state) had not been rash enough to do so, but this new action could be a precursor to a blockade. Clearly some closer observation was in order.

A small flotilla of American warships was ordered to report to the Persian Gulf and monitor Iranian naval activity in general and particularly to shadow her Kilo-class diesel-electric submarines. The group was led by the 10,000-ton *Arleigh Burke*-class guided missile destroyer *USS Cook*. There was also another destroyer – an older, slightly smaller *Spruance*-class – the *USS Morris*. The two big warships packed enough firepower to take on the entire Iranian Navy and level several major cities by themselves.

They were accompanied by two 4,000-ton *Perry*-class frigates, and were trailed underwater by a *Los Angeles*-class attack submarine, the *USS Topeka*. Frigates specialize in anti-submarine warfare – that is, finding and sinking enemy submarines. And the American sub is also exceedingly good at finding other underwater warships and killing them with advanced torpedoes. And like the destroyers on the surface, the attack submarine carries a large load of cruise missiles that can strike very far inland with devastating effect. Of course the US Navy wasn't in the Persian Gulf to destroy anything – they were just keeping an eye on a couple of old second-hand subs.

With all of this gear in such a small area, one might expect the Navy to turn up the two stolen submarines as well. But no one noticed that all four subs were being shuffled. One would leave port, proceed on the surface out to the gulf, submerge and run silent. Then one of the subs at sea would start making noise and eventually move back to port in the first subs place. The Americans followed the subs as closely as they could, but because the Kilo is so quiet, the watchers never realized they were being tricked. They were also in great danger. The two hidden subs could have easily fired on the US warships and taken them completely by surprise. But for the time being, the Iranians were content to shuffle their cards under the table, while the Americans watched, unsure of what game they were going to play.

## NEAR THE TOWN OF ALAGIR, CHECHNYA
## 0200 LOCAL, APR 2ND

Hundreds of trains run across the largest country on earth every day using Russia's highly efficient railway system. Most are civilian freight or passenger services, but many are operated by the military. Lacking in advanced heavy airlift capacity like the US Air Force Air Mobility Command, the Russians rely on the railroads to transport hardware from the vast depots and storage lots in Siberia to bases around the long borders. One such train rolled through the quiet town of Alagir late at night, heading toward the more beleaguered cities in Chechnya. The train was over two miles long. Six powerful diesel engines hauled nearly two hundred flatcars, loaded with tanks, infantry fighting vehicles, armored personnel carriers, self-propelled artillery, and shipping containers filled with fuel, ammunition, food and medical supplies. Fifty sleeper cars at the end of the train were filled with soldiers and tank crew. It was a full armored brigade, riding on rails.

Chechnya has been a curse to the Russian leaders since the collapse of the Soviet Union in 1991. The small mountainous region is home to a large minority of ethnic Islamic rebels who demand autonomy, and resort to notoriously violent means to express their demands. Many of the sub-groups of rebels have connections to al-Qaeda and other terrorist groups. The Russians wage a constant war to suppress the rebels, which of course incites even more violence from the radicals.

As the reinforcement train entered a rural forest, an old van drove out of a side road and ran down the gravel ballast bed alongside the tracks. The aged vehicle had little trouble keeping up with the train, which was only moving at thirty miles an hour. Two commandos jumped from the van onto the rear-most flatcar, occupied by a huge T-80 main battle tank. The van ran ahead at forty-five miles an hour, slowly gaining on the locomotives in the front of the train. Two more commandos jumped over to the catwalk on the side of the lead engine. They were armed with silenced submachine guns, and they entered the cab and subdued the train's crew.

The van drove ahead at full speed. It crossed a bridge over a deep gorge, and went on ahead to a switch crossing. The driver got out and changed the switch to align the tracks to a southern line. He radioed to the man now driving the train, who accelerated it up to fifty miles an hour. Once it reached that speed, the men on the flatcar overrode the mechanism that coupled the train cars and separated the fifty passenger coaches at the end of the train.

A young army lieutenant was dozing restlessly in the front of the first sleeper car – the only one awake out of the forty-six troops in the coach. Periodically he sat up, stared out the window at his T-80 tank on the flatcar ahead, taking strange comfort in its presence, and went back to sleep. He woke up again, and noticed that the train was moving a little faster. He looked at the huge tank he would be commanding against the rebels, and then lay down. Before he closed his eyes, he felt the train start to slow. He sat up again, and looked at his tank, and was astonished to observe it slowly moving away from him. He looked at the half-empty 750ml bottle of Stolichnaya vodka he'd smuggled with his luggage, and then he rubbed his eyes and looked back at his tank. It was accelerating away from him and was now over twenty yards ahead of his train car. In actuality, the rest of the train – including that tank – was traveling steady at fifty miles an hour and the passenger cars were gradually slowing down.

Soon the tank and its flatcar had vanished from sight. The lieutenant had just convinced himself he was dreaming when he saw something on the tracks ahead across a trestle. A van drove out onto the middle of the bridge, and parked on the westbound tracks directly in the path of the train. The driver got out, unlashed a dirt bike that was tied to the roof, and sped off into the darkness. The runaway passenger cars coasted onto the bridge at forty miles an hour, still carrying enormous momentum. The lieutenant stared blankly through the van's windshield. As he got close he could see two big metal drums in the back, marked "flammable." He stared at the unfamiliar English word as the train cars slammed into the van. The explosion blew a thirty-foot gap out of the double-tracked bridge, and launched the leading car high into the air. The second sleeper dropped through the gap and sailed across the gorge, ripping out bridge supports and collapsing half of the remaining structure before slamming into the opposite wall and tumbling into the deep, dark chasm.

Forty-six of the remaining coaches followed, crushing the hundreds of soldiers inside. The last two and the caboose ran out of momentum at the edge of the shattered bridge. The second-to-last sleeper dangled over the precipice, hanging at a sharp angle with only the weight of the other two cars to hold it up. The crewmen in the caboose were wide awake by now. As soon as they realized that something was very wrong they engaged the brakes, but without the connecting hydraulic lines from the engine the brakes were useless. Once their car came to rest they jumped out to see what had happened. They gaped in horror; they could see only two cars out of two hundred and forty-five in the train. The rest, they assumed, was at the bottom of the gorge. Soldiers were beginning to crawl out of the rear coach. The crewmen shouted at them to wait, and to balance the cars until the coach in front of theirs could be evacuated. The troops slowly moved out of that car, which still dangled precariously. Many of them were seriously injured from being launched out of their beds. The ninety-six survivors gathered back on the cliff edge. Once they regrouped, the able-bodied troops scrambled down the slope to try to reach the fallen coaches. The two trainmen and a medic tended to the thirty-one injured. Only these would live.

Three minutes later, a tanker train came along the opposite way. The engineer of this train was extremely edgy. He had just seen the last

44

cars of the military train cross a switch in front of him onto the southbound branch line. His train had narrowly missed hitting the giant tank on the last flatcar. Then he saw a dirt bike driving like mad along the gravel bed. Then he saw the sky light up in the distance, and heard a noise like a million beer cans being crushed. When he came around the bend and saw that half of the bridge had been destroyed, it was too late to prevent his train from adding to the wreckage. His 30,000-ton load would require a mile and a half to stop, and he had only four hundred yards. He and his conductor jumped from the cab, taking their chances with a forty-five-mile-an-hour leap into the trees. They did not survive landing. Their locomotive and its two slave engines disappeared over the cliff, followed by eighty tanker cars filled with refined petroleum from the Caspian Sea. The train flew into the canyon, impacting at the base of the remaining supports and dropping the rest of the bridge and the last three cars of the military train into the abyss.

Millions of gallons of fuel became a massive inferno that raged for days over the crash site, and left nothing but unrecognizable pools of molten metal. The death toll was listed at two thousand, two hundred and sixty-eight military personnel and eight train crew. Only thirty-four men survived, all with various injuries. The citizens of Alagir would later build a memorial for those that perished in the worst rail disaster in history. Investigators found no trace of foul play, but by then the wreckage was so hopelessly annihilated it was not possible to tell that two trains were ever there to begin with. Railroad officials thought it was almost beyond belief for the two trains to have collided head-on in the exact middle of the bridge, and pulled their entire loads into the gorge after them. They decided that sabotage was the most plausible cause of the disaster. The media quickly pointed blame at the Chechen rebels, who of course had motive and probably an opportunity, even though the scene of the catastrophe was over a hundred miles away from the heart of the fighting. The leaders of the rebel organizations quickly denied any culpability, claiming that even they could not support or condone so heinous an act of terrorism.

But terrorism was the only likely explanation for a well-built bridge and two huge trains suddenly vanishing into an immense, hellish nightmare. However, no one was ever quite sure whether or not two hundred armored vehicles were at the bottom of the amazing scene of tragedy and destruction. All of the vehicles were, in fact, quite intact although very much in the wrong hands as the stolen train sped southeast through Georgia, Armenia, Azerbaijan, and finally into northern Iran.

## TSANXIANG AIRBASE, XINJIANG A.R., CHINA
## 2100 BEIJING CENTRAL TIME, APR 5TH

Americans familiar with security procedures at US military bases would be astounded by the practices employed by the Chinese. In a country where the populace lives in terror of uniforms, one would think that a few armed guards would be a sufficient deterrent, but that is not the way of the Chinese Red Army. Tsanxiang Army Airbase is remote, located in the steppes of the Xinjiang Uyghur Autonomous Region in the northwest corner of the country, over 100 miles from any notable population center. But there has been a major rebellion movement among the Islamic population of the region, and so this installation was heavily guarded even by Chinese standards. Miles of razor-wire-topped chain link fence surround the facility, patrolled by dozens of People's Liberation Army regulars, attack dogs, armored cars and helicopters.

Security was iron-clad to say the least. No one entered the base unless they could prove they had orders permitting their presence. Anyone suspected of trespassing was simply shot. All possible entrances were covered, including maintenance and sewer tunnels. Approach by air would be noticed by attentive young radar technicians, deliberately trained to be jumpy and nervous in the theory that they would err on the side of vigilance. Unauthorized aircraft were used as target practice by the air wing stationed at Tsanxiang. For all intents and purposes, an attempt to illegally enter Tsanxiang Airbase was an act of suicide.

Suicide is not an unattractive proposition for the Islamic jihadist, who fights for his leaders with the firm faith that his glorious death would earn him eternal reward in paradise. So for the twenty Iranian commandos, sneaking into Tsanxiang was not as much suicide as opportunity. Besides, commando raids were not contingencies that the Chinese guards trained for. Suicide bombings and riots, yes; but most terrorist groups don't use highly trained special ops soldiers. These were from the Quds Force of the Islamic Revolutionary Elite Guards, a Special Forces unit trained in similar fashion as US Army Rangers or British SAS, though hardly to the same proficiency. They are just as the name says – an elite unit of the Islamic Revolutionary Guard, which is the volunteer frontline army division of Iran.

An IREG sniper took point as the attackers neared the fence. He killed a dog and two sentries, and then waited to make sure the area was clear. Two young soldiers ran forward, setting aside their silenced AK-SU carbines and attacking the fence with tin snips. The raiders moved silently into the base, constituting the most significant security breach in Tsanxiang's thirty-nine-year history.

The first objective of the IREG team was to raise an alarm far from their true objective. Three expendable operatives wearing unmarked uniforms were assigned to carry a bomb into the base guard barracks and blow it up. The rest would hijack a pair of transports scheduled to take off from the base in two hours. The trick would be getting across the base unnoticed. Mauressh Ballid was a senior sergeant in the IREG party, and he was scared. He had studied the security procedures at this base for days, watching the guards through binoculars, and he knew it was only a matter of time before they ran into another patrol. The snipers kept the way clear, though, and before long the team had reached the massive hangars of the main airstrip.

Commander Beiruz gave orders. "Okay. The transports should be in these two hangars. We wait for the explosion, and then we go in. Whatever guards are in there will run out the other doors, so we should be able to take the planes pretty easily. Mauressh, what's happening?" the team leader asked.

The sergeant followed his men with binoculars. "They're eighty yards from the barracks. No guards in sight. I think they're going to make it... yeah, they're in. Flashes... looks like gunfire. All they have to do is arm the bomb..."

The blast ripped through the ground floor of the building, scattering bodies and debris in all directions. The building collapsed a second later, a full thirty seconds before anyone could trigger an alarm.

"Let's go! Let's go!" Beiruz led the way into first hangar. In the dim lighting, the Antonov-124 Condor transport looked even more enormous than it really was. Beiruz took a moment to get his bearings, and then led his younger comrades to the front of the big plane and into the cargo bay. Like most big military cargo planes, the Antonov's nose swings open to allow easy loading of outsize cargos. Beiruz's team entered through this gaping maw, and quickly accosted the crew.

"Get this thing into the air as quickly as possible," the IREG officer ordered in practiced Chinese. "Don't try to be a hero. We will let you go once we reach our destination, just as long as you cooperate. Understand?"

"Commander!"

"Yes, Sergeant Ballid?"

"Team Three is dead, sir. Only one of them got out of the barracks before it blew, and he just got cut down."

"It is the will of Allah. You, pilot," he switched to Chinese again, "get clearance from the base tower to take off." He turned to Ballid again. "What's happening with team two?"

"They have their plane under control. We're ready to go, sir."

Beiruz took the plane's radio from the fear-frozen hand of the Chinese co-pilot. "Tsanxiang tower, this is Mountain Brother One. Can we get out of here?"

"Mountain Brother, we don't think there is any risk of further explosions. We have things under control."

"Copy, but I'd feel safer if we got all this expensive cargo away from this base."

"Affirmative, Mountain Brother. You and Brother Two are clear for take off on westbound runways."

The IREG commander turned off the radio and snapped at the cowering pilot. "Move it. Follow your scheduled flight path until I tell you otherwise"

The huge jets flew 800 miles south before the commander spoke again. "Mauressh, find and remove this plane's transponder and black box. Pilot, you're supposed to fly this cargo to Myanmar, right?"

"Correct," the Chinese pilot answered. "Artillery pieces and ammo, sold to..."

"I know what it is, that's why I'm stealing it. In five minutes we will be out of the Chinese radar cover, over the middle of the Himalayas. You will send an appropriate mayday signal, and then Sergeant Ballid will toss your transponder off the plane. Brother Two will do the same after about three minutes. Then you shall turn west across Nepal and Kashmir. It would be good if you mention sabotage in your mayday transmission. We're trying to pin this on the local Islamic rebels."

"Were it not for the gun held to the back of my head, I think I would almost be enjoying these spy games. Where am I to go when this is over?"

"A motel for a couple weeks, and afterward you may go anywhere you want. We have no plans to kill you. You could even tell the Chinese what happened. By then it will no longer matter. My government will compensate you for the inconvenience." The IREG commander was lying. The Chinese would all be dead shortly after landing at the remote Iranian airfield they were heading for.

## ALBORZ MOUNTAINS – DAWN, APRIL 6$^{TH}$

Rannovich sat in the back seat of his heavily-modified, bullet-proofed Brabus Mercedes S-Klasse Biturbo, gazing out the windows at rows of tanks and self-propelled artillery as his driver toured him through the newly completed bunker complex. Over forty square kilometers of parking had been excavated from under the mountains; over four hundred million cubic meters of rock removed to form a series of huge tunnels and caverns, even an underground airfield. The complex was already over half-filled with stolen hardware, and more armored vehicles, aircraft and munitions continued to arrive every day. *Soon*, Rannovich thought, *this will be the fourth-largest army in the world, and no one will know it exists until I use it.* A small, rare smile crossed his scarred face. *Soon. Very soon.*

# CHAPTER 3: UFO'S AND IOU'S

## CHEYENNE MOUNTAIN, COLORADO – 1400 MST, APR 5$^{TH}$

Most of those civilians who have heard of NORAD think of it as an ultrasecure, top-secret facility, like Area 51 or a missile base. The perception among the public is that NORAD would be America's command center in the event of nuclear war. None of this is actually true, but like so many other matters of national security, the government allows the general public to believe whatever they make up for themselves.

NORAD is a poorly constructed acronym for North American Radar Defense Command. It does little more or less than the name suggests – monitoring military radar stations across North America. The original Cold War purpose was to watch for Soviet missiles and bombers, and to relay any information to the real nuclear command centers: the White House or Air Force One, the Pentagon, and the underground Strategic Air Command bunker complex outside of Omaha, Nebraska. Today there is not as much of a threat of nuclear war, and so the huge, sophisticated network of computers and radar are mostly put to work tracking and monitoring satellites.

The facility itself is under Cheyenne Mountain, a small rise near Colorado Springs. It is only fifty feet underground, which is rather insufficient to protect it from a direct nuclear strike. The security is no different from any ordinary military base. In fact, the staff offers guided tours to school groups and tourists on an almost daily basis. The facility is jointly operated by the Army, Air Force and Department of Defense, with extensive assistance from NASA owing to the nature of NORAD's current line of work.

Lt. Colonel Gene Wheeler, USAF, was a veteran of those frantic Cold War days when NORAD was the first line of defense against a Soviet first strike. He was a graduate of the Air Force Academy, with a degree in aerospace engineering specializing in orbital mechanics. He was posted to Cheyenne Mountain, not an hour's drive from the Academy. During his twenty-five years of service he was moved around a lot, but always to work with missiles in some aspect – Vandenberg AFB in California, Redstone Arsenal in Alabama – and finally brought back to Cheyenne Mountain to do the mundane task of tracking satellites.

Space is getting crowded. By 2012 there were no fewer than four thousand satellites in low earth orbit, with more being constantly launched to expand DirecTV's service or to provide satellite phone coverage to New Zealand or to track hurricanes in the South Atlantic or whatever. That's just active devices, not counting dead satellites that never reentered or bits of space junk that had fallen off. Nuts, bolts, solar panels, even tools and gloves dropped by astronauts float around the earth in stable orbit, posing a hazard to satellite navigation. Wheeler tracked and catalogued everything, defined orbital paths and advised the Air Force, NASA, SeaLaunch, and others on what orbits are available. He made sure nothing bumped, or even came close. Since your average satellite costs over five million dollars to build and launch, bumps would be a big problem.

Wheeler faced precisely such a problem, as displayed on his computer. His technicians had alerted him to a series of launches from Russia, each of which parked a small satellite in orbit dangerously near that of an American military satellite - specifically, the KH-12's or Keyholes. These are basically small Hubble telescopes, except they're aimed back at earth instead of out to deep space. They constantly take video and still photographs and transmit the pictures for American military intelligence. There are twelve of these machines, crossing the globe and systematically watching every trouble spot for signs of terrorist or aggressive militant activity. They cost just over half a billion dollars apiece, and so the military defines very private orbits for the Keyholes – a privacy the mysterious Russian satellites were now violating.

Wheeler's concern was somewhat offset by the prospect of challenge. His job had seemed trivial when he was first assigned back to NORAD, and after two years under the mountain he was continually amazed at how boring it could be. He had made every possible request for another transfer, had actually been considering an early retirement when this new incident cropped up. He actually had to do some math – the only part of his job that he still enjoyed – to project the new orbits and pinpoint their intersection with the military Keyholes. Then he had to explain the situation to the people at Vandenberg who controlled the birds, and at the National Reconnaissance Office in Virginia who owned them – it was kind of fun to whip some urgency into the techs and spooks who were usually just as bored as he was. Next he had to go through several different channels to gain authorization to view the exact position of the satellites; normally he could only access the approximate orbital paths.

The results were not dramatic. Although each of the twelve Russian mystery objects intersected the orbit of one of the KH-12s, the satellites rarely actually approached each other. The computer projected that they would not actually be in collision danger during the next twenty years – five years longer than the expected life span of the KH-12s When the satellites did actually approach each other, there would be about a mile clearance, which is hardly cause for panic. Wheeler did note, however, that in just six weeks all twelve satellites would cross just in front of their new neighbors within a two-hour span. Twelve near-misses in two hours would not please Vandenberg or the military intelligence agencies that relied on the satellite data.

Wheeler discussed the situation with his superiors at NORAD and the Pentagon, who also felt that this situation would not be acceptable. He was instructed to contact the Russian space center and request that the mystery satellites be moved. Wheeler's call was transferred to centers around the old Soviet Union before finally being put through to someone who both spoke English and knew what he was talking about.

"Spaceflight sub-director Andre Turbalov speaking, how can I help you, Colonel?"

"Mr. Turbalov, I'm sorry, I got a little lost with all of the transfers. Where exactly are you and what do you do?"

"I am in charge of all launch operations at the Kosmodrome in Kazakhstan. For my part, I was only informed that I was speaking to an American Colonel. What exactly, please, is your name and position, sir?"

"Forgive me. Lieutenant Colonel Gene Wheeler, USAF. I'm in command of NORAD Orbital Operations, Cheyenne Mountain, Colorado."

"Orbital Operations? Ah, you are a rocketman, just like myself. Excellent. How can I help you?" the Russian asked again.

Wheeler explained the situation, omitting the details of the American spy satellites. "Basically, we would like to request that the orbits of your satellites be altered, and we seek assurances in the meantime that your devices will not interfere with our systems."

"Well, I think they are not radioactive if that's what you mean. Are the objects in immediate danger of collision? And would it not be possible for you to move your own satellites yourselves?"

"That is possible, of course. But they are locked in to schedules and timetables that their owners have no desire to alter. To your first question, no, there is no danger of collision, but our systems are very sensitive in nature and their controllers have established boundaries we prefer not be crossed. Your satellites are crossing those boundaries."

Turbalov was silent for a moment. Then he said "We are talking about spy cameras, yes?"

"I am not permitted to comment on the nature of our satellites." *I suppose it's pretty obvious, anyway,* Wheeler thought.

"I am thinking, Colonel, that I know more about your not-spy satellites than the ones I launched myself. I will be candid with you, sir. I have no idea what those devices were, or who owns them. They arrived by train under armed guard, and I was faxed launch orders authorized by the Air and Space Marshal himself. I have no control over the units, and I don't know who does."

Wheeler was alarmed by this revelation. "Isn't that unusual?"

"Not so much as you may think. If it is a secret military device, it is done this way. If it is a commercial unit owned by a foreign company, it is done this way. If the owner simply wishes to remain anonymous and if the Marshal is not above taking bribes, then it is done this way."

"How likely is that?" Wheeler asked. That last part was very unsettling.

"Quite likely, I am sorry to say. I have known the Marshal for many years, and I would not call him a man of upright character. And I have it on good authority that he is living beyond his means."

"I see," Wheeler said, even though he didn't. *How can anyone get away with this? The Air and Space Marshal is like the Secretary of the Air Force and NASA Administrator combined!*

"Listen, I know that this sounds like bad news for you, but I will sort this out. As I said, the Marshal and I have history. I will take this up with him and he will get the satellites' owners to make the adjustments as you request. How much will they have to be moved?"

"Just raised or lowered five miles in altitude. That will take them out of our defined perimeter. Thank you, Mr. Turbalov."

"No problem. Happy to help you. You have good night, yes?"

## MOSCOW

Andre Turbalov sent a memo up to the Marshal, outlining the American's request. The Air and Space Marshal knew exactly what satellites his friend Andre was referring to. The owner of the satellites did indeed wish to remain anonymous and was actually much more secretive than those that the Marshal had dealt with in the past. Two weeks ago a man in an expensive suit had walked in to his office, dropped a thick, unmarked manila envelope on his desk, and walked out without saying a word. The envelope contained explicit instructions regarding the launches, and two hundred thousand dollars, American, cash. There was also a business card that bore only the words *New Patriotic Enterprises* in English and a Postal Service box number for Moscow. There was no listing for such a company anywhere in Russia. The Marshal asked the security personnel to check the identification of the visitor. The papers were all in order, but they could have easily been forged. The name the man had given was the Russian equivalent of John Smith.

Now the Marshal wrote a letter addressed to that P.O. Box and fake corporate entity reiterating the request, explaining in no uncertain terms that he would do everything possible to ensure his client's privacy, and attached a copy of Turbalov's memo. He gave the letter to his secretary to be included with the outgoing mail. Two days later he was informed of the death of Andre Turbalov, who was apparently the victim of a mugging gone awry. Before he could do anything else, the same man named "Ivan" walked in to his office, placed an identical, thick, unmarked, manila envelope on his desk and left without saying a word. The envelope contained $300,000 US in cash, and two typed words on a single sheet of paper. *Kakie Sputniki?* – What Satellites?

The Marshal called the director of the Federal Security Bureau, one of the successors to the old KGB and the equivalent to the American FBI. "I just received a..." He looked again at the pile of money on his desk and changed his mind. "...A phone call, and was told that my friend, the sub-director of space flight operations at the Kosmodrome was murdered. I want to know how you plan to proceed with the investigation."

"Well, Marshal, I have just seen that report myself, and I am sorry in a personal way, but we of course have no official capacity in the Republic of Kazakhstan. We will be in touch with local authorities, of course."

"You do have unofficial channels of persuasion, yes?"

The Marshal could feel the other man bristle across the telephone lines. "I do not like what you are implying, comrade. These are not the old days of the KGB."

"I am all too aware of that, but a senior official of my administration and a personal acquaintance has been killed and..." he hesitated, but continued before his greed overrode his conscience again "I suspect there may be something more sinister than a petty thug behind this murder."

"What are you suggesting?"

"There may have been blackmail involved," he blurted. *Careful now.* "Something about mysterious satellites he was talking about the other day. Something smells of a cover-up to me." *And I know what it is. It's the smell of those freshly printed US hundreds all over my-*

"Very well sir. We will be very much involved with the local authorities and assist their investigation as needed. Off the record, I will personally see to it that we get to the bottom of this."

The Marshal realized too late that his phone line was probably tapped by the "New Patriotic Enterprises" people. As he drove back to the Kremlin from his bank, a twenty-year-old black Volga sedan ran a red light and rammed his Mercedes limousine broadsides. He woke up in the state hospital, and discovered a manila envelope on his bedside table. The sheet of paper inside read *Posalujcta ne poprobjte to cnova.* – Please do not try to do that again.

## BAGHDAD, IRAQ – SAME DAY, APR 7<sup>TH</sup>

The man known as Kahlil walked fearlessly through the Jadiriya suburb of the ancient capital of Iraq. Before Saddam Hussein came to power, this had been the Beverly Hills of Baghdad: the finest section of a prosperous and elegant city. Under the Hussein regime, the city decayed into squalor. Only the neighborhood of Jadiriya had held on to the wealth of Iraq's glory days, and only then because it had become the home of Hussein's entire administration. He and each of his sons had palaces there, and mansions once owned by trade magnates and oil sheiks were seized by generals and yes-men.

In the aftermath of Operation: Iraqi Freedom, Baghdad had undergone another transformation. Jadiriya cowered while the rest of Baghdad celebrated the fall of the tyrant. The Ba'ath insurgents, who were mostly Saddam loyalists anyway, had made Jadiriya their home base for the Baghdad area. Consequently, many of the grand homes had been bombed beyond all recognition during the many months that the Americans had fought to rout the remnants of Saddam's army in firefights with American and Iraqi security forces. Then later as the insurgents and sectarians began targeting civilians, Jadiriya became quiet and the rest of the city was engulfed again in waves of violence. Those few who remained living in the mansions that still stood were mostly from the old elite and had switched sides as power changed hands.

Kahlil sought out two such men: brothers, both former captains of the Republican Guard – Saddam's secret police – who had advanced into the Mukhabarat – the General Intelligence Directive – and who made contact with the Americans in the early days of the fighting to help the Americans track down important members of Saddam's regime. These two had later been instrumental in helping American and Iraqi Special Forces infiltrate and destroy the Ba'athist insurgent network. Now they lived in their old luxury condos, secure in their safety but little else.

Kahlil had been their primary contact when they wished to go to the Americans. They supposed he was involved with the CIA in some capacity, which he neither confirmed nor denied. They only knew for certain that whenever they told him a secret, the Americans acted upon the information quickly. He may have been an Arab, or he may have been in disguise – he was rumored to be a man of many faces. The Iraqis thought he may have actually been an American Indian, but if that were the case he spoke exceptionally fluent Arabic.

Kahlil found the two former Iraqi agents eating dinner together, as they often did, in a once-popular restaurant across the street from their condominium complex. The proprietor had held on to his business in hopes that the rebuilding of Baghdad would quickly reach his neighborhood. If nothing else, it was the only open restaurant on that particular street. The staff recognized Kahlil, although they were surprised to see him, and led him back to the table where the only two other guests were dining.

The two agents were also surprised, and as Kahlil sat their sullen moods turned darker. "When we last saw you a few years ago, you left us with only a warning to stay out of trouble and an I.O.U." The taller man on the left spoke, in lightly accented, educated English. "I certainly hope you have brought us a more tangible token of your government's appreciation tonight."

"I am very sorry about that, Ellirat," Kahlil answered using the Iraqi's old code name. "You and Elessar must think very poorly of me and those you think I work for. I really am sorry, but you see, these rewards you were seeking are not for me to give."

Elessar, the younger of the two responded: "Yet you either have something for us or you want something from us, or else you would not have come here."

"Yes, and while we are stating the obvious, you two look like you could use a drink." Kahlil pulled a bottle of The Glenlivet from inside his coat, to the obvious delight of his associates.

"But we are Muslim; we can not partake," Ellirat said with utter insincerity, as the attractive waitress placed three glasses on the table.

Once she moved off, he said "Pour."

"Still not very good Muslims, are we?" Kahlil smiled.

"We try, we try, but we are corrupted by Western influences; single-malt Scotch whisky of course being one of our favorites." Elessar took a long swallow, than became serious once more. "But this is not all you have brought for us, is it?"

"Why not? I'm sharing a drink with old friends, in this charming café, reminiscing of past exploits. But I see you grow weary of this. I have more gifts." Kahlil produced two sheets of official-looking paper, checked them, and handed one to each man. "I believe this is what I promised you, when we last met."

"Unconditional pardons, signed by the Prime Minister of Iraq? Please, do not pull my leg, Mister- Oh, my holy God." Ellirat stopped smiling as he read the document. It was, in fact, an unconditional pardon, signed by Prime Minister Nouri Al-Maliki himself, and dated only the day before.

Kahlil smiled. "Assuming you two delinquents haven't done anything felonious in the last twenty-four hours, you're officially no longer fugitives."

Elessar read his pardon, identical to his brother's except for one detail. "How did you find our real names?"

"Never mind that."

"No, that scares me a little," the Iraqi operative said. "I know your name is not Kahlil, and I knew that you knew our names were not Ellirat and Elessar, but how in the world did you find out our real names?"

"He probably got them from the Mossad." Ellirat guessed. "Surely they have a pair of thick files on us. My brother, are you not familiar with the American proverb, 'never look a gift horse in the mouth'?"

"I already knew you were brothers," the American operative explained. "There were not a lot of guys with the same last name in the Mukhabarat, except for Hussein's relatives of course. And there are even fewer former members of your organization who are not confirmed to be dead. You were identified by elementary deduction, my dear Watsons. So, does this even us up a little bit?"

"Does it ever. My friend, I am so very sorry that I ever doubted you or the CIA," Ellirat answered

"That's good, because my employer wants to hire you now."

"We are to be agents like you?"

Kahlil shook his head. "No, you are going to be *assets*. Field agents like me eventually have to pay taxes."

"So you *do* work for the CIA."

"I work for one of the US intelligence agencies, obviously. But who we are does not matter. We need information from people you used to work with. We are most interested in your Iranian contacts. I know you have a lot of friends in the National Council for Resistance in Iran. Are they still reliable?" The NCRI was one of the largest and most well-organized resistance groups in the country. Officially disavowed by the US government because of alleged terrorist activities, they still drew considerable financial support under the table from the US and other western nations.

"We have tested them, every now and then, partly to keep our hands in the NCRI's business, and also so they would know we are not dead."

"Tell me what you know about the current power struggle."

Ellirat leaned back in his chair, sipped the whisky, and took on the air of a history teacher. "After the re-election of president Ahmadinejad in 2009, rumors began to circulate that the voting had been rigged. People took to the streets, protesting the outcome. After the massacres in Tehran in June, the protesters quieted down. Nevertheless, the majority of the educated Iranians feel that the election's outcome did not reflect the will of the people.

"President Ahmadinejad was swift to shut down all talks with the UN and US, especially regarding the nuclear programs. It was revealed that the president was involved in the terrorist group that attacked the American Embassy in 1979. He may have even participated. At any rate, the US does not officially recognize his presidency. UN levels sanctions on Iranian oil, and all imports into the country, very nearly making the same mistakes they made with our Iraq after the first Gulf War.

"President Ahmadinejad recently selected a new oil minister and is keeping him behind closed doors. This guy has sidestepped the embargo and opened the country to foreign oil development. Now Russia, China and France are pumping oil out of the country, and pumping money in. The UN is powerless to enforce the restrictions because three key members are not cooperating."

Kahlil nodded. This turn of events had gone completely unnoticed by the American public, who called for more cooperation with the UN to reopen lines of communication, unaware that the UN had shot itself in the foot and that no one in Iran's government really cared to hear what the US wanted.

Elessar continued: "We are hearing that the Guardian Council and foreign parties have formed a coalition, and may be orchestrating these events. The president may have started all of this, but it seems now that things have moved beyond his control. He can be counted on to fight American interests, and side with the religious leaders. But as it was before, it is the Ayatollah, and now also these foreigners, who rule the country."

"What foreigners?"

"Russian mafia, it seems, or a Chinese conglomerate, or maybe some renegade general, or, most likely, a combination thereof. We've heard the name Rannovich a lot. We don't know who he is, but he appears to be at the center of this cabal."

Kahlil stiffened. He'd also heard the name before. "What about the military?"

"We hear of purchases, and of weapons being moved in to the country, but as far as we know, no new hardware is showing up at their bases. We have friends who would see such things. So do you. If they were stocking up on new tanks and airplanes, people in your NSA would be the first to know."

"I have no knowledge of such things," Kahlil lied.

"Of course you don't. Anyway, large sums of money are changing hands and someone is buying weapons. These weapons then disappear in Iran."

"How are they being brought into the country?"

"Some of it actually comes through Iraq. Now that our esteemed Prime Minister decided to reopen the borders, they can get through almost unimpeded. All they have to do is dismantle everything and pass it off as farm machinery. Our friends at the railroad say that a lot of farm machinery is being railed in to Iran."

Kahlil nodded in tacit judgment of the Prime Minister's decision. Over late 2007 and early 2008, the Americans had launched a major undertaking to close Iraq's borders and interdict the flow of weapons and foreign terrorists entering the country. This allowed the American and Iraqi forces to overwhelm and destroy many of the more organized insurgent militias. But after a few months the Prime Minister had decided to exercise some independence and reopen the trade routes. Suddenly there were more bad guys running around with rocket launchers, despite the new Iraqi Army's best efforts to search every vehicle entering the country.

"Another disturbing rumor," Elessar spoke now, "concerns the IREG – their Special Forces. They have been making 'distance training' expeditions that may be covers for raids on Chinese and Russian military bases. Reports come of military equipment being destroyed by random terrorist strikes, or disappearing without explanation, and then a few days later we'll hear of equipment being sneaked into Iran. IREG goes out, a Russian or Chinese base goes dark, and half a dozen tanks are seen driving through the desert a week later."

"Why?" Kahlil asked. "They're buying, stealing and smuggling military gear, and it just vanishes? What are they planning to do with it?"

"I'm sure we are not going to like it when we find out," Elessar said. "But considering what they have already done-"

"I forgot, we did not tell you the worst." Ellirat interrupted. He pulled a folder out of his very old attaché case. "We just got this information today." He placed several photographs of trains on the table, all time-stamped from the third of April.

"These came from an Armenian fellow, who has the peculiar hobby of watching, documenting and photographing railroad activity," Elessar explained.

"That's not too unusual; lots of people do that in the US. Well, actually, those folks *are* kind of weird…"

"Well, you don't have many trains like this. Do you remember, about a week ago, hearing about a big, awful train crash in Chechnya?"

"Of course. But what does that have to do with Iran?"

"Iran's M.O. for military theft appears to involve terrorist acts that can easily be pinned on someone else. That is why they have gotten away with it. Look, I have here the consist table for the military train that was involved in the wreck. There were six engines, one hundred and ninety-five cargo cars, and fifty bunk coaches. These pictures were taken of six trains that passed from northern Armenia to Iran on the day after the crash. They total six engines and one hundred ninety-five cars. All the cars are covered with tarpaulins, but look here:" Ellirat pushed one of the photos forward. Kahlil leaned down to examine it closely, and immediately saw that on one of the cars the tarp had ripped away from one corner, revealing a BMP-2 infantry fighting vehicle on a flatcar.

Elessar selected two more prints. "The lighting was pretty bad when these pictures were taken, but on these two you can see the markings on the locomotives – they are Russian military. And on this one you can make out the numbers, here on the cab. Number 5995 – which is one of the engines from the military train that was lost."

"Gentleman, you are telling me that the hideous carnage I saw on the news was a cover to steal a brigade's-worth of tanks? The Iranians jacked a train, disposed of over two thousand troops, blew a bridge and the next train that passed by, and then let their fellow Islamic radicals in Chechnya take the fall?"

"Well, the Chechens are Sunni and so are the Muslim separatists in Xinjiang, so the Iranian Shiites don't really give a damn what happens to them, but you've got the big picture. The evidence is somewhat circumstantial, except for those engine numbers. But the pattern is clear. They are buying or stealing hardware any way they can, and they are definitely building up to something, probably even more heinous."

"What? Short of starting a world war, what could they dare to do that is worse than this?"

For that the Mukhabarat brothers had no answer.

# CHAPTER 4: CHANGING GEARS

## NAS FALLON – APR 7<sup>TH</sup>

Finishing TOPGUN meant enduring all of the ceremony that went with it, which included being alternately roasted and lauded by classmates and instructors. Roche, Nick Santos and fourteen other pilots were graduating, and Deuce was finally retiring, which made the ceremonies longer than usual. Each of the aviators took turns on the podium, accepting their "diploma," which is actually a thick folder of papers and certificates, and their new call-sign. The nicknames Navy pilots get stuck with are always assigned by their peers, and it is an honored tradition at TOPGUN for a graduated pilot to retire his handle and receive a new one concocted by the faculty. Santos, formerly known as "Santa Claus," became "Toymaker." Roche, who had been "Polar Bear" since his Pop Warner football days, was now officially "Sharkey."

"Your approach to combat, Commander," O'Wools had told him, "is most closely compared to the cold, instinctive, and efficient aggression of a shark. The shark is the ultimate hunter-killer: stealthy, focused, mechanical, lethal, and always on the move."

The ceremony and ensuing party lasted long into the night. Late the next morning, Roche went to the commandant's office for his new orders.

"What, you're leaving? Just like that?" the captain teased. "I know we spent all night saying goodbye to you guys, but don't you want to linger just a little longer?"

"Nothing personal, but its getting hot up here, and I would like to seek a milder climate for this summer."

"How about Florida?"

"Please, no."

"Virginia?"

"Not ideally."

"San Diego?"

"That would be perfect, I think."

"Good. Door number three it is. Seriously, every squadron commander in the service wants you. You have your pick."

"San Diego would be perfect."

"Ya know, the TV weather guys down there have the best jobs in the world. You get a six-figure income to be on TV for twenty seconds a night. '...So what's the weather like, Al?' 'Uh, nice. Really, really nice. Back to you.'"

Roche laughed, and looked at the transfer papers the captain showed him. "VFC-233 *Stingrays* – I haven't heard of that squadron. Air Wing Thirteen, that's on the *Reagan*, right?"

"Yep. That's where Deuce is going, too. He'll be your new CAG, so you better kiss and make up to him."

"That's okay. I like the old guy. Is this a Super Hornet squad?"

"Yeah, they're getting the newest planes. You'll have the block-2Cs; the very latest production batch. The Rhinos we use here are 1B versions. 2Cs have newer avionics and some really nifty countermeasure technology. The squad is brand new too; essentially it's two squads being reorganized into one. VA-23 *Rays* were a reserve squadron flying old A-6 Intruders – they're actually the last to use those birds – had them for thirty-five years. Long before that they were the first squad to use the old Douglas Skyray. VFA-113 *Stingers* was originally the first Hornet squadron. They were just retiring their 'C-models when someone got the idea of combining the two squads."

"VFC stands for 'fighter-composite,' right? I haven't seen or heard of many of those. This isn't an aggressor squad, is it?" The only two VFC squadrons Sharkey knew of were made up of F-5 Tigers, F-16n Sea Falcons and modified Hornet-As. They were based at Fallon and Pensacola and were used for other squadrons to train against planes that didn't look like other Navy jets.

"No, this isn't anything like that. You'll be on a carrier deployment. This is sort of an experimental thing – one single squad doing everything from fleet intercept to long-range strike – like the Tomcats used to do – along with all the odd jobs that Hornets usually get. They're gonna have four Fs and twelve Es plus two spares, with sixteen pilots and four wizzos, downsized from what used to be three dozen total crew in the two squads. Apparently a lot of the older guys are retiring, because they need a few bodies in senior squadron positions. That's where you come in." O'Wools showed Roche another page from the folder.

"They want me to be their new XO?"

"That's the idea. They think it would be good to have a Top Gunner be in charge of all the interceptor stuff. I was happy to recommend you."

\*        \*        \*

Roche left the office and walked across the tarmac to the TOPGUN hangar. He walked around his Super Hornet and found a maintenance technician on the ladder. He was spraying gray primer over his name where it was stenciled on the side of the cockpit. He watched the words "Polar Bear" get erased and nodded to himself. "Well, that's that." He stroked the wingtip pylon, running his fingers down to its needle-sharp point, and then he turned away. He went to the lockers to collect all of his gear out and found his friend Lt. Santos doing the same thing.

"So, what's the story, Sharkey?" he asked.

Roche smiled. "I'm still not sure I like that name."

"You don't like sharks?"

"Sharks are awesome. But I've never really identified with them."

"It'll grow on you. 'Karl "Sharkey" Roche.' It sounds better, anyway."

"Maybe. What about you, Toymaker?"

"Ha. I like it. It sounds like a Batman villain. Santa Claus is supposed to be some fat jolly old white guy from way up north, and me, well..." The lanky, devious young aviator from El Salvador shrugged. "Anyways, where'd they send you?"

"San Diego."

"Lucky. You got that XO slot for the new Rhino squad on the *Reagan*?"

"Apparently."

"I'm in the VAQ-138 *Yellow Jackets*. They just got the new EA-18g."

"The Growler? That's a sweet ride."

"*Grizzly*," Santos corrected, using the new electronic warfare aircraft's unofficial nickname. "I hate the name 'Growler' – sounds like you're talking about taking a crap."

"Definitely inappropriate for a plane that awesome," Roche agreed. The Growler is an extremely capable and specialized derivative of the Super Hornet, intended to replace the EA-6 Prowler, which itself was derived from the Vietnam-era A-6 Intruder.

"Anyway, it looks like we'll be shipmates. I'm in the same wing as you, but my squad's stationed at Lemoore."

Roche furrowed his eyebrows. "Lemoore? That's nowhere near San Diego."

"No, it's a few miles south of Fresno. Horrible place. You lucked out, buddy."

64

"So how are you planning on moving all your stuff from here to Fresno? Your motorcycle is awfully fast, but it doesn't offer much payload capacity."

"I planned ahead and reserved a U-haul truck. I got one of the big ones so I can load the Suzuki in the back."

"Good thinking."

"Just one problem. I went to pick it up a couple hours ago and brought it back, and loaded it already. The thing's huge. My stuff is gonna slide all over the place because there's nothing to hold it in."

"I got an idea. If I threw my stuff in the truck, would it fill up the floor space?"

"Probably. You want to follow me over to Fresno?"

"Sure. What's a wingman for? I'll trail you in my car and that way if you crash the truck trying to make it over Donner Pass I can call your mom and tell her you died screaming like a little girl."

"She doesn't speak English."

"*No problema,*" Roche replied. "*Yo hablo mejor Español que usted, baboso.*"

"*Chingatu, cabron.* I forgot you were a linguist."

"So, you carry my stuff over the mountains, I ride on your six, I help you unload and move in, and I pack my stuff in my car and head south by lunchtime tomorrow."

"You gonna help me pay for the truck rental too?"

"No way. I'm doing this as a favor. I could head south on the 395 now and be in San Diego in time to plug my TV in and watch the Tonight Show. I'll tell you what; you can keep anything of mine that I can't squeeze into my car."

Santos nodded. "Deal."

## NAS LEMOORE – 28 HOURS LATER

Roche closed the trunk of his Oldsmobile 442, relieved that almost everything had fit. He ended up leaving his TV with Santos, but the rest of the contents of his old room were stuffed inside his cavernous trunk and back seat. *I hate moving,* he thought, *even if I'm moving to the beach, I hate the whole process.* He opened the driver-side door and tossed his last bag – a flight duffel – into the passenger seat. As he sat down he looked at the bag. The patch sewn on to the flap bore his old "Polar Bear" moniker and a caricature of the animal. A similar patch was on his flight jacket. That reminded him he'd have to get his mother to redo them. *I should call her now. I'll be driving pretty close to the house anyway.* He checked the clock before he dialed – 2:30PM on a Saturday – he was sure his mother would be around the house. "Hi, mom."

"Karl! How nice to hear from you! I wish you'd call more."

*Here she goes. I just called home last weekend.* "Yeah, well, sorry. It's been a busy week for me."

"Oh, yes, yes, you had your graduation ceremony, right? How did that go?"

"Well they don't call it that, but it went fine."

"First in your class again, weren't you?"

*One thing I hate about always being number one. She's going to have a stroke as soon as I come in second place at anything.* "Yeah, but there were only twenty-six people in the class, and ten of them dropped out…"

"Even so, I'm very proud of you."

*That goes without saying. You haven't stopped talking about how proud you are of me since I was born.*

"You probably broke a few more records, didn't you? Someone told your dad you were really shaking up the instructors."

*And there's another thing. Half of dad's old Navy buddies are keeping tabs on me…* "Well, they don't exactly hand out awards for that sort of thing, but I did give them a scare or two."

"That's my boy. One of these days you'll be an Admiral…"

*I* have *to get her off this track.* "I got my next assignment, mom. They're sending me to San Diego."

"Oh, wonderful. You won't be too far from us at all. Are you going to be on a carrier?"

"The *Ronald Reagan.* That's the one of the newest ones in the fleet. I'll be living on the airbase in Coronado, and I go for a cruise in a couple months."

"That's wonderful. It will be so good to see you; perhaps you could stop by on your way down there, even."

"I was actually thinking of that. I'm on my way down today. I'm actually about twenty miles south of Fresno right now. One of my friends got posted here. Anyway, I thought maybe we could go out to dinner…"

"Oh, you don't want to eat out."

*Yes, I do.*

"I'll make you something myself. I haven't made you a dinner since, well gosh, I don't remember. We were at your uncle's house for Thanksgiving, and Oma's for Christmas, and the last few times we saw you down here we'd always go out. Nobody let's me cook"

*Nobody let's you try to cook because you always use the smoke detector to tell you when the casserole's done.* His mother had grown up in an embassy, the daughter of the naval attaché to the British consulate. She had never learned to cook. And since it was a British embassy, the few things she could successfully prepare tasted terrible.

"I have this new lasagna recipe I want to try out..."

*Giving her a recipe is like giving a power tool to a three-year-old. It's going to be messy and someone'll get hurt.* "I'm not really in the mood for Italian."

Mrs. Roche didn't miss a beat. "Or I could always make a shepherd's pie. You must miss my shepherd's pie."

*Maybe if I was stranded on a frozen Antarctic island and I ran out of penguins. I have to talk her out of this.* "Mom, please. I don't want you to spend all day cooking. Besides, I thought we might want to celebrate a little." *That should be enough of a push...*

"Ooh! I could make a cake! And we have some champagne..."

*No, no, no.*

"And I could invite the Allisons and Richie and Lance..."

*No, no, no.* "Maybe you should talk to dad about this."

"Oh, he won't mind."

*There* has *to be a way out of this.* "It's real short notice to invite friends."

"Actually, we were going out with Allisons anyway. We had thought about going to Claim Jumper..."

*Perfect.* "Well, you don't have to change your plans on them. I'll just meet you at the Claim Jumper."

"Well. If you're sure you're okay with that, I'll just call the Jordans, then."

*Of course I'm okay with it.* "Yes, that's totally fine. I can be there by six. It's the one near the Brea Mall, right?"

"Right, but are you sure you'll be here that soon?"

"Yeah, no problem. It's mostly a straight shot down Interstate 5. It's not that far." *Only 250 miles. She won't figure that out though-*

"That's two hundred and fifty miles, isn't it?"

*DAD! Stop showing her how to read maps!*

"Well, I suppose the way you drive it's not so far. Just be careful, will you?"

"Don't worry, mom."

"Oh, I know I shouldn't. You fly fifty-million-dollar jets upside-down at a thousand miles an hour. You can handle a road trip down the valley."

*Am I hearing correctly or did she actually say something totally reasonable?* "Okay, well I'll see you at six or so."

"I need to get your bedroom ready."

*Uh-oh.* "No, mom, I'm not spending the night."

"But it will be so late, and you'll be tired after driving all the way down here. And we could go to church together in the morning."

"It's only an hour and a half further for me to go on to San Diego. And I need to move in to my new house, and report to my unit, and besides, I'll be up a couple of times next week to get all of my stuff out of the garage."

"Well, if you're sure you can't spend any more time with us…" she trailed off. Her disappointment was palpable.

*Why does she do this to me?* "Well, I guess I'd have enough time if we went to the early church service."

"It's settled then. See you soon, sweetie."


Just looking a Karl's car, you wouldn't believe it was capable of attaining the speeds he drove it at. But that's assuming you wouldn't recognize a cleverly concealed monster. It was a 1970 Oldsmobile 442 – one of the last of the great GM muscle cars from the heady days before the oil crisis. The 442 is derived from the Olds Cutlass coupe, and the number refers to the package of optional features that made the original '64 Cutlass 442: four-barrel carburetor, four-speed manual transmission, dual exhaust. The feature list changed over the years, but the name stuck. When Larry Roche had bought it new in 1970, the 455 cubic-inch engine with the rare W-30 performance package made 370 horsepower and over 500 pound-feet of torque, and could do 0-60 in six seconds flat. For its time, it was an undercover superfighter. It wasn't so showy as the Chevrolets and Pontiacs or the Ford Mustangs or the outrageous Dodge and Plymouth muscle cars. Yet it could outrun just about anything and was a fairly luxurious model.

Karl got the car from his dad on his fourteenth birthday, and had spent the last fourteen years modifying it extensively. He even used it as his senior project at UCLA to develop a turbo-supercharger system for the car. Karl had replaced or modified nearly every part of the 442, but was careful to make sure it looked even more unobtrusive than the original. Even the big shaker scoop that would feed his turbo-supercharger at high speeds was retractable so it wouldn't draw attention around town. A giant spoiler, which was also an engineering project at school, also retracted flush with the trunk lid. The car was painted flat matte gray, carefully shaded in order to disguise the more muscular lines of the car. The result was an incredibly powerful hot-rod, effectively disguised as an unrestored classic. As intended, the car rarely got the attention of traffic police.

Before getting on the Interstate, Roche had a fifty-mile stretch on State Route 41. Karl decided it would be safe to shift into flight mode on the sleepy highway. He switched the engine onto full activation (normally the big-block V-8 only ran on four cylinders to save gas) and engaged the supercharger assembly and twin turbochargers. This instantly tripled the engine's power. Then Roche deployed the spoiler in the back and ram-air scoop on the hood. The angular scoop popped up and extended three long, 4" PVC pipes which bypassed the supercharger and directly force-fed cold air to the turbos and intercooler. The arrangement looked so much like a battleship turret that Roche had taken to nicknaming the car "the Battleship." He even bought personalized plates designating the cruiser as "BB-442." The paint scheme matched as well, flat military gray and dark red along the rocker panels.

Running in this mode, the car accelerated effortlessly to 120 mph. Roche relaxed, confident that the modified suspension could deal with the excessive speed. On a straight stretch of roadway he diverted his attention to the stereo. He was beginning to lose the signal from Fresno's classic rock station, so he checked which CDs he had loaded into the ten-disc changer and selected one to play. A second later his favorite Avenged Sevenfold album was blasting through the twelve-speaker Alpine surround sound stereo and 800-watt Rockford Fosgate amplifier, triumphantly loud albeit slightly muffled by the bags of clothes he'd piled into the back seat.

Enjoying the extremely loud music, he failed to notice the warning of his radar detector as he approached a small side road. He saw the road, and slowed to a mere 90 mph as he passed it, and only then did he notice the Sheriff's patrol car waiting for him to speed by. He immediately dropped down to the posted speed limit but the cop already had him doing thirty over. The deputy only had to flash his lights once and Roche pulled over, careful to keep his hands on the wheel and not immediately reach for his license – a move a cop may mistake for going for a weapon.

"Please turn down your radio sir." Roche complied. "Sir, do you know why I pulled you over?"

Roche took a wild guess. "Something to do with violating the speed limit, right?"

"Do you know what that limit is, son?"

"Last sign I saw said '65'"

"Then why were you doing ninety-five?"

"To be honest, it was because I didn't think I'd see anyone out here. And I didn't see any particular harm in blasting along an empty stretch of highway at ninety-five. I was actually going a good deal faster, but I slowed down for the cross-street."

The deputy was amused. "I believe you. This is quite a car you have here. Let me see your license and registration."

Roche slowly pulled his wallet out of his back pocket, and then reached for the glove compartment. "The registration papers are in glove box, but you should know I also have a pistol in there."

"Okay, I'll need to see your permit for that too."

Roche removed the documents, careful not to touch his 9mm, and handed them over along with his driver's license and the Special Forces military ID that permitted him to carry a concealed firearm in any state.

"And is that a radar detector I see under your dash?"

Roche looked where the officer was pointing. "Yes. Yes it is. It's legal in both Washington State, where this car is currently registered, and in Nevada, where I lived until yesterday. I disabled it when I crossed the state line." Roche didn't actually know whether it was on or not, but the indicator lights on the device were dark. Anyway, he knew it wasn't technically illegal in California either as long as it wasn't mounted on the windshield. He wasn't sure whether the deputy was aware of that letter of law or not.

The deputy didn't press the matter, and began studying his papers. "Mr.- no, Commander Karl Roche?"

"That's me."

"Driving down from Fallon?"

Roche nodded. "I was just transferred to San Diego."

"You're kinda out of your way here."

"I made a side-trip to Lemoore, helping a friend move in."

"I see. Could you please remove your sunglasses?" Roche whipped off his gunmetal aviators, and the officer stared at him, then the license photo, then back at him, then at the military ID again, then back to him for a few seconds before handing everything back. "You were almost right about missing us. I was coming back from a call, but everyone else in the county is napping at their desks. Try to keep it below takeoff speeds, and slow down to about fifty or so when you go through towns, okay?"

"Will do, sir." Roche turned the stereo back up and drove off, waiting until the cop was out of sight behind him before he accelerated back up to triple digit velocity. *Military service benefit number 263, you never, ever get a speeding ticket.*

## BREA, CA

Karl pulled into the Claim Jumper parking lot at 5:54 PM; his car was back in stealth mode and it growled quietly through the crowded parking area. Roche noticed first a heavily modified Chevy Avalanche that he knew belonged to his oldest fiend, Jeff Allison. He also saw his dad's new Cadillac CTS-V, and two new silver AMG Mercedes coupes that he correctly guessed belonged to his second-oldest friend, Rick Jordan and his father, Lance. He walked in to the Gold Rush-era-themed restaurant and told the hostess he was with the Roche party. He was escorted back to a table set for nine and found six of the seats full. He spent the next few minutes hugging his friends and family, and in that time Wayne and Carrie Allison – Jeff's parents, arrived. The party settled into their seats, leaving Karl to take the remaining chair at the head of the long table.

Karl regaled them with slightly understated descriptions of his TOPGUN dogfights. They discussed his new assignment, and congratulated him on his new job. Karl turned conversation toward his friends, asking about Wayne's job with the County Sheriffs Department and Lance's car dealerships. Wayne had long since retired from his front-line duties as part of an elite anti-gang unit comprised of police forces from several different cities in northern Orange County. Now he did public relations for that task force. Lance had just opened his sixth car dealership, this one a Dodge dealer in Burbank.

Then they talked about Jeff's business. He had built a custom four-by-four shop that had become highly successful and garnered a large clientele among rich adventurers. The company was called TerraForce Industries. Jeff's huge Avalanche mod – which he renamed the "Landslide" – served as the flagship model in his growing catalog of custom off-road vehicles. Richie worked for ESPN, doing play-by-play for college football games during the fall and producing rebroadcasts of old games on ESPN Classic during the rest of the year. He had been a star receiver for USC while pursuing a degree in broadcast journalism. He had been drafted by the San Diego Chargers but he never played a regular-season game. His current job suited him perfectly.

The conversation wound down when desert came, as everyone indulged in the Claim Jumper's famous seven-layer chocolate cake. By 9 o'clock everyone was heading out.

The Roche family left church together at a little after 12:30. The pastor had given an inspiring if somewhat long-winded sermon on releasing your focus on your own ambitions and seeking God's will. Karl made a good effort to pay attention but lost all trace of interest about halfway through the second point in the lesson. After the service, he waited patiently while his parents socialized and reintroduced himself to people who wondered how he was getting along in the military. When it was all finally over, Karl hugged his parents and drove on south to San Diego.

He left Orange County on Interstate 5 and drove down the coast through the huge Marine base called Camp Pendleton, and entered the suburbs of San Diego. Just south of downtown, he exited at Dewey St. for the San Diego Bay Bridge – an enormous blue-painted steel causeway that spans the harbor. On the other side, he hesitated for a moment at an intersection. Every time he'd been here before, he had turned left, which led to the Naval Amphibious Warfare Training Center, and SPECWARCOM – headquarters of the Navy SEALs. Now he turned right, and drove up to the gates of Naval Air Station North Island.

The gate guard asked for identification, which Roche presented, along with his transfer orders. "And do you know where on the base you are headed, sir?"

"Actually," Roche answered, "I was hoping you'd be able to tell me. I'm supposed to move in to my house today, and find my CO tomorrow, but I have no clue as to where to look for either. I've never actually been here before."

The MP guard looked at his computer for a few minutes, and then presented Roche with a visitors' map of the installation. "We're at the main south entrance, here, okay? Your billet puts you here, on McClusky Street, unit 507, which is only a few blocks in from here. All the squadron HQ offices are in these two buildings here, next to runway 18 behind the main hangars. Your CO will be somewhere in here and your plane will either be in there, or the Air Wing 13 hangers across the runway. I'll give you a temporary vehicle pass for now, but you'll have to go to the security office to pick up a window decal tomorrow."

"Great. Thanks." Roche took the marked map and found his new house. All of the officer housing units were two-story town-home dwellings. The architecture was typically bland as most structures are on a base. The stucco walls were pained a khaki-greenish color which was fittingly military but not at all attractive. The trim was painted a shade of blue that simply didn't match.

Roche found two identical keys under the doormat and let himself in. The house was furnished with comfortable-looking leather sofas in the living room and new appliances in the kitchen. There were two bedrooms upstairs, both of which were about the same size, both contained a large dresser and a queen-size bed with new linens, and both had a private bath. Unsure of which one would actually be a "master" bedroom, he tossed the flight bag into the one with the better view and went back downstairs. Roche was making a mental list of the furniture he would need to buy as he moved through the rooms. *Big computer desk for my big computer, new TVs for the bedroom and living room (I shouldn't have gotten rid of my old one; well, I'd had that old twenty-inch tube since college; I'd want to upgrade anyway.) Entertainment stand for the living room, a bookcase or two, and a coffee table. Weren't mom and dad talking about getting new furniture? Maybe I can get some of this from them.*

Roche went back outside and looked at his car, and tried to work up the necessary enthusiasm to unload it. As he stood there, someone shouted "Howdy!" Roche looked and saw a guy ambling over; he was about five-nine, lightly built and hid his hair under a Texas Rangers baseball hat. "You movin' in?" he asked.

"No, I just like to carry most of my possessions around in my car."

The other guy laughed. "Right, well now that I've made an ass outta myself, how do you do? Lieutenant Jack Masterson, at your service."

"Lieutenant Commander Karl Roche at yours," Karl answered, offering his hand. "You fly?"

"Yep! In the new *Stingrays* squad."

"Were you in the *Stingers* or *Rays* half?"

"*Stingers*. Hornets, you know."

"Right. Well I'm your new XO. What's your callsign?"

"I'm called Blackjack," Masterson replied. "So you're the Top Gunner? Wicked cool. I hear you can do amazing things with a Super Hornet."

"Well, what can I say, it's an amazing plane," Roche shrugged.

"They say you never lost against an instructor. I'd heard it was almost impossible to beat them!"

"Don't buy the hype."

"If you say so, sir. Hey that's a nice car!"

"Are you in to cars, Jack?"

"Yeah, I drive a blown '02 Camaro. Did you restore this yourself?"

"And modified it heavily. I call her the Battleship." Roche reached across the driver's seat and toggled the switch to deploy the hood scoop and spoiler. Masterson whistled appreciatively. Then Roche popped the hood and waved the Lt. over to admire his handiwork. "As much as it killed me to destroy a rare work of automotive art, this old W-30 was run almost to the ground and way too far gone to properly restore. So I saved the block and squeezed everything I could out of it. I re-bored it from 455 to 480 cubes, and the headers, pistons and camshaft I had custom-fabricated from aircraft-grade aluminum. I built in an intercooler and twin turbos by Rajay, and a supercharger of my own design, all ram-air fed. But the chargers can be taken offline when I don't need the power. There's an exhaust bypass to cut off the turbos, and the pulleys that drive the supercharger can be disengaged." Roche showed him how everything under the "Battleship Turret" worked, which left Masterson quite impressed.

"Holy smokes. That makes the bolt-on setup in my car look like a toy. How much power does all that make?"

"1120 brake horsepower at 5500 rpm with everything running. Normally I cruise with the turbos engaged and only half the cylinders activated. That gets me 380 hp, which is still more than the whole engine made stock. The torque curve looks like Ayers Rock. I get a little over 900 pound-feet at 2000 rpm and 1050 at 4000. I have a custom-built six-gear transmission with a racing clutch and limited-slip differential to handle it."

"That's insane. What do you use that kind of power for, drag racing?"

"Occasionally. I usually run a quarter in less than nine seconds on slick tires. Once I almost got down to eight and a half. It does zero-to-sixty in well under three seconds without me even really trying, and with a perfect launch I'll nail two flat."

"Why haven't I seen this thing on the cover of Hot Rod Magazine?"

"I never bothered to show it off, but it's been on TV. Some guys from the Speed channel got me at Laguna Seca once."

"Yeah? How does it handle on a course?"

"It handles beautifully," Roche said, now genuinely pleased to have met this fellow muscle car enthusiast. "There's an aluminum space frame I built myself to reinforce the chassis. The suspension is all-new: Bilstein coil-over springs in front, rear leafs borrowed from a new Corvette, and custom-fit Koni dual-stage shocks for both axles. Then at the wheels I've got racing-grade compound brake pads, six-piston calipers, slotted and drilled carbon-ceramic rotors, all by Brembo. Everything's wired to a stability-control computer, which I can adjust to several driving modes, sorta like the setup in a new Ferrari."

"So, what kind of mileage does it get? That big ole engine must suck unleaded like a tank."

"It does at full power," Roche admitted. "But I get about the same mileage as a Honda Accord when I have it in street mode." Roche closed the hood and opened the driver's door. "Here, take a seat and fire it up."

Blackjack eagerly settled himself in to the front bucket seat. "Are these custom seats, too?"

"Naturally. Sparco racing seats, carefully disguised to match the original upholstery. I tried to keep the interior looking stock, but there's a lot of tech under the skin. An aluminum roll cage is hidden in the pillars, and I added a little insulation so I don't deafen myself with the engine. Speaking of which..." Roche handed him the keys, and Masterson started the big motor. The big-block engine growled quietly, then slightly louder when Jack revved the throttle. "Go ahead and hit those switches there next to the gearshift," Roche suggested.

Masterson looked down at the center console, and saw a row of switches labeled "super," "turbo," and "cyl. deac." He flipped them together and the engine brought its other half to life and forced extra air down through the huge carburetors. The engine roared with unnatural fury when Blackjack revved it again. "Yikes!" He shut off the ignition quickly. "I almost ruined your seats. I think if this thing was in gear it would have gone right through your house!"

Roche laughed. "That's a great exhaust note though, right?"

"Hell, yeah. What kind of system do you have back there? Borla? Magnaflow?"

"Custom-built Venom."

"I almost look forward to you waking me up with that thing."

"Nah, I always keep it sleeper mode unless I'm racing. If I were you I'd be more worried about my stereo."

Jack spotted the Alpine system in the dash and turned the key backwards to hear it play. "Man, isn't there anything here you haven't tricked out?"

"The interior trim is just restored original, that's it."

Jack looked around and nodded appreciatively. "Well sir, I think you're my new hero. This is by far the sweetest car I've ever seen."

"Thanks."

"You need any help unloading it?"


Roche was about to call his mother again to ask about the furniture, but she beat him to it. He answered his cell phone without checking the caller ID, and was more surprised than he should have been to hear his mother.

"How's the move-in going, honey?" she asked.

"Wow, mom, I just left, what, three and a half hours ago?"

"Is it a nice house?"

"Uh, yeah, well it was when I got here. Now it's full of empty boxes, but…"

"Do you need any furniture? Anything we can help you out with?"

"Yeah, actually, I think you can. I remember you were talking about getting new living room furniture. I could use your coffee table and entertainment center if you're getting rid of those."

"Well sure! And do you want a TV?"

"Which one?"

"Well, your sister is coming home for the summer, and she wants to bring her own TV. You know, the flat-screen one you got her for Christmas?"

"Oh, yeah."

"Well, she loves it so much she's driving back from Colorado with it. So I guess you can have the twenty-four-inch box, if you need it."

"Sure, I could use that in my bedroom. It's got a built-in DVD player right?"

"I think so. It's pretty heavy."

"Okay. I also need to get my little armory out of your garage. I'll come up there on Tuesday with a U-haul truck and get everything."

"I have a better idea. I'll call Jeffery and ask him if he wouldn't mind doing it."

"No, mom…"

"Please, dear. He said last night he'd love to help you move in if he could. He could just come down tomorrow and then you two can go hang out or something."

"Okay, mom. But let me call him, alright?"

"Sure, Karl."

Karl called Jeff at home.

"Yello, Allison residence."

"Jeff, it's Karl."

"Hey man, what up?"

"I could use a favor, if you have time in the next couple days. I need some stuff brought down from my parent's house, and it won't fit in my car. But you have those big trucks, so…"

"Right, no problem. What do you need moved?"

"The armory, a coffee table, that big wall unit in the family room, and a TV."

"Uh, well there's no way I can get that wall unit into the Landslide, but maybe I can borrow my wife's pickup. It's a lot lower and it has a bigger bed."

"That's what I was thinking."

"When do you need it?"

"Hopefully sometime this week."

"It's spring break for the school district, so she won't be teaching, obviously. I'll talk to her tonight and see if I can borrow it for an afternoon."

"I don't want to interfere with *your* work schedule either."

"Karl, I'm the boss. I can take a day off whenever I want."


Early the next morning, Karl drove across the base to the Air Wing 13 HQ building. He found the office of Cmdr. William Burke, CO VFC-233, on the second floor of the building, and knocked on the open door. "Good morning, commander."

Burke looked up. "You're early for your appointment. I just got here myself."

"I don't have an appointment, sir. My orders just said to report to you earliest."

Burke flipped through calendars and organizers until he found Roche's posting. "Oh. You are Karl Roche, my new XO?"

"Yes, sir." Roche's subconscious was sizing up Commander Burke. He reached the conclusion that he was probably a very good pilot and leader, or at least very well liked by someone up in the brass. There had to be something exceptional about him, because there weren't very many black guys in squadron command positions.

"Excellent. Pleasure to meet you. Call me 'Hannibal.' What's your callsign?"

"They call me 'Sharkey.'"

"Alright then. Now the whole squad's on leave until next Monday when we officially become an actual unit, so you can just hang out until then. We'll have a squad meeting at 0900 Monday morning in our hangar, which is 36E, right across the runways there," Burke pointed out the window. "They're repainting the emblem on the door right now. We're a brand new squad, as I'm sure you know. Most of us were from the old crews, but everyone is going to get introduced to everyone at the meeting. Then after that we're just scheduled to do training flights until our next deployment, which is supposed to be five weeks from now. Eh, since you've been up at TOPGUN for the last couple months, you can probably wave most of the training flights until we start the CQ gear-ups. You know the routine."

"Yes, sir. Thank you sir."

"You were flying Rhinos up there, right?"

"Yes, sir, there and with another squad on the *Lincoln*. I did the whole crossover training deal at Whidbey before that. I have about eighteen hundred hours in the Supers."

"You certainly know what you're doing then. Most of us are just starting with the crossover training. Okay, Sharkey. I'll see you in a couple days. Enjoy San Diego."

## LATER THAT DAY

With the official check-in taken care of, Roche was free to finish moving in. His arrangements with Jeff and his parents secured most of the furniture he needed, but he still didn't have a computer desk or a TV for the living room. Roche sat on his couch with his laptop on a wireless connection, and started shopping. He had worked for Best Buy stores on and off during high school and college, and he always used his store credit card whenever he bought anything from them, so over the years he'd racked up several thousand dollars worth of credit. He blew half of that bank on a 50" HDTV and a new home theater audio system which would be delivered to his house along with a technician to put everything together.

After another half hour he found just the desk he wanted, available from Office Max, and was informed that he could either pay twenty dollars additional for shipping which would take not less than ten business days, or he could pick it up that day from a store in La Mesa, northeast of downtown San Diego. Roche called the store and asked them how big the box would be, and confirmed his pick-up for around one o'clock. The rear bench seat of his car could tilt and slide forward to access the trunk, and that would provide just enough space for the big box.

Roche got to the store at 12:59, and left forty minutes later after wrestling the box into the trunk and avoiding crushing his car stereo components. He ended up having to remove his subwoofers in order to not smash them. The unassembled desk weighed about 150lbs, and on the way home he was trying to figure out how he would possibly get it up the stairs. He considered calling Lt. Masterson and asking for help, but he wouldn't use his cell phone while on the freeway.

Traffic was thickening on Interstate-8 as he approached downtown, so he decided to take his chances on the surface streets. As he entered the far right lane for the next exit he saw a car ahead of him in trouble. A double-semi was changing lanes, but the trucker couldn't see the Mini Cooper in his blind spot. The Mini's driver accelerated, but ran out of room and was unable to get in front of the truck, so the driver slammed on the brakes and pulled in to the shoulder to try to let the truck squeeze past. But the second trailer sideswiped the Mini and pushed it into a sound wall. The trucker drove off the freeway, unaware of the accident he had caused.

Roche pulled over on the narrow shoulder behind the trashed Mini. He watched for an opening in traffic on the busy freeway before opening his door. The Mini's driver stepped out at the same time. Roche was facing an amazingly beautiful young brunette, who appeared to be only in slight disarray after the dangerous accident. "Are you alright?" he called out.

"I think so. *I'm* not hurt, anyway, but look what that jerk did to my car!"

The girl looked back at him, and made eye contact. Her eyes – hazel, green-tinted eyes – were literally staggering. Roche felt like his knees would buckle. He took a deep breath and swallowed hard, before asking his next question. "Can you still drive it?" Roche found it helpful to look at the car and not at the girl. "We should get it off the freeway if we can."

"Yes, I think I can do that. It looks like nothing's really busted but sheet metal."

"There's a gas station right off the ramp down there." Roche was raising his voice now to talk over the noise of a passing SUV. "I'll follow you down there and we can call the highway patrol." She nodded at got back in her car, and drove down the off-ramp with Roche right behind her. Once they had parked, Roche called the non-emergency number for the California Highway Patrol while the young woman called her insurance company.

"CHP, how can I help you."

"Hi, I need to report a non-injury, hit-and-run traffic accident and request patrolman assistance." Roche knew it was standard procedure for them to send a car to the scene of any car accident on a highway.

"Sir, were you directly involved in the accident."

"No, I was not."

"But you did witness the collision, and the at-fault driver fled the scene."

"Yes."

"Describe the incident, please." Roche did. "And there are no injuries."

Roche looked the young woman over, taking a little bit more time then he needed. "None that are apparent, and she says she doesn't feel anything."

"Thank you sir, now are you still on the freeway."

Roche noticed that the dispatcher was delivering the questions like statements. "Just off I-8 at Morena Blvd. in the parking lot of a Shell station."

"Okay. I am sending a car there now. Can you describe the vehicles involved. You said a semi hit a Mini…"

"Right. A blue Mini Cooper S, and I only saw the second trailer on the semi…" Karl gave the dispatcher the plate numbers.

"Thank you sir. A patrol car will be on the scene in about three minutes."

Roche hung up and watched the girl talk on the phone. She was done with her insurance agent and had called a friend at school, asking her to explain to the professor why she would miss class. When she finished, Roche asked "what time is your class?"

She checked her watch, and answered "twenty-five minutes. I'm taking med classes at USD. Hey, thanks for all your help. My name's Tracy, what's yours?"

Again their eyes met, and Roche felt physically weakened by their spell. "I'm Karl. Karl Roche. And I hope you don't mind me saying, you have the most extraordinary eyes I've ever seen."

"I was thinking the same thing about you," Tracy Davis replied. The man who had stopped to help her was staring at her with a pair of eyes so deep and blue, they were like looking into an ocean. She took a moment to examine the rest of him. The eyes were set in a chiseled and tanned face that belonged in the movies; hard but handsome features, topped by light blond hair – almost white – combed back and slightly spiked. The head was mounted on a solid frame – a little less, she guessed, than six feet and around a hundred and eighty pounds. He wore a black t-shirt and blue jeans and white sneakers, but also an expensive-looking watch on his arm and aviator sunglasses pushed back in his hair. He had stepped out of an old muscle car that had been carefully restored, and probably modified – her father worked on old cars; she knew of such things. He was a man with money who did not bother to show it off with stylish fashions or new cars, but had his own tastes and indulged them. And he was quick to help people in trouble, and he had those eyes... Tracy wondered what the odds were of meeting someone like this, and she reminded herself that she did not believe in coincidence.

Roche had leaned back against his car, looking Tracy over. She was exquisitely beautiful, he realized when he tore his gaze out of her eyes. Her hair was exactly the same shade of brown as walnut wood. Her skin had the natural tan of a life spent in the Southern California sun, but under that was an ingrained darker tint. He guessed at least one of her parents was of Mediterranean extraction, and that matched with her body of a Greek goddess. *Stop staring at her, you idiot,* he scolded himself. *Talk to the girl.* "So, USD, huh? What are you studying?"

"Physical therapy and chiropractics. Right now I work part-time as a massage therapist at a day spa in La Jolla."

*Massage therapist. This is looking real good.* The CHP car arrived right then, interrupting Roche's opening.

"I hope this won't take too long," Tracy said. "Maybe I can still make it to my class at three."

The cop got straight to business. "Which one of you was involved in the accident?"

"That was me," Tracy replied.

The patrolman looked at the license plate on the Mini, then back to Tracy. "You are Ms. Tracy M. Davis?"

"That's right."

"And you, sir, you were a witness to the incident? What is your name and your employer?"

"Karl Roche – that's Karl with a 'K', R-O-C-H-E; – US Navy." The cop looked up for a moment, then back down to his notepad. Karl observed a very positive body language reaction from Tracy. *I guess she likes guys in uniform.*

"What is your rank, sir?"

"Lieutenant Commander."

"And I assume you're stationed on one of the bases around here?"

Roche nodded, "North Island Air Station."

"You're a pilot?"

"Yeah, fighters off the *Reagan.*"

"Cool," he said, and Tracy seemed to think so too. The patrolman went back to his notes. "So the truck cut you off on the exit ramp," turning to Tracy, "and you got sideswiped."

"Basically, yeah. I couldn't speed up or slow down fast enough to let him go by."

"And are you sure you aren't injured, ma'am?"

"Positive. I'm a physical therapist, so I know crash injuries and I'm very sure I don't have any."

"Good. I don't think we need any more evidence, then. If no one's injured, this is a pretty simple property case. They shouldn't need you two to come to court. We'll track down that truck and your insurance company should take care of everything at your end. Have you called your agent yet?"

"Yeah, first thing."

"Good. Let me get his contact information."

Tracy pulled a business card out of her purse.

"Now, you live at 171 Lemon in Santee, right?" the officer confirmed.

"That's it."

"And what's your address, Commander Roche?"

Roche frowned suddenly. The patrolman had wrongly pronounced his name with a soft CH sound. "It's Roche, with a hard 'kuh' sound. Rhymes with Coke."

"Ah, Dutch, not French," Tracy remarked.

Karl smiled at her. "German, actually."

"My apologies, sir," the patrolman said patiently. "Your address please?"

"507 McClusky Street, NAS North Island."

"Okay." The officer wrote that down. "Like I said, we probably won't need anything more from either of you, except maybe pictures of your car before you send it to the body shop, Ms. Davis. That'll do it. Have a good day."

The patrolman left, and Roche said, "It's probably a little late for this to be a good day for you, isn't it?"

"Well, it's only mid-afternoon. We'll see what happens next," she smiled meaningfully. She called the auto club next to get a tow truck sent out, but they told her that the insurance agent had already made arrangements.

Roche waited until she had hung up again and offered to give her a ride to the university.

"Thank you very much, but I don't know if it's necessary. It's only a few blocks away." She acted dismissive, but only to test him

"It's over a mile, which is long way to lug all those books. You'll get there way late for your three o'clock class, all tired and sweaty, you wouldn't like that. I could drop you off there in just three minutes, and you wouldn't have to miss class at all."

Tracy thought about it for only a moment. "Okay, I'll let you give me a lift now if you let me take you out to dinner tonight."

Roche was surprised, but agreed without hesitation. The flatbed tow truck arrived a minute later. Tracy told the driver how to get to the BMW-Mini dealer where she usually had the car serviced. Then Karl opened the passenger door of his Oldsmobile for her and they drove off to the university. After fastening her seatbelt, Tracy leaned over and gave Karl a peck on the cheek. "Thank you very much for your help. It's not often you find a Good Samaritan type around here."

"Anything for a beautiful woman."

"Ha! I'm flattered, but you pulled over to help before you could see what I look like. You have a kind spirit, Karl."

"And keen eyes and a taste for brunettes." Despite his light response, Roche was blushing red when he stopped at the medical building on the campus. "Obviously you're not going anywhere without me, so should I just meet you here?"

"Yeah, that's fine, at about 5:30, okay?"

"Will do."

"Thanks again, Karl."

\*      \*      \*

Karl returned to that exact spot at 5:25, wearing a gray button-down shirt and a blue tie, hoping to roughly match Tracy's level of dress. He had a wool sport coat in the back seat in case the restaurant required him to wear one. Tracy appeared at 5:29, wearing a cardigan over her dress and toting a book bag over her shoulder. "Hey, you don't have to dress up for me," she said.

"Well I wasn't sure where you'd be taking me, but I'm guessing it wouldn't be Taco Bell."

She laughed, and said "You look nice cleaned up. You like seafood?"

"Absolutely."

"Oceanaire Seafood Room. Reservation for 6:15."

"You're taking me to the Oceanaire?" The restaurant in the historic Gaslamp District is justly famous for serving the best seafood to be found anywhere in San Diego. Consequently, it was very expensive. "I would have been happy with Red Lobster."

"I wouldn't. Don't worry, I actually make some money, you know. Thirty bucks an hour, which is pretty good for a college student. And here you are getting us in to our first argument, and we've only started our first date. Time's wasting."

Roche obeyed, trying not to show the grin he felt. He liked Tracy more every second he spent with her. He turned up the stereo and drove south to Pacific Highway.

"Is this Muse?" Tracy asked.

"What, the CD? Yeah, it is."

"I *love* Muse. But I don't think I've heard this song before."

"This is their first album. They didn't sell it in the US."

At the next stoplight, a kid driving a tuned-up Mitsubishi Evolution pulled up next to him. The kid waved at Roche and revved his engine. Roche smiled and shook his head, and the kid shrugged disappointedly. Tracy asked, "You're not going to race him?"

Roche was surprised. "You think I should?"

"This thing has to put down, what – six, seven hundred horsepower? Why would you have that kind of power if you're not going to use it?"

"More than that," Karl answered. "But I only use it legally, at a racetrack, and only against cars in my class." The light turned green and the Evo peeled out down the street. Roche followed at a leisurely pace. "Well, maybe I'll occasionally run a street race if there are no cops around and some punk really needs to get schooled, but not here in downtown."

Up ahead the kid slammed his brakes to avoid running a red light just as a police car rolled by the other way. Roche could see the cop glaring at the young driver, but the officer ignored the Oldsmobile when he passed them. Roche stopped gently next to the Mitsubishi again. "It would be no contest with ricer-boy over there anyway. He thinks his stickers and that carbon-fiber park bench of a rear spoiler make him go faster. I've got at least three times as much power as he does."

Tracy looked into his eyes and said in a soft voice, "You should know that I am turned on by fast cars." Roche raised his eyebrows at that and revved his engine in response to the Evo's challenge. The kid pushed his throttle to the redline, and grinned at the sound made by his own whining turbocharger. He flashed his smile at Roche, who suddenly flipped all his switches and revved his own engine one more time. The enormous V8 – now running on all cylinders and being force-fed twenty psi of extra air – made its thunderous sound, startling both Tracy and the kid in the Mitsubishi. Roche's eyes darted up and down the streets, making sure it was clear of police. He made a tire-smoking launch when the light turned green, leaving the Evolution choking on a cloud of scorched Goodyear rubber.

Tracy shrieked in delight as they crossed the next intersection only seconds later and half a block ahead of the Mitsubishi. Roche shifted gears and let off the gas, and let the thoroughly embarrassed ricer catch up. "What the hell *is* that thing?" the kid called out. Karl just waved and shot away again.

They made it to the restaurant with six minutes to spare. Tracy ordered shrimp and scallops over linguine alfredo. Roche had the seared ahi tuna steak and the lobster bisque. They shared a bottle of California Zinfandel while they ate their appetizers; Tracy finished it with her pasta and Karl had a glass of Shiraz with his fish. After the waiter delivered the main course Tracy looked up at Karl, eyes wide with interest. "So tell me about the planes you fly," she asked.

"Well, ever since I started flying six years ago I've been in the F/A-18 Hornet – that's a fighter-attack jet." Roche's tone and expression gave away the fact that he presently regarded the very juicy and succulent piece of fish on his fork with far more import than his fifty-million dollar fighter. Tracy was showing an unusual level of interest in his jet, however.

"My dad's an engineer for Boeing, and he works on the Super Hornets. Are those the ones you fly? The new E/F models?"

Roche swallowed hard. He had never met a woman who knew anything about military jets. "That's right. I've flown in those for a couple of years now. What does your dad do on the program?"

"He works at the old McDonnell plant in St. Louis. He does something with installing the on-board computer and calibrating the interface, I think. I have no idea how it works."

"Well, you know more than most people, it seems. Tell your dad I said thanks, next time you talk to him. That computer is a wonderful system."

"How exactly does it work? I mean, how does it improve the plane?"

Roche sipped the Australian red wine while he thought about how to phrase it in layman's terms. "You know how a plane flies, right? Pitch, roll, yaw, thrust, drag, lift and Bernoulli's principle?" She nodded. "Basically, the Hornet's got more control surfaces than I can keep track of. You know, rudders and ailerons and flaps and slats and stuff. It's got two control surfaces for each axis of motion, plus the strakes, which work in roll and pitch, and the engines, which can alter pitch, roll and yaw all by themselves as well as obviously controlling thrust. I'd lose my head trying to make that all work for me while I'm trying to shoot someone down. The SHOC, the computer your dad works on, takes my basic input from the stick, throttle and pedals," he pantomimed his hand placement in a cockpit, "and translates that for all the different control surfaces. If I pull the stick faster, it adjusts the strakes to make me climb faster. It adjusts everything so the Hornet can do tricks that I can't tell it to do myself, and keeps me in control when I try and make the plane do something crazy."

"That makes sense. So it's sorta like the electronic all-wheel-drive and traction control systems on certain cars."

"Exactly." *Wow, she's sharp.* "It also connects with my navigation and targeting systems, and it links me with the other Hornets in my flight."

"So if your wingman has a radar contact that you can't see, the link up can show you what he's got on his screen, like a pix message on a cell phone."

"You catch on quick."

"Well, I'm sure dad will be glad to know how much you guys appreciate it."

"So, did you grow up in St. Louis?"

"No, actually, my parents moved back there in '02. Before that, my dad worked in Anaheim, where they designed the SHOC."

"You're an Orange County kid then," Roche said. "Me too."

"Oh, yeah? Where'd you live?"

"Yorba Linda."

"My old house was in Brea, just off Harbor, north of Imperial."

"I used to work at the Best Buy right there, when I was in high school."

"So what do your parents do?"

"My dad's a cardio surgeon at CHOC."

"Children's Hospital? So he helps sick kids? That's wonderful!"

"Yeah, he loves his work."

"Okay, now this may seem like a silly question, but when did you first realize you wanted to be a fighter pilot?"

"You know, it was such a gradual thing I'm not even sure myself when exactly I made the choice. Well, when I was nine I discovered I really liked cars, and all the way through high school I didn't enjoy anything so much as playing with cars. So when I was a senior I realized I would either be a mechanic or an engineer if I was going to play with cars for a living. So I went to UCLA on a football scholarship and studied mechanical engineering. Then I discovered aerospace, and I enjoyed that whole aspect of engineering so much more, so I made a switch."

"Then how did you get from designing airplanes to flying them?"

"I took Navy ROTC classes to make up a few credits, and then they offered me a scholarship when I decided I wasn't going to be a pro football player. After I graduated I went into Special Forces, but I got hurt in Iraq. The injury made it hard for me to swim, so I left the SEALs and took up flying instead."

"You were in Iraq?" Tracy's interest suddenly intensified. "For how long?"

"I wasn't even over there for a month before I got hurt."

"What happened?"

"I got some shrapnel in my shoulder."

"So, now you can't swim at all?"

"Well, I can dog paddle well enough to escape from a sinking ship, but that's about it. I can't rotate my left shoulder all the way, so I can't swim fast or far enough to qualify for the SEALs."

"That's too bad."

"Well, I wish I hadn't been injured, but I am glad I ended up in aviation. It's a lot more fun. Maybe it's more dangerous, statistically, but definitely a lot more fun. So how about you? How'd you get in to physical therapy?"

Tracy laughed. "That's not as exciting as your story. I graduated from high school without any college or career aspirations, so I went to Fullerton Junior College and took random classes until I found something I liked. That turned out to be massage therapy. So I got licensed in that and transferred to USD, and that's where I am."

"What do you want to do when you finish?"

"Open my own practice somewhere, or join a big hospital office. I'm not sure."

"But you're not planning to marry a rich doctor."

"Not at this point. That's plan B, I guess. Do you want dessert?"


After they finished eating, Tracy paid the check with her American Express card. "This is the first time I ever let a woman buy me dinner," Roche said. "To tell you the truth, I don't mind a bit."

"See, you can be a gentleman without having to worry about all the details of chivalry."

"Speaking of which, I suppose you need a ride home."

"Karl, I've had a great time with you today. You are a wonderful man, and I would like to continue seeing you."

*Thank you, Lord.*

"But I need to apologize for maybe giving you the wrong impression with some of the things I said. I... I don't believe in getting physical, I mean all-the-way physical, until after marriage, or at least until I'm with the man I know I want to marry. Would you be okay with that?"

*Well, now, I think I should be feeling disappointed, but for some reason I'm not. This actually makes her even more attractive.* "Yes, Tracy, I'm okay with that. I totally respect that you want to go by that principle. It's a rare and beautiful thing, especially when you're this upfront about it."

"I'm glad you see it that way."

Roche drove her home and walked her to her door. He was rewarded with her phone numbers and a goodnight kiss on his cheek. He drove back to the base with a funny feeling in his chest. He was sure it wasn't the wine he'd had with dinner. He suspected it may be something like love.

# CHAPTER 5: BRIEFINGS

## THE WHITE HOUSE, OVAL OFFICE – 0900 EDT, APR 11TH

"Deputy Director Casey, my favorite spook. Pick a chair. Do you want coffee?" Brett McNeil, the new President of the United States rose and walked around the desk to shake the visitor's hand

Jarrod E. Casey had delivered the weekly Presidential Intelligence Operations briefing every Tuesday morning for the last six years. After the first five weeks under the new administration, he stopped accepting the President's coffee. Maybe it was just the way they liked it in the Southwest, but Casey thought it was awful. It was too bitter, too strong, and too hot. "No thank you, sir." Casey plopped down in the same leather sofa he always sat in, and the President came around the desk and sat in his favorite armchair, right in front of the *Resolute* Desk and within easy reach of all of his papers.

Casey liked a lot of things about these briefings. They made an excellent reprieve from his other duties as the Central Intelligence Agency's Deputy Director of Operations. As the Agency's number-two man, and a lifer, he was in charge of all the dirty work the Agency carried out around the world. It was a messy and thankless job, and although he was exceptionally good at it, he was glad he got to take a weekly break. For one hour each week, he had the undivided attention of the most powerful man in the world, and the one man who was allowed to know what Casey and his people really did.

The DDO was still feeling his way around the new President. After five years under George W. Bush, he had grown to like the guy. The former President really wasn't nearly as dumb as a lot of people thought. Even though Casey often disagreed with many of his policies, he approved of the job he was doing overall. Perhaps this was because he had the benefit of insight into what went on behind-the-scenes on the foreign policy issues. The new man in the Oval Office was a very different character. He certainly looked better on camera and he certainly knew the wet work of geopolitics, but he wasn't always easy to get along with. He put up a friendly façade, but he could turn on his friends and advisors in an instant if he didn't like their ideas.

Casey put his personal thoughts aside and got to business. He had 58 minutes to bring the Commander-in-Chief up to speed on the latest crisis. "I want to brief you this morning on the Iran situation, Mr. President. Did you get the last memo I sent you?"

President McNeil reached into his inbox and rifled through the stack for a moment before drawing out the faxed message. "Signs of foreign influence in Iran's power structure."

"That's the one. Our agents in Russia confirmed what appears to be the source of that influence." Casey pulled a very slim folder out of his attaché case and dropped it on the table between them. "That is our complete dossier on a man we know only by the name 'Rannovich'."

The President opened the file and picked out the man's picture: a scowling face with dark eyes and a knife scar on his chin. "That's an unpleasant-looking character."

"Trust me, sir; he's far more unpleasant than he looks. The Russians fingered him in a series of violent murders among the upper echelons of the Russian Mafia. We think these murders have given him complete control over several key factions of the mob, and their various spheres of influence. We know for sure that he used to be a young general – a rising star actually – in the Soviet Army. Then he was disavowed for some reason and his files were buried. We can't find any records that refer to him by name. Anyway, he maintains extremely strong connections with the Russian military. His industry connections are, if anything, stronger. He's a silent partner in KUPEC – the largest petroleum producer in Europe – and United Aircraft Corporation, which was recently formed to bring all the formerly independent Soviet aerospace design bureaus back under one roof. And then, of course, he has access to all the mob-controlled companies and workers' unions in the country."

"I assume Rannovich is some sort of alias, right?" McNeil was still looking at the man's file. "What's the significance of that name?"

"All we could come up with was that it's the name that Carlos the Jackal supposedly used when the KGB trained him during the sixties."

"Okay, so he's a major player in Russian organized crime, military and industry, and likes to identify with an infamous hit man. What's he got to do with Iran?"

"Oil. He's very definitely orchestrating oil deals with the Iranian government."

"That's old news," McNeil said. He knew this particular side of the situation very well. "KUPEC's been developing Iranian oil reserves since the nineties, ever since Clinton screwed up our chances to get in. And the Mafia connection with KUPEC is also well established. After they bought out LukOil, they became the second-

90

largest petrochemical company in the world, and the way they do business makes Exxon-Mobil look like a Girl Scout troop. They're drilling up cheap crude around the planet and hoarding most of it."

"That's all true, and in the last decade KUPEC has established quite a line of credit with the Ayatollahs. That influence has let Rannovich proceed to the next stage. This is a picture of the new Iranian Oil Minister, appointed a couple weeks ago." Casey handed the photo over.

"Okay, this guy looks like any other cabbie to me. Who is he?"

"The Four of Diamonds."

The President looked up. "It's been a while – remind me which Iraqi scumbag you're talking about."

"It's Sheik Akandhras."

"Saddam Hussein's finance minister?"

Casey nodded. "Saddam made a lot of money on oil before we busted the whole regime. But somehow this guy disappeared with all the account numbers. We weren't the only ones looking for him. This picture was taken in Montenegro, six days after the fall of Baghdad. On the left you see Akandhras. One of these guys on the right is a Russian Mafia underboss, the other two are midlevel peons. They caught our eye because these three have no business in Montenegro. They're from the Baltic sector, and are notable only for being part of Rannovich's original crew. Four days later, they all walk in to the Orient Exchange Bank in Geneva, and leave hours later carrying two armored cases apiece." Casey produced more photo printouts. "Here they are getting off the plane in St. Petersburg, the day after they were seen in Geneva. They are met by more Mafia chiefs, including someone who appears to be Rannovich. Later that day, the whole party goes in to KUPEC's headquarters in St. Petersburg."

The President looked over the pictures in sequence several times, as if trying to piece together what had happened over the five days they represented. "Did the Russians apprehend him or was Akandhras seeking them out on his own?"

"At the moment that is unclear, but also irrelevant."

"But this all happened years ago. What's the relevance now?"

"We don't know exactly what he was doing with KUPEC for the last few years, but we know he's deeply and enthusiastically involved with their game now."

"Okay. So Saddam's main money man skips out with all of Iraq's cash, goes to the Russians, and now somehow after several years of manipulation, KUPEC has installed him as the Oil Minister of Iran. I do not like this, Casey."

"I didn't think you would. Neither did most of the Iranians. No one outside President Ahmadinejad's inner sanctum and KUPEC's board of directors was told about the appointment. I don't think even the Mossad has found out about this."

"How did *you* find out?"

"You're not supposed to ask."

"I don't actually want to know. Are you going to let the Mossad know?"

"Not until we need something from them. You know how that works."

The President shrugged. "I guess they still owe us a couple of favors after the whole Lebanon thing anyway."

Casey smiled. "It really is better if you don't ask."

"If you say so. Now, was it Rannovich's idea to let the Chinese and French oil developers into Iran? Because right now I'm trying to get the UN to shut that whole discourse down, and I'm getting blocked at all levels."

"Yeah, the funny thing about UN sanctions is that you can't enforce them when three out of five members of the permanent Security Council are violating them. I don't know why France is involved, but Rannovich does have connections with several senior Chinese military staff, and a conglomerate called New Patriotic Enterprises. That conglomerate, in turn, controls three major defense contractors, a giant shipping firm, and two major oil companies which are both drilling in Northern Iran and the Caspian Sea as we speak. By the way, all of the actual drilling and construction on Iranian oil projects is being done by Mafia-controlled Russian companies."

"Dear God. This guy actually bought Iran."

"Yes, he did. And he's put together a little cabal to help him run the place. There's the NPE people, a half dozen Chinese Generals and Admirals, and more Russian mafia and ex-Soviet Army types. Then in Iran we got the sheik, the mysterious new Supreme Ayatollah who apparently has no name, President Ahmadinejad, the head of the IRG – General Rezai, and Iran's leading nuclear scientist – guy by the name of Saburi. The whole bunch is orchestrating quite a game over there. Now are you ready for the really bad news?"

The President leaned back, massaging his forehead as though fighting a headache. "Does it have anything to do with a series of deadly terrorist attacks on Russian and Chinese military targets?"

"How, may I ask, did you leap to that conclusion?"

"I had dinner with the Israeli Ambassador last night. He told me that you might be bringing some really nasty news about the train crash in Chechnya last week, and two missing Russian subs, a couple Chinese transport jets that crashed in Tibet…"

"Figures the Mossad would beat us to it," Casey said. "They have more agents in Chechnya than the Russians do. Anyway, we have very good reason to believe that the Iranians were involved with those incidents. The NSA says that there was an increase in signal traffic between the Iranian military high command and the IRG Special Forces precluding each incident you mentioned, and half a dozen more, lower-profile attacks. Most of the evidence is circumstantial. Like a dozen retired submariners flew from London to Murmansk the day before the subs went out. But on that Chinese plane crash, there was a terrorist attack right before they took off that may have been a cover for a hijacking. Three dead Persians were left on the scene at Tsianxiang airbase. Here are their coroner's reports."

"How lovely." The President didn't bother to look over the photos of the Iranians that had been dug out of the rubble of the Chinese guard barracks.

"And there was never any wreckage found from the planes. Of course that was way up in the Himalayas so they'd probably never find anything anyway, but they did find the transponders from the planes just sitting by themselves, and nothing else. That makes it look a lot like a hijacking."

"That makes sense."

"Then the Chechnya incident is quite the figurative train wreck. They can't identify any actual wreckage because everything was completely melted down. That gorge was a blast furnace for several days after the fuel train fell in. But we think someone stole the front end of the military train with all the heavy equipment and dropped the passenger cars and the fuel train off the bridge to cover their tracks, pun not intended. We got pictures from Armenia that look like what was left of the military train going through toward Iran."

The President summed up. "Chechens take the rap, Iran gets a free armored brigade, and two thousand soldiers die. I've never heard of an uglier robbery."

"Not all the thefts were that violent, fortunately. For instance, a Malay-registered container ship actually owned by New Patriotic Enterprises loads up at a naval weapons depot in Canton instead of at the cargo terminal, and unloads in Bandar Abbas instead of Mumbai.

Then a shipload of disassembled Sukhois which was supposed to go to Shanghai somehow ended up in Bandar. All of these cases, whether it's misdirected traffic or an actual terrorist attack, had inside help. Obviously Rannovich has partial control over United Aircraft Corporation, and NPE can send their ships anywhere they want. As for the military attacks, in each case the commander responsible for the base or the train or whatever was a rival of one of Rannovich's friends."

"Naturally."

"In all, we think the Iranians have stolen about four divisions'-worth of armored vehicles and maybe two hundred aircraft, not to mention a pair of Kilo-class submarines, but those may well have sunk unless they are being very cleverly hidden. The NSA and ONI haven't been able to find them, as far as I know. And then there's Dassault."

"The French aircraft company?"

"They opened a plant a year ago in Lebanon to build Defiant fighters and export them without the French government restrictions. We think large numbers of their product is being sold to Iran."

President McNeil glanced at what was now a foot-high stack of the documents they'd covered so far. "All this is confirmed information?"

"Nearly. Some of it's just deduction and some of it's only preliminary reports. But my point man will be in Tehran tomorrow, meeting with our best asset. He promised information that should confirm everything I told you, and a lot more."

"What in the world are the Iranians going to do with all that hardware?"

Casey's normally blank face betrayed his concern. "I wish we knew, but I don't think we'll like it when we find out."

**TEHRAN, THE CAPITAL OF IRAN – 1540 LOCAL, APR 12<sup>TH</sup>**

Ellirat and his brother and partner Elessar were in a city they knew only from intelligence reports, but thanks to the detail of those reports they felt they knew it intimately. They were dressed like many modern Iranians in conservative western suits, carrying briefcases like any of the other professional businessmen that populated the city. Tehran has a rich and often violent history that is reflected in its architecture, but in modern times it has evolved into a thoroughly modern metropolis. The country's exports, especially oil and carpets, make for lucrative trade and in recent years the nation's leaders had wisely learned to exploit it for benefit of the people. And so despite the

94

deceptions and corruptions of the government, the capital city offered at least the strong illusion of prosperity. And with the modern developments came modern problems, like pollution magnified by a complete lack of emissions regulation, and traffic jams resultant of streets designed three thousand years before the automobile.

Yet the city and its scenery are beautiful in their own way. The huge Imam Khomeini Mosque is the religious center of the entire nation. The Azadi Monument arch in downtown is perhaps the most striking example of modern architecture in the Middle East. The city itself is nestled against the Elburz Mountains, with the peak of Mount Damavand, the highest point in the country, visible in the distance.

The two Iraqis entered the expensive and cosmopolitan Café Artaxerxes, looking for the American spy who they knew only as Kahlil. They knew he'd probably spot them first. They had applied a small amount of makeup to disguise their more distinctive Arabian features, but they still were clearly not Persian. Kahlil, on the other hand, had the reputation of being a chameleon. It was said that he could change his features from American to Arab to Persian to Russian with nothing more than an eyebrow pencil. The Iraqi agents were skeptical about the claim, but at any rate the American had the sort of face that you forget as soon as you looked away from it; that you would be unable to describe if you saw it every day of your life.

As they looked around the restaurant, maitre d' approached and asked in English "Are you the Mukhab brothers?"

The two often referred to themselves as such – alluding to their former employer. Ellirat said yes.

"The gentleman you are looking for has invited you to his booth. Follow me please." He led them toward the back of the restaurant – which was decorated like a museum and filled with ancient Persian and Babylonian artifacts – to a table where Kahlil had been waiting.

Ellirat recognized the tactical perfection of the American's stakeout immediately. The booth was invisible from the front door, hidden by shadows and misdirected lighting. But from where the agent sat, he could watch the entire café. Furthermore, he was not three yards from the kitchen door, which meant he could make a hasty exit if necessary.

"Would you gentlemen like some coffee?" An attentive waitress spoke in English, correctly assuming it would be a more comfortable language than Farsi for the new arrivals. They requested lattes and when she left they waited for Kahlil to speak.

"I have another friend coming," he said, "so we shall say nothing of importance until he arrives. He goes by the name Kujet, or Kujetski. You should know of him."

Ellirat shook his head. "Never heard the name before."

"That's rather surprising. He used to be a Russian double-agent, but now he is an international arms dealer. My employers have worked with him since we helped the Afghanis kick the Soviets out in the eighties. I met him inside the *Mafya* after that. Anyway, he's very famous in our line of work."

"He is a Russian who works against Russians?"

"No, he is a Cossack who works against communism and organized crime, and he makes huge amounts of money selling weapons around the world to people that my employers want to have well armed."

"Sounds like just the sort of person the CIA would recruit," said Elessar.

"Actually, you would not believe how useful he is. He literally keeps track of every single firearm in the Middle East. I doubt he was directly involved in the weapons thefts we were talking about, or he would have given me a heads-up a while ago, but I guarantee he knows who's running that show and what they've acquired so far. I expect our conversation to be extremely enlightening."

The waitress returned with the lattes. As she went back through the kitchen door, a man in a well-cut suit came the other way and walked straight to their table, sitting next to Kahlil. "How ya doin', man?" He spoke in casual American English.

"You find me well. And you, my friend?" Kahlil responded in Russian.

"We live in interesting times." Kujetski completed the coded greeting in Farsi as he took a hand-rolled cigarette from a silver case and lit it.

"You do not look Russian," observed Ellirat.

"And he doesn't look American," Kujetski answered, indicating Kahlil. "I'm not the sort of Russian you normally see anyway, at least not White Russian, or Belarusian, or Bolshevik. I am a Cossack, the True Russian." He struck his chest with his right palm as he said the word *Cossack*; obviously he was very proud of his heritage.

"Even though much of your homeland is no longer a part of Russia," Kahlil said.

96

"Yes, and the name of the country is badly misspelled. Anyway, my very obviously Arab new friend, Kahlil and I don't look like ourselves because we are in disguise. Really, if you two plan to stay in the country after a month or so, you'll need a professional to touch you up." He placed an irritating emphasis on the word *professional*.

"They are closing the country to foreigners?" Kahlil asked.

"They will in a short time. We will all soon be at war, you know."

"What do you mean by that?"

Kujetski took a long drag on his cigarette. "All of us – the US, Russia, Iraq, and probably Israel and China, too – are about to be very pissed off by Iran."

Kahlil turned to the Iraqis. "See, guys, I told you he had a bombshell."

Kujetski grinned. "I do at that, in several different sizes, ready for immediate delivery with your choice of warhead."

"Now I recognize you," Elessar said. "You are the one the Israelis call 'Kushaiah' aren't you? The Bow of God?"

"Oh yes; they are such good clients, the Israelis. They are much quicker with payment than the blasted Palestinians." Kujetski snickered at his own pun.

"It is interesting that you only know him from the Israeli circles," Kahlil said.

"Hey, we were too young for the Iran-Iraq war and for most of our careers we were far more concerned about what the Jews were up to than the Persians," Ellirat said. "Actually I'm wondering why we never came across you working in Iraq, Mr. Kujet. You did work for Saddam at one point didn't you?"

"Of course. But everyone in your office who ever heard of me or my activities in Iraq was killed or imprisoned by your old boss."

"Ah."

"I am sure that there are not many people still alive – besides Mr. Kahlil here – who know more than one of my aliases," Kujetski said reflectively, "but that is business."

"Speaking of which…"

"Just a moment. Waitress!" The other agents waited while Kujetski ordered a very specific variety of Russian tea. "Anyway, I already told you that there is an imminent war. You could have guessed that if you knew anything about the military buildup over here. You must know about that else you would not have come to see me."

"Obviously," intoned Ellirat, who thought that this Cossack was much too cheerful in the face of serious danger to be sane.

"Well, you are in luck. You see, my good Iraqi fellows, I collect fine information with nearly as much enthusiasm as I collect fine weapons and fine art such as the pleasant things here." He indicated the priceless artifacts of ancient Persia that decorated the restaurant. The brothers realized that Kujet owned them, and the restaurant itself. He went on "Good for me that the information is so much easier to store. You wouldn't believe the overhead I have to pay, renting warehouses, hiring guards, hiring informers to make sure the guards aren't working for my competitors and so on. Sometimes, if I go too long without checking my account balances, I wonder why I got in this business."

"Let's talk about your other inventory now."

"Apologies. I digress. Item number one." Kujetski produced a CD jewel case and handed it to Kahlil. "That's a complete list of every single item of hardware Rannovich and Co. have obtained to date, and several alternate lists of what he plans to acquire within the next month."

"How in the hell..." Kahlil started to ask as he took the disk.

"Item number two." Kujetski cut him off and produced another CD. "The money trail. You would have found out by now, I suppose, that Sheik Akandhras is bankrolling the whole thing."

"What!?" The two Iraqis just had their minds blown.

"KUPEC, the Russian Mafia, and some Chinese outfit called New Patriotic Enterprises are contributing, but the money begins and ends with Akandhras, the new Oil Minister of Iran."

"WHAT!?" The Iraqis were extremely unhappy about the news, but as Kujet guessed, Kahlil already knew this, and had passed it back to the CIA days ago.

"Quiet down," the American said. "Did you think that snake would have just gone to ground in the Bahamas or something?"

"That is what I would have done," Elessar said.

"He planned to," Kujetski told them. "The mafia actually kidnapped him in Montenegro. They kinda convinced him to invest in this scheme. Item number three: Rannovich's general plans. I won't give you all the very gory details now, because I'm afraid you'd all scream and run out to the streets in stark horror. But Mr. Kahlil's employer should pay close attention to my bit on American intelligence satellites."

"What about them?"

"The Chinese have a plan to take them out  I have no idea how, so I checked out everything that New Patriotic Enterprises has to do with space and put it on this disc for your analysts to figure out.  But I think that, shortly before the war begins, all of your KH-12 satellites will be disabled."

"Hmph. That would suck."

Ellirat had another question.  "Now, Kujet, I am curious, how close did you have to work with these guys to get this information?"

"I didn't get close at all.  I never met Rannovich or anyone in his cabal personally.  I am only supplying small arms for their soldiers; AKs, Uzis, RPGs, Stingers, the usual crap.  That is the extent of my direct involvement.  To be honest, acquiring major hardware on the scale that Rannovich is moving on is a ways out of my league.  I can get you a couple dozen tanks or a squadron of fighter-bombers, but not whole regiments and air wings.  I just don't have the connections – or frankly the guts – that Rannovich has to pull that off.  But I know plenty of people in the Russian mafia, and most of the Iranian military commanders are friends of mine.  So I hear things, and other people hear the same thing, and they call their friend Kujet to confirm what I hear.  And also I have this Indian kid I keep in my attic with the best computer I can get hold of.  He's what you call in America an Uber-Hacker.  If I need to see things I can't hear, he finds them for me."

"This is hot stuff, Kujet."  Kahlil was looking at the CDs.  "We need to take them to the bank right away."

"I was going to do that when you called.  I thought I should brief you and the Mukhab brothers first.  Let's go together.  I am sure Sam would like to finally meet you."  Kujetski got up to leave without further ado.

"Uh, you two" Kahlil looked at Ellirat and Elessar, "aren't allowed to go to the bank yet.  I need to get you guys a higher clearance before you can see that operation.  Do you have anything you can do without me for the next couple of hours?"

"We're supposed to meet one of our NCRI contacts tonight," Ellirat answered.  "He has a safehouse for us."

Kahlil nodded and slid out of the booth, following Kujetski.  "Good.  I'll call you in the morning so we can discuss the next step."

"And don't forget to change your makeup," Kujet said, leaning back through the kitchen door and pointing at the Iraqi brothers with his cigarette.

*        *        *

99

Ten minutes later, Kahlil and Kujet entered the downtown office of the Central Bank of Iran, and were allowed to proceed directly to the office of Mr. Samadad. "Sam," as the agents called him, was a perfect go-between. He oversaw the bank's international investments, which made him an ideal channel for moving sensitive material in and out of the country. He also managed Kujet's large accounts personally, and often arranged for transporting his wares. His two grown sons were also employed by the firm as security handlers. They were often allowed to handle CIA field runner assignments.

As the two men went up the elevator, Kahlil asked in English "How's pest control in a place like this?"

"Not so good." This meant that it was entirely possible that the offices were bugged, and no sensitive information should be spoken. That is why Kujet and Sam had scripted conversations, entirely in code.

They got off on the fourteenth floor and Kujet led the way to Sam's corner office. A secretary politely waved them in. "Mr. Samadad, good to see you again." Kujet said.

"Ah, my favorite client. You have brought your associate with you?"

"This is Kahlil, a good friend of mine who works for your uncle."

"I have heard much of you. It is an honor to see you at last." Although Sam, Kujetski and Kahlil had all worked closely together for many years, this was the first time Kahlil and the Iranian banker had actually met in person. "My dear uncle. How is he?"

"Worried as always by foreign affairs," Kahlil answered. Sam's Uncle, of course, referred to Uncle Sam, who was extremely worried by certain foreign affairs.

"There is so much to worry about, these days," Samadad said. He turned to the Cossack. "You are here to make a deposit, Kujet?"

"Yes, if you could please convert this to Swiss Francs and send it to my account at the Royal Bank." Kujet placed his briefcase on the desk. It contained his most recent payment from the Iranian Army.

"Immediately."

"And also," Kahlil placed a gift bag containing the CDs on the table, "here is a present for your uncle. He is a great lover of music."

"I think that will do for today," Kujet said.

"I will see that my uncle gets this right away. Please, my new friend, do not hesitate to come see me if ever you need anything. Perhaps you would like to open an account here?"

"Perhaps, when my account outgrows my local branch."

That evening, Sam's oldest son took a Swissair flight to Zurich carrying a metal briefcase and a small gift bag. He also carried a silenced SIG P228 .45-caliber pistol, which he checked with the airline and was allowed to carry once he left the airplane. A limousine took him to the Royal Bank, where he deposited the contents of the suitcase in the capable hands of a CIA asset by the name of Hans Albrecht, along with the gift bag. The next day, Albrecht ran a trace on Kujet's money, and of course it connected through several known Russian Mafia companies and all the way back to Saddam Hussein's oil accounts. Albrecht dutifully completed the deposit of Swiss Franc notes into Kujet's own account, and included his newest findings in the gift bag before passing it off. The present was given to a US Embassy staffer who was going home for the weekend. He was met at Dulles Airport by a midlevel CIA analyst who was just returning from vacation with his family. He carried the bag straight to CIA headquarters, and left it on the desk of Deputy Director of Operations Jarrod E. Casey.

Despite what people have seen on TV shows like *The West Wing* and *24*, it is extremely unusual for the President to call a full-blown emergency meeting with the senior cabinet members and the Joint Chiefs of Staff, especially on less than an hour's notice. Casey's team had analyzed the contents of Kujet's disks, and when they reached the third one Casey had gone straight to his boss, Carter Grayson, the Director of Central Intelligence, and said, "Call the President." There was zero hesitation. The DCI had known Casey long enough to know that if he ever looked as upset as he did now, they were facing a real crisis. He read Casey's notes with growing alarm while he waited to be connected with the Oval Office. He was of course, familiar with the Iran situation on the same level as Tuesday's Presidential briefing. But the mere summary of the new information was more frightening in its implications than he could have imagined. When the President came on the line, he requested the first full military situation briefing since the planning for the Iraq offensive began 2003.

## THE SITUATION ROOM – 1500 EDT, APR 14<sup>TH</sup>

The Situation Room had seen many urgent meetings since it opened during the Truman administration, but none on such short notice. Grayson and Casey set up at one end of the long table in the middle of the room. The Joint Chiefs of Staff – the senior commanders of the four armed forces – arrived next by helicopter from the Pentagon. Commandant of the Marines General Albert Schilling, Chief of Staff of the Air Force General Joshua Caleb, Chief of Naval Operations Admiral Terrence Marsh, and the Chief of Staff of the Army and Chairman of the Joint Chiefs General Paul Chappelle all sat down on one side of the table. Secretary of Defense Michael McLeary, Secretary of State Janice Rand, National Security Advisor Richard Harmon and Vice President Hal Bowman arrived one at a time and filled the other side of the table. President Brett McNeil arrived last, and took the head of the table. "Alright, Deke, what's going on?" he asked the DCI as he sat.

Grayson "Deke" Carter passed twenty-page double-spaced outlines around the table. "Deputy Director Casey's team has uncovered disturbing details regarding the Iran situation. I've asked him to deliver this presentation."

Casey launched right in to a thorough recap of his Tuesday briefing. By now it was old news, but it was still altogether shocking to the Joint Chiefs and the Secretaries. The VP and NSA had already heard this, so they waited patiently for the "emergency" part. "We have just received new data from our agents in Tehran. First, it is absolutely confirmed that Iran now possesses the fourth largest army in the world, consisting largely of stolen weapons. This army is hidden in underground bunkers masked by the construction of oil projects all over the country. You will find the complete inventory on pages eight through seventeen in your notes." The military people displayed various expressions of shock and amazement as they skimmed the lists of weapons. Secretary McLeary also looked very concerned.

"Second, we have a decisive paper trail linking Sheik Akandhras to the money being used to finance the whole thing. We also have the Russian Mafia and the Chinese firm New Patriotic Enterprises tied to the capital funds being used to finance the operation. We should use this data to push our case when we eventually go to Russia and China for support."

"Why will we be going to them for support?" the Secretary of State asked.

Casey stared at his notes for a very long time.

"Tell them, J," prompted the DCI.

Casey raised his eyes slightly, looking at the center of the table. "We will need their support because we will want China and Russia to be on our side when Rannovich tries to start World War Three."

For several moments, nobody said anything. Casey and Grayson looked down at their notes, waiting for the President or anyone else to offer a comment or ask a question. Janice Rand flipped rapidly through her copy of the outline, as if looking for something among the CIA data that would contradict what they had just said. Then she got to page twenty, which summarized Rannovich's apparent plans. The rustling of papers stopped. She and everyone else just let it sink in.

Rick Harmon – the National Security Advisor and a man gifted with infinite skepticism – made the first attempt to challenge the report. "Gentlemen, I say this with all due respect, but the CIA's track record of providing reliable intelligence in recent years has been less then perfect. I need hardly give examples, but you will understand if I find your credibility lacking and find your analysis somewhat doubtable."

DCI Carter Grayson was not a CIA lifer like Casey. He was a political appointment with at least as much connection and experience with politics as he had with the intelligence community. He was used to, by now, being called in so many polite words a dirty rotten liar, and he had already anticipated the challenge and had his response. "Gentlemen, I am sure that the NSA has voiced a concern many of you share. I agree our public credibility took a hit following 9/11 and the War in Iraq, but in this case, we consider our source to be impeccable. We received most of this information from an agent we consider to be our very finest, and his number one asset. We trust that asset, because he is the same man who smuggled Saddam Hussein's weapons of mass destruction out of the country prior to our invasion."

The dead air in the Situation Room broke into a buzz of conversation that rapidly crescendoed in volume and intensity until the voice of the President spoke up over the others. "Mr. Grayson," he said – for the first time in memory he had not called the DCI "Deke" – "I had not authorized the release of that information. I believe it was Delta-level material, which requires my specific consent for dissemination."

"Actually sir, everything in this briefing is Delta-Classified. You authorized me to provide any and all information relevant to the Iran situation, and the Iraq WMD thing is actually very relevant."

Vice President Bowman had turned his usual glare up to a withering level and aimed it at Grayson. "Why?"

"Because some of those weapons may now be in Iran."

If Grayson was trying to induce heart attacks, he was rolling along in the right direction. Nine of the most important people in the world just felt their hearts skip a beat.

Once the group had calmed down slightly, Casey offered an explanation. "You all know that our soldiers didn't find any actual, usable WMDs after we invaded Iraq. And some of the evidence we had used as a pretext for the war turned out to be either misleading or falsified – some by the sources who provided the information, some by officials within the Bush administration. Everybody knows that. But there's a lot more to the story.

"As a matter of fact, prior to our invasion, Saddam did have in his possession eleven complete nuclear devices and enough weapons-grade fissile nuclear material to make perhaps twenty more. He also had several tons of weaponized anthrax and other biological agents, as well as a few dozen tons of different types of nerve gas."

"*WHAT??*" six people gasped at once. The President, who at the time had sat on the Senate Armed Forces and Select Intelligence committees and had been in President Bush's personal confidence, knew this story. So did the Secretaries of State and Defense, who had both been on the National Security Council. They listened patiently and tried to imagine the fresh shock the others must have felt now.

Casey went on. "Here's what happened. In the November 2002 National Intelligence Estimate, we determined that Saddam Hussein would be very likely to use his arsenal against us, either immediately before, or during, or shortly after our planned invasion. President Bush ordered us at the CIA to find some way to get the weapons out of Saddam's hands. We contacted this weapons dealer we've worked with in the past and put together an operation to remove the weapons from the country. He worked with our agents to set up sting operations and take down several terrorist organizations that wished to acquire the weapons, and if all went according to plan we would later present the weapons and the information from the terrorists as evidence to incriminate Saddam.

"Unfortunately, our own military moved faster than we expected and ended up forcing us to change our plans, and we were unable to reach the final phase of the operation. The chemical and biological materials were all safely destroyed, but our weapons dealer ended up having to store the nuclear materials in Iran. We never got to expose Saddam's WMD operations or terrorist dealings, and now everyone thinks we invaded his country for no good reason."

The President and the Secretaries nodded in somber agreement with Casey's analysis. The Joint Chiefs were stunned – none of them had been in a position of privileged information back in 2003 and they had never been told any of this. The Vice President had run two unsuccessful presidential bids on a support-the-war platform and was now shocked beyond all comprehension. The National Security Advisor was livid. "Why haven't I heard this before? Why weren't the people told? This is insane!"

The President responded with a degree of calm that was frightening, and eerily reminded several of the older men of Ronald Reagan's manner of dealing with such situations. "You weren't told because you were not at this level of seniority in the Bush administration and frankly, you did not need to know. We have not and will not let this be exposed to the American people because it would look really awful for us. Imagine their reaction, if you will, if the media picked up the story. The CIA conspired with an international arms dealer with known terrorist connections, who stole enough WMDs to kill everyone in the Middle East and stored them in Iran – a country whose government has apocalyptic ambitions and which, as it turns out, is being puppeteered by a Russian mafia don. With all due respect to my staff, we'd never be able to put a positive spin on it or explain our justification. And I agree entirely with your last comment. It is insane. It makes me physically ill just thinking about it.

"But at the time, we had agreed it was the right thing to do. All of us in this room knew that Iraq was by far the mostly likely trigger for another major war. And WMDs or no, Saddam *had* to be removed. We made it our national policy back in '98 with the Iraq Liberation Act. With what we knew in 2002, we felt that it was time to make that happen. We didn't pull it off smoothly, obviously, and we've paid for the mistakes we've made every day since we went in. However, had we not done exactly what we did at the start of the operation, we'd now have weapons of mass destruction in the hands of terrorists. These are facts that the American public simply cannot deal with, and so they never will. The book on Iraq has been closed. The question we must now deal with is what the hell do we do with Iran?"

There was a very uneasy silence for half a minute. The Joint Chiefs slowly realized that everyone was looking at their side of the table. "We have contingency plans, Mr. President," General Chappelle finally said.

"I know you do. Tell me about them."

The Chairman of the Joint Chiefs had this moment well-rehearsed. "First sir, we should establish a position of containment while simultaneously deploying all the forces we can spare to the METO. By containment I mean we increase our naval forces in the Gulf and deploy armor and air patrols along the Afghanistan and Iraq borders."

"Fine. What about the troop levels?" The President asked.

"At this point we're running a little lean," Chappelle answered. "We have sixty thousand ground troops in 'Ghanny and a little over twenty thousand in Iraq. We have very little in armor in either of those countries, a fair number of helicopters, a few tactical fighters, plenty of AWACS and UAV assets."

"So we need more troops in Iraq," McNeil said.

"We *had* more troops in Iraq," General Schilling, the Marine chief reminded him. "You took them out."

"I'm aware of that. I'm also aware that part of the reason my predecessor invaded and occupied Iraq in the first place was so our troops could be a buffer between Iran and Israel in case something like this situation arose. But you are all of course aware of the issues that overrode that concern."

"Yes, Mr. President. Regardless, we need to get ready to redeploy to our forward bases in Iraq in order to confront this threat."

"I'm not going to gear up to invade Iran," McNeil said. "That's not an option."

"We wouldn't want to do it anyway sir," Chappelle said. "Our thinking is more along the lines of a Desert Storm-style operation. If we need to lay the hammer down on Iran, we use air power. And we use armor and mechanized infantry on the borders to make sure Iran's big shiny new army stays on their side of the fence. If we can get enough firepower over there, we can handle Iran pretty easily. If necessary, we're confident we can dismantle their military with casual effort, no matter how much they've built it up. This is what we do best. No invasion, no occupation, no winning of hearts and minds or any other crap like that. We just beat down until the bad guy calls uncle."

"Basically you're describing Desert Storm Two," McNeil summed up, grinning slightly at the CJC's choice of words.

"That's where we're coming from." Chappelle pulled a thick folder out of his briefcase. "We call this contingency 'Operation Perfect Storm.'"

106

# CHAPTER 6: CLOSER TO DANGER

## NORTH ISLAND – 1030 PDT, APR 11$^{TH}$

"So, what is there to do around here?" Karl asked Jack Masterson. They were in Blackjack's living room after breakfast on Tuesday morning, playing on his XBox 360.

"You mean besides getting your ass kicked at Halo?"

"I'm thinking about clubs, bowling teams, things like that."

"Well there is a bowling league," Jack said, "but since we're gonna be taking a cruise in a month that wouldn't work for you. You any good at bowling?"

"I average 160."

"That's good enough. You'd have to wait till we got back before you joined. There's a bowling alley on the *Reagan*, believe it or not, so you can practice."

"Does that work ok? I mean with the rolling?"

"It takes a tidal wave for you to feel it on a ship as big as the Gipper. Besides, they put it on the waterline and right in the middle of the ship. It's as good as dry land."

"Sweet."

"Anyway, there's a golf league here," Blackjack went on, "but you got the same problem. I can't think of anything that's good for short-term. What else are you in to?"

Karl listed several favorite activities. "Scuba diving, martial arts, fishing…"

"I think there's a martial arts club that meets at the gym on Tuesday nights. Either that or weird gymnastics. I never hung around long enough to figure it out."

"Okay. I'll check that out."

Karl found the gym schedule on the base services web site. There was in fact an amateur martial arts club on Tuesdays at 1900. Karl drove over and checked it out. There were about ten people sparring each other on practice mats, and another thirty or so watching. And there was a guy sitting at a table with a stack of papers on one side. That, Karl guessed, was the office. "Hi, there. I want to join."

The guy behind the table stood up and offered his hand. "Happy to have you. I'm Lieutenant Hank Miller. You can call me Hacksaw."

Karl accepted the handshake. "Karl Roche, Lt. Commander. Sharkey, they call me. What do I have to do?"

"Just help me fill in this form." Hacksaw pulled a sheet of paper off the top of the stack. He wrote down Karl's name, rank and callsign. "Address?"

"507 McClusky, here on base."

"Phone and email?" Karl gave them. "Now, physical. Male, obviously... six footer ballpark?"

"Five-eleven."

"Weight?"

"One-eighty-eight."

"Any heart problems, blood pressure issues, respiratory conditions, back trouble or nervous disorders?"

"No."

"Old injuries that might be an issue?"

"My left shoulder doesn't rotate properly. I mean, it will rotate if someone grabs it and pulls it, but I can't physically raise it over my head myself."

"Huh." Hacksaw made a note, flipped the page over and went on. "What disciplines are you in, and at what experience level?"

"Advanced Jujutsu and intermediate Kung Fu."

"Okay, um..." Hacksaw had a long table listing various martial arts categories. "Kung Fu, and... Brazilian Jiu Jitsu..."

"Not BJJ," Karl corrected, "traditional Jujutsu."

"Oh, okay." Miller scanned the table. "I don't have that. I guess I'll write it in on the bottom. Uh, you might have trouble finding someone to spar with."

"Every Asian-influenced grappling martial art, including BJJ, evolved from traditional Jujutsu. It also influenced several schools of Karate. I'll be fine."

"Alright," Hacksaw shrugged. "I'm just a kickboxer, myself; I never learned much about martial arts history, and no one else seems to know what influenced what."

Roche smiled a little. "Maybe I could give a lecture."

Hacksaw shrugged again. "Maybe. For now, just sign the liability agreement. Basic lawyer crap – if you get hurt it ain't the club's fault."

"No worries." Roche signed the form.

"Okay, welcome to NIASMAC." He pronounced the acronym *knee-smack*. "Follow me and we'll find you a locker."

Roche picked up his duffel and followed Hacksaw to the locker room in the back of the gym. Once there he changed into his old ryu gi; black pants and tunic with a polar bear in a fighting stance on the back, and a black belt with four red stripes at the ends. "Is that for Jujutsu?" Hacksaw asked.

"Yeah, but I've been out of practice since college." They went back out to the main floor.

"This end of the room is all ours from seven to ten. We have a couple experts who give lessons at nine, and the rest of the time it's just sparring and showing off. That guy in the red is Commander Wilkes; he's our resident BJJ and MMA expert. He'll warm you up nicely. Hey, Hardcase." He called. "Got a new victim for you."

LCdr. "Hardcase" Wilkes did look like a convict, right down to the bright red uniform with matching red belt – the highest belt attainable in Brazilian Jiu Jitsu. He looked Roche over and said "Take your stance, buddy."

"My name's Karl."

"You're about to be takedown number five hundred and some-odd. On guard." With out further ado, Wilkes attacked with a low sweeping kick. Karl jumped back and took a defensive posture. He blocked several grappling attempts and kept his distance.

"Don't hurt him, Danny," someone called out. Karl tried a couple of punches that were easily slapped aside. Clearly Danny Wilkes was skilled and practiced. Karl had no doubt in his own skills but he was rusty and didn't want to get overwhelmed by his opponent. If the fight was brought to the ground, it would likely end very quickly in Wilkes' favor. Karl stuck to basic attacks and studied Hardcase's moves.

Jujutsu is among the most balanced of the martial arts, practiced by Samuri warriors since at least the 16th Century. It is built around a variety of hold and throw moves, but includes plenty of other attacks such as kicks and punches. The defensive forms are complex and wonderfully effective, and are designed to create openings for an endless repertoire of counterattacks. The desired end result is a submission hold – either a joint lock or a choke hold – immobilizing the opponent and either forcing him to tap out in submission or suffer crippling pain. The Brazilian method, which evolved through Judo, forgoes most of the balance of traditional Jujutsu and focuses on ground fighting, and wrestling the opponent into submission.

A skilled BJJ practitioner is next to impossible to stop in a ground fight, so Karl wished to remain standing for as long as possible.

He worked through the forms and remained on the defensive, keeping his distance so that Danny could not get a hold. But Danny's footwork was better than Karl's, and soon Roche was having trouble maintaining his distance as they danced around the mat. So Roche abruptly switched tactics. He stepped under a high arm strike and began attacking at close quarters.

Wilkes was quick to respond, but his defensive pattern was disrupted long enough to give Roche the opening he needed. Sharkey went for an open punch to the ribs, but instead of just striking him he reached his left arm under Danny's right armpit and grabbed his shoulder. Then he spun around, pulling Danny with him, and yanked his arm back causing Danny to drop hard on his side. Hardcase knew he was going down as soon as Roche got the handhold. It was a powerful drop attack for which there is no effective counterthrow. As soon as he landed, he rolled to his left, causing Roche to miss the kick aimed at his stomach. Danny rolled into a pushup stance and was on his feet in an instant. He expected Roche to resume his close-in approach and set up his own throw move for as soon as Roche stepped up.

Roche saw the spacing of Danny's feet and recognized the set-up, so he checked his approach and tried another classic move. He aimed a kick at Danny's knees, which Danny parried easily and responded with an extended kick in return. This was the correct move, but Danny's stance was wrong, and he was slightly off-balance. Roche grabbed the extended foot with both hands and flipped his opponent back to the ground. Karl stepped up again, but this time Danny made a sweeping kick that connected with both of Karl's ankles, bringing him down. In the same motion, Danny wrapped his legs around his opponent's torso and seized his arm.

Roche was caught in an armbar – one of the classic joint locks which threatened to hyperextend his elbow if he didn't submit. He quickly tapped out on Wilkes' right leg, and was released. Wilkes rolled away and came to his feet. Karl stood as well, a bit shakily. Hardcase's sudden kick had caught him unawares, and he realized he'd have to be prepared for unexpected moves from a mixed-martial-arts expert.

"Best of three?" Wilkes offered.

Roche nodded, and resumed his stance.

This time Wilkes simply dove for Roche's legs, knocking him down before he could react. Karl recognized the tactic – he had used it himself in the past, as a quick if reckless way to take down a larger opponent. He caught his fall and pinned Danny with his knees against his hips. He now had Danny in a reverse back-mount, which is a dominant position but the weakest one possible. Danny quickly crossed his legs, preventing Roche from isolating one for a leg lock. Then he reached his arms back over his head and seized the collar of Karl's gi, and pulled him down until they were back-to-back. Roche rolled to his left, hooked his right leg over Danny's legs and attempted to get a good hold on his right arm.

Danny knew he was trapped unless he could free his arm from under Roche's body. He rolled the opposite direction, locking his legs around Karl's right and trying to pull his arm clear. But Roche held his wrist with both hands and applied a simple rotational wristlock. Danny tried to apply a leg slicer, crushing Karl's thigh muscle between his legs, but Karl was hurting him far more than he could hurt Karl. He tapped out on the mat, and the excruciating pain in his wrist was instantly released. Karl rolled off of his arm and helped him to his feet. "You know what you're doing, I'll give you that," Wilkes said.

Roche just shrugged, and resumed his starting position. They had bruised each other, but so far the fight was a draw. By this point the entire club was gathered around their mat, making wagers and cheering wildly. Wilkes gestured for his opponent to resume. Sharkey fake-stepped right and then charged. Danny grabbed him at the waist and shoulder and stepped into an off-balance throw. Roche had set this up – he kicked his foot down in front of Danny's ankle, tripping him up. At the same time he put his arm around Danny's neck. Suddenly he had leverage and Danny didn't. Wilkes was pitched onto the mat, with Karl falling on top of him and into a side control position known as the kesa-gatame – or scarf hold – with his legs braced for stability, one arm around the opponent's head and the other up against his chest.

Wilkes tried to use his legs to get leverage, but if the kesa-gatame is correctly applied by a larger opponent it is next to impossible to escape from. Fortunately for Wilkes, it also difficult to gain a submission hold from that position. Danny had time to consider his options. He had his right arm free, and he could pry his held arm free if he worked his right fingers under Roche's right elbow. He tried that, and then transitioned into a bridge-and-roll maneuver to attempt to roll over Karl and get side control on him.

But Karl had anticipated the escape attempt, and as soon as Hardcase got his left arm free Karl seized his right, and pushed it down across his own neck, transitioning from kesa-gatame to kata-gatame or single-arm hold, and linking his own arms together and forcing

Danny's arm into his windpipe. This was a classic arm-triangle choke. Danny knew he could not escape and disgustedly tapped Karl's shoulder.

Karl released him and helped him up again. "Three out of five?" Karl offered.

Danny agreed, warily. It had been a very long time since he was beaten twice in a row. He resumed his stance, took a deep breath and nodded. Karl approached again, more confidently this time. He utilized his Aiki-Jujutsu repertoire of strikes, forcing Wilkes to block arms swung at him from unexpected directions and leaving himself open for a handhold. Roche landed a blow against a nerve bundle in the side of Danny's neck, momentarily paralyzing his left arm. Roche quickly stepped up and seized the arm, placing his back against Danny's side, preparing an over-the-shoulder throw.

But Wilkes recognized the tactic instantly and used Roche's leverage against him, dropping to the mat first and pulling Roche down. Karl tried to step out of the pull, but Danny hooked his left leg and grabbed his ankle with his right hand. Roche had to release Danny's left arm to try to get out of the reversal, and by now the paralyzing effect had worn off. Wilkes grabbed the left sleeve of Roche's gi, and now had him in the De La Riva guard position – one of the most difficult BBJ positions to escape from, and one of the easiest from which to apply a submission hold. In this case, Wilkes simply pulled Roche toward him while applying increasing pressure on his leg, employing a thigh crusher technique like he'd tried to use earlier. Karl was forced to tap out. The crowd cheered Wilkes as he rose to his feet.

"Last point," Hacksaw Miller announced. Roche and Wilkes both nodded.

Emboldened by the crowd, Hardcase came on with combo attacks drawn from kickboxing and Karate that quickly wore through Sharkey's defensive forms. He had give up parrying and just kept up with blocking Danny's fierce moves, and tried not to give him an opening for a takedown. Wilkes eventually got a handhold on Roche's collar, but Roche was able to use his longer arms to push away. Wilkes then immediately seized both of Karl's wrists and pulled his arms out to their sides. This was a very dangerous position for Karl. Danny only had to choose which way he wanted to transition and put Karl on the mat or straight into an arm lock.

Then Karl remembered a powerful Kung Fu kick-throw he had learned that could be used in very close quarters. He leaned back, planted his right foot on Danny's chest, and pushed with his back leg to remain upright. This put the collective force of Roche's leg muscles against Danny's body. Simultaneously he thrusted both of his arms forward, while rotating them out to break Danny's grip on his wrists. The sudden transition from Jujutsu – which literally translates as the "way of yielding" – into the immensely powerful kick attack caught Wilkes completely off guard. There was no way to resist the kick-throw anyway. Danny was launched off his feet. He landed on his back and slid clear to the other edge of the mat. Wilkes was momentarily stunned, and that moment was all Karl needed. He pounced on him and pressed his knee to Danny's throat – a finishing move that signaled the end of the contest.

The crowd went nuts, mobbed Karl and made it clear he was welcome in the club. Karl helped Danny to his feet. "Good match," he said.

"Yeah, whatever, man. I've never seen that kick before."

*There's got to be an easier way to make friends around here,* Karl thought.

## NORTH ISLAND – APR 15<sup>TH</sup>

Tracy came by on Saturday and found Karl sitting on his living room floor surrounded by handguns and half-watching a baseball game. They'd gone out again on Wednesday night, and that time Karl had treated her to the Old Spaghetti Factory. Tracy hadn't been to a Navy base yet, and asked if they could just hang out on the weekend. It now appeared to Tracy that they had different ideas on the concept of "hanging out."

"Oh, hi." Karl looked up sheepishly. "I thought you were coming in the afternoon."

"It's two o'clock."

Karl looked at his watch. "So it is. 1405, actually."

"So, what are you up to?"

"Cleaning my gun collection. Later, I'll probably rob a bank or something; maybe shoot up a post office." Tracy laughed at Karl's dark joke and leaned down and picked up his SIG 9mm. She checked it to make sure it was empty, and sighted at one of the baseball players on Roche's new big-screen TV. Roche watched her, noting that she took a marksman stance and not the fake-cop posture people usually try when they aim a gun for the first time. "Have you ever done any shooting?" He asked.

"I took a self-defense seminar once. They taught me how to fire a gun, but I've never owned one or shot anything since."

"Is it something you'd ever do again?"

"Come to think of it, it was a lot of fun. I just never met someone who had a gun collection; otherwise I might have made a hobby out of it. I assume you play with these things all the time?"

Karl was still rubbing a disassembled gun barrel with a soft cloth. He looked at her reflection in the shiny, polished black metal. "I don't ever play with them. They're not toys. But I do frequently use them all at a firing range. Are you asking me to take you to the shooting range here on the base?"

"If you wouldn't mind."

"Not at all." He blew the lint off the gun barrel with a can of compressed air, and reassembled the Glock automatic pistol from a dozen pieces in ten seconds. Then he packed all four of his guns into two foam-lined cases and carried them out to his car. He saw the Ford Focus hatchback that Tracy arrived in. "Is that a rental?"

"Yeah, my insurance company gave me that. My Mini will be out of the shop on Tuesday. While it's dismantled anyway, I'm having them add the John Cooper Works performance kit."

"Nice. That makes, what, an extra fifty horsepower?"

"Yeah. Next time I'll be able to outrun the stupid trucks."

Roche laughed. He drove them to the indoor gun range on the other side of the base, pointing out various administration and support buildings along the way.

"I thought this was an airbase. Where are the runways and hangars?"

"Northwest end. It's a bit out of the way, but let's give you a look anyway." He turned in to an alleyway and accelerated hard. The squealing of the tires echoed off the walls and prompted Tracy to laugh.

"Who's chasing us, Mr. Bond?"

"I don't know, but if you don't want to find out you'd better stick with me," Karl growled in his excellent Sean Connery impression. The alley led into a maintenance lot, which was strewn with partially dismantled aircraft. Roche drove past the planes and the work crew, who were used to pilots using their lot as a shortcut. Roche drove through a giant hangar, under the wing of a C-130 and emerged on the tarmac apron of the runway complex. He drove around the runways, staying off the active taxi zones. "This is runway eighteen," he raised his voice over the noise of planes landing and taking off. "It's the main north-south runway. That building is my squad HQ. I supposedly have an office there, but I haven't needed to use it yet." He drove around the edge of the runway, right at the shore. "If it wasn't for the noise, this

114

would make a nice picnic spot, don't you think?" They had a view of the entire harbor and downtown San Diego. "You only get to see this when the *Nimitz* is out. She docks there," he pointed to a long, low pier, "and blocks everything to the right of the Hyatt Tower."

Tracy could see another carrier further down the docks. "Is that the *Reagan*?"

"No, actually that's the *John C. Stennis*. The *Reagan*'s parked behind her." He continued northwest along the perimeter of the airfield until he reached the end of runway 18. He turned south, following that runway along a parallel taxiway, and pointed ahead to a slim tower. "That air control tower is a dummy. The radar and stuff is all real, but the traffic controllers are in a bunker somewhere. A few years ago, a big C-5 transport came in on runway eleven, a little wide right. It was having engine trouble, and eleven is a pretty narrow strip anyway. It clipped the old tower, knocked it down and killed everyone inside. So the new tower's empty, seventy yards away from the runways, and the heavy transports can't land on runway eleven anymore."

"Does runway eighteen cross eleven?"

"Yeah, actually, that junction is where eighteen ends and runway thirty-six begins. And eleven becomes twenty-nine."

"Oh, I get it. The numbers are like compass points. 'Eighteen' means a hundred and eighty degrees, and 'thirty-six' is for three-sixty."

"Exactly." Roche stopped in front of a big hangar. "This is where my squad parks its planes." He pointed out the emblem above the door: a mean-looking stingray with its fins wrapped around several missiles. The huge door was partway open, but the interior lights were off, so Roche pointed the Battleship toward the opening and flicked on the high beams.

Tracy gasped at the sight of the two Super Hornets sitting just inside the doorway. Invisible in the dark, they shone brilliantly in Roche's headlights. "They're beautiful," Tracy said. Karl had never heard of the deadly warplane being described quite that way, but he agreed. The fighters were painted a deep, cold blue, and a special anti-radar coating produced a pearlescent shimmer.

"That paint's expensive," Karl explained. "It's more than a pretty skin. The color actually changes a little in different light. It's bright blue in direct light, dark blue in dim light, and a steely gray in shadow. Even subtle changes make it shift. Watch." Karl switched the headlights to low beam and the Hornets darkened noticeably. He drove forward and to the right, and the color scheme distorted eerily. "You can see how confusing that would be to an enemy pilot. It's

115

supposed to mimic the way ocean water reflects light. Sort of an adaptive camouflage."

"That's a neat trick."

"They say it will fool radar the same way. It throws off the return as the Hornet moves around, which should keep a missile from getting a terminal lock and actually hitting the aircraft. That, plus the ECM makes this thing almost untouchable."

"Well, that's just incredible. I didn't know anti-missile technology was so advanced."

"They say in ten years, the radar-guided anti-aircraft missile will be practically obsolete." Karl drove back to the end of the runway.

"What's that?" Tracy pointed to an angular metal object sticking out of the water.

"That is the wing of a Hornet that rolled off the runway. There're about twenty older-model Hornets out there."

"Why so many?"

"Bad brakes. Hornets don't use their brakes when they land on a carrier; they rely on the tailhook to drag them to a stop. But the impact force of landing on a carrier overpressurizes the hydraulics. So sometimes when an old Legacy Hornet flies in from a carrier and lands on a big runway like this, it's using those brakes for the first time in a hundred landing cycles. The hydraulics blow, the plane can't stop, the pilot jumps and the Hornet just rolls into the harbor."

"Huh."

"Here's the sad part. The new Super Hornets don't have this problem, because they have a separate hydraulic system for the brake lines. When the Navy figured it out 1998, Boeing offered to retrofit the Super's brake hydraulics on to the older Hornets. They tested them on a few old A-models, and it worked perfectly. The Navy says 'great, problem solved, let's refit all these planes. How much?' Boeing said they'd fix all eight hundred or so active Navy and Marine Corps Hornets for a hundred and eighty million bucks. That's just over twenty grand a pop – a pittance. That's not much more than I spent on the chassis in my *car*."

"So what went wrong?"

"Congress shut it all down, of course. Some retard Democrat from Rhode Island thought it made no sense to spend that kind of money on new brakes for an aircraft they had just authorized replacing. 'Why spend millions on the old Hornets when we're spending billions on the Supers?' Why, because those old Hornets are still going to be serving the frontlines for the next fifteen years, that's why. But

116

congress accuses Boeing of trying to gyp the military when they just wanted to sell brake lines at a fraction over cost. So now, another Hornet goes in the drink or off into the woods a couple times a month, for the last twelve years. Almost seven billion dollars' worth of modern jet fighter wasted, not to mention dead pilots. A friend of mine back at Whidbey Island in Washington broke his leg jumping on the runway at fifty miles an hour. The Navy paid twice as much for his hospital treatment than they would have for his Hornet's brakes."

Tracy stared at the aviator. "That's quite a rant."

"I've got more. I've been in the service long enough. Ask me about hazard pay for air wing maintenance crew."

"Maybe later."

They continued down through the carrier docks, which consisted of three piers placed parallel to the shore, each 500 yards long. The first one, the *Nimitz's* berth, was empty. Roche drove along the entire quarter-mile length of the *Stennis* and pointed to the next ship. "That's the *Reagan*."

"It looks even bigger than the other one."

"She is, by twelve percent. And that one is bigger than *Nimitz* by a fifth. They're all technically in the same class, but each ship is unique from the keel up." Roche was driving slowly now – both ships and the adjacent docks were crawling with traffic. Forklifts and flatbeds were dashing across between the piers and the warehouses on shore. "Join the Navy, and you could end up working here, for the busiest moving business in the world. They spend three weeks unloading a carrier when it comes in, and six weeks loading it back up when they go out. *Stennis* goes in three weeks, and I go with *Ronald Reagan* the week after that. *Nimitz* comes home in between. You think this is crazy now, watch on the day *Nimitz* gets back."

Roche stopped the car to let a forklift through carrying a rack of AMRAAMs. "What would happen if those missiles blew up in front of us?" Tracy asked.

"Are you morbid or what?"

"Just curious."

"That's sixteen missiles with a twenty-seven pound shaped-charge warhead on each. They'd spend the next few days picking our teeth out of the *John C's* fantail."

"Eew."

"You asked." Karl turned inland once they were past the docks. "Do you still want to play with guns?"

"Are you kidding? After seeing all that hardware, I'm hooked."

The shooting range was empty, which suited Karl and Tracy just fine. The range was fifty yards long – or half a football field – and fifty feet across. There were six stalls for shooters to use, each with a motorized track for setting up paper targets at different ranges. Karl led Tracy to the stall furthest from the door and unpacked his weapons. "What kind of gun did they teach you to shoot?" He asked.

"It was a revolver. Not a big magnum like in Clint Eastwood movies, the smaller thing that cops use on TV."

"A thirty-eight special?"

"That sounds right."

"Well, I have the gun that real cops use these days." Roche handed her his SIG-Sauer P226. "And SEALs use it too. It's a nine-millimeter. See how you like that one."

Tracy aimed it down the range, looked it over, and aimed again. "This feels pretty good to me."

Karl handed her a clip. "I'm giving you five rounds, subsonic, hundred-and-fifteen grain. Same thing the police use."

"Cool." Roche put up a man-shaped target and moved it twenty yards out on the track. Tracy loaded the gun, chambered a round, and clicked off the safety. She fired once as if testing the weapon, and then fired the other four rounds in rapid succession.

"Not bad at all," Karl said, as he brought the target back. "Your first shot was a six, and then you got three eights and a nine. I don't think you've forgotten a thing."

"I guess it's like riding a bike, right?"

"I wouldn't know. I practice constantly."

"Can I try a forty-five?"

"That's a lot bigger than a 9mm."

"I know."

"Okay. This is a Heckler & Koch model 23, subsonic .45 ACP with an integrated silencer. It's the SEALs' other standard issue pistol, intended for stealthier applications."

"Does the silencer make any difference when I'm shooting it?"

"No it just makes the gun a little heavier, that's all. But it's designed to be balanced with the silencer." Roche loaded the larger pistol and passed it to Tracy. "The safety is the red switch on the left side. The button on the trigger is for a laser sight, but that's not attached."

The big bullets made almost no noise as Tracy fired. But even using a two-handed grip, she seemed to have trouble controlling the heavier pistol. "It's weird," she said. "I feel it kick, but I don't hear a thing."

"If you think that's a surreal feeling, you should try shooting a fifty-cal rifle with a suppressor. Huh." Karl read the target as it was automatically returned. "Two, four, four, five, and the last one's outside."

"I think this gun is a bit too heavy."

"That's what it looked like to me. You shouldn't shoot a gun you don't feel comfortable holding. Why don't we stick with the SIG?" He put the .45 away and gave the Swiss 9mm back to her. "This time I'll give you full-power military rounds. Normal cop bullets, you know, aren't actually intended to kill. You have to shoot a guy right in the heart or brain for instant lethal effect. But these babies," Roche held up a 9mm parabellum cartridge out of a new box, "are full metal jacket bullets, one-twenty-three grain, with high-speed charges. They'll punch right through a man."

"Excellent; gimme." Roche put five fresh parabellum rounds in the magazine and gave it to Tracy, who eagerly loaded the gun and started shooting as soon as the target stopped.

"Uh, looks like you're missing wide right. You got a couple on the paper, but you're definitely going a little wide here." Karl felt that gentle understatement would be the most constructive form of criticism. Tracy had actually missed very badly.

"What's wrong? Are the sights off?"

"No, it's just the recoil. Can you feel your shoulder pull back when you shoot?"

"A little."

"That's throwing off your aim right at the moment the bullet leaves the barrel."

"So, is there a different grip I can use?"

"That might help some; try standing sideways, like this." Karl held the empty gun in his right hand, stood facing Tracy on his left, and held his arm away from his body. "This way, the pistol, your arm, and the mass of your torso are all aligned. The recoil won't affect you so much." He reloaded the gun and gave it back to Tracy. She mimicked Karl's posture, and he helped her position her arm parallel to the floor. "Keep your wrist loose; you need to use it to correct your aim after each shot. Try not to move your arm at all."

This time, she got all five rounds in the target's chest. "I think I'm getting the hang of a 9mm."

"You're a fast learner."

"I though the G.I. sidearm was a Beretta."

"That's right, but SEALs don't use it. The Beretta has an open slide, and that tends to snag on loose fabric and it jams if it gets dirty. SEALs are always getting dirty. The SIG doesn't have a problem with dirt. I could pull it out of the bottom of a swamp and turn around and shoot."

"So, that's what you used in Iraq?"

"Actually, no. Officers had a slightly wider selection that we could pick and choose from. I went for the biggest handgun they had in stock." He took his Desert Eagle out of the other case and handed it to her. "I used that bad boy in the field. Fifty-caliber Action Express, the most powerful automatic in the world. Dirty Harry's .44 Magnum has nothing on it. Now this also has an open slide but it's a much different design that never gums up like the Berretta. It's got a free-floating magazine that can jam if you hold it wrong, but it's never failed me yet. And its ability to knock anybody down with a single shot makes up for minor flaws."

"This thing is *huge*. Its half again as big as the .45, and I could barely hold that. How do you shoot something like this?"

"I shoot it very well," Karl said. "Better put on ear protection for this one." The target Tracy had used was still in place, so Roche moved it back to the far wall, fifty yards away. He took the big gun from her, slapped a full clip into the handle, pulled back the slide and kept his eyes on Tracy the entire time as he fired off all seven rounds. Roche shot a perfectly straight line, right to left, across the target's forehead.

"You weren't kidding," Tracy said. She took off the foam ear pads and asked offhandedly "how many people did you shoot with that thing?"

Karl Roche stood still for a moment, staring at the end of his gun before answering. "A lot."

"Oh, jeez, I'm sorry. I shouldn't make you talk about people you've killed. That's horrible."

"Don't worry about it. It was just eighteen months after 9/11. I didn't feel sorry then, and I don't feel sorry now." There were several months in between when it made Roche sick just to think about it, but he didn't let that come up.

"So, now you carry this big gun in the plane with you?"

"Sometimes, but usually I just carry my Glock." Karl put the Desert Eagle away and pulled another gun out of the case.

"Where did you get all these guns?"

120

"The other three were parting gifts from the SEALs, and this one was given to me by a friend in law enforcement." He handed her the Glock 18C. "Now, the 'Deagle' is a one-shot killer, but it only holds seven cartridges. But this guy uses either a seventeen or thirty-three round clip, and fires full automatic. You hold the trigger down, and it keeps shooting, like a machine gun. It's just a 9mm, but being able to empty the whole clip in less than two seconds makes up for that."

"Is this the gun that can supposedly go through airport x-rays?"

"That's just a myth. The slide, magazine and grip are made of plastics, but all the moving parts inside, not to mention the barrel, are old-fashioned steel. They see it just fine on x-ray. It does have the advantage of being completely water-proof, however, and that makes it an ideal companion for a SEAL or naval aviator."

"Okay, show me how quickly that thing shoots."

Roche packed the 33-round extended magazine with ammunition. Then he positioned a fresh target forty yards down the range. He fired a continuous stream of lead that sliced the target clean in half, perfectly straight down the middle.

"You're dangerous," Tracy said.

Karl gave her a sly grin. "Only on paper."

She shook her head. "Is there anywhere we can get a cup of coffee around here?"

There are those who believe that the Starbucks Coffee Company is trying to take over the world. This conspiracy theory is of course irrational. After all, why would a café franchise chain try to claim political domination? But if the conspiracy turns out to be true, then truly nothing on earth could stop them. They already have at least one franchise in place on every military base in the US, and NAS North Island hosted three. Karl drove to one of them and he and Tracy ordered a couple of blended iced coffee drinks.

"So, the Killer-SEAL-Top-Gun-Fighter-Jock likes his mint mocha chip frappachinos," Tracy teased.

"I do like mint, and I also like the little chocolate chunks blended in. It's like mint chocolate chip ice cream with coffee poured over it. I like it."

"Mmm, that's my favorite ice cream flavor."

"Well, what do you know, it's mine too."

\*　　　\*　　　\*

Back at the house, Karl excused himself to put the guns away, and Tracy had a look around his pad. He'd moved himself in pretty fast. His idea of decorating was pretty minimal, but he did have a few framed paintings of WWII air battle scenes. There was also a row of framed photographs on top of the television cabinet. Tracy found one of his family – him standing with his parents and little sister with a mountain background. Karl came back in and told her about the picture. "We took that last year, when my sister Dannae started school. That's Colorado Bible College."

"Looks like a beautiful campus," Tracy said. She put the picture back and picked up a photo of a different family. "Who's this?"

"That's my dear, dear, dear friend, Jeff Allison, with his wife and little girl. They'll have another kid in a few months."

"Awesome. Is this you and Jeff?" She held up a high school graduation picture.

"Yeah, and if you could see under the hat, I had the same haircut back then. That guy on the other side of me is Rick Jordan. He was a year behind us, but the three of us were always hanging out together."

"He looks familiar, somehow, but I can't place him."

"Are you a fan of college football, by any chance?"

"Yes, I am."

"Then you recognize USC's star wide receiver, 2000 to '03."

"I remember now. Doesn't he do commentary on TV, these days?"

"Yeah, on ESPN."

"He was nominated for the Heismann in '02, wasn't he? Why didn't he go pro?"

"He was drafted by San Diego, but they never put him in a game. He just played on the practice squad and they released him after a couple of seasons."

"That's too bad."

"Eh, he landed on his feet, which is more than can be said for the Chargers."

"Uh-oh, I sense a disgruntled fan."

"I'll spare you my rants. They're coming back, anyway."

"Sure, they are," she said sarcastically, aware that the Chargers had been in decline for the last seven seasons. She found a group photo of some exuberant young men wearing a variety of wet suits, jungle fatigues and Navy uniforms, each proudly displaying long flippers and golden trident pins. "Who are the sea monkeys?"

122

"That would be the BUD/S class of fall 2002, or at least the quarter of it that made it through without cracking."

"So why do you have- oh, hey, that's you!" In the picture, Roche's face was covered by black grease paint and a dive mask, but the spiky white-blond hair and piercing blue eyes identified him.

"Basic Underwater Demolition / Swimmer is the SEAL training course."

"Oh."

"Everyone in that picture is extremely happy for two reasons. First, we just finished the toughest twelve weeks of our lives, and second, we were about to go to Iraq."

Tracy nodded, and looked up at the man standing next to her, expecting more of the story. But Commander Roche just stared at his one-time buddies. Tracy tried to read his eyes, but saw only distant coldness that was at once sad and frightening. Karl caught her look and gave her a little smile. Tracy knew she wouldn't open him up and moved on to a more comfortable memory. "This one is more recent, I think."

Karl put down the Grinder picture and picked up the frame that Tracy had pointed out. "This actually just came in the mail yesterday. This is my class at TOPGUN." The photo showed sixteen pilots, including Roche, wearing their flight suits and standing under a banner that read "TOPGUN Congratulates: Sharkey..." and the callsigns of the other graduates. That was the last photo on the shelf.

"What do you want to do for dinner?" Tracy asked, after glancing at the clock. It was a quarter past five.

"I was about to ask you the same thing."

"I can't decide, so you choose."

"I have no ideas or preferences, so you choose."

"Compromise: I tell you what options I'm thinking of, and you pick."

Karl shrugged. "Okay."

"Steak, Japanese, salad, or we could order in."

"That's an extremely wide range of options. We could go to a restaurant that serves steak and salad, or Benihana does Japanese steak, or I can have sushi delivered here, or..." Karl trailed off as he went to his refrigerator. "Or I could make steak salad for you here using Japanese preparation methods."

"Well, that sounds terrific."

"Tracy, party of two? Welcome to Karl's Kitchen. We can seat you here at the counter. Can I offer you a cocktail while you wait?"

Tracy had noticed that Karl had a well-stocked wet bar. "I'd like a cosmo, shaken, with a twist, if you can do that."

Karl's bartending skills had made him an honorary brother at several fraternities at UCLA. He produced a martini glass filled with vodka and cranberry juice with a slice of lemon, poured the mixture into a shaker, and back into the glass.

"You shake it with the lemon?" Tracy asked. She had never seen a drink mixed that way.

"It's the only way to evenly distribute the lemon juice throughout the drink. Otherwise a twist is just a decoration, right?" After Roche handed her the cosmo, he squeezed the rest of the lemon into a tall glass of ice, then added a shot of Captain Morgan's Private Stock rum, a dash of sweet-and-sour and a can of Diet Pepsi.

"I can see what you mean about the lemon," Tracy said, after sipping the cosmopolitan. "Hat's off to the barkeep. And what do you call that concoction you've made for yourself?"

"This is just a minor improvement on a Cuba Libre. I don't really have a name for it." He went outside and lit his hibachi grill, came back in and started emptying the fridge. In a minute, he had the kitchen counter covered with salad fixings and two frozen steaks. "I haven't practiced this recently, so I should warn you that you are watching me cook dinner at your own risk. Do you promise to waive any liability?"

"Uh, ok…" Roche disappeared upstairs, and returned a moment later carrying a pair of either long knives or short swords in decorated scabbards. Tracy had no idea what he was up to. "What in the world are you doing with those?"

"I told you I was cooking Japanese-style."

"I thought you meant the hibachi."

"Minor detail. What I meant was cooking the way they do at places like Benihana – preparing the food at your table with long, dangerous blades." Roche drew his own blades and bowed from the waist.

"I see. And are those proper Japanese cooking utensils?"

"These are called tantu, the traditional Samurai short sword and preferred alternative to butcher knives on the Iron Chef TV show."

"And do you often use the tantu in the kitchen?"

"No, I usually keep them with the rest of my collection. Remind me after dinner to show it to you." During the conversation Karl was rather casually hacking a head of lettuce, a cucumber, three tomatoes and a bell pepper to tiny bits. Now he took a pair of large

124

plates from the top of the refrigerator, set them on edge and spun them, then loaded his pile of salad evenly on the plates as they settled on the counter. Tracy applauded the trick. "Intermission," Karl said. He went outside and put the steaks on the grill.

"Are those sirloins?"

"New York strip, actually. How do you want yours?"

"Medium-rare, please."

"Alright." He went back to work on the salads, adding shredded cheese, raisins, sunflower seeds and bacon bits, then he cut open a pair of avocados.

"You save those for last?"

"They brown if you cut them too soon. You have to hit them with salad dressing right away to keep them fresh."

"You certainly have your cooking honed to an art form."

"Do you want honey mustard, ranch, or vinaigrette?"

"Vinaigrette, please." Roche applied the dressing, and then he went back to the bar and poured generous shots of sake and bourbon. "You haven't finished your first drink," Tracy noted.

"This isn't for me," Karl explained. He emptied the shot glasses into another cup, and poured in a couple of ounces of Worcestershire sauce, and took the odd mixture out to the grill. Tracy watched him flip the steaks, and abruptly splash the contents of his cup into the grill. The alcohol exploded in a small fireball, startling Tracy and causing her to think for a moment that her new boyfriend may have killed himself. But when the flames cleared, he was still there, calmly poking the burning meat and drizzling the dregs of his combustible sauce on the steaks. After a minute he brought the sizzling beef inside. "I hope I didn't frighten you a moment ago."

"Well, you could have warned me you were going to blow something up."

"I think you will be pleased with the explosive flavor." Karl went to work with the swords again, carving and chopping the steaks down to bite-size, before finally adding them to the salad plates and sitting down next to Tracy.

She eagerly stabbed her fork through the salad, collecting as many different ingredients as possible, and tasting it all at once. "Fantastic," she said as soon as she swallowed. "Karl's Kitchen gets five stars."

"Better make it four," Karl said, as he got up again. "A five-star restaurant would have remembered napkins."

*     *     *

After dinner, Roche took her upstairs to the spare bedroom.  He opened the sliding closet door to reveal his collection of firearms and blades.  On one side he kept the all the guns – six weapons he'd been issued while in the SEALs, plus his own Glock machine pistol and a shotgun.   An enormous McMillan .50 caliber rifle was mounted proudly at the top, complete with an expensive scope and a heavy suppressor.  Below that, a pair of MP5 submachine guns; one a slightly smaller "k" model, the larger one sporting a laser/optical sight, both with silencers.  Then there was a Mossberg 590 12-gauge pump-action shotgun.  It is used by the Navy and Coast Guard when they board ships suspected of smuggling drugs, but Karl had bought his own gun commercially.  On the floor there were the two large cases Roche used to transport his pistols.  The case that he used to carry the .45 and the 9mm was empty.   Roche normally kept the SIG in the glove compartment of his car, and he left the silenced SOCOM pistol under his mattress.

"That's quite an arsenal.  You actually shot that huge rifle in combat?"

"Scored my first kills with it.  I can hit a playing card a mile away with that gun."

"At what point is a rifle no longer a rifle, but actually a cannon?"

"Technically, at twenty millimeters, you advance from the small arms category to what is considered artillery."

"So what's that?"

"Fifty cal, or twelve-point-seven mil.  It uses the same ammo as an M2 Browning machine gun.  At a thousand yards it can punch through a quarter-inch steel plate like it was a soda can."

"Very cool.  Now where are your swords?"

"Other side."  Roche moved the doors to reveal the other half of the closet, which contained a number of swords and knives protected by a plexiglass case like a museum exhibit.  He opened the case to put away the tantu, and removed a larger weapon in a similarly designed scabbard.  "This is the katana, the big brother of the tantu.  The tantu are replicas I purchased from a company in Atlanta, but this is the real deal."  He drew the twenty-nine-inch sword, which was polished to gleam like silver and engraved with Japanese characters.

"Beautiful."

"This was made by a master swordsmith in the fourteenth century for a samurai who served as the emperor's chief bodyguard. Generations later, the samurai's descendants became lords in their own

126

right. This sword was passed down through that family until the 1860's when it was presented as a gift to a Russian industrialist, who was my great-great grandfather."

"I thought you were German."

"Mostly in name. I am, in fact, equal parts German and Russian on my dad's side, and Scottish and Scandinavian on my mom's side. I'm the only grandson of four different families, so I sort of inherited all of their military heirlooms."

"I see. So these have all been in your family for years, other than the samurai steak knives."

"Those I bought by mail-order, and this little baby I bought in the Philippines a few years ago." Roche presented a balisong – also known as a butterfly knife – which is illegal in most states because it can be whipped out almost as fast as a switchblade. Roche demonstrated how the two-part handle swings open to expose the four-inch blade sandwiched inside. Next he showed off a wicked-looking seven-and-a-half-inch bowie-style semi-serrated black-finish blade. "And this is a SOG combat knife, which is SEAL issue. The rest of these are from the Roche-Kranov-McLain-Larson heritage collection."

"Wow."

"This sword here," Roche pointed to an old-fashioned but strong-looking blade, "is a Royal Navy Officer's saber that first belonged to my great-great-great-great-great-great grandfather, Robert McLain. He was the first leftenant on the British heavy frigate *Serapis*, which sank the *BonHomme Richard* but was captured by John Paul Jones in the last and greatest warship duel of the Revolutionary War. Jones actually knew the McLain family from his childhood in Scotland. Robert later died of the wounds he received in the battle but Jones had his sword inscribed before the *Serapis'* crew was released in France."

Tracy looked closely and read the engraved writing on the blade. "To Once and Future Friends – Jn. Pl. Jones."

"Pretty cool, huh? The next six generations of McLains were Royal Navy officers, including my Granddad, a retired Admiral and former Ambassador. This sword had been in every major war from 1776 to 1943, and then it was almost lost. Granddad was a navigation officer on the cruiser HMS *Charybdis*, which was sunk during the war. He escaped, but he didn't have time to get dressed, let alone find his sword. Twelve years ago a diving expedition snooped the wreck of the *Charybdis*, and recovered this and a few other artifacts. Now, when the London Historical Society saw this, they immediately called up my Granddad, who was at the time the Ambassador to Jamaica – sort of a retirement posting. Anyway, he was of course delighted beyond words that they found the family saber. Finally, when I was commissioned in 2001, he presented it to me to keep the tradition alive. I keep it here, so it doesn't get sunk again."

"That's an incredible story."

"I know. To think, some people just collect stamps or commemorative plates." There were two other swords in the collection, both medieval broadswords. Roche explained one belonged to a Viking chieftain and the other to a Teutonic Knight of the Order of St. John, both of whom were his ancient ancestors.

"So, lemme get this straight. You're part Viking, part Knight of the Holy Cross, part Royal Navy Admiral, and what's your Russian side again?"

"My Oma was KGB agent," Roche explained, using the German word for grandmother, "and her parents were an old-school Cossack cavalry general and an industrial heiress. My German side also has a Nazi rocket scientist, a gentleman pirate, and the guy who built the first railroad in continental Europe. My Scandinavian quarter is all Vikings and lumberjacks, and one fashion model."

"So *that's* where you get your good looks."

"My maternal grandmother. I never met her. She died before I was born. That was actually how my parents met."

"How did that happen?"

"Well, at the time, granddad was the naval attaché for the British consulate to the States. He worked at the embassy and lived there along with his wife and daughter, my mother. His wife suffered a heart attack and was brought to the US Naval Hospital at Bethesda, Maryland. My dad was a Navy doc at the time, and was the cardiologist on call that night. He saved her for the time being, but she was diagnosed with congestive heart failure, which in the seventies meant she wouldn't live much longer. These days there are all kinds of drugs that can reverse the damage but back then, none of that was around. But my dad did his best to make her comfortable, and my mother ended up being enamored with him."

"Wow."

"My whole family line is full of unlikely pairings. Take my Dad's parents; Opa was rocket scientist working for Werner von Braun, who developed the V-2 ballistic missile and then came to the US to design missiles and rockets for the Air Force and NASA. Oma was a KGB agent who was supposed to kidnap him and take him back to the Soviets. Instead they fell in love and defected to the US together."

128

"Well, we seem to fit that profile too, with you meeting me by pulling me out of a car wreck."

"I was just thinking that." Karl said, and he saw something in her eyes that made him feel very happy that he had met her.

"He's a real nice guy," Tracy told her mother on the phone that night. "He's funny, sweet, sensitive…"

"Is he cute?"

"Well, he's cute like you think a bear is cute. Kind of soft to the touch but very tough and strong underneath."

"So maybe he's a kind of dangerous nice guy? Best of both worlds?"

"He certainly leads a dangerous life. Besides his job, which he says is second-most dangerous in the world next to Alaskan crab fishermen, he has some thrill-seeking hobbies and a past he won't talk much about."

"Ooh, a little dark mystery added to the formula. Sounds like everything a girl could want. Wait, can he cook?"

"Believe it or not, he's an excellent cook and bartender. I just had a very unique dinner experience at his house. Oh, and he keeps his place nice too."

"So, where do you see this going, honey?"

"It's a little soon to say, but I am definitely going to keep seeing him until he has to leave. And unless I see something seriously wrong with him I'll be waiting when he gets back."

"How long will he be on deployment?"

"Three to six months, maybe longer if a war breaks out."

"That's quite a commitment, Tracy."

"I know. At this point, that's exactly what I want. I just really hope he wants the same thing…"

# CHAPTER 7: THE SHOC

## NAS NORTH ISLAND – 0720, MONDAY APR 17<sup>TH</sup>

The *Stingrays'* squadron briefing room had all the comforts of a solar oven. It was built into a loft in the back of the hangar. The large skylights did an excellent job of letting in the California sun, and the corrugated steel roof did a better job of not allowing a single photon of infrared radiation to escape. The air conditioning had no effect on this room twenty feet above the ground floor, owing to the simple thermodynamic principle that cool air sinks and hot air rises. Only an hour after sunrise, the briefing room was twenty-five degrees warmer than the air outside. Conditions would worsen as the twenty flight officers arrived for the hour-plus-long introductory meeting.

As per the skipper's request, Roche arrived early with nineteen copies of a very detailed technical document that would introduce the Super Hornet to the other aviators.

Hannibal was already there, organizing his stuff. He took one of Sharkey's thick folders. "You didn't write this yourself, did you?"

"Absolutely not. I merely compiled excerpts from Boeing's project report, NAVAIR's test data, and some less technical descriptions from a web site."

Hannibal looked at the bottom of the last page where Roche cited his three references – Boeing, Naval Air Warfare Center, and "GlobalSecurity.org? Who's that?"

"That's a privately funded military database and think-tank. They are claimed – by more than just themselves – to be the most comprehensive public source of defense and intelligence information in the world."

"I'm not a fan of people who share information that ought to be classified freely over the web."

"Well, be that as it may, they had almost all the data I needed. Design specs, system analysis, and most importantly, a complete technical comparison between the Super and the Legacy Hornet. I only needed to go to Boeing for their reports and to NAVAIR for the test specs, and that actually *is* classified. I had to fax them a copy of my DoD security clearance papers before they let me see the data."

"What's the difference between design specs and test specs?"

"About fifty percent. I'll explain that in my lesson."

"Okay. Good work."

The crew started to trickle in gradually. Roche had already met "Hardcase" Wilkes and "Hacksaw" Miller, and of course Lt. "Blackjack" Masterson. He was introduced to the rest of the squad as they walked in. Some were from the old *Rays* and *Stingers* squadrons, others were new transfers like he was.

Lt. Cmdr. Jules "Hunter" Hidelmann had joined the VA-23 *Rays* as a pilot in 1989. He flew several combat missions during the beginning of the Gulf War, but was shot down over southern Iraq shortly after Desert Storm commenced. His Bombardier/Navigator was killed and he was captured by the Republican Guard, and held for seven weeks as a POW. He sustained injuries during the bailout, gun battle on the ground and subsequent torture, which left him temporarily crippled. He hopped desk jobs in the Navy for three years before he had recovered enough to fly again. His pilot status would elude him forever, but he rejoined VA-23 as a B/N. He was offered promotions several times, but he turned down any advancement that would have moved him out of flight ops. Navy bureaucrats refer to this behavior as "planting," and their typical response is to ignore the plant. So now, at the age of 45, Jules knew he'd never advance in the Navy and he couldn't have been happier about it. Even flying in a reserve squadron was enough for him. In the new squadron he'd fly in the back seat of a Super-F as a Weapon System Officer (WSO, pronounced Wizzo) where his vast experience with precision bombing would be invaluable.

Lt. Dennis "Hawk" Collins had studied criminal justice in college and originally planned to exit the active service and go to law school as soon as his minimum four years were up. Apparently he changed his mind, because he had now been flying for six years and had voluntarily returned to active duty with the *Stingrays*. He started off in the Hawkeye AWACS service, moved to Prowlers, and from there to the Intruders in the *Rays*. He was double-rated as a pilot and WSO.

Lt. Amber "Blaze" Worthy was widely regarded as the best one-night-stand and the best female aviator in the Pacific fleet. The Navy had long recognized that due to their smaller stature, female sailors and aviators had certain advantages in tight shipboard quarters, especially on submarines and in aircraft cockpits. But the process of allowing women to serve in combat roles was completed grudgingly and with considerable resistance from a percentage of the male population. Aviators especially, tend to be a conservative group and reacted with strong opposition to the inclusion of "aliens," as female aviators are often called. Women like Blaze who loved to flirt and sleep around didn't help such matters, but her skills in the air certainly did. Once behind the controls of a warplane, she had nothing to prove. She was extremely popular with the men she served with and no one had called her an alien in years. She had just been transferred to the *Stingrays* from a Super Hornet squadron based in Japan.

Lt. jg. Maggie "Mystique" Banning was a different case. She had joined many activist causes while in college, and supposedly had joined the Navy on a dare to push for women's rights in the military. She was a cold fish by nature and seemed shy, but it turned out she was an excellent Wizzo. Her practice of Zen Buddhism gave her a level of concentration that was almost inhuman.

Lt. John Henry "Doc" Holliday shared more than just his name with the legendary OK Corral gunslinger. Doc was all Wild West swagger, with plenty of shootin' skill to back it up. He was a TOPGUN alum, and he had spent a tour playing aggressor at the Air Force's counterpart fighter school also. His favorite thing in the world was to dive into the fray of a dogfight shooting off missiles in all directions and whooping and hollering like a drunken cowboy on open channel. But he had never flown a combat tour and his antics didn't lend well to a leadership role.

Lt. Reginald "Beowulf" Stamper and Sub-Lt. Ian "Claymore" Bruce were British Royal Navy pilots. They had been seconded into the US Navy as part of a co-op training program. The RN would soon be taking delivery of the F-35 Lightning II joint strike fighter as a replacement for its Harriers, and the pilots who would be flying it had no experience with supersonic fighter-attack jets. So Beowulf and Claymore and a hundred-plus other Brits were sent to the States to fly Hornets and learn a new style of combat.

Lt. Darren "Rooster" McCoy appeared to be a wild-eyed hillbilly from the hollers of Tennessee. He actually had grown up in Knoxville, possessed a genius-level IQ and graduated from the University of Tennessee with an electrical engineering degree, but he carefully cultivated his backwater-rural image. He was in fact from the same McCoy clan that had a legendary feud with the Hatfields. His antics had added plenty of color to the *Stingers*, and he was an extremely competent pilot to boot.

Lt. jg. Jake "Gator" Palmer was born in New Orleans, and grew up in Tampa, Florida. He was prone to taking long midday naps and had a few other odd habits, but he was very highly regarded for his weapons skills.

Lt. Joe "Hitman" Armani had been Hardcase's wingman in the *Stingers* for several years. He was fiercely loyal to his friends, particularly Wilkes, and was well known for making difficult missile kills.

Lt. jg. Mike "Ronin" Shinano and Lt. jg. Kevin "Creep" MacGregor had grown up together in Seattle and had stuck close all the way up to their first flight assignment, which was with the *Stingrays*.

Lt. Eugene "Bulldog" Harris was a large black man who was both an excellent pilot a devious character. He weighed in at well over the Navy regulation 195lbs, which is mandated by the maximum load of the Mk. 9 ejection seat. For a month before his annual physical, he would go on a diet of raw vegetables and water and run as if training for a marathon. Somehow it always worked, and right after the doctors cleared him for another year in flight ops he'd go back to eating pizza and donuts until he was at his "normal" 240lb weight.

Lt. Sherman "Shredder" Ferraby was Hannibal's pick as wingman. His claim to fame was being the best shot in the Air Wing with the Vulcan cannon, or at least he had been before Sharkey came to town.

Lt. jg. Bobby "Buzz" Edwards was the youngest member of the *Stingrays*. He was an electronics genius and his superiors believed he would evolve into a highly talented weapon systems officer.

Hannibal stood in front of a folding table, setting up his laptop and a projector. After Buzz helped him connect the two, Hannibal began the meeting. "If you guys could all find a seat now, let's start this. As of now, the A-6 Intruder, which several people here have been flying, is officially 100% mothballed. VA-23 no longer exists, and the Intruder therefore has no squadron flying it. Also, another historic squadron, my own VFA-113 *Stingers*, which flew Hellcats, Cougars, Avengers, and the first-ever Hornets, has entered its last line in the history book. We are one squad, now. *Stingers* and *Rays* don't exist; everyone here is a *Stingray*, so I will tolerate no cross-squad rivalry, got that?

"As I said, both former squadrons had a long and glorious history, but that's all it is now – history. We are being catapulted into the future of naval aviation with the very newest and most powerful carrier-based strike fighter in the world. Also, by combining a group of bomber pilots and a group of fighter pilots, we are something called a composite squadron. We are a great experiment, because this has never been done before with mixed Super Hornets. We will be the *Reagan* battle group's first option for dealing with any threat. The *Reagan* itself being the most powerful carrier in the Pacific fleet, this sort of makes us the tip of the spear for the entire military. This means a lot of brass will have their eyes on us, so do good.

"We're organized into four divisions, led by Sharkey, Hardcase, Blackjack and myself. Each division leader will be piloting a Super-F. The theory is that a single Wizzo can coordinate air and ground attacks for the entire division. Since two of our Wizzos are rookies, we'll have to see how well that will work in practice. I want to pair Hunter – our most experienced Wizzo – with Sharkey. I'll take Buzz – who's the least experienced and will have the most to learn from me. Hawk goes to Hardcase so we have a second division with well-balanced leadership. That leaves Mystique to Blackjack. If that doesn't seem to work out we can always make adjustments later. Sharkey's wingman is Hacksaw, Hardcase keeps Hitman, Blackjack gets Creep, and I've selected Shredder. Second section leads will be Bulldog in my division, paired with Doc; Beowulf and Claymore under Sharkey, Rooster and Gator under Blackjack, and Blaze and Ronin under Hacksaw." Hannibal used PowerPoint to show the organized squadron in simulated formation. Then he moved on to another org chart.

"Here's the command breakdown: I'm the CO obviously, and I'll be handling S-1 administration duties. The XO is Lieutenant Commander "Sharkey" Roche. He's been with Rhinos the longest – with VFA-151 and TOPGUN – so he'll be the one training us and he'll pick up all the S-3 position jobs. S-2 intel will be handled by Hunter; Hardcase will be S-4 mechanics and logistics, and Hawk is S-5 comms and requisitions. They can all pick they're own assistants. I'll assign my own assistant duties to whoever gives me the most trouble. Questions."

Blackjack raised his hand. "Who are the op leaders?" Op leads take command of different missions depending on the objective. Usually the CO and the XO each had one op lead responsibility, but other senior pilots were picked as second-option leads.

"I'll lead strike ops, and Hardcase can be my second. Sharkey is the highest-scoring Top Gunner in history and supposedly the best pilot in the world, so I think we'll let him do the fighter ops. I'll let you pick your alternate, Commander."

"Blackjack can be fighter-two if he's up to it," Roche said. "And TOPGUN is just simulations. It doesn't mean anything in real life."

134

"Yeah, sure. Anyway, we have a training schedule for the rest of the month. First two weeks, we have crossover training to teach us how to fly the new Super Hornet. Sharkey doesn't have anything to do with that – Boeing and NAVAIRPAC S-3 put that together. Sharkey and Blaze have had this so they get a little extra leave while the rest of us go back to school. Unless, Sharkey, you want to throw in a few pop quizzes."

"I'll give you a week to get used to the planes, and then I'll give you a few surprise aggressor exercises to keep you sharp. Trust me, by the second week, crossover starts to get boring otherwise."

"Okay. After that we are going to start carrier qualification. Now, for some reason, the *Reagan* is on rapid gear-up and the fleet command wants the squadrons to start CQ as soon as possible. So when the *Stennis* is going out in a couple weeks, we'll do a few traps on her, and then again on the *Nimitz* when she's coming in the week after that. That way, we'll be almost finished with CQ by the time we deploy, and the carrier won't have to wait near shore for us to finish all the qualifiers, and we can all just go straight to the Middle East Theater of Operations."

"What's going on in the METO that requires our urgent attention this time?" Hardcase asked.

"There's some intel chatter that the Iranians are up to no good. Again. Having an extra CVBG in the gulf should make 'em keep their heads down." The Navy always keeps a CVBG in the Arabian Sea as a highly visible reminder of America's interest in the region. Placing *two* carriers in the area – each with enough firepower to destroy entire countries – was an unmistakable sign that Uncle Sam meant business. "Anyone else have a question about our schedule or deployment? No? Okay, then the crossover training begins now. The XO here is going to give a little lecture introducing us to the Super Hornet."

Roche got up and started talking. "The Super Hornet is a fourth-and-a-half-generation multi-role superfighter, widely regarded as the best strike fighter in the world. It is not the fastest, stealthiest, hardest-hitting or most agile fighter, but it's the one that best blends all of those attributes into a single package. It's also by far the smartest plane ever built – I'll explain what I mean by that in a minute. It's earned a few nicknames, ranging from the derogatory 'Big Bug,' popularized by the Tomcat crews that the Super's replacing, to the more affectionate 'Rhino,' as in 'how do you stop a charging..?'"

Sharkey passed out his folders. "This is the Reader's Digest condensed edition of the Super Hornet project summary. This is mostly optional reading, and you won't understand much of it anyway unless you took engineering in school. Pages five through nine, however, you should pay attention to. That covers the test limit specs of the aircraft. They won't tell you this during the training program, but the performance limits you will have set on the ground simulators are not the same as the real thing. The simulators are programmed with the design specs as constraints – that's the specs the Navy asked for when the Super Hornet program began in 1993. But the production aircraft has been tested to exceed all design limits by twenty to sixty percent. The top speed, for instance, is about two hundred and sixty knots better than design spec. The airframe is supposed to handle up to eight-and-a-half Gs, but it will actually take over twelve without any problem. So look that over and keep it in mind when you get to the simulators, and be ready for it when you try the real machine. Nobody told me about the test limits when I started on Supers, and I scared myself to death when I hit a ten-G turn the first time. So make sure you understand the capabilities of the Super.

"Otherwise, it's a real easy plane to fly. Those of you who were flying Hornet-Cs in the *Stingers* shouldn't have any trouble. I included a comparison sheet in your folder. The cockpit is laid out a little differently, but the flight mechanics are almost identical. 'Truder pilots will have much to learn, but you'll probably get used to it quickly. It will be like driving a new Corvette instead of a '66 Impala. The first thing you'll all have to learn is using the sidestick. It just sits comfortably in your right hand and it feels a lot more natural than a center stick, but the first few times you get in you'll be reaching between your knees and there's nothing there. It's all fly-by-wire, so you can one-hand it through anything. No more fighting the airframe. This also gives you full-time HOTAS – hands-on throttle and stick. You can reach pretty much any button on the panels without moving your hands away from the controls.

"The fly-by-wire system goes through the SHOC, (pronounced 'shock') – that's the Super Hornet Onboard Computer. This computer is the single biggest evolutionary step in military aviation technology since the jet engine. It controls seventeen different subsystems that you would never be able to simultaneously monitor on your own. The fly-by-wire system will interpret your control input from the force-feedback sidestick, and translate that for more control surfaces than any human can manage. Elevators, rudders, elevons, ailerons, flaps, slats, strakes, all respond precisely as you intend, directed by only subtle movements of your right hand. By the way, the rudder pedals are part

136

of that input, but you can also twist the sidestick from side to side to give a little more precise rudder control." Sharkey spotted someone with his hand up. "Yeah, Ronin, you have a question?"

"Does the computer ever make a mistake and misread you? Like you're just trying to do a roll-on and it pulls you through a corkscrew instead?"

"That's not a problem. The control is very precise. It will never move beyond what you input. Besides, this is an extremely well-educated system. Boeing test pilots spent years literally teaching SHOC how it's supposed to perform. It is very good at predicting your intentions, so you probably won't ever confuse it. Also, it learns from you. Even if you have an eccentric style of flying, it will catch on quick. And its memory can be transferred to any other Rhino you fly. When I get into my new plane, I'll be uploading my accumulated eighteen hundred hours with the type and Blaze will be able to do the same thing. And along the way, if any of you switch to one of the two spare Es, you can load all your hours from your own plane.

"The SHOC will also have a few ideas of its own that you may want to take advantage of. The software can analyze a target or a threat and give you guidance on how to deal with it. It's called CEI for computer evasion and intercept. If you select a preloaded strike option on your computer or press the CEI button on your stick, SHOC will display a series of flight path gates on your HUD, which will appear in different colors depending on where your airspeed needs to be. They'll be red if you need to slow down, green if you need to speed up, blue if your airspeed is okay, and blinking if it wants you to use afterburner. This can be very useful in a dogfight if you're not sure where an incoming missile is or where an enemy aircraft is heading. The SHOC will tell you exactly what you need to do to evade a missile or intercept your nearest target.

"Furthermore, we have SHOClink, which is a dedicated, secure Wi-Fi channel we can use to share data with each other and any other Super while in flight. It can also be patched in to the radar picture from any AWACS assets in range. Among other things this lets the SHOC put together a composite multi-source radar picture which can let us defeat stealth aircraft by hitting them with radar from different angles. Are there any other questions about the SHOC?"

"Does it control the ECM suite also?" Buzz asked.

"Thanks for reminding me. It does have a dedicated processor which works in conjunction with a separate and even more powerful ECM system. The block 2-c production model that we have is equipped with the last word in ECM technology – the AN/ALQ-214 IDECM block 3." (Roche pronounced it "Ann-Alk-two-one-four-I-deck-'em") "SHOC provides the IDECM computer with all the radar and signals input it has, and from there IDECM sets up a full range of countermeasures. It's got full-spectrum jammers, a false-return-generating RFCM system, and something called an FOTD, which is a towed decoy on a fiber-optic cable, like a submarine uses, and it will throw off even the smartest missile. Also, instead of old-fashioned flares and chaff, the ALY-50 decoy launcher is equipped with flare-shells, which explode in your wake in a cloud of white-hot, razor-sharp aluminum shrapnel. It's irresistible to infrared and radar guided missiles alike, and destroys anything that flies through the cloud. And by now you've noticed the fancy paint job. That's got a special coating that throws off radar at close range. Altogether, this plane's virtually immune to missiles, especially radar-guided weapons. But don't put all your money on the automatic systems. There's still nothing more effective than a well-timed turn-and-burn, and again, the SHOC can help you with that timing. Anything else I can tell you? Hawk?"

"What's the Rhino's actual top speed at full military thrust?"

"There's a chart on page fourteen that has that. It's 620 knots at sea level, 650 at 30,000 feet – at which point you are well into the supersonic – and 700 at 50,000 feet. That's flying clean. Subtract about five knots for every hardpoint you load. Top speed with afterburner at altitude is around Mach 1.95 – quite a ways beyond design spec. They say it will do Mach 2 and a bit of change in a dive, but I've never tried that."

No one else had questions, so Hannibal stood up and called it a wrap. "Okay, thanks, Sharkey. We need to assemble at the COMNAVAIRPAC HQ in ten for the beginning of crossover. Sharkey and Blaze are dismissed. Feel free to get some practice hours in on your free time, but remember, that fancy skin cost half a million for each plane – don't scratch the paint."

**NAVAL MEDICAL CENTER SAN DIEGO**
**TWO HOURS LATER**

Captain Joshua Thompson let his eyes wander around the office while he waited. On either side of LCdr. Dr. Herbert Tobias' framed letter of recognition from the Navy Medical Board were his diplomas from UCLA and the Naval Academy. These were surrounded by pictures of all the ships he'd served with over his thirty-year career. The new supercarrier USS *Ronald Reagan* was at the top.

"Well, the stress-echo results came back," Dr. Tobias said as he entered his office. He walked around the desk and sat down in his chair, studying the contents of a folder he was carrying.

Deuce waited, leaning back in his chair, deliberately appearing unconcerned. He waited until Tobias gave him an expectant look over the top of the chart. He obliged the doctor. "And?"

Tobias set the chart down. "Your ejection faction is still at thirty-percent, so your condition appears to have been stabilized by the medication. It's not any worse, but it hasn't improved either since your last round of tests."

"So I'm still okay to go."

Dr. Tobias sighed deeply, making a great show of his discomfort. "Again, you shouldn't even be cleared to fly at all. I'm going to give that to you because we're old friends and I really don't want you to twist my arm."

"Thanks."

"As Commander Air Group, you're traditionally expected to lead from the air. You will not be able to do that, unless by some miracle you show dramatic improvement between here and the METO. And it *would* be a miracle, since you're at the maximum dose for the medicine. So you won't be up there leading the charge."

"It's not an issue," Deuce said. "Commander Burke, the *Stingrays*' skipper, is being groomed for promotion. I'm supposed to let him lead the charge anyway."

"Burke is a good officer," Tobias affirmed. "I met him on the *Nimitz*."

"Who's running our ship?" Thompson asked.

"You haven't met them yet?"

"I've been in and out of doctors' offices all week, and moving my family into a nice house in Clairemont. I haven't been on a Navy base until today."

"How are Loraine and the boys?"

"They're doing well; happy to leave the desert. So who's running this ship?"

"The CO is a guy named Brian Young. Remember him?"

"No."

"He was on the *Enterprise* with us, in the Med. Skippered a Viking squadron."

"Oh yeah, they called him 'Nuke.'"

"Right, 'Nuke' Young. Hopefully he'll remember you better, and all the favors he owes you."

"Who's the flag?"

"New assignment. I don't think he's arrived in town yet. Do you remember a Wally Krause, who was on the *Ranger* while we were on the *Midway*, in the Gulf?"

Deuce frowned. "That the guy who was a squad S-2 and got bumped up to Wing Intelligence Officer and got a medal for accidentally sending a flight of 'Truders to bomb a parking lot full of artillery and got half of his planes shot down in the process?"

"That's one version of the story, but you have the right guy. He kept moving up; made Admiral in '99 and was Deputy Director of the National Security Agency until a few months ago."

"Our flag is a spook," Deuce said unhappily. "And not just a spook; he's a spook with connections to more spooks, and worse, politicians."

"That might not be a bad thing, you know."

"We'll see," Thompson shrugged. "I have a good wing, anyway. As long as the skipper keeps the boat pointed into the wind, and that spook doesn't make me do anything stupid, I'll be happy."

"And as long as you take care of that ticker, I'll be happy. Have you been cutting back on the cigars?"

"Yeah," Thompson sighed.

"Well don't. If they help you relax and keep your blood pressure down, they'll help your heart recover."

Captain Thompson raised his eyebrows at that. "Is my hearing failing on top of everything else? Because I think you just told your heart patient to smoke *more*."

"Yeah. Well, it's not a typical prescription, obviously, but you're not a typical case. You're showing no symptoms of congestive heart failure yet; what you really need is something – anything – to help chill you out. Smoking occasionally will do you more help than harm, at this point."

Deuce grinned and pulled a Macanudo from his shirt pocket. "I love you."

**FIVE DAYS LATER**

Tracy came over to visit Karl again the next Saturday. By now her Mini was out of the shop, good as new and sporting a fresh coat of shiny blue paint. Karl came out of the house to meet her as she pulled up. She let him examine the car. "I could never tell that this thing used to be a sound wall sandwich. And that's a great paint job."

"I was inspired by your planes. They just looked so pretty." The Mini's pearlescent paint finish shimmered in the sunlight, similar to the *Stingrays'* new Hornets.

"So, what do you want to do today?" Karl asked.

"I was thinking you could take me to see that new Brad Pitt movie."

"That's fine with me." Roche opened the sliding keyboard on his cell phone and consulted the web browser while they continued talking. "What about dinner?"

"Could we go to In & Out?" Tracy was craving the world's greatest hamburger.

"You bet. There's one right next to the Bayside Edwards theater, and... we now have tickets for the six-forty showing." Roche snapped the phone shut.

"Okay, cool. Now how do you want to kill the next five hours?"

"Well, I really should get some flight hours in this weekend. Would you want to go for a little ride with me?"

"In a Hornet? Are you kidding? That would be so awesome."

Karl unlocked his Samsung smart phone again and hit the speed dial key for the *Stingrays'* hangar office. "Hey there Chief, it's Sharkey. Is there a Fish left in there?" The *Stingrays* had eighteen planes – fourteen Es and four Fs. The variants were designated Eels and Fish for easy reference.

"Yeah, they left one for you. Hawk is flying in the front seat today, so they only took three of the Fish." Chief Petty Officer Terry Newman was the squadron's senior non-commissioned officer – the maintenance crew chief. He was directly in charge of the team of mechanics that kept the Supers lubed and tuned. Of course, since the planes were brand new, he didn't have much to do yet.

"Alright, good. Could you roll that out for me, and find a small helmet please?"

"Taking a lady friend up sightseeing sir?"

Karl didn't much like the way Newman asked that question. "Inasmuch as it is entirely within regulations for an unrated observer to be allowed to be a passenger on a non-combat training flight when not on carrier operations, yes, I am."

"Right, well, no problem here, Commander. Fish Two will be waiting for you on the tarmac, and I'll find you that helmet and a spare suit."

"Thanks."

"Can I drive over?" Tracy asked.

"Sure, as long as you drive fast. You remember how to get there?"

"Past the Starbucks, behind the warehouses at the carrier dock, around the end of Runway eighteen, fifth hangar on the right." Tracy took off as soon as Roche buckled in. The tiny car is surprisingly roomy; Karl had no trouble getting his 188lb frame into the passenger seat. "Are you sure it's okay for me to drive this fast?" Tracy asked as she entered the back of the dockyard at fifty miles an hour.

"This deep into the base, the SPs would be suspicious if you *weren't* going at least this fast. Only an aviator has any business driving around back here, and all aviators ignore the speed limits. If you stuck to the roads and the posted limits you'd look like a lost tourist or maybe a spy." Tracy skirted the main runway and screeched to a stop in front of the hangar. "Fourteen seconds off my personal best," Karl said, checking his watch, "and you weren't even trying. Not bad. You can just leave the car here."

One of the maintenance crew was towing a Super-F out into the sunlight with a Quiktug. Tracy got out and looked at the gleaming fighter, and back to her car. "The color looks like a perfect match."

"Yeah, it does." Karl walked up to his plane and helped the guy driving the tug disconnect from the nosegear. A gray-haired, muscular man came out of the hangar a moment later carrying two helmets and two pairs of khaki coveralls. Karl made introductions. "Tracy, meet my mechanics, Chief Terry Newman and Petty Officer Hector Domingo. Gentlemen, this is Miss Tracy Davis."

"How do you do?" Tracy shook their hands.

"I brought you a new suit, Miss Davis," Newman handed her one of the coveralls. Roche took the other pair and quickly pulled them over his jeans and t-shirt.

"It looks a little too big," Tracy said, as she stepped into the pants. It was an understatement. When she pulled the sleeves up her shoulders and zipped it up, the baggy coveralls hung off her like a clown costume.

"It's one size fits all," Roche said. "It just needs to be tailored." He squeezed a tab on the zipper, and the outfit miraculously shrank until it fit Tracy perfectly.

"What the-"

"It's called thermagel," Newman explained. "It expands and contracts dramatically with small changes in temperature. And it's incompressible, like water. It fills the whole suit, between layers of

142

neoprene. In high-G maneuvers, it contracts a little more to squeeze blood out of your legs and back into your brain. In the old days – well, four years ago – they used air bladders on the pants to keep pilots from blacking out. These work much better. The same gel stuff lines the helmets, so you don't 'red out' in a negative-G maneuver. It lets these pilots pull even crazier stunts than before. Here, try this on." He handed Tracy a white helmet with a black visor pushed up on the crown.

"This is just a little bit loose."

"Say when." Newman pressed a small two-way switch on the right temple.

Tracy felt a slight warming sensation as the gel lining expanded and tightened on her head. "Okay, no, wait, that's a little too tight."

"It's supposed to be a little snug."

"Okay, but it could be a little less snug." Newman clicked the switch the other way and the helmet released a little. "Perfect." Tracy looked at the helmet Karl had put on. It was black, with a blue shark painted on each side and blue and red stripes running across the top, front to back.

He was checking over the plane with Domingo while Newman was getting Tracy squared away. "Are you ready to go?" He asked. She nodded and approached the plane. She hadn't gotten a sense of how big it was until she stood next to it and realized her seat was above her head. She looked under the wing, to the huge parallelogram-shaped air intake, and caught a glimpse of the turbofan blades deep inside the machine. She had thought the machine looked beautiful from a distance, but standing this close, she began to feel the menace of the aircraft.

"Just go up the ladder," Karl told her. "I'll come up behind you and help you settle in." Domingo had pulled the ladder out from under the port-side strake for them. Tracy climbed and stepped into the back seat. Karl knelt on the carbon-fiber-composite strake next to her, and helped her adjust the four-point harness. He took an oxygen mask, connected it to a hose built in to the airframe, and clipped one side of it to her helmet so it hung off her left cheek. "If you get light-headed, lean into the hose here for a shot of oxygen. Before we start any kind of radical maneuver I'll say 'mask on,' then you need to clip the other side of it here so it covers your mouth and nose, and pull your visor down to keep it in place. You may want to slide that down about halfway anyway, to keep the sun out of your eyes. And if you start to feel sick-"

"That won't be a problem," Tracy interrupted. "I never get airsick."

"This isn't like a 737 you know. How do you do on roller coasters?"

"I've ridden every coaster on the West Coast and haven't chucked yet."

"Okay, well, just in case, there's a little bag under your left armrest."

Tracy looked at the array of controls and displays; the back seat is where the WSO normally sits, and the imposing spread of avionics made Tracy nervous. "What if I push the wrong button while I'm back here?"

"I'll lock your controls once I power up. Just sit back and enjoy the ride."

Tracy sat back like he said and discovered that the big military ejection seat was very comfortable. She had plenty of leg and elbow room, and was very contented by the time Roche had powered the engines on. Lights flashed across the panels, then went dark, leaving only three LCD screens illuminated. One showed the Hornet's current position on a map display, along with a list of flight data numbers that all read zero. The middle screen was mostly blank blue except for the Boeing logo in the upper left corner and *F/A-18f* across the bottom. The last one, on the right, showed Roche, looking into a camera in the front of the cockpit. "Are you comfortable back there?" he asked her.

Tracy couldn't have heard him through the thick helmet or over the dull roar of the idling engines, but a microphone in the air mask transmitted his voice wirelessly to speakers built into the ears of her helmet. "Yeah, I'm just fine."

"Your camera is right above me." Roche pointed up. Just above where is finger was on the screen, Tracy could see a small black lens with a little red light next to it. She waved to him, and Roche nodded and went back to his checklist. After making sure all the systems were go, he called the tower. "Island control, this is type Rhino, callsign *Stingray* Fish Two requesting takeoff clearance on one-eight, over."

"*Stingray*, thought you guys were on a day trip to Pensy, over."

"Yeah, Island, a couple of us stayed behind; I already got that merit badge."

"Roger, Fish Two. We have a heavy coming in on three six in about ninety seconds. Once they're off the porch, I'll let you out to play, over."

"Thanks, mom."

"So, do I get any kind of safety demonstration or what?" Tracy asked when the exchange was over.

"I'm sorry. I forgot I was supposed to be your flight attendant also. In case of an emergency the exits are located directly over your head. To begin an emergency exit procedure, reach down on either side of your seat and pull upward on the large yellow handles. Try to keep your knees and elbows as close to the seat as possible. Do not attempt the emergency exit procedure unless instructed by a member of the flight crew. If you are seated in an exit row and are unwilling or unable to perform the duties outlined, please inform your flight attendant at this time. In the unlikely event of a water landing, there is a life raft located under your seat. If your seat sinks before you deploy the raft, your pilot may also be used as a floatation device."

By now Tracy was laughing out loud, but Karl kept going. "Our in-flight movie this afternoon is a rare post-release cut of Top Gun, which has been edited for offensive content. This removed the gratuitous high-fives, Val Kilmer's poor attempts at sarcasm, the homo-erotic volleyball game, and of course the scene with Tom Cruise in his underwear leaning on a sink and crying, reducing the runtime to about ten minutes."

Tracy was laughing so hard she thought she'd pass out. She took a deep breath of oxygen from the mask and asked "What about the scene just before that, when Tom's plane spins out of control and the guy in the back seat gets killed?"

"Ah, we do not expect any turbulence on this flight, ma'am, and again, in that unlikely case you will be instructed to execute the emergency procedure." Roche then plugged his phone into the Hornet's audio system and started playing "Mighty Wings" by Cheap Trick, from the original movie soundtrack.

By now the C-17 they were waiting for had landed and was turning off the runway. The tower called down to them. "Fish Two, this is Island; that heavy is clear, confirm your departure request, over."

"Roger, Island, Fish Two is awaiting clearance."

"Right, off you go then."

Roche pushed the throttle gently, and the fighter rolled down past the center of the airbase where all four runways meet. He coasted down the center of the runway until he was clear of the traffic area, then he accelerated more. After fifteen hundred feet he was doing 150 knots. He rammed the throttles to the stops, he and Tracy were slammed into their seats, and the Hornet left the earth. Roche pulled back on the stick with his right hand and retracted the landing gear with his left, allowing the Hornet to climb to twenty thousand feet in thirty seconds.

Roche eased the throttle back and settled into a cruising speed around 350 knots, and looked at Tracy in the camera. "Still back there, baby?"

"That was fun!"

"Some ride, huh? You should try it off a carrier."

Tracy noticed that a small group of buttons under the display screens was still backlit, indicating that they were enabled. "There's some buttons here that are lit up still. What do they do?"

"That's just the display controls. They cycle different screens. The camera screen has about a half-dozen different views you can check out."

Tracy pressed the button furthest to the right and the screen that showed Karl's cockpit switched to a camera facing at a downward angle under the nose. Tracy cycled through and got cameras looking ahead over the gun barrel, backwards behind the canopy, and forwards from each wingtip. "What do the other two show?"

"The one on the left is a fixed Nav/Fly display."

Tracy correctly guessed the interpretation of the abbreviation as navigation and flight data, which explained the map and the airspeed and altitude numbers.

"The one in the middle you can also cycle. It's an MFD. It can show radar, TacOps, WepCon, or EWOC."

Tracy had no idea what he was talking about, but when she pressed the tab button under the multifunction display she got self-explanatory radar, tactical operations, weapons control, and electronic warfare operative control screens. These were all mostly blank.

"Once we get past the marine layer I'll drop down closer to sea level," Roche said.

Tracy looked around out the canopy and could only see blue sky above and gray clouds below. According to the nav display, however, they were over the Pacific Ocean heading south.

Tracy switched the MFD back to the radar picture, wondering if it could show clouds. It didn't, but Tracy noticed a text box in the corner explaining that this was the target radar. Maybe it only showed targets, and there were other radar modes that showed different things. Tracy tried another button she hadn't pressed yet, and the three LCDs got brighter. She pressed the only other active button and the screens dimmed. Tracy then noticed, with screens slightly dimmer, there was a

146

faint red glow around the edges of the MFD. It was an infrared touch screen. She tapped her finger on top of the wording that said "Target radar." The fiber optic grid in the plastic screen was disturbed by her touch; the computer processed the motion, and changed the screen in accordance with the WSO's implicit command. To Tracy's delight, the wording changed to "Weather" and the picture showed the cloud bank underneath the airplane. Another text box appeared in the other corner of the screen. It said "nav/sat overlay." Tracy tapped that and was rewarded by a map and satellite image superimposed over the false-color radar picture. The display now looked almost exactly like a TV weather map. There were small plus and minus icons in the bottom corner of the screen. Tracy discovered she could use those to zoom the radar and satellite in and out. She was enjoying herself so much she almost didn't notice when the plane started to descend. She did notice the edge of the cloud cover on the screen, which quickly rolled away beneath them.

"We are now descending below ten thousand and if you are looking out your window you can see nothing at all except the ocean," Roche announced, still using the airline voice.

Tracy looked around. There was nothing but bare blue ocean for miles in every direction except for one white object far away. "What's that over there?" she pointed.

"Over where?"

Tracy remembered that the pilot could only see her head on his screen. "Sorry. Left, way off on the horizon."

"Surface contact at ten o'clock, range twenty miles," a disembodied female voice announced.

"Who's that?"

"Bitchin' Betty 2.0," Roche answered, "our built-in stator of obvious facts. As for that contact, I think it's a cruise ship coming back from Mexico. Let's go take a look." He banked the plane to the southeast and continued his descent.

Tracy's radar switched back to target mode, and a message from the computer explained that the pilot was manipulating the system. It then entered scan mode, and soon created a composite 3-D image of the cruise ship. The MFD automatically switched to WepCon and listed attack options, which amounted to nothing since the Hornet was unarmed. It went back to the main radar screen with another line drawn across it to describe their intercept vector. "Are you doing that?"

"Doing what?"

"Switching my MFD around."

"No, if you're a passenger it will automatically show whatever I'm doing."

"How does it know I'm a passenger?"

"Because I locked the rest of your controls so you wouldn't worry about pushing the button that makes the wings fold in half."

"There's a button that does that?" Tracy asked in genuine alarm.

"Yes there is, but it's up here on my console," Roche answered honestly. Like most Navy aircraft, the Hornet's wings can fold up part way to save space on the carrier deck. It doesn't work with the landing gear up or the engines above idle power.

"Range to civilian passenger vessel, ten miles," Betty announced.

"Did you tell the computer it's a cruise ship?"

"Nope. SHOC figured that out all by itself from the scan image."

"That voice sounds vaguely familiar."

"It's Cortana from the 'Halo' video games," Roche explained. "One of the Navy's better ideas. They figured we'd respond most quickly to a female voice we're used to taking tactical input from."

"A video game character, from the game every guy has been playing since 2001."

"That's right," Karl confirmed. "I hear the Navy actually got the voice-overs pro bono. The actress works for Microsoft and when they heard what the Navy wanted her for they decided not to charge us for her work."

"That's awfully nice of them."

"Microsoft also gives away free software and XBox games to soldiers, sailors and aviators. They get a tax write-off for the wholesale value, so it isn't exactly a sacrifice on their part, but a splendid gesture, nonetheless."

Tracy could now see the Carnival Lines cruise ship over Karl's right shoulder. The pilot had settled his approach to 200 knots and 100 feet altitude. "Are we going to give them a flyby?" she asked

"Oh, yeah. This is going to make their day." Roche began to circle the ship, maintaining a hundred yards' distance. Tracy could see crowds starting to gather at the rails to watch the Hornet. Sharkey made a couple of passes at higher speed, doing barrel rolls and corkscrews. A couple of times Roche came alarmingly close to the surface; Tracy could see waves rush by right past the wingtips. Then

148

Karl approached from the rear to the starboard side, pulled a loop above the ship and came down on the port side.

"That got 'em off the shuffleboard court," Tracy commented. "It *is* legal for you to do this, right?"

"I have to give them standard high seas maritime clearance, which is about a hundred feet for a ship that size, and I can't charge them head-on or go supersonic anywhere near them. But I can get them a little wet." Roche turned the plane perpendicular to the trailing wind and across the ship's path. He dove to wavetop level and went full throttle, kicking up a spectacular rooster tail of spray and steam that drifted over the ocean liner. "That ought to be enough for them." Roche climbed away and turned back toward shore.

Tracy was laughing hysterically. "I can't believe we did that."

"Cruise ships get buzzed all the time; they're used to it. We play with ferries and whale watchers too."

"Do you guys ever go up and chase airliners?" she asked.

"Sure. The same rules apply for keeping a certain distance, and we obviously can't bother them on a landing approach, but at cruising altitude they're pretty much fair game. I like to just hang out off their wing and let the passengers wonder why they have a fighter escort. You can see them in the windows. If you stay long enough they start to freak out."

"Oh, that is so mean."

"I know, so I always give them a thumbs up to reassure them before I break off. And I chat with the pilots too, so they at least know that nothing's wrong." They were heading due north now, under the cloud cover at high speed. When they passed Point Loma – the edge of San Diego harbor, Roche turned toward shore and flew over Mission Bay. "There's Sea World, down there." Karl rolled the plane upside-down so Tracy could get a better view of the park.

"Have you ever gone there?" She asked.

"Not since I was a kid."

"There's a girl in one of my classes that works there. She could sign us in if you want to go sometime."

"That would be fun." Roche went over the Wild Animal Park, then turn south around Miramar Marine Corps Air Station and right over the USD campus.

"Hey, we're flying over my school!" Tracy noted.

Roche continued east, over Qualcomm Stadium and following I-8. "We'll be over Santee in a moment. You can probably see your house from here."

"There's Lake Murray, and Navajo Road; I think that's my apartment complex there, with the green roofs."

Roche climbed and accelerated, and was soon heading out over the desert.

"Where are we going now?" Tracy wondered.

"Now we're going hunting."

"Hunting for what?"

"Sitting ducks." Tracy stared blankly at her camera. Roche caught her look and decided to explain. "Everyone in my squadron – except me and one other pilot – has to do something called crossover training. They're new to the Super so they have to take something like a two-week drivers' ed class. One of my jobs on the squadron is to provide a training curriculum, and like all teachers I like to throw in a few surprise exams. Right now, the other eighteen *Stingrays* are flying fifteen planes on their way back from Pensacola, Florida. I am going to pretend to shoot them down, and see how well they can try to stop me."

"Just when I thought you couldn't get any crazier."

Roche was still flying east, now at 30,000 feet and 500 knots. He checked his watch periodically, and right at a quarter past four, he began a long, wide turn to the south. As the nose of the plane swung to the right, the radar picked up a group of contacts to the south. The computer identified the contacts as four friendly Super Hornets traveling west, at 25,000 feet and 520 knots. Roche accelerated as he continued his turn, and approached above and behind them. The SHOC picked up identifier tags from the computers in the other Hornets, and identified them as Hannibal's division.

"They're leading the pack," Roche explained. "They can't see me or sense me right now. I have all my transmitters disguised as a civilian jet." He typed a few commands into his computer. Tracy saw the radar contacts on her MFD change from blue for friendly to red for enemy. Then the display switched to WepCon. The previously empty weapons slots now were packed with over a dozen missiles. The computer reminded her that this was only a simulated exercise.

Roche locked on to the two planes on the sides of the diamond formation – Shredder and Bulldog – and fired two imaginary AMRAAMs. Their computers were alerted by Roche's and the pilots were immediately aware that they were being engaged by radar-guided missiles, but they didn't know how. Roche accelerated again and got within two miles of the formation. Hannibal by now was aware of the attack and ordered the division to split up, but the aggressor was too close to miss. Roche shot a sidewinder at Hannibal and another one at

150

Doc Holliday, who was bringing up the rear. Roche counted down the time it would take the missiles to find their marks. He had synchronized his shots so they'd all hit at once. "Fox-three! Fox-three! Fox-two! Fox-two!" He announced the kills on open channel.

"Sharkey, what in God's name is going on?" Hannibal yelled back.

"Ambush-evasion exercise, sir. Your division failed. Now stay off the radio; you're dead."

Tracy enjoyed the little battle but wondered "You're not getting in trouble for this, are you? Your boss sounded mad."

"He's just a little cheesed because he didn't think to shoot back. Like I said, I was supposed to do something like this to them. They just didn't know when or what."

Blackjack knew now. He was leading the next group of four, trailing fifty miles behind Hannibal's division. He had heard the exchange on the radio, and told his wingmen to keep their eyes open. He made the mistake, however, of looking for a radar warning to tip him off on Roche's next attack. Sharkey wasn't using radar anymore, however. After trouncing Hannibal he dove toward the ground and turned around again. He let Blackjack fly obliviously overhead, and then he came up from behind.

"You're making a shark attack," Tracy observed.

"That's right. I come up from below, using only visual and thermal imaging, which they can't detect, and then I bite their legs off." Roche climbed until he was directly under Gator, the number-four man in the formation. Tracy looked up and saw a belly tank only ten feet over her head. She realized they were in a total blind spot. The other four Hornets couldn't possibly detect them despite being so close. The dual exhaust on each jet burned hot on the forward-looking infrared scope, providing a target that the heat-seeking sidewinders couldn't possibly miss. Roche fired his imaginary wingtip sidewinders at Rooster and Creep, who were holding the sides of the diamond. Then he dropped back and pulled his nose up a little, and simulated cannon fire on Blackjack and Gator. "Fox-two, fox-two, fox-one, fox-one!"

"Aw, *hell* no!" Blackjack complained ineffectually. Roche came up above them so they could see he was there the whole time.

"Was I a –one or a –two?" Rooster asked. "'Cuz I ain't been hit by a cannon yet, and I don't want to start that now."

"You took a Sidewinder up the pipe," Roche answered, "which might be a little more embarrassing. Now hush up kid, daddy's busy."

Tracy saw the MFD light up. "What's going on now?"

151

"That's the EWOC display. We're getting searched out by Hardcase's Division Three. I'll let the RFCM take care of that."

"The what?" Before Roche could answer, the MFD showed a simulation of an enemy's radar picture – a picture of their Super-F, mysteriously surrounded by eight false contacts. The radio frequency countermeasure unit created fake contacts by transmitting weaker, distorted copies of the Hornet's real radar return. "Will that fool them?"

"For the moment."

Hardcase and Hitman each fired two AMRAAMs, but they had locked on to fake signals. Tracy watched, amazed, as six of the artificial contacts broke away as if taking evasive action, while Roche continued flying steady. Three more radar sources showed up on the EWOC board now, and when SHOC calculated their positions all seven fighters appeared to be forming up in a semi-circle behind them.

"It looks like there's more of them now."

"Yeah, the Fish caught up with us. They've got us surrounded, poor fools."

"What do you mean, 'poor fools'? All they have to do is use scanning radar on the fakes and figure out which one is us..."

"They already did that. Right now they're overpowering my jammers and are about to get weapons lock."

"Then how-"

Karl interrupted. "Mask on."

Tracy obeyed. She noticed in the camera that Roche left his mask off, and there was a big smile on his face as he pulled back hard on both the throttle and the sidestick. The maneuver is called a "breach stall." The plane pops up to vertical, stalls, and flips on its back like a breaching humpback whale. This takes advantage of the SHOC's pattern recognition software. When it sees a contact stall like that, it makes the reasonable assumption that it's been hit and informs the pilot that the contact is dead. For several seconds, Wilkes and the other six pilots were asking each other who'd shot Sharkey, and they stopped paying attention to what the XO was actually doing to them.

For a moment the Super Hornet was flat on its back, dropping like a rock, with no engine power or any control whatsoever. Tracy knew that with all control surfaces perpendicular to the wind flow, there was no way of maneuvering the plane. She briefly wondered how long it would take to fall five miles before smashing canopy-first into the Mojave Desert. Roche let them fall for only a second longer than was necessary to fool the SHOCs, then he simply moved the stick to

152

the right. A vent opened up in the left strake, allowing air to flow through. Simultaneously, the right wing extended its flaps and slats, increasing the surface area and catching more wind resistance. This slight imbalance flipped the plane over, delivering airflow into the gaping intakes on the underside of the plane. Roche restarted the engines and put the throttles to the max, and just like that the Hornet was fighting ready again.

By the time Hardcase and the others saw what was happening, Sharkey had already them in his sights. He flew behind their semicircle locking on and shooting in sequence, and they were all down before they could react. Roche turned the radio off so he didn't have to hear any more fitful cursing or angry complaints.

"Holy smokes," Tracy said, watching the other Hornets limp off. "I can't believe you took them all out just like that."

"I know; that was way too easy. I'm gonna have to whip these guys in to shape."

## UNIVERSITY OF SAN DIEGO – 1220, APR 24TH

Tracy was having lunch at the cafeteria with her friend, Angela, who worked at Sea World. "I can sign you and your boyfriend in on Friday or Saturday," Angela said, "As long as you get there before noon. So what's this fighter pilot of yours like?"

"He's a kind man, a little mysterious, a bit dangerous, and very funny."

"Oh, that's a good mix. Funny how?"

"He's got a darker sense of humor. You know, like he's seen war and violence and anything else is some sort of joke. He doesn't take anything too seriously."

"Does he at least take *you* seriously?"

"I'm not sure. I think so. I'm serious about him, at least."

## SAME TIME, 70 MILES NORTHWEST OF NORTH ISLAND

Karl was eating lunch in a place he'd never been before, in the *back* seat of a Super Hornet. Lt. "Blaze" Worthy was flying the jet high over the California coastline. Roche was a comfortable passenger, relaxing in the spacious cockpit and eating a turkey sandwich while the squadron flew up toward their exercise area.

Today's curriculum called for "weapons training at squadron S-3 discretion." That meant Roche could plan anything he wanted. He organized a little wargame with Destroyer Squadron 23, which would be escorting the *Stennis* when it embarked on deployment later that week. The *Stingrays* would attempt to attack a *Ticonderoga*-class missile cruiser, two *Perry*-class frigates, four *Arleigh Burke*-class destroyers and an imaginary aircraft carrier. The seven surface ships would of course try to defend themselves. The destroyer group was supposed to get a test of its air-defense ability anyway, so this joint exercise worked out nicely.

"There seems to be an endless list of awesome features that you have to love the SHOC for," Sharkey told the team. "Tack on this item: a vast repertoire of attack profiles that make every job easy. Hit F2 for the target approach menu, press three for the air-to-surface submenu, and get ready to sink some warships."

"Ah, Sharkey, I don't have any kind of weapons load on my computer, here," Hannibal reported.

"Hit F6 and select ASM Train from the load menu."

"Got it. Four Harpoons and standard air-air?"

"That's it. Note that the SHOC will automatically retard your performance to imitate the added weight and drag."

"Thanks."

"Okay, now the cruiser *Vella Gulf* is trailing the formation. Division Four will start with her. An Aegis cruiser is a formidable air defense platform, but we have a system to beat it. Rooster and Gator, you get to be rodeo clowns. Fly back and forth across her wake, about ten miles astern, and practice low-level missile evasion. Blackjack and Creep, while the clowns have their attention, approach from dead astern at wavetop level and initiate attack pattern two-tango-six."

The four aviators acknowledged and engaged. Rooster and Gator let *Vella Gulf*'s radar lock on to them, and then they dove to sea level to break the lock, and then popped up again. This kept the sophisticated Aegis system preoccupied and let Blackjack and Creep approach unnoticed. Their computers directed them to split up and release two Harpoon missiles apiece in a spread pattern. By fanning out the four missiles they overwhelmed the lone CIWS cannon protecting the stern of the cruiser.

"Two hits," Roche announced. "Nice work; *Vella Gulf* is out of commision. Next up, we have the frigates *Kaufman* and *Bale* on perimeter screen positions. Hannibal and Bulldog get to take them one-on-one, using one-yankee-six. Shredder and Doc, trail at five hundred meters to cover your section leads but do not engage unless they have a missile failure."

The CO and his wingman came in behind the *Kauffman*, while Bulldog split off his section and went after the other frigate. They

154

stayed at wavetop level, and once they got close the radar could see them but couldn't ever lock on. Both attackers fired one Harpoon, but continued flying along the target line to mask the missile. This "umbrella" tactic hid the deadly missile from the radar with the fighter's own radar return. The frigates didn't know the missiles were there until it was too late. Hannibal and Bulldog then broke off just beyond CIWS range and let the Harpoons make the kills.

"I honestly didn't think that would work," Bulldog said.

"It's a weak spot on the *Perry*-class that you also see on a lot of Russian designs: their rear-facing radar is no good at picking up low-level targets. Now we move on to the destroyers. Hardcase, your division is going to take on the *Lassen* to start with. The destroyers and the carrier are all close enough to cover each other, so I'm going to simulate an EW platform. I'm going to screw up the air-search radar on the other three ships, and *Lassen* is going to be completely blind for about twenty seconds. That gives you enough time for my personal favorite air-to-surface attack: the 'bat swarm.' It's called three-papa-eight in your computers."

Wilkes led the attack under the cover of simulated jamming. His four Hornets surrounded the destroyer and fired two missiles apiece from eight different directions, overwhelming the *Lassen*'s diminished defenses. Next, Roche and Blaze joined Division Two (which Roche would normally lead) and led Hacksaw, Beowulf and Claymore on another "Bat Swarm" attack on a second destroyer. At this point, the commander of the escort group, who happened to be the captain of the last ship that got sunk, was ready to call it quits.

"I'd call that a good day's work," Roche said.

The *Stingrays* returned to base where Hannibal opened the debriefing. "As we've just demonstrated, the Super Hornet is a fearsome attack platform. But we've also demonstrated that our own carrier group is not immune to coordinated air attack. Our squadron will be counted on to defend the battle group as well as lead its strikes. I think this would be a good time for Sharkey to brief us on our defense tactics."

"The most important tactic is actually counter-intuitive," Sharkey said as he passed out notes. "Our goal is not to control the high altitude. That is already well-covered by the missiles of our surface ships. As we've shown, the best way for an enemy air attack to succeed is to approach at low level. That's where we need to defend. If we can control the wavetop level, we eliminate the only vulnerable avenue of approach to our carrier." Karl went on for several minutes describing how to engage and disengage enemies while maintaining an effective patrol pattern.

After the debriefing, the aviators milled around for a while chatting. A few small groups discussed going out for dinner. But Hardcase Wilkes marched straight out, followed closely by his wingman, Lt. Armani. As he passed Roche, Wilkes fixed the XO with a hard glare. Roche caught the look and was about to say something when Hardcase turned and went through the door. "I wonder his problem is," Roche to himself.

Hacksaw Miller overheard. "You mean Hardcase? He's got an issue with you."

"I noticed. Is it because I beat him up at NIASMAC a couple weeks ago?"

"Maybe partly. But also he thinks you're in his seat."

"You mean I passed him up for XO."

"He's been a division leader for longer than you've been a fighter pilot."

"Huh."

"Don't worry about him, sir," Hacksaw said. "Everyone else knows by now that you're the right man for the job."

Roche typically didn't care what his peers thought of him, and he didn't mind that Wilkes didn't seem to like him. But open disrespect was another matter. He spoke to Masterson about it. "Blackjack, how long have you flown with Hardcase?"

"Last coupla tours; I was his second section leader on the last one."

"So you know him pretty well?"

"Not as well as his wingman, but better than most, I guess. Why?"

"I'm sensing a lot of hostility from him."

"Well, he thinks you jumped his assignment to XO," Blackjack said with a shrug. "It'll take him a while to get over that."

"Do you think he'll come around on his own?" Sharkey asked. "Because I just can't tolerate his disrespect. How do you think I should deal with him?"

"Just do what you're doing until you earn his respect," Blackjack suggested. "He probably won't ever like you, personally, but then he doesn't like most people. But if you impress him enough, he'll fall in line behind you."

That made sense to Roche. "Okay, thanks, buddy."

"Sure thing, sir."

Roche stood outside the hangar doors and watched his squadmates get in their cars and leave. He could tell a lot about their personalities by what cars they drove, and what condition they were kept in. Hardcase rolled out in a black Dodge Charger SRT-8 that was waiting to star as the bad guy's car in a remake of "Bullitt." Hitman followed in a Chrysler 300 SRT-8, also in black, with the same engine and even meaner body styling. They were a pair that you knew not to mess with. Hacksaw departed in his BMW M3 – he was a man who liked to be in control of his machine, and demanded a lot from it. Blackjack took off in his modified Camaro – he was a bit of a show-off, but then he knew it, and he also knew what he was doing. Beowulf had his eight-year-old Jaguar XKR – traditionally British to the core, but always up for a spot of fun. Claymore had bought himself a used '05 Pontiac GTO – he possessed an understated sense of the dramatic. Doc Holliday owned an old Ford Bronco – a cowboy born a century too late. Blaze drove in her '68 Plymouth Fury convertible, fireball vinyl graphic decorating the front end, 426 Street Wedge V8 rumbling, flames shooting out the exhaust every time she changed gears – she wanted your attention and she knew how to get it. Mystique, meanwhile, drove an old Honda Accord that appeared to be held together with bumper stickers – she didn't care what you thought about her, but she wanted you do know her thoughts about apparently everything. Creep and Ronin peeled out on a pair of motorcycles; Creep riding a Suzuki GSX-R1000, Ronin astride a Honda CBR1000RR Fireblade – these two were speed freaks who liked to live on the edge. Gator followed them on his Harley-Davidson Super Glide – laid back and nonchalant, but not shy about his sense of style. Rooster had an early-'90s Chevy pickup that had been supercharged and jacked up on massive tires and was about one step away from being classified a monster truck – he considered himself an ambassador of redneck culture. Shredder appeared to enjoy living up to his callsign with what he did to the tires on his Saleen-tuned Ford Mustang. Buzz had to have been every bit the electronics wiz he was reputed to be in order to keep his Saab 900 Turbo in working order. Hawk was a madman hiding behind his veneer of sensible responsibility – he drove a 365hp Ford Taurus SHO. Hunter was a family man and made no effort to hide the fact, driving his Chevy Suburban with his *my kid is an honor student* stickers displayed with pride. Last to leave was Hannibal in his Mercedes G550 SUV – he was the boss and he knew it, and he let you know it too.

Roche let a smile of satisfaction grow across his face. He had a good squadron, and they would all be much better by the time they started their deployment. *If the biggest problem in my life is a disgruntled division leader,* he thought, *then I should consider myself fortunate.*

# CHAPTER 8: LAST NIGHT ASHORE

## NORTH ISLAND – 1800 PDT, SATURDAY, MAY 10$^{TH}$

Karl and Tracy had spent the last three weeks together as much as possible, between her school schedule and his carrier qualification flights. They went to Sea World one weekend, the Zoo and the Wild Animal Park the next. On weekdays they went swimming, surfing, SCUBA diving, and deep sea fishing. Right now Karl was grilling up a couple filets from a three-foot thresher shark that Tracy had landed on their last fishing trip. "I thought you'd never want to eat fish again after what that dolphin did to you at Sea World," Tracy said with a bit of giggle.

"Aw, that was just an open-mouth kiss. It was a little awkward, and it certainly tasted fishy, but it won't stop me from eating tuna. Besides, thresher shark doesn't taste like any other fish. Have you ever eaten shark before?"

"No."

"Don't expect a fishy flavor."

"Looks like you have plenty of other flavor going in there anyway," Tracy observed. Karl was splashing tequila and lime juice all over the fish. "What did you do with the rest of the filets?"

"I let the boat captain sell most of it at the fish market for us, and I ziplocked up the rest and stuck it in your freezer with all the yellowfin we kept from last week."

"How much is there?"

"About three times what I've got cooking here."

"Maybe you should have sold all of it, and more of the tuna too. What am I supposed to do with fifteen pounds of fish? Without you around I don't have anyone to grill it for me."

"Don't worry, it'll keep."

"For six months?"

"At least." Both were aware of the double meaning their conversation held. They shared a smile, until a small explosion diverted their attention

"Your shark's on fire!" Tracy exclaimed.

"It's supposed to do that," Karl said unconvincingly as he rushed over to flip the blazing steaks.

"This is the second time you've grilled for me and both times you've blown something up."

"I'm cooking with gas."

"Cooking with alcohol, anyway."

"Bam!" Karl didn't look or sound anything like Chef Emeril, but Tracy discovered the results were no less spectacular. Roche brought the seared shark inside, and placed it on his kitchen dining counter next to the garlic-cheese mashed potatoes and steamed asparagus that Tracy had prepared.

"What sort of wine would go with this? I mean, it's fish, but it's meatier, right?"

"Yeah, a mild red would go with this best. I think there's still a half a bottle of a good California merlot in my bar."

"Okay." Tracy found the wine and Karl poured as they sat down to eat. "Oh, wow, this is delicious," Tracy said after her first bite of thresher. She quickly cut herself another. "You're right, it doesn't taste like seafood at all. It's more like... chicken... no there's an aftertaste, it's more like steak now."

"I wouldn't bother trying to identify the flavor. After the party tonight, you won't remember any of this."

"You think it will get that out of hand?"

"I guarantee it."


The Last Night Ashore party, or LNA, is a Navy tradition dating back to the days of John Paul Jones. It is encouraged – to a certain extent – by Navy regulations, on the theory that one solid night of excess would limit a sailor's craving for sex and alcohol during the voyage. It usually has that effect for at least the first couple weeks of the trip.

As a general rule, Karl never got drunk. He drank, but always in moderation and he could pack away quite a few before he became noticeably inebriated. LNA's were the only times he ever really cut loose. His first LNA party, which was also a celebration for surviving the Grinder, was like every single frat party he'd seen in his five years at college condensed into nine hours. At least, that's what he thought he remembered. Somewhere between staring up through the bottom of an empty glass that had contained a mix of beer, bourbon and scotch and waking up twenty-four hours later in a C-5 transport over the Indian Ocean, he was sure there was one hell of a party he drank through.

Organizing a party for an entire Carrier Battle Group about to go on deployment is an overwhelming task. Over ten thousand men and women had to find a place to tear up; *Reagan* alone has 5700 personnel in its crew. No building in the city short of Qualcomm Stadium or PETCO Park could house that many drunk and disorderly sailors and aviators. The only way to do it was to split everyone up by ship, watch section, and unit among the hundreds of bars in San Diego. Usually a total of 120 or so establishments were rented out for the evening and each was occupied by a hundred or so sailors. Civilians found it hard to find a place to get a drink on the night before a carrier went out, but this was accepted as a normal occurrence in the Navy town.

The flight officers of Carrier Air Wing 13 had landed themselves the most coveted LNA party joint in the city: the Kansas City Bar-B-Q. Having been used as a location scene in the movie "Top Gun," it was destined forever to be a favorite hangout of naval aviators. Only five of the eight squadrons in Air Wing 13 were actually stationed at North Island; the rest were at NAS Lemoore, just south of Fresno, CA. But the *Stingrays*, VFA-97 *Warhawks* (Super-Es,) VF-24 *Renegades* (Tomcats,) VAW-117 *Wallbangers* (E-2c Hawkeyes) and HS-14 *Chargers* (Seahawk and Strikehawk helicopters) filled the saloon to fire code capacity.

Karl and Tracy were picked up by a limo, along with Blackjack and everyone else on that block going to that particular party, which included two Renegades and a Warhawk. Roche was following the LNA dress code – no Navy attire. He wore an old Hawaiian shirt and old jeans and old, dirty white sneakers, fully expecting to get something spilled on his clothes before the night was over. Tracy wore a casual dress that covered her well but accented her feminine features in a way Karl found alluring. The limo had a mini bar. Karl already had an elevated blood-alcohol content by then, after the wine with dinner and the three bottles of Dos Equis he'd downed since lunch time. He fixed himself a rum and cola anyway, as did nearly everyone else in the car.

They got to the bar, which is in downtown San Diego a few blocks from the train station, at about eight o'clock. It was already packed with aviators. There was a cover band playing mostly eighties metal songs, and they had cranked their own sound system and the house PA to redline to make themselves heard over the raucous crowd.

"This place is crazy!" Tracy yelled to Karl.

"I know! Isn't it great? Go get a drink and enjoy yourself."

Tracy hadn't ever been a party person, and she worried that she wouldn't mingle in with the Navy people very well, but once she adjusted her senses to the bar scene she realized she wasn't the only girlfriend or wife or one-night pick-up in the room. There were at least as many disoriented dates as there were aviators. She took advantage of the well-stocked open bar and ordered a hazelnut martini. She started a few conversations with the line "Hey, who are you here with." She talked a little with Blackjack's girlfriend Jennifer, whom she had already met in the limo, but Jennifer was more interested in getting sloppy drunk then chatting.

After thirty minutes, Karl found her again in company of a short, skinny bald man he seemed to know pretty well. "Karl Strauss Red Trolley," he ordered from the Kansas City's extensive selection of local microbrews.

"Make it three," said the friend.

"Tracy, how's it going?" Karl asked, as if he hadn't seen her for several days.

"Pretty good. I was just talking with Jenny here…" she nodded to the empty stool next to her, but realized Jennifer had wandered off and was now stumbling through the bar calling for Blackjack.

"Tracy, this is Commander 'Worm' Bellbrook. He's in charge of the *Warhawks* now, but we used to be in the *Vigilantes* together, up at Whidbey Island."

"How do you do." Tracy shook the shorter man's hand.

"This guy is the only guy I know who can pound more tequilas than me," Sharkey continued. "That's actually how he got his name."

"That, and my appearance," Worm added.

Karl went on. "We were making a port call at, where was that? Mazatlan, I think. Anyway, this guy drank an entire bottle of tequila in about a minute, including the worm at the bottom."

"That's revolting," Tracy said, involuntary scooting back on her barstool, away from Bellbrook.

"In addition to being a world-class alcoholic, though, he also knows more trivia then anyone I've ever met."

"I was a once Jeopardy champ," Worm explained.

"I'm putting together a 'Stump the Worm' contest," Roche continued. "Five bucks in the pot to ask him a question; if he can't answer it, you win the pot. He and I split whatever's left at the end of the night."

"Sounds fun," Tracy said, suddenly wishing she'd hurry up and get buzzed.

"Stay here, Worm, I'm going to get this thing promoted. And don't drink too much. It won't work if you can't think."

162

"Relax, I'm only on my fifth," he said as he picked up another bottle Red Trolley ale. "I'm in the green zone now."

Tracy noticed her level of enjoyment going up with every sip of a drink she took. By 8:30 she was finally in a party mood. Roche quickly got everyone at the party excitedly queued up to try and stump Worm. Someone got fifty bucks out of the pot when Worm drew a blank on something to do with ancient Chinese history, but after that he rolled on, slowly draining his glasses of booze and everyone else's imagination.

Tracy went out to the patio at ten, mostly to let her ears heal. The band had just finished playing all nine-and-a-half minutes of Iron Maiden's "Dream of Mirrors" and nearly melted the amplifiers with overload and feedback. Tracy found someone else taking refuge from the heavy rock music. It was Deuce Thompson's wife, Loraine, who was holding a margarita glass and enjoying the respectful compliments of junior officers. Tracy struck up a conversation, hoping to find out more of what it was like to be in a relationship with a Navy pilot.

Loraine had met Josh Thompson in 1990, waited for him to come back from the Gulf war, and dated him through several deployments until he finally proposed. They were married in 1994, and he had gone right off within a year to fly combat missions over Bosnia. Over the years, Josh's postings had moved them from Norfolk, Virginia to Lemoore and back, then up to the Nevada desert and back down to San Diego. Loraine had raised their two boys and kept the family together while Deuce spent three to nine months at a time at sea.

"That must be tough," Tracy said.

"Of course it is, but Josh more than makes up for it with the time he's home. It just took some getting used to. The first time he went out after we were married, I'd sometimes roll over in the middle of the night, wake up and wonder where he was. Then I'd remember he's in the Mediterranean, doing a job that has one-in-thirty odds of getting him killed, and I'd spend the rest of the night praying. I still pray for him, but by now it doesn't keep me up at night anymore."

"I see."

"How long have you been with Karl?"

"We've been dating about four weeks. We met the day after he moved here."

"Have you talked about long-term stuff?"

"A little. At least I made it clear I'll be waiting for him when he comes back."

"I hope it works out for you guys. Unless he gets himself killed, of course." Mrs. Thompson was loosened enough to let that slip, but Tracy wasn't put off.

"Well, that's always the thing, I guess, in this business. One-in-thirty odds, you say? Karl gave me twenty-nine. One bad landing, or a bump with a tanker, and that's it."

"If Karl gets killed, it won't be a plane crash. He's been laughing at the odds too long for that. Did he tell you about the stunts he pulled at TOPGUN?"

"He said he used some unorthodox maneuvers."

"Honey, that guy scared my Josh half to death. He did things no one had ever tried before, at high speed and low altitude. He once made Josh chase him through the bottom of a canyon at full throttle." Tracy smiled as she imagined the CAG – the big bald guy, she remembered, not the skinny bald guy – thoroughly unnerved after a Shark encounter. "No, what's gonna get him is all his thrill-seeking activities," Loraine continued. "Skydiving, car racing, motorcycles…"

"Don't forget shark diving."

"Oh, that's new. When did he pick that up?"

"Two weeks ago. He said he needed to study his persona. The shark exhibit at Sea World was too tame for him, I guess. We went scuba diving Tuesday before last, and after a couple hours of teaching me some basic stuff he went down by himself with a bag of chum and started hand-feeding hammerhead sharks."

"Now that's just crazy."

"Maybe. But he had his big SEAL knife with him, and I just had a feeling that he could win a fight with any fish that gave him trouble."

"Well anyway, I wish you both the best of luck and all God's blessing. But I'm just afraid he'll never stop taking risks with his life for kicks."

"Well I guess I'll just have to provide enough thrill at home so he won't have to."

Admiral Wally Krause came by shortly after ten o'clock to say hello to the aviators who would be at the business end of his fleet. Someone called out "Admiral on deck!" and a few men even snapped to attention before Krause put them at ease.

Hunter Hidelmann looked over his shoulder and muttered "Aw, hell."

Deuce was sitting next to him. "You know that spook?"

164

"Know him? I flew with him for two years, before he tried to get me killed."

"Oh, right," Deuce said, recalling Hunter's file from memory. "He was in the *Rays* with you way back then. He got a medal for that mission when you get shot down."

"Thanks for reminding me," Hunter mumbled. "Yeah, him and his pilot hung back and cheered us on as we bombed the wrong target and happened to catch a whole artillery battalion napping. Then about half of us wind up getting knocked down by SAMs that we all knew were in the area. I got caught, my best friend got *shot*, and that asshole goes home and gets fast-tracked to Admiral."

Krause approached. His eyes appeared to light up as he recognized Hidelmann. "Hey there, Hunter! It's good to see you again! How long's it been?"

Hunter looked at the admiral's extended hand, then looked up into his face. "About twenty years, Admiral," he muttered, then turned around and picked up his beer.

The admiral shrugged, and patted Hidelmann's shoulder. He looked at the man seated next to him. "And you must be Deuce Thompson, my new CAG."

"That's right, sir," Deuce replied, accepting the offered handshake. He made a conscious effort not to show any expression. The admiral's hand felt clammy and weak. He squeezed it hard.

Krause was clearly trying hard not to wince. "Well, it seems your boys and girls are all enjoying themselves, Captain."

"Yes sir, just getting it all out of their systems," Deuce said with a nod as he released the admiral's hand. "They'll all be shipshape by tomorrow."

"No doubt, no doubt." Krause looked around the room as he flexed his pulverized hand. "And where is the man who defeated you up at TOPGUN? I'd like to meet him."

"He's taking the stage right now," Deuce pointed with his beer bottle. "I think he's about to sing his squadron's new theme song. Tradition, you know."

Karl Roche climbed up on the stage, borrowed the microphone from the band's lead singer and screamed "Lemme hear all the *Stingrays* out here!"

"Yeeah!" Hidelmann exclaimed, joining a smattering of cheers and whistles from around the room. A dozen or so fists were raised up in the air.

"Alright!" Sharkey gripped the microphone and launched into his passable imitation of Metallica frontman James Hetfield. *"Gimme fuel, gimme fire, gimme that which I desire!"* The band joined in with thrashing guitars and pounding drums while Karl charged through the lyrics. Four and a half minutes later, he finished the last line with a guttural *"OOH!"* and dropped the mic and dove into the crowd. Several *Stingrays* were there to catch him, and they passed him over their heads back toward the bar. Sharkey was dropped to the ground at the edge of the mosh pit. He landed on his feet and staggered up to the bar next to his friend Worm.

Krause walked up to him. "Lieutenant Commander Karl Roche, I presume?"

Karl looked at him for a second. "That's me. You're Admiral Krause?" Sharkey looked down at his clothes, soaked in sweat and spilled beer. "I hope you'll disregard my appearance as part of my first impression."

"Ah, don't worry about that. My first impression of you is you being a rock star." Krause was chuckling. "That's quite a set of pipes you have there."

"Thanks," Karl said with a shrug, "but that's pretty much the limits of both my vocal range and my musical talents."

"Somehow I doubt that."

One of the bartenders approached them. "Lemme have a Stone Ruination," Roche requested, switching his local microbrew brands and selecting the strongest beer available. "Admiral?"

"Oh, nothing, thanks," Krause replied. He changed subjects abruptly. "How did you beat Deuce Thompson?"

"Ah, so that's why you want to talk to me," Karl surmised as he picked up his bottle of extremely hoppy India pale ale. "Had I known just how notorious that would make me, I woulda let him win." Sharkey described his maneuver as trivially as possible.

Krause saw right through him. "I used to be an aviator myself, you know. I was a Tomcat RIO for a few years before I moved to 'Truders. You're not fooling me with that 'it was nothing, really' line." Krause's face suddenly broke into a wide grin. "Thompson was a real hotdogger back in the day. The first and only ace since Vietnam. We all thought he was the best we'd ever see. But you..." Krause poked two fingers into Karl's left shoulder. "I know you're better. I expect you to prove me right."

Sharkey wasn't sure what he meant, but he said "I'll do my best over there, sir."

166

"I know. Have a good night, Commander. I'll see you around the boat." Krause slapped Karl's shoulder, turned and left. His intended dramatic exit was thwarted by the crowd, who had just gotten a new song to start dancing to.

Worm stared after him. "Why didn't he say 'hi' to me?"

"Well, did you kill Deuce when you were at TOPGUN?" Karl asked him.

"No, but-"

"There you go then." Karl drained the rest of his beer. "I'm gonna go find Tracy. Don't get stumped, buddy. There's at least three hundred bucks in the pot now."

## THE NEXT MORNING

Karl's radio alarm clock went off ten minutes before noon. Roche opened his eyes for only a fraction of a second before squeezing them closed. "Whoa, too much light," he moaned. With the blinds closed the midday sun barely illuminated the room. Nevertheless Karl kept his eyes in darkness as he fumbled for his clock radio. 91 X was blasting a new Foo Fighters single and as much as he liked that particular song, the pounding beat was synchronizing with Roche's throbbing headache and quickly driving him insane. He finally got his hand on the device and started whacking the buttons on top until the music stopped. He lay there for anther minute, and then carefully opened one eye to check the time.

*Reagan* was scheduled to clear the docks six minutes ago, but the Air Wing wasn't supposed to fly aboard until the giant vessel had cleared the shipping channel and was well out to sea. This gave the pilots an extra three hours to recover from the LNA, except for the squadrons stationed at Lemoore. They had to leave at 12:30 for their two-hour flight to rendezvous with the carrier.

Roche's superhuman eyes grudgingly adjusted to daylight, and Roche approached the window. Looking northeast through the blinds and over the rooftops he could see the mast of the *Ronald Reagan* towering two hundred feet into the air, and slowly moving up the harbor. The light was still too much for his head, and Roche turned away.

Roche went to the bathroom, and grabbed two ibuprofen pills from his medicine cabinet and popped them in his mouth. He splashed cold water on his face and looked in the mirror, and realized he didn't look as bad as he felt. He put on clean clothes and went downstairs. He walked straight to the bar, mixed a Bloody Mary, drained it and made another in a clean glass. He had never figured out how it worked – curing an alcohol-induced headache with more booze – but as he discovered during his college days, it usually helped. He drank a glass of orange juice and brought the second Bloody Mary back upstairs to the second bedroom where Tracy was sleeping.

She was sprawled across her bed, and apparently had tossed off the covers in the middle of the night. He set the drink and the bottle of ibuprofen on the table next to her and pulled the covers back up to her shoulders. He went back downstairs and started thinking about brunch. The headache was fading, he could think clearly now. He had two objectives in making breakfast. The first was to eat as much protein as possible to purge the alcohol from his system – and Tracy's too. Second, he had to clear as many perishables as he could from his refrigerator. He had eggs, sliced ham, cheese and an avocado that all had to go. He would make a couple of big omelets – objective complete.

The smell of cooked eggs wafted through the house and soon brought Tracy down to the kitchen. She wore only one of Karl's t-shirts a baggy pair of sweatpants, and had the half-empty Bloody Mary in hand, and looked very sleepy. She still looked beautiful. "Good morning, gorgeous," Karl said, "would you like orange juice or cranberry juice with your omelet?"

"Both. And coffee, please. And technically, it's the afternoon isn't it?"

"Not around here. This is a little separate dimension we're in. The rest of the base has been working all morning to get an aircraft carrier underway. An aircraft carrier designed to get planes and aviators to the enemy's own shoreline. But the aviators themselves, if any of the others are even up yet, are just making eggs."

Tracy laughed. "That does seem a little weird." She sat down on one of the kitchen stools.

Karl put the two juice glasses in front of her. "Drink the orange first; you need the vitamin C."

Tracy sipped the juice and watched Karl move around the kitchen until he turned back to her with two plates of steaming eggs.

"As you can see, I *can* cook a meal without making a sudden fireball. Eat up, and please eat as much fruit as you can. I have to throw out any leftovers."

"Do you want me to clean out your refrigerator for you?"

"I only had the ingredients of this omelet, the juice from the bar, and the fruit, so that's all done. But thanks for offering."

168

"What about your laundry?"

"That can wait."

"I could do it for you while you're gone. That way you when you come home there won't be a smelly pile in the closet, and you can have clean sheets on your bed."

"If you want to do that for me, I'd really appreciate it."

Roche was just coming to terms with how serious Tracy was about their relationship. He had always had a "take-it-or-leave-it" personality. He had thought that if Tracy was there to meet him when he came back, that would be great. If she wasn't, it wouldn't bother him too much. So he thought. But after a moment of reflection, a moment of thought more than he had ever given a relationship, he realized the last five weeks had been the happiest of his life. Love had never been something he looked for. He almost failed to recognize it when he found it. He had realized only the week before how much he wanted this to continue, and how much he craved her companionship. Even without sex – or maybe it was *because* they hadn't gone all the way – she was the best romantic relationship he had ever had. He didn't know how to best express his feelings to Tracy, but he had an idea.

"Go get dressed and then bring all your laundry down here," Tracy instructed. Sheets and towels too. I'll take it with me after you go."

"Okay." Roche went upstairs and put on one of his khaki number-two uniforms. Then he dug his dirty clothes out of the closet, packed them into the big drawstring bag that he used as a hamper, added his sheets and towels, and rolled the whole thing down the stairs into the living room. He stayed upstairs to pack the rest of his things.

He was allowed to take whatever luggage could fit in the plane with him, which amounted to his flight duffel, a hanging garment bag with his uniforms, and his leather laptop case. He could also pack one cardboard box which would be loaded into a C-2 Greyhound and flown out separately. He packed up his coffee maker, his pistol cases and a few personal items. The coffee machine was actually for the squadron ready-room. Each squad had their own ready room – an office-lounge-suite – and these were served by a little ten-cup Mr. Coffee with a glass carafe that usually broke at an inconvenient distance from shore. Roche's machine could grind beans and brew up to twenty individual cups of coffee or espresso and even make cappuccinos, with no vulnerable external container. As executive officer, he was responsible for maintaining the morale of the squadron. The coffee maker would help.

Roche finished packing, leaving out one small item that he brought downstairs to Tracy. She had done up the dishes and started watching Saturday Night Live, which his DVR had automatically recorded for him the night before. Karl sat down on the couch next to her. "I got something for you," he said, handing her the black velvet jewelry case.

"Oh, Karl..."

"I'd ordered it for your birthday knowing I wouldn't be here for that, but I decided I'd give this to you early." It was a silver chain necklace, with heavy pendant. Tracy held it up and saw that it was cluster of small sapphires and diamonds held together with silver wire in the shape of shark tooth.

"How pretty," Tracy said, too amazed to say anything else.

"It's a locket." He showed her the secret clasp and she gasped when she saw the picture inside. It was the two of them on a fishing boat at sunset, with the light reflecting off the skyscrapers of San Diego behind them. On the other side there was an inscription: *I don't do catch and release. ~ Karl*

"This is so unbelievably sweet," Tracy said as she rolled over and hugged him. "Were you afraid I'd forget you?"

"Not at all," Karl answered between kisses. "I just wanted some way of always being close to you."

An hour later, Karl was sitting in the front seat of his Super-F. The plane was officially his, now. His name had been stenciled under the canopy on the left side of Fish-2. Jules "Hunter" Hidelmann had his name on the back seat. He was sitting there, behind Roche and in front of the small storage compartment that contained their luggage. Three thousand feet further up runway eighteen, the Tomcats of VF-24 were leading the long line of aircraft waiting to take off. They started to go, two-by-two, with screaming engines that could be heard a mile away. Roche was paying no attention to the action. He stared across the tarmac to Tracy, who was parked with other families and friends watching their loved ones fly out to sea. She sat on the hood of her blue Mini, looking at each of the blue Super Hornets but unable to identify Roche through the reflective canopy of his fighter. Roche closed his eyes for a moment, relishing the last ten minutes they spent in the house together ...

170

"Green light, buddy." Hunter snapped him out of it. Bulldog was in front of him, and he'd moved up another ninety feet. Roche eased off the brake lever and let the idling engines push them forward to close the gap. As soon as he stopped the line moved again; this time he followed closely. The *Renegades* were gone, and the *Warhawks* were up next. Hunter asked "Is that your girlfriend, the lovely brunette with the Mini that you're staring at?"

"Yes."

"She's got good legs." Tracy's long legs extended from her shorts and were indeed very pretty, even across a runway.

Roche rolled forward again, stopping with the nose of the jet twelve feet behind Bulldog's tail. "She does have quite a figure," Roche agreed.

"How long have you been together?"

"Ever since I came down here, a little over a month ago."

"Is she going to wait for you?"

"Oh, yes," Karl said with absolute conviction. He rolled up again and continued, "She says she's very committed to me."

"Mm hm." Hunter sounded unconvinced.

"I know what you're thinking. I know there's plenty of girls that just hook up with whatever man in uniform is in port at the moment and dump them as soon as their boat sails. Tracy is very different."

"They always are," Hunter commented as Roche eased off the brakes again.

"What about your wife? She's stuck around for you."

"Well, once you're married and you've had kids together, that limits their options. But my wife hasn't always been there for me either."

Karl pivoted in his seat and stared at Hidelmann. "You know that for a fact?"

"We've worked it out," he replied with a shrug. "This was years ago, when we were both a lot younger. Just saying, you can't trust any woman until you both know each other a hell of a lot better than the two of you know each other now."

"Tracy's different," Karl insisted again.

Hunter fell silent. They kept rolling. Now the *Stingrays* were in front of the line. Hawk and Deuce would go first, flying the spare Eels, followed by Hannibal's division, then Sharkey's. After the first two *Stingrays* took off, Hunter spoke up again. "What makes you so sure about Tracy?"

"I don't know how to explain it," Karl said, looking back at her over his shoulder. "It's not something I've ever felt before."

Tracy guessed Karl was in the second of the blue two-seat Hornets she saw lined up on the runway. Shielding her eyes from the sun overhead, she could count the letters stenciled under the canopy. She couldn't read them, but the letters and spacing could have spelled out "Lt. Cmdr. Karl 'Sharkey' Roche." She kept her eyes locked on the plane, thinking about Karl.

Ever since adolescence, Tracy had kept boys at a physical and emotional distance. It had been easy to end relationships with pushy boyfriends, once she made it clear she had no intention of rounding first base. She had been teased by other girls in high school, and earned the reputation of being frigid, but she had always been firmly committed to saving herself for marriage. But she had always wondered to herself, was she missing out? Did her physical barriers prevent her from making the emotional connection with the man she was supposed to fall in love with? She had struggled with that question for her entire adult life so far.

Until she met Karl. Everything with him was different. He didn't press her, he didn't pry at her, and he didn't coerce her. He just loved her, and brought her into his world. There was no need to shield her affections from him. It was obvious to her that they were meant to be together. But now he had to go away. Tracy hoped she had been able to communicate to him, in their last few minutes together, how much she wanted him to come back to her.

"*Stingray* Charlie Zero Five," the tower called, "you are departure clear on one eight left side, Zero Six will be taking off behind you on your right. Safe flying."

"Roger, Island," Roche answered, "don't change the locks on us." He left the brake engaged and throttled up to half-power, then let the brake out and the Hornet jumped forward. He looked over his shoulder one last time at the beautiful woman staring back at him, and then she receded beyond his field of vision as the plane shot down the runway.

"*Stingray* Charlie Zero Five, passing off your flight control to Nancy," Island tower said once Roche reached cruising altitude.

"*Stingray* Charlie Flight, this is Nancy." The new voice was coming from the *Reagan*'s flight ops control center. The senior flight ops officer was called the Air Boss. "We have your cousins from up north down here already, and *Renegade* Adam is beginning to make approach. Proceed to orbit two and await further instruction, over."

"Copy," Hannibal answered.

"Charlie One Seven, you are to accept new call sign Frenchie One, and take orbit station eight." This was another tradition. Deuce, the CAG, was trailing the squadron formation in one of the *Stingrays*' two spare F/A-18e "Eels." Flight ops would push him through hoops, give him embarrassing official callsigns, make him change orbits every few minutes and finally let him be the last plane to land. All the torment would be on open channel, so the entire wing could enjoy it.

"Frenchie?" Deuce called back. "I'm not going to let you call me Frenchie One. I hate the damn French."

"Frenchie One, I did not copy your last. Please proceed to orbit five while I resolve your communication difficulty." Through the joking, other officers in flight ops were talking down the Tomcats and lining Worm's Super squad up for approach. They were landing a plane every twenty seconds, so it took only four minutes to land a squadron. Eight minutes later the *Stingrays* were placed on approach. "Charlie Zero Five, you are T plus one-eighty seconds, approach track two and advise your LP."

"Copy, Nancy." Roche tapped his chronograph to synchronize the landing procedures and banked into his approach vector. "Charlie Zero Five is T plus one six eight, now on track two, landing payload is…" Karl summed up his remaining fuel, the weapons that he carried (in order to use every bit of airlift capacity available to load the ship, the fighters all flew aboard fully loaded) and his and Hunter's weight and luggage. "…two-six-four-seven-zero pounds. Current weather please."

The Air Boss checked his display for *Reagan*'s sophisticated weather data system. "Weather Channel says wind eleven knots nor'nor'west, barometer twenty-nine-point-eighty-nine rising, bright sunny day, over." Roche adjusted the computer for the wind and air pressure, which then factored in the Hornet's rate of speed and descent relative to the position of the moving warship on the radar. The heads-up display gave the aviator his vector, and he settled into his final glide path. He ran through the landing checklist quickly. Flaps and slats out, gear and hook down, everything was working just like it had when he had landed fifteen times on the *Nimitz* last week and thirteen times on the *Stennis* the week before.

In order to get his CQ, or carrier qualification for a deployment, he had to make twenty landings and eight bolters. A bolter is a touch-

and-go move. The Navy pilots practice these because almost every time a Navy plane crashes, it's on a near-miss carrier landing. By hitting full throttle as soon as they touch down, pilots can just bounce back in the air instead of going over the side and into the sea. If the tailhook catches the wires on the deck, the plane is yanked to a stop; if it misses, then the pilot bolters.

At T+60, one minute from touchdown, Roche was passed to the arresting gear officer, who is a senior CPO responsible for every plane that touches the deck. Roche followed his verbal directions and watched the "meatball," which is an array of colored lights that indicate a plane's position relative to desired approach. Roche came in slightly higher and slower than the "ok" approach, using the SHOC's auto-leveling feature to keep him on his line, and made a perfect three-point landing with the hook slapping the deck right behind the two-wire. He punched the throttle unnecessarily and then screeched to a halt, safely on the *Reagan*'s deck

He wound the engines back to quarter-power and rolled off the landing deck as soon as he was taken off the wire. He followed a yellow-vested aircraft handler to elevator 3, which would lower them down to the hangar deck. Hacksaw rolled up next to him twenty seconds later, and the elevator inched down thirty-eight feet to the hangar level. Two Quiktugs rushed out to get them off the platform. Another yellow-shirt crewman waved at Roche to get his attention and made a weird signal that Karl didn't recognize. He had his arms straight out, then he bent them up at his elbows at a right angle and repeated the gesture. Hunter caught the meaning first. "Wings," he said.

"Oh, right." Roche hadn't used the folding wings on a plane since his last carrier deployment almost a year before. He found the red knob on his panel, pulled it out, twisted it and pushed it back in. A sophisticated locking mechanism opened the joint two-fifths of the way toward the tips of the wings, and the outboard segment of the trapezoid-shaped wings tilted up to a position just past vertical and locked again. The tug dropped them off in the stern section of the deck, and crewmen swarmed the plane to strip its weapons, drain its fuel, and as an afterthought, pull the ladder down for the two aviators still inside.

Roche let Hunter get out first while he finished the power-down routine. He unloaded the luggage, carefully tossing the bags to the WSO, and then he jumped down himself, as always ignoring the ladder. He carried his bags to the large opening in the back of the hangar, which provided an unrestricted view of the ship's wake. He looked back, over the churning water, under the incoming planes, to the distant shoreline. He couldn't see exactly what he was looking for, but he stood there taking his last look at a place and a memory of a woman that he wouldn't see for a long time.

# CHAPTER 9: MONSTER UNDER THE MOUNTAIN

## ALBORZ MOUNTAINS, 240 MILES NW OF TEHRAN
## 0000 LOCAL, MAY 19<sup>TH</sup>

Rannovich had every clock in every bunker in his entire network synchronized to the millisecond. In the command center, where he stood now, there were fifteen different clocks, including a countdown timer superimposed over one corner of the twenty-foot-wide display screen. Rannovich stared at his own Rolex, as if he didn't trust the multimillion-dollar supercomputer to tell time for him. The hour, minute and second hands on his black and gold UTC-Master lined up on the 12, and simultaneously digital watches belonging to everyone else in the room chirped their alarms. The computer display flashed red, and broke up into four quadrants showing different activities that were taking place in accordance to Rannovich's plan. "It is time," he said, unnecessarily.

## NORAD – SAME TIME, 1330 MDT, MAY 18<sup>TH</sup>

Lt. Colonel Wheeler's computer was also set on countdown alert. He had been tracking the unidentified Russian satellites for six weeks now. So far they appeared to be benign. The Air Force, NSA and NRO had all been concerned at first, but Wheeler made an orbital projection for the next thirty years – double the KH-12s' expected service life – and reported there would never be any collision danger. The State Department had been trying to resolve the matter with Russia, but at this point they had dropped it with a reminder to inform NASA and NORAD before placing any more satellites in orbit.

Wheeler hadn't stopped worrying about it. The things that Andre Turbalov had told him before his death made it clear that this was more than an orbital coincidence. Someone powerful and shadowy operated those devices, and had arranged their orbits to intersect with US military satellite systems. There had to be some sort of sinister plan at work. But despite Wheeler's suspicions, nothing happened. After six weeks he almost stopped paying attention when the satellites crossed paths. But today, between 1930 and 2100 UTC all twelve Russian satellites would each close within a mile of a different Keyhole. Wheeler would have to keep an eye on that.

The alarm sounded at 1:30 PM. Wheeler was at his desk eating a late lunch, and he loaded the radar view on his monitor to watch the intersection. High above the Northern Pacific Ocean, the KH-12 and the mysterious stranger approached each other on perpendicular vectors. The small Russian satellite, which was actually built in China by New Patriotic Aerospace, passed five hundred yards in front of the American bird and abruptly exploded. Wheeler saw the radar contact vanish and immediately guessed it was a bomb, sent to destroy the American satellite. But the bigger contact on his radar screen was still there and still stable, not blown out of the sky or even disturbed by a blast.

Wheeler dropped his sandwich and grabbed his keyboard, and quickly adjusted three different radar transmitters to provide a high-resolution 3-D scan of the satellite. The American bird appeared to be unharmed. He looked at the Russian's track and found debris – larger objects like a solar panel and pieces of the steel casing. The little device had obviously suffered a small explosion, but the force was barely sufficient to break it up. If it was supposed to be a bomb to destroy the American, there should only be very tiny pieces left over from both satellites.

Wheeler started to think it was another coincidence. The Russian had malfunctioned or been hit by a micrometeorite or something; no foul play. Then the phone rang. "Wheeler, Orbital Tracking."

"Ah, hello, this is Colonel Parker at Vandenberg spaceflight."

"What can I do for you Colonel?" Wheeler guessed what this was about and didn't like it. *There are no coincidences...*

"We just lost telemetry from one of our satellites. Diagnostics checks out on our end, so we were wondering if you could check and see if it's still there for us."

"Is it a KH-12 over the Aleutians?"

"Um, yes, yes it is."

"I have it on my screen now. I was actually about to call you guys. Do you remember those Russian satellites that we told you about last month?"

"Yes..."

Wheeler told Parker what he'd seen on the radar. "If you've lost all telemetry abruptly there are only two things that could cause that. It was either completely destroyed, or it was damaged by an electromagnetic pulse. It's still on my radar in a stable orbit, which leaves only one explanation. The Russian satellite was an EMP bomb sent up to intercept and disable that satellite."

Parker swore.

"If you think that's the bad news, brace yourself. In the next eighty minutes, the eleven remaining Keyholes are going to get very close to unfriendly Russians. If they are EMPs, I think we're going to lose the remaining satellites one by one."

Parker swore again. "Which one's next to go?"

Wheeler checked the computer. "Eastern Indian Ocean in ninety seconds."

"Watch the telemetry from Keyhole Eight," Parker yelled to someone else in his control center.

Three hundred miles above the west coast of Australia, the KH-12 cruised in its silent orbit. Another small and dangerous object approached at an oblique angle, passed behind it, and suddenly disintegrated. The KH-12 was half a mile away when the invisible EM pulse fried every bit of electronic hardware that was packed into the quarter-billion-dollar camera. "The data feed crashed," Parker reported, "just like the last one. It was stable, and then zap, nothing."

"Same story on my end," Wheeler confirmed. "The Ruskie popped, and the Keyhole's just drifting."

"You'd better notify the NRO."

"My department is calling them and the Pentagon right now."

"Oh man, I would not want to be the on the phone with the brass. The entire intelligence community is gonna go ape over this."

## NATIONAL RECONAISSANCE OFFICE HQ, FAIRFAX, VA
## SAME TIME

Captain Johnny Mendez was one of the few Army personnel that worked at the NRO. The Office occupies a massive complex twenty miles south of Washington DC, on what is technically Army property, but only a tiny percentage of the staff are in fact US Army soldiers. Most of those are part of the security force. Half of the NRO's 10,000 employees are civilians, and most of the others are from either the Navy or the Air Force. Mendez worked in a room full of Air Force geeks, analyzing endless streams of satellite images, most of which came from the KH-12 Keyholes.

At 1530 someone asked his computer screens "What the hell?" when a bird over the North Pacific stopped transmitting. There was nothing interesting there to look at, so it was just in idle mode as it floated over the top of the western hemisphere, but it wasn't ever supposed to cut its feed entirely. Ten minutes later there was a state of mass confusion when a satellite watching Singapore conduct naval exercises also blacked out. NORAD and Vandenberg called a minute later to explain what was going on. The information prompted all the NRO analysts to panic.

Mendez didn't have the time to spend panicking. If they were going to lose all the satellites in an hour, then he had work to do. Iran was the highest priority for collecting new photos, and one of the Keyholes was just coming into position to take shots. Mendez scanned the wide-angle pictures for anything interesting. The Keyhole was pre-programmed to take close up shots of certain targets, like Bandar Abbas naval station, the nuclear facilities at Natanz and Bushehr, and government buildings in Tehran. Johnny switched it to a scan mode, covering as much ground as possible, flagging and filing anything remarkable that showed up.

Then he spotted something as one of the cameras made a quick sweep across the desert. He took manual control and zoomed in on what appeared to be a military convoy in the middle of nowhere, miles from any Iranian Army or IRG base. The camera took hundreds of close-up stills and continued shooting constant video footage while Johnny panned the length of the convoy. Tanks led the way – big, old, Russian-built T-72s and T-80s that ran over the desert brush and pounded the ground flat for the vehicles that followed. Mendez counted a hundred and twenty tanks, making a whole armored regiment. BMPs – Russian light armored troop carriers – followed next, then heavy trucks carrying hundreds of infantry. Finally there was artillery. Self-propelled M1973 howitzers and bigger guns towed behind trucks, mixed with heavy vehicles to carry ammunition. All in all, it totaled up a full armored brigade with sufficient firepower to start or finish a major war.

Mendez finally reached the end of the convoy and couldn't believe what he saw next. The vehicles were coming out of a hole in the ground. Just sitting in the middle of the desert, twenty miles from the nearest town and a hundred more from any known military base, here was the end of a secret tunnel and almost five hundred vehicles had just used it as their expressway. The video feed went black. The bird had been hit by whatever was knocking out all the others. Mendez had expected that to happen and kept working, compiling all of the image files into one serious block of data for the Pentagon to look at. Out of curiosity, Mendez plotted the course of the convoy to try to guess where it was going. He discovered that if it continued in its last known direction, almost exactly southwest, it would cross the Iraqi border a hundred miles away and go straight to the Tigris River port city of Al Basra.

## THE WHITE HOUSE – THIRTY MINUTES LATER

"All I know is what the Air Force and the NRO is telling me," the President had the Secretary of State on the phone. "But from what they say it sounds like the Russians have started a war in outer space and the Iranians are trying to sneak half their army into Iraq. Now I'm asking you, does the State Department know anything about why any of this is happening?"

"We're trying to get some answers from Moscow right now," Janice Rand answered, "but keep in mind that it's the middle of the night over there."

"I'm pretty sure the freakin' Kremlin has people working a night shift," McNeil said. He stood in the middle of the Oval Office, pacing the room with a cordless phone. Lane Bender – his chief of staff – was sorting a flood of phone calls and reports from seemingly every military and intelligence service in the country, either bringing more bad news or trying to find out what was going on. She picked Colonel Wheeler's report out of the printer and handed it to the Commander in Chief, who skimmed as he talked and got angrier with the SecState. "NORAD knew about these EMP things for a month and a half and submitted all kinds of requests for your people to do something about it. They're telling me you made no progress with the Russians. Explain that to me."

"Honestly sir, I don't know much about that matter. Getting Russia to move some satellites seemed like a fairly low priority at the time, and I did not deal with it directly. That obviously was a mistake."

"It's painfully obvious, Jan. Let me read to you from NORAD's original report, which you should have seen about six weeks ago. 'Our contact with the Russian space agency confirmed they were launched as part of a secret project on the authority of the highest level of the military and space command structure... The satellites are in an orbital pattern that intersects with our KH-12 Keyhole military ImInt satellites, and violates the established margin of clearance imposed and enforced by the US Air Force... there are twelve of these Russian satellites and twelve Keyholes, and while there is no foreseeable danger of collision the coincidences are alarming enough to be considered a possible national security threat.' Was that not enough to act on, Ms. Rand?"

180

"We tried to get the Russian space administration to see it that way-"

The President read from another report. "'In addition to costing three billion dollars to build and launch and over a hundred million a year to monitor and maintain, the Keyhole program is our first and best line of national image intelligence defense, allowing us to see threats before they develop and take swift action. This remote intelligence system must be protected at all costs, as it is vulnerable to anti-satellite weapons that may be developed by our enemies in the near future.' The Air Force sent that to you five weeks back. Calling up the Air and Space Marshal and letting him jerk your chain around is not my idea of protecting our national security assets at all costs."

"But Mr. President, surely you must understand that this is an unforeseen development and-"

"No, I do not think so at all," Brett McNeil interrupted again. "This guy at NORAD, what's his name, Colonel Wheeler, he saw this coming, and he got more answers from the Russians in six hours than you have in the last six weeks. And then a couple weeks ago, the CIA actually warned us that Rannovich was going to try and blow up our satellites. Somebody should have put two and two together and come up with a hell of a lot more than the big fat nothing that you've produced.

"Now, let me tell you what I think you should have done, and what you should be doing now. You need to call Moscow again – you, yourself, personally – and raise all sorts of hell 'til they tell you what they're up to. You may yell, you may sweet-talk, you may coerce, seduce and bribe. You may threaten *immediate military action*, because Mike McLeary is across the river with the Joint Chiefs planning that *right now.*" The President had raised his voice to deliver that line. "You may piss them off so long as you convey to them exactly how pissed off we are. Understand? I don't care if you have to drag Vladimir Putin himself out of bed to calm you down. You are going to drive Moscow insane until they explain themselves, you got that?"

The Secretary was stunned for a moment. She had never heard the President talk to her – or any other cabinet member – like that. "Yes sir. I'm sorry, and I understand sir. Now what about the Iran situation? I need to get people on that right away."

McNeil calmed down a little. "I'm forwarding everything I have to your office, which isn't much. All we know is they're moving an Army brigade around their southwestern desert, which could be an exercise or the beginning of a real shoot-out. We can't do anything until we know more about what they're up to, and you need to figure that out for yourself with the intel you have. I'll make sure you're kept up to speed." The President hung up and turned to his Chief of Staff. "Is the Vice President still here?"

"Yes, sir," Lane Bender replied. "He cancelled his other plans as soon as he heard what's happening."

"Good. Then tell Hal to get online with the SecDef and Joint Chiefs start going over our contingency plans. If Iran *is* declaring war on Iraq I want to know what we can do about it. And I also want a full briefing on what ideas they've come up with to rattle Moscow's cage if that becomes necessary."

The National Security Advisor walked in just then followed by the Director of the National Security Agency. DNS David Martin had a heavy briefcase manacled to his wrist. He nodded to the President and dropped the case on the giant square coffee table in the middle of the room. The President took a seat and motioned to the two newcomers to do the same. "This is our preliminary report on that armored convoy, sir, including all the pics the NRO could grab before we lost the birds." the Director opened the case and handed a thick stack of notes and photos to the Commander in Chief. "This is no exercise. You don't dig a tunnel under the Zargos mountains and drive a whole brigade into the middle of nowhere for target practice."

"That does seem a little insane, even for the Iranians," McNeil acknowledged. "What's their likely target? They're not heading for Baghdad, are they?"

"No, they're going further south. They're actually on a beeline to Al Basra."

"That's the third biggest oil-producing city in the world – a good target to grab if they're trying to start a fight."

"Yes, sir," the NSA jumped in. Thanks to the government's chronic acronym abuse the National Security Advisor had to share his abbreviation with the agency, which often confused things because he had to work with the agency so much. "My Army analyst says they'll be there in three and a half hours."

"Okay. I'll make sure our ambassador in Baghdad is notified, along with their people here in Washington. Now, what's the news on our satellites?"

"Eight down, four to go," Martin said. He checked his watch and modified the statement. "Actually we have nine down now, if they're on schedule."

"Now, this isn't completely blinding us, is it? We have more satellites than just these twelve, right?"

"Of course," Harmon said. "We have tons of them, mostly top-secret. But they are mostly in geosynchronous orbits over North America, Russia and China. We have two in the Middle East, but one's watching Palestine, Syria, Iraq and that whole neighborhood, the other one's above the Pakistan-Afghanistan border. Neither can provide high-resolution coverage of central Iran. We can't see anything in Bandar smaller than a major warship, and we can't make out Tehran at all. Because these satellites can't move, we can't get a bigger viewing angle. We never worried about it, because we always had another KH-12 flying over every forty-five minutes."

"Can we see Al Basra?"

"Yes. It's not a great picture, but we'll be able to track the vehicles when they make an attack."

"What are we doing right now to get new image intel?"

"The NRO is going through all our other options, which is pretty much limited to aircraft. The Air Force is mobilizing our Global Hawk and Sentinel drones and Aurora spy planes..."

"Those are not going to fly over Iran," the President flatly stated. "No aircraft will penetrate Iranian airspace unless we actually reach a condition of war, and definitely not the Aurora. We've spent billions to keep that thing a secret and if it gets shot at..."

"Understood, sir. The first Auroras will be in-theater by dawn local time. We'll keep them at maximum altitude over the Gulf and the Caspian Sea. They should be able to provide at least limited coverage of the northern and southern provinces. We are also looking into refitting new digital cameras, communications, and ECM gear into the SR-71's we've mothballed. They'll be able to supplement the Auroras in a couple of days."

"Okay. Keep me posted on what develops, gentlemen. If Iran starts a war, I don't want to be the last to know."

## IRAN-IRAQ BORDER – 0430 LOCAL (0000 UTC, 2000 EDT)

Major Anju Duhamad could see well enough in the predawn twilight that he didn't need his night-vision goggles anymore. The oil refineries surrounding Al Basra bathed the city in a permanent glow anyway. Duhamad stood upright in a T-80 tank at the head of a long column that was spreading out as it neared the invisible line separating his country from Iraq. The outskirts of the city were only seven miles past that line.

They had begun their journey during late evening the day before, moving the vehicles out of a huge storage bunker built into the foothills of the Zargos Mountains. They reached the surface at midnight, exiting from the tunnel driving across the desert. They passed oil fields, crossed the highway and railroad tracks south of the city of Ahvaz, crawled across a railway bridge over the Karun River, and finally reached the border, halfway between Basra and the Iranian town of Khorramshahr.

The tanks were getting low on fuel, so the first thing they would do when they attacked the city would be to capture an oil refinery. The huge BP complex on the eastern edge of the city would work nicely. Somewhere in the middle of the formation there was a general planning all of this. Major Duhamad just had to lead his tank battalion. One fourth of the big Russian battle tanks were his responsibility, and he would be the spearhead of the assault. Rannovich had told him this yesterday. His tank would officially start the war when he drove it across the border at the head of the brigade. Duhamad didn't know why the Russian man had been put in charge of building Iran's secret army, or what the ayatollahs hoped to accomplish by capturing Al Basra and the nearby seaport of Umm Qasr. He was only told that it was the will of Allah, and that made it his command.

The specific command was to cross at sunrise, when he could clearly see the shadow of his gun on the cyclone fence marking the border. He was then supposed to run over the fence and the brigade would follow, along with two squadrons of helicopters that would be taking off soon from the Khorramshahr airport, fifty miles away. The Americans would not see it coming and the Iraqis would surrender immediately, he was told. This was Duhamad's first experience with a war, so he believed whatever his commanders told him.

## USAF E-3 SENTRY 30000' ABOVE AL BASRA
## THIRTY MINUTES LATER

"Major, I think I've got some movement." The AWACS plane, along with almost every aircraft the US still had stationed in Iraq, was patrolling the border to watch for the Iranians making a sneak attack.

"Watcha got there, son?" The major came back to the radar booth and sat down next to the Specialist 1st Class who was operating the powerful AN/APY-2 radar system.

"Down in the grass, sir. See there, and there? I think they're choppers trying to sneak over the border. Fifty knots, two hundred feet, heading 270."

184

"Use TerCom overlay to filter out some of the ground clutter."

"Yes sir." The young radar operator flipped a switch. The CRT screen reset itself and resolved to show two dozen slow-moving contacts.

"That's choppers alright. Call it two squadrons. Good work. Sergeant, call Snoop Dog Flight to check them out. Lieutenant, call Army Air Command and ask if they've got any whirlies down there."

Two of the Sentry's crew got on the radio. They made the calls as the Major ordered. "Snoop Dog is inbound, ETI six minutes."

"Army Air says there are no friendly choppers in our immediate airspace, sir."

"No IFF tag response either, sir," the Spec1 added. "They're definitely not friendlies."

"Okay. Tell Snoop Dog they are looking for two squadrons of Iranian attack or light transport helicopters. Intercept and discourage by use of non-lethal force."

## SNOOP DOG FLIGHT, USAF F-16 FALCON DIVISION

"Roger that, Studio One, we'll scare them off for you." Snoop Dog-1 had the targets on his radar. His three wingmates were close behind and were locking on also. "Set radar to full power, flight, give their warning receivers a good buzz." The choppers must have known they were being searched but gave no response. The Falcon pilot switched to open channel, broadcasting across all useable military radio frequencies. "Iranian aircraft, this is a US Air Force fighter squadron. You are violating sovereign Iraqi airspace. You must turn around immediately or you will be fired on."

The helicopters still ignored them. The F-16s flew right between the two helicopter squadrons, and identified one group of Mi-24 Hinds and another of smaller Mi-28 Havocs. "They're not listening, Captain," Snoop-2 observed. "They'll be in missile range of the BP refinery in a minute."

Snoop-1 turned around to lead another pass. "I'm firing one safe-locked Sparrow missile. Do not join fire, Snoop Flight." Snoop Dog-1 launched the missile past the leader of the Havoc squadron. The helicopters slowed down and pulled up, startled by the warning shot.

"That got their attention," Snoop-3 observed.

"Come right to ninety, we're gonna fly right over their heads at full throttle. They can't possibly misread that." Snoop Dog Flight blasted passed the Iranian helicopters, heading into the sun. Snoop-1 looked over his shoulder as he passed the Hind squadron, and saw something else on the ground. "Uh, Studio One, this is Snoop Dog, I see some armor down there, we're going to take another look, stand by. The Falcons turned around again, and made an approach lower and slower with the sun at their backs. Now they could clearly see the huge formation of tanks and trucks moving toward the city behind the helicopters. "We found the armor brigade, repeat this must be the armor brigade command had us looking for. There must be, oh crap, there're hundreds of them, and their lead units are about two miles from the edge of town. We are requesting instructions, Studio, please get command on the line to advise."

Major Duhamad couldn't hear the jet engines over the tanks and helicopters, until they made their full power pass directly overhead. The Mi-28s above him broke formation and scattered, and the tankers broke radio silence with chatter. Duhamad was terrified. The surprise attack had failed; surely the Americans would kill them all. He'd seen video from the first Gulf War and knew what the Americans were capable of. A squadron of USAF A-10 Warthogs could wipe out this entire brigade in a single pass.

Someone in the end of the column said they were coming back. Duhamad turned around to look, but couldn't see into the sun. When they flew over his head again, much lower this time, he was able to identify the single-engine, single-tail fighters as F-16 Falcons. He got a glimpse of the racks of bombs under their wings and realized that they wouldn't have to wait for the Warthog tank-busters to wipe them out. These Falcons could take them apart anytime they wanted. The helicopters had no air-to-air weapons, and Duhamad's tanks only had .30 caliber machine guns for air defense. The mobile SAM units could protect them once they reached the city, but they'd take half an hour to set up. Duhamad didn't think they had that long. He decided they were doomed.

But he'd forgotten about the infantry in the middle of the column, who had stopped and dismounted and set up their GA-16 man-portable missiles. Similar in size to the US Stinger, the GA-16 is often called the "Stingerski." The Falcons came around again, this time from the south, and now started shooting at the helicopters. Four of the Mi-24 Hinds were taken out as the Americans made another pass over the column. Then the BMPs fired upward with their 25mm automatic guns, and the infantry contingent launched a dozen Stingerskis.

*　　*　　*

"Missile! Missile! They're everywhere!" Snoop Dog Flight was in big trouble.

"Drop flares and go to afterburner," Snoop-1 ordered, but it was too late for his wingmen. There were just too many missiles. They were all hit and the pilots bailed out somewhere north of the tanks. Snoop Dog-1 hit the afterburners and tried to outrun the missiles that were locked on to his hot exhaust. "Mayday, mayday! Snoop Flight is down, request SAR at grid-" a missile went up his tailpipe and exploded, blowing his single engine inside-out. Somehow the fuel tanks held. The pilot tried to give his coordinates before bailing out, but the radio was dead. He listened to the Doppler pitch of the wind rushing past his shattered airplane. A sharp drop in the note indicated he was subsonic and could safely eject. He did so, and let the plane crash into the rocks below.

### THE WHITE HOUSE SITUATION ROOM – 2105 EDT

"Al Basra is under attack from the Iranian ground force we spotted earlier," the President announced. The Joint Chiefs and all the senior cabinet members except Secretary Rand were seated at the table in the Situation Room. President McNeil was much too agitated to sit. "They started shelling the city soon after we caught them crossing the border, and their tanks are rolling through the city right now. They are indiscriminately attacking military and civilian targets. They captured a BP oil refinery and blew up another one belonging to some Polish company. Prime Minister Al-Maliki wants to know what we are going to do about it."

Everyone looked up at him. Then General Paul Chappelle, the CJC asked, "So? What are we going to do about it?"

The President threw his hands up. "Nothing! There's not a damn thing we *can* do! You told me this morning we're still three days away from a re-deployment. We have three divisions of Army infantry and Marines, but practically no armor. And we have four- now make those three-and-a-half Air Force squadrons. We can't fight off an armored brigade with artillery support and air defenses with the force we have in the field now. The Iraqis will just have to deal with this mess themselves for the time being. Did we at least get our pilots out of there, Josh?"

"Yes, sir, we did," Joshua Caleb, the Air Force Chief of Staff answered. "They went down five to ten miles northeast of the city, and we were able to get a Pave Hawk full of parajumpers in there to rescue them before the Iranians noticed."

"Good. So there haven't been any US casualties so far?"

"We haven't had any troops in Basra since 2003," General Chappelle answered. "That was always one of the more stable of the major cities. The Brits had security duties in that province until they turned it over to the Iraqis in 2008. Now there are no coalition soldiers down there at all. There may be Americans working at some of the refineries though, but I think the Iranians will try to capture those facilities intact."

"But they've already blown one up," McLeary noted

"Not exactly," Lane Bender corrected. "They only fired one shot at it, apparently by mistake. It happened to hit a condenser tower, which exploded and set some other stuff on fire. All our news from Basra right now is coming from a local TV station, so we don't know much else, but it from what we do know it looks like they're not trying to target any production facilities."

"Anyways," the President continued, "I'm not about to get us in the middle of a war with Iran and Iraq when we don't even know what's really going on. And we don't have enough troops on the ground in the Middle East to do anything about it. Not yet, anyway. And we have no image intel to see what they're up too, so we don't know how to engage them. I'm going to sit tight until we know what Iran's game is. Getting in a gunfight in the middle of Al Basra won't work out very well for anyone."

"So what are we going to tell the Iraqis?" McLeary asked.

"The truth. We tried to get the Iranians to turn back, but now there's not a lot we can do to kick them out. Iraq has its own army – 200,000 troops we armed and trained. If they want learn to live without us babysitting them, then they need to use that army."

"Has the State Department heard anything from Iran?" Chappelle wondered. "Where's Rand anyway?"

"Iran's not saying nothin' to nobody," Bowman grumbled. "Everyone that's supposed to be running that country has been hiding in the mountains for the last week. As for Jan, at the moment she is on the phone with Moscow, I believe in a conference call with Putin and the head of the FSB and the three of them are grilling the living hell out of the Air and Space Marshal, who apparently allowed Rannovich to fry all twelve of our best spy satellites for half a million greenbacks."

"So we're sure Rannovich was behind that? How did we establish this?"

The President responded, matching the VP's gloomy tone. "It's obviously no coincidence that we lost all our visual intel an hour before

Iran started a war. And we already know that's what Rannovich wants to do, jump-start a major war in the Middle East. As for the satellites, Rand updated me half an hour ago..." McNeil found a page in the stack of papers he'd left in front of his empty seat. "Here it is. The Marshal admitted that the satellites and the money came from someone calling themselves 'New Patriotic Enterprises.' There is no company by that name in Russia, but it is the name of a Chinese conglomerate that has financial ties to Iran and the Russian Mafia, and owns among other things an aerospace company that is China's leading manufacturer of satellites and has invested a lot of research into EMP weapons technology."

"Well, that's a pretty clear-cut case then," McLeary said. "So Russia's government is off the hook?"

"For the moment. As you can imagine they are royally embarrassed that this happened under their noses and they seem to be trying to help. But they don't yet fully appreciate how deep the conspiracy goes."

"So if Rannovich is orchestrating Iran's attack and has blinded our satellite surveillance, how are we supposed to respond?"

The President finally sat down. "I haven't decided yet, but we're definitely not going to jump feet-first into a war. That would be playing right into his hands."

## THE COMMAND BUNKER

Rannovich had a much better view of the events in Al Basra than the Americans did. Two of the Mi-24 helicopters carried camera crews and were providing extensive video coverage as the attack was carried out. President Ahmadinejad stood next to Rannovich, watching the huge screen in the bunker. His phone rang, and he stepped away to take the call.

"Sir!" an officer ran up to Rannovich a moment later with a typed dispatch. "General Palinov reports that his forces have captured another refinery and are preparing to cross the Tigris."

"Good. Tell him to proceed. Are the SAM batteries operational yet?"

"Three SA-6 systems and one SA-10 are online. The others should be set up in a few minutes."

Ahmadinejad lowered his phone and looked up at the Russian. "My Foreign Minister has been contacted by Baghdad. What message shall he pass on to the Iraqi Prime Minister?"

"Exactly what we discussed. Tell him to play our game or learn how to swim."

Ahmadinejad went back to his phone, and hung up a minute later. "Maliki isn't buying it. He says he already reported the attack to Washington and asked for their assistance, and he apparently said a few other things that were most unbecoming of a head of state."

"The Americans aren't going to join the game with the stakes where they are set now. Maliki's going to sweat it out for a while, and then we shall send him a video."

"What video?"

"The one we are going to shoot right now. Lights!" The room was illuminated only by the giant computer screen. Suddenly huge fluorescent lights came on overhead, making the control center brighter than the set of "The Price is Right." Ahmadinejad scrunched his eyes shut. Rannovich was already wearing Roberto Cavalli wraparound sunglasses and seemed unaffected by the intense luminosity.

A camera crew had been standing by, and they came to the center of the room. "Ready when you are, sir."

Rannovich nodded and made a speech in English. "This message is for Prime Minister Nouri Al-Maliki and his senior staff only. It concerns the future of your country and your very lives, so listen up. You have already informed the world that Iran has attacked the city of Al Basra without warning and is wantonly assaulting your civilians. This may be the truth, but as you are aware as a politician, the facts are whatever you make them. The fact is, in this case, that you allowed us to pursue and engage a large force of NCRI rebels that are operating in your country with mutual assistance from the local insurgency. They have been trapped far from their support base and our army will soon eradicate them all. It is necessary to place the cities of Al Basra and Umm Qasr under martial law until this process is complete.

"Now, I know that this version of the truth will be openly questioned, especially by the Americans who have already decided not to help you. But if you only repeat these facts, this will ensure that no one interferes with my plan. Who I am or what my plan entails is none of your business. It is unfortunate that my designs have to involve you and your country, but this is mainly a result of location rather than any personal issue.

"Now obviously I can't order you to cooperate without making a threat, so here it is. Iran's foreign minister already told you that we placed a small atomic device behind the largest dam in your country,

190

the Samarra Barrage. The device, which you could call a 'suitcase nuke,' will vaporize the dam, as well as one of Saddam Hussein's favorite palaces, and empty all twenty-three cubic kilometers of water stored in Lake Tharthar. The flooding would reach Baghdad in just under an hour, and raise the level of the Tigris River by forty feet. Your bulletproof office window, which overlooks the river, will become an aquarium, affording you an excellent view of your citizens drowning in the surge. Anyone who can swim will be swimming in heavily contaminated water, which will do awful things to anyone who survives after the flooding recedes. I have a remote trigger in my hand, and my thumb on this red button is all the power I need to drown a good percentage of your population and ruin a million square miles of arable land for a hundred years.

"I am basically holding you and anyone else downstream of the Samarra Barrage hostage. The only option you have is to do whatever I ask of you. Right now that isn't much. All you have to do is restate the facts as I dictate and not interfere with my forces in your country. Okay? Thank you for your cooperation." The camera operator removed a freshly burned DVD from the back of the Sony digital camcorder and gave it to Rannovich, who turned and gave it to the President of Iran. "Dmitri will help you encrypt the video so it can only be viewed on Al-Maliki's computer. You can add your own message before you upload it."

"Your ruthlessness as always amazes and pleases me, Mr. Rannovich."

The Ayatollah looked concerned. "You wouldn't actually do it, would you?"

"Do what," Rannovich said, "drown half of Iraq? I'm not planning on it. It wouldn't work anyway. The town of Samarra would be destroyed, but Baghdad will only get five or ten feet at the most. Loss of life would be severe, but nothing on the Biblical scale I just described."

"What about the radiation? To destroy the sacred Tigris-"

"Relax. Do the math, holy man. There's thirty kilograms of uranium in the bomb, about half of which will be converted directly into energy. The rest will be diluted in twenty billion metric tons of water; that's just about oh-point-four parts per trillion on a mass basis. There's more radioactive material than that in Perrier."

"So what are you saying, Ruskie?"

"I'm saying, your holiness, that if the Prime Minister decides to call our bluff I will have no hesitation to blow up the dam. The effect will not be quite as spectacular as what I told him it will be, but it will make our point."

"But even if the flood only wipes out the cities immediately down river, it would be a disaster of phenomenal scale," The Supreme Ayatollah now protested. "And the holy shrines in Samarra are sacred to all Shias, Arab and Persian alike."

"Are they holier than our greater cause?" Rannovich asked.

For that the religious leader of Iran had no answer.

"The outcome of our war will be determined by who puts more on the line," Rannovich declared. "If you want to win, you need to be willing to lose a little, okay?"

"He's right," Ahmadinejad said, as he came back to the room. "Revolutions are fueled by sacrifice. Besides, who cares if a few mosques get flooded? The damned Sunnis already blew up one of them a couple years ago. They're just buildings. Someone will rebuild them. And it's not like we can go there to pray anyway."

"Did Dmitri send the video?" Rannovich asked the President.

"Yes. I have no idea how the encryption thing works, but it should only be accessible by Maliki himself."

"Good. I don't want the Americans to know about the bomb until it goes off."

**TEHRAN**

Iran's Information Ministry is an entire government service dedicated to restricting the public's access to the internet. To a government as repressive as Iran, the World Wide Web is a quagmire of free speech and western attitudes so shockingly counter-revolutionary and offensive in the eyes of Allah, the national web servers must filter out ninety percent of it. The government did embrace the use of email, however, which does help ease the strain on Iran's woefully inefficient postal system. There are restrictions there too, however. Personal email use is aggressively monitored, especially if a message appears to contain a large file attachment. And any message leaving the country is opened and censored, and deleted outright if the sender had encrypted it. Unless it was sent by the Security Council, of course.

Albie, the Indian Muslim hacker that worked for Kujet, had much better internet access than the average Iranian. He had bypassed most of the filters in the national servers, allowing him to access illegal web pages. Hacking his way out of the email system was a little more difficult. He would never be able to get past the screening that guarded international data transfers. But the system worked both ways – he could use the Information Ministry's own network to monitor government email. So when he found a direct data transfer from the President of Iran to the Prime Minister of Iraq, he was able to covertly intercept and copy it.

The encryption system that Dmitri employed was child's play to the twenty-year-old New Delhi Tech drop-out. The supercomputer Kujet had bought for him ran a program of Albie's own design to analyze the encryption algorithm, and then Albie worked the algorithm backwards to break the code. Five minutes before Iraq's Prime Minister saw the message in his computer, Albie was already watching the video. "Oh holy hamburgers," he said to himself. He dug his phone out of the pile of candy wrappers on his desk and called Kujet.

## THE BUNKER – 1336 LOCAL

"Mr. Rannovich!" An Iranian officer called from the entrance of the command center. "Mr. Sun is here. He's waiting in the anteroom."

"Very good. Did you see to his accommodations?"

"Personally."

"Good." Rannovich left the command center and followed the officer down the short hallway to the anteroom. The tall, silver-haired Chairman of New Patriotic Enterprises was sitting in an overstuffed chair. He remained seated while Rannovich approached to shake his hand. "Mr. Sun, welcome to my little castle. I trust you had a pleasant journey?"

"I did, up until the point where your pilot appeared to steer our plane into the side of the mountain. That, I was not prepared for. Otherwise, yes, quite comfortable."

"What do you think of my army and air force?"

"Impressive," Mr. Sun answered. "I'm sure I saw only a fraction of your forces on my way in through the tunnels, but they looked ready to take on the entire American military machine."

"And with any luck, they will, in only a week's time," Rannovich said.

"So you are on schedule?"

"Yes. I have an Iranian brigade launching an apparent invasion on southern Iraq, which Iraq's Prime Minister will actually deny, and I've blinded the American's spy satellites. This should get Uncle Sam's undivided attention."

"Excellent."

"Once the Americans commit, all we have to do is draw them in, and keep them fighting. And we know what happens whenever there is fighting in the Middle East."

"Yes we do." Sun removed an Apple iPhone from his suit pocket. He showed Rannovich the screen. "Oil prices closed up ten dollars in Tokyo, another six in Hong Kong. London just opened and they are skyrocketing."

"Beautiful. We'll be back to record prices in no time. Much more, if we get to the final stage."

"And there we are," Sun said, "sitting on our three-quarter-trillion-barrel stockpiles in Siberia and Inner Mongolia – enough oil to fill the world's needs for twenty years, while the Middle East is a smoldering radioactive wasteland… twenty years and the world must pay whatever we ask for our oil."

Rannovich stood, his smile fading. "Keep dreaming those trillion-dollar dreams my friend. There is still work to do to make them reality. I must attend to this work."

"Of course."

"Your room is-"

"The Major told me," Sun interrupted. "Thank you, Rannovich, for everything."

## CIA LANGLEY HEADQUARTERS, MCLEAN, VA
## THREE HOURS LATER

"I know I bypassed the proper channels, but this is too urgent to sit on a plane from Tehran to Zurich to Washington."

Casey listened to Agent Caspian on the phone. The field operative was explaining why he'd uploaded a fifty megabyte video file directly to the CIA's FTP servers instead of sending it through Sam's chain of banks and embassies. "If Rannovich encrypted this video he obviously doesn't want us to have it," Casey surmised. "If he finds out you sent it to me your cover will be blown."

"Kujet got it out of the country on a disc using our local field runners. I sent it from an internet café in Bahrain, using a free access account under an alias I made up on the spot. And the video itself is spliced into the middle of a Simpsons episode. Albie walked me through the whole thing, and if he's sure Rannovich can't find it or trace it, then I'm sure it is quite safe."

"Okay. What am I looking at here?"

"Fast forward fifteen minutes into the video, right after when Homer and Ned Flanders get arrested by the Canadian border patrol."

194

"Okay." Fifteen minutes and two seconds into the video, the cartoon was abruptly replaced by Rannovich's message. Casey watched in silence until the Russian signed off. "Well, I'll be damned. That would explain Al-Maliki's press conference."

"Yeah, that was a riot. Iran and Iraq, working together to open a new front on the war on terrorism? Hilarious."

"I'm not laughing now."

"No sir."

"I'm going to have one of my analysts confirm that threat. Forty feet of water in downtown Baghdad is an awful lot."

"I remember reading that we'd looked in to knocking down that dam with a few cruise missiles during the first Gulf War. We gave it up because civilian casualties would have been so high, and that was looking at winter water levels. Doing that now, in late May after an extremely wet rainy season, I can't imagine what it would do."

"I don't want to. The radiation threat seems a little overstated though, unless he's got about three tons of plutonium sitting down there."

"Does this change my other operation?"

"We haven't discussed it with the President yet, but I don't see how it would. You got the packages, right?"

"Yeah, and they are way heavier than you said they would be."

"Sorry about that. Someone decided to give you the new model with the bigger battery pack."

"Okay, I'll be back in Iraq in twelve hours. I'll call you for an update on Operation Mouse Hunt then."

## THE WHITE HOUSE SITUATION ROOM – 1700 MAY 20<sup>TH</sup>

Brett McNeil was sitting down now. He wasn't nearly as agitated as he was last night when everything had gone to hell all at once. He was now looking at solutions, not problems. The new twist with the threatened deluge had moved him into "fix it" mode. The group at the table was the same as last night, with the addition of the Secretary of State and the Deputy Director of Operations for Central Intelligence. The President began the meeting. "Before the CIA gives us another scary bit of news, let's get an update on the other crises. State?"

Janice Rand looked up and down from the President to her notepad. "The Russian Federal Security Bureau has literally beaten a confession out of the Air and Space Marshal. It is very clear from his testimony that this was planned months in advance, by a secretive organization that is undoubtedly working for Rannovich. The timing on this and the attack on Iraq makes it obvious that he is behind both events. Further, he still has some nastier surprises waiting for us. Knocking out our satellites was a costly, high-risk venture. He's got a lot more up his sleeve than just occupying a couple of Iraqi oil towns."

"That's a sound assessment," The President said.

"As for that actual standoff, you all must have heard that Prime Minister Al-Maliki is pulling some sort of ostrich maneuver, saying that it's a joint operation to eliminate several NCRI and Sunni separatist terror cells in the area."

"Ridiculous," said the CJC.

"Maliki's Foreign Minister is feeding me the same line, and Iran is of course not talking, so I really have nothing further to report."

"Okay, thank you," the President said. "NSA? What's up with our ImInt blackout?"

Harmon had his comprehensive notes spread out before him. "We have all six of our operational Auroras canvassing the northern and southern borders of Iran, operating from Diego Garcia and Incirlik Air Force Base in Turkey. They can each remain on station for at least thirty-six hours with two aloft over each zone at any given time, operating with two crews and receiving aerial refueling every twelve hours. They orbit at an altitude of one hundred and twenty thousand feet and provide essentially the same quality of imagery as our missing Keyholes. The only thing is, they're staying over water and can only see about a hundred and fifty miles in from the coasts."

"So, they can see Tehran," the President observed, looking at the map, "and obviously the Gulf ports, but they won't be able to see if they make another move on Iraq or Afghanistan?"

Harmon shook his head. "Not from the Auroras. However, we do have Global Hawks and Sentinels patrolling both of those borders, and at seventy thousand feet they can see about eighty miles in. That would give us two-to-three hours warning."

"What if they make an air strike?" General Caleb asked.

"Uh, our E-3s would give us a heads up in that case, and we'd have half an hour's notice. But we don't expect any air strikes. Iran doesn't have much of an air force."

"Yeah, well, they didn't have much of an army either, until the CIA noticed they've begged, borrowed and stolen every spare military vehicle in Eurasia."

"According to our sources," Casey spoke up, "Rannovich has acquired a large number of aircraft, but mostly fighters, not bombers.

196

And he hasn't deployed them yet. At least he hadn't twenty-eight hours ago when we got our last satellite pictures of Iran's air bases."

"We're not very worried about the air threat," Harmon said. "The worst thing they could do is run a few dozen strike fighters over Baghdad and cluster-bomb the market district. We'd see them and probably intercept them before they made it that far."

The President nodded. "Okay, does that cover the bases so far?" No one had anything else to add. "Okay. Now I've got bad news and worse news. The bad news is that if Iran's forces are not withdrawn in the next forty-eight hours, we will have to take military steps to remove them. We are forced to do this because Iraq's government is not taking necessary steps to protect its citizens and our interests. Iraq is cooperating with the Iranians for reasons you've all been guessing at, but for the real reason and the worse news, I give you the CIA."

Casey pressed a button on the table in front of him and pushed his chair away so the others could see the screen on the wall behind him. Rannovich's video ran for about three minutes, at the end of which everyone in the Situation Room wore mixed expressions of shock and outrage. "Are there any comments before I give you the CIA's analysis?" Casey asked.

"Well, obviously Maliki bought it," the NSA said. "I guess I'd do the same thing if I didn't know any better."

"You seem to be of the mind that Rannovich is bluffing," the President noted. "Would you care to elaborate?"

"Mr. President, I've been discussing this with you on a frequent basis for the last three-and-a-half months. Iran does not have either sufficient quantity or quality of weapons-grade material or the technical expertise to build a working nuclear device at this time. Dirty bombs they can do, no problem; they have tons of enriched uranium, but nothing in the purity range needed to achieve critical mass. Furthermore, if they had a suitcase nuke, they would not deploy it twenty miles up-river from three of the holiest shrines in all of Shiite Islam lore. They would rather try to smuggle it in to Tel Aviv Airport and blackmail the Israeli government."

"Reasonable, and well put, sir," Casey said, trying hard not to sound patronizing and failing. "But the CIA has reached a different conclusion. Ahmadinejad and the Ayatollah do not control Iran's weapons anymore; Rannovich does, and he will put a suitcase nuke wherever he damn well likes. And, no, Iran won't have the capability of building and deploying a nuclear weapon for at least five years, but they didn't build this bomb. Iraq did."

"You're not suggesting Iraq's in on this now are you?" the SecState asked.

"It would explain a hell of a lot," Vice President Bowman muttered.

"No, I'm not talking about the current government. Saddam's own program was much more successful at producing nuclear weapons, because they didn't screw around with repeating the Manhattan Project and developing their own material. They stole it from us, from China and from Russia. Now you were all here when we discussed this last month, about our involvement in removing those weapons prior to the invasion." Heads around the room nodded, and one or two faces grimaced in disgust at the thought. Casey looked to the other end of the table. "Mr. President, just for the record, I still have your approval to tell the rest of the story?"

"Proceed." McNeil and SecDef McLeary both leaned back in their seats with their arms crossed. They were the only ones that already knew what was coming.

"The DCI implied during that briefing that the WMDs are safely in our possession. That is mostly true. Our asset directed the smuggling operation through Syria, Lebannon, and back to Iran. Along the way he exposed several terrorist organizations that had negotiated to acquire the weapons, including an al-Qaeda cell that wanted to purchase enough anthrax to infect all of North America and Europe. All of the chemical and biological agents were destroyed. The nuclear devices are stored in, of all places, a bank vault in downtown Tehran, safely disarmed and partially dismantled. The original plan to expose Saddam had failed, but we had the idea that if the time came to take preemptive military action against Iran, the devices could be planted at Iranian sites for the UN to discover and make it seem like Iran was further along in its program than it really was."

"As heinous as it is to be working with an arms dealer and smuggling WMDs, that does sound like a pretty clean operation," Rand said. "So what's the problem?"

"Not all the weapons were actually accounted for," Casey said. "Our asset directed the transport and brokered several sales and stings, but one of Saddam's nephews was also involved, and he moved several devices beyond our reach. We recovered one very dangerous dirty bomb that had been sold to Hezbollah, and the Mossad intercepted another one before it was delivered to Hamas, but there were several

198

full-scale nukes that completely disappeared en route to Iran. Until last month we had no idea where to look for them. Now we know to look in a bunker under the Alborz Mountains and the bottom of Lake Tharthar."

"You'd better run down the list," Harmon said, plainly furious with the man from the CIA. "I am the National Security Advisor, after all, and it would help me in my job if I knew about these particular threats to our national security."

"Very well. There are four devices that would be classified as suitcase nukes. Three of them are extremely low yield, containing the very least amount of plutonium necessary to achieve critical mass. These were developed by us as part of a bunker-buster program that got sidelined in 1994. Since we're the ones who built them, we know they work. Exactly how they got into Saddam's stockpile we don't know. The Chinese stole them from us in '95 and either sold them to Saddam or he stole them too. Anyway, these things could take out a football stadium or an airport terminal pretty easily but fortunately will be nearly impossible to smuggle back into the US. They have identifier tags integrated into the plutonium core, which were originally designed to interface with whatever plane was carrying the bunker-buster bomb. Every port, airport, and border crossing has devices to pick those things up if they ever come back to us. The Brits and Israelis have the same gear. Also, it can only be armed by the interface panel on a B-2 stealth bomber. Any attempt to reprogram the weapon's chip will render it useless. For all intents and purposes, those weapons are harmless.

"There's a fourth suitcase bomb which I suspect is the one at the bottom of Lake Tharthar. This one is a fairly crude uranium device which any high school kid could build with plans found on the internet, as long as he had about seventy pounds of highly enriched U-235 on his hands. This one scares us because not only is it easy to transport and activate, it's a powerful little bastard. We estimate twenty kilotons yield, which could knock down everything between the Capitol building and the Lincoln Memorial. One-and-a-half Hiroshimas, if you want to use that reference."

"I guess that would knock down a dam pretty easily," General Caleb noted. "How big is this dam by the way?"

"Stick to the bombs for a minute," the NSA said. "What else is missing besides the suitcase nukes?"

"One more, or two, actually," Casey said. "There was Soviet strategic warhead with a spare primer. This thing is huge. It can only be carried by a big transport plane or by special train cars or very large and slow trucks."

Harmon continued jotting down notes. "What's the yield?"

"Twenty megatons."

Harmon dropped his pen. "Holy mother of God!"

"The primer itself is about the size of a car engine. Very cumbersome device with all sorts of safety features. It has a seven kiloton yield – half a Hiroshima."

"How long was Saddam sitting on a twenty megaton H-bomb?"

"Fifteen years. It drove the guy crazy that he couldn't ever use it. He brought in experts from all over Russia to try to arm the thing, but it can only be done with a special computer from a missile base – same problem as with the little bunker-busters. And then there's delivery. This thing won't even fit in a 747. There's only three or four different planes in the world that could hold it. Saddam actually tried to build a giant cannon out of oil pipe to lob it at Israel. You know something funny, it actually turns out that a well-built nuclear bomb in the wrong hands isn't really that dangerous, because only the right hands can arm it."

"So, that leaves the twenty kiloton uranium suitcase nuke," Caleb concluded.

"Hold it," The Secretary of Defense said, "isn't it possible that Rannovich could have stolen or acquired the arming system for the big nuke? He does have Russian military connections after all."

Casey shrugged, as if stolen nuclear weapons were only a trivial matter to him. "It's certainly possible, and it's even likely that he's got a hold of other stolen Soviet warheads. But that's just conjecture, and we can only operate on what we know to be fact. We know that there are six bombs that disappeared somewhere in the Middle East and we know only one of them can actually be used by anybody. That's what we can expect to be dealing with."

"Okay, now tell us about the dam and the flooding effects," McNeil instructed.

"Yes, sir. The dam itself is a large concrete and earthen embankment dam similar in size and design to the Oroville dam in California. It doesn't make the list on the History Channel's "Engineering Marvels" shows; it's only somewhere around the fortieth or fiftieth biggest dam in the world. What's remarkable is the reservoir. Lake Tharthar is almost two-thirds the size of Lake Meade, making it the fifth or sixth biggest artificial lake in the world. The whole point of building the dam was to divert the seasonal flood waters

200

which occasionally overflowed the Tigris by a good five feet around Baghdad. If the lake was suddenly emptied, you'd get one of those floods in a hurry."

"Rannovich said forty feet in Baghdad. Is that accurate?"

"I've had my analysts make an estimate based on the current water level in the lake and accounting for the amount that would be vaporized by the blast. In the initial surge, there could be a wave thirty to fifty feet high. The total flooding would probably be closer to ten feet above the normal river level, which is still pretty devastating. Samarra is the nearest major city to the dam, and that would be wiped away entirely. The city of Al Kut – which is a hundred miles or so downriver from Baghdad – would get a twenty-foot surge and six or seven feet of floodwater. After that there wouldn't be much. The flood would just spread across the plain between the Tigris and Euphrates, wash out some farms and stuff, but there shouldn't be any significant casualties below Al Kut. "

"What about radiation?"

"Well, that part was a bunch of crap. Detonating the twenty megaton bomb at high altitude wouldn't even produce the kind of fallout as he's claiming. In reality, we're talking about a mere suitcase full of uranium evenly distributed through *five cubic miles* of water. Considering how contaminated that country already is, they'd barely notice it."

"Even so, this has to be averted," the President said. "We cannot allow Rannovich to destroy the dam. We also can not allow the Iranian army to continue occupying Iraq's only two port cities. Let's discuss our military options, people. How can we get them out the two cities without actually blowing the cities up?"

"We were hoping you'd ask that, sir," General Chappelle said. "Caleb and Casey and I have worked something out that we think will almost certainly work." The three of them described "Operation Mouse Hunt," which the President immediately approved.

Long before the President had reached his decision on addressing the Iran-Iraq issue, the military had started looking at their own solutions. If the President decided to take direct action against the invading Iranians, the military would need to have a plan already in shape. The plan was called Operation Mouse Hunt. The problem was that two cities were infested with enemy armored vehicles. Any attempt to assault them from the air or ground would cause a lot of collateral damage to the cities. The only way to attack the vehicles with enough precision to avoid unnecessary ruin would be to use laser-guided smart bombs. Laser-guided bombs lock on to laser light of a specific wavelength and pulse frequency reflected off of a target. If the bomb acquires its target at a sufficient altitude, it is guaranteed to hit not more than three feet from where the laser is pointing. The laser itself is generated by a device the size of a chalkboard eraser, and must be fixed in position by someone on the ground unless the target is clearly visible from the air. Operation Mouse Hunt was an elaborate scheme to smart-bomb the entire invading army.

## SOUTHERN IRAQ – 2200 LOCAL, MAY 21<sup>ST</sup>

Three men met at a gas station on the highway between Al Basra and Umm Qasr. Agent Caspian – aka Kahlil – came in an old 4x4 Chevy pickup that bounced across the desert without using its headlights. The Mukhabarat brothers arrived by car from opposite directions. "I told you to find a car with a big trunk," Kahlil admonished the Iraqi agent named Elessar, who had brought a battered subcompact. "That piece of junk won't carry half the load you need."

"It was hard enough to get a car out at all. I got shot at twice and had to ditch a vehicle that would have been much more suitable. It's got a roof rack, though; I can tie things to the roof if I need to."

"How many targets did you count in Umm Qasr?"

"One hundred and thirty-seven."

"That's all? Well, you might be okay then. Ellirat, you have how many?"

"Four hundred and twenty-three."

"That accounts for all the vehicles. Good work. Okay, I have twenty LTD's in each of these boxes," Caspian lowered the tailgate with a squeak. "Seven hundred and twenty units total, so help yourselves." He helped the Iraqis load the boxes into and upon Elessar's Volkswagen Polo and Ellirat's Ford station wagon. The VW managed to carry nine boxes. Ellirat took the rest.

"What's the battery life on these things?" Ellirat asked.

"Twenty-four hours. Conveniently, that's about how long your people have to place them. Remember, they have to be aimed at the top of the vehicle on a spot visible from the air. If they're parked in a garage or something, aim at the roof of the building. If they have more than a meter of cover, make a note of the laser unit's code and location so the Air Force can assign a bunker-buster. You need to provide me with a report telling me which part of the city each box-load of units is used in, and the total number of targets in each area. I'll relay that to the Air Force so they'll know where to drop each bomb."

"What about the infantry? They're holed up in hotels and apartment buildings alongside civilians."

"That's where the Rangers come in." Kahlil showed them spots on their maps. "They'll drop here, here, here, and here in Al Basra, and at both ends of this street in Umm Qasr. You and your people will need to identify the troop concentrations, command posts and guard stations, and provide English-speaking guides to lead the Rangers to each target. If they're mixed in with civilians, you need to identify beforehand which doors to knock down."

"That part's already taken care of," Ellirat said, "I have Basra's entire police department working with me."

"Good."

"When do the bombs drop?"

"Tomorrow night. The President gave the Iranians a deadline for 6PM Greenwich Mean Time, which is 10PM here. If the tanks aren't on their way back across the border by then, we will undertake the biggest precision bombing mission ever."

## LAKE THARTHAR – SAME TIME

Iraq is not known for having clean water. The Tigris River is one of the most polluted bodies of water anywhere in the world. The giant reservoir is even worse. It was so contaminated, the Geiger counters the Navy SEALs were using to look for the nuclear device were constantly chirping with reports that the water around them was only marginally in the "safe" zone. Lt. Lance Nathan had been swimming in the cold water at the base of the dam for an hour now. In thirty minutes he'd have to return to the surface to recharge his advanced Draeger re-breather system. It couldn't be soon enough for Nathan, whose arms ached from carrying a heavy Geiger counter and a heavier floodlight through the cold water. He could hear another device carried by one of his pals, about a hundred and fifty yards away. Because the water was so murky, he could hear a lot further than he could see, even with the five-million-candlepower floodlight.

Suddenly the needle jumped, wavered and jumped again. Nathan turned back and forth to find out what direction the radiation spike was coming from, and spoke into the tiny microphone built into his facemask. "I got something. EE40-31KS." Three other SEALs swam to the military-coded mission grid cell he indicated, and their Geiger counters also read the radiation source. Nathan's needle was steady at the low end of "moderate," indicating he was currently receiving the same radiation dose he'd get from a chest x-ray. Not that he cared; he was wearing a fully CBN-compliant dry-suit that could protect him from very high levels of radiation, but not the cold, for some reason.

The four SEALs cautiously swam forward, sweeping their floodlights in a synchronized pattern until they found the nuke. It wasn't actually in a suitcase. It was in a cheap wooden coffin loosely wrapped in heavy chains. Nathan swam around the coffin to confirm that it was indeed the radiation source. "Carter – go on up and get the winch." The rookie SEAL nodded, released his weights and floated up to the surface. He ascended in stages, slowly adjusting to the reduced pressure as he approached the surface. If a diver goes up to quickly he experiences something called "the bends," when the gasses in his bloodstream expand rapidly and painfully and often lethally.

While he waited for Carter, Nathan pried up a corner of the coffin with his knife. He could see the device inside; it was a simple "gun barrel"-type atomic device consisting of two separate blocks of uranium that would be slammed together with high explosives and form a critical mass. There was no shielding apart from the length of steel pipe used as the weapons case. Obviously the coffin itself did nothing to contain the radiation. One of the other SEALs documented the whole thing with a camera.

Nathan heard a voice in his earpiece. It was Commander Clark, who was running the mission from the surface. "Carter's coming down," he said. "Any booby traps?" Nathan called to his explosives expert, Petty Officer Louie Morris, and brought him over to check out the device. Morris reported there was only a VLF radio detonator, no automatic gadget that would blow the bomb if it was moved.

Carter landed four feet away, with a thick steel cable and a heavy clip, which was connected to the Super Stallion helicopter that had carried them and lifted their boat all the way over to this lake. The other three SEALs lifted one end of the coffin while Carter wrapped the cable securely around it, crisscrossing the bulge in the middle. He gave it two tugs and the line went slack as Clark disconnected it from the Pegasus fast-attack powerboat. The line went taut again as the big helicopter winched it up. The SEALs ascended with the nuke, checking that the line was secure before surfacing and boarding the Pegasus. Fifty feet below the surface the coffin stopped going up, and started to move laterally. The helicopter was dragging it through the water rather than carrying it away, to avoid exposing itself and anyone else nearby on the lake surface to the radiation. Fifty feet of water provides as much shielding as three and a half feet of lead.

The Marines had marked off a small bay halfway up the lake, warning swimmers and boaters to stay away. The helicopter slowly moved over the bay, followed by the five SEALs on the boat. Morris and Nathan went back in the water and helped the chopper lower the coffin another thirty feet to the bottom. They disconnected the winch and Morris went to work disarming the device. He didn't bother messing with the detonator. It was a modern commercial system and probably would detonate automatically if he tampered with it. Instead he just took a big pipe wrench and some Teflon-powder lubricant and unscrewed one end of the atomic pipe bomb. As he expected, the end-cap was packed with plastic explosive, intended to launch the adjacent uranium slug into another mass of uranium with tremendous force. Nathan tilted the other end of the pipe, and two heavy cylinders slid out into Louie's arms. Separated from the conventional trigger explosives, the two chunks of weapons-grade U-235 couldn't possibly reach critical mass and set off a chain-reaction.

The helicopter winch came down again with two large cases lined with memory foam and shielded with lead. Morris packed the uranium away and the SEALs swam back up. On the surface, Commander Clark helped them climb back on the boat. "Congratulations, Louie," he said. "You're the first man to ever dismantle a live atomic bomb underwater."

## THE WHITE HOUSE – FIVE MINUTES LATER

The Chairman of the Joint Chiefs and the Chief of Naval Operations made a report directly to the President. "Our SEAL team successfully relocated and dismantled the atomic device in Lake Tharthar," Admiral Marsh reported. "It was a simple uranium suitcase nuke, like the CIA predicted, except it was packed in a coffin, not a suitcase."

President McNeil let himself chuckle at that. "So the whole thing's contained?"

"Yes, sir. The radioactive core materials are being transported to the aircraft carrier *Abraham Lincoln* for safekeeping."

"Terrific." The President picked up an ivory-colored phone on his desk. "Get me Prime Minister Al-Maliki on his hotline. I've got some good news for him." McNeil looked back up at the Joint Chiefs. "Now that a wall of dirty water is no longer hanging over his head, let's see if this guy will stand up to Iran. Have a seat, guys. This'll only take a minute."

The Admiral and the General sat down and watched the President have a one-sided conversation. "Mr. Prime Minister, I hope I'm not disturbing your rest but I have something fairly important to talk to you about... Good, good... Well, I have good news and bad news. The bad news is you need to call up your friend Ahmadinejad right now and cancel that joint counterterrorism thing you're playing with. The good news is my Special Forces troops found and disarmed that little nuke he'd dropped behind the Samarra Barrage to blackmail you... Never mind how we found that out, you little weasel. The point is there's no longer any reason for you to put up with the Iranian Army occupying your ports. Now, you call up Ahmadinejad and you give him the same deadline I already gave him. Ten o'clock tomorrow night, your time... I already told him he needs to get his dirty hands off our commercial property in the area, namely the half-dozen oil refineries we've built there."

McNeil listened to Al-Maliki's protests for a minute with the expression of a parent listening to a child complain about a decision that had already been made. Finally he interrupted. "Look, buddy, you seem very unappreciative of the fact that we just pulled a twenty kiloton nuke out the lake for you, in all probability saving you a very expensive swimming lesson... You don't believe me? You want to see for yourself? Okay. Terry?" The President looked over to the Chief of Naval Operations. "Can you have that chopper swing by Baghdad? Mr. Maliki wants to see some sort of evidence."

"No problem." The CNO pulled out his cell phone. "They don't have the bomb itself, but they have the uranium core materials and a photo record."

McNeil spoke into the phone again. "Okay, buddy, our dive team will come over and show you some before-and-after pictures and the uranium core they took out of the bomb. Look for a big Marine helicopter landing on your front lawn in-"

"Fifteen," the CNO said.

"Twenty minutes. Call me back when they get there." The President hung up the phone with a very smug look on his face.

Admiral Marsh hung up a moment later. "Why'd you tell him twenty?"

"It adds a little dramatic emphasis if we move faster than he expects. Okay, Paul, where are we with Mouse Hunt?"

"General Caleb has twenty B-1s and B-2s at Diego Garcia all ready to go," Chappelle answered, "and CNO here gave us the Prowler squadrons off the *Roosevelt* and *Lincoln* to provide EW support. The bombers will each be packing a max payload of 500lb GBUs, and they'll be able to clean out the entire area with a single pass, as long as the CIA gets the designators in the right place."

McNeil had just gotten that report a few minutes earlier. "Our field agents should be distributing the targeting devices now. According to Casey, they've also got the local police forces working with them."

"Good. After the bombers finish their part, we have six planeloads of Rangers and Army Airborne jumping in. There's a little snag right there, apparently one of the C-17s we allocated doesn't have the new ECM gear. If they can't get that refitted at DG we'll use a couple of MC-130s instead. Once the troops are on the ground, they'll rely on the locals to help them locate and capture the enemy soldiers. Again, that's up to the CIA to organize; my boys don't have any actual plan beyond getting to the DZs."

The President looked thoughtfully at the CJC as he called the Army paratroopers "his boys." Chappelle had entered the Army as a grunt in the 101st Airborne midway through the Vietnam conflict. After completing OCS in the early eighties he asked to join the Rangers. He had led a platoon with distinction in the Gulf War, and led a company in Somalia. He was still leading his boys on the ground – as the CO of the famed 2nd Ranger Battalion – during the invasion/liberation of Afghanistan in 2001. After that he was promoted to Major General. During the invasion of Iraq he had commanded the entire 101st Airborne Division with adjunct authority over Special Forces. He was immensely proud of his boys, and justly confident in their capabilities. The President was a Vietnam Special Forces vet himself, in the Navy SEALs. Despite their inter-service rivalry, the new President got along very well with the new CJC.

The President picked up his note pad. "They're supposed to coordinate with the local contacts organized by the CIA. Casey just called me two minutes before you walked in and said their side of the op is going even better than expected. They have targets picked out and local resistance is ready to lead your boys right on top of the enemy bivouac areas and command posts. Apparently only a quarter of the enemy units are parked in Umm Qasr, which we expected because it's a smaller city. But you have your paratroopers split accordingly, right?"

"Yes, sir. We have two DZs in Umm Qasr and four in Basra, with one Ranger platoon and one company of the 502$^{nd}$ Regiment of the 101$^{st}$ Airborne landing at each, and an extra Ranger squad for each of the Basra drops. We'll also be using non-lethal weapons wherever possible – flash-bang grenades, rubber bullets, things like that."

"Excellent. Minimize civilian casualties and let the Iranians have their soldiers back for the right price. Good thinking." The ivory phone rang, and McNeil waited a few seconds before he answered it. "El Presidente speaking... Why, hello, Mr. Prime Minister... Yes, that's right, even in a highly enriched, weapons-grade form, U-235 only emits about as much radiation as dental x-ray machine... Okay, so you're convinced; what are you going to do now? Okay, good, and what will you do if he refuses? Don't know? Well we have a little plan for that ourselves. Why don't you send a few of your best battalions down there to bivouac just outside artillery range, and talk to the Pentagon about how they can support our operation, okay? Well, yes, you're welcome. We're happy to do it. We do things like this all the time for our friends, you know that? All you had to do was ask. Remember that next time someone threatens to blow up the Samarra Barrage, okay? Alright, take care." He hung up the phone and let himself chuckle a little.

"The Iraqis could secure the perimeter for us and help process the prisoners," General Chappelle said. "But we can't let them participate in the strike itself."

"That's okay," the President said, "as long as they can at least pretend they're actually defending their own country for once."

## AL BASRA – 2200 MAY 22$^{ND}$

Major Duhamad Eschewed the command officer's billet in the King's Hotel downtown. He preferred stay with his tank, and the others in his battalion, out under the mild night sky. His tank had been backed into a smashed storefront, half-concealed by the old building. Other tanks up and down the street were wedged into alleys and sitting under awnings, as if it was possible to hide a seventy-one-ton battle tank. Duhamad was settling into his sleeping bag on a cot behind the counter in the wrecked store. He and his crew did not notice the tiny red point of light that had appeared on the exposed hull of their tank four hours earlier, aimed from a rooftop across the street at the driver's hatch.

He did notice a noise, a high-pitched rush of jet engines softened by distance. He got up and grabbed his night-vision binoculars, and ran out to the street. He looked up and saw the terrifying form of an American B-2 stealth bomber; a black silhouette against the green glow of the night sky. He did not see the bomb that another plane had already dropped, plunging through eleven miles of atmosphere, locked on to the reflection of the tiny laser beam on the T-80 tank. It missed the laser point on the driver's hatch by a foot and a half, instead hitting the hull just in front of the turret joint. The five-hundred-pound armor-piercing bomb punched clean through the tank and detonated on the concrete floor below it. The tank's gunner, sleeping on top of the turret, was crushed against the shop's ceiling when the huge vehicle bounced three feet off the ground. The driver, lying on the floor under the rear treads, was incinerated.

Duhamad was blinded by the bright light that filled his binoculars. He dropped them and squinted at his tank, which was now burning from the inside out. There were more explosions all around – he could feel them in his feet and see the fiery blasts, but he could no longer hear. But his senses told him enough to realize that the Americans were systematically wiping out his battalion. He ran to his command post in the basement of a dry-cleaner's around the corner. "The Americans are bombing us!" He yelled.

"We noticed," one of his company commanders replied.

The ground-shaking impacts suddenly stopped, and survivors trickled in to the command center. Duhamad tried to organize medical assistance for the wounded, and ordered his communication unit to get ahold of the General on the radio.

"What happened to our air defenses?" he wondered. "We had all those mobile SAMs that were supposed to protect us from bombers." Nobody knew anything. Major Duhamad decided to take action. "Captain, organize an armed search party. There must be more survivors and we are going to find them. And then I want you to go to the hotel and contact the General directly."

But before anyone could go anywhere, the tense situation ended rather anticlimactically for the First Armored Battalion. A US Army Ranger kicked in the unlocked door, than stepped aside as another sprayed the stairs with automatic shotgun fire that hit no one. Then they tossed a metal cylinder down the stairs which went off like lightning and thunder knocked all the Iranians out for the night.

Duhamad woke up eight hours later with a massive headache, handcuffed and sitting upright in the back of an army truck that was packed full of officers from his regiment. He looked around and saw he was surrounded by American and Iraqi soldiers. A US Army medic was walking through the truck, checking on the prisoners, who were all still unconscious besides Duhamad. An Iraqi was following the doctor, checking the identification of each of the Iranians. He noticed that Duhamad was awake.

"Good morning, Major Anju Duhamad of Shraz, you rug-selling pile of camel dung," The Iraqi agent known as Elessar said in Farsi in a very polite tone. "When you get back to your commanders, assuming they don't execute the lot of you, I think you should recommend to them that they not try and pull a stupid stunt like this again."

# CHAPTER 10: RAISING THE STAKES

## USS *RONALD REAGAN*, SOUTH PACIFIC OCEAN
## 0950 LOCAL, MAY 23RD

Lt. Cmdr. Karl Roche had three spaces on the ship he could call his own. He had his own stateroom: a six-foot-by-seven-foot little room, just big enough for a long-twin bunk, a desk, and a wardrobe and very little else. He had his locker in the men's shower room next to the gym area, which was basically a cubby hole with a door and a name tag where he could store towels and a clean change of clothes. He also had a much larger closet among the Air Wing lockers, where he stored all of his flight gear and weapons.

As an aviator, Roche's schedule was dictated by his next flight. But right now the *Reagan* was charging at full speed to the Arabian Sea, and couldn't be bothered with zigzagging into the wind for flight ops. This meant Roche and the other aviators could actually develop some semblance of a routine for the first two weeks of the cruise. This also meant Roche had very little to do with his time. His major responsibility in the squadron was limited to training the other aviators. There was little for them to learn without actual flight practice. All Roche could do was schedule some simulator time with pre-loaded scenarios, and he was sharing *Reagan*'s one Super Hornet flight simulator with the *Warhawks*. He could also assign reading homework, and give lectures that parroted his TOPGUN classes, but after a week of this he and his squadron were completely bored.

Roche's routine was almost lazy compared to all the work the rest of the *Reagan*'s crew had to do. He woke up at 0800, two hours after the daytime work shift was supposed to start. He would roll out of bed, do fifty pushups and fifty sit-ups, stretch and put on the half-dirty clothes he'd worn yesterday. He'd proceed to the gym, which is the largest and most crowded non-combat space on the ship, but at 0815 it's mostly deserted. Roche would work out until 0900, and then toss his dirty garments down a laundry chute, shower, and change into clean clothes he'd left in his cubby hole. He shaved his stubble, spiked his hair, and went up to the officer's mess for breakfast.

The "Dirty Shirt" officer's mess, as opposed to the "Clean Shirt" wardroom, was where the air wing officers ate most of their meals. Roche could eat some combination of eggs, waffles, cereal and fresh fruit at the dirty shirt any time between 0500 and 1000. His schedule got him breakfast toward the end of the shift. As a squadron executive officer he had access to the wardroom, but in order to enter he had to be in uniform, and they only served meals at the traditional mealtime hours. Also there was a cultural barrier between the shipboard officers – typically career officers and Academy grads – and the aviators, who were generally college-bred and more laid-back than the "brown shoe" officer corps. But the food was somewhat better in the wardroom, so Roche would eat there whenever his schedule allowed it. A step above the wardroom on an aircraft carrier was the Flag Table, but dining there was by the invitation of the Admiral. And obviously it was invitation that was never turned down.

After eating he would go downstairs to his squad's ready room, located on a deck between the flight deck and hangar deck but miraculously soundproofed from the persistent clamor above and below. The ready room usually served as a lounge when there were no flight ops. Roche would make small talk with his squad mates while pouring himself coffee. He Eschewed the nasty brew upstairs in favor of the gourmet coffee his own machine produced. As he had expected, the high-quality coffee maker he provided endeared him instantly to the squadron. Roche used one of the computers in the ready room to check his Microsoft Outlook account and make sure nobody had scheduled a surprise meeting for him. From that point on he'd spend the day puttering around the ready room, air wing lockers, and the squad maintenance space in the hangar.

Today there was something to break the routine: organized target practice. The one thing a *Nimitz*-class carrier didn't have was a shooting range, but with no flight ops the front end of the hangar deck could be rigged up for that purpose. Open shooting would begin at noon, followed by a 9mm marksmanship tournament. That gave Roche two hours or so to clean his guns.

Roche sat down on the bench in front of his locker and got out his pistol cases. The locker assignment was, as far as he could tell, completely random. On his left he had a guy from the other Super Hornet squadron, an Australian named Nelson McGee who went by the handle "Bonzer." The door to his locker was identified by an old Outback Steakhouse poster of Ayer's Rock. On Roche's right, marked up with flame graphics, was Amber "Blaze" Worthy's locker. His female squad mate was just walking down the isle. Like the rest of the pilots there wasn't any real work for her to do so she also just spent a lot of time "puttering around." Apparently she'd been puttering around the jet engine shop, because her coveralls were covered with oil and grease.

She looked straight at the XO as she started to unzip her suit. Roche sensed what was coming and leaned behind the open door of his locker. Sharkey's locker was branded by a photoshopped "Jaws" movie poster that Buzz had made for him, with the swimming female victim replaced by the profile of a MiG-29. Karl put the poster between him and the woman undressing next to him. He could see the coveralls hit the floor under the gap on the bottom the door. He continued working on his Desert Eagle while Blaze sat down on the bench next to him. "What are you up to, XO?"

"I'm cleaning my sidearms," he said. He could dismantle, clean and reassemble his gun blindfolded, but he needed some light to inspect his work and he couldn't hold all the oily parts of the pistol in his hands. He decided it was futile to avoid her and sat up. She was brushing her hair, wearing only her sport bra and panties, and sitting in what could only be described as a seductive pose. Lt. Worthy had made it clear to the eighteen males in her new squadron that she expected not only to be treated as an equal, but allowed to behave like their equal also. That meant, apparently, walking around the locker room in her underwear like all the guys did. Roche couldn't get used to it.

"What are you doing that for?" She asked.

Roche blasted compressed air down the eight-inch barrel of the big pistol. "They're setting up a firing range today. I try to practice shooting at least once a week. I always clean my guns before and after I shoot them." He put the fifty-caliber handgun back together, worked the slide, took it back off, added a little bit if oil, and reassembled it. He rammed the slide back again, and now satisfied that the double-action mechanism was as smooth as possible, set it down beside him.

"Why do you clean it so much?"

"Three reasons. One, I like to. I like to work with mechanical things, and that's all that an empty gun is. Two, I'm a borderline neat freak, and I want my favorite things to be squared away at all times. And three, I don't want my guns to back-blow on me."

"What's that?"

Roche picked up the Desert Eagle. "The barrel of this gun is precision-engineered to very fine tolerances. If a bit of debris gets in the barrel, and it's larger than the gap between the bore and the bullet, the bullet will get stuck. At that point, all the propellant gas of the magnum cartridge will seek a new path of least resistance, which will blow out the breach of the gun and launch the slide into my face."

"That would hurt." Worthy picked the huge gun and looked it over. "This thing is huge. What is it, a fifty-cal?" Roche nodded. She double checked the chamber to make sure it was empty and looked down the barrel. "I hope you're not compensating for anything." She watched Roche while she said that, to gauge his reaction. He ignored the innuendo. She put the gun back down next to the commander, brushing against his buttock. He still ignored her completely. With undisguised disappointment, she stood up and put on a pair of running shorts.

"Lieutenant," Roche said, "how you conduct yourself with the other guys is none of my concern, but I'd appreciate it if you stop making advances on me."

"I'm sorry, sir, I wasn't, I mean, I didn't mean to. I was just playing around."

"Fine, that's as far as it goes, though. The Navy has regulations on this sort of thing for a reason, you know."

"Is it only because of regs?"

"No, it's not. And by the way, you're trying to hard."

"What do you mean?"

"You know exactly what I mean. If you want my respect, just do whatever it is you do best, okay? I hope it's flying fighter planes, because locker-room talk isn't it."

With that Blaze got up and left. Roche didn't watch her go, but Bonzer did, as he came up the aisle from the other end. "Oowhee, she's somethin' there, ain't she mate?"

"She certainly is."


By now, of course, Roche and the entire crew of the *Ronald Reagan* were aware that a small war had already started in the Middle East. The whole point of their hurried departure was to get on-scene to deal with the impending crisis. Their battle group was spread out all over the ocean, having left different ports at different times, all racing at top speed to meet somewhere near the tiny island of Diego Garcia in the middle of the Indian Ocean. The *Reagan* could cruise at a sustained top speed of thirty-eight knots, and was running with its reactors redlined along the great circle route from San Diego, through French Polynesia, past American Samoa and Fiji, between New Zealand and Tasmania, and across the roaring forties of the southern Indian Ocean, which is a terrible place to be during this time of year. The huge carrier could handle anything up to and including a category ten Pacific typhoon, but the flag escort – the new destroyer USS *Halsey* – wouldn't be having as much fun.

Three more *Arleigh Burke*-class guided missile destroyers were following them: the *Fitzgerald*, the *John Paul Jones* and the *O'Kane*, steaming from either San Diego or Pearl Harbor. The powerful destroyers could make forty-one knots at flank speed, and they were heating up the ocean as they raced toward Diego Garcia. They went around the north coast of Australia, though, through the Strait of Malacca, avoiding the scary weather down south.

Somewhere ahead of the *Reagan* and the *Halsey* the slower ships were making their way to the rendezvous, having left their home ports with a four-day head start. Two old *Oliver Hazard Perry*-class frigates – the *Vandegrift* and the *McClusky* – would serve as screen escorts for the battle group. Two *Ticonderoga*-class missile cruisers – *Shiloh* and *Bunker Hill* – would stick close to the carrier and coordinate air and missile defense. The second biggest ship in the CVBG was the new combat replenishment ship *Lewis and Clark*, which would shuttle back and forth between DG and the battle group and keep the other nine surface ships topped off with fuel, food and ammo.

There were two more ships in the battle group, but they could have been anywhere just then. The *Los Angeles*-class attack submarine USS *Tucson* would be the CVBG's best defense against enemy subs. The second sub was part of the *Seawolf* class but it had been extensively modified and was really in a class by itself. The USS *Jimmy Carter* would supplement the *Tucson*'s defensive duties but it would also serve as a base of operations for any covert SEAL missions in the coming campaign.

The entire CVBG – twelve ships in all – carried enough firepower to meet any conceivable threat and defend itself against any possible aggressor. There is nothing a carrier battle group has to worry about except another carrier battle group.

**THE PENTAGON – 0900 EDT**

Admiral of the Fleet Terrance Marsh, the Chief of Naval Operations, was thinking about that match-up as he looked at the Pentagon's Big Board. The eighteen-by-thirty-two-foot display screen showed every single military unit in the world. Or at least it was supposed to; without the Keyhole satellites it was difficult to track foreign movement. However, a few older geosynchronous satellites were still watching certain targets, including Russia and China's major military ports. Over the last several hours, both countries had begun deploying the bulk of their fleets from Shanghai, Zhanjiang, St. Petersburg and Murmansk.

"We count thirty-two Chinese warships, sir, including almost every destroyer they have, a couple of either *Yukan* or *Yuting*-class tank landing ships, and their aircraft carrier. Two destroyer flotillas and what amounts to a CVBG." A dozen officers were on the phones with the NSA and the NRO and constantly updating the information.

"That carrier hasn't even had sea trials yet," the CNO said. "Why are they sending it out with a full battle group?"

"Beats me sir, but the last pictures show they're running west at flank speed."

"What are the Russians doing?"

"We count twenty-three ships total sir, again mostly destroyers, with three capital ships. The carrier *Kuznetsov* just cleared the St. Petersburg harbor an hour ago, and the heavy cruisers *Peter Velikiy* and *Marshal Ustinov* are preparing to get under way."

"Admiral, we have two more Russians clearing docks," someone else reported. "The amphibious assault ship *Moskalenko* and the Akula-B attack sub *Yaguar*."

"Another Chinese ship is coming up also, sir. It's that new LPD we don't have a name for."

"You mean the copy of our *Tarawa*-class assault ships?" Marsh asked.

"Yes, sir."

Admiral Marsh turned to his aide. "Call a meeting with the Joint Chiefs and SecDef right now. And get someone from the State Department on the line. If Russia and China are thinking of doing what I think they're doing, this little war in Iran is about to go global."

"It would obviously be a very dangerous situation to have sixty foreign naval vessels sharing the Persian Gulf with two of our CVBGs," General Chappelle agreed. The senior military commanders were in a conference room on the E-ring. "From what we know of Rannovich's plan, this is going to fall right into it. If anything goes wrong, a ship accidentally gets sunk, we could have Russia and China shooting at us and each other. Then Iran starts attacking again while we're all distracted, it'll be a nightmare."

"And I hate to be the voice of doom," Secretary of Defense McLeary said, "But some of those ships may actually be under Rannovich's control."

216

"What do you mean?"

"Well, he's got several senior officers of the Russian and Chinese Navy in his network, right? Where's that list the CIA gave us..." The Secretary rifled through his briefcase. "Here it is. Yeah, Admiral Bussolari of the Russian Navy, Admiral Laido of the Chinese Navy, half a dozen Russian captains, nine PLA/N colonels..."

"Colonels?" Marine Corps General Schilling asked.

"The Chinese Navy is organized as branch under the People's Liberation Army," Marsh explained, "so the Navy uses army ranks for everything up to admiral. A colonel is a captain."

"We need to get the CIA to find out if any of these guys sailed out in these fleets," the Secretary of Defense said. "Because that's at least fifteen warships that will be against us from the start."

"I'll have them get on it," General Chappelle announced. "Meanwhile, we need to figure out how we're going to deal with them. What's the situation with our CVBGs?"

"The *Theodore Roosevelt* is there now," Marsh said, as he placed a tablet PC on the table showing the locations of his ships. "We let the *Lincoln* head home once we got the cease-fire agreement. The *Reagan* will be there to take over by the time the cease-fire expires."

McLeary asked "Have you considered bringing the *Lincoln* back to the METO in light of the new situation, and maybe bringing another carrier in as well?"

"I've only had an hour to think about it," Marsh answered, "but yes. *Link* has two months left in her deployment. We were planning to send her on a little goodwill tour when all hell broke loose, but I can keep her in the area for another month or so. I have a blue flag scheduled on Tuesday for the *Link* and the *Reagan*, after that I'll just move them both back up to the Gulf. Also, I have the *Stennis* in the Strait of Formosa. With the PLA/N's Eastern and Southern Fleets leaving town, it doesn't look like we need a CVBG to guard Taiwan, so I'll send the *Stennis* and half of its escorts to shadow the Chinese Southern Fleet. That will give us forty ships – three and half carrier battle groups – with enough firepower to completely destroy the navies of Iran, Russia, China, and the rest of the eastern hemisphere if we feel so inclined."

"Well I doubt it will come to that, but I think that will give us total control of the region," McLeary said. "Where's State Department at right now, Ed? Any progress on the negotiations?"

Ed Helms, the Undersecretary of State was there and he answered. "Iran only agreed to the cease-fire because we'd captured two thousand soldiers and that was not the way they wanted to start a war. So far they have not given us any terms for standing down or explained why they attacked in the first place. We have until Friday to work something out, but right now the Iranians are just stonewalling."

"You're not in touch with Rannovich himself are you? Or their president?"

"No, the highest government official we've spoken to is the Minister of Foreign Affairs. Apparently he's the highest ranking man in Tehran right now. Ahmadinejad and the Ayatollah and the generals are all in some undisclosed location."

"Well, I think they'll start talking to us soon enough. Paul? You have our contingency plans ready?" The SecDef asked the CJC.

"Yes sir. Our mobilization is almost complete. If Rannovich tries another foray outside his borders he'll have half the Army, Air Force and Marines coming down on him. We have a little 'Shock and Awe' bomb show for Tehran, bunker busters for all the suspected nuclear facilities, and the Navy's going to help us with cruise missiles. The only thing we don't have is intel. We still don't know exactly where they've hidden their army. But once we do engage, we should be able to roll them up pretty easily."

"Good. Then it will just be up to the Navy to keep the Chinese and Russians from getting in the way."

"I think we may have a way to do that with out a direct confrontation, sir," Admiral Marsh said. "We could announce that one of our subs – say, the *Jimmy Carter* which is invisible anyway – sank in the Strait of Hormuz after suffering massive reactor damage. We could establish quarantine in international waters and close the Strait. Our ships are CBN-compliant, so they could go through, but the Russians and Chinese would be locked out of the Gulf."

"What about tanker traffic? Oil prices are going berserk as it is. If you shut down the tankers..."

"They could use the Omani side. But the Oman government and the UAE won't let warships in their waters."

"Well then, couldn't the Iranians let the Chinese and Russians through their own territorial waters?"

"No, not if we position it right. Look:" Marsh got up and walked to a large map of the Middle East on the wall. "Maritime law stipulates that a nuclear vessel recovery zone is closed for fifteen nautical miles around the site of the sinking. We could say the *Carter* went down somewhere in this five-mile radius," he tapped a point on the map, in the narrow strait between Oman and Iran, "and that gives us a twenty-mile-radius circle to quarantine. Right here the Strait's only thirty-seven miles across. We can close Iran's national waters and leave only Oman's three-mile stretch open for tanker traffic."

"That is so devious, so simple," McLeary said. "I love it."

"Ah, that's not going to fool them," said the Undersecretary of State. "If we lock the Strait of Hormuz they'll see through any cover."

"Maybe," The SecDef said, "but if we're using international maritime law there will be nothing they can do about it. What, you think they'll come out and insist that we're faking the whole thing? That would be perfect. Then we get to hold a press conference and say 'how dare they accuse us of skullduggery, we just rescued a hundred men from a foundering steel coffin, all of them recovering from radiation sickness, and these guys accuse us of lying about it?' We'd be untouchable."

"What do we tell the families of the crew?" Chappelle asked

"Same thing we tell the press," Marsh said. "We got everyone off, but we have to keep them in isolation for treatment. *Carter*'s on Black Ops anyway, so the crew can never tell anyone what really happens during their deployment. Then after a month we can say we salvaged the sub and we can refit and redeploy it."

"Okay," Helms conceded, "but I think we need to get the President's approval before we even pretend to dump a hot nuclear reactor in the one of the world's busiest waterways and then lie about it on TV."

McLeary stood up. "I'll get his approval in two minutes. Terry, the *Carter*'s in the *Reagan* battle group right?"

"Right."

"As soon as your blue flag is over, send her up to the Strait. Have the captain make distress signals on open channel and make it graphic. I want to have independent sources reporting the accident before we announce it. Actually, have him say there are fatalities on the radio, and we'll deny that in our press conference."

"A strawman cover-up."

"Exactly."

"I'll have it all set up by Wednesday, just in time for the evening news."

### *REAGAN* – 1300 LOCAL

"Attention, registration for the marksmanship tournament will begin in five minutes, open only to nine millimeter users. Open range closes in thirty minutes." The announcement repeated over the hangar deck PA, far louder than necessary to be heard over either gunfire or jet engines. Roche combined ear protection with entertainment, playing mp3s through his cell phone over his noise-canceling headphones, but he still heard the announcement over the external noise and the jazz music he was listening to. He emptied his Desert Eagle one more time and stepped away from the firing line, letting a young petty officer take the spot. He walked back to the folding table where he left his other guns and his ammo. Another man was standing there, rubbing his Kimber 1911 Gold-Match .45 with a soft cloth.

"Excuse me," Roche said. The other guy stepped aside and looked down at the gun Roche was holding.

"That thing's ridiculous," he said.

"Pardon?"

"The Deagle. Fifty-cal, right? What are you gonna use somethin' like that for?"

Roche was tempted to say "Killing dozens of terrorists in Iraq" but he didn't. He just shrugged and said "It's all about stopping power."

"Huh, well it only packs seven rounds, and those things have jamming problems."

"Only if you hold it wrong. Besides, you only have seven rounds in yours."

The other guy put his .45 down. "Yeah, but I only use it for fun. This is the real deal, right here," he said as he picked up a modified Browning Hi-Power. "Custom built right down to the barrel. This is what I fly with."

"I see. I usually fly with this." Roche opened the case to put away the Desert Eagle and showed off the Glock. "Full auto."

"Oh, that's a nice piece. You can't use that in the tourney though."

"No, I'll be using the runt in my collection." Roche took out his SEAL-issue SIG, glistening with oil. He wiped it down carefully. "I don't think we've met, by the way. My name's Karl Roche." He extended his hand but the other pilot didn't take it.

"Sergei Unther. But you can call me Deadeye, if you're an aviator."

Roche decided to ignore Unther's attitude. Odds had it that Roche outranked him but he didn't bring that up. One thing he hated about the military was the way everyone, especially junior officers, tried to pull rank on each other. Roche tried to match the name and face to the Air Wing roster he'd partially memorized. VFA-25, the

220

legendary Fists of the Fleet, was one of the Pacific Strike Fighter Wing's last remaining Hornet-C squadrons. Roche remembered the name Deadeye from that list.

The PA speaker crackled again. "Registration for the tournament begins now. Please be prepared to allow your gun to be inspected, unless it is a G.I. M9. Ammunition will be provided at the firing line. First one hundred names only, and have your five dollar entry fee up front."

Roche locked his gun cases. "After you," he said to Unther. He followed the shorter pilot to the sign-up table.

Unther handed his gun to the petty officer that was inspecting the non-G.I. weapons. "Lieutenant Sergei Unther, VFA-25."

"What kind of gun do you have, L-T?" asked the warrant sitting at the table.

"Browning Hi-Power custom."

The warrant looked up at the PO, who nodded and handed the pistol back to Deadeye. "Okay, you're in group one. We start in fourteen minutes."

"Thanks." Unther started to walk off, but was hemmed in by the queue of people.

Roche stepped up and surrendered his sidearm, checking the safety even though it wasn't loaded. "Lieutenant Commander Karl Roche," he said it just loud and clear enough to be sure Unther heard, and he saw the lieutenant turn sharply out of the corner of his eye. "VFC-233, and that's a SIG-Sauer P226."

The PO removed the gun's magazine. "This is a fifteen-round mag, right?"

"Yeah."

The PO replaced the clip and handed the pistol back to Roche. "We're only firing thirteen shots per group, because that's all that a Beretta carries, so only load thirteen rounds, okay sir?"

"Got it."

"Group six, Commander," the warrant said.

"Thanks." Roche walked sideways through the line.

Unther wiggled through the crowd and caught up with him. "Sir, I'm sorry, I didn't know you were a-"

"Hey, forget it. All ranks are equal out of uniform. Now go practice. You'll need everything you got if you want to beat me."

Unther lost his air of false humility immediately. "I'm the defending champion, Commander, three straight deployments."

"Not for long."

"Hey, Sharkey!"

Roche looked around to see who was calling him, and spotted Hannibal waving him over. He walked up to him. "What is it?"

"Palerider, Deuce and I each put a Benjamin on you," Hannibal said. He gestured across the hangar to where the CAG was standing with the half-Navajo CO of the *Yellow Jackets* squadron. "If you lose to that Deadeye punk, we're coming after you."

"What kind of odds am I getting?" Roche asked.

"Hardcase gave us four to one," Burke answered. Wilkes was the *Reagan*'s unofficial bookie. "But Deuce and Toymaker say you're a sure thing."

Roche looked for and found LCdr. Wilkes, with a crowd gathered around him, punching numbers into a caclculator and consulting with Hitman Armani, who was writing furiously in a notebook. "I sure hope Hardcase has his bets covered."

The way the tournament was organized, ten participants were in each group, and the top three from each group would advance to the second round, then the top ten of those thirty would be in the finals. Roche and Unther were both first in their groups in the first two rounds. For the final round they stood next to each other, pistols unloaded, waiting for the ordnance techs to set up the new targets. Once they got out of the way the announcer said "Load." Roche, Unther and the eight other finalists slapped fresh clips into their pistols. Roche looked up and down the line quickly and saw there was only one Beretta left. Everyone else had a non-GI sidearm, like his SIG and Deadeye's Browning. "Ready." The shooters clicked the safeties off and rammed the slides back on their pistols. They aimed down the range at paper targets thirty yards away. Roche stood sideways with his back to Unther, with his gun in his right arm fully extended toward the target. Unther held his gun close to his face with two hands. "Fire!"

Deadeye grimaced with concentration, lining up each single shot carefully with steady, mechanical rhythm. Roche looked almost bored, as he casually emptied the pistol's load while holding his rock-solid aim. In a few seconds the gunfire stopped, and the announcer called "Clear!" The shooters clicked their safeties and removed the empty clips, while the ordies went out to examine the targets. They reported to the announcer after a minute's discussion. Unther sweated and stared at Roche. Sharkey watched the ordies, still wearing an expression of only casual interest. "In third place, with one hundred and twenty-six points, Petty Officer first class Hector Domingo."

Roche cheered the *Stingrays* maintenance crewman, as he walked up to the table to accept his award. "Ah, we have a tie at first place, between Lieutenant Sergei Unther" – Deadeye looked up at the announcer – "and Lieutenant Commander Karl Roche." Deadeye looked back at Roche, now with a fierce glare. Roche didn't change expression at all. He already knew the score. His keen eyes had counted his own shots and Unther's as they hit the targets, and he knew both had a perfect 130.

The crowd of aviators and sailors cheered wildly, quieting only slightly when the announcer spoke again "I... guess we'll have a tie-breaker now, so, sirs, if you'll just wait right there while the ordies put up fresh targets-"

"Set them up at fifty yards," Roche called out. He doubted either of them would ever miss at only thirty.

The announcer hesitated then called back "Lieutenant Unther? Is that acceptable?"

"How far back can they go?"

"Sixty," an ordie called back.

"Make it sixty yards then." This was beyond what's supposed to be the maximum effective range of a 9mm. The spectators cheered and hollered even louder.

"Sixty is fine," Roche yelled over the noise without waiting to be asked, "and only five shots each." Now he looked right at Unther, who nodded in agreement. Two ordies came up to them and packed five fresh parabellum rounds in their magazines.

"Load. Ready." The guns clicked in unison. Then Roche turned sideways, facing *toward* Unther and holding his pistol with his *left* hand.

"I didn't know you were left-handed," Unther muttered.

Roche smiled. "I'm not."

Unther's eyes went wide. The announcer called "Fire!" and Unther did, but Roche saw his adversary had lost focus. Deadeye swore and tightened his grip before firing his second shot. Roche continued smiling as he gazed at the target through his sights. He fired all five rounds from the SIG-Sauer before Unther's Browning shot its last three. "Clear!"

Roche whirled the pistol in his hand, flipping the safety and dropping the empty clip in a single motion. He heard Unther mutter something and asked "What was that?"

"I said you fucking cheated."

"No, I don't think so."

One of the ordies carried a bullhorn to the end of the range and checked the targets. "Lieutenant Unther, forty-eight out of fifty!" There was a round of applause from the spectators. Sergei's face twitched as he tried to smile. He knew his first shot had gone low.

The ordie announced the other score. "Commander Roche, fifty out of fifty!"

Roche half-expected the other aviator to explode, but he didn't. He just slouched forward, tucked the pistol into his waistband, and shuffled to the table to accept his second-place prize. Roche turned and saluted the cheering crowd before following him. "Hey, don't feel too bad. No one ever beats me."

"Yeah, that's what I hear. You're that guy who beat Deuce at TOPGUN, right?"

"Uh, yeah."

Unther's mood brightened. "Well, if I had to lose, it might as well be to a famous guy like you. Besides, I'm still getting a chunk of the pot."

# CHAPTER 11: FREE RIDE

## USS *REAGAN*, 1200 MI SE OF DIEGO GARCIA
## 0300 LOCAL, MAY 25<sup>TH</sup>

Roche was in the officer's mess, sitting alone, which was not surprising given that it was three o'clock in the morning. He'd been flying night ops practice all evening and had nothing to eat since 1700 except for a Snickers bar. The *Reagan* had caught up with its escorts and could slow down enough to do flight ops, and all the pilots needed the practice. This blew their routine apart, and they had to be up at random hours. Fortunately the dirty shirt is always open, offering a special meal for night fliers called midnight rations, or MidRats. Roche sat at his favorite table, overlooking the front half of the flight deck, eating lukewarm ham and pineapple pizza and reading all the paperwork that had piled up on his desk while he'd been sleeping or flying that day.

"Good morning," a short, stocky, bald man said as he sat down suddenly at the table. "Mind if I join you?"

Roche looked up quickly, expecting a prank. He didn't recognize the new guy, so he let his guard down. "You can take a seat, but I don't think you're allowed to say 'good morning' before sunrise," he said.

"Does it matter around here? Something's always going on, even at this ungodly hour." To demonstrate, a pair of Tomcats launched off the deck below them. "Like them. What other kind of job has the potential to kill you before breakfast."

Roche grunted. "Tell me about it. I just came down from there."

"Yeah? What do you fly?"

"Supers."

"Really? That's my plane."

"You're an aviator?" Roche asked skeptically, doubting the older man would pass a physical.

"No, I don't fly them, I build them. I'm sorry, let me introduce myself. Marty Silverman; I work for Boeing."

"Karl Roche. I work for the Navy." The two shook hands and Karl asked, "so what are you doing out here?"

"I'm here to keep an eye on the new Hornets and Growlers. Make sure they're working out for you guys, take performance evaluations and sort of show a little connection between the company and the customer."

"I see. That's awfully thoughtful of the company."

"Which squadron are you in?"

"*Stingrays.*"

"Oh, so you have the new block 2-c models."

"That's right. And may I say that is a fantastic airplane you guys put together."

"Well, thanks. I just hope the government is getting its money's worth. You know, that paint job alone cost upwards of a quarter of a million dollars."

"If it fools missile radar like it's supposed to, it's worth it."

"Hopefully you won't have to find out."

"So, what are you doing up this late? Or early?"

"I'm trying to stay somewhere between local time and Central Daylight Time. That way I can communicate with my people in St. Louis and Chicago. They're ten hours ahead of us out here."

"Actually they're fourteen hours behind us. But either way, I see your point."

"Anyway, I'm sort of eating breakfast right now. And my intern is getting dinner." Silverman pointed across the mess to a tall young man wearing a backwards USS *Ronald Reagan* baseball cap, who was loading his tray with grilled cheese sandwiches and chicken fingers.

He came over to their table with his tray balanced on top of a stack of papers and a Dell notebook computer. "These just came in from Paula's team," he said, handing Marty the paperwork. "They want us to find out how often the landing lights are replaced on the Grizzlies, I guess to compare to the replacement rate on concurrent Rhino blocks."

Silverman looked at the documents. "Well, she's got the wrong part number on these request forms. The LED groups are 214011 series. I don't know what this is for."

"No the ones on top are for the clip switch in the nosegear. Sorry, I should have been more specific," the kid swallowed the half-sandwich he had in his mouth. "They want the entire LRU package, not just the lights themselves. The LEDs are on the bottom." He opened his computer so Marty could read an email explaining the request.

Roche had no idea what the young man was talking about, so he just studied the newcomer instead of trying to follow the dialogue. The intern was built like Roche, heavy but athletic. He was about two or three inches taller with dark hair and a lightly tanned face with Anglo-Norman features. He was wearing an unzipped windbreaker bearing the Boeing logo, and underneath that, a blue T-shirt that read *It is as bad as you think, and they are out to get you.*

"That's a great shirt," Roche said.

"Thanks."

Silverman looked up. "Oh, right, I'm sorry. Karl Roche, meet my superstar assistant, Greg Sander."

Karl reached over and shook the kid's hand. "Hi. I fly the Rhino 2-c."

"Es or Fs?"

"Both."

"Cool."

"Now, you're an intern, right Greg? Still in college?"

"Yeah. I go to Embry-Riddle in Arizona."

"So how did they get you on an aircraft carrier on a combat deployment cruise?"

"I don't even know. Marty snuck me out somehow."

"He's actually supposed to be in someone else's department," Silverman explained, "but I took over the project they had him on and got him as a bonus. Now, his internship contract says he's basically supposed to work directly for the head of his department and shadow him everywhere he goes. That means he gets to follow me on a little field trip."

"What's your major, Greg?" Roche asked

"I'm getting dual-BS degrees in Aeronautical engineering and aviation science."

"So you're learning to build planes *and* fly them."

"Right."

"That's the other reason why he came with me," Marty said. "He's the only one in my department allowed in the back seat of fighter."

"I'm in the ROTC," Sander explained. "For Air Force, not Navy – please don't hold it against me – but I've got some flight training and that makes me a rated observer."

Roche raised an eyebrow. "Do you fit a fighter plane?"

"I'm six-two and one-eighty-five; I can squeeze in."

"Have you ridden one of our Supers yet?" Roche asked.

"Actually, no. I've spent the whole week looking up part numbers for Marty."

"I do want to try to schedule some flight time for him at some point," Marty explained, "but so far we've had too much to do."

"Well, Greg, when you get some free time this week, call me. I can arrange a ride in one of my squad's F-variants. I'll probably be taking you up myself. That's one of the XO's jobs – tour guide and VIP chauffer. Actually, on Tuesday, we'll be doing a BFX and you can see a little bit of mock combat."

"A what?"

"Blue Flag Exercise is a simulated attack on another CVBG; in this case, the USS *Abraham Lincoln*."

"That sounds like fun," Silverman said. "What do you think, Greg?"

"Absolutely, if the folks back home stop asking for reports, I should have Tuesday morning free."

"Alright then," Roche said. "Just come down to the *Stingrays'* ready room at around 0700 on Tuesday. Do you know where that is?"

"No."

"Follow me then. You might as well do some of the paperwork now."

"Oh, great."

Sander and Roche bussed their empty trays and headed for the ladder. Roche took them to the gallery deck between the flight deck and hangar, down the main starboard corridor.

"Have you figured out how you find your way around the ship?" Roche asked.

"Sorta. I picked up the frame numbers pretty quickly. Keeping track of which corridor I'm in is a little more difficult."

They stopped at a door marked "VFC-233 AVIATORS RR." Roche entered a six-digit code on the keypad on the door and opened it. The room was dark. Roche hit the light switch, and went straight to a coffee maker.

"Do you want any coffee?"

"No thanks. I don't much care for the coffee here."

"But mine is better." Roche held up a bag of Givaldi brand dark roast grounds.

"Well in that case, yeah, I'll take a cup."

Roche loaded a filter basket and started the brew. Then he went over to one of the four computers in the room which was glowing softly on screensaver. He logged on and pulled up a few files. "Just the basic 'don't sue us if we accidentally kill you' nonsense," Karl explained as he printed out release forms. "And a non-disclosure form promising

228

you'll keep quiet if we say that anything you saw or heard is classified. And this one is an authorization for a civilian to participate as an observer in a training exercise, which I can approve, but I need all your personal info. I can type it all in for you while you read and sign those lawyer papers."

"Okay." Sander took the other forms.

"Full name, please."

"Gregory Lewis Sander."

"Address?"

"Which one – my home, my school, or the room I rent in St. Louis?"

"Your permanent home address, I guess."

Sander gave him a street address in Villa Park, California, a town Roche knew well.

"Orange County kid, huh?" Roche asked

"Right. But it's nothing like the TV show."

"I know. I grew up in Yorba Linda."

"Really? Did you play football for Esperanza, by any chance?"

"Yes, I did."

"My cousin was on your team, I think. J.J. Hudson. He played strong safety."

"Hudson… yeah, I remember him. He was a sophomore when I graduated. I ran him over more than a few times in scrimmage. Okay, what's the phone number at the house, there?"

"We don't actually have a house line. We just use our cell phones."

"Do both your parents live there?"

"Yeah."

"What are their names and cell phone numbers? I assume you'd want them notified in case of emergency." Sander gave them. "I also need your social security number and birth date." Sander gave those too. "And, uh, what's the name of that school of yours again?"

"Embry-Riddle Aeronautical University in Prescott, Arizona."

"What year are you in?"

"I'll be starting my senior year when I go back in the fall."

"Okay." Karl printed two copies of the form and signed them. "If you could just autograph those, and I'll take the ones you already signed… and you wouldn't happen to know the fax number for Boeing's legal department, would you?"

"Not off-hand, but I have the whole directory in my phone." Sander pulled a large Nokia smart phone out of his pocket. He found a number for Roche to fax the legal forms to Chicago.

"I guess that's it. See you on Tuesday, Greg."

"0700 sharp, I'll be here."

## USS *RONALD REAGAN* OPS INTEL CENTER
## 0550 LOCAL, MAY 27<sup>TH</sup>

"You know you can't smoke in here," Admiral Krause looked pointedly at the cigar jutting from the CAG's mouth.

"It ain't lit," Deuce Thompson growled a reply with the Macanudo clamped between his right molars. After ten days he was tired of the two-star spook running this fleet. The Admiral had signed himself on as Wing Intelligence Officer instead of waiting for another senior aviator with an intel background to be assigned to the wing. Krause liked to think he was a hands-on leader. Thompson thought he was just butting in.

Krause, for his part, almost laughed in the CAG's face the first time he saw him. He thought the bald, square-shouldered, cigar-munching fighter jock was a perfect caricature of the stereotype of an old-school wing commander. He certainly had the correct CAG attitude – an ingrained belief that the entire battle group existed to put his planes in the target area. In a sense that was of course true, but wing commanders like Thompson always failed to see the bigger picture. They were all about linear combat. No strategy. "Where are your squadron commanders?" Krause asked.

"I told them to be here at six. I also told them to bring their execs and S-2s."

Krause shrugged, turned away from Deuce Thompson and went back to studying his computers. He had been plotting probable courses for the "enemy" battle group all night and well into this morning, preparing attack and counter-attack scenarios, playing it like a chess game.

Thompson looked on over his shoulder wondered if he and his aviators would be expected to memorize the entire playbook Krause was cooking up. *Damned useless spook,* he thought to himself.

## GALLERY DECK – 0700

Greg Sander knocked on the *Stingrays* ready room door, and Lt. McCoy opened it from the inside. "Howdy. Are you here to see the exec?" The aviator asked.

"Yeah, he said he's going to take me for a spin today."

"He told me to tell you he's runnin' late. The exercise strategy/ROE meeting was supposed to end fifteen minutes ago, but Sharkey, Hunter and the skipper are all still up in the Ops-Intel center."

"Okay. What am I supposed to do in the meantime?"

"Meet some of the guys. I'm Rooster, the guy sleeping in the comfy chair is my wingman Gator, and that unhappy fellow next to the fridge is Hardcase."

"Greg Sander. No callsign."

"Ya want any coffee?" Rooster offered.

"Don't do it, kid," Lt. Cmdr. Wilkes warned. "It's disgusting. These southern redneck guys like it, but it tastes like Rooster filled the bean grinder with manure."

"Gator made it, not me, and it's called chicory. It enhances the flavor of the beans."

Wilkes rolled his eyes. "This is what happens when you let some hick from Their-Kansas watch Martha Stewart Live."

"*Their*-Kansas?"

"Yeah, not *Our*-Kansas. We don't want it."

Rooster glared at the other aviator. "I'm from Tennessee, not Arkansas you ignorant jackass. You just don't appreciate regional culture and cuisine, seein' as how you come from Ohio, the blandest state in the whole country."

"Inbreeding, Confederate flags and monster truck rallies don't make a culture, and mixing septic tank dredge with perfectly good coffee grounds isn't cuisine."

"Why you damned Yankee-"

"Let the guy try it for himself and decide," Gator growled from his curled-up dozing position. "Use my mug, Greg."

Greg correctly guessed it was the University of Florida Gators mug and poured himself half a cup. He cautiously sipped it and spat it out quickly. "Gaaa! Like poison, it tastes!"

"I told you," Wilkes sighed as he opened the fridge. "Here, have a Pepsi and wash that crap out of your mouth."

Roche walked in right then. "Hi, Greg, sorry I'm late. As soon as the crew gets here I'll start the briefing, and after that I'll take you downstairs and get you rigged up. I got us scheduled to take a Fish on our first exercise flight. What's the matter? You look sick or something."

"I tried the coffee."

"I tried to stop him," Wilkes said.

Roche glared at Rooster. "I thought I told you to clean that awful sewage out of my coffee maker."

"Why does everyone keep comparing my coffee to shit?" Gator wondered.

"Because that's what it tastes like," Roche, Sander and Wilkes all said together.

"You said to clean it out when I was done drinking it," Rooster explained to the XO, holding up his half-full mug, "and I ain't done yet."

"Well, clean it out now. The rest of the squad will be in here in a minute looking for caffeine and I don't want them all hemorrhaging right before we start the op."

"Can I leave it out for the skipper? Please?"

"Oh, alright."

Commander Burke walked in half a minute later and marched straight to the coffee pot. "First op is an escort run," he said, not breaking stride. He continued to speak while selecting his personal mug and filling it with the toxic brew. "Sharkey will lead a flight with three divisions. Hardcase and Jack will be the other division leads, and- OH MY GOD!" The other five men in the room watched with rapt attention as the CO took a long swallow of the awful beverage and reacted explosively. The ensuing laughter lasted several minutes.

## AIR WING LOCKERS – 0930

The name of the Rigging Room referred back to the days when pilots would need to strap their parachutes to themselves before going out to their planes. The straps were complicated and could become fatally tangled if not properly secured, so in the rigging room there resided a rigging crew to maintain the parachutes and help the pilots get rigged. These days, parachutes are built in to a military airplane's ejection seat. All a pilot needs to do is buckle his six-point seat harness. The rigging room is now a large closet adjacent to the shower facilities in the locker room, which is where pilots keep all their flight gear and change before and after their sortie. The last vestige of the rigging crew is one petty officer who sits at a counter in front of the rigging room and checks helmets in and out. He also keeps track of extra suits and gear bags and things like that.

Karl and Greg went straight to the Rigger, PO1 Weller, to get the visitor the right equipment. "Hi, Sharkey," Weller greeted them. "I got your helmet cleaned for ya."

"Thanks." Roche took his black helmet and looked it over. Yesterday a hydraulic test valve had failed while he was examining a sluggish control cluster. Hydraulic fluid is difficult to clean off high-gloss surfaces, like a custom flight helmet. "This is Greg Sander; he'll be flying with me as an observer. He needs a suit, a vest, a helmet, boots and a bag, plus a basic overwater survival kit."

"Do you need a gun?" Weller asked Sander

"I don't think so."

"You're supposed to have one on any kind of combat sortie," Roche explained, "even if it's just an exercise. But you can just borrow one of mine. My locker is down row two, the one with the 'Jaws' poster. Come find me when you're done here."

Sander was given a light gray helmet with "CIV/GOV OBSERVER" stenciled on it, an XL-size combat flight vest, a pair of size-twelve flight boots, a nylon gear bag, and a very baggy flightsuit. He found Sharkey's locker, easily identifiable by the famous monster fish. "Are the pants supposed to be this big?" he asked Roche, who was changing out of his khaki uniform.

"Yes."

"Weller says it's one size fits all, but I don't quite see how he's arrived at that conclusion."

"It shrinks to fit." Roche's undershirt came off, and Sander saw the scarring on his back, side, forearm and shoulder. He looked away when Karl turned around. "Put it on, Greg, and I'll show you."

Sander took off his New Balance running shoes and stepped in to the baggy suit. After adjusting the sleeves and zipping it up, Roche squeezed the power tab on the front to contract the Thermagel and suddenly the suit was tailor-fit. "That's a pretty good trick," Sander remarked.

"Put the vest on over the pressure suit," Roche said, while he pulled his empty SIG-Sauer pistol out of its case. "You can carry this in one of the holsters."

"Thanks." Sander fiddled with the reversible holsters for a minute before finding a way he could carry the gun comfortably. Roche was still wearing only his boxers, and Sander couldn't help starring at the scar tissue that seemed to cover the whole left side of his torso. "What happened to your shoulder, sir, if you don't mind my asking?"

"Old shrapnel wound," Roche said, "I got it in Iraq."

"Were you shot down?"

"No, I wasn't a pilot at the time. I used to be a SEAL. It's kind of a long story, but the punchline is, I got my arm almost blown off. So now I can't swim well enough to be in the SEALs, and I fly Hornets instead." Roche put on gym shorts and a t-shirt, put his flightsuit on over that and assembled his gear quickly. He gave Sander a couple clips for the SIG. "You won't need these unless we go down on a shark-infested reef or right next to a pirate ship, but the regs say you need to carry at least twenty rounds of ammo. There's little elastic bandolier loops on your vest; you can put these there or just else just stash them in your gear bag."

"Okay." Sander stowed the magazines in the bag. "What's in this survival kit?"

"SAR radio, inflatable raft, water-wing floaters in case the raft sinks, water, dehydrated rations that will make you waste all your drinking water if you want to eat, flare gun, pointlessly cheap utility knife, shark repellent that doesn't work, sunscreen lotion that isn't waterproof, fishhook and line in case you're hungry or bored enough to try snaring mackerel."

"Which ones did you say were useless?"

"Take out the water-wings. Those are for toddlers learning how to swim, they don't even fit most normal people and they're redundant anyway because your vest is inflatable. Swap the sunscreen for this," Roche gave him a tube of Bullfrog waterproof roll-on. "The shark repellent looks like a giant bar of soap. Get rid of it. All it does is you make you taste a little worse; it won't stop a shark from taking a test bite. Here's a real multi-tool knife to replace that Gerber toy that's standard issue."

Sander thought the Gerber Military Provisional Tool was a decent piece of hardware, but then he saw Roche's SOG PowerLock Assist. Without opening the handle, he was able to flick out a lethal four-inch blade using only his right thumb. The SOG also housed multi-link pliers, a variety of screwdrivers, a can and bottle opener, a saw, a file and an odd hook-like tool with a sharp blade on its inner edge – also outside the handle to be flicked out quickly. "What's this, and what's it for?" he asked.

"That's a V-blade. It's designed to cut wires, but it works great at cutting away seatbelts and parachute harnesses."

"I see." Sander found a small pocket for the multi-tool on his vest and made a mental note that he would have to replace his well-worn Leatherman at home with one of those SOGs. "The bag is only half-full now," he observed.

"You can use the extra space for these." Roche handed Sander an extra 1-liter water bottle and a trio of Snickers bars. "That's for you to snack on during the flight. We'll be up for at least four hours today."

"Thanks."

"And you might want to take one of these." Roche produced a small green pill from a bottle.

"What's that for?"

Karl phrased it as delicately as possible. "There are certain things you can't do in a Super Hornet. Each seat has a relief tube, so you can pee in-flight, but any other business has to wait until you're back on the deck."

"I see."

"The Navy calls these metabolism regulator pills. Really though, it's just extra-strength Imodium. It totally shuts down your lower G.I. tract for a good eight hours after you take it."

"I'd better take it then. I had the enchiladas last night."


The locker room is on the hangar deck directly under the "island," so it's actually part of the superstructure. Roche led Sander out to the hangar itself, toward the stern section where the *Stingrays'* maintenance sector was located. "Yo, Sharkey!" Petty Officer Hector Domingo called out to them.

"Hey, there, Ming. Did you and Terry figure out why my Eel decided to squirt hydro fluid all over me?"

"I think the system was still charged for some reason, which shouldn't be possible once main power is down," the technician replied.

"How soon do you close the control group after landing?" Sander asked.

"Immediately," Roche said.

"And how long were the engines running after that?"

"About five minutes."

"I think what might have happened was the landing gear hydraulics were locked in an overpressurized state when you cut the flight control, and since the power was still up for so long, the system couldn't equalize right away."

"Oh, well that makes sense."

"How's that guy know so much?" Hector asked.

"He works on the program," Roche answered. "Now where's Fish Two?"

Hector pointed across the hanger to a pair of blue Super-Fs. "On the right, the one with your name on it."

Roche gave his gleaming fighter a once over, and made sure the practice missiles that the ordies had loaded an hour ago were the ones he'd asked for earlier that morning. "Okay, hop in, Greg," Roche said, and he pulled the ladder out of the port wing strake. "You don't need me to help you strap in, do you?"

"If it's the same as a T-38, I'm fine." The Mark 9 ejection seat is indeed similar to those on all current US fighter and trainers, except this model has extra shoulder room and padding. Greg had himself squared away just as quickly as Sharkey himself was strapping in. Domingo drove the Quiktug that moved them across the hanger on to elevator four. This brought them up to the landing strip across the *Reagan*'s stern.

Roche's Super-F would actually be the second plane to launch that morning, after a Hawkeye that had launched at 6AM. When the elevator came to rest, he powered up the engines and followed the yellow-vested traffic cop to Cat 3, outboard on the port side of the ship. Hacksaw, Blackjack, Creep, Hardcase and Hitman were all lined up behind them on the landing strip. The second section of each division (Beowulf and Claymore, in Roche's division, Rooster and Gator in Blackjack's, Blaze and Ronin in Hardcase's) would launch from the bow cats, followed by the strike and EW aircraft for the mission. The E-2d Hawkeye already in the air would report to them as Quarterback. The *Stingrays* flight would call in as Blocker, and would cover for Touchdown, the strike package led by Worm and consisting of his entire *Warhawk* squadron. Commander Scott "Palerider" Tachini led half of the eight Growlers in his squadron. That group was designated Punter Flight and would jam Diego Garcia's defenses and help deal with any other defensive threats.

The *Lincoln* battle group's objective for the Blue Flag was to defend not only themselves but the island base of Diego Garcia as well. *Reagan* would be on the offensive, and Admiral Krause wanted to take one primary objective as quickly as possible. A major air strike on Diego Garcia's defensive grid would leave it open for a cruise missile bombardment which would destroy the objective buildings on the island. That assumed Worm left anything for the cruise missiles. The only "objective" buildings were the HQ building, the flight control tower, and a pier. Worm's twelve bombers carried more than enough firepower to wipe out the radar/SAM network and the objective buildings.

Fish-2, now designated Blocker-1, was locked into place on Cat 3's shuttle. The plane sat there facing off the side of the ship at six-degree angle and watching the Indian Ocean race by. The green-shirt launch crew was just standing around on the deck, waiting. "What are we waiting for?" Sander asked.

"Noon," Roche answered. "The exercise doesn't start until noon, so no strike can be launched until then."

Greg checked his Fossil Multifunction Blue Dial watch. It was 11:40. "So we just sit here for twenty minutes?"

"It may look like a hurry-up-and-wait situation, but actually by sitting here we're letting the rest of the strike get assembled so we can all launch as quickly as possible. Oddly enough, by sitting here we're staying out of everyone else's way and then we can all clear the deck in about five minutes."

Sander looked around. The rest of the carrier deck was indeed busy – Hornets and Growlers were coming from different elevators and forming lines up and down the *Reagan*'s 1,092-foot length. He changed the camera view on his cockpit display so he could see the ocean; Roche blocked his view forward and the other Hornet blocked his view over the side. The ocean swells had grown to about twenty feet. Normally you couldn't feel any seas on a *Nimitz*-class, but sitting here, a hundred and twenty feet to the side of the center of gravity, Sander felt the fullest effect of the ship's roll.

Roche saw him on his camera screen. "You're not going to get seasick on me, are you, Sander?"

"Not at all," Sander lied. He was feeling the first signs of nausea, but he figured that once airborne he'd be alright.

"That's good. Because if this makes you woozy there's no way you'll handle what I'm going to put you through in a few minutes."

*Oh, that's just wonderful,* Greg thought, but he said "Don't worry about me. I'll be fine."

"I know you've been in a Talon before, and maybe a Falcon-D, but those are toys compared to this plane. It's like going from Thunder Mountain to Ghostrider."

If Roche's rollercoaster analogy was accurate, than Sander knew he was in over his head. The T-38 Talon he'd ridden in twice had made him vomit, and that was only in a five-G dive.

"Veteran NASA pilots have puked their guts out when they've gone up in a Rhino for the first time."

*Shut up already.*

"But then, I took my girlfriend for a pretty wild ride and she did okay."

*Well, that's probably a good sign.*

"Anyway, if you do end up tossing your breakfast, take your hose off at least. There's a little baggie under your left armrest."

Sander noted the location of the barf bag, anticipating its use in the near future. "What about the control panels?"

"Don't worry about the console. The whole cockpit is waterproof. I'd worry most about Ming making you clean it up."

*I'm holding on to this bag.* He almost had to use it when the *Reagan* turned sharply to port, dipping into a huge wave and dropping the edge of the deck fifty feet. Roche ignored the pitching motion and watched the launch crew. They were anchored in place and had started giving signals. Sander felt, rather than heard, the Super Hornet's massive engines rev up. He checked his watch and saw that it was forty seconds short of the hour, assuming his timepiece was still synchronized with the Navy Atomic Clock. It dawned on him that, while he had seen several takeoffs in the last week and was aware of the violent forces necessary to launch a thirty-ton jet, he had never actually experienced this himself and was suddenly terrified. "Oh, boy," he whispered.

Roche heard him over the microphone and reassured him. "This is the fun part. You remember the Xccelerator ride, at Knott's? It's just like that, times three."

Sander looked at his watch again. Twelve seconds. The Hornet was shaking; the engines were at full throttle now and the furious power of the aircraft tensed against the restraints. Sander could see over the pilot's left shoulder – his hand rested on the throttle, flexing his fingers, thumb poised over the fat red button on the end.

The launch was actually synchronized to a heart beat. At 11:59:57 the *Reagan*'s roll would reach horizontal, and the greenie on the deck would get the go-ahead to launch the first Hornet. A slight time delay in human reaction time would release the catapult at 58.2 seconds, and at noon on the spot *Stingray* Fish-2 would be vaulted off the deck at a slight upward angle, right before the ship hit the apex of its bank. Hacksaw would follow a split second later as the angle was just starting to decrease. Simultaneously, Beowulf and Claymore would be thrown off the bow cats.

Roche's eyes flicked from his watch to the greenie on the deck. "Here we go," he said, right before the crucial moment, "hold on to your socks."

238

The 19-year-old greenie extended his fingers, instructing Roche to go to afterburner. Roche responded instantaneously with a jab of his left thumb. Simultaneously, in the glass bubble on the edge of the flight deck, the launch officer pressed a button to open a massive valve holding back nearly a hundred thousand pounds of steam pressure. That force was concentrated into the shuttle set in a groove in the deck of the carrier. That shuttle was locked to the Super Hornet's nose wheels. It blasted down the track, dragging the Super Hornet with it until the thrust of engines matched the momentum of the aircraft. The acceleration was beyond Greg Sander's comprehension. He felt like some unseen force was compressing him and his seat together. It was a sensation he literally felt in his gut – his internal organs were pressed against his back muscles and ribs.

12:00:00.00 exactly Cat 3's shuttle slammed into the end of the track, releasing the lock on the nosegear assembly and pitching the screaming machine over the side of the ship. Screaming machine and screaming passenger. Roche used the 1.8 seconds that plane was entirely out of his control to shut off Sander's microphone. The launch was flawless, and the Super Hornet continued to accelerate smoothly as Roche rolled up and away from Hacksaw's flight path and settled into a steady climb.

Once Greg realized he'd been yelling his head off he shut up. Once the moment of pure, elemental terror had passed, he realized that it was actually fun. Roche clicked his mic back on in time to hear him say "I guess that wasn't so bad."

"You took what I said about roller coasters too literally. It is considered poor form to scream at the top of your lungs during a liftoff. It's a process that requires a lot of concentration, you know."

"Sorry," Sander said, feeling embarrassed.

"No worries. Everyone likes to let out a yeehaw now and then."

Sander noted that the Super Hornet was still climbing rapidly and accelerating through 500kts. "How long will it be until we're in position?"

"Eh, twelve minutes. We'll take an orbit station roughly middle of the triangle between *Reagan*, *Lincoln* and DG; that way we can engage any fighters that come after our strike team or the battle group." Sander's MFD showed a blue circle on the TacOps screen that indicated their intended station. "Blackjack and Hardcase will be here and here" – two more circles on the screen – "north of the island. Our division won't actually get in a fight unless absolutely necessary. Sorry to disappoint you."

"No, that makes sense," said Sander, who was actually relieved that they wouldn't be engaged in high-G combat. "You need to hang back and command the squadron."

"Right. And actually, with you here, that could be a little easier."

"In what way?"

"Do you know how to read a radar screen?"

"Sure..."

"I'll set up your MFD so it shows radar or TacOps whenever I'm *not* looking at one of those screens. That way if something changes on a screen I'm not watching, you can warn me."

"Okay."

"Nothing's happening now, but once we get some bad guys up here, things will be popping off fast."

"So I'm an extra pair of eyes for you. I definitely can watch a screen for-"

TacOps suddenly lit up. "Quarterback calling all Scrimmage flights, SHOCLink is online with the Skycam, please check your tactical." The E-2 had updated all the Hornet MFDs with its own radar scope. SHOC integrated the new data with each Hornet's own radar and tactical overlay. Roche obeyed Quarterback's order and checked his TacOps screen, swapping with Sander who now got the radar picture. The sky was swarming with blue blips representing the twenty-nine aircraft in Mission Scrimmage.

"Blocker Lead, this is Blocker Nine," Blackjack called to Sharkey. "I am detaching my division and moving to my assigned orbit point."

"Copy, Nine, proceed to Coverage Zone Weak."

"Lead, Five is separating also," Hardcase said.

"Five, you may take your division to Zone Strong. Lead division, holding at Cover Zone Deep."

"Punter Flight is at Cover Safe, no contact," Palerider reported.

"Touchdown, this is Quarterback, you are clear to engage all End Zone and Hail Mary targets. Hut, hut, hike!"

Roche kept switching between radar and TacOps, but the action was visible on both screens. Touchdown flight, consisting of an entire squadron of fully loaded Super-Es, dove from 40,000 feet toward the tiny atoll of Diego Garcia. The radar grid on the ground was active for three seconds before it was completely jammed by Punter, who then killed them for good with simulated HARMs. Touchdown had the coordinates of all the SAM emplacements on the island. They dropped

240

JSOW glide bombs, which were independently guided to their targets by GPS. Touchdown flight hadn't even dropped below the cloud cover yet, and the defenses of the island were already crushed with extreme redundancy.

"We have company." Hawk saw them first. He was in the backseat of Hardcase's plane, and he saw the unidentified contacts on the fringe of Quarterback's radar coverage even before anyone on the E-2 did.

"All flights, we have a twelve-man rush."

"Roger, Punter is standing by for full coverage jamming." Their work on the island was already done; they were free to devote twelve ALQ-99 pods to jamming twelve fighters. Total overkill.

"Blockers Five and up, when Punter says it's safe you may engage bogeys at will," Roche instructed.

Just then they all lost the radar feed from Quarterback. "Hey, who forgot to pay the cable bill?" Palerider asked.

"We have pass interference," Quarterback answered. "Prowlers, probably hiding in the enemy formation."

"Stick with the plan, guys," Roche ordered. "We know where they are. Punter, do you have them?"

"We're looking at ten Tomcats and two Prowlers," Tachini replied. Sander could see this information on TacOps before Roche changed the display to see for himself. Palerider went on, "We're going to cover the '71's frequency range. They'll be blind in six seconds." Sander looked at the EWOC display and could see the threat radar pattern becoming weak and disorderly.

"Take them, Blockers." Blackjack and Hardcase led their divisions out against what would be the bulk of the *Lincoln*'s air-to-air forces. Without their radar, the Tomcats were sitting ducks. The Prowlers picked up the incoming Hornets but could not effectively jam them in time. The Supers locked on in a synchronized dance of death, penetrating the opponent's formation and easily overwhelming the would-be interceptors. Except...

"Sharkey, this isn't right. My missiles are showing no return. We're chasing ghosts up here!" Blackjack's missiles were locked on to false targets.

"Mystique, overlap your radar picture to filter out shadow contacts."

She complied. Six contacts in the formation were real, six were ghosts generated by the Tomcats ECM gear.

"Quarterback, there are eight more Tomcats out there. Find them!" Sharkey knew he'd been fooled, and didn't like it. "Blocker Nine, handle the bandits you have. Five, return to zone to cover Touchdown." Sharkey steered out of his orbit pattern in the southeast zone, and his division followed him to the northwest without having to be told.

With the Prowlers out of the way, the Hawkeye could see again, but it was Worm who found the rest of the Tomcats first. He had just made a low-level pass on the Air Force hangars at the airbase, when his threat receiver warned him he had enemy radar looking for him. "Radar traces from the west. Blockers, I need cover on the weak side!"

Sharkey and Hardcase were on the way. Quarterback finally got the rest of the Tomcats on radar. "Sixteen repeat sixteen enemy contacts, 40 miles from DG."

"That's not possible," Roche said. "*Link* only has fourteen 'Cats onboard, including two spares." The legendary VF-2 *Bounty Hunters* had to be their opponent here. It was the only Tomcat squad *Lincoln*'s air wing had – the only other Tomcat squad left in the Pacific Fleet besides the *Reagan*'s *Renegades*.

"Maybe they mixed in some Rhinos," Sander suggested.

Roche considered that. It was possible, but more likely that the extra contacts were ECM ghosts again. "Punter, give me a signal search, tell me who's looking at the strike package." By analyzing the radar signals, the Growlers could tell if they were dealing with Tomcats, Hornets, ghost contacts or some combination thereof.

"Eight broadcasting on APG-71 range, eight blank." The Growlers were to far away to analyze the signals themselves, but they were able to remotely process the information from Touchdown's SHOC systems. "Eight Tomcats, eight silent contacts."

"I thought so," Roche said.

"Advise," Palerider added, "Punter is not in range for jamming."

"No matter," Sharkey said. "We outnumber them two to one."

"How do you figure?" Greg asked. "Assuming those other eight contacts aren't just running passive, you only have your division and Hardcase's on intercept."

Roche's next instruction resolved the confusion. "Touchdown Lead, this is Blocker Lead. Detach your second and third divisions to my command." Worm complied with the junior officer's instruction. "Touchdowns Five and up," Roche continued, "Jettison all air-ground stores and revert to fighter mode." Eight of Worm's bombers, which had never actually dropped their heavy dummy bombs on the real targets, released their load over the lagoon and switched their weapons mode as ordered. "Now, it's sixteen-to-eight in *our* favor."

The Touchdowns, Blockers and the Tomcats all closed within AMRAAM range right then. Punter had separated the real Tomcats from the ghost contacts, but still couldn't jam their radar. It would be up to the IDECM-RFCM self-protection jammers that each Super Hornet carried, and those were only of limited effectiveness against imaginary missiles.

"This is going to be messy," Bonzer predicted. He didn't identify himself, but everyone on the command channel recognized the Australian pilot's accent.

"Engage your own shadow gear," Roche ordered, referring to the false contact generator. "Use their trick against them." It worked; as the Tomcats and the Hornets stared shooting at each other with AMRAAM missiles, the *Lincoln*'s fighters mostly targeted the ghosts that the Supers had generated. The *Reagan*'s pilots could tell who was who, and were more effective. One of the *Warhawk* pilots got hit, but that was it. Only two *Bounty Hunters* survived the barrage and turned northwest, trying to get away. "Blocker Five, return your division to station. Touchdown fighters, cover the rest of your squad. The rest of you, we're going to catch those two 'Cats."

"Oh, goody," Claymore said.

"Passive approach. Quarterback will provide radar data." The two Tomcats were making a high-speed getaway but so far hadn't gone to afterburner. If they did, they would outrun the Hornets and probably lose them. Sharkey didn't want to scare off his prey with his own radar. "Were going to do a bird claw spread. Stay right on their tail. I'm going to get in front of them and make them slow down."

"Wouldn't it be easier just to get back in AMRAAM range?" Hacksaw wondered.

"Where's the fun in that?" Beowulf countered.

"I'm not going to risk letting them run away from a fight," Roche said. "And Three is right, this way is a lot more fun." Roche dropped ten thousand feet below the Tomcats' altitude and hit full afterburner. Sander thought the carrier launch was a shocking jolt – he was utterly unprepared for the plane suddenly doubling its already high flight speed. The world outside blurred as the Hornet jumped to 1200 nautical miles an hour. He didn't see the pair of F-14s flying backwards overhead, but Roche did. Still in rocket mode, he pulled back on the stick until they were in a vertical climb. Sander felt the full pull of earth's gravity adding one extra G to the weight on his chest, and again thought of the bag. And just in time, because suddenly everything spun around, the Hornet slowed to almost a stop, and Sander was abruptly weightless. His stomach felt the effect immediately.

The Tomcat pilots recoiled in surprise when the Super-F jumped up right in front of them. They instinctively slowed and pulled back on the stick, allowing all four Hornets to quickly close within Sidewinder range and finish them off.

"Blocker, that's the end of the drive," Quarterback called. "Touchdown has hit every available target and is heading home. Your flight is assigned to CAP cover northwest quadrant at Battle Group perimeter until relieved at 1600 hours."

"Copy, Quarter. All Blocker elements, turn to 120 degrees and cruise while I plot new patrol orbits." Roche clicked off the radio. "Three more hours," He said to Sander, "talk about working through lunch. Aren't you glad I gave you some candy?"

"Yeah," Greg answered as he wiped the vomit off his chin with the back of his hand. "Thanks a lot."


Roche and Sander had basically nothing to do for the next three hours. *Lincoln* launched two cruise missile strikes with minimal effect, neither of which came close to Roche's patrol zone. Once Sander's stomach had settled, Roche started to run a few maneuvers like he'd done with Tracy, starting with gentle loops and working up to serious high-G stunts. Slowly, Sander became more comfortable with the wild flight.

Roche and Sander were able to keep track of the exercise over the radio. It sounded like *Reagan* was winning. The loss of the *Bounty Hunters* made it easy for the Hornet-C's in VFA-25 to pick off two of *Lincoln*'s escorts. *Link* responded with another cruise missile barrage that did no damage. *Reagan*'s destroyers then fired their own missiles through the hole in the other battle group's perimeter and sank a cruiser. None of the action came anywhere near the *Stingrays*' patrol area. Finally, a group of Tomcats from the *Renegades* relieved them and they were allowed to land at four-thirty.

"You'll get two hours off while your plane is refit, Sharkey," Deuce told him after he returned to the carrier. "Then I'm sending your squad up with full Grizzly support for a run on the *Link*. But your passenger can't see how we can sink one of our own flattops."

"That's okay," Sander said. "I've seen enough."

## CHAPTER 12: EYES OF THE STORM

### THE PENTAGON, OFFICE OF THE CNO
### 0900 EDT, MAY 28TH

Admiral Marsh was on the phone with Admiral Patrick Caldwell, the Commander-in-Chief of the Pacific Fleet (CinCPAC) and both Admirals were very unhappy with the report on the blue flag exercise. "The *Lincoln* was on defense, Pat. Defense always wins these games, because our CVBGs are supposed to be invincible. Now tell me, does this mean that our battle group defenses are inadequate, or does it mean that Admiral Dempsey and his commanders are a bunch of morons?"

"Sir, my analysts are telling me that *Lincoln*'s command staff didn't make any tactical errors. They reacted appropriately to the situations presented by *Reagan*'s attacks. But *Reagan*'s strike fighters were able to exploit the weaknesses of individual warships on the battle group perimeter, and slowly wear down their air wing. By nightfall, Dempsey's BG had lost both their cruisers and all their interceptors. Then a composite squadron of Super Hornets backed by a Growler division was able to make a final breakthrough and hit the *Link* with enough heavy gravity bombs to write it off. Really, it was a brilliant attack to exploit their weakened low-altitude defenses."

"So our carrier groups do not have adequate air defenses?"

"No, it just means that the Aegis system isn't quite a match for a combined air force of Super Hornets and Growlers. *Reagan*'s Air Wing 13 is the only group of planes in the world that could possibly pull this off. No one else has the Growlers yet."

"I still think there had to have been a way for Dempsey to defend himself better."

"Sir, Dempsey and Krause are my two best fleet commanders. They were very evenly matched. My staff and I can't see any mistakes in Dempsey's plan. It looks like the equipment won this one, sir."

"Okay, but just in case, I don't want the *Link* to be anywhere near the Chinese carrier when the time comes, you understand? The Gipper gets that show."

"You got it."

"Where are the carriers now?" Marsh could have looked on his computer, which displayed a miniature version of the Big Board downstairs, but he wanted Pat's analysis, and not just his report.

"I'm sending the *Lincoln* down toward the Cape of Good Hope to intercept the Russians and escort them into the METO, and they should get there by noon on Friday. *Reagan* is cruising north, and by mid-morning Thursday that battle group will be over the supposed wreck of the *Carter* and enforcing the quarantine zone. *Roosevelt* is holding its patrol pattern in the Gulf itself, going back and forth between Bahrain and Dubai. She's providing air support to help the Air Force enforce the no-fly zone. *Stennis* is running at flank to catch up with the Chinese fleet. They'll be entering the Strait of Malacca in about an hour, and they and the Chinese will reach the Arabian Sea in forty-five hours."

"So Friday's when it's all going down, huh?"

"Yes, sir. And if it all does go down the way we're afraid it might, this will make the Battle of Midway look like a bumper-boat fight."

## THE OVAL OFFICE – 1500

"The President will see you now, gentlemen." The Chinese and Russian Ambassadors had just arrived, along with their naval attachés. Ambassador Chaun Li, Colonel Vong Cho, Ambassador Pavel Dubovski, and Rear Admiral Alexei Myasnikov, had all been summoned to the White House half an hour ago. As they prepared to meet the President, their televisions and radios informed them that an American submarine had experienced a reactor accident of some sort, and the US Navy had closed the Persian Gulf until the rescue and clean-up operation was complete. The diplomats figured out why they were being brought in to meet the President.

"Thank you all for coming on such short notice," President McNeil said, as he came to the door of the office to shake their hands. "Please, have a seat." The President took his favorite armchair once they were seated. The chief of staff offered them beverages, and the guests all took hot tea.

"Mr. President," Li began, "I would like to formally express the sympathies of the People of China with regard to your lost submarine."

"Moscow has asked me to pass along our condolences as well," Dubovski said. "Your sailors are in the prayers of our people."

"Thank you both," the President said, with a tone and expression of carefully measured gravity.

"Informally," Li continued, "we want to know just who you think you're fooling."

McNeil feigned confusion. "I beg your pardon?"

246

"Mr. President, it seems a very unlikely coincidence that one of your extremely advanced submarines has experienced a major reactor leak just in the time and place where it provides a perfect excuse to lock us out of the Persian Gulf, allowing you and your Navy to do whatever you please to Iran. Our governments have even more invested interest in that country than you do, and it appears to us that this is a ruse to prevent our Navies from securing our interests."

"You can make of it whatever you want," President McNeil said, playing coy. "Officially, I'm surprised too. As you may know, we have not lost a submarine under any circumstances since 1963, and I don't think our submarine fleet has ever had any reactor accident of any kind since then. But you can understand how these things can happen unexpectedly, in anyone's navy."

The two navy attachés looked down at their feet. Russia and China both had dismal safety records with their nuclear submarine fleets, and they felt the President's subtle insult. "Unofficially," McNeil continued, "no good could possibly come of your fleets interfering in the Gulf. Having your ships and ours all packed in that little bit of ocean is just asking for trouble. We feel that to avoid friendly fire, your ships should stay outside the quarantine zone."

Ambassador Dubovski glared at the President. "Moscow will not sit idly by while you invade Iran and seize our oil fields."

"Neither will Beijing," Li added with the same tone and expression.

McNeil tried to placate them. "Gentlemen, I can promise you, your oil is the least of our concerns. We're trying to stop a nuclear war here. I've had to talk Israel's Prime Minister down from nuclear alert twice this week, I had to stop Iraq's PM from surrendering outright, I've got Afghanistan begging us to redeploy our troops to help secure their western border, and I have four more Arab countries asking how we plan to keep the tanker routes open. Having your battle fleets in there to do a three-way tango with our carrier groups in the middle of all that would be way too complicated. So please, let us handle it, okay? We promise not to bomb or capture your oil fields."

Dubovski said sarcastically, "I guess it sounds reasonable when you put it that way. There are just too many children pestering Uncle Sam right now."

"I wouldn't put it quite that way," the President said, "but you're exactly right. Do you guys even realize how bad this could get? Israel launching a first strike on Iran with their sizeable nuclear arsenal is an absolute worst-case scenario. That's going to touch off a firestorm

247

that will consume the entire Middle East and leave the three of us and the EU fighting over what little is left of the oil reserves. We'll need your cooperation here to prevent that from happening. And by cooperation I mean non-interference."

"But Mr. President," Li persisted, "we don't want to interfere with your operations. We're perfectly happy to cooperate. We only want to have our ships in the Gulf to remind the Iranians we mean business too. The Persian Gulf is over four hundred miles long. Surely there is room for our warships to share with your battle groups."

McNeil shook his head. "Not from where we're standing. Look, if you can get Oman and the United Arab Emirates to let you use their territorial waters, we can't stop you from getting in to the Gulf. But we *can* quarantine the rest of the Strait, and we will use any force necessary to keep your ships outside that perimeter, okay?"

Li snorted, which in the Chinese culture is an expression of incredulity and contempt. Dubovski verbalized the same sentiment with a Russian curse, the equivelant of "Horseshit." The two naval attachés looked warily between their emissaries and the American President. It seemed all three governments were ready to throw down the gauntlet over this.

"Okay," the President sighed. "So, I put our cards on the table and you don't want to play. Let's see if we can change your mind another way." He looked up to his chief of staff, Ms. Bender, who was standing by the door. "Bring Marsh and Casey in here, please." The CNO and DDO had been waiting in the outer office for only a minute. The President had actually wanted them to talk to the diplomats right away, but the CIA man thought they should try to push the cover story first.

"Mr. President, Ambassadors." Casey sat in a chair next to President McNeil. Admiral Marsh sat on a couch next to Admiral Myasnikov, who was an old friend of his.

"Mr. Casey, please give them copies of your list, and explain to them exactly what they are looking at," the President instructed.

"Yes sir. Gentlemen, our intelligence indicates that your militaries have been infiltrated at the highest level by a criminal cabal led by a Russian Mafia don named Rannovich."

Ambassador Dubovski paled, but Li became even more annoyed. "What fresh tripe is this? There is no Russian Mafia operating in China."

"They don't need to. Your lack of corporate regulation makes an unscrupulous but legal business venture potentially even more

248

profitable and efficient than organized crime. You know about New Patriotic Enterprises, right?"

Li became silent. Dubovski became even paler.

Casey switched to a softer tack. "Look, I know this is a lot to assimilate. I brought a couple files with me that contain all the information we can share with your respective governments. But long story short, your barely-legal conglomerate and your mafia are backing this character named Rannovich who's pulling the strings in Iran. They've bought and stolen tons of weapons from you, and they have corrupted several key officers in your armed forces. This includes your Navy. We believe that the entire Chinese carrier battle group and a flotilla of six Russian warships are under their control. We further believe that upon reaching the gulf, they will defect from your fleets and start shooting at you and at us, trying to get us all in a big high-seas battle against each other."

The Ambassadors said nothing. The CIA's allegation was so far out of left field, they had no idea how to respond. The naval attachés looked at the lists of the warships involved, and they looked very concerned.

"We want to use the quarantine zone as a line in the sand," the President explained. "If your ships are ordered not to cross it, and these fifteen ships do anyway, that will prove they have been turned by Rannovich's people."

"If that is the case," the CNO joined in, "then like Casey said, they will probably start shooting at all three fleets in hopes of drawing us all in to a full-scale conflict."

"And at that point our warships will use preemptive self-defense and sink any non-American vessel on, under or above the water," the President added.

"By the time your fleets arrive," Marsh continued, "we will have four aircraft carriers, five submarines, six cruisers, fifteen destroyers, and five frigates in range of the quarantine zone. We'll be somewhat outnumbered but with our four carrier air wings you will be way outgunned even if you team up on us instead of shooting at each other. Surely you are familiar with our capabilities. I can guarantee you that none of your ships will survive if they choose to fire on a United States vessel."

"Obviously, we don't want to have to go that level," the President concluded, "but if it does come down to your ships or ours, there's only one answer: not ours."

"Let us say you are right," Li said shakily. He had lost his air of indignation and was now genuinely afraid of the Americans. "What can we do stop us all from shooting at each other?"

"Just have your leaders order the admirals to stay outside the quarantine zone. International law dictates that it be enforced by NATO, so that's what we'll do. If any of your ships do cross the line, we will order them to turn back. If they fire on us, we will respond with lethal force. If all fifteen compromised warships get in a fight with us, we will handle it ourselves. You just have your ships stay back and let our Navy handle this, and we'll try to make sure no one else gets hurt."

Casey indicated the folders he had given them. "Pass this information back to your intelligence agencies. They should be able to confirm most of it."

"If you decide to believe us, decide quickly," the President said as he stood. "You guys only have thirty-six hours to choose how many of your ships you want us to sink."

## USS *REAGAN*, 10 MI. INSIDE NATO PERIMETER
## 1130 LOCAL, MAY 30TH

When Karl turned off the water for the shower, he heard nothing, which was extremely unusual. The men's shower and locker room next to the gym always had dozens of sailors and aviators cleaning up after their workout. There had been at least fifty men in the room talking and running water when Roche had stepped into the shower stall five minutes ago, and now he could hear nothing. He stepped out and looked around, and the room was indeed deserted, except for another sailor who was leaning out of a shower stall and looking just as confused as Roche did.

"What happened, sir?" The eighteen-year-old seaman recruit safely assumed the other naked man outranked him.

"I have no idea." Roche wrapped his towel around his waist and checked the gym, but it was also empty. Roche had never seen that either. There were always a hundred or more people using the gym at all hours unless there was a battle stations drill. But in that case there would've been a klaxon alarm also. Roche went back and checked the rows of small lockers and spotted a CPO adjusting his uniform. "Do you know what's going on, Chief?"

"Some kid ran through here about two minutes ago and said we had the Chinese and Russian fleets in sight. Everyone just jumped and

250

ran upstairs to look. I figured I had a couple minutes to get dressed before those ships went anywhere."

"Oh, good idea," Roche said. The younger seaman didn't think so, and he ran out in his towel like several other sailors already had. Roche put on clean gym shorts and a Hard Rock Café t-shirt and ran *down*stairs to the air wing lockers to grab his Zeiss binoculars. Then he went up to the flight control lookout bridge, sixty feet above the flight deck. Worm and Hannibal were already up there with their own heavy binoculars. "What are we looking at?" he asked.

Hannibal pointed out four dark shapes on the horizon. "The *Stennis*, the *Link*, the Russian carrier *Kuznetsov*, and the Chinese carrier they call Zen-ye or something."

Roche looked at two of the only three non-American supercarriers in the world. They looked very similar, and he remembered that the Chinese had bought the *Kuznetsov*'s unfinished sister ship several years before. They had just recently finished modifying it and fitting it out. With his slightly more powerful glasses, Roche could make out the lettering on the Chinese carrier's bow. "*Zheng He*," Karl read.

"That would be named after a sixteenth-century Chinese Muslim Admiral who established China's first ocean trade routes with the Middle East," Worm announced as if he were reading an entry out of the Encyclopedia Britannica.

Roche glanced at his friend without lowering his binoculars. "You've studied up on your Chinese history, I see."

"Well, I think *Zheng He*'s here for something else, now," Hannibal remarked.

"You got that right," Deuce said as he came up behind them.

"What's going out there, sir?" Roche asked.

"*Lincoln* and *Stennis* are going to come to our side of the quarantine line. If anyone follows them, we'll all turn around and chase them off. If they start shooting, we sink 'em. Basically we're all playing a big game of 'red light, green light.'"

The senior officers of the battle group had already been told about the faked accident on the *Carter* and the possibility that fifteen Russian and Chinese ships were under the control of rogue commanders.

"Have we made contact with them yet?" Roche asked.

"Admiral Krause has been on the radio with Admiral Zihao, who's commanding the Chinese fleet, and Admiral Doshka from the Russian fleet. They've both been ordered by their superiors to hold up outside our perimeter, and Beijing and Moscow have authorized us to use whatever force is necessary if those orders are violated."

"Wow."

"Well, it's only fifteen ships we're worried about right?" Worm asked. "We could take care of that in a couple of minutes."

"It might be that easy, but only if they're all dumb enough to charge across the line when the rest of their fleet stops. But the guys at the Pentagon think they're gonna try and get us all shooting at each other."

"You mean by standing in the middle and firing off missiles in both directions?"

"Something like that. Then we might have a helluva lot more than fifteen targets to worry about."

Roche had been counting warships. In addition to the four carriers, there were dozens of smaller ships approaching the perimeter, which was marked by *Reagan's* own escorts. "I count nineteen Chinese ships and eleven Russians."

"There's thirty more that will be up here by midnight."

"Wait, isn't this exactly what we wanted to avoid, having all these ships so close together?" Hannibal asked. "I mean, I'm looking at a Russian cruiser carrying nuclear-tipped cruise missiles, and with our escorts all spread out they could probably sink us right now."

"We're here as a visual deterrent right now," Deuce explained. "After sundown our three carriers will move out of their missile range, and leave just a few destroyers and our fighters to guard the perimeter, along with our subs, but of course they won't know about those. Anyway, they know they're outgunned, and they'll wait until all of their ships are here before they start anything stupid."

Roche trained his binoculars on the Russian cruiser, which he identified as the Atlant-class missile cruiser *Marshal Ustinov*. It was close enough now that he could see sailors crowding its rails, looking back at the American supercarrier. "They're almost close enough to see us on the decks, and they can see the *Fitzgerald* and *O'Kane* for sure. Our people aren't wearing any protective clothing. Won't they figure out that we're lying about the radiation?"

"They've already guessed that," Deuce answered. "Right now we're just testing to see who's on our team and who's not. They just have to respect the line."

"What about the Iranian Navy?" Worm asked. "They're already on this side of the line, up at Bandar Abbas."

"What, you're worried about them hitting us from behind, Worm?"

"Yeah, a little, especially with those sneaky little subs of theirs."

"Don't worry. We already took care of them."

The USS *Jimmy Carter* had two missions on Wednesday night. First, the skipper called for help on the radio and pretended to sink somewhere in the Strait of Hormuz. Then the big sub continued north, and settled on the seabed just outside of the harbor of Bandar Abbas. Four full 12-man squads of Navy SEALs deployed in a pair of high-speed swimmer-delivery submersibles, and proceeded into the Iranian naval base.

Lt. Nathan's unit had the assignment to attach magnetic limpet mines to the hulls of the two Kilo-class submarines that were docked right then. US intelligence still believed these were the only two working subs the Iranian Navy had – they didn't know where the two that were stolen from Russia had gone.

Nathan and the other SEAL commandos worked fast, spreading out across the harbor and mining every military vessel they could find. By sunrise, they had rigged the entire Iranian fleet, and escaped back out to sea with the *Jimmy Carter*.

## THE SITUATION ROOM – 1500 EDT, MAY 30TH

"Our carriers are in a Mexican standoff with the Chinese and Russians, sir." Admiral Marsh pointed to a satellite map display on the big computer projection screen. "The suspected renegades haven't broken away yet, but I'm betting they will as soon as the last squadron of frigates gets there at around midnight, their time. That's just half an hour from now."

"That's also when the cease-fire agreement expires," the President noted.

"Yes, sir."

"State, any luck getting that extended?"

"Nothing," Rand said. "They've taken the phone off the hook, offered no apology or explanation, and made no demands. We won't know what they'll do next until it happens."

McNeil nodded. "Okay. Now, Terry, you're sure the Iranians can't hurt our fleet? Not even with those new weapons they were testing a couple years ago?"

"They can't touch us. Their anti-shipping missile is a joke, they don't have enough cruise missiles to overwhelm Aegis, and that rocket torpedo is useless except at close range and they never figured out how to modify the launchers on a Kilo-class sub. Besides, our SEALs went in earlier and rigged all their ships with limpet mines. If they come after us, we'll blow them all up remotely."

"What about those two missing Russian subs?"

The Admiral shook his head. "We have no idea where they are, but our ASW teams on the battle group escorts will be watching for them. They're only quiet if they're very slow, and that limits their ability to attack us. A Kilo is a defensive submarine, you know, not a hunter-killer like ours. We'd literally have to trip over them for them to attack our ships."

"Okay, so we don't have to worry about the Iranian Navy. Deke? Did the Chinese and Russians follow up on the intel we gave them?"

"They didn't like what they found," the DCI reported, "but they were able to confirm that those officers we found out about are most likely renegades."

"Admiral Krause has been in contact with the Admirals in charge of both fleets," Marsh added. "They're playing along with us, and they won't shoot at us under any circumstances."

"Alright. Now do we have any idea what the Iranian army is up to?"

"We suspect they're building up their army units along the Iraqi border," General Chappelle said. "But they're still using the pipeline tunnels to stay hidden and we just don't have enough cameras to watch the whole desert. If we catch them trying to-" The Chairman's pager went off, and then the rest of the Joint Chiefs found their phones or pagers vibrating. "Excuse us, Mr. President."

The President suggested they put General Chappelle's cell phone on speaker, and they did. "Sirs," the Pentagon watch officer on the line said, "we have confirmed reports of several dozen armor platoons that have crossed the Iraqi border and are firing on multiple civilian and military targets."

"Where, exactly," Chappelle asked, as he stood up to look at the map of the region displayed on the wall behind him.

"All along the border, sir. They're outside the towns of Banjwin, Halabjah, Khanaqin, Mandali, and Zurbatiyah."

"Jeez, Mandali is only sixty miles from Baghdad," the President noted.

"Looks like they jumped the gun on the cease-fire agreement," McLeary observed, checking his watch.

"Mr. President," Paul Chappelle sat back down in his chair and leaned forward on the table. "I recommend that we respond immediately in accordance with our stated intentions, and proceed with Operation Perfect Storm."

"I agree," the Secretary of Defense added. "We should immediately transition from Perfect Firewall to Perfect Storm."

"This is exactly what Rannovich wants," the Secretary of State protested. "There's no reason for Iran to attack Iraq or anyone else except to goad us in to a war."

"If all he wants is a war he'll get one sooner or later," the President said. "If we just ignore them they'll start inflicting more and more civilian casualties until we are forced to respond. Or worse, Israel responds for us and sets off a nuclear apocalypse. We need to take steps to stop this from getting out of our control. I am authorizing fully all planned stages of Operation Perfect Storm. Push them out of Iraq, push them as far as we can into Iran. General Caleb, send in your bombers and scare Tehran to death. And Terry, tell your Admirals in the Gulf to get ready for all sorts of hell to break loose."

## THE LALEH HOTEL, TEHRAN
## SAME TIME (1148PM LOCAL)

Kahlil was lounging on his bed watching CNN when someone started pounding on his door. "What the hell," he muttered to himself. He called in Farsi "One moment, please." The pounding stopped. Kahlil took his silenced pistol off the nightstand and went to the door. He looked through the keyhole and saw his friend Kujetski staring back at him. He put the gun behind his back and unlatched the door and jumped back as the Cossack slammed it open.

"We need to go," he said, speaking English. "Pack your stuff and change your disguise." He turned to a frightened man in the hall behind him. "Don't just stand there, idiot," Kujetski barked in Russian, "get inside before someone sees you."

The CIA agent already had his makeup case out. "What's going on?"

"Rannovich jumped the gun – he's attacking Iraq again. We have about two hours, maybe less, before your Air Force starts bombing the crap out of this town."

"Who's your friend?"

"He's one of the Russian mafia contractors." Kujetski was going around the room gathering up his friend's clothes and dumping them into a suitcase.

"What am I disguising myself as?"

"A Russian. We have to take refuge in the Russian embassy until your military can get us out. We'll use our usual cover story."

"My military is going to get us out?"

"Oh, yes. When you tell them who we're bringing with us, they'll pull all stops."

"Who is he?" Kahlil asked again. "What does he have? What does he know?"

"The command bunker," Kujetski explained. "He built it. He's the only man who knows where it is, how deep it is, and how your guys can blow it up. Your CIA friends will need his information so your people can put an end this war before it gets completely out of hand."

"It hasn't even started yet."

Kujetski turned up the TV so the American agent could hear. *"...Reports are piling up from all our sources; apparently Iran has made another incursion into Iraqi territory and is already being engaged by the US Army and Air Force units that have deployed to the border in the last week. And now the US Navy is also engaged in a major battle in the Persian Gulf; we go live to Melissa Kerrigan on the USS* Abraham Lincoln*..."* The CIA man came out of the bathroom with makeup drying on his face and watched the screen.

*"Yes, I'm on the* Lincoln *now,"* the reporter could barely be heard over the noise of rockets and jet engines.

"She's cute," Kahlil said.

Kujetski waved him off as Kerrigan continued. *"The* Lincoln *battle group has engaged several warships from the Russian fleet, exchanging salvos of missiles with them... That cruiser is firing now!"* Melissa pointed to her left. The camera panned hastily to see what was actually an *Arleigh Burke*-class destroyer launching a pair of Harpoon missiles off into the night. *"Oh my God, those must be Russian missiles, heading this way..."* The camera blurred for a second, than focused on dozens of points of light trailing columns of fire skimming above the ocean surface. Warships lit up briefly around the screen as they fired more missiles to intercept the Russian weapons. The flag escort launched missile after missile out of its VLS launchers and brought down the last Russian weapon just before it reached the range of carrier's own defenses.

"Oh man," the American sighed. "Those guys are in for it."

## PERSIAN GULF QUARANTINE ZONE – SAME TIME

Roche cruised at an altitude of 20,000 feet, within radar contact of the *Zheng He* but out of the missile range of its escorts. Hunter sat behind him, tracking all the other fighters in their group under command of Sean "Pain God" Mullen. Pain God's Tomcat squadron and half of the *Stingrays* were waiting to engage the *Zheng He*'s MiG-29s. Hannibal had the rest of the *Stingrays* and Worm's squadron to engage the warships. The Chinese battle group had been cruising in a circle just outside the NATO quarantine line. *Reagan* and *Stennis* waited over the far horizon, leaving their escorts and the *Reagan*'s planes up front to engage the renegade fleet, while their cruisers and the *Stennis* air wing held a second line of defense. At midnight exactly, A Chinese Luda-class destroyer turned and crossed the line.

"This is it," Hunter said. "*Zheng He*'s launching fighters, and they're all heading for the line." Roche watched the situation unfold on his computer screen as the destroyers and frigates from the *Reagan* and *Stennis* battle groups jockeyed to physically impede the Chinese warships. The Chinese jets circled north to avoid the missiles of the American warships.

"Stonewall Flight," Pain God called to his team, "this is Stonewall Lead. Move to intercept bandits at maximum range. Do not enter Iranian airspace." The *Roosevelt*'s air wing had launched to take out Iran's air defenses along the coastline, but they hadn't reached that area yet. The cruisers *Shiloh* and *Bunker Hill* had launched Tomahawk missiles to take out most of the fixed radar and missile systems, but without the satellite coverage they couldn't engage smaller mobile defenses. "Turn on the high beams and all your flashers, guys," Pain God ordered. Roche complied, cranking the radar to maximum search power and activating every gadget in the IDECM suite.

"The Grizzlies will have their hands full with the junks," Hunter said over the flight's secure channel. "Don't expect any jammer support."

"Right," Pain God confirmed. "We're on our own. Twenty of us versus... I count thirty-six of them."

"Well that's hardly even odds," one of the Tomcat crew commented.

"I know," Blackjack replied. "Those poor bastards must be suicidal."

"Can the chatter," Roche ordered. He had lost his radar view of the confrontation on the surface and was listening on the radio command channel to keep track of what was going on.  The USS *Russell* – one of the destroyers from the *Stennis* battle group – came within inches of being rammed by a smaller Chinese destroyer.  The battle group's admiral immediately ordered a warning shot to be fired across the bow of the offending ship.  It returned fire, launching a missile right at the *Russell*'s superstructure at point-blank range.  Another Chinese destroyer opened fire on the frigate *Vandegrift* and quickly sank it.  The remaining Americans responded with lethal force.

The Chinese MiGs hit their afterburners and made a run to west, apparently intending to attack the American carriers.  Deuce perceived the move from the *Reagan*'s command center.  "Kill 'em," he ordered.  Stonewall Flight kept pace with the MiGs and fired dozens of AMRAAMs.  The Chinese pilots made the mistake of trying to run and paid dearly.  Stonewall Flight chased them straight toward the six Aegis warships and two Super Hornets squadrons from the *Stennis* defending the two carriers.  It was a massacre – a perfect "hammer and anvil" maneuver.

Roche was the first to hit the afterburners and he closed in at the lead of the US Navy fighter group.  His AMRAAMs leapt from his wings as fast as his computer could switch targets.  The other Hornets and Tomcats joined fire, and then the cruisers fired dozens of Sea Sparrow SAMs from the other direction.  "Break off," Pain God instructed.  "Don't get in the crossfire."  Roche throttled back and watched his missiles bore in.  He counted four explosions, corresponding to his computer telling him that four of his six AMRAAMs had scored hits.

Only five MiGs made it out of the crush of missiles.  They were running like mad to get back to their carrier.  Roche split his division off to run them down.  The MiGs went to wavetop level, hoping to hide from the all-seeing Aegis radar, but Roche had them glued into his sights.  The hot exhaust of the big RD-33 engines stood out sharply against the cold sea on his infrared scope.  The Russians were watching their backs, but they couldn't see the *Stingrays*' Hornets.  Their paint blended with the sky.  Sharkey got as close as he dared before firing a pair of Sidewinders.  "Fox-two!  Fox-two!" he called, as his missiles went straight up the tailpipes of the trailing MiGs.

His wingmates followed, taking down the MiG-29s one by one.  "That was way too easy!" Hacksaw said when the last flaming wreck of a Fulcrum splashed into the sea.

Roche switched his radio back to the command channel to see how the other end of the battle was going.  The firefight had been short and fierce. The Chinese had sunk the *Vandegrift* and left the *Russell* a flaming derelict, but many of the crew were rescued form both ships. The American bombers and warships had sunk four Chinese vessels and downed dozens of missiles. The *Zheng He* had fled into Iranian waters with its remaining escorts and Admiral Krause ordered the battle groups to disengage. Meanwhile the *Lincoln* had annihilated the renegade Russian flotilla. The Iranian Navy had launched all of its available warships to join the fray, but those were blown out of the water by the remote mines the SEALs had placed the night before. "Sounds like we won," Roche commented to Hunter.

Then a fresh burst of excited chatter crossed the airwaves. "What's going on?" Hacksaw asked.

"I don't know," Roche replied. "I keep hearing '*Teddy*'s hit, *Teddy*'s hit,' and 'where's the Kilo?' It sounds like one of those missing subs just turned up."

"Sharkey, your division's closest," Deuce called a minute later. "I need you to provide aerial recon for the *Roosevelt* BG. New callsign is… uh, Longstreet Flight."

"Longstreet One copies. What happened?"

"*Teddy* got hit from behind by a couple of torpedoes. She's dead in the water. They're looking for the sub and could use your ATFLIR systems to help."

"Roger."

The USS *Theodore Roosevelt* had actually been hit six times. It cruised right past a Kilo that had waited motionless for three days, and fired from every torpedo tube it had at a range of only a thousand yards. The carrier was listing badly to starboard and taking on tons of water.

"Oh, boy, that doesn't look good." As Roche's fighters approached, they could see the huge ship, powerless, eerily illuminated by floodlights from its escorts. It was listing fifteen degrees already and getting worse. "This is Longstreet Lead," he called on the command channel. "Who's in charge down there?"

"Longstreet Flight, this is the cruiser *Port Royal*. Estimated firing position of the sub is a click and a half dead astern of the carrier's present position. We're keeping our subs away right now, so if you see anything down there, it's a target."

"Got it." Roche could see four Seahawk helicopters over the indicated area, dropping their dipping sonar hydrophones to try and pick up a sound from the lethal little sub. More choppers were heading that way, followed by two frigates and three destroyers to help search. "Do we have Vikings?"

"*Reagan*'s launching theirs now," the *Port Royal*'s officer said.

"What about the *Roosevelt*'s Sierra threes?" Hunter asked.

"They can't launch planes because of the list," Roche explained. "They've got all their Hornets and Prowlers out on strike ops, but it looks like their other planes are pretty much stuck down there."

"She's not going to sink, is she?"

Roche shrugged. "It's not supposed to be possible to sink a *Nimitz*-class without a nuclear weapon. But that ship is not looking good right now."

Longstreet Flight spread out as it approached the target area, and the Advanced Tactical Forward Looking Infrared sensors scanned the ocean for any sort of temperature variation. Hunter checked all four feeds for anything that could indicate a submerged vessel. He transmitted the images to the *Port Royal* so their technicians could double-check the scans. "Nothing," Hunter reported when they made their first sweep. "Let's move a little further up the line."

The four Hornets turned around and made another low sweep. This time, Hacksaw's scan picked something up. "That's either a sub or a blue whale in heat," he reported. Hunter confirmed the target and forwarded the grid coordinates to the surface commander. The closest destroyer immediately fired an ASROC, which is medium-range vertical-launch missile with a mk46 torpedo for a warhead. The helicopters swarmed the target to check it out. As soon as the torpedo splashed down, the enemy sub's captain made the mistake of trying to move away. The sensitive sonar gear picked up the movement and allowed the Seahawks to guide their own torpedoes precisely on target. The Kilo's explosion was marked by a luminous burst of spray from the surface. Roche and his division returned to their own ship, leaving the *Roosevelt*'s escorts to get to work rescuing the crew of the crippled carrier.

The *Nimitz*-class is designed to be unsinkable, but as the designer of the *Titanic* Thomas Andrews himself had observed, "If it's made of metal, it can sink." And whoever fired the torpedoes knew exactly how to capsize a supercarrier. The weapons had been programmed to go shallow, and they all hit only ten feet below the waterline, leaving massive holes evenly spaced all along the ship's right side. The vast spaces of the lower levels were flooded, drowning the unlucky sailors below the impacted decks and adding tens of thousands of tons to the carrier's ballast. The ship's huge pumps were overwhelmed – the influx of water was more than they could handle, more than any marine engineer or naval architect would have anticipated. Within in an hour it was listing so badly the edge of the flight deck was almost touching the water. The crew was forced to give up their valiant efforts to save the ship and abandon the giant wreck. The nine escorts surrounded the derelict and pulled the survivors from the water – 5,780 men and women in all, out of over 6,000 that had sailed from Everett, WA.

Finally at 0600, the huge vessel rolled over completely. The large elevator openings in the sides of the hanger deck allowed water to quickly flood the rest of the ship. The *Port Royal* fired several rounds from her five-inch guns into the keel of the sinking ship, allowing the trapped air to vent and eliminating the last bit of buoyancy in the vessel. The rescued crew watched from the rails of the escorts as their beloved *Teddy* sank out of sight.

## E-3 SENTRY 32,000FT ABOVE IRAQ/IRAN BORDER
## 0100 LOCAL

Lt. Dave Richards watched the screen that showed every airborne contact within range of the powerful AN/APY-2 radar system. It was covered with blips. Cruise missiles launched from bombers to the north and warships to the south were converging on a point he knew represented Tehran. Helicopters were closing in on the border from both sides, followed by heavily-armed close-air-support attack jets. Dozens of American fighters swarmed across northern Iraq to secure the airspace at the border and across northern Iran, where more bombers were headed to continue pounding the capital city. And even though he couldn't see them, he knew that B-2 stealth bombers from Diego Garcia were already flying across Iranian airspace to drop very powerful bunker-busters on Iran's suspected nuclear weapons facilities.

The blips moved closer together. The fireworks were about to begin. And from his vantage point, Lt. Richards could watch the whole show. He wished he had a more comfortable chair, and a cold beer. *Here we go,* he thought.

## RUSSIAN EMBASSY, TEHRAN – SAME TIME

The American spy, the Cossack arms dealer and the Russian engineer stood in the lobby, waiting for the night watch security guard to find someone on the staff while they discussed their cover story.

"Let me do all the talking," Kujetski reminded the others. "They know me here. The Ambassador and his security chief are good friends of mine."

"They'd better be *very* good friends," Kahlil said as he looked over a document. "Because this passport you found for our contractor friend is the worst forgery I've ever seen. Did you have Albie make this at the local copy shop?"

"Photoshop on his PC, actually," Kujetski answered.

"You're kidding, right?" Kahlil stared at his longtime associate and did not like what he saw. "Dammit, you're not kidding."

"No, I'm not."

"Damn." Kahlil looked at the phony ID booklet again. "And where did you come up with the name 'Arvydas Sabonis'?"

"Albie suggested that too. Why?"

The American looked up. "That's the name of a former NBA player."

"Oh."

"That reminds me, Kuj," the CIA man said with a smile, "make sure you get us a room that has cable TV. Game Four of the Western Conference Finals starts in a few hours. I want to see if the Thunder can finish the sweep."

"We'll get our room, we'll get your TV, and we'll get this guy through without a second glance at his papers. You'll see." Kujetski turned to Antonov, the contractor. "What's your name?"

"I am Arvydas Sabonis, from Volgograd," he said. "I am a civil engineer who's worked twenty years for LukOil. I am in Iran to take tours of the new oil refineries."

"Good, but only answer one question at a time. See?" Kujetski smiled at Kahlil. "No problem with him. How's *your* paperwork?"

"If I was any more legitimate, it would look suspicious," he said. "Roman Kalinov entered the country on an Aeroflot flight from Moscow three months ago, cleared customs, and has been working legally on a business visa with your company ever since. I have all the documentation to prove it."

A pretty blond woman came to the reception desk and turned the lamp on to illuminate her counter. "I can help you over here, gentlemen."

Before the three men could take a step another man entered the lobby. He was a tall, thin Russian in a cheap suit, and he spoke with a voice that sounded like gravel being crushed. "Natascha, I can see to this. You can go back to bed."

"But it is no trouble-" Natascha started to say, but the tall man cut her off.

"No, please. I have been expecting Mr. Kujetski's visit and I should attend to his business personally. Please. I'm sorry that the guard brought you down here."

"Whatever you say, Mr. Lysenko," Natascha shrugged and left.

Lysenko greeted Kujetski warmly. "It is very good to see you, my friend."

"I'm also pleased to find you well," Kujetski said. "These are my associates, Mr. Kalinov and Mr. Sabonis. Gentlemen, this is Mr. Lysenko, embassy chief of security."

"Pleased to meet you," Kahlil – now Kalinov said.

"Likewise." Lysenko shook their hands before leading them to the desk. "Now, what can I do for you tonight?"

"We've come to seek asylum in the embassy," Kujetski said. "As you know the airports have been closed and Iran is now at war with at least three different countries, including ours. We think this would be the safest place for us."

"And it would be. We would only be too happy to make accommodations for three of our country's citizens at a time like this. But I must wonder why you didn't fly out last week when the Russian consulate recommended that all Russian nationals including non-essential diplomatic staff should leave Iran immediately."

"My credit card miles were blacked out last week," Kujetski answered, deadpan.

"Of course." Lysenko said, matching his friend's tone and expression. "I only need to see your passports then." The three guests surrendered their documents. Lysenko flipped through Kujetski's and Kalinov's and handed them back. He paused when he saw the third. "Is this a newer issue?"

"Yes," Kujetski answered. "Yes it is."

Lysenko thumbed through the phony passport and looked up at Antonov. "What is your name, sir?"

"Arvydas Sabonis."

"You're not as tall as I would have expected," Lysenko deadpanned again, obviously recognizing the assumed name. "Where are you from?"

Antonov was sweating. "Stali- I mean, Volgo- Volgograd. I work for LukOil and I am in Iran for-"

"I don't need to know of your business, sir." Lysenko handed the photoshopped passport back. "Your papers seem to be in order. I can take you all to your VIP suite now. Would you gentlemen prefer a view overlooking the courtyard or the gardens?"

"Courtyard, please," Kujetski said. He would have actually preferred to see gardens but the outside wall of the building might be vulnerable to snipers. Kalinov cleared his throat and Kujetski added "Oh, silly to ask, but do we get cable?"

"Satellite, even better than the local cable service," Lysenko smiled as he picked their room key off the wall. "We even have free HBO." Right at that moment a cruise missile whooshed overhead and exploded a moment later in a distant rumble. More blasts quickly followed. "Just so you know," Lysenko added, "to get to the bomb shelter you just take either of the two central stairways or the main elevator all the way down to the lowest level of the building."

"We'll keep that in mind," Kalinov said.

## THE COMMAND BUNKER – SAME TIME

"They're tearing into our fixed air defenses around Tehran sir."

"Cruise missiles?" Rannovich asked.

"Yes sir."

"Good. How are their fighters dispersed right now?"

Rannovich's chief of staff, General Mikhail indicated the map display on the big screen. "They're covering these corridors, running north and south across our airspace, directly across Tehran and all of our nuclear facilities."

"They'll be following with bombers soon," Rannovich said. "B-2s from the south, B-1s and B-52s from the north."

"Sirs!" an Iranian Air Force Captain called from his station. "Reports from our facilities at Bushehr and Fasa – they're being carpet-bombed!"

"Anything on radar?" Rannovich asked.

"No sir," the General answered. "That would be the B-2s then. That would put their attack wave here…" A line appeared across the map, just north of the two cities that were just hit. "Our mercenary fighters in the camouflaged bases can catch them from behind if I launch them now."

"No, don't do that," Rannovich ordered. "I want to save that particular surprise for later. Besides, our fighters can't catch what they can't see. Ignore the stealth bombers. Instead, I want you to send out reserve squadrons of Sukhoi Flanker-Ms armed with KS-172 missiles and try to take out as many of their AWACS planes as they can. Then send up four squadrons of MiGs to harass the fighters and bombers to the north. But I want the Americans to think they have gained air superiority, especially over the southern portion of the country."

264

"As you say, sir."

"Zoom the display in on our forces in Iraq."

"Yes sir. As you can see they've already sustained heavy losses. The Sixth Brigade was decimated by American aircraft as they advanced on the city of Ba'qubah from Mandali."

"So they didn't get in range to shell Baghdad?"

"No sir."

"That's too bad."

"The Fifth and Eleventh Brigades are retreating across the border, in a running fight with American helicopters. They were repelled at the Nahr Diyala River. Three American armored regiments will have them flanked before they can make it back to our fortified positions. Our air cover will not be able to help them either."

"Okay."

"And the Ninth is in a pitched fight with the Americans southeast of Al Kut. They are completely surrounded so I think they'll be a total loss."

"Okay. Go back to that line of retreat. Can you order what's left of the Fifth and Eleventh north toward Sanandaj?"

"Yes sir."

"Good. Then do that, and draw the Americans within range of our artillery."

"We won't be able to hit their tanks with any accuracy, sir."

"I know, but they'll turn around in a hurry anyway. Then order two Defiant squadrons to be ready to intercept American attack planes over the artillery batteries."

"Yes, sir."

President Mahmoud Ahmadinejad looked on with a vacant expression. "You appear to be throwing my army units away like old rags," he said to Rannovich. "I hope this is necessary to fulfill our plan."

"It is, my friend. The Americans must believe they have the upper hand right now, otherwise they will not fully commit to their attack."

"But when the Americans are fully committed to war then no army on earth can stop them," the president said.

"That's what they think, anyway. That's why this will work."

### *REAGAN* – 0800 HOURS LOCAL

Roche found the *Stingrays* RR the same way he found it almost every morning. Bulldog was eating. Ronin and Creep were reading their motorcycle magazines. Gator was dozing in the recliner. Buzz was playing on his Gameboy. Mystique was on the internet, reading through a blog article. Beowulf and Claymore were on another computer, looking for English Football scores. Everybody else was watching a wrestling match on TV – WWE, actually. Roche watched the screen long enough to see John Cena hurl some unlucky opponent over the ropes.

He thought it slightly odd that everyone had settled back into routine immediately after participating in the biggest naval battle in over sixty years. But as he thought more, what else could they do? They had won, they had survived, and there would be more missions to follow. Another day at the office. Roche turned his attention to the coffee maker. "Hey Rooster, you guys didn't make that nasty chicory stuff again, did you?"

"No sir. The Skipper dumped all of Gator's beans overboard. That's your uh, Kenyan Mocha, I think."

Roche filled his Sea World Shark Encounter souvenir mug and tested the liquid cautiously, confirming that it was indeed a chocolate-laced Arabica blend and not some sort of culinary prank.

Hannibal walked in right then, proceeding directly to the coffee maker like usual, but he paused with his mug under the spigot, and looked at Roche. "Is this safe?"

"Yes sir. This is the good stuff." Roche took a large sip of his coffee to prove it.

Commander Burke filled his mug, tasted it himself, and gulped the coffee down. "By the way, Sharkey, you're officially an Ace."

"Really?"

"Yeah, someone went over all the stats from last night and figured you got six kills all by yourself."

The squadron broke in to applause, as Roche modestly bowed his head.

"So, good shooting, Sharkey. I don't know what else to say." Hannibal looked around the room and did a quick headcount. One aviator was missing. "Where's Blaze?" he asked her roommate, Mystique.

"I think she's still in bed," Lt. jg. Maggie Banning replied.

Hannibal's eyes narrowed suspiciously. "With who?"

Mystique shrugged.

Hannibal looked like he wanted more of an explanation, but he let it go. Instead he turned his attention to the TV. "Whoever's got the

266

remote, put the news on," he ordered. "There's more important stuff going on outside than Friday Night Smackdown."

Hardcase looked at him funny. "No there isn't."

Hunter waved the remote over his head. "I'll switch to a news station on the commercial break."

"Alright." Burke sat down on the couch and waited for John Cena to finish pounding another challenger's skull into the mat and be declared the "winner." Then Hunter finally started changing channels.

"By the way," Beowulf asked, "not that I care about this World Wrestling thing of yours but why do we get Friday Night Smackdown on Saturday morning?"

"Our satellite service comes from San Diego," Hawk explained. "We get whatever's on the regular west coast schedule, and at the moment that's eleven-point-five hours behind us."

Hunter settled on CNN. Melissa Kerrigan was live again from the *Lincoln*. *"We still don't know how many people went down with that aircraft carrier when it sank but the Navy had their smaller warships surrounding it and it looked like they rescued several thousand people before it finally capsized and sank about two and a half hours ago. In the meantime the Navy forces are waiting to see if the Chinese fleet decides to make another attack..."*

"I thought it was impossible to capsize a *Nimitz*-class," Bulldog said.

"It depends on how far off the keel-line you're sitting," Blackjack joked.

"It also depends on how many torpedoes hit and how close they are to the waterline," Sharkey brought some intelligence to the discussion. "In theory, the athwartships pumps should be able to transfer water from side to side and keep the ship balanced on an even keel, and even if she floods to the hangar deck she'll float on the flight deck. But when *Teddy* got hit last night, she apparently took six torpedoes right below the belt. Too much water coming in too fast on one side. You can't beat physics."

The aviators fell silent as the reporter finished describing the current situation in the Persian Gulf.

*"Okay, thank you Melissa,"* the anchor in Atlanta said. *"The calm in the Persian Gulf at the moment must be the eye of the storm. The fighting still rages fierce on the ground in Iran. According to the latest reports the US army has stopped the Iranians' second assault on Iraq after a fierce night battle, and they are now engaged in scattered tank skirmishes all along the western edge of Iran. Meanwhile the US*

*Air Force claims they have destroyed all known and suspected Iranian nuclear production and storage facilities, and are continuing to hit military targets around the vicinity of Tehran."*

The screen now showed a green city – a night-vision view of Tehran from several hours before. *"This view of Iran's capital city comes to us courtesy of the BBC's Iranian correspondent."* The video played for a few minutes, while an Iranian reporter with a British accent described the numerous explosions that lit up the night sky.

"Looks just like Baghdad in '03," Shredder remarked. Roche's jaw clenched at that. Hunter noticed out of the corner of his eye, but didn't say anything.

The screen switched to a daytime view and the CNN anchor continued. *"The BBC lost that audio feed but they're still providing live video footage of Tehran. You can see columns of smoke from last night's cruise missile strikes- oh my."* The camera panned upward suddenly and focused on a B-52, just as it released four heavy bombs. The camera blurred as it tried to follow them and it refocused just in time to see them explode in the distance behind the downtown skyline. Four massive mushroom clouds towered over the skyscrapers.

"BLU-96 fuel-air bombs," Hardcase observed. "That target must have been something important."

"Or maybe they're just trying to scare people," Mystique said.

"Either way, it worked," Hunter noted.

## THE RUSSIAN EMBASSY, TEHRAN – SAME TIME

"What the hell was that?" Antonov exclaimed, as the quadruple thunderclap shook the windows.

The American was stretched out on a sofa bed reading an old Clive Cussler novel. He glanced over the top of his book at the Russian. "You know, Mr. Sabonis, it's been a really long night and I'm really getting tired of you jumping and yelling every time you hear a loud boom."

"I'm sorry, but believe it or not this the first time I've been hiding from people who want to kill me in a city that's being bombed by the people I want to rescue me."

"Yeah that takes some getting used to. But don't worry about the bombs, okay? The US Air Force is being very careful to avoid hitting the middle of the city and if by chance they do end up blowing us away, we'll never know what hit us."

"That's comforting," Antonov said sarcastically.

"Kuj," the CIA man called across the room. "How's it coming with my phone?"

Kujetski had a cellular phone in one hand and a disassembled satellite phone in the other. "Albie finally found a frequency that the Americans aren't jamming and that he can also patch us in to," he said. "Now he's going to walk me through the process of resetting the phone to that exact frequency."

"Okay, no hurry. I'm very comfortable here."

"Yeah, I noticed. It's only the fate of the world that rests on getting Mr. Sabonis here out of the country and into the hands of your employer."

"Sabonis" jumped again when someone knocked on the door. Kalinov was on his feet with his pistol drawn in an instant, and he checked the peephole. "Who is it?"

"Your breakfast, sir," a young Russian man in a steward's uniform said from the other side of the door. The CIA man slipped the gun back into his waistband and let him in. "Fresh fruit, scrambled eggs, sausage, toast and tea," the steward said, while he pulled in a service cart.

"Great, thanks." The spy helped the steward set the table.

The young Russian noticed Kujetski and the dismantled satellite phone. "Did you break your telephone, mister?"

"I'm talking to tech support to fix it now," Kujetski said with a thin smile.

The steward nodded cheerfully, and turned to leave. But he stopped and stared when he saw Antonov. The American agent sensed danger and reached for his gun again, but the steward spoke after a moment's hesitation. "You do not look well, sir. Shall I send for the doctor?"

"I'm just a little nervous because of the bombs," Antonov said, honestly. "The tea should help me relax, thank you."

"Very good, sir."

As soon as the steward was out the door, Kalinov asked Antonov "Do you know that guy from somewhere? Do you recognize him at all?"

Antonov looked confused. "No, I've never seen him before. Why?"

"I think he recognized you," Kalinov answered. He went to his bag and took a small tool like an airport security wand and swept it over the breakfast spread, checking for electronic bugs, but found nothing. Then he picked up the room phone and dialed the security chief's extension.

"Security." The voice sounded even more gravely on the phone.

"Mr. Lysenko, this is Kalinov."

"Oh yes, Mr. Kalinov. What can I do for you? Feel free to ask for anything."

The American took that to mean the phone was clean and Lysenko was alone. "It may be nothing, but I'm a little suspicious of someone on your wait staff."

"Who?"

"He didn't have a name tag. Young guy, blond hair. He just brought food up to our room."

"Okay. I'll ask the kitchen people who that was and I'll watch for him with the cameras."

"Make sure he doesn't make any phone calls."

"Right. I'll take care of it. Have you been in touch with your people yet?"

"Not yet. Kujetski is working on my sat phone. That's the only way we can get a secure connection with the outside right now."

"Okay. I told the ambassador about your plan. Let me know as soon as you get in touch with the CIA, and I'll have him call Moscow and formally request a rescue. Moscow won't be able to help, but Kujetski has a friend in the state department who will recognize this as a signal and recommend they ask Washington to get us out. So we should have this working from both ends."

"Good. They should be able to arrange a rescue within twenty-four hours after I make the call."


The steward had plugged his earpiece into his tap on Lysenko's phone line just in time to hear the description of the rescue plan. The steward immediately grabbed his cell phone and called the only number in its contact memory.

"Rannovich," said the powerful man who answered that number.

"Sir, this is Number Five, at the embassy."

"Yes? Be quick. I'm very busy."

"You sent me a message last night, with a picture of a contractor named Antonov. Remember?"

"Of course I do. Do you have a question about my order?"

"No, sir, I found him! Antonov is here, in a VIP suite at the Russian embassy, with two American agents. They are being protected by the security staff here, and they're trying to arrange for the CIA and the US military to rescue them right now!"

Rannovich was silent for a moment. "Okay, very good work, Number Five. Do you know how much time we have?"

"They said twenty-four hours after they make a call."

"Have they made the call yet?"

"No."

"Can you stop them from calling the Americans?"

"I don't think so. I'd have to stop the security chief and the CIA agents at the same time."

"On second thought, let them try to launch a rescue. That will be amusing. Okay, you just keep an eye on them and let me know if they change any details in their plan. Otherwise I'll call you when something changes on my end."

"Yes sir."

"You did very well, Number Five. There will be a substantial reward for you when this is over."

"Thank you, sir."

Lysenko had just hung up the phone after talking to the kitchen staff and identifying the steward. Then he saw on his signal security display that someone was making a cell phone call from the old switchboard room, which had long since been automated and closed off. He watched the camera feed from up the hall as the steward stepped out. "Hello, there."

"Testing, testing," Kujetski spoke into the sat phone. "You hear me, Albie? Yes, you're coming in fine, five-by-five... Okay, you can connect us to Langley from there, right? Okay. I'll give the phone to Mr. C then."

"You got it to work?" The American asked as he took the phone.

"Albie says we did, that's good enough for me."

"Great work, kid," the spy said into the phone.

"I'm putting you through to the main switchboard," the Indian hacker said. "I don't think you want me to know your boss's extension."

There was a hiss of static, a series of tones, and then the static cleared and the other end of the line rang once. "You have reached the

Central Intelligence Agency," a recorded voice said. "To speak to an operator, press zero."

Kalinov pressed the key and told the operator "Office of the Deputy Director of Operations, please. Tell him Caspian is calling." DDO Jarrod Casey was soon on the other end of the phone. "Sir, we have an emergency situation. I need ASAP extraction for K and me, plus a Monster House-level contact."

Monster House meant the command bunker. Casey was on top of it immediately. "Alright. That's you, Special K, and I'm calling your new asset Contact Red. Where are you guys?"

"The Russian embassy. We have the ambassador and the security chief on board with us. They're in K's network. We're trying to put together a cover scenario where they'll call for an emergency evacuation of the entire embassy staff."

"You mean the Russians will ask our government to rescue them?"

"Right."

"I like that idea. I'll call you back as soon as we have a plan, Caspian."

"Okay, thanks, boss."


Number Five was waiting in the telephone room with his earpiece in the tap when Kujetski called Lysenko. "Hey, we got our call in to Langley."

"Okay, good," the security chief said. "I'll have the ambassador call Moscow in a few minutes. By the way, you know that steward you thought might be spying on you?"

"What about him?"

Lysenko opened the door of the switchboard room, holding a cordless phone in one hand and a huge pistol in the other. "I found him."

# CHAPTER 13: HELL IN A HANDBASKET

## 40,000 FT ABOVE IRANIAN COASTLINE
## 1130 LOCAL, SUNDAY, JUNE 1ST

"Halo One is feet dry. Feet dry and ready op." Roche called over the command frequency. Five other pilots called "Feet dry, ready op" behind him, as Halo and Shade Flights crossed the Persian Gulf coast. The two groups consisted of four Super-Es and two Growlers. Roche had four other friendly contacts on his radar – Lifeboat, Monitor, Dropship and Pelican, which were a KC-10 tanker, an E-3 Sentry AWACS, an MC-130 Combat Talon transport and an MV-22 Osprey respectively. These ten aircraft were the air support for "Operation Bungie Boss."

Operation Bungie Boss had been assembled in the last twenty hours in response to Agent Caspian's request to extract himself and the assets codenamed "Special K" and "Contact Red" under the cover of a mission of mercy to rescue those trapped at the Russian embassy. In addition to the collection of airplanes swarming over the country, there were ten SEALs ready to parachute out of the MC-130 and secure the Russian embassy. Roche's Halo flight would provide close support and be there to defend against enemy aircraft, which were not expected to be a problem because the Air Force was simultaneously engaging the Iranians to the west of the city. Shade flight was supposed to be the real defense – the two Growlers carried enough HARMs to blow whatever was left of Tehran's air defenses apart. The E-3 would of course watch for air threats, the KC would keep everyone fueled up, and when it was all over, the Osprey would swoop in and pull out the SEAL team and the occupants of the Russian embassy, which Caspian had reported to be not more than twenty-five. It would be a comfortable load for the long-range heliplane. The MC-130 was also hauling three troop-carrying Light Armored Vehicles which could be parachuted in with Marine drivers in case the SEALs needed to get the Russians driven to an alternate pick-up site.

The whole plan was foolproof, complete with the cover story that they were rescuing the trapped Russians at Moscow's request, which was partially true and would be readily confirmed by Moscow. The White House decided also that this mission would make a much needed success story for the media, and so the whole thing was being closely followed by reporters.

Roche felt uncomfortable with the media attention. He wasn't in the limelight himself, of course – he'd just be an anonymous fighter pilot – but a high-profile mission could become embarrassing if things went wrong. The story wasn't being announced to the public yet, of course. All the reporters would kept under guard until the Osprey was "feet wet," safely back over international waters. But even though they weren't allowed to broadcast, the media would be following every detail of Operation Bungie Boss and if anything went wrong, the consequences would extend far beyond those directly involved.

Sharkey put aside thoughts of the ramifications and concentrated on his job. Moving at 520 knots, the six attack jets made short work of the 800 mile distance between the shoreline and the capital city. They overtook the much slower Osprey and Combat Talon, as was planned. The KC-10 took station 100 miles south of the city limits, and the E-3 positioned itself just southwest, which was the mostly likely approach vector for defending Iranian fighters.

Lt. Nick Santos was commanding the EW strike from the back seat of Shade-1. As soon as the fighters started drawing radar attention, the Toymaker went to work jamming the defense network around the city. When necessary, he guided a HARM into a SAM radar on the Dropship's line of approach. The op went like clockwork. The city had absorbed punishing air strikes all weekend and seemed almost lifeless. Sharkey ordered Halo flight to spread out and fly in a 50-mile-radius circle around the embassy. There was no contact except intermittent radar from the defense grid which seemed to have been pummeled into total ineffectiveness. "Okay, Dropship, this is going even better than we hoped," Santos called on the command channel. "I'd say you're clear for insertion on vector oh-fifteen."

"Copy, Shade. Bungie Jumpers inbound, ETA twenty-one minutes."

## THE BUNKER, 240 MILES NORTHWEST OF TEHRAN

"The New York Times guy says the paratroopers are twenty minutes out." General Mikhail reported to Rannovich.

"Excellent. They are definitely going for our embassy, then?"

"The radar confirms that the Navy fighters are in an orbit pattern centered exactly on the Russian embassy's coordinates."

"How many fighters?"

"Four, sir, plus two 'Wild Weasels' which are rather casually dismantling what little is left of the fixed radar grid. They seem to think we have insufficient defenses."

"So they haven't found the camouflaged SA-10 batteries?"

"No, sir. Or the armor platoons in the underground garages."

"Perfect," Rannovich said. "And the fighters are looking for other aircraft, right? Not ground forces in the city."

"Right. They're patrolling over the outskirts in a wide loop."

"They are much too spread-out. But we must reward their erroneous tactics. Send a couple squads to engage the fighters, and try to get their transport if you can."

"What about our man in the embassy?" Mikhail asked.

"I shall alert Number Five myself."

## THE RUSSIAN EMBASSY, TEHRAN

Number Five was at that moment bound and gagged and tied to a chair in one of the large closets in the VIP suite, so he wasn't able to answer his phone when it rang

"Is that your Blackberry, Kuj?" The American agent asked.

"No, it's not. Where the hell is that coming from?"

It took the agents a few moments to find the source of the ringing. They found the phone in a pile of stuff they'd taken from the mole. Kalinov took the phone and opened the closet, and growled in Russian. "Your boss is trying to call you. You will speak to him, and I will listen. If you say anything that gives us away, I will hang up the phone and shoot you in the crotch, like this." Kalinov took out his silenced 5.7mm pistol and fired a bullet at the floor between the mole's legs. It didn't hit the man, but it was close enough to show how serious the American was. The mole's attitude became very cooperative. Kalinov ripped the duct tape off the other man's face and hit the speaker button on the phone.

The mole said "Da."

"Number Five, what took you so long to answer?" Rannovich demanded.

The man called Number Five fearfully eyed the American's pistol as he made up a lie. "I had to find some place quiet so I could talk. I am on the wait staff, you know? I'm supposed to be in the kitchen right now. There were people everywhere-"

"Shut up and listen. The Americans are trying to get their spies and our traitor out of the embassy."

"When?"

"Right now. They have tactical fighters circling the capital and a big transport full of paratroopers is on its way."

"What are you going to do about it?"

"We are launching interceptors and we have armored vehicles on the ground. But if they do succeed in landing their Special Forces, you need to silence that traitor."

"I understand. Now I must get back to work or I will arouse suspicion."

"Never mind them and their suspicion. In fifteen minutes you will have paratroopers on the roof. Be alert."

"Okay."

Rannovich terminated the call from his end.

Kalinov took the phone away. "Good boy. Did you hear any of that, Kujetski?"

"Everything. Should we tell the ambassador?"

"No point. He'd just get angry and panic. He's unhappy enough with what he knows about this operation. If we told him the SEALs are going to be shot at…"

"I see your point. But you should tell our rescuers at least."

Agent Caspian took the satellite phone out of his pocket and called the number that Casey had given him.

## NORTHERN OUTSKIRTS OF TEHRAN, 20,900 FT

"Halo One, this is Monitor, I've got contacts coming up in the grass, a hundred clicks off your three o'clock."

Roche tapped his MFD to display the E-3's telemetry. Eight aircraft showed up, fuzzy contacts approaching low and fast from the northwest. "I see your bogeys, Monitor. Can you resolve?"

"Neg, Halo, they're a little too low for me to get a clearer image, over."

"Toymaker," Sharkey called on a direct channel, "how about we try that telephoto lens of yours."

Santos directed his pilot to fly across the city airspace, pointed directly at the contacts. The super-high-resolution tandem radar his Growler carried scanned the incoming bogeys until 3-D images became sharply defined on his display. "We got ourselves eight Sukhoi thirty-five Flanker-Mikes headed right toward… no, wait, they're banking south. Oh, shit. They're goin' for the Echo-three."

"Not this again," someone sighed onboard the E-3. Su-35s pack an ultra-long-range missile designed specifically to take down AWACS aircraft, and had been devastatingly effective in the air battles the day before.

"Not to worry, Monitor, we'll keep 'em busy," Roche said. "Halo Three, Four, take anti-missile stations on the Echo's quarter. Hacksaw, stick with me. We're going to kill some jackals."

"Monitor, what's your sniffer reading?" Santos asked, in Air Force slang, if they knew what radar frequency the Flankers were using.

"Between 1980 and 2020k."

Santos dialed the kilohertz range into the jamming pods and blinded the Flankers.

The confused interceptor pilots slowed down and tried resetting their radar, but Shade-1 had all the frequencies in their range covered. They climbed up to fifteen thousand feet to try to engage the Americans visually.

"All too easy," Roche muttered to his weapons panel in his Darth Vader voice. As the Flankers climbed, he and Hacksaw went down, approaching above and behind the big Russian jets. "Fox-three, fox-three," he called as he fired both his AMRAAMs at the two Sukhois in the front of the formation. Hacksaw accelerated to close quarters and fired all four of his missiles at the trailing division. The Flankers probably could have dodged the AMRAAMs, but their pilots had been badly trained and were caught totally off-guard. The two survivors turned and split to the west, leaving half a dozen flaming wrecks and only two parachutes in their wake.

"Great work, Halo," Santos cheered.

"Strike leads, this is Dropship Command," a voice belonging to the SEAL commander addressed the aviators. "Tune on secure comm band theta three."

Roche obeyed. "Halo Lead checks on theta three."

Santos called in as well. "Shade Lead checks on theta three."

"We got a call from our man in the embassy," Commander Clark told them. "The enemy knows of our approach and will attempt to intercept."

"No, kidding?" Toymaker said sarcastically. "You mean like they might send a bunch of Flankers after us? What other brilliant intel does that spook have?"

"Expect ground resistance. I'm adding another channel for you guys. Spartan One and Two are ground assets, and will act as forward air control."

"I don't like you guys changing the mission on me, Dropship Command," Santos complained.

"Try being flexible, Shade. Spartans, comcheck."

## THE *REAGAN* AIR OPS CENTER

"What happened to 'No appreciable resistance,' Admiral?" Captain Thompson gave Admiral Krause a sidelong glance after overhearing the communication with Commander Clark. "Sounds like some pretty serious resistance to me."

"The Air Force assured me that virtually all air and ground defenses in the city were wiped out," Krause said. "I suppose a handful of small units could have remained in hiding."

"Hiding? No, waiting. They're waiting for us."

## OVER TEHRAN

"Halo Flight, this is Spartan One. I have a target for you."

Roche thought he detected the accent of an Arab who had been educated in England. "Go ahead, Spartan."

"Abandoned hotel, ten stories, occupied by an infantry company with Stingers and light triple-A on the roof," Spartan-1, the Iraqi agent known as Ellirat reported. "Target is five blocks north of Embassy complex. GPS reference four-eight-delta-November and mike-Quebec-five-five."

Roche plugged the coordinates into his tactical display and got the target superimposed over a city map. "Got it. Give us two minutes, Spartan, and that building will be strictly past tense. Blackjack," Roche switched channels, "you're closest. Go ahead and toss-bomb it with a JDAM."

"Piece of cake." Lt. Masterson accelerated at low level on a beeline approach to the target, then pulled up at a range of two miles, released the bomb at the apex of the climb, and rolled away. The Joint Direct Attack Munition – a thousand pound bomb with a GPS guidance kit – continued upward in a parabolic arc, then as it descended tiny fins on the tail steered it to the GPS points. It punched through the roof of the hotel and exploded between the fourth and third floors. The building collapsed on itself, killing the soldiers inside but not harming any other civilian structure on the block.

"This is Spartan Two. I've got another one, Halo. Light armor in a parking structure at five-oh-gamma-kilo and Oscar-Romeo-four-eight."

"Same drill, right?" Blackjack tossed his other JDAM and brought down the multi-level car park on top of a company of armored vehicles.

"Halo and Shade, Dropship is on final approach. LALO drop in T minus 132, on fifty-double-A and M-Z-ninety-nine." LALO means low-altitude/low-opening. The SEALs would jump at the lowest safe altitude with minimum exposure to ground fire.

"We got another contact cluster," the E-3 reported. "Aw, hell, how did they get so close? Halo, we have semi-stealth fighters, on track oh-five-oh. They're going right past us and intercepting Dropship."

"Halos three and four, engage bandits!" Roche ordered. "Shade, what're we dealing with?"

Shade-2, under command of Lt. Dane "Fozzy Bear" Foster was closest to the new bandits. "I'm not sure, Halo, I never saw anything like these guys before."

Roche looked at the 3-D scan on his MFD, but he'd never seen a Dassault Defiant before either and couldn't identify the targets. "Take 'em out, whatever they are."

"Halo Three has steady lock on Bandit Four, fox-three, fox-three." Blackjack fired his AMRAAMs on a pincer spread at the trailing Defiant. The nimble little fighter rolled away from one and right into the path of the other. The missile punched clean through the fighter and detonated on top of the long, yellow drop tank strapped to its belly. The two Defiants on the sides of the diamond pattern turned around and fired two missiles apiece toward the Hornets. "Aw, shit. Taking evasive." Blackjack hit the brakes and rolled out of the line of fire, but Rooster, piloting Halo-4, stood his ground a couple seconds longer to shoot back.

"Fox-two-two-three-three," he yelled hurriedly as he shot down the onrushing French-built fighters. Then he cornered sharply and threw the enemy missiles off, but two of the weapons found him again and closed on his tail. The ALQ-214 active countermeasure system mounted in the Super Hornet's tail automatically launched two flare-shells in the path of the missiles, and the shells exploded in a hot shower of aluminum shrapnel. One of the Matra missiles took the bait and flew straight through the lethal cloud and self-destructed. The second ignored the new target and stuck with the Hornet. Rooster pulled another tight turn, and the missile sailed past his plane, missing by thirty feet. But at the instant the missile lost its lock it detonated the fragmentation warhead and managed to severely damage the F/A-18's tail surfaces. "I'm HIT!" Rooster squawked. "But it ain't too bad. I gotta bug out, guys."

Roche was vaguely aware of Rooster's heroic duel, but he had to focus on the last Dassault. The Combat Talon transport was flying directly over downtown now, at only three thousand feet, and there was a little red jet hot on its tail. Roche's Super Hornet screamed toward them on a perpendicular vector. He only had Sidewinders and cannon to engage the Defiant, so he had to be close. Just as the IR seekers on the AIM-9 missiles locked on to the French jet, it fired its own missile at the Combat Talon. Roche split his lock between the red fighter and the black missile and fired at them both the instant he got the indicator tone. The enemy missile was blown out of the sky just over a hundred feet behind the MC-130's tail. The enemy pilot snapped a barrel roll, but the accurate Sidewinder caught him under the left wing tip. The Defiant continued to roll, out of control for a minute, but this pilot was very skilled. He leveled his fighter and lined back up with the cargo plane. Karl had now turned in almost directly behind the Defiant, slightly above and trailing at a distance of two thousand yards. "The Force is strong with this one," he muttered. He lined up his cannon to finish it off, but could only watch incredulously as the tiny fighter suddenly hit the afterburners. Roche tried to get back in range, but he could tell the Dassault would catch the MC-130 first.

At that moment the big transport was right on top of the embassy complex; the back door gaped open and the ten SEALs in the jump team were beginning their LALO skydive. Roche could see what was unfolding and there was nothing he could do about it. He tried anyway. He dove to the deck, flying below the rooftops of the skyscrapers to gain precious speed, closed just enough on the Dassault, pulled up the nose just a little to aim between the other planes and he held down the gun trigger. He felt the vibration through his entire body as the Vulcan cannon spat a long stream of lethal 20mm shells at the enemy jet. The shots scattered widely over the two-mile distance, but some still punched through the Defiant's wings and the deadly missiles still racked on their frames. The two Magic short-range missiles were destroyed just as the pilot tried to fire them. But the enemy pilot ignored the warnings and stuck to his suicidal approach, guiding his supersonic jet right into the tail of the transport.

The last SEAL had just leaped clear when the tinted canopy of the Defiant crushed itself against the base of the Combat Talon's tail. The pilot died instantly, but the moment of his death passed like an eternity for the eleven men in the Combat Talon. The Jumpmaster, a

SEAL NCO who directed the synchronized leap out the back of the plane, clutched to a hydraulic piston supporting the ramp and prayed to God that the searing fireball he knew was coming would not hurt too much. The SEAL mission commander, who was supposed to direct the entire ground op from his computer station on the passenger deck, spent the last seconds of his life erasing the hard drives on his computer so that the mission data could not be captured and compromise his team. Five Marines sitting behind him put their heads between their knees and kissed their butts goodbye. The last LAV driver got up, floated through the cabin as the plane made a zero-G dive, and grabbed a spare parachute. He had no idea how he would get out, but he figured his chances were better in a parachute than in the plane. The flight engineer, pilot and co-pilot clung to their controls as their precious bird went crazy on them.

The exploding fighter tore the entire tail section clean off. The impact pushed the plane into a dive, and with no way to correct the pitch, the massive aircraft simply somersaulted in mid-air. It slammed down in an industrial park about two miles from the embassy, upside-down and backwards. All nine men on the upper deck were flattened instantly. The three 20-ton LAVs strapped to the cargo floor were thrown clear through the gaping hole in the tail and rolled away like dice. That much Karl Roche saw, as he flew directly over the ruin.

"NOOOOOO!!!" The scream escaped on open channel before he realized it. That old transport was the mission critical, and he had watched it go down right before his eyes.

"What happened, Commander?" Blackjack asked.

"Dropship got fox-zeroed," he said, fighting back the rage. "It came down on its back about three clicks north of target."

"Did the Bungie team get clear?" Santos asked.

Roche remembered seeing the SEALs jump. "I think so. Most of them, at least."

"Damn," Rooster said, "tough break sir, but, ah, I got a little emergency too."

Sharkey shook his head to clear it. "Right, Four, what's your fuel status?"

"I've got enough to go feet wet, but my tail's shot up. I'm shakin' too bad for a carrier trap and I can't tank up neither."

"Okay, head for the divert field. Can you make it there?"

"Uh, yeah, no problem."

"Monitor, advise the Air Force patrols between here and the Iraqi zone we have a wounded Rhino Echo going to Subakhu Airbase."

"Copy, Halo."

One of the Arabians on the ground came up on the radio. "Halo, this is Spartan Two. If you have a minute, I'm watching enemy vehicles in target vicinity, but they are too far away for me to identify."

"Shade Two, here, I'll check it out." The Growler made a quick pass and Fozzy Bear confirmed the sighting. "Sixteen heavy vehicles, two clicks southeast of target. I have no idea where they coulda come from."

Hacksaw was closest to the vehicles at this point. Blackjack, who still had two missiles, was covering the AWACS, and Roche was following Rooster to check on his damage. "I'll get them. I have plenty of bombs," Hacksaw reported.

"They're on the Avenue of Victory – that's a wide boulevard that goes east-west four blocks north of the bypass highway," Spartan-2 said.

"Roger." Hacksaw identified the landmarks and approached straight down the road. Then his radar-warning alarm went off an instant before missiles were launched in his direction. "Where the hell did those things come from?" He was forced to abandon the bombing run and evade a pair of SAMs, swearing profusely as he ran.

"Damn it all, I thought we cleaned that sector." Santos and his pilot made a pass and launched their last HARM at the hidden SA-10 site. They flew straight past the vehicles and Santos got a good look at the target. "Uh, that looks like artillery down there. I think they're gonna try and blow up the embassy!"

"Well, we can't have that now." Roche had circled around and lined up for a bomb run of his own. He selected his Sensor-Fused Weapon – a highly advanced anti-armor cluster bomb. He dove to twelve hundred feet and settled in to a perfect approach. Using his forward camera to get a better look at the target, he could see four M1973 self-propelled artillery tracks, screened by several tanks and an infantry company. As he watched, one of the artillery pieces fired, and there was a huge explosion in the gardens behind the Russian embassy building. "No, that won't do at all." Karl's computer counted down to a release point; he just had to remain steady on his approach.

"Halo One," Santos called, "there's another SA-10 in your area."

"For crying out loud, Nick, can't you do anything?" Roche's radar warning gave him the alert a second before a missile was launched right on his tail. "Well, that stinks." He looked over his shoulder and saw the Grumble-class missile shoot up behind him, big as a telephone pole. It locked on with its onboard radar and spiraled down toward him. Roche looked forward again; the artillery was now firing in a barrage. They would level the embassy in short order, unless Roche carpeted them with dozens of armor-piercing bomblets, as he had planned to do before the missile came up.

"Break off, Sharkey," Hacksaw called. "It's too close. I'll come around again."

Roche looked at Hacksaw's position on the tactical display, and considered it. A split-second passed in minutes in his mind while he weighed his options. It would take either Hacksaw or Blackjack at least two minutes to line up another pass on the artillery battery, which would be far too late to stop them from flattening the embassy. But the SA-10 missile would catch him if he maintained course and speed to make the drop himself. "No time. I'm committing. I'll take my chances with that missile."

There were about forty Iranian soldiers operating the artillery, two dozen more in the tanks, and almost a hundred ground troops. They all heard the planes flying low around them, and looked up nervously each time they approached. But this one was coming straight at them, lower than the others. The artillery crew stopped firing, and watched the terrifying warplane swoop toward them. It passed right over their heads; the noise was deafening. A missile followed, about to hit the Hornet, but the soldiers now watched the objects dropped by the American fighter. A fat cylinder had peeled from its underwing pylon and broken up in midair, showering a deadly confetti pattern of tiny bombs over the artillery position. The bomblets locked on to the heat signatures of the vehicles and detonated overhead, blasting a slug of molten copper into each vehicle with lethal accuracy. In seconds, the huge vehicles were blowing themselves inside out, and men were being killed and maimed by the blasts and shrapnel. The entire fire team was ripped apart by the lethal American weapon.

Roche did not enjoy the luxury of watching his little smart bombs take their toll behind him. As soon as he released the CBU he climbed up and rolled away from the dangerous missile. The IDECM system that was supposed to protect him wasn't working. It had been damaged when he had flown through the debris cloud when the Defiant and Talon collided. The missile bored in despite Roche's desperate maneuver, and got as close as it could before the radar return was distorted by the anti-radar paint coat. Its big shaped-charge warhead exploded forty feet behind Roche's tail, close enough to tear up his control surfaces, perforate an engine and blow a hydraulic line.

"Sharkey! You hit?" Toymaker called.

It felt just like hitting a speed bump with his car at eighty miles an hour, something he'd only done once. "I'm okay, oh wait, no, I'm not." Alarms spread across his panel as his starboard engine flamed out and his main hydraulics went dead. Bitchin' Betty read off a list of warnings that Roche didn't bother to listen to.

"You think you can land?" Lt. Santos asked.

"I can barely fly." Just like that time he hit the speed bump when he was seventeen, it felt like the controls were dead in his hands.

"Try to get back to the safety corridor," Santos advised. "You can ditch there and someone will pick you up in a few hours. I'll call a chopper now."

"Excuse me, this is Spartan Two again," the Iraqi agent interrupted. "If anyone's still up there, there's another artillery battery that you need to destroy *right now*."

"Where?" Hacksaw asked. He was moving further south to cover Sharkey's proposed exit.

"I have them." Roche could see the new threat a few miles down the same street he'd just bombed. The artillery pieces had their barrels angled up and aimed toward the embassy. "Nick, cancel that chopper. I'm landing right here."

"WHAT?"

"I'll crash my Rhino into that battery. I'll ditch over the city and hook up with the SEAL team for evac."

"Sharkey, no! Just get the hell out of here!!" Hacksaw called desperately.

"Don't worry, buddy. Just cover that Osprey and I'll be fine." Roche armed his JDAM bombs and lined up on the Avenue of Victory. The Hornet wobbled as he tried to hold a steady approach. The plane kept trying to dip to the left, so Roche shifted his line of approach to the right of the artillery position. The artillery battery hadn't fired yet. Roche wondered if the gunners were all just standing there watching him. Eight blocks away, he released his controls, grabbed the straps at his sides, and blasted out of his damaged fighter.

The Super Hornet banked left, drifted down, and came straight toward the tank at the front of the column. Major Anju Duhamad, having survived his first encounter with the Americans, stood up in the open hatch of his new T-80, right in the path of the out-of-control fighter. The sharp pylon on the left wingtip stabbed through his stomach, caught the hatch lid behind him, and held fast. The Hornet picked up the enormous tank as it began a cartwheel. The nose hit pavement, smashing the radar but the airframe held. Duhamad's tank was launched straight up as the wrecked plane continued to tumble. The right wing came down on an M1973 artillery track, and the Hornet spun around that. Now facing forward, still moving with tremendous momentum, it crashed down on its belly right on top of an ammunition carrier. The two armed JDAMs ripped free and buried themselves in the pavement below. The huge double blast ripped a giant hole out of the middle of the road, and set off the entire load of artillery shells in the ammunition carrier, followed by *Stingray* Eel 13's load of jet fuel. Duhamad's T-80 dropped on top of another tank just as they were both caught up in the massive blast wave.

### *REAGAN* AIR OPS

"Holy damned Christmas!" Deuce literally reeled in shock as he watched Roche's plane explode, live via the camera feed from Shade One. He leaned his torso back as far as his chair allowed, as if trying to get away from the image. He held his hands against his head as if trying to contain the explosion in his mind.

"What the hell was that?" Admiral Krause asked from behind him.

As he turned in his seat, Captain Thompson's facial expression morphed from absolute shock to unrestrained rage. "That, *that* was my *boy*! You just got him *killed*, you goddamned *useless* motherfucking *spook*!"

### OVER TEHRAN

"Holy shit, they've gone nuclear!" Hacksaw yelled.

"Calm down, Halo Two." Santos took charge immediately. "Halo lead is down. Did anyone see a 'chute?"

"This is Spartan Two. Your man got clear. His plane hit an ammo truck – that was the blast you saw. Halo One is in a parachute about six blocks from the crash site, three blocks south of the embassy. I'll cover him while he moves north."

### *REAGAN*

Krause stared back at Thompson, unsure of what to do, while the CAG glared daggers at him. They heard the exchange on the radio, and Deuce turned back to his screen. Krause cleared his throat. "He bailed out, Thompson. He's alive."

"For the moment. But he's coming down in a fucking *war zone*, where you said there would be *no resistance*."

Krause cleared his throat again. "Apparently our intel report was erroneous."

"And who's our intel officer?" Deuce turned again, with a glare that could melt steel. "That's *you* isn't it? You sent Roche in to get killed. Isn't this sort of thing your specialty, just like with the *Ranger* in '91?"

"What the hell are you talking about?"

"You know damn well-"

"Excuse me, sirs," Commander Burke spoke up. "May I suggest that we do something to recover this SNAFU?"

Deuce nodded. "They need more air cover. All I have in the area is Palerider's Grizzly flight spotting for armor near Qom. I'll send them up to Tehran but they need at least two more squads of fighter-bombers, ASAP. It'll be two hours before I can assemble a new package and get it up there."

"I'll call the Air Force," Krause said. He went to a secure comms booth.

Hannibal sat down next to Deuce. "You're damn lucky he didn't throw you in the brig for that little show."

"You think? What about you? That's your XO who just went down."

"Hey, I'm not saying you were wrong. I'm actually glad you were the one to yell at the Admiral. You saved me from having to do it. I kinda like working here."

"He'll hear more – from me at least – if Roche doesn't get out of there alive."

**TEHRAN**

Roche briefly lost consciousness as the ejection seat launched him into the sky. He'd never actually used an ejection seat before, and had not tensed for the jolt. The parachute popped open and settled him into a slow descent. The shockwave of the blast jolted him awake. He looked at the raging inferno under a towering mushroom cloud that marked his Hornet's crash. He looked behind him to the first target. He could see scattered smoke, but he was too far away to see just how thoroughly he had destroyed that threat. He detached himself from the heavy ejection seat to further slow his descent, and steered for the roof of a building as close to the embassy as he could get. As he passed over a street, an Iranian soldier with an AK shot at him. He was

286

moving fast, and the bullets only caught the fabric of his parachute. Another bullet whizzed by from the side, faster and more accurate – a sniper. Roche whipped out the V-blade on his SOG PowerLock and cut his parachute lines in mid-air and dropped ten feet onto the roof of a building. As soon as his boots touched the roof he tucked and rolled and went straight over the side. Luckily he dropped onto a fire escape. Another sniper round cracked the top of his helmet and hit the wall next to him. Roche dove into a window, dragging the gear bag strapped to his harness behind him.

He threw his split helmet away and grabbed his binoculars from the bag and went to another window to try and spot the sniper. He found him three rooftops away. He wasn't aiming with the rifle now; he was reaching for a radio on his belt. Suddenly he lurched forward, clutching his chest, and slid off the roof. The sound of a gunshot reached Roche a second later. He realized a friendly sniper, either a SEAL or one of the Spartan spotters, was covering him. He went back to the fire escape and looked around. He couldn't see the embassy roof from where he was. He looked across the rooftops to the south and saw Elessar – Spartan Two – on the minaret of a mosque with a heavy rifle. Roche waved, and the Iraqi gave him a thumb's up. Roche looked down to the street but he couldn't see the guy who'd shot at him with an AK, and figured he must be out of the Spartan's line of fire.

Roche stripped off his heavy flight suit and put the vest back on over his street clothes. He stowed the binoculars and took his pistols out of the flight bag, checked them, loaded them, cocked them, and slipped them into the holsters in his flight-combat vest. The Desert Eagle went on the left side of his vest, where he could grab it quickly with his right hand, and his Glock automatic went on the other side. He loaded extra clips into the bandolier loops on his vest – .50 cal on the right for the Desert Eagle, 9mm on the left for the Glock. Then he reversed the straps on the gear bag to wear it like a backpack. Finally he looked down to the street again, checked that it was still clear, and went down the fire escape.

He was three stories up when four soldiers came around the corner, led by the one who had shot at him earlier. Bullets zinged off the metal framework around him as Roche crouched and pulled his Glock free. He fired back, hitting two of the men, and the others ducked back behind the corner. Roche jumped to an awning and rolled to the ground. He advanced with both pistols drawn, finished off one soldier who was merely wounded, and waited. A soldier leaned his head out and Roche blew it away with a shot from his Desert Eagle.

The last one jumped out and fired from the hip, but Sharkey held his ground and put a fifty-cal bullet in his chest.

More soldiers would come soon, he knew. He ran to the wall surrounding the embassy grounds, watching each street and alley he passed for more threats. He got to the wall unmolested. He found a bus stop lean-to that let him climb up and grab the top of the twelve-foot wall. It was topped with razor wire. The handy SOG multi-tool came out again; Roche used the tough compound cutter-pliers to snip a few feet out of the obstacle. As he pulled himself over the wall another bullet ricocheted off the concrete next to him. He figured it came from behind him somewhere, but then another sniper bullet hit the wall behind him as he landed in the garden on the other side. He instinctively dove for cover, and ended up in the crater made by an artillery shell earlier. He realized the SEAL team sniper was the one shooting at him this time. He pulled off his white UCLA Bruins Football t-shirt and waved it over the rim of the crater. Then he pulled a Sharpie marker out of his gear bag and wrote on the back of the shirt *I'M A USN AVIATOR – DO NOT SHOOT*. He held the message over his head and stood up slowly, facing the embassy building.

A door opened up and a young SEAL ran out to meet him. "Sir! Petty Officer Morris says he's sorry for trying to shoot you."

"I'm glad he's such a lousy shot."

"Yes sir, he is. Our designated sniper was injured on the drop." The SEAL offered his hand and name. "SEAL second class Carter, Second Battalion, Team Three."

"Lieutenant Commander Roche, Air Wing Thirteen, USS *Ronald Reagan*." He accepted the handshake before putting his shirt and vest back on and gathering his gear. "Who's your CO?"

"Lieutenant Nathan, sir. We got a CP set up in the dining room on the second floor. I'll take you there."

Roche followed him inside. "Your CO's name is Nathan? Lance Nathan?"

"Yes sir. You know him?"

"We finished the Grinder together, first and second place."

"You were a SEAL?"

"I was until I got hurt in Iraq. Now I fly Hornets."

The younger man stopped, and stared at the aviator in awe. "You're *Karl* Roche? The *Polar Bear?*"

"That's what they called me. Am I supposed to be famous or something?"

288

"Sir, every SEAL knows who you are. And this is your old squad! Half of the guys are from your old crew. Morris, Williams, Ramirez, Yao, Sherman, Coles... and Master Chief Bowers is our Jumpmaster – was, I mean." Carter looked at his feet. Roche didn't register the news that his old Chief had been on Dropship when it was hit.

"I'd love to see them again. Do we take this stairway?"

"Uh, yeah. Follow me, sir. It's easy to get lost in here. All the signs are in Russian and Farsi."

Roche followed up to the second floor, down a service hallway, through an office and into a main corridor, which lead finally to an opulent dining room where the occupants of the embassy had gathered and eight members of the SEAL team stood guard. SEALs don't wear insignia in combat, but Roche was still able to easily identify his old Grinder buddy, Lt. Lance Nathan. At six feet, seven inches, he towered over the other SEALs.

"Somehow I always knew I'd find you like this," Sharkey announced,
"hiding in some half-bombed-out building waiting for my boys to rescue you."

"Oh, for God's sake, Roche, do you always have to make a grand entrance?" The two men extended handshakes that closed into a hug.

Roche was instantly surrounded by his former brothers in arms, including expert sniper Chief Travis Williams, who had bandages around his shoulder and his arm in a sling. "What happened to you, Trav?" Roche asked.

Williams pulled a seven-inch shard of metal out of his pocket. "This stabbed me in the right shoulder when we dropped. I can't move my arm at all."

"Ouch." Roche examined the shrapnel. It was a guiding fin from a French Matra Magic missile. "So what's the plan here, Lance? How close are you to being ready for the Osprey?"

"We can leave here any time. Problem is there's no LZ. An artillery round blew the helipad off the roof, and another one put a fat crater in the driveway. By the way, thanks for taking care of those guns. Another hit on the roof woulda killed us. Morris says you took a missile for us, in order to shut them down."

"Yeah, that's how I got here. So, wait, you're saying there's nowhere for the Osprey to put down around here?"

"Not inside the complex, no. And there's infantry crawling all around us over the wall. And without radio, we have no other intel besides what Morris can see."

"What do you mean, 'without radio'? You *all* have radios."

"But the only outside band we know is the secure channel for Dropship Command – that's Commander Clark – and he's dead. Unless you know what frequencies and encryptions your flyboys are running."

"Not off the top of my head. It's all managed by the onboard computer. Wait a minute, I have an SAR radio." Roche pulled the small walkie-talkie device out of his pack. It didn't turn on. Roche opened the battery compartment, and found it empty. "Oh, the battery – I took it for my phone."

Nathan rolled his eyes. "You gotta be kidding me." The aviator looked up sheepishly and shrugged. Nathan sighed. "Well, that sucks. Any more ideas?"

"Yeah," Roche said, "We can go to the crash sites. Your Combat Talon and my Hornet have everything we need. Dropship went down in an industrial park, which is another wide-open and walled-off area, and it's easy to see from the air so it's an ideal alternate LZ. And there should be plenty of emergency supplies in the wreck. And the onboard computer from my plane can interface with your laptop and use the flight channels to give us a complete tactical display, and new radio frequencies."

"Okay, but the Combat Talon went down two miles from here, and your Super Hornet was blown to very tiny pieces."

"The computer might have survived. It's in an armored compartment under the cockpit with heat shielding. It's supposed to be nuke-proof."

"If it's indestructible, what's to stop it from falling into enemy hands?"

"Each component self-destructs if you try to take it apart," Roche explained, "or if you try to hack it, unless you know exactly what you're doing."

"Which you do, I suppose. Okay, it's worth a shot. Now, how do we get out of here without being spotted?"

"This is a Cold War-era Soviet government building. There has to be a secret escape tunnel." Roche turned to the embassy staffers and asked *"Kto rabotalo zdes samoe dleennee?"* – *Who's worked here the longest?* An old man in a steward's uniform stood up. Roche asked him several questions in Russian, which none of the SEALs

290

understood. He made notes on the SEALs' map while the elderly steward spoke. "Okay Nathan, there's a tunnel leading from the wine cellar to a warehouse about three blocks west of here. The warehouse is owned by that guy," Roche indicated Kujetski, "who's an old friend of the ambassador's, and it should be pretty secure. I say we move there. You hole up with the Russians while me and a couple of the guys run down to my plane, then we can go north, to the MC-130. There are just warehouses and factories all along these roads," he indicated lines on the map between the warehouse and the crash sites, "so we shouldn't run into too many enemy patrols. And once we have my tactical module we'll have a bird's-eye view so we can avoid them altogether."

"Okay, let's do it." Nathan tapped his earpiece and called Morris downstairs. When he arrived he apologized personally to Roche for shooting at him. Nathan then described the plan to the entire team. "I'm going to make Commander Roche our acting mission controller, so we'll defer to him on all command decisions."

One of the staffers was translating for the other Russians. "Is he the only guy here besides me who speaks both *Russki* and English?" Roche asked, quietly.

"Apparently. He's an economic analyst or something. He's been translating for us the whole time. Someone should have thought about that before we got here, but this whole thing was thrown together a little hastily."

"I noticed. What about the American agent?"

Nathan looked puzzled. "What agent?"

"There's supposed to be a CIA guy among this crowd," Roche said. "That's what this whole mission was all about."

"That's news to me." Nathan looked at the civilians. "Are you sure? They all look like Russians to me."

"Maybe I'm thinking of another op," Roche lied, realizing that the agent must still be undercover. "That punchout must've jarred my memory a little. Okay, forget about that. Let's get out of here." The old steward led the group down to the hidden door in the cellar. Roche did a headcount as they entered the tunnel. Twenty-six Russians, eight SEALs, and himself. "There are thirty-five of us, Nathan, remember that."

"Got it."

"And keep an eye on that guy in the wheelchair. Make sure no one leaves him behind." The man in the chair was actually Rannovich's mole. Caspian had tranquilized him when the SEALs arrived, so he appeared to be passed out. *"On v chorosheech zdorofach?" – Is he in good health?* Roche queried the American agent who was pushing him along.

"He's fine," Agent Caspian answered in Russian. "He was having a panic attack, so the doctor gave him a shot of something. He'll be out for a few hours."

"Hey, do any of you guys have a Samsung cell phone or handheld computer?" Roche asked the Russians. One did, and surrendered the battery, which miraculously fit both Karl's own phone and the SAR radio. Roche was now able to call the aircraft overhead. "This is Halo One, anyone listening up there?"

"Halo, Monitor reads you. Are you ok?"

"Yeah, I linked with Bungie team. Can you patch me through to Pillar?"

"Yeah, just a second." The E-3's comm officer connected the SAR band to the *Reagan*'s air-ops center.

### REAGAN

"Sharkey, what the hell happened?" Deuce demanded as soon as he found out who was on the line, masking his relief with a flash of anger.

"Hey, Deuce. Sorry I didn't check in earlier, but I had to find a new battery for my radio. Don't worry, I'm with the SEALs. What's going on out there?"

"All hell broke lose; there's bad guys all over the place. Pelican is holding with Lifeboat at the outskirts and is waiting for this shitstorm to clear. We're sending another four Grizzlies up there to replace Shade and what's left of Halo. The Air Force is throwing in some Strike Eagles and Raptors to deal with any more surprises. Monitor will assign new callsigns when they come on station. What's going on with your end?"

"Right now this channel is our only comlink. What's the command frequency for Monitor? The SEALs need that band for tactical comms." Deuce gave it to him, and he passed it on to Nathan. "We're leaving the embassy now. There's this tunnel that connects to a secure warehouse somewhere around five-one-alpha-alpha-Lima-golf-zero-zero. From there were going to go to the Dropship wreck and secure for dust-off there."

"That sounds like a good plan."

"Okay, the SEAL commander's on the horn to the AWACS, so I'll save my battery. By the way, did you remote-destruct my SHOC?"

"It doesn't appear to be necessary."

"Well don't do it. I'm going to try and recover the tactical module."

"Roger. Good luck, kid."

"Why's he going to do that?" Hannibal asked when Deuce closed the call.

"Do what?"

"Recover his computer? You saw the video. There is absolutely nothing left of that plane. He's taking a big risk for nothing."

Thompson shrugged. "I don't know about that. The SHOC is supposed to be indestructible. Besides, there's no one alive near the crash site to bother him."

"It's a waste of time and effort though," Cmdr. William Burke insisted.

Deuce gave him a somewhat patronizing smile. "Will, you're going to figure out sooner or later that Roche never wastes his time or his efforts. He's always on an objective, even if he's the only one who can see it. If he thinks he's got a good idea, I wouldn't try and second-guess him." Thompson put another cigar in his mouth.

## CHAPTER 14: THE GAME GETS REAL

### SPECWARCOM, CORONADO, CA – 1900 PST, OCT 15$^{TH}$, 2002

The Chief Petty Officer was screaming at the young men who lay in the sand, shivering in their wet swim trunks. "If you fairies think you're gonna break my heart by flopping around like a bunch of overdosed crack addicts, then you all got mental problems. You all get your sorry asses up. You got a five hour break, now double time it to the canteen while you have the option. Five hours and you're back in the water for night ops. You want dinner, and some water and a bunk, then you better get on over to the canteen. Or just lay there and die. I don't really give half a fuck."

Ensign Roche and the other thirty-seven surviving SEAL recruits were in day five of "hell week." Their original class of seventy-two had been cut nearly in half in the last month. Statistically, it would be cut in half again by the end of the course. Basic Underwater Demolition/Swimmer is the name of the curriculum. BUD/S to the recruits, "the Grinder" to the initiated. Whatever you wanted to call it, it is officially the most brutal Special Forces training program in the world. It is designed to weed out all but the most physically, emotionally and mentally fit soldier-sailors. The majority of applicants will fail under the strain and be carted away sobbing on stretchers to a Navy hospital and reassigned to less demanding tasks. Karl Roche would have none of that.

Roche had applied for the SEALs on September 11, 2002, four months after his graduation and commissioning. At the time he had only wanted to strike back at the evil scum who'd killed nearly three thousand American civilians exactly a year before, and he figured the SEALs would give him a shot. The Navy's Sea, Air, and Land Special Warfare Command is the most elite combat unit in the entire world. SEALs are known for a deadly skill set rivaled only by the British SAS and perhaps by Delta Force, but even they don't dare challenge the SEALs claim to martial superiority in the aquatic realm. Roche already knew how swim, shoot, run, and think on his feet, and he was just mad enough to join up with the meanest hit squad in the world. Someone in the brass liked what he saw in the young officer's file. Roche had participated in a special ops training camp during his last summer in the ROTC, his fitness report was outstanding, and his leadership qualities were highly advanced. Roche's assignment was approved without any hesitation, bypassing the normally required tours of duty. Thirty-two days later, Karl wondered if this had been such a lucky break.

BUD/S consists of a training regimen involving armed and unarmed combat, weapons, ropes, and of course demolition and underwater swimming, interspersed with "exercises" which involved some combination of running, rolling, more swimming and rowing along Coronado beach. SPECWARCOM (the official acronym for the Navy Special Warfare Command) owns two and a half miles of priceless beachfront property on the Southern California coast, called the Naval Amphibious Warfare Training Center. But for the recruits, these shores of paradise feel like the gates of hell. Especially during week five, when all normal training curriculum is suspended and the recruits exercise on the beach for eighteen to twenty hours a day, for eight days straight. Somewhere along the way, most of the recruits will drop in the sand and refuse to move, curling up into little balls and crying. Or else they will pass out trying to swim or row through the surf and need to be rescued by their trainers. Only those who defiantly push their own broken bodies onward will earn the right to wear the coveted trident badge and the custom flippers inscribed with their serial numbers – the only identification of a SEAL.

Now Roche ignored the screamed instructions from CPO Fred Wilson. The canteen was half a mile away. He needed water now. He lay still on the sand, ignoring the pain signals his body was sending him, focusing only on the movements of the instructor. When he turned away, cursing at the few men staggering up the beach, Roche lunged forward and grabbed the chief's water bottle. He drank half a liter of cold water before he got caught.

"What the *hell* are *you* doing?"

"I just thought I'd have some water."

"I done *told* you where you could get your water son, that bottle's *mine*. Boy, are you gonna pay for that."

"Aw, c'mon, Chief. What's the big deal?" asked Ensign Lance Nathan, who had drunk the rest of the chief's water while he was yelling at Roche.

"Oh, you two think you're real funny, doncha? You know what I do to comedians I don't like? I drown 'em. Take out a boat. You leave it with Bob – he's in the same spot, three-quarters of a mile out. Then you are gonna *swim* for your miserable lives back here. You make it back by sundown, you'll earn another drink. Comprende?"

Roche was already up and moving. He and Nathan shoved a rigid inflatable Zodiac boat into the surf, jumped in and started paddling. Paddling a six-hundred-pound boat through four-and-a-half-foot surf is difficult enough with eight men. Doing it with two is ridiculous, and Roche was well beyond where he thought he should have collapsed from sheer exhaustion. To make matters worse, they were heading toward the setting sun, making it impossible to see. After half an hour, they finally made it past the breakers. Nathan collapsed as soon as they got over the last wave. Roche kept paddling. His arms ached more than he had previously imagined possible, but he ignored that. He stood up, cupped his hands over his face, and stared into the western horizon to find Bob's boat silhouetted against the sunset. He found him and struck out, moving faster now, with the tide. He coasted alongside ten minutes later.

"Kid, you look like hell." Bob said, as he tossed Karl a rope. "Why don't you two rest for a few minutes before I have to throw you back in."

"Thanks." Karl lashed the rafts together, and then prodded Nathan awake.

Bob was playing the nice guy today. Tomorrow he'd be yelling along with the other Chiefs. Roche watched him warily as Bob picked up his radio and called the instructor on the beach. "Yeah, they're here."

"That was too fast." The radio squawked back. "Let 'em rest a minute."

Roche suddenly jumped from his boat to the rear of the other, bouncing the chief, who was sitting on the bow, into the water. He ignored Chief Petty Officer Robert Allain's sputtering and cursing as he collected the chief's water and sandwich, and passed them over to Nathan, who devoured half the sandwich and drank slightly over half the water. Then Roche picked up the radio Bob dropped and called "Man overboard." He tossed paddles over the side, and then pulled out the locking pins on Bob's outboard motor, which instantly sank. Bob, by now, had grabbed the side of his zodiac, but he had no success pulling himself in. It's extremely difficult to pull oneself into an inflatable boat. Even for a SEAL, the upper body strength demanded was incredible. Roche thought Bob could probably do it eventually, so he let the trainer hang there. "No hard feelings, eh, Chief?" he asked after he ate the rest of Bob's sandwich and guzzled the last of Bob's water bottle.

"Go to hell!"

"That's the plan."

"Why'd you drop the outboard?" Lance wondered. "We coulda stolen his boat."

Roche shook his head. "It'd be pointless. Wilson would just send us back out."

"What, you think he won't throw us back in anyway, after we've thoroughly ruined Bob's evening?"

"Nah. He hates Chief Allain almost as much as we do."

"Yeah, good point. Okay, let's go." Nathan dove into the water and swam for shore. Roche dove after him, and quickly passed his friend.

Roche felt refreshed, both by his stolen snack and his mischief, but the swim quickly became more difficult than he expected. Swimming had never really been his forte to begin with, but he was normally very good over long distances. This wasn't normal; it was like nothing he'd ever experienced before. Waves of pain coursed through his body in sync with the ocean swells. But as bad as he felt, he knew Nathan was feeling worse. His concern for his friend augmented his reserves of strength and stamina. "C'mon, buddy," he called back between swells. "We're almost there."

"Yeah, right," Nathan coughed. "Don't worry about me. I'm right behind you."

Swimming against the outgoing tide, Roche estimated he was being pushed out at a rate of fifty feet per minute. He settled in to his most efficient stroke and just went for it, checking his position against particular sand dunes on the shoreline, checking back on Nathan to make sure he wasn't slipping too far behind. But Nathan kept up the pace despite his agony, trying for nothing more than a strong finish alongside his friend.

The swim took a little over an hour, but every minute that passed seemed like thirty. By now all of the instructors except the stranded Bob – four chief petty officers and a veteran lieutenant commander – had gathered on the beach. Five minutes before the sun disappeared over the horizon, Roche washed up ten feet from where he entered the water – a superb feat of navigation, considering the circumstances. Nathan crawled up the sand five yards behind. They flopped on the beach, gasping, while the instructors surrounded them.

"Okay guys, give 'em some air."

"Give Nathan a drink before he passes out!"

"Here, kid." Chief Wilson crouched and gave him a Gatorade sport bottle, which Lance Nathan grasped weakly and sucked dry. Karl

Roche was already on his feet, and he accepted a water bottle from the commander.

"I can't believe you guys did that," Lt Cmdr. Pastis declared. "Bob should have followed you guys back."

"Bob... might need some help..." Nathan said, still gasping for air. "He fell out of his boat..."

The chief who sent him out looked down at the young ensign in amazement, then turned his stare to Roche, who only shrugged. "Crazy bastards. I don't see we have any choice, Commander. We gotta give these kids a couple sets of tridents and flippers."

## 40 MILES WEST OF AL KUT, IRAQ
## 1924 LOCAL, MARCH 19TH, 2003

*"Just like a video game," they said. Point, shoot, move. It's like Halo, or Counterstrike. Just relax, but be alert. Like you're playing a video game.* Roche had his crosshairs centered on a man with a white hat and an old Republican Guard camouflage jacket. Roche had been watching him through a sixteen-power scope for the last quarter of an hour, and it was obvious he was a leader. Holding his twenty-three pound rifle steady, Roche zoomed out to the 2x power setting. Forty-six Iraqi soldiers were in his view, along with a van carrying an old, but functional Soviet-made air-search radar set, as well as an ancient half-track, and an SA-6 missile battery on a trailer. This mobile SAM unit had downed an Air Force A-10 Warthog and at least two Marine helicopters in the area recently. In a very few minutes the entire unit would be wiped out.

Roche made sure his rifle was steady on its bipod, and then raised his left hand to tap his earpiece. He whispered into the microphone on his jacket collar. "Lead has shot. Travis? You have the radio?"

Petty Officer Second Class Travis Williams, the squad's best sniper, answered. "Affirmative; sparks will fly." Williams was further west along the ridge, in a position to shoot the equipment inside the van.

This squad of twelve men from second battalion, SEAL Team Three was under Lt. jg. Karl Roche's command. They'd been in-country for three days, and spent most of it riding helicopters and Humvees to get to this ridge in the middle of nowhere. But this area was strategic, because at least one Iraqi mixed brigade of armor and mechanized infantry was taking cover in the surrounding hills, and the main highway to Baghdad went right through them. The invasion force could not proceed without air support, and air support would not be available until the mobile SAMs were knocked out. The Iraqi army had learned a lesson from the first Gulf War, keeping their SAMs moving and only activating their radar when they had visually acquired a target, in order to hide from the Wild Weasel strike fighters that had decimate the air defenses over a decade ago.

Roche's squad had spent the afternoon planning this attack. It was a fairly orthodox plan by SEAL standards. Roche and Williams would snipe from cover, and take out the leaders and the communication equipment. Then the squad would advance downhill and fill the gully with sub-machinegun fire. The maneuver was textbook – or it would have been if the Grinder had ever been a textbook course. Roche relied on input from his top NCO, Senior Chief Petty Officer Matt Bowers. The experienced chief walked the rookie lieutenant through the planning stages and set him up for a fool-proof first op. Bowers had never trusted the word "fool-proof" – he'd learned long ago that the only way to make something fool-proof was to keep it away from fools. Roche was no fool, though – Bowers saw that immediately. The freshly minted officer had all the right stuff for the SEALs. The senior commanders saw this to, and felt confidant enough in his ability to put him straight to work against the enemy.

The sun had just set. It was time to kill. Roche focused again on the white-hat officer. He was facing away, talking to the technicians inside the van. Roche had the crosshairs on his ear, adjusted for the slight west wind and the depression of the bullet's trajectory over two hundred and twenty yards. That distance was nothing for the gun he was holding – an M87 ELR McMillan .50 caliber – it could kill a man from ten times this range. The shot would be almost impossible to miss with such a powerful and accurate weapon, but Roche took no chances with his work. *Video game.* He double-checked his settings, held his breath, and forced his right eye to stay open as he pulled the trigger.

The delayed gas operation, muzzle brake and padded stock minimized recoil, but the gun still had enormous kick. But Roche was practiced, and held his aim on the target. For the fraction of a second that the bullet was in flight, he watched the man. It is impossible to completely silence a fifty-caliber bullet leaving a gun at 3000 feet per second, but the huge cylindrical suppressor screwed over the barrel did a pretty good job. The officer couldn't have heard the shot, anyway – the supersonic bullet reached him long before the crack of sound did –

but perhaps he felt a pang from his sense of danger as he turned his head to face the oncoming bullet. His eyes widened, and then crossed as he watched the huge slug spiral toward his own forehead. Roche watched with morbid fascination; the facial features were distorted hideously by the torque of the spinning shard of metal. The hollow-point round shattered on impact, ripping out the entire contents of his skull. Blood and gore splattered in a wide circle around the body.

It took Roche's mind a moment to realize that he had just caused the gruesome carnage below. *I just killed that guy. Horribly. The video game is real.*

Ping! Ping! The sound of fast bullets hitting metal snapped Roche from the moment of remorse and reflection. *Travis got the van. Kill the other officers.* Roche zoomed out to 4x power and found a man in a tanker's helmet, running toward the van. Time slowed in his mind as he tracked the target, leading the crosshair just in front of the officer's chest. He worked the bolt-action loading mechanism as he refined his aim. *Shoot. No, I can't, not now that I know what it looks like, what it feels like... forget what it feels like! This is your job! You signed up for this, remember why!* An image came through the noise in his mind: the American flag draped above the gaping hole in the side of the Pentagon. Roche tightened his grip on the gun and squeezed hard on the trigger. Roche watched, this time without pity, as the running target bent in half, somersaulted in mid-air, and tumbled to the ground with an empty ribcage.

*Next target.* Roche remembered a guy that was inspecting the missiles a few seconds ago. He was now standing in the same place, shouting and waving his pistol. The man died before Roche pulled the trigger. Travis had fired first, and his bullet was an armor-piercing incendiary round, which sliced through the back of the officer's head and punched into a missile casing. The old warhead and its frayed electronics absorbed the shock without any resistance; it detonated and took the other five missiles on the trailer with it. The fireball blinded Roche's right eye for a moment, but he didn't miss a beat. He switched the weapon to his left side, picked out a moving shape silhouetted against the fire. The bullet hit the man's leg above the knee, and a massive spurt of blood indicated that he was missing a good chunk of his femoral artery.

A flurry of activity grabbed Roche's attention. He moved the gun back to his right side after making sure his eye could focus again, and zoomed on the half-track. Two men were standing in the back of the vehicle, tossing assault rifles to the soldiers who had started to

300

organize themselves. Roche zoomed all the way in with the scope to find the vehicle's fuel tank, loaded an incendiary round in the chamber, and fired. The explosion was not quite as spectacular as the simultaneous detonation of half a dozen missiles, but it had quite an affect on the enemy. The rear end of the half-track blew apart, launching bodies and guns in all directions.

About thirty surviving soldiers, mostly armed with AK-47s, now stood around the encampment, leaderless, unsure of what to do. Some fired blindly into the hills; others ran heedlessly away from the destruction. But a few figured out what was going on and concentrated their fire in the general direction of the two snipers.

Roche called to his team over the radio. "Okay, guys. Stick to your zones and watch your ammo. And for crying out loud, don't get killed." The other ten SEALs responded with their Heckler & Koch MP-5/sd5 submachine guns. The German-made 9mm weapon is widely regarded to be the finest in its class. The SEALs hidden near the base of the ridge tore through the Iraqis with accurate automatic fire.

Roche watched for a few seconds before bullets started bouncing off nearby rocks. *Time to move.* Roche slid down the slope on his belly, holding the rifle above his head with one arm, dragging his gear bag in the other. He crawled twenty yards down the hill to a new spot he'd picked out in advance and pulled the five-round magazine from the rifle and reloaded. Somewhere off to his left, Williams was doing the same.

Despite the fresh shock of the attack and the loss of leadership, the Iraqis regrouped quickly. As soon as the SEALs started shooting, the Republican Guard soldiers figured out basically where the enemy was. They charged up the hill, shooting at moving shapes, guessing where the silent 9mm slugs were coming from, blasting back with the noisy Kalashnikovs. One rookie SEAL took a bullet in the arm, and a veteran petty officer received a glancing blow off his body armor. The SEALs own fire, guided by night vision gear and shooting downhill, was far more effective.

Roche watched his men through his scope, saving his ammo for major threats. He got one about thirty seconds into the firefight. A SEAL stopped shooting, dropped his MP, and raised his arms. Roche zoomed out and saw an enemy soldier aiming an AK at the SEAL. Roche recognized his man as SEAL 3rd class Patrick Sherman – they were classmates in the Grinder. Without a shred of hesitation, Roche took a snap shot that hit the enemy's right shoulder at three times the speed of sound, abruptly separating about five different bones and ligaments. Sherman jumped up, whipped out his sidearm and finished off the wounded soldier that had jumped him.

The SEALs were thorough, but three Iraqis broke through the perimeter and moved up the hill. "Check fire," Roche ordered. He couldn't risk his men hitting each other with cross-fire, or shooting up the hill toward him. Likewise, he couldn't fire downhill with the McMillan, for fear of hitting his own SEALs. "Flanking maneuver, come up the hill toward my position. Do not shoot without pos-ident."

He set the rifle aside and pulled his Desert Eagle .50AE out of the bag, checked the ammo and clicked off the safety. He'd had a long debate with Lance Nathan while the two new SEAL officers were selecting their personal sidearms. They had a lot of choices besides the two pistols that were SEAL-standard-issue, and Roche picked the most powerful handgun in the world. It was true that the American-designed, Israeli-built Desert Eagle had plenty of drawbacks. It was too big and heavy to carry comfortably, it only had a seven-round magazine, it had a notorious design flaw that caused jamming if it was held wrong, and the massive recoil made it very difficult to fire on the move, which Roche was now trying to do. *On the other hand,* he had said, and now repeated the thought, *it only takes one shot to put someone down permanently.*

The twilight was fading into evening darkness as Roche moved slowly downhill, with his night-vision goggles over his head and holding the big pistol with both hands. He listened and watched for movement as he himself moved silently and invisibly. He spotted a hunched figure eighty yards down the hill, cradling an assault rifle and moving up the slope. His men all carried smaller submachine guns, so this was definitely a bad guy. *That's Pos-ident.* Roche took a few steps to the right to get a better line of sight on the figure, then crouched and waited. When the soldier closed within fifty yards, Roche fired the powerful pistol. The Iraqi walked right into the huge bullet, which entered just below the collar bone and knocked him flat on his back, with a shattered spine and a bisected windpipe.

The other two Iraqis following the first man saw him go down and they dove for cover. Roche shot one in the leg before he disappeared behind a bush. He ignored the screams and moved toward the last one, who had gone under a rocky outcropping. Roche sidestepped to get below him, lifted his goggles off his eyes and squinted into the dark space under the rock. A gleam of moonlight off the stamped metal Kalashnikov gave away the frightened warrior. He

302

aimed a little to the left of the shiny metal and fired twice. The man staggered out, clutching his shattered elbow. He took one last bullet between the shoulders and died.

A few seconds later he other man's screaming was cut off by the signature, soft *bap!bap!bap!* report of a silenced MP-5. Soon the SEALs came out of the shadows around their leader, each grinning widely under their goggles and black face paint. "Area secured, sir."

## SEAL TEAM 3 HQ, COBRA BASE, ABU GHURAYB
## THREE WEEKS LATER

Roche and Lt. Commander Ames, his battalion's commanding officer, discussed Roche's next assignment. Roche had just returned from an extended recon mission. Ames brought him up to speed. "What's left of the Republican Guard has linked up with the Ba'athist militia and they're fighting us guerilla-style all over Baghdad. We need to locate and secure a weapons depot in the Jabbur industrial district."

"Okay, what's the situation in the target area?"

"I don't know. The CIA is sending one of their agents to give us their intel. They've apparently infiltrated the Ba'ath resistance pretty well."

A helicopter approached the building to land outside and the noise quickly made conversation impossible. "This must be him!" the CO shouted to Roche.

The chopper was a Marine AH-1w Cobra attack model, one of the fastest helicopters in the world. The intel man jumped from the front seat – where the gunner normally sat – as soon as the gunship landed. He followed a Marine guard inside to the SEAL commander's office. Roche noted he was dressed for the field, wearing cargo shorts and a khaki windbreaker. His skin was darkly tanned, and Roche guessed he may have also been part American Indian. He carried thick folders and a satchel case for a notebook computer – obviously he had plenty of new data. "Hi, I'm from intel. Agent... uh, you can call me 'Mr. C.'"

"What, your real name is classified?" Roche asked.

"Matter of fact, it is, kid. The CIA does try to protect its field agents." Mr. C had many names, each as real as the expertly forged passports that identified him. The only documents that had his real name on them were buried in a vault at Langley. He used a dozen other names depending on the cover he was using. No cover was needed at the moment. He could operate behind American lines ostensibly at the service of the military, but he still avoided using names. "I've got a briefing to deliver. Who's in charge here?"

"I am," the CO said. "Lieutenant Commander Arnold Ames, second battalion, SEAL Team Three."

"I'll just call you 'Commander.' Who's this?"

"This is Lieutenant junior grade Karl Roche, who will be leading the strike based on your intel."

Mr. C gave Karl a funny look and asked Ames "How old is he?"

"I'm twenty-three, sir," Roche answered.

"He's new, but he's proven to be very good at our line of work," Ames added.

The man called Mr. C knew all about Karl Roche. He was talking down do the young officer only to test a man whose career he'd followed closely. The Agency had actually marked him as a potential recruit during his last summer in college. They scouted him at a special CIA/SOCOM cross-training camp, where cadets are taught covert-ops, unarmed combat, explosives, and special weapons, all unaware that the CIA was monitoring them. All of Roche's scores were unbelievably high, which facilitated his inclusion to the SEALs. Roche was also highly intelligent; his IQ at the lower end of genius-range. He could learn languages very quickly, and spoke three besides English almost fluently. Furthermore, he could cope phenomenally well in highly stressful circumstances. The CIA needed only to look at Roche's college career to learn this.

The Agency also considered his medical report, and discovered him to be a remarkable specimen. In addition to all-around athleticism at near-Olympic levels, Roche possessed a few highly beneficial physical abnormalities. Roche had practiced martial arts since the age of six, and did breaks – smashing bricks and two-by-fours. This repeated strain, if carefully checked, causes the bones to form tiny fractures that heal rapidly and gradually increasing the density of the skeletal structure. The bones in Karl's limbs were now six times denser than the average person; almost unbreakable. Beyond this, Roche had extremely keen visual acuity, especially at night. His eyes adjusted to changing light conditions rapidly and he could see better in the dark than any normal person, with or without light-enhancing goggles. Also he had a curious mental condition that eliminated normal fear-based inhibitions. He could react in extremely dangerous circumstances without being influenced by fear.

304

The CIA wanted Roche. They were extremely disappointed when he turned them down without a second thought and later joined the SEALs. They would pursue him later, perhaps, if he left the service at a relatively young age. But the Navy would be getting Roche at his prime. Already, he had personally killed dozens of terrorist operatives and Iraqi soldiers, and led his squad with distinction. Mr. C was far more impressed by the young man standing in front of him than he would ever let on.

After leading the op on the SAM site, Karl Roche's squad had participated in fifteen different patrols and raids, all successful. They had quickly distinguished themselves as the most effective Special Forces squad engaged in Operation: Iraqi Freedom, having killed or captured hundreds of enemy troops in just over three weeks. Roche's SEALs themselves had suffered no casualties or injuries worse than minor flesh wounds. This was thanks in part to their weapons and their training; but mostly, the men all agreed, thanks to Lt. jg. Roche's unique approach to mission planning. He approached every situation with the assumption that his men could overcome any odds, and they did, because they believed him.

CPO Bowers, the senior NCO in the squad, was tasked with analyzing and reporting the individual abilities of the squad members to SEAL Team HQ. When he was assigned to the rookie L-T, he assumed he would have to babysit Roche until he felt his way into a comfortable combat role. Bowers had been prepared to virtually run the platoon himself. He found out that first night at the SAM site that this would be unnecessary. In his op reports, Bowers praised Roche's cold, clear and efficient leadership. Bowers found himself looking up to the rookie, who already seemed more comfortable with combat than Bowers ever had. This was coming from a veteran who had been through Desert Storm, Bosnia, Yugoslavia, and Afghanistan. Mr. C had seen all these reports; he knew all about Lt. Karl Roche.

"I'm sure he's good," the agent said. "All you guys are supposed to be the 'best-of-the-best,' right? Twenty-three, that's not much younger than I was when I started working in the field. Okay, Lieutenant, let me show you what I have." The briefing took two hours, as Mr. C pored over maps, satellite and camera drone pictures, and a thorough description from memory of the neighborhood. He narrowed the target down to a six-block area. "One more thing: we need to know exactly what they've got in there. After your team secures the site, and before you blow the warehouse inside out, we need you to take an inventory."

"That might take a while, and leave us vulnerable to counter-attack. We were thinking more of a hit-and-run sort of mission."

"You don't need to count every thing. Just list what types you find and kinda estimate how much they have. You can still blow it up as you leave. Make sure you bring a couple of guys who specialize in weapon identification."

"Sir, we're all experts," Roche told him. "Any of us could tell you whether an AK was license-built in Slovakia or Singapore just by looking at it."

"Okay. Just try to be careful down there. There's no way of knowing if there's anybody in there or not, but I wouldn't advise firing blindly."

Roche became sarcastic. "Oh, I hadn't realized that shooting in a warehouse full of munitions would be a bad idea. I had actually planned on bringing some flamethrowers and thermite grenades to clear the place out. You really think that might be dangerous?"

"Sorry."

"We can handle it, sir. Don't you worry about a thing."

## JUBBAH, SOUTHERN BAGHDAD – FOUR HOURS LATER

"We've got the perimeter, L-T," Bowers reported. "Wild Turkey reports no movement."

Roche looked up as one of the Whiskey Cobras clattered overhead. "That doesn't mean anything. The bad guys are gonna be staying indoors while those choppers are here. Okay, bring the squad in. We'll check these warehouses one by one." Roche's team had set a closed perimeter around the first block. Bowers sent the order by radio.

Williams had something to report. "One of the warehouses on the south side of the block is boarded and nailed up shut, but there were fresh tire marks and oil spills in the loading dock. I think that might be our target."

"Okay, good call. Did you see any activity around it?"

"Nothing. The Iraqis are keeping their heads down. And they're staying down as long as those Cobras are here."

"Bowers and I were just discussing that. The complete lack of activity out here means precisely nothing. Maybe the overheads will tell us something though." Roche turned to Bowers. "Where's our laptop, chief?"

306

"Cabbage has it." SEAL 1$^{st}$ class Bernie "Cabbage" Coles was a big, black man with a very round head. Bowers called him up to their position with the squad's Panasonic Toughbook computer – a powerful laptop with a rugged carbon-fiber frame.

"Bernie, pull up all the drone photos from the last twenty-four hours." Roche ordered. Then he watched as Coles scrolled through megabytes of still and video footage from the all-seeing Predator and Global Hawk drones. He scanned the data as quickly as the satellite link could download the files. Some of the stills he recognized from his briefing, and he saw some new images that showed Iraqis entering and leaving the building. "Three guys walk in at 1500, three guys leave an hour later, they look like the same people. A truck drives out at 1945…"

"I told you," Williams said.

"…and that's it. This helps confirm the target, but it doesn't tell us much about what's going on inside. Let's check it out ourselves."

Williams led the way to the warehouse. It wasn't a very large building; just a single-story, about twenty yards square. Bowers knocked on a door and got no response. He kicked it in. Still nothing. "They don't want to come out and play," he observed. "Do we get to use the scout, sir?"

"I guess we have to. I am not walking in there unless I know for sure it's empty. If anyone's hiding in there they could have more weapons on hand than the entire Canadian Army."

The "scout" was actually a remote-control car – much like a toy from Radio Shack – armed with a digital video camera and a spray can of incapacitating nerve gas. Bowers unpacked it and used the computer to drive it inside. The front of the building was deserted. Bowers drove along the wall until he found a circuit breaker. Bowers manipulated the scout's arm to extend and flip the switches. All the lights came on in the warehouse. Bowers backed up and panned the camera.

"Would you look at that!" Coles exclaimed. The warehouse was packed with weapons, but there was no sign of life.

Bowers drove around a little longer and fired bursts of gas into dark corners, but the little remote control car found no guards. "It looks like it's clear, L-T."

"Let's move in then. Travis and, uh, Yao," Roche selected a 19-year-old rookie SEAL 2$^{nd}$ class, "stay out here and watch the road. That little guard shack there will give you good sightlines."

Four Iraqis were watching the American helicopters from an abandoned factory up the street. They knew their comrades would be returning to the weapons dump shortly to arm for a raid on the American camp at the airport, but the helicopters made it impossible for a large group to approach the building in the open. After a brief deliberation, the four men decided to sneak in and get some RPGs, and hopefully bring down the Marine gunships.

The weapons stockpile inside was impressive. Orderly piles of AK's and Uzis and crates of ammunition constituted the bulk of the supply, but there were also drums of fuel, RPG-7 rocket launchers, and stacks of bigger missiles all over the place. "Okay," Roche called, "who wants to play accountant while the rest of us check these crates?"

SEAL 1st class Mike Ramirez used to work in a warehouse in Long Beach – he elected to sit down with the computer and make an inventory while the others rummaged through the stash and called out weapon types and estimated quantities.

"You know," Bowers grunted as he moved a heavy crate, "If I'd wanted to do this kind of work, I would have just kept working for Schick when I left high school."

"The careful movers," Patrick Sherman laughed as he gently lowered a fragile missile casing.

"Hey guys," Yao called on the radio, "I hate to interrupt your house-warming party, but we got uninvited guests."

"What's that, Yao?"

Williams answered: "We're tracking movement. They're being really sneaky, moving through the buildings on this side of the street, watching the choppers. I don't think they've noticed us quite yet."

"Trav, it would be excellent for them not to ever know about us."

"Copy." Williams sighted with his McMillan, waiting for the enemy soldiers to come out in the open. One of the Iraqis peered out of a doorway, looked for the helicopters, and waited until both were facing away. Then he led his men out into the street. Williams fired four shots in rapid succession.

The crack of the fifty-caliber rifle echoed through the warehouse. Roche picked up his radio. "Did that take care of our problem Trav?"

"What problem?"

The gunshots were heard by another group of Republican Guards, also hiding from the Marine choppers. These ones were right across the street from the guard shack where Williams and Yao were staked out. Their leader peered at them through a window for a few seconds, and then reached for a grenade.

The window behind Williams shattered and a small object struck him in the back. "What the hell?" He turned and saw the grenade rolling into the corner of the shack. "Oh shit, get down!" He grabbed Yao, knocked over a desk, and dragged himself and the rookie behind it. Two walls blew out and the roof collapsed on top of the SEALs. The heavy sheet of corrugated metal fell on the sniper's leg, pinning him in place.

"Thanks for saving my butt. Are you okay?" Yao asked.

"Yeah, I think... no, my leg is stuck." Travis swore as he tried to move. "Where did that grenade come from?"

The SEALs in the warehouse had heard the explosion. "What's going out there?" Roche asked on the radio.

"I don't know," Williams answered. "Someone threw a grenade at us. Were okay, but my leg is pinned and I think it's broken."

"Yao, if you can, look around and see who's out there."

Yao had been lying in the doorway so he was free to move. He crawled out and looked across the street. A hail of bullets drove him back behind the wrecked shed. "Four RGs with AKs. They got us pinned down."

Roche overheard on the radio and accurately imagined the scene. The two SEALs were outgunned, armed as they were with only two SIG-Sauer pistols and Yao's MP. The big bolt-action sniper rifle would be almost useless with Williams stuck under the wreckage. "Wait there," he ordered. "The Cobras will come back and cover you."

Yao didn't want to wait. "I'm making a break for it."

"Don't move, dumb-ass!" Travis snapped, but the rookie ignored him. Yao could run pretty fast, but he couldn't outrun bullets. He took two in the back and went down hard, rolling across the pavement. One of the Iraqis closed in quickly and stabbed Yao in the chest with his bayonet.

Williams didn't see what happened to the rookie, but he heard the shooting. *That dumb kid.* He peered out through a crack and pulled his rifle into an awkward firing position. One of the soldiers walked into his sights and Williams fired a bullet through his abdomen. The other three soldiers saw their friend disemboweled, and they emptied their guns on the guard shack. Williams knew he was in trouble. He screamed loudly, and then abruptly silenced himself. He stayed motionless, letting the Iraqis assume they'd killed him.

Roche assumed the same thing, listening to the radio. "Oh my God, I think they're both dead."

Bowers and Coles were at the front door. "We can't get out there sir. We have no cover and they'll have us ranged."

"Okay," Roche was thinking fast. "Cover the doorway while we figure out how to open the doors at the loading dock. Maybe we can flank them. And where are those choppers?"

"Wild Turkey, this is Jägermeister. We're pinned down in the warehouse and we have two men down outside. We need you back here, now!"

"Copy that Jäger. We're right on top of you." The SEALs could already hear the noisy helicopters moving in over their heads, and soon they heard the 20mm rotary cannons firing away.

The Iraqis scattered and ran for cover. Two got cut down. The third ran straight for the warehouse. He got five steps into the door before he realized he was surrounded by armed men.

"Waqafa!" Roche shouted, using the most basic Arabic command he knew. *Stop right there!*

The Iraqi looked around, dropped his AK-47, raised his hands, and abruptly dove behind a pile of sandbags. The SEALs followed him with streams of gunfire. Before he died, the Iraqi soldier tossed something over his makeshift wall.

Roche heard the distinctive metallic *clink* sound of the grenade bouncing off the cement floor. He watched in horror as it rolled to a stop next to a 55-gallon drum of gasoline and a crate of explosives. Roche's thoughts moved at light speed; he considered that he had maybe three seconds before the warehouse went up in a mushroom cloud taking him, his other nine men, and the two helicopters with it. Without further calculation, he pounced on the grenade, slapped it away from the combustibles, and drove it into the sandbags with his left shoulder, burying it under his own body. In the instant before the charge went off, he looked up at Matt Bowers. The shocked expression on his chief's face was the last thing he saw.

As the doctors later explained to him, the concussion of the grenade knocked him unconscious before he could feel the intense pain.

310

The other SEALs watched, horrified, as the muffled blast tore through their leader's body. But the hot shrapnel never touched anything that could burn. The instantaneous reaction and sacrifice of Lt. Roche saved their lives. Bowers recovered his composure quickly, and worked fast to regroup the squad. He carried out the lieutenant himself, and ordered Coles and Sherman to find Williams and Yao. Williams had a broken leg, and was bleeding from several minor bullet wounds and several more cuts. The other SEALs dug him out of the hut. Yao had passed out from shock and blood loss. The hole between his ribs made a sucking sound as blood drained into his punctured lung.

Bowers got on the radio. "This is Jägermeister, calling command. I need immediate, repeat, *immediate* extraction of wounded!"

A big Marine Super Stallion helicopter was waiting nearby, and arrived within five minutes. While they waited, Bowers ordered PO2 Louie Morris, the team's explosives expert, to rig a small charge to blow up the munitions dump behind them. Louie used a radio detonator once the chopper was safely clear, and the whole block disappeared in a passable imitation of Hiroshima, 1945. "Nice firework show, Louie." Bowers said. He turned to the Marine medic attending to the wounded. "How are they?"

"This guy will be okay," the Medic replied, indicating Travis Williams, who looked up and gave a weak wave, then grimaced and tightened his tourniquet. "But the other two are in trouble. We have to get them straight to one of the carriers. I don't think the local hospitals can handle this." Many of the hospitals in Iraq's capital had been flattened in the Shock and Awe bombardment, and those still standing in the Green Zone were deemed woefully inadequate by the coalition military doctors. Most of the critically injured Allied troops were being flown out to the aircraft carriers *Abraham Lincoln* and *John C. Stennis*, which were stationed as close to the shore as possible in support of the continuing operation.

"Pilot! How fast can you get us out there?"

"Two hours. I'm running full tilt, Senior Cheif. We'll have to slow down to refuel though. My cope is arranging for a tanker now." Over his big headphones, which made communication barely possible in the noisy, three-engine helicopter, Bowers could hear the copilot calling to a temporary Marine airfield to rendezvous with an MC-130 multi-purpose transport and arrange an aerial refueling.

Bowers turned back to the medic. "How are their chances, doc?"

"Bad," the medic said, indicating Yao before pointing to Lt. Roche, "and worse." He looked grimly at the lieutenant, who was completely soaked in blood and appeared to be held together only by the wet red dressings that barely covered the holes in his body, and the two SEALs applying pressure to the most critical wounds. "I've used up every inch of gauze in my medkit and he's bleeding right through it. I honestly can't believe he's still alive, but I don't think he will be for long. I gave him some Remifentanil to slow his heart rate and drop his blood pressure. That'll give him more time before he bleeds out, but without more dressings, there's really nothing else I can do for him."

Bowers tore up his t-shirt and then attacked the nylon seat fabric with his knife. The other SEALs caught on and did the same. The startled medic took a minute to figure out what they were up too, but he understood when the fabric began piling up next to Roche's stretcher. He plugged the lieutenant's wounds with the rags, still expecting the young man to die on him at any moment. But the improvised dressings staunched the blood flow, and Karl Roche still clung to life when the big chopper landed on the *Stennis*.

Roche was on life support for three days while doctors slowly added blood to his damaged system. He spent a total of sixteen hours in surgery while Navy doctors removed gravel, wood splinters, metal shrapnel and bone fragments from his shattered body. His skull was split apart, and the whole left side had to be replaced with a ceramic plate. He also needed extensive work on his left lung. Half of the *Lincoln*'s medical staff was flown to the other ship to assist with the surgeries. Yao had been saved by the tube the medic had placed in his knife wound to keep him form drowning in his own blood, but he wasn't in much better shape than the lieutenant. He was put on a respirator while awaiting a lung transplant. The rest of SEAL squad never left the sick bay while waiting for their comrades to recover.

Roche woke up after spending four days in a concussion-induced coma. The first thing he saw was Bowers, again. "Ooh, that really stings. Where am I?" He asked.

Looking at SEALs – tough, impassive, professional soldiers – you would think it impossible for them to weep. Yet occasionally they do, sometimes under the trauma of the Grinder, and then sometimes in situations like this. All ten conscious members of the squad were streaming tears as their lieutenant returned from his near-dead state.

*    *    *

After Roche was stabilized, he was flown to Bethesda Naval Hospital in Maryland, where his dad used to work. A specialist from Stryker Orthopedics in New Jersey installed an artificial shoulder made of high-stress plastics, over which one of the best reconstructive surgeons in the world grafted blood vessels and nerve, muscle and skin tissue. By Memorial Day, he was finally able to move his arm again.

But the new shoulder would never be able to rotate properly, which meant he couldn't swim, which meant he was physically disqualified as an active SEAL. At first, this news hurt him more than his wounds. He also started having nightmares, remembering the people he had killed, seeing their gore splatter and their corpses twist unnaturally as his .50 caliber bullets punched through them. He was sliding dangerously into depression, and it took several months of counseling with a Navy therapist, a chaplain, and the pastor of the church he grew up in before he could be at peace with his actions and look toward his future.

He had other visitors. Mr. Jarrod E. Casey – the new Deputy Director of Operations of the Central Intelligence Agency – dropped by. He personally – although, Roche thought, somewhat insincerely – expressed the gratitude and concern of the CIA in general, and the anonymous Mr. C in particular. Later he got a whole boatload of brass in his hospital room for a little ceremony. His battalion CO, Commander Ames; Rear Admiral Dale Hawes, the head of SPECWARCOM; the C-in-C of the Pacific Fleet, Admiral Terrence Marsh; and finally some senator all crowded around his bed. The senator was Brett McNeil; he had once served in the SEALs himself, and now served on the Senate Armed Forces Committee. They informed him that he was hereby promoted to full lieutenant, and that he had been awarded several medals. They presented him with the Purple Heart, for being wounded in battle, and the Navy Cross, for conspicuous bravery and sacrifice above and beyond the call of duty.

He'd always hated hearing that phrase "above and beyond the call of duty" in connection with any of his actions, no matter how heroic anyone else deemed them to be. He had always considered his duty to be whatever it takes to protect the lives of the men he was responsible for. Because after all, only two things really matter on the battlefield: the mission, and the man next to you.

And sometimes, not even the mission seems all that important.

# CHAPTER 15: HELL BREAKS LOOSE

## SAFETY CORRIDOR, 180 MI. SOUTH OF TEHRAN
## 1500 LOCAL, JUNE 1$^{ST}$

Six B-52s waited in a racetrack pattern, packed with enough ordnance to flatten a small city by themselves. The bombing of Tehran had been suspended during the joint extraction operation, but they still had several targets left to destroy.

"Warhammer One, this is CENTCOM," the radio called.

"CENTCOM, Warhammer reads," Major Jesse Bermudez replied from the cockpit of the lead B-52.

"Warhammer, new targets identified: one hidden airstrip northwest of city, one crashed C-130 in an industrial lot north of city center. Coordinates are being uploaded."

"Huh." Lt. Presley, Warhammer-1's bombardier looked over the coordinates in his target list. "This crash site is at the same coordinate grid as a couple of our secondaries. Looks like it's right between a couple of factories we're supposed to knock out. Any chance we can kill three birds with one mother of a stone?"

"You mean that big momma in our forward bomb bay?"

"That's what I mean."

Bermudez went back to the radio. "CENTCOM, we have a target area overlap at that crash site. We suggest MOAB deployment, over."

"Ah, roger, Warhammer. Massive Ordnance Airburst would be considered an expedient measure for that target area. Stand by for strike order, over."

## TEHRAN – SAME TIME

It could be difficult for someone to imagine the aftermath of thirteen and a half tons of high explosive and a few thousand gallons of jet fuel blowing up all at once, but it is pretty nasty. In this case, the two JDAM bombs had dug a crater out the middle of a city street, and the Hornet and the ammo truck had fallen into that and then exploded together. Most of the energy of the ammo truck's blast was directed upward, but it took the whole military convoy with it. This left a massive hole in the middle of the road, and absolutely no visible trace of the American jet that caused the explosion of the first place.

Roche, Carter and Coles moved six blocks through the bombed-out city, sneaking through alleyways and empty buildings, and finally stumbled across a scene of nearly-unimaginable destruction. Carter walked out the front door of small restaurant and fell into the crater yelling a curse.

"Are you ok?"

"No. Yes. Yeah, I can stand up."

Roche looked over the edge of the hole and saw Carter standing on a broken pipe twenty feet below. "We'll get you out of there, kid. Okay, Cabbage, find a couple tablecloths back there and let's make a rope." Coles didn't answer. He was staring up at a T-80 turret sticking out of a fourth-floor window. "Bernie!"

"Right, make a rope outta tablecloths. Got it."

"And Carter, next time you find a door blown off its hinges from the other side, be more careful about walking through it."

"I'll remember that."

Coles came back to the door with sixteen feet of makeshift rescue line and helped Roche haul Carter out of the pit. "You didn't happen to see a black ceramic case the size of a cereal box did you?" Roche asked.

"Are you kidding? The ruins of the Lost City of Atlantis might be down there and you'd never pick out an identifiable piece."

"He's got a point, Commander," Coles said. "Your plane got blown eight ways from Sunday, and if that computer did survive, it could be anywhere."

Carter brushed the dust off of himself. "As likely as not it's in a thousand tiny pieces each individually buried under a pile of rubble and melted like a-"

"It's over there." Karl pointed to a hole in a wall up the block.

"WHAT?"

"Based on the mass of the section of the aircraft forward of the main fuel cell, forward momentum, orientation of the-"

"Okay, rocket scientist, let's check it out." Carter led the way to the building that seemed about to collapse, but was propped up on one corner by the hulk of some sort of tracked vehicle. He cautiously stepped through an enlarged window and swore loudly once more.

Roche winced. "Tell me you didn't fall down again."

"No! It's here!"

"Really?" Roche and Coles followed Carter and saw, in all its glory, the titanium bathtub-shaped piece of airframe that protected the Super Hornet's cockpit. In the same room there were several other bits of airplane. Coles picked up a piece of shiny blue composite material that had been part of the skin. "Nice paint job," he said.

"Yeah, it was."

"Sorry your ride got all messed up like this, sir."

"Eh, don't worry about it. I got a bunch more just like it." Roche removed the half-melted display panels inside the cockpit and started rummaging through computer parts. "Here we go." He held aloft what looked like a solid piece of black ceramic.

Carter stared. "Well, I am very impressed that you found that thing. Now, explain to me again how that helps us get out of this god-awful country?" Roche ignored Carter and removed the outer case with his SOG. "And now you tell me that thing survived something just short of a nuclear blast, and you can take it apart with a knife?"

"This, my funny little friend, can interface with Nathan's laptop and receive realtime tactical data from the EA-18's flying overhead-" a roar of jet engines cut him off. "Like that one."

"How could you tell what plane that was?"

"Engine noise. The GE F-414 engine has a unique signature that-"

"Okay, okay, I'm sorry I asked. Can we get the hell outta here now?"

Roche had been right. Using the computer they were able to patch in to the tactical picture generated by the Growlers' computers, and find their way through the city to the MC-130's crash site while avoiding Iranian patrols. Everything the sophisticated Navy warplanes could see, the SEALs saw. Roche had led the entire group through a maze of alleys, warehouses and industrial lots until they came to the loading yard where the transport plane had crashed.

But even after seeing the disaster left by the Hornet's impact, the SEALs were unprepared to comprehend the scale of the devastating wreck of the big transport plane they had just bailed out of. The SEALs said nothing; they just gaped at the ruin and tried to comprehend their narrow escape from the transport. The plane was facing them, upside down, and surrounded by the debris and wreckage it produced when it came down and skidded backwards across the lot.

The area was eerily silent, which made the atmosphere all the more disturbing. Roche had the SEALs cautiously advance and secure the yard. It was surrounded by an industrial plant on one side, a locked-up warehouse on the other, and high walls on either end. The only way in or out was through the narrow road they had just walked

316

through, which was now clogged with wreckage, or through a hole in the wall of the factory knocked out by the Combat Talon's wing. "It looks secure, sir," Nathan reported after the team made a brief survey. "Morris and Yao will cover the road, but I think we're pretty safe here for the time being."

"Good. Call up Monitor and let them know we're ready for Pelican to get us. While we wait for them to get here, we should try and get the bodies out of the MC-130."

The upper deck of the Combat Talon was crushed, and the nose was entirely smashed in, so all the doors were jammed shut. The only point of entry was the rear cargo hatch, which had been torn away when the Dassault had collided with the bigger plane. The entire tail had been sheered off, leaving the huge cargo bay wide open and easily accessible even though the plane was upside-down. The three LAV troop carriers that had been carried inside were tossed on impact and were hopelessly wrecked, but at least they were clear of the cargo bay which made the SEALs' job easier now.

"We got a body," Coles reported, "or at least, it *was* a body."

The Marine who had tried to escape with a parachute had been flattened when the LAVs came loose; flattened as in completely mashed by a 35-ton armored vehicle landing on his chest.

"I... I don't think that he's recoverable," Nathan said shakily.

Roche, who was not so squeamish, picked up an arm, which was no longer attached by anything but some stringy muscle tissue. "Any idea who he was?"

Part of the face was still recognizable, but none of the SEALs remembered his name or anything except that he was part of the vehicle crew.

Roche removed a wedding band and a watch from the arm he was holding and found the man's dog tags among the pulp of his chest cavity. "Let's see if there's anyone in the cabin deck."

The passenger seating area, formerly the upper deck of the aircraft, was now a narrow crawl space under the forward cargo bay. Ramirez and Sherman ducked into the three-foot-high enclosure with flashlights and looked around.

"Eh, they're all here," Sherman called back. "The other five Marine drivers and Commander Clark. Mostly head and neck trauma, no crushing like that last guy."

One by one the SEALs dragged out the dead, and wrapped them in tarps they found in a storage locker. Then Ramirez went back in to try to get to the flight deck.

"No good," he hollered, his voice muffled by the mass of bent metal around him. "It's completely crushed. The cockpit took the brunt of the impact, I think."

"Can you reach them at all?" Roche asked him.

"I can reach one guy – I think he's the flight engineer. I'll get his dog tags and any jewelry, but I'll need the Jaws of Life to get his body out or for me to climb any further in there." Mike came back with the tags, a watch and a class ring. "We could try going through the windscreen to reach the pilots, but I gotta warn ya, they make that guy," he indicated the pulverized Marine sergeant, now covered by a tarp, "look like he died in his sleep."

Mike Ramirez was hardly exaggerating. Roche and the SEALs went outside to the front of the plane to look through the windscreen, which was now at ground level. The pilot's skull was mashed against the glass; his aviator sunglasses identified the gory mess as having once been a man's head. The copilot was bent in half, pinned to the controls by his own chair. Roche kicked the windscreen in and lay prone on the ground to reach the bodies. He got his arms completely covered with blood and gore but managed to secure two more piles of dog tags, rings and watches.

"Okay, does that account for everyone?" he asked as he wiped his arms on his already-ruined t-shirt.

"Everyone except Bowers," Nathan answered.

"Right, Bowers." Karl tried not to remember his former chief.

"He was our jumpmaster," Travis said. "He was standing at the ramp when I went out, right before the fighter hit."

"He must have been incinerated," Carter said.

"…Or he could have been thrown out when the plane crashed," Nathan suggested.

"More likely he fell out somewhere between here and the embassy," Coles stated.

"Let's look over by the Light Armoreds, then we can search the rest of the yard," Roche decided. "But if we can't find him by the time the Osprey arrives, we'll have to write him off as MIA."

"Sir-" Travis started.

"I know, no SEAL has ever been left behind, dead or alive, but once the V-22 gets here we'll have maybe five minutes to load up before the IRG finds us and tries to shoot us down. At that point it's either we look for a dead body or we save our own skins."

"Yes, sir." They went back around the plane and another hundred yards north of the wreck, where the three LAVs had ended up in a heap. One was standing upright, but had been crushed to half its height. The other two were on their sides and bent at weird angles. The SEALs looked around, hoping they'd find Master Chief Bowers and also hoping he wouldn't be quite as mutilated as the marine.

Suddenly, the hatch popped open from the upright LAV and a ghost appeared. The SEALs drew their guns and the surprising occupant of the vehicle yelled in alarm "I surrender! Don't shoot!"

"Bowers?" Karl asked in utter amazement.

"ROCHE?" Bowers was even more amazed. "What the hell are *you* doing here?"

"Never mind that; how did you survive that crash?"

"When I saw that little fighter about to hit our tail, I just grabbed the hydraulic supports on the ramp and held on for dear life. I remember fire, everything was spinning, there was a horrible smash, and then I woke about halfway between here and the plane."

"Are you hurt?"

"A little." Bowers hoisted his legs out of the hatch. His left leg was twisted funny and there was a nasty-looking gash above the knee. "When I came too I still had this in my hand," he held up an aluminum piston from the ramp hydraulics, "and I've been using it to hobble around. I checked on the other guys, all dead, went outside and threw up, and started thinking about escaping. I figured to get out of here I'd need a radio. The cockpit and the commander's gear were all smashed to bits, but I thought I might find something from the LAVs."

"Well, we're all really glad to see you, Master Chief," Nathan said. "We squared away all the bodies, but we couldn't find you and we were starting to think we'd have to leave you behind."

"I'm glad to see you too. So what's going on? Why aren't you at the embassy?"

"It got too hot," Nathan explained, "and the LZs were artillery bait, so we made our way over here."

"How'd you make out? Any injuries?"

"Just Williams."

Master Chief Bowers saw CPO Williams' arm in a sling. "Dammit, Trav, you already have a purple heart. Give it to someone else, why doncha. And you," he turned to Roche and asked again "What are *you* doing here? Aren't you supposed to be shooting down enemy planes before they hit us?"

"That's the idea. I did hit that fighter, but I couldn't stop him from hitting you. Then I got shot down myself and decided to hook up with these guys."

"Ah, he got shot down only because he was focused on bombing the living daylights out of the artillery that was about to kill us," Nathan added.

"So, what now?" Bowers asked. "Is Pelican coming here?"

"Any minute now."

As if on cue, a whisper of rotor blades became audible in the distance and slowly crescendoed into a thunderous roar. The MV-22 Osprey came into view over the buildings, and slowly circled the crash site. Its pilot spotted the crowd of embassy refugees and slowly set the ungainly-looking aircraft down near them.

"Wrap the bodies together in a tarp," Roche instructed the SEALs. "There won't be room inside the Osprey, so they'll have to be secured to the cargo hook. There should be plenty of tie-down lines in the MC-130." Then he ran over to the heliplane to explain the situation the Marines. Once they were up to speed, he directed the Russians to get aboard the Osprey.

The SEALs followed in two minutes hauling the six corpses on a canvas sheet along with a bag containing the personal effects of the other four men. "Is that all of the bodies?" Lt. Anderson, the Marine pilot asked.

"Everyone we could move," Nathan answered. "The others are pretty much closed-casket cases anyway. We got their tags and rings and stuff."

"Okay. We've got the cargo winch out. Just hook them up and make sure the ropes are double-knotted."

"Quickly, people," Roche urged, "we don't have a lot of time here."

"The Air Force is going to drop a big bomb on this site as soon as we're clear," the Marine Lieutenant said, "so the enemy doesn't recover anything from the wreckage."

"Actually, I'm more worried about-" a burst of gunfire cut Roche off but validated his concern. Yao and Morris, who were covering the gate to the compound, were suddenly in a firefight with IRG troops.

"Never a dull moment," Nathan sighed. "Cabbage, break out the SAW."

"With pleasure." Bernie "Cabbage" Coles finished securing the winch and ran over to where the SEALs had left their gear. The M249 Squad Automatic Weapon is a compact light machine gun. Coles propped it up on a trash dumpster just outside the gate and started blasting 5.56mm rounds into the Iranian troops. The rest of the SEALs grabbed their MP5's and joined the battle.

Roche started to follow, but the Marine held him back. "Listen," the Osprey pilot said, "if the bad guys get in here and start shooting at this bird we're in trouble; especially if they bring an RPG or a Stinger. And if they keep us here long enough, they'll start using mortars and you guys won't be able to stop them. If you don't win this gunfight in a hurry, we're history."

"Don't worry. Just keep the engine running." Roche drew his heavy fifty-caliber sidearm and sprinted to the gate, sliding into cover next to Nathan. "We need to make this quick," he told the SEAL, "or we're going to lose our ride."

"I know," Nathan said, "but these guys keep coming. We've killed twenty already but they're not letting up."

Roche fired single shots with his long-range Desert Eagle but the SEALs were doing the most damage with their automatic weapons. It was soon evident that Nathan was right, the IRG was going to keep charging up the road until they got a crack at the Osprey. "Listen, you guys need to go. I'll hold them off while the Pelican gets clear."

"What? We're barely holding them back now with ten of us. You want to try this by yourself with two pistols?"

"Leave the SAW and an MP. In my hands, that's enough firepower to keep their heads down for a few minutes."

"Forget it, sir. We already discussed leaving a SEAL behind, and I'm telling you it's not going to happen."

"I'm not a SEAL."

Nathan glared at the man he'd crawled through the Grinder with. He poked his finger into the golden trident pin on Roche's flight vest. He pressed it hard. "This says you were, you are, and you always will be a SEAL."

Roche looked down at the little pin he was given on October 28th, 2002, when he and Nathan passed the BUD/S course. He had pinned that little trident on his uniforms and flight suits every time he'd put one on for the last six years. It was the only way he let himself remember those seven months... He took the pin off and placed in Nathan's hand. "Not now, I'm not. You hold that for me until I get out of here, but right now you're not leaving a SEAL behind, you're just following the orders of a ranking officer."

"Damn it all, Commander-"

"We have no time to discuss this further, Lieutenant," Sharkey said firmly. "Now take your men and get out of here. And remember to count heads before you take off. I don't want you to leave anybody down here with me."

Nathan felt a massive mental conflict of emotion and reason, but in true SEAL form he closed his mind to all thoughts except the mission. "Okay. Troops," he spoke loudly enough for all to hear, "we are going to fall back on my command. Get your gear and get on board on my say so; this is going to have to be fast in order for it to work."

There was a slight break in the action when an IRG soldier dropped a live grenade and the Iranians scattered before it exploded among them. "GO!" They drew back quickly, each holding his gun in one hand and gear bag in the other. Nathan stopped Coles for a moment as he passed. "That stays," he said as he took the machine gun and handed it to Roche. Chief Travis Williams noticed and looked questioningly at the L-T. "Just go!" Nathan yelled as he sprinted to the Osprey.

Williams understood immediately. Like Nathan he felt the conflict for only a moment before he gave Roche his own MP5 and said, "Tell me you're not going to get yourself killed trying to save us again."

"I'm not planning on it." Roche clapped his friend's good shoulder and the SEAL ran off, following the other men to the Osprey.

As he boarded, Nathan asked the pilot "how many civvies do we have on board?"

"I counted twenty-five before your guys got back," Anderson answered.

*Twenty-five and nine is thirty-four*...he did a quick headcount to confirm the number as Travis entered and closed the rear hatch. *There were thirty-five of us,* he remembered the count from the embassy tunnel, *minus Roche is thirty-four.* "Okay, lift off! Get us the hell outta here!"

"Roger *that!*" The Marine revved up to full throttle with the rotating engines at full tilt, and the big aircraft took off vertically in helicopter mode.

"Where's Commander Roche?" Carter asked. Nobody answered him.

Roche crossed the road while under fire, shooting back from the hip with the Squad Automatic. He ducked behind the heavy dumpster and checked the gun's ammo. He could hear the Osprey revving up behind him, and he felt the wind as it lifted off. He came back up just

322

in time to see an Iranian soldier aiming an RPG over his head at the transport. Roche fired a burst from the SAW that cut the shooter down just as he was about to fire the rocket. Instead of hitting the MV-22, he fired it back the way he'd come into the middle of the IRG formation. This gave the Osprey the opening it needed to escape into the clear. The Iranians came back a few seconds later, now trying to capture or kill the squad of Special Forces troops that had thwarted them, not realizing that they had all escaped too. Almost all of them.

Roche continued shooting in methodical bursts as more of the enemy came into view. When he stopped for a moment to load a new belt into the machine gun, he noticed that someone was shooting a gun behind him. It wasn't a noisy machine gun or assault rifle, and it wasn't the distinct bap!bap!bap! report of an MP5 that he heard. It was the whisper of a silenced pistol. He swung around and saw a man aiming a small handgun past him and shooting at the IRG. Roche was astonished at first and doubly so when he realized the shooter was the Russian guy who had been pushing the wheelchair back in the embassy. "Who are you?" Roche asked in Russian.

"I'm your backup," he replied in English. "Less talking, more shooting from your end. You have all the big guns."

Roche faced forward again and swept the road clear with the M249, then turned back to the mysterious stranger. "You're supposed to be on the Osprey with the others."

"Yeah, and you're supposed to be back on the *Reagan* already. But in this business, some damn thing always goes wrong."

Roche finally figured out who it was. "You must be the CIA agent we came here to extract."

"Bingo. Hey, would you mind tossing me that MP if you're not going to use it?"

Roche complied, and Agent Caspian started snapping off very accurate three-round bursts at the weapon's maximum range. Roche recognized his small pistol as a Belgian Fabrique Nationale 5.7mm. It was made by the same company that made the SAW machine gun. Roche was going to ask the spy a question but a burst of automatic fire slammed into his dumpster. Roche fired back, clearing the alley again.

The agent spoke. "You're probably wondering why I stayed behind to help you." Roche was. "First of all I thought it was pretty cool that you'd sacrifice yourself for everyone, and I felt I owed you something. Also I've actually got another errand I need to run, and it would be useful if you were alive to assist me. Now that my ulterior motive is on the table, I sincerely do admire your bravery."

"Well, thanks, but I was under the impression that the whole point of this very costly operation was to get you out."

The Iranians sent another wave of men into the kill zone, but the CIA man was able to shoot them and carry on a conversation at the same time. "Me? Oh, no. At this point any other mission I may have is just a sideshow. The SEALs were sent in to secure a real Russian with valuable information. That was done, and I'm free to pursue other tasks. I wasn't actually planning on leaving at all until we all had to clear the embassy."

Roche had to space his words between bursts from the noisy machine gun. "Okay, well... I do appreciate your help, but... I think I could handle this myself... and I still plan on making my own escape."

"Really? You have maybe five or ten minutes before a B-52 drops something on that Hercules back there and incinerates everything in this lot. How did you plan to get out?"

"As soon as these guys let up a little... I'm going to run to that hole in the factory wall... and hide in the basement until they drop the bomb. And when I was flying over I remember... seeing a parking garage a few blocks from here. I'll hotwire a car and drive myself... to the southern edge of the city... where I can be picked up safely."

"Good plan, except you'll be baked alive by the two-thousand-degree fireball, and if you did somehow get past that the IRG would catch you before you could make it to the highway." Caspian emptied the magazine on the MP5 and asked "Do you have another clip for this thing?"

"Sorry, no."

"Do you have any 9mm ammo for your pistols?"

"Here, you can just use this." Roche tossed him the Glock automatic and the agent resumed shooting.

"Anyway, the whole city is on lockdown, if you haven't noticed, and it has been ever since the bombing started the night before last. No one is allowed out of their homes. Any moving vehicle will be stopped and its occupants arrested."

It briefly occurred to Roche that this was an odd conversation to be having in the middle of a gunfight, but if the spy hadn't brought up the issue it probably wouldn't have occurred to him to take cover from the bomb. "Okay, then I'll just hide out until they open the streets again. I've got plenty of provisions."

"Have you ever camped out in a strange and deserted city with half of the national military looking for you? I have. It's no fun.

Besides, that doesn't solve the problem of escaping the impending explosion that will flatten this entire block."

"Fine. So what's *your* plan?"

"First I need you to trust me, Karl."

"I don't even know your name."

"You can just call me 'Mr. C.'"

Roche stopped breathing. *It's the spook from Iraq that almost got me killed. I thought he looked familiar.*

"Yes, that Mr. C," he said, reading Karl's mind. "I'm sorry about what happened to you in that warehouse, but I can make up for it now if you just trust me."

The machine gun clicked when Roche pulled the trigger again. He looked down without expression as the last link of the ammo belt fell out of the receiver and in to the dirt. Roche had been bluffing to the spy; he actually was very pessimistic about his chances of living. He knew that surviving the bomb was unlikely and getting away from Tehran was even more of a gamble. But this agent did seem to have a good idea of how to escape, unless he too was trying to bluff through their desperate situation. "Okay, Mr. C. What are we going to do?"

Cannon dropped Roche's empty Glock and stood up with his arms raised. "Hold your fire!" he called in Farsi. "We give up. We have valuable information if you take us to your commanders alive."

Roche didn't understand what the spy was saying but he didn't like the way he said it. "You'd better just be taunting them, or I swear, I'll-"

"Relax, I'm turning us in," he said cheerfully. "If they follow IRG standard procedure, they will take us straight to the only place around here that could protect us from the bomb blast."

"Oh, man, was this the worst mistake of my short life, or what."

"Put your other pistol down the front of your trousers, and dump your ammo in your gear bag. They won't search us yet. If we show them the empty machine guns, they'll think we're unarmed."

Roche hoped that was true, because even if they could escape both the bomb and IRG custody, he wouldn't last long on the run without the contents of his gear bag. Twelve heavily armed soldiers cautiously approached them. They kept their AK's leveled at the Americans but didn't fire. Roche had laid the SAW on top of the dumpster lid and held his hands behind his head. He was shirtless, wearing only a nylon and leather flight vest and camouflage pants. There was blood all over his arms and torso, the holsters, ammo loops and pockets on his vest were empty. Unless they checked the large bulge in the front of his pants, he offered absolutely no threat. The soldiers pushed him down on his back, looked him over briefly and patted his pockets. Then one soldier guarded him at gunpoint while the others approached the spy.

The agent had placed the empty MP5 on the ground in front of him and tucked the Glock and the FN pistol into his pants also. He knelt on the ground with his hands on top of his head and jabbered excitedly in Farsi. The soldiers didn't touch him. After he answered a few of their questions they lowered their weapons and allowed him to stand up. He spoke to Karl in Russian. "I told them I'm the Russian ambassador and you are my bodyguard, and that the Americans assaulted the embassy in order to rescue a spy."

"You told them *that*?"

"Shut up! Let me do all the talking. The IRG command already knows that. I told them the Americans abandoned us here to cover their escape. They told us to shoot until we ran out of ammo or they'd kill my family." Cannon also looked his part. He was wearing an inexpensive suit that looked like he'd been dragged through the streets in it, and he was tearing up a little bit as he spoke which obviously sold the story. "I think they bought it. They're taking us to their superiors, but they won't hurt us."

The guard covering Roche shouldered his weapon and helped the pilot to his feet. The Iranians led them back down the road in a protective circle and even allowed Roche to carry his bag. They escorted them to an armored car and told them to wait inside while they consulted with their superiors. Roche realized quickly the sheer brilliance of the agent's plan. They were surrounded by nearly fifty enemy soldiers, and despite having killed at least that many by themselves they were now being protected by them; moreover, they were sequestered in an armored vehicle that would shield them from the imminent fireball.

"Here's your Glock back," Mr. C said, reaching inside his pants.

"Hey, I don't want to touch it after you had it down your-!"

"Relax, it was outside the shorts."

Roche took the gun, holding it by two fingers, and dropped it in his bag. He put the Desert Eagle away also, and took out a Snickers bar to snack on. "So, now what?" he asked, still speaking in Russian in case anyone was listening, "we wait here for the bomb to blow everyone away and then we just waltz off?"

"Pretty much, and unless they open the door right as it goes off, we'll be fine."

**40,000' OVER TEHRAN**

"Warhammer One, extraction package is clear; you are go for MOAB deployment, over."

"Roger, CENTCOM." Bermudez guided the bomber across downtown Tehran.

Presley, behind him, watched his bombsight crosshairs until they were centered on the upside-down C-130. "Releasing." The huge bomber jumped as the 28,000lb weapon separated from its belly. As the GBU-43 fell from the sky, its onboard GPS steered it toward its target. The bomb detonated three feet from the belly of the C-130. The plane, the wrecked vehicles, and the two buildings on either side were instantly buried under a colossal ball of flame.

The MOAB, unlike most other bombs, is designed to detonate its enormous high-intensity explosive warhead a few feet above the ground. The result is a very passable imitation of a half-kiloton low-yield nuke. A pressure wave on the ground flattens buildings and tosses vehicles, and is followed by a searing fireball. The airburst blast effect of a MOAB can flip a main battle tank parked five hundred yards from ground zero. Roche and Mr. C were half that distance away.

The little armored car was picked up and thrown against an office building, which collapsed under the shockwave. The Americans had the foresight to fasten their safety belts but were still very shaken up by the ride. They came to rest upside-down after a moment of violent motion, half-buried by the ruin of a three-story commercial/light-industrial complex. They struggled to open the door, but after a few kicks from Roche it yielded and let them escape. They dug their way clear of the rubble and crawled out to a place that was very different from the place they remembered coming from.

Roche had thought the two plane crashes he'd witnessed that day were the most devastating things he'd observed in his life, but now he'd seen what the most powerful non-nuclear bomb in the world could do. The MC-130 was gone, replaced by a smoking crater that also included the factory he'd considered hiding in. As for the armored car they'd just taken for a wild ride, what was visible was charred and smashed beyond all recognition. The entire neighborhood was devastated; every building within a three-block radius of ground zero

327

was leveled. Their polite IRG captors were probably part of the ash that was raining down on them.

"Holy cow," Roche was finally able to say. "I was not expecting this."

"Well, that's the Air Force for you," the CIA man said. "Never use a little bomb when a fricking huge bomb will do just fine."

# CHAPTER 16: HOT WAVELENGTH

## USS *RONALD REAGAN* – 1800 LOCAL, JUNE 1^ST

"Admiral, one of the Chinese ships is making blinker contact with the *Fitzgerald*," the Battle Group Operations Officer reported

Krause came over to the plotting board in the Combat Information Center. The BGOO, Captain Marcus DeTomaso, was writing down the message as the captain of the *Fitz* was reading the International Morse Code signal from the Chinese ship. "XXX – US DDG – DO YOU COPY – WE INTEND TO MAKE PEACEFUL CONTACT – PLEASE RESPOND BY IMC – XXX."

"*Fitz* wants to know what to tell them," DeTomaso said.

Krause looked at the message. "Which ship is sending this?"

Captain DeTomaso pointed to the board. "*Luhai 063*, the ship that sank the *Vandegrift*. It's been in standoff with our perimeter escorts since the fight."

"Tell them we will continue dialogue by Addis lamp contact. Obviously they're trying to talk to us without the rest of their fleet knowing."

The BGOO passed the instruction to the *Fitzgerald* and copied the message returned from the Chinese. "*LUHAI 063* AND *LUDA 202* ARE NOW UNDER PLA/N CONTROL – JUNIOR OFFICERS SUCCESSFULLY MUTINIED AND SUBDUED TREASONOUS CAPTAINS – UNABLE TO CONTACT ADMIRAL ZIHAO OR OTHER PLA/N AUTHORITY – WE WISH TO JOIN YOUR FLEET AND BE ESCORTED BACK OUT OF NATO PERIMETER."

"Where's *Luda 202*?" Krause asked, looking down at the map board. "Oh, wait, I see it. They're the flank escorts. If they've reverted back to the good guys' control, that kind of leaves the *Zheng He* wide open, doesn't it?"

"You want to take another crack at the carrier, sir?"

"Not yet. I'm not going to start another firefight while that Osprey's on its way here. Besides, we only have two Growlers at the moment, right Deuce?"

The CAG had just walked in to the CIC. "Toymaker and Fozzy Bear are rearming and could go back out in about half an hour," Thompson reported. "That will give us full EW capability. The other four are following the Osprey, and they can tank up when they get to feet-wet in fifty minutes. In another ten they can be in position to help deliver pure overkill."

"And in seventy-five minutes the Osprey will be safely onboard," Krause said. "Okay, Deuce, work up an air strike option for the last two escorts and something that will disable – disable but not sink – the *Zheng He*."

"I already have it," Deuce said, coldly. "Just let me alert my commanders." Thompson went out to the Air Ops Center next door.

"Admiral, *Fitzgerald* wants to know what to tell the Chinese," DeTomaso said.

"Give me Commander Edmunds," Krause told the comm officer. The connection went through to the Admiral's headset. "Jim," he called the *Fitzgerald*'s skipper, "this is Wally. Tell them we have processed their information and are preparing to help them re-defect to the PLA/N fleet. But first we need a signal of their intent. In a little over an hour an aircraft is going to come within their range, and the traitors would very much like it to be shot down. If they ignore it, we will accept their allegiance. And tell them to repeat to *Luda 202*."

"What's the point of that, sir?" DeTomaso asked. "If they're trying to get two destroyers in range to shoot missiles at the Gipper, they'll happily pass up an Osprey."

"The Tehran mission was compromised, Marcus, they know we got our agents out, and they went to a lot of trouble to try to stop us. That bird is more valuable to them than just about anything. Plot a course for the Osprey that takes them within missile range of both of these Chinese destroyers, and make sure those Growlers that are escorting them are fully alert."

"We're gambling with the mission critical, there, sir."

"Relax. The Growlers can protect the MV-22, and if anyone shoots, *Fitz* will take them apart."

Deuce updated his op plan while he scrambled the *Warhawks*, *Yellow Jackets* and *Stingrays* that hadn't participated in the Tehran mission. When he wasn't looking at the computer screens or the map board he was staring at Krause through the door to the CIC. He was still somewhat surprised that he hadn't been sidelined or even locked up for insubordination, but he realized that Krause had taken his diatribe to heart and accepted full responsibility for the Tehran SNAFU. They had stood side-by-side in anguish when they heard the Osprey report in and say that LCdr. Roche was not on board. At that moment, Krause swore to his CAG that he would pull all stops to save

Sharkey Roche. Deuce accepted the promise and the truce. He hoped this second round with the Chinese wouldn't take too long. He really wanted to get back to working on Sharkey's rescue.

## ONBOARD CHINESE CARRIER *ADMIRAL ZHENG HE*

"At sundown, we will make our final attempt to take down the *Reagan*. We will launch our remaining attack aircraft, the *Sovremenny*s will fire their remaining missiles, and the last Kilo will make its sneak attack. If the wind remains steady and the *Reagan* holds its course, it will go right by the Kilo just as we unload our missiles into the battle group. Bear in mind, we will likely be destroyed when the Americans return fire, but if we sink another one of their carriers it will even the score and allow China to save face."

"The *Luhai* and the *Luda* are still out of contact, sir. What are they to do?"

"Obviously the Americans are jamming their radar and radios, but they will see our weapons being launched and could fire their own cruise missiles and guns without the use of their radar."

"Admiral, it will be as you order. The loss of our fleet and the Russians' is not too dear a price to pay for sinking two American supercarriers."

## BETWEEN THE BATTLE GROUP PERIMETERS
## 2005 HOURS

"We are powering down our jamming gear, Godfather," Palerider called to the *Reagan* from the lead Growler. "Standing by to cover for Package Boy as needed."

"Roger, Wiseguy One. Maintain formation. Package Boy, advise you are in missile range of a possibly hostile Chinese warship, be ready to take evasive."

"No problem, as long as Wiseguy keeps the jammers warmed up," Lieutenant Anderson responded from the cockpit of the Osprey.

Lieutenant Nathan was sitting behind him and leaned forward. "Why are they moving us into the danger zone like this?"

"Apparently two of the surviving Chinks are running up the white flag. The Admiral is putting us in their shooting range to prove they aren't still working for the Iranians. If they are, they'll try and hit us with a missile. If they aren't, we'll help them get back to Canton."

"Go back to the part about them hitting us with a missile."

"Relax. The Grizzlies have us covered. They won't let a seagull get within squawking distance of us."

"Mobster and Scarface Flights stand by for strike runs," Thompson ordered. The two squadrons of Super Hornets were orbiting over the *Reagan* Battle Group, beyond the *Zheng He*'s radar range. "Remember, destroyers first, and then go for the carrier's tail. Just try not to sink it."

"No promises," Worm answered. The *Warhawks* were designated as "Scarface" and would be making the ASM air strike. Hannibal and eleven other *Stingrays* that had stayed home so far that day, were designated "Mobster" and were going to provide air cover for the *Warhawks* and the surface ships.

"Seriously Worm," Deuce intoned, "the Chinese are just starting to play ball with us here. It would do a lot to promote our relationship if we could keep their capital ship and the five thousand sailors onboard afloat."

The Chinese aircraft carrier *Admiral Zheng He* began life as a sister ship to the Soviet carrier *Kuznetsov*. It was to be called the *Varyag*, and had it been finished it would be the only strike-ops-capable carrier in the Soviet fleet. (The *Kuznetsov* does not have catapults, so its aircraft can only carry fighter and light-attack loads.) The *Varyag* was not finished before the Soviet Union collapsed in 1991. It sat in dry dock in the Ukraine, and a dispute arose between the Ukraine and Russia over who actually owned the ship. In 1994 Russia was allowed to continue construction on the vessel. Three years and two-and-a-half billion dollars later, the *Varyag* was less than three-quarters finished and the Russians realized that it was just a money pit.

At that point the Chinese made an offer to buy it. The Ukraine, who had adopted a peacenik attitude since the fall of the Berlin Wall, insisted that the Chinese not use the ship for military purposes. The Chinese Navy backed away, but a few months later a private Chinese company made an offer, claiming they would dock it at Macao and convert it into a floating hotel and casino. The Ukrainians and Russians took the deal, and sold it for two billion, splitting the money between the two countries.

Now a dispute arose with Turkey, who controlled the only way to get the ship to China. The narrow Bosporus Strait is the only outlet of the Black Sea, where the *Varyag* was. The strait cuts right through Istanbul harbor, and the Turks had never been too keen on letting large military ships pass through. A sixty-five-thousand-ton aircraft carrier under tow and in the hands of a bunch of Chinese junk pilots was right out, as far as the Turkish Coast Guard was concerned. Eventually the Chinese paid up a quarter-billion-dollar damage deposit and the Turks allowed the ship to make its way out to Macao.

It never went to Macao. It went to the port of Shanghai, the headquarters of the Chinese People's Liberation Army / Navy Eastern Fleet. It spent five years being rebuilt into a modern supercarrier and in 2009 it was rechristened *Admiral Zheng He*. The namesake was an explorer-statesman from the 1400s who built the Chinese Navy into the largest in the world. For one-quarter of the 15th Century, the five hundred ships of the Chinese Fleet ruled the Eastern Pacific and Indian Oceans, and protected a vast maritime trade empire that kept China's coffers full for centuries to come. When Zheng He died in 1433, the emperor dismantled the Navy and China didn't build another blue-water fleet for the next five hundred and fifty years. The new carrier was a fitting statement that China was back in the navy game.

"With all due respect, Captain, they sank the *Roosevelt*, and it seems fair that we get a carrier for ourselves." Worm still argued over the command frequency.

"They didn't sink the *Teddy*, Worm, that piece of crap Russian sub did. And that took six hours to sink and almost the entire crew got away. Our weapons are a lot more effective than the obsolete torpedoes those Kilos carry. We will minimize damage to the carrier, and attempt to disable its engines only. If you have a problem with those orders, you fly your skinny ass back down here and argue with Admiral Krause."

"Okay, sir, Scarface Flight will attack with skip-bombs only and attempt to damage their machinery spaces. No superstructure damage or anything below the belt."

"Glad you're onboard."

"Package Boy, you are clear of the missile zone, please make tracks to rendezvous with Godfather."

"Roger that," Lt. Anderson answered the call from *Reagan* air ops. "It looks like those boys from Chinatown are playing nice."

"They sure are," Krause said, even though the Marine pilot couldn't hear him. He got online with Commander Edmunds on the *Fitzgerald*. "Jim, blink that Chinese guy the following. 'Your compliance in ignoring the Osprey target confirms your intent. We are preparing to engage the remainder of the traitor warships. Proceed immediately within our perimeter and rendezvous with cruiser *Shiloh*.

*Shiloh* will escort you to NATO safety line. Any attempt from you to fire on any ship, ours or yours, will be met by swift and merciless armed response. You are welcome. Repeat to *Luda 202*.'"

"*Shiloh*'s only ten miles off our beam, sir," DeTomaso noted. "If they're still trying to get a shot at us, they'll be in missile range."

"For crying out loud, Marcus, have a little faith. Deuce, get your boys in there and finish this game."

Thompson looked up from his console. For the first time in several hours, a slight smile was playing at his mouth. "They're already locking up their targets. Those junks out there haven't got a prayer."

"Scarface, engage close escorts. Ignore repeat ignore perimeter escorts. Mobster, spread out and proceed to cover stations. Wiseguy, remain on station and provide full EW support for air strike." There were a total of thirty-two Supers and Growlers in the air. They spread out across the sky and came after the three Chinese ships. The enemy radar operators were allowed to see what was coming for only a minute before the Growlers jammed their systems, but the image of thirty-some fighters coming to get them was burned in their minds.

## THE *ZHENG HE*

"The Americans are coming after us!" The *Zheng He*'s radar officer screamed. The admiral saw the picture for only two seconds before the radar was blacked out, but it was long enough.

"Launch all our fighters, and fire all our missiles!"

"We are early, the Kilo will-"

"Forget the Kilo. That pig-boat willfend for itself until-" A massive explosion cut him off. A pair of Harpoon missiles slammed into the Russian-built *Sovremenny*-class destroyer that was screening off the *Zheng He*'s port bow, ripping the stern wide open. "Quickly, tell the other destroyer to fire before it is destroyed!"

"They cannot fire without radar, Admiral. They have no target solution." It didn't matter. Two Super Hornets flew straight over the *Zheng He*'s deck and unloaded another set of Harpoons at the other destroyer. The last escort was sliced in half and sank in five minutes.

## SCARFACE FLIGHT

"The destroyers have been fitted with cement shoes and are sleeping with the fishes," Worm reported. "Preparing a skip bomb run on the carrier."

334

"This is Wiseguy One. Enemy aircraft are in play. Repeat, they're launching fighters from the carrier," Palerider warned. A pair of MiG-29k's took off and went looking for the Hornets. "Scarface, break off and wait for Mobster to clear the airspace."

"We're on it," Hannibal said. "Nine, take your division after those first two. The rest of us are going skeet shooting."

Beowulf had been put in charge of the leftover pilots from Sharkey and Blackjack's divisions. He and Claymore caught the attention of the Fulcrums while Gator and Creep caught them unawares with AMRAAMs. "Splash two," Gator reported.

Hannibal had the next two MiGs on his radar before they even took off, and fired at them while they were rolling. One got slammed just as it reached the edge of the deck. The missile came in from above and blew it apart, and the explosion damaged the catapult. The other one got three hundred feet further before an AMRAAM hit it between the tailpipes and ripped it in half. But more Fulcrums had gone off the side catapults unmolested.

"Radar warning," Bulldog reported. "Someone's behind me."

"Not for long." Bulldog's wingman, Doc Holliday, whirled around and spotted the two Fulcrums. In half a second a pair of Sidewinders were in the air, followed by Doc's open-channel report. "YEEEEEHAAW!! Fox-two, fox-two!"

After another minute of frenzied shooting, the radar screens were clear of bandits. "I count eleven splashes," Toymaker said, "no friendlies hurt."

"Confirmed, eleven kills and zero losses," Hannibal said. "Scarface, get back in here and beat up this Chinaman." Worm's squadron came back around, approaching from the *Zheng He*'s stern.

It would seem to the untrained observer that if you are going to drop bombs on a ship, the best way to attack would be from the side, where you'd have a wider target. However, the bombs are going to fall in a fairly straight line, and the real difficulty is timing the release so the bomb does not overshoot the target. Therefore, it is best to line up with the ship lengthwise, so you have the entire deck of the ship to aim for.

"Release about five hundred yards short," he instructed the flight. "The bombs will skip to the target. Two bombs each from five hundred feet." The Hornets came in at low level, at four hundred knots. They dropped a total of twenty-four bombs in the water and flew right over the *Zheng He*. The bombs hit the waves and bounced crazily. A few detonated on impact, others ricocheted vertically off the waves, but half of them skipped straight toward the carrier. Eight of them hit the stern of the ship, punching through the hull and detonating in the machinery spaces in the stern half of the carrier. One hit a freak wave and bounced sideways, hit the starboard hull and exploded against the thick skin just above the waterline, blowing open the tank of diesel oil that fueled the big ship.

The fuel didn't burn, it only leaked out at a very fast rate. The cold oil itself isn't flammable, so five hundred pounds of explosives couldn't set it on fire. It's the diesel fumes, not the actual liquid, which burns and even explodes when tightly compressed. The hole was letting fuel out and water in, and the heavier sea water went to the bottom of the tank and was effectively pumping out the diesel.

"I see an oil slick," one of the Warhawk pilots reported. "We got his tanks."

Worm looked at the trail of sludge that shimmered iridescent in the light of the setting sun. "Would you look at that? It's bleeding like a stuck pig. At that rate her tanks will be dry in no time."

"Should we make another pass, sir?"

"I don't want to risk burning her," Worm said. "If we accidentally drop a match on that slick who knows what will happen. If I blow that ship up, Deuce will convene my court-martial with me hanging by my toenails from the *Reagan*'s radar mast."

"That's probably not much of an exaggeration."

"Let's let her run out of gas. That's all we have to do, is disable her. Man, look at it go. There must be water pouring in the tanks and floating it out."

Bonzer was watching the shiny oil slick, when he saw something else shining in the distance. "Bogey, two o'clock, low level," he reported. "No radar return, no radar emissions. That oil slick is bollocksing up the radar somehow."

"It's the fumes," Worm said, "it makes the air really dense. It's like an invisible smoke screen." He squinted toward the southern horizon. "I see the bogey. Looks like another MiG, coming in on a landing approach... Oh, hell."

"Crikey, he's gonna fly right through those bloody diesel fumes and ignite them with his exhaust." Bonzer and Worm realized at the same time what would happen. The MiG, which had somehow escaped being massacred by the *Stingrays*, was a match flying toward a fuse.

"We have to shoot it down," Worm said. "Bonzer, come with me. Someone get the *Fitz* and the *McClusky* over here and prepare to put out a big fire." Worm hit afterburners and Bonzer followed, careful to fly around the oil. The MiG kept coming, oblivious to both the danger it was in and the danger it posed to the carrier. The *Warhawks* only had Sidewinders, and had to close in to five miles to make the shot. This wasted precious time. "Fox-two, fox-two" Worm fired both of his missiles as soon as he was in range.

The MiG pilot seemed to suddenly wake up, and he took evasive action. "No you don't, mate, ya stupid wombat." Bonzer kept the throttles pegged and crossed the MiG's trail. He launched his own AIM-9's from the other side. The four missiles converged on the target, but the Chinese pilot dropped flares and barrel-rolled away, somehow dodging three of the missiles. The fourth one hit it in the side of the port engine, right under the trailing edge of the wing.

The plane seemed to take forever to die. Huge chunks of metal flapped in the wind and peeled away, and the entire wing was almost sheared off. The engine was belching fire and smoke as it burned itself inside out, but that pilot was determined to limp as close to the ship as possible before he ditched. Too close. The flying wreck passed right over the edge of the oil slick, and right then the damaged engine blew up. The intake fan tore itself free and spun away from the plane, then boomeranged back and sliced through the tall vertical rudders. The pilot decided this would be a good time to bail and he punched out, letting the torched fighter plunge into the sea like it wanted to. Then the pilot looked down and realized his catastrophic mistake.

The fumes did not ignite instantaneously, like the Americans feared. This far away from the ship, the oil had evaporated most of the way before beginning to break down in the seawater. Most of the way. The flaming Fulcrum ignited the residue, which burned fairly unimpressively, but the flames quickly spread. The Chinese pilot splashed into the oily ocean and choked and sputtered as the toxic fuel entered his mouth. The heavy seat sank immediately, dragging him down with it. He finally got free and swam back to the surface, and found himself surrounded by burning oil. The heavy chair had disturbed the film on the water, leaving a little ring that was briefly clear of oil. But the ring closed, and flames were now coming closer to the half-drowned aviator. He knew from what he'd seen from the parachute, that he was surrounded by a hundred yards of oil on all sides. There no way he could swim that far on one lungful of air. The flames closed in, and the heat was torturous. All he could do was decide whether he'd rather drown or burn alive. As he swallowed foul, oily seawater one last time, his last thought was a sickening realization that he had doomed his shipmates to make the same choice.

## ZHENG HE'S BRIDGE

"Damage control reports that the fires are out," Colonel Shin, the ship's captain announced. "The damage from the bombs was confined to the machinery spaces in decks three through six. Only five dead, twelve injured. And we've lost engine number two."

"What about the fuel leak?" Admiral Laido asked.

"It's bad. Water has flooded the starboard tanks and it's pumping them dry. We've lost, I estimate, three hundred and twenty tons already, and the one hundred tons that's still floating in the port tanks is not usable, because it's floating above the intake valves. We're maintaining power on reserve fuel, but that's going to run out in half an hour and leave us dead in the water. At that point, we can only hope the Americans will allow us to live."

"Living to face Beijing is not an attractive option for us, Colonel."

"No, sir, but at this point I must think of my crew. We have no offensive weapons, no fuel, and no aircraft. Our radar and communications systems are useless, as are the defensive weapons which require radar to operate. We are at the mercy of the US Navy. One of their destroyers is closing on us, doubtless to offer assistance in exchange for our surrender. I suggest we take their deal."

The elderly Admiral sighed. Rannovich would be disappointed in him, but not nearly as disappointed as the ancestors he had disgraced. He had acted, always, in China's best interests, or so he thought. If Rannovich succeeded, his plan would secure the energy needs for China's bright future for centuries to come. But that promise was slipping away like the oil pouring from his stricken flagship. They had lost the battle at sea. If Rannovich's own forces were doing any better on land and in the air, there may be some hope, but surely the war he created could only hurt China in the short term. And no amount of cheap oil would replace the loss of the better part of the Eastern Fleet. "You may surrender the ship to the American destroyer, Colonel. I am going to go decide how to kill myself. Maybe you can use my logs to clear your name with Beijing."

The Admiral went out to the aft bridge and looked back over the stern of the ship. His eyes followed the trail of oil toward the southern horizon, and then he saw his last Fulcrum trying to fly home. He realized immediately what would happen. The others on the bridge joined him at the rail as the Americans were trying to shoot it down. He and the other officers found themselves rooting for the Hornets,

338

unashamedly cheering when they finally hit the MiG-29k and dropped it into the sea. Then they saw the flames spreading away from the wreckage and across the ocean surface. They were spreading toward the *Zheng He*.

Commander Jim Edmunds saw it too. He was half a mile off the carrier's port quarter, watching the final air battle while dictating a Morse code message to the Chinese ship. "*Zheng He*, US DDG *Fitzgerald* offers assistance and emergency aid on condition that- oh holy shit. WAIT! Don't blink that last part!"

The Chinese captain was already blinking back, "WE SURRENDER – PLEASE HELP US."

A watch officer holding huge binoculars was watching the trail of fire. "Sir, estimate five minutes before the fire reaches them." The slick was six miles long, and flames were spreading as fast a car driving on the freeway.

"All ahead emergency flank. Helm, cut us across her stern. We need to make a fire break." The *Fitz* charged through the oil at thirty-five knots, and its wake cut cleanly across the treacherous trail, but it closed itself back up before the destroyer could turn around and make another pass. The ship cut across the bigger vessel's wake again, but Edmunds could see it was useless. The oil just spread across the water too quickly. "Tell the Growlers to stop jamming their mayday frequency."

"Aye sir, they already did, sir." The comm officer tossed the skipper a headset.

"*Zheng He*, this is US escort ship *Fitzgerald*, do you copy? *Zheng He*, this is-"

A voice answered in unaccented English. "We read you. This Colonel Shin Wai, commanding officer. What can you do to assist us?"

"We tried cutting through your oil slick but it isn't working. Is there anything you can do to stop the spill on your end?"

"I wish. We're trying to pump the oil out faster, but there's still a hundred and fifty tons left and we are only discharging about ten tons a minute."

"You have four minutes." Edmunds looked at the flames. "Make that three and a half. You need to get everyone on the port bow of your flight deck and be ready to abandon ship."

"My officers are organizing that now. They're throwing the munitions over the side as they go, so nothing else will blow up. Only a skeleton crew is manning the pumps and damage control stations, and the Admiral and I are remaining on the bridge."

"Colonel Shin, this is Admiral Wally Krause of the *Reagan*," the *Reagan*'s comm watch had alerted him to the exchange on the mayday frequency. "Let me talk to Admiral Laido."

"This is Laido." The Chinese officer was standing on the bridge like a statue, watching his men huddle up on the flight deck.

"Admiral, we tried to stop the plane from hitting the oil slick. I'm sorry, we only intended to disable the *Zheng He*, not sink or critically damage it."

"I know, I saw that. And for what its worth I am sorry for the damage I have caused to your battle group. I have betrayed China and her allegiance with your country, and I take full responsibility for the losses my Navy incurred in face of your firepower."

## *REAGAN*

Krause muted his microphone and glanced at the comm officer. "We're recording this, aren't we?"

"Yessir."

Krause clicked the mic back on. "Admiral, the *Fitzgerald* and the frigate *McClusky* will assist your men in the water and fight the fire. Were there survivors from the *Sovremennys*?"

"We launched boats for them. Most of their crew made it off. Oh, God, the Kilo! Admiral, you must avert your course! There is a fourth Kilo submarine waiting to ambush the *Reagan*, about five miles in front of you!"

"I wouldn't worry about us," Krause said.

## USS *TUCSON*, 200 FEET BELOW USS *RONALD REAGAN*

"Conn, Sonar, the Gipper's overhead now, sir."

"I noticed," Commander Parsons said. The carrier's noisy propellers were clearly audible without being amplified by the highly advanced equipment that Petty Officer O'Brian was using in the sonar room. "Okay, let's sprint again. Forty knots, three minutes, and don't float up when we stop this time."

The *Los Angeles*-class attack sub *Tucson* had been operating close to the *Reagan* ever since the attack on the *Teddy Roosevelt*. If a Kilo was waiting to ambush the pride of the carrier force, they would have to deal with the pride submarine force first. One of the last of the 688-Improved-series submarines, *Tucson* had been modified as a stealth technology testbed for the new propulsion and sonar systems that would be built into the Navy's next generation of subs.

The *Tucson* was employing a tactic called sprint-and-drift, which is a very efficient way to both cover a lot of ocean and find anything hiding along the way. The *Tucson*'s passive sonar is extremely effective, but not when the ship is moving fast. The sensitive BQQ-10 sonar array is mounted in the bow, and the noise of water being parted by the bullet-nosed hull drowns out the noise of other ships in the sea. So by charging a short distance at full speed and then slowing down to listen for contacts, the attack sub could hunt more effectively. The *Tucson* spent most of the time drifting in this case, mostly waiting for the *Reagan* to catch up.

After three minutes running flat-out, Commander Parsons called "all stop." The helmsman adjusted the planes a little to keep the ship from rising up as it burned momentum. The CO noted the depth gauge was staying flat at 200 feet and nodded his approval. The *Reagan* was now two miles behind them, cruising at a steady eighteen knots into the wind. PO1 O'Brian could hear it behind them, and so could anyone else listening in the area, including the stolen Kilo-class submarine hiding on the bottom of the Arabian Sea not a thousand yards from where the *Tucson* had drifted to a halt.

The sonar operator on the Kilo did not hear the *Tucson*, which even at flank speed was about as noisy as a deaf-mute ghost. But he heard *Reagan*, and he deduced that its course would pass too close to them for an optimal firing position. He notified the captain, who started the battery-powered motor and wound it up to five knots, just fast enough to get to the correct position in time, but slow enough to avoid detection. At least, theoretically avoid detection. American sonar gear was designed to listen for reactor and turbine noises, not direct-drive electric motors.

But the huge ball of electrostatic gel and electrodes that served as the *Tucson*'s ear could hear a seagull sneeze from twelve miles away. The swelling electric hum and sudden thrash of the seven-bladed propeller did not escape the BQQ-10 sonar system's attention. With the instincts of a shark looking for lunch, the signal processor automatically isolated the distinctly man-made noise and brought it to O'Brian's attention. "Conn, Sonar, transient contact."

"What? Where?"

The computer had both answers an instant after O'Brian had already guessed them. "It's a Kilo-class on electric power; it just made jackrabbit start, nine hundred fifty yards on our oh-twenty. It's making turns for five knots heading oh-eighty." As he spoke, the weapons officer dialed the data into the torpedo computer. They could've fired a Mk. 48 Advanced Capability torpedo right then and probably gotten a hit.

"Launch a distress flare rocket," Parsons ordered. The weapons officer reached back without looking and hit a button on the bulkhead behind him. A rocket the size of a two-liter soda bottle was ejected in a column of bubbles, and shot to the surface launched exactly like a tiny version of a sub-launched ballistic missile. The flare and rocket motors ignited together when the device broke the surface, clearly visible a mile and a half in front of the USS *Ronald Reagan*.

## *REAGAN*

Just as Admiral Krause was saying "I wouldn't worry about us," the CO of the *Reagan*, Captain Brian Young, spotted the signal rocket. It was a prearranged warning from the *Tucson*, and Young reacted instantly.

"Sound collision," he ordered.

Someone hit a big red button and klaxons all over the ship blared the alarm.

Young pointed to the helmsman and barked more instructions. "Port hard rudder, starboard impellers quarter thrust, port full reverse."

The helmsman sat at a control console not unlike the cockpit of a commercial airliner. He cranked the wheel hard to the left and adjusted the throttle settings. Just like an airliner, the enormous ship banked into the turn at fifteen degrees. Any unsecured crewmen, who were only given four seconds' warning by the collision alarm, were thrown to the deck. The *Reagan* wheeled a one-eighty away from the Kilo, only two miles away but totally safe from danger.

The klaxons didn't sound in the CIC, because human voices would need to be heard in order to direct the battle, but Krause guessed what was going on. He held on tight to the railing around the map board and continued directing the operation to save the *Zheng He*. "What's the status on that fire? How much time do they have, Jim?" Krause called to the captain of the *Fitzgerald*.

"It's a thousand yards behind them. Ninety, maybe ninety-five seconds."

## SCARFACE FLIGHT

"There has to be something else we can do," Bonzer insisted.

"I don't think so," Worm said. "We're fighter-bombers, not *fire*-bombers."

"Wait, that's it! Why don't we drop bombs in the oil slick behind the ship?"

"What are you talking about?"

"Look mate, *Fitz* ran through the slick and tried to separate it right? But it didn't work, because his wake couldn't push the oil back far enough. What if we drop a few bombs in the water right behind the chink, yeah? They make a much bigger splash, and they'll explode underwater so it won't restart the burn."

"It's worth a shot. Let's do it." Worm, Bonzer and two other *Warhawks* dove at a forty-five degree angle and dropped bombs right into the carrier's wake. At such a steep angle, the bombs couldn't skip. They simply exploded under the surface of the water. The splash cut a hundred yards out of the slick, but it started closing up again.

"That slowed it down, at least," Edmunds told them. "Do it again."

Worm sent another division in. "I can only make a few passes before we run out of bombs," he said

"Try bombing the fire; the splash might extinguish some of the burning oil."

Worm's third division tried that and two hundred feet of fire was splashed out. "We can make six more runs," Worm said, "but you'd better try and evacuate that ship."

## *REAGAN*

"My bombers have bought you some time," Krause told Laido, "But the oil just spreads back and once we run out of bombs the slick's going to burn toward you again. You need to have your men abandon ship."

"I understand."

"They can line up all the rafts and boats on a hawser and our ships can tow them to a safe distance."

"Very good. I will instruct the sailors to do this. What about you and the submarine, though?"

"Yeah, what about it?" Krause asked DeTomaso.

"We're three miles from its last known and moving further away. The *Tuscon*'s between it and us. As soon as they reacquire it, they'll sink it."

## TUCSON

"He's hiding on the bottom somewhere, Commander. Active can't separate his return unless it's in high-res mode, and that's taking forever to scan the last known area."

"Mr. O'Brian, we're in no particular hurry here," Parsons answered. "He can't hear us, so he can't shoot us. And *Reagan*'s too far away, so he can't shoot them. He's like a little kid playing hide-and-seek and we're babysitting 'safe.' Keep looking."

The *Tucson*'s active sonar was disguised to sound like natural ocean noise instead of making the usual mechanical "Ping!" sound. It made high-frequency clicking noises, imitating a bottlenose dolphin, and using that sound the return signal actually comes back in greater detail than normal active sonar. O'Brian used this system to map the bottom of the Arabian Sea, five hundred feet below them. Metal makes a sharper return signal than sand and stone, but like American subs the Kilo's hull was sheathed in a material that mutes the sonar reflection. So O'Brian watched for not a strong return off the seabed, but for a weak and distorted area. "Got 'em!"

Parsons looked at the screen. A cigar-shaped space of color represented a very weak sonar return, clearly giving away the sneaky diesel sub. "That's got to be it. Yankee-lash the target, and plug the solution."

The dolphin clicks were replaced by a shrieking pod of orcas, originating signals from several different parts of the sonar dome and creating a field of sound energy that identified every detail of even the stealthiest of subs. There was the Kilo, bouncing the sound waves right back at them, floating twenty feet above the ocean floor.

"Flood tubes one and two and fire as soon as solution is set," Parsons ordered the weapons officer.

"He's flooding his own tubes," O'Brian said. "He's going to try and shoot back."

Parsons smiled, amused by the Russian's late attempt to defend itself. "Good for him; he finally figured out we're not a school of whales."

"Dolphins, you mean. Orcas are big dolphins, not whales."

"Whatever."

The bigger sub shuddered as fourteen thousand pounds per square inch of air pressure blasted a pair of ADCAP torpedoes into the water. The launch force is equivalent to a steam catapult on a carrier, and the torpedoes were immediately moving at forty-five knots. The

Kilo was a thousand yards away, giving the crew of the smaller ship twenty-two seconds to say their prayers. They tried to launch their own torpedoes but they had no accurate fix on the *Tuc*'s position. The Mk. 48s struck together, hitting the Kilo square on the nose and peeling it open like a banana. The entire ship flooded in five seconds. The two torpedoes it fired back had no guidance, and just went off into the ocean until they ran out of fuel.

### REAGAN

Young had his binoculars trained on the patch of ocean where the Kilo had last been heard. He saw a plume of water, steam and oil marking the cataclysmic sinking of the little sub. He keyed his microphone to the ops center. "They got him. We're resuming previous course."

Krause passed the news on to the Chinese. "Our sub bagged that Kilo you were worried about, Admiral Laido."

"Well, that's good. Our crew is almost evacuated. In about a minute and a half the only people left on the ship will be Colonel Shin and myself."

Krause realized that the Admiral and the commanding officer of the carrier intended to go down with their ship. He didn't know what to say to that, so he changed the subject. "Okay. Right about that time the oil you are still leaking will catch up with the patch that's still burning behind you, and we estimate it will take no longer than four minutes for the fire to reach you when that happens.."

"So, we have about five and a half minutes left altogether."

"Approximately."

"The First Officer is in command of the crew and is in contact with the destroyer. At this point I am going to sign off and the Colonel and I will record personal messages for our families and our commanders. We will then upload the files to you, if you would please pass them on to our families."

"You are no longer being jammed. You may transmit directly to Beijing or Shanghai as you wish."

"I know, but I want my family to hear the truth from me before the government tells them their version of what happened out here."

Krause swallowed hard. "I understand. We will forward all files to your families and the Eastern Fleet Command separately."

The *Shiloh* brought the two Chinese destroyers back to help with the rescue. Between them, the *Fitzgerald* and the *McClusky* they were able to get half of the Chinese crew out of the water. The other half was in lifeboats and rafts securely fastened to the warships. The odd little flotilla was gathered a mile from the *Zheng He* when the trail of fire finally caught up with the carrier.

The tanks were all but drained of diesel fuel, but filled with fumes compressed by the seawater that had flooded in. The hole in the ship was directly under the rear edge of the island superstructure. Laido and Shin stood right above it, on the aft bridge railing, and watched with placid acceptance as the inferno kissed the side of the ship. The fumes flashed off with the intensity of a bomb. The Chinese officers saw blue flames rush up to meet them and nothing more. The five-and-a-half thousand men watching from other ships saw the *Zheng He* silhouetted against a titanic ball of fire. The carrier rolled toward them, pushed by the blast, and then it rolled away as water poured through the breached inner hull. The fumes in the port tanks cooked off next, and the hull on that side was blown out in a dozen places.

The carrier settled lower in the water as the ocean flooded compartments, but the watertight doors contained the flooding before it filled the lower decks. The fuel burned out within minutes, and the carrier struck a balance with its new ballast. It didn't sink. It was thoroughly ruined, but it was still afloat.

Krause, DeTomaso, and Young watched aerial footage of the whole event, courtesy of the *Warhawks* that were still covering the ship they'd hit. "Update Admiral Zihao and tell him to send rescue ships and some heavy tugboats," Krause instructed. "Then they all need to go home."

# CHAPTER 17: UNFORESEEN COMPLICATIONS

## USS *RONALD REAGAN* FLAG QUARTERS
## 2330 LOCAL, JUNE 1<sup>ST</sup>

"Admiral, we uh, we have a problem."

Only three hours had passed since the incident with the Chinese carrier. Admiral Krause was not in the mood for more problems. He looked up at Hunter Hidelmann. "What kind of problem?"

"Mr. C was not among the embassy hostages." Hunter, as the *Stingrays* intelligence officer, was one of only a handful of people on the *Reagan* who knew the details of the mission they had launched that morning to rescue a CIA agent.

"He's got to be. Sharkey made sure they all got out."

"Apparently he missed one while he was off machine-gunning the IRG."

"Damn." Krause left his desk and followed Hidelmann down to the gallery deck. The rescued hostages had been sequestered in an empty ready room. The SEALs were temporarily being put up in the one belonging to the *Stingrays*. Krause checked in on the Russians. "Hello," he said. "Welcome aboard. I am Admiral Krause, the battle group flag officer." As he spoke one of the Russians translated. He looked at the picture that Casey had faxed him from Langley. Mr. C was definitely not among the Russians.

"We want to know, how long before we be able to go home," the economic analyst acting as translator spoke for the group.

"Good question," Krause said. "I'm making arrangements with the Russian government. In the morning we will have a better answer but I don't expect you will be here longer than forty-eight hours. We will find cabins for you to sleep in shortly. Now, can any of you tell me about this man?" He handed the picture to the translator. The Russian immediately passed it to a dark-haired man who looked particularly despondent. He brightened visibly when he saw the picture.

"I know him," he said in English. "I should talk to you in private, Admiral."

Krause nodded. He turned to Hidelmann. "Find us a private place to chat." He stepped out into the passageway and followed the rabbit warren trail to the *Stingrays'* ready room. The SEAL team inside saluted him. "Hello again, guys." Krause closed the door. "Seems you missed someone."

"Beg pardon, sir?" Nathan looked puzzled.

Krause handed him Mr. C's picture. "This guy was not aboard the Osprey."

Nathan smacked his forehead and swore. "I counted everyone when we got out of there, but I forgot we'd picked up Bowers after the headcount in the embassy."

Bowers saw the photo. "I know I've seen that guy before."

"He was in the embassy," Krause said.

"But I wasn't. No, I saw that guy years ago, in Iraq."

Something clicked with Nathan. "He's one of our agents, isn't he?"

"Yeah," Krause said. "Didn't anyone tell you about him?"

Nathan shook his head. "We were sent in with pretty basic orders. Our whole mission was assembled in only eight hours. I guess they didn't have time to brief us properly. But Roche knew. He said something about picking up an agent. This must be the guy he was talking about."

"It's not your fault," Krause assured them. "He probably stayed behind voluntarily. He must be with Roche now."

"He'll be fine, then." Nathan said. He looked away, trying hard to choke back the emotion in his voice. "You'll get him out, won't you Admiral? Roche, I mean."

"I'll do everything I can." Krause thanked the SEALs and left.

Hidelmann was waiting at the bulkhead. "I put Mr. Kujetski in Sharkey's stateroom."

"Lead the way."

Kujetski was sitting on the edge of Sharkey's bed watching TV. He had found CNN and was watching repeating coverage of the botched rescue attempt. "There is nothing more useless than the American media," he remarked, "with the possible exception of the Russian government."

Krause sat down in Sharkey's desk chair, holding Mr. C's picture. "How do you know this man?"

Kujetski didn't look at the picture again. "That's Mr. C, a.k.a. Agent Caspian – the CIA's lead field operative in the Middle East. I know him because I'm his favorite contact in the region. I got him and his package into the embassy where we could hide from the Iranians and wait to be picked up."

"Package?"

"There's a man in the other room who will answer to Arvydas Sabonis. He needs to be brought back to Langley as soon as possible to be debriefed. He's got… valuable information. And there's a man in a wheelchair who should be held under armed guard."

"I see," Krause said. "So why wasn't Mr. C on the Osprey with you?"

"He was, briefly, but when he saw that your fighter pilot wasn't coming back with your commandos, he told me he had some more work to do and he jumped out. You should be glad about that. Your pilot will need help to survive in Tehran."

"What makes you say that?"

In response, Kujetski changed the channels to the Iranian national news station. "I must say, I'm impressed that you guys show the local channels, especially since I'm probably the only guy on this boat – apart from some of those embassy staffers – who understands Farsi."

"The men like to make fun of their cartoons," Krause explained. He watched for a few seconds before he realized what he was seeing. It was video from the ground in Tehran, showing Sharkey's plane getting hit by a missile and tumbling to the street, and the aviator punching out at rooftop level. "Oh my God."

"In between the rhetoric and the grossly inflated damage and casualty reports," Kujetski said, "they're saying that this guy single-handedly destroyed two platoons of artillery assigned to defend the city and he also bombed a hospital full of sick orphans." The screen showed what was actually an abandoned hotel full of IRG infantry collapsing after being bombed by one of the other Super Hornets.

"The first part is true."

"They're saying there's a ten billion rial reward for his capture. That's over a million bucks, US. Now, the state news is about as trusted by the people in Tehran as Fox News is trusted in San Francisco, but you can see how all this may be bad news for your pilot."

"Yeah, I do."

"Speaking of which…" Kujetski switched to Fox News. Somehow they had picked up the Iranian report and drawn very different conclusions, calling the downed aviator a hero and announcing that in the process of getting shot down he had single-handedly saved the rescue operation.

"I don't know how they reached that conclusion, but they're actually right for once." Krause watched for a few more minutes. "But that's not going to help him hide from the IRG."

"No, but Mr. C will."

Krause opened the door and found Hunter waiting outside. "I'll bring him up to my flag conference room. You find Deuce and have him meet us there. He needs to talk to this guy."

## TEHRAN – 0100 LOCAL, JUNE 2<sup>ND</sup>

It took Agent Caspian and Sharkey Roche over six hours to sneak back to the warehouse where everyone had been hiding earlier. The MOAB bomb put the city's entire garrison on high alert. Both the spy and the aviator were very good at hiding, but hiding and moving at the same time is always tricky. After midnight the IRG seemed to relax a little, and the two Americans reached the warehouse under the cover of darkness.

Once safely indoors the CIA operative reintroduced himself to the Navy pilot. "It really isn't right," the spy said, "that I know almost everything about you and I haven't even given you my name. So let me introduce myself. I am the CIA's lead field operative for the Middle East Theater of Operations. My controllers call me Agent Caspian, the locals know me as Kahlil, the Russians call me Kalinov, but my real name is Robert Cannon."

"That's your *real* name?"

"It must be, because it's the only one I've never used. The only documents that prove it are in the CIA's NOK vault. I've got about half a dozen legal names that I use, all as authentic as the passports they're printed on – American, British, Russian, Jordanian – but if you want the name on my birth certificate, my high school and college diplomas, the one my parents gave me, that's Robert Cannon."

"Okay, well thanks for sharing that. Now, what do you mean when you say you know everything about me?"

"Oh, I've memorized your file. I'm your recruitment officer."

"My what?"

"Once you get tired of flying fighter planes, the CIA is going to try and recruit you again."

"I turned them down the first time," Roche said. The CIA had approached him before he joined the SEALs and he rejected their offer out of hand. "Why would I have changed my mind in the last eight years?"

"I don't know that you would, I'm not a psychologist. But I know the Agency hasn't changed its mind about you either."

"What, I'm that special?"

"Actually, you are. The CIA saw your potential a long time ago. That's why you were sent to our camp."

"What camp?"

"Camp Peary, Virginia. Summer of 2001, Karl."

"Oh, that camp. That was a SOCOM thing."

"Wrong. That is a CIA scout camp. Much like the scouting camp college football players go to before the NFL draft; that camp is where the CIA sends all its potential recruits for old spooks like me to study."

"I don't remember seeing you there."

"You weren't supposed to. You were supposed to think it was all a Special Operations introduction course, so I guess it worked. Anyway, you were by far the most impressive young man we'd seen in over a decade. The CIA has been tracking you ever since, and sending me regular updates on your file."

"So, when we met in Iraq, you already knew all about me."

"I'd known you for over a year. I had actually insisted to your superiors that you lead that mission for me. Again, I'm very sorry about how that turned out."

Roche didn't want to think about it. "I don't know why you guys bother. I'm really not cut out to be a spy. There's nothing really all that extraordinary about me."

"Don't give me that crap. You are exceptional. You know it, and everyone around you, anyone who's ever met you knows it too. Do you think they let just anyone in to UCLA? Do you think they let normal athletes play starting offense on the football team as true freshmen? Do you think the Navy gives just anyone a type-1 ROTC scholarship after they've already been in school for two years? Do you think they let just anyone even try out for the SEALs? Do you think they let any rookie lead a platoon by himself, especially in combat? Do you think they'd normally let a guy with a plastic shoulder start flying jet fighters? Do you think they send every pilot to TOPGUN? Do you think they take any officer and give him command of a whole fighter-attack squadron, twenty men's lives and a billion dollars' worth of aircraft?"

"Wait a minute; I'm not commanding a squadron."

"Not yet, but you will be after you get back to San Diego. I think I've made my point here, Roche. You are in the very top percentile of America's most elite warriors. And you have everything the CIA looks for in its agents. You are extremely smart, very adaptable and resourceful, you have good instincts, quick reflexes, you are a superb athlete, you speak four languages and could learn several more, you know guns, you know explosives, and you can lie convincingly and think fast in a stressful situation. And you're single."

"Not anymore."

"Oh, right, I forgot about your new girlfriend. But other than that, you're a perfect candidate."

"What about the fact that I have absolutely no interest in wiretapping foreign embassies, consorting with weapons dealers, assassinating foreign government officials, and playing both sides of international terrorism?"

"Is that what you think we do?" Cannon asked with a mock-defensive attitude. "I've never wiretapped a- oh, wait, yes I have."

"It's just not a life I want to live. I want to do something normal once I'm finished with the Navy."

"Roche, I hate to break it to you, but you're never going to be normal. You're meant for greater things, kid. The longer you keep selling yourself short, the harder it is going to be for you to meet your true potential."

"What are you now, my life coach?"

"Maybe," Cannon said with a shrug. "Just my professional opinion. I've been around enough people like you and me to know what makes us different from everyone else. You're one of those born killers you see in the movies. It's taken you a while to grow in to it, but that's what you are."

Roche was getting annoyed. "I don't know what you're talking about, and I don't think I like it either."

"Look, you just killed a couple hundred people today. That fact has no effect on you. Most people wouldn't be able to do that and then stand there holding a water bottle without shaking so much they spill every drop." Roche looked at his right hand, holding a half-empty Aquafina bottle. There was no tremor. "That's the ice in your veins that makes you so good at what you do," Cannon said. "That's the sort of person the CIA wants. And that sort of person doesn't do well selling cars later in life."

"Look, I appreciate all the time and interest you guys have invested in me, but this isn't the time or place to be discussing my future. I won't have one unless we get back to working on getting out of Tehran."

"We're staying here, for tonight at least."

"What, in the middle of a warehouse?"

"It's also a safehouse. Come on, I'll show you around." Cannon led the way to an office, and a room behind that contained two cots, a microwave oven and shelves of food and supplies.

"This is your setup?"

"Not really. This whole warehouse belongs to my associate. You may have seen him talking to the ambassador – they're good friends. His name is Kujetski. He's in the import-export business."

"You mean he trades weapons for information."

Cannon sighed. "I guess you can't help me if you don't know what's going on around here. This is all above top secret. You can't ever talk about anything you see hear or do here, got it? You don't tell your superiors on the *Reagan*, don't tell Tracy, don't even tell my boss at Langley, ok? I could get in serious trouble for exposing you to the operations, and God knows what they'll do to silence you."

Roche nodded. "If there's one thing I'm good at, it's clamming up. Now tell me why the CIA sponsors a weapons dealer. Is it just so you can keep tabs on terrorists?"

"It's more complicated than that, but basically, yes. This warehouse is actually part of his barely legitimate front; it's full of Persian carpets and antiquities that he'll send out of the country. He's got another warehouse across town that's packed with European cars, furniture, fine wines and liquors and other luxury items that he brought in to sell to the upper-class Iranians. The rest of his business is weapons. He uses that tunnel under the embassy to get smaller things to and from Russia."

"So he works for the Russians?"

"Sometimes. He mostly works for us. We've helped him the most, but the Russians supply most of his merchandise. He's set himself up as the biggest and best weapons dealer in the Middle East. We use him to control the weapons trade, and he also provides us with priceless information on terrorists and governments that buy from him. And the money he makes supports resistance groups here in Iran and in Syria and elsewhere. He's helped us take out many terror cells before they could mount attacks on the West. He also helped us circumvent a major war situation in Iraq."

"I can see how well *that* worked," Roche said sarcastically.

"No, really. That insurgency and the gang war with the Sunnis and Shiites and stuff was a real mess, but nothing compared to our worst-case scenarios before the invasion. Kujet stopped Saddam from making a major counterattack and killing thousands of Americans and many more of his own countrymen."

"How?"

"Remember the WMDs we never found?"

"Yeah…"

"Suffice it to say that without Kujetski's smuggling expertise and inside information, that little war would have been much bigger."

Roche sat down on one of the cots. "That explains a lot, I guess…"

"And until yesterday, Kujet was inside the cabal that's running the whole situation over here. He put his life, reputation and business on the line to deliver us one man who knows how we can get to the Iranian leaders. So, yes, he does play to three or four different sides of the war on terror, but he's always working things out in our best interests. And right now, he's provided us with a decent place to hide out."

"Hang on, if this is connected to the embassy by a tunnel, what happens when the IRG searches the embassy and finds the door on that end?"

"Your SEALs wondered the same thing. While you went out looking for your computer, and the rest of us were waiting here, they booby-trapped the secret door at the embassy and sealed the tunnel on this end."

"Okay," Roche decided to accept that he had no control over his situation. "I'm not going to worry about anything you and this Kujetski character are up to. If you think this place will be safe for the night, then I'm going to get some rest while I can." With that, Roche rolled over on the cot and fell asleep

## *REAGAN,* FLAG CONFERENCE ROOM – SAME TIME

Kujetski pulled his silver cigarette case from inside his coat. "They told us we can't smoke in here, but perhaps I can get special permission?"

Krause nodded. "Go ahead."

The Cossack fumbled in his pockets. "I can't seem to find my matches."

"Here." Deuce Thompson held out his Zippo.

"Thanks." Kujetski puffed one of his cigarettes to life.

"Sure." Thompson took the lighter back and finally lit the cigar he'd been chewing on all night. He caught the Admiral's sidelong glance. "Might as well, right?"

Krause shrugged.

Kujetski sniffed the air and frowned across the table. "What is that disgusting thing?" he asked the CAG.

Deuce matched the Cossack's stare. "It's a Macanudo."

"Dominican?" Kujetski shook his head in disdain and pulled out his Blackberry. "Give me your address. I'll send you a case of Montecristos from Havana. If you're going to completely destroy your lungs by smoking cigars, you might as well smoke something that's worth the grief."

Krause was amused. "I thought you said you were an antiquities dealer."

"I deal in many things. I have a lucrative little side venture running old Chevy parts into Cuba and swapping them for cigars."

Hidelmann answered a knock at the door. A young female ensign stood there. "Yes, Hammil, what is it?"

"Sir, Admiral, you are requested in the secure comms booth."

Krause sighed. "Washington, Arlington or Langley?"

"Er, Washington this time, sir."

Krause followed Ensign Hammil upstairs to the comms center and stepped into the secure booth. When he closed the door, the Telepresence screens activated. President Brett McNeil was looking at him. Krause looked down self-consciously at his rumpled uniform. "Mr. President, sir. I apologize for my appearance. I've been in these clothes since this time yesterday."

"No apologies needed, Admiral. You've been leading the fight out there and I have nothing but respect for the job you're doing."

"Thank you sir."

"Have you been watching the news?"

"Yes sir."

"Seen this?" McNeil turned his chair so Krause could see the big flat screen behind him. The President's TiVo was paused on a shot of Sharkey Roche bailing out of his wounded Super Hornet.

"I saw that on Fox about an hour ago, sir."

"The others will pick it up soon." President McNeil let the clip play, and listened to the commentator reiterate the act of heroism that it represented. "I got your report on the rescue attempt, so I know that for once Fox and Friends are right on the money." McNeil held up a folder. "It says here that's a Lieutenant Commander Karl 'Sharkey' Roche on my TV."

"That's right."

"Now, that name sounded pretty familiar when I read that, so I checked out your report on the first engagement with the Chinese renegade fleet and I found him again. He shot down about a sixth of the Chinese carrier air wing by himself, making himself an ace in the process."

"Yessir."

"That got me interested, so I did some more digging and I found out I'd actually met this guy before. A few years ago, when I was still in the Senate, I visited him in the hospital while Terry Marsh, who was CinCPAC at the time, gave him the Navy Cross for heroism in battle. He had jumped on a grenade to save a platoon of SEALs. I checked some names out and for the most part it's the *same* platoon of SEALs he's just saved twice in Tehran."

"I didn't know that."

"Those guys are still on your ship, right? Ask all the senior enlisted men. They served under Roche in Iraq." McNeil looked back at the TV. "And now this guy is missing in action after fighting off the whole IRG to get these SEALs and the Russians out of Iran."

"I promise you he'll get home sir. We don't want a media sensation about a man left behind."

"Actually, yes, we do."

"Sir?"

"We absolutely do. Roche not only saved that mission; for the moment at least he's also stolen the spotlight from the whole fiasco that rescue was, and from the sinking of the *Roosevelt*, and from all the other losses we've suffered. Bad news has been piling up and in about an hour and a half, people are going to turn on the evening news over here and say 'What the hell have we gotten ourselves into?' Roche is going to change that."

"How?"

"By being our Twenty-first Century Sergeant York. I want the broadcast networks to lead the evening news with that video you have from onboard Roche's plane, and a statement from you of how and why he got shot down. Then by primetime, CNN will get shots from the Osprey taking off and an announcement that Roche volunteered to stay behind. Sometime later, Fox gets interviews with those SEALs.

"People here are sick to death of Iraq and Iran. We've got over two thousand casualties in the last twenty-four hours and the American people will not swallow that easily. This war needs a hero, a symbol. And we've got him right here."

Krause looked at the President a little differently than he ever had before. "I'll do anything you ask, sir, but something tells me your hero might not be too thrilled with this idea of yours."

## TEHRAN – SEVERAL HOURS LATER

Roche woke up in the exact same position and immediately grabbed his gun. He looked around the little room, found it empty, and relaxed slightly. He thought a noise had woken him up, but he heard nothing now. His watch said it was 0844, but he couldn't remember what time zone it was set in. He went to Kujet's office, and the clock on the wall also said a quarter to nine. Roche had slept for seven hours. Cannon didn't seem to be anywhere around, but Roche didn't bother looking for him. He found a bathroom, which was rather dirty but he used the facilities anyway. He went back to the safehouse room and looked over the stores of food, deciding on what to eat for breakfast.

Cannon found him half an hour later, sitting on his cot eating out of a can of peaches. "Good morning, Commander, I see you slept well."

"Morning. Where'd you go?"

"I was shopping for clothes for you. You can't go out in public looking like *that*." Roche had washed the blood off of himself, but he still had nothing to wear except his vest and camouflage cargo pants.

"I thought the city was on lockdown."

"Not anymore. They figured it's been twelve hours since the Americans had dropped any bombs on the city, and they let people go back to work. There are people everywhere now."

"Good, that means we can make our escape."

"Not so fast. You're forgetting my other errand."

"Oh yeah, I almost forgot. What do I have to do to earn my keep?"

"Don't worry, you're going to like it. We have to rob a bank."

"Oh, for the love of God." Roche slumped forward and put his head in his hands.

"I'll explain later. First we need to get you into a disguise, and then we need to secure transportation, and I don't remember how to hotwire a car."

"Okay, I can do that." Roche stood up. "What about those clothes?"

"Khaki pants, two checkered shirts, a dark green windbreaker, clean underwear and socks."

"Oh, thank you, Auntie," Roche muttered as he took the shopping bag.

As Roche examined his new clothes, Cannon produced a makeup kit. "First, though, it's time for your Extreme Persian Makeover," he said.

"Eew, do I have to wear makeup?"

"Yes, unless you'd rather be wrapped in gauze and pretend you're a burn victim. Don't think of it as makeup; call it 'disguise elements.' I have to wear it all the time, so don't complain about one day."

"Alright." Roche noticed that Cannon's face looked several shades darker than it had yesterday, when he was disguised as a Russian. His facial features also looked slightly different. "I see you already have yours on."

"No, this is my real face. I look different because I washed off what I was wearing yesterday." Roche thought Cannon's natural skin tone was very dark for a Caucasian, and he pointed that out. "Yes, I know," Cannon said. "I get this from my Cherokee blood. It does come in handy, because my natural tone is about half-way between normal white and normal Middle-Eastern. Okay, let's start with some putty." Cannon applied a little bit of mask putty to Roche's face to extend his eyebrows and add a little bit of a hook to his nose. Then he brushed on a coloring agent that darkened Karl's light tan to a shade of light brown. A little bit of eye shadow changed the apparent shape of his eye sockets and completed the illusion.

Roche looked at himself in a mirror. "That actually looks pretty convincing."

"Now for your stink."

"My what?"

"Your body odor, which you stopped noticing long ago, is very distinctly western. It's produced by your diet, you know. You live off breakfast cereal, bananas, pizza and cheeseburgers, but around here people eat mostly meats and rice stewed in exotic spices. If anyone gets close to you, your B.O. is a dead giveaway." Cannon produced a stick of deodorant and a bottle of cologne. "Roll this anywhere you have body hair, except your face, and then I'll spray a little bit of this on you."

"Okay." Roche applied the deodorant to most of his body, and then Cannon sprayed the back of his neck and his underarms with the cologne bottle. "Ugh, what is that, eu de New York cab driver?"

"Basically, yes. It's the CIA's secret formula. I don't know what's in it, but it does make you smell exactly like you would if you lived here. Okay, now I need to put the color stuff on your arms. It takes half an hour to dry, so don't touch anything." Cannon applied more of the coloring agent to his arms. "Now for your hair." Cannon produced a black wig.

"That looks ridiculous."

"Trust me, despite their ancient Aryan ancestry, there are no such thing as blond Persians. The hair is essential." When he finished with Roche, Cannon applied his own makeup and soon was also a very convincing Persian.

"Do I have to be worried about getting my hands or face wet and accidentally washing any of this stuff of?" Roche asked.

"No, it won't come off with just a little moisture. You have to soak it in hot soapy water for two minutes and then scrub it off. But after twenty-four hours it will start to separate and you can just rinse it or rub it off."

"Okay. What about the putty? It itches a little."

"That will go away in about an hour, once it dries."

"Okay. Now since we can't go anywhere for half an hour, tell me about the bank we have to rob."

"Well, we don't actually have to do anything but pretend to rob a bank in order to protect a bank robber named Sam."

Sam, as Cannon explained, was about to be investigated by the Iranian government. This unpleasant process would reveal that he had been managing several accounts for Kujet and the mysterious Kahlil, who would soon be identified as traitors and spies. Sam would be sent to prison, and about ten million US dollars that rightly belonged to Sam, Kujetski, Cannon, and the CIA would be seized from the accounts as evidence.

The only way Sam could save himself from going to prison was to close the accounts and erase any record of their existence. The problem would be in getting money out of the accounts first, and manipulating the records so that the accounts and cash would be gone without a trace.

"Can't he just transfer it to Switzerland or something?"

"The originating account has to remain open for at least a week after the transfer; otherwise the Swiss report it as a possible illegal money exchange. Then if Sam gets investigated in the next week, those accounts will still be there.  They'd be empty, but they would have a record of the transfer and he'd be just as screwed."

"What about the Cayman Islands or somewhere else that doesn't have those kinds of laws?"

"Any international bank has to operate under those laws.  Sam's been going over this backwards and forwards for the last couple of days, and he's telling me the only way it will work is if we stage a robbery."

"Exactly how will that help him, if police find out he was involved?"

"Nobody will find out if he doesn't actually do anything.  If we do all the work and disappear, he'll be in the clear.  And apparently, he'll then be able to clean up the records and he and Kujetski and I can keep working here."

"If that's all this is about, then what's the point?  Once we win this war the government will collapse and the FDI or INF or NCRI takes over with a new, friendly, pro-US leadership.  Your work here will be complete at that point, right?"

"In a perfect world, yes, but there's no guarantee any of that will actually happen the way we want.  It's just as likely that the next bunch of people to run this country also end up on the crazy side.  If you remember history, it seems half the time we try and help someone over here they turn around attack us a decade later.  Politics aside, before this war is over, Sam and his family will be in grave danger. One look at those account records and the SAVAK security ministry will be all over the Samadad family."

"So, why don't we take them with us when we extract?"

"We'd be talking about his whole frickin' extended family. SAVAK is very thorough – they'll arrest and imprison and maybe torture and execute anyone who they think may be helping Sam.  We'd have to extract all of them in order to protect them from the government, and that means rounding up hundreds of people scattered all over the country.  Right now we're only looking at a solitary chopper to rescue the two of us.  Sam's already looked over the options, and he says this is the only way everyone keeps their jobs, their necks, and their account balances."

"I still don't understand how armed robbery helps him with the law."

"Neither do I, and that's why I think it's going to work.  Sam will explain when we meet him."

At 10:30 AM Cannon and Roche went shopping for a car. They found a two-story garage nearby and looked for something worth stealing. "I'd prefer something that's rear-wheel drive," Roche said, "with a good strong engine, so we can outrun a pursuit if we need too. But it should be an older model that won't attract any attention." He passed up several older European cars but stopped to examine a twenty-year-old Jaguar XJ8.

"What do you think?" Cannon asked, differing to the amateur mechanic's opinions and tastes in automobiles.

"We'll come back to this if we don't find anything better, but I'd be worried about this thing breaking down at an inopportune moment. Besides, Jaguars don't have good air conditioning."

Cannon spotted a car that might have met Roche's criteria. "How about that old muscle car?"

"Where?" Roche looked over at the car Cannon was pointing to. "Not just any muscle car, it's a 442! *Now* we're talking!"

"Well sir, I think we'll take this one for a test drive."

"Let me check the engine." Roche opened the hood and exclaimed "And not just any 442, it's a 1970 W-30, just like mine! Man, talk about hitting pay dirt. You know there were only just over a thousand of these things ever made?"

"No," Cannon answered, "I did not know that."

"It's got factory air conditioning, which is a plus." Roche quickly took the air cleaner off the engine block and inspected the vital parts. "Whoever owns this car knows what they're doing. I really feel bad about stealing it from him."

"He's insured. Everyone around here is. Tehran leads the Middle East in car theft." Cannon put his head under the hood even though he had no idea what he was looking at. "Yeah, this engine looks like it's in great shape."

"It's a pretty recent re-build," Roche said. "Custom headers... Edelbrock carbs with large-diameter downpipes..." Roche shined an LED penlight deeper into the engine bay to inspect the suspension underneath. "...And he installed Koni sport springs and shocks that look brand new. And it looks like he upgraded the brakes..." Roche knelt to the floor and looked behind the wheels. "Oh, yeah, we've got stopping power here. This is a complete Brembo GT system. These tires look pretty worn though..."

"Yeah, yeah," Cannon muttered, as he unlocked the door with a coat hanger. "Just hotwire the damn thing already."

"No need." Roche pulled a piece of electrical tape away from the underside of the hood, and unwrapped a spare set of keys. He closed the hood and came around to the driver's seat. The engine turned over and started right up. "Four hundred and fifty-five cubic inches of Detroit muscle. That's a beautiful sound, isn't it?"

"Yeah, terrific. Now let's go; we're going to be late."

Roche drove out onto the street and frowned when he shifted roughly into second gear. "Huh. I forgot about that."

"I thought you had the same car," Cannon remarked.

"Yeah, but I've been driving it with a custom six-speed racing tranny for the last ten years. This one is original, and a little worn. Let's see if I remember how to double-clutch..." Roche pushed the clutch in and shifted into neutral, let the clutch out and revved the engine to match the rotational speed of the driveshaft, hit the clutch again and dropped the gear selector into third. The drivetrain realigned seamlessly. "There we go."

A moment later they left the warehouse district and Roche saw a very different city. Despite the many hits that American bombs and missiles had scored in the last two days, the city of Tehran appeared largely unfazed. People were going about their lives as if nothing had happened, ignoring the bombed-out buildings and wreckage in the streets. Roche drove slowly toward the city center, amazed by how little the Americans' firepower had affected the city. He drove past a department store that was still open, even though the top floor and the radar station on the roof had been blown apart by a HARM missile. A grocer in the next building over was calmly sweeping broken glass and shards of metal off his sidewalk, and people were entering and leaving both stores with shopping bags, seemingly oblivious to the fact that they standing under what had been considered a military target.

A few blocks further, Roche saw a side street blocked off by the police. He looked past the yellow tape and traffic barriers and saw the crumpled wreckage of a Defiant fighter that one of his squadmates had shot down. A man in an old Buick was arguing with the police, pointing past the barriers to the garage where he wanted to park his car, just across the street from where the plane had taken out the front of an apartment building. "It's kind of like London during the Blitz," Cannon commented. "If it didn't land on you, you just go around it. What else can you do?"

"Man, this is so weird," Roche said as he looked at another building that had been hit by a cruise missile earlier. "Yesterday I was dropping bombs on these people."

"This is modern war," Cannon shrugged. "It's a complicated thing."

# CHAPTER 18: SMOOTH CRIMINALS

**TEHRAN – NOON**

The dark blue Oldsmobile blended with traffic just like Roche wanted. The streets of Tehran were clogged with American-made cars from the sixties and seventies, along with a number of European and Japanese imports. Suzuki seemed to be well-represented; they manufacture cars in Pakistan and they sell well in the Middle East. There were also some late model Chevrolets and Buicks, imported by the Chinese. "It would appear that the Iranians aren't too concerned with conserving fuel," Roche noted. "I see a lot of old gas-guzzlers out here."

"Why would they be concerned? They pay about a buck-fifty a gallon."

"That's it?"

"Of course, it's a lot of money compared to what they make, but most Tehranis are pretty well-off."

"I noticed." Roche wasn't sure what to expect from the residents of Tehran, but this sure wasn't it. Nearly all of the men he saw were wearing western clothing, mostly suits. But what few women he saw were wearing more traditional robes, or some other sort of outfit that managed to cover everything except their faces. Anyway, everyone he saw seemed to display some semblance of wealth. The people with new cars, especially, had to be doing all right.

"Iran is being westernized right under the Ayatollah's nose. Two-thirds of the population lives in urban centers, and a good chunk of those folks are like this, upper and middle-class businessmen, merchants and professionals. The live like us, they drive cars like ours, they dress like us, they're starting to eat like us…" Roche drove past a McDonalds and a Starbucks, more surprised than he should have been. "…They even talk like us. You could pull over and talk to any of these people in English, and they wouldn't bat an eye. It is the language of international business, not necessarily the language of the Great Satan, so the government actually demands that it be taught in the schools. And you notice these women are wearing more traditional clothing, but once we get closer to the market district and downtown the dress code is a bit more relaxed. The women of Iran are in many ways leading the national reform movement, and are becoming much more involved in the workforce and in government."

"So if they're so sophisticated and western-thinking, why did they elect a known terrorist as their president in '05, and re-elect him four years later?"

"That second election is so disputed, it made Bush and Gore 2000 look like a game show. Basically, everyone with a backbone voted for the other guy, a liberal reformer by the name of Mousavi. But the religious freaks who run this country intimidated a lot of the devout into voting for the terrorist nutcase, and in the end, the Ayatollah just declared Ahmadinejad the winner without ever releasing the vote total."

"So you're saying it was rigged."

"Officially, the parliament and the judiciary oversaw the whole process and said all ballot proceedings were conducted legitimately in accordance with the national constitution. But both the parliament and the judicial branch are dominated by the same bunch of religious fundamentalists."

"Oh, great."

"Of course, the free-thinking urbanite citizens didn't buy it, and took to the streets in protest. Probably as many as half a million people were right out here in downtown Tehran, voicing their dissent, crying foul, demanding a recount."

"Yeah, I remember seeing some of that on the news."

"That went on for about a week and a half before the Guardian Council called in the IRG to restore order. The Islamic Revolutionary Guard is awfully good at guarding against revolutions. They shut the whole city of Tehran down and used some pretty serious force to clear away the more riotous groups; killed maybe a hundred and fifty people and arrested thousands more. Mousavi was declared a religious dissident and imprisoned, and later secretly executed."

"That I didn't hear about. I know there was a police crackdown, but I had no idea it was so brutal."

"The Iranian government thoughtfully expelled all the foreign press before they unleashed the IRG, and they don't usually advertise what amount to war crimes committed against their own citizens in their own capital. What we have here is a representative system of government that does not actually represent the people in any way. The majority of these people here have no ill feelings toward America or the West or even Israel. They hate terrorists, they love democracy, and they would love to give our system a try. Right at this very moment they're rooting for us to kick their government's butt until it collapses, like you said earlier, and the resistance groups will then try to take over. Before 1979 these people were our best friends in the Middle East. As soon as we take out the mullahs, they will be again. At least, that's the theory."

"If the people resent their government so much, why haven't they done anything about it yet? I know there are about a hundred organizations that say they're trying to reform this country, so why don't they make any progress?"

"Fear, mostly. Since long before the 2009 election protests, the IRG has been quick to fire on any crowd that starts to look like a protest march. You may remember an incident like that a couple of years ago? One American kid was killed along with about thirty Iranian students in Esfahan. There's been another dozen demonstrations in the last few years that ended with shootings. So that keeps the more vocal reformer groups quiet. And then the clerics keep about a third of the population afraid of Allah."

"That's it? I thought Iran was something like 99% percent Muslim."

"Sure, in the same sense that something like 80% of Americans are Christians. But only a fraction of them are really devout. It's a larger fraction over here, but most people just treat it as a ritual. They go to the mosque once a week and kneel toward Mecca at the call to prayer, like they are required by law, but they're not really religiously motivated. At least, not motivated enough to go all jihad on us."

They were in downtown now, surrounded by skyscrapers and expensive hotels and fine restaurants, and there was nothing to indicate that the business and financial center of Tehran had ever come under attack. Roche drove past an especially showy joint, advertised in Farsi and English as the Café Artaxerxes.

"That's where we're going," Cannon said, pointing to the restaurant. "Better find a place to park."

Roche found a space on the curb near the end of the block and parallel-parked, carefully backing up close to the car behind them so that the license plate on the rear bumper couldn't be seen. He wasn't sure how long it would take before the authorities started looking for the stolen car, but he figured they should be careful.

Cannon was thinking about the same thing. "We'll have to get clean plates for the car before we drive it on the highway. They've got tollbooths at every onramp and the cops often use them as checkpoints."

Roche felt self-conscious walking into the café. It was decorated with priceless antiquities, and had the atmosphere of a five-star hotel's coffee lounge. "Aren't I a little underdressed for this place?"

"Not if you're here with me. You're my bodyguard, remember?" Cannon was wearing a clean Italian-style pinstripe suit that was much more expensive than the one he wore yesterday. Whoever he was disguised as, he'd make a good impression. Roche would obviously be assumed to be a bodyguard, especially if anyone noticed the bulges of the pistols under his light jacket.

The maitre d' approached them as though he'd been waiting all day to be of service to the American agent. "Ah! Monsieur Kahlil, how good to see you today." He spoke English with a thick French accent, exactly like Roche would expect in a snooty restaurant in the US. "Your party is waiting at your usual table."

"Thank you, Jacque," Cannon said, signing the guest book as 'Kahlil and staff.'

"I will take your coats, please," Jacque said.

Cannon shrugged off his suit jacket, but Roche didn't bother to unzip his windbreaker. He figured it would be a bad idea to display a pair of handguns in the classy coffee bar. "I'll keep mine, thanks."

"It is our policy during lunch hours-" the maitre d' started to insist, but Cannon cut him off.

"My personal security escort would like to wear his coat, Jacque."

"Of course, Monsieur Kahlil." Jacque was immediately obsequious.

"And please make sure that the tables adjacent to ours are unoccupied for the next couple of hours," Cannon added, as he handed the maitre d' his coat with a small wad of cash protruding from his fingers.

Cannon found his own way to the nine-seat curved booth in the back of the room, where Sam, his two sons, and Ellirat and Elessar were already seated. They were chatting idly, drinking iced beverages, and looking over the menu. Sam stood up and greeted the CIA field man. "Hello Kahlil, I am so glad you were able to join us. Did Kujet and your contractor make their flight?"

"Just in time. Kujet sends his best, but your uncle's business was most pressing."

"I understand," Sam said. "Please, I do not believe you have met my sons, Razi, and Nima." The two young men, who appeared to be in their early- to mid-twenties, stood and shook Cannon's hand. They wore name-brand casual western attire, unlike their father, who was wearing a tailored suit. All three spoke English with moderate British Public School accents. "Who have you brought with you today?"

"This is... uh... Mr. Sharki. He flies planes for your uncle. Sharki, these are the Samadads, and those surly fellows in the corner are Ellirat and Elessar, brothers from Iraq and longtime partners in crime." Roche recognized Elessar as Spartan-2, the sniper/spotter who'd covered him when he was shot down.

Elessar recognized him as well. "We haven't actually met," the Iraqi said, "But I think we were working together yesterday."

"Yeah, it's good to see you in a safer setting." A waitress came by to offer drinks to the Americans. She was wearing an outfit that would be scandalous by modern Iranian standards, but probably not so much in ancient Persia. When she moved off, Roche asked Cannon, "How safe are we here, by the way?"

"We're totally safe, as long as no one overhears us say anything important. Sam and I are good friends with the owner."

Roche took a quick look around at the priceless artifacts and made a guess. "Kujetski?"

Sam nodded. "Museums around the world have offered him a fortune for these pieces, but this is his personal collection, and he's not about to part with it. He keeps them here, where they are much safer than any museum, and free to be viewed by anyone who can afford to spend fifty thousand rials on a cup of coffee."

"Fifty thousand what?"

"Rials. Local currency," Cannon explained. "Fifty thousand is about five-and-a-half US dollars. In Kujet's defense, it is very good coffee." The waitress returned, bringing the iced latte Cannon had ordered and a black iced coffee for Roche. She took lunch orders, and left again. Roche wondered who was picking up the check, considering the sandwich he'd just asked for cost 180,000 rials.

The people at the table closest to theirs got up to leave. Sam waited until the staff had bussed it before he started talking business. "Kahlil, I'm assuming you've told the pilot what I've already told you?" The American agent nodded. "Good, then you all have the same understanding of my problem. I am the international accounts manager for the Central Bank of Iran, which is the country's largest. I am directly responsible for every single rial, dollar, yen, pound, franc, ruble and euro deposited in the bank by our foreign clients. I have been accused of laundering money through five accounts, which is true. One belongs to Kahlil, one belongs to Kujet, another to my uncle," – Roche

368

nodded, finally catching on to the "Uncle Sam" allusion – "and the other two are my own. Now, I have covered my tracks in such a way that I cannot be proven guilty of any *financial* crime; however nothing will prevent those accounts from being investigated until every detail of every transaction is scrutinized by the Ministry of Commerce. This would expose Kahlil, Kujet and I in all of our dirty deeds on behalf of my uncle.

"The only way I can protect us is to completely eliminate any record of those accounts. I can renumber five other completely legitimate accounts, and SAVAK and the Commerce Ministry will examine those and be none the wiser. I could do this whenever I please from my own office. The problem is, once I erase the accounts, the process will also erase all the money inside. Now this would be a small price to pay if it were the only way I could ensure that Kujet, Kahlil and my sons and I could continue operating here, but I would still like to make every reasonable effort to keep those funds. So I need you all to help me make a large, covert withdrawal."

"By robbing your own bank?"

"Not exactly. The robbery itself will fail. All it will do is shut down the bank's entire system while I manually withdraw ten and a half million and close the accounts for good. You see, if anyone attempts to rob my bank, all the computers will lock up so the robbers can't access anyone's information. The only computer that won't lock is inside the vault, which will also be sealed automatically. That computer, and the vault itself, will be completely isolated during the staged robbery. I simply time it so I am trapped in the vault, and anything I do in there will never be known by anyone but me. Once the robbers escape empty-handed, everything returns to normal. The floor manager will let me out, people get back to work, and we can move the actual cash at our leisure."

"That's the easy part," Nima said. "Razi and I move money out of the country every week. We just pick up ten and a half million dollars that doesn't belong anywhere, and we can take it anywhere we want. No one will ever ask questions."

"But even with the account records erased, won't someone notice that there's a lot of money missing?" Ellirat asked.

Sam shrugged. "My bank does ten *billion* dollars worth of business every quarter. When they total up our assets at the end of this month, an eight figure shortfall won't make a difference, especially if there is no account that the money is missing from. I'll leave my accountants to try and sort it out if the auditors ever notice. Someone clever may eventually trace the missing money to me, but I don't plan on working here much longer anyway."

Cannon nodded. "Okay, so if you three will take care of the money itself and erasing the accounts, what exactly do the rest of us do?"

"You all pretend to rob the bank so I can work on the system unseen. You need to give me half an hour, at which point the police will be there and you will have a hostage situation. You will be able to escape out of the parking garage if you use my personal elevator. It goes straight from my outer office on the 14$^{th}$ floor to my personal parking space, where you can leave the getaway car."

"Why do you need all four of us?" Ellirat asked. "One man can try to rob a bank and fail all by himself."

"Oh come on," Razi jumped in. "Haven't you ever seen a heist movie? You need at least four men. One to crack the safe, one for crowd control, one guy to wait in the getaway car with the engine running, and one last-minute replacement that someone vouches for but goes psycho in the middle of it and starts a gunfight with the SWAT team. That would be Sharki, I suppose."

"I'd rather be the driver," Roche said. "Going 'psycho' really isn't my style."

"The driver needs to know his way around town, Sharki," Sam said. "I am sure you're good behind the wheel, but you will need to navigate also."

"I studied the city street maps pretty thoroughly before I flew over here yesterday. I know my way around. We're on Revolution Boulevard right now, between Seventeenth and Eighteenth Avenues, two blocks from the Central Bank Tower, which is the third-tallest building in the city, and we're two blocks from the north edge of the market district, which is a good place to evade police pursuit."

"Okay, so you can drive. My elevator goes to the executive parking area, which is separated by tinted, bulletproof glass from the rest of the parking garage. The police will surround the building and set up guards in the garage, but not in the executive area. You can park your car in the space next to mine. It belongs to one of our VPs, but he had left the country last week and now he can't get back in. So look for my black Audi and park next to it. These guys will come out of the elevator, and you can drive straight out even if the police seal off the rest of the garage."

"This sounds like a good plan," Cannon said. "When do we start?"

370

"It's best to hit a bank at closing time, so right at five PM you three," Sam indicated the CIA agent and the Iraqis, "come in and order everyone up against the back wall, open the safe or we'll start shooting, etcetera. They won't be able to open the safe for you, but you can get whatever's in the counter and what the customers are carrying on them. You can also bust up the ATM's in the outer lobby if you have time before the police show up. After half an hour goes by, you pick one of my sons out of the rest of the hostages and order him to show you a safe exit. He takes you upstairs to my elevator and you're out of there."

"I have a question," Elessar said, "how common are bank robberies in Iran?"

"Extremely common. It happens every week here. Iran is pretty homogenous, and the minorities here face a lot of hardship. Anytime you have an oppressed minority group with limited economic opportunities a few will usually turn to crime to feed themselves. There are several organized gangs representing different ethnic groups that specialize in big things like drugs, car theft and bank heists. You guys should modify your disguises to look more like Kurds or something, and you'll just be business as usual as far as the police are concerned."

"Kurds?" Ellirat said with a grimace of undisguised racism.

"...Or something. Anything but Persians. And wear clothes that are a little more working-class. Sharki's fine just the way he is. The gangs will often hire a local thug to drive for them."

"I'm actually hoping no one will see me at all," Roche said.

"That will be the case if it goes according to plan. Um, you obviously don't speak Farsi, do you?"

"I know how to say 'I am an American pilot, please help me hide from the IRG,' and 'I need food and water,' but that's it."

"Well, the authorities will only speak Farsi, and those phrases won't get you far. So if you run in to any of them and you don't have one of us with you, you're in trouble. For casual conversation, at least in this neighborhood, you can get away with English. You should try to affect a European accent, though."

"I could do a German or Russian accent, I suppose."

"He does speak nearly fluent Russian," Cannon added helpfully.

"Stick with English," Sam said, "but a Russian accent would fit well. You'd come off like you've been working for the Russians in the mountains. A lot of unemployed locals went up there last year and they've been trickling back now that the projects are finished. That would make a plausible cover."

"Okay."

"Hey dad," Nima jumped in with a suggestion, "How about if I stay with him in the garage? That way he won't have to deal with the police."

"It's tempting, but I'm afraid it will definitely look like an inside job if you and I both disappear in the middle of it, especially if Razi leads the others right to where you are hiding with the getaway driver."

"Good point."

"He should be okay. He'll be totally separated from the main garage. Nobody will bother him."

"Do you have a book to read or something while you wait for us to do all the work, Sharki?" Ellirat asked in jest.

"Very funny. Actually, I was going to tune up the car while I wait. If we get in a real car chase, I should have quite a surprise for the police."

"Just make sure you're ready to go at 5:30," Cannon warned.

"Sharki, you should go now," Sam instructed, "and take Nima with you for the moment. You can pick up whatever parts and tools you need to modify the getaway car, and be back in plenty of time to do your work in the garage."

"Okay. I also need clean license plates."

"I know where to get that," Nima said.

Nima and Sharkey drove to a junkyard on the other side of the market district. Nima paid his friend who ran the place 100,000 rials and got his pick of huge stash of old plates pulled from totaled cars. They took one with up-to-date tags and drove back north through the district. They stopped again, this time at a specialty auto-parts store where Nima was a regular customer. Roche picked out a direct port nitrous injection system, a bolt-on supercharger that would fit the big-block engine, new tires which they had installed at the store, and a calibration kit that would let him adjust the custom suspension already installed on the Oldsmobile.

"Do you think we can do all this work in just three hours?" Nima wondered. It was already half-past two.

"Yeah, no problem. I know my way around this car. I have one of these bad girls back at home."

"Really?"

"Yeah, except it has quite a few more modifications than what I'll be putting into this one."

"I figured you American military pilots would all drive new Corvettes or something; you can afford it, right?"

"Sure, I could, but this old thing has more character, and I can have my way with the engine. If I wanted to modify a new ZR1, for example, I wouldn't know where to begin. It's already tuned to about the highest possible level of performance. But if you take an old muscle car, you're starting from scratch. You can do anything you want to that engine, and eventually get a lot of power out of it."

"What does yours run?"

"Eleven hundred and twenty horses, with a thousand and fifty pounds of torque."

"Holy shit, are you serious?"

"Yeah, it's quite a monster." Roche admitted.

"What can you do with this one?"

"Uh, I'm not sure. It's already got a custom carb, plus the supercharger... probably around six hundred horsepower, and another hundred at least with the nitro boost. What do you drive, by the way?"

"A 2001 BMW M3 CSL," Nima said.

"Very cool. What does your brother drive?"

"He's in to motorcycles. Every couple years he'll either total his bike or trade it in and get a new one. Right now he's got a Buell street bike, whatever their top model was last year."

Roche was impressed. "Awesome. I've always wanted one of those. Where do you guys get your vehicles? I don't see any new car dealerships around here."

"These days if you want a car in Iran, you either buy it used or import it. Nobody sells new cars here; it's one of the UN sanctions, for some reason. Anyway the three of us travel to Switzerland on business all the time, so we buy anything we want there. Kujet brings us parts sometimes, but his business is too backlogged for us to wait for a whole car."

"I see." They reached the CBI building, and Nima directed the driver to a gate that was separate from the main parking entrance. Nima used his ID badge to open the security barrier, and Karl drove down a long, straight, descending tunnel to the executive parking spaces. It was just as the banker had described – the left wall was a thick pane of darkly tinted glass, separating them from the main garage, and along the right was a row of private elevators. Roche spotted a big, black Audi sedan and took the empty space next to it.

"We've been trying to get dad to buy a new car," Nima said as Roche stepped out and took a closer look at the Audi.

"What's wrong with this S8?"

"Nothing, it's just twelve years old and it's a bloody bitch trying to get new parts for it. The damned thing coughed up a turbo last month, and I had to rebuild it myself."

Roche took the jack from the trunk and raised the rear end of the Oldsmobile. "So what's he going to replace it with?"

"I don't know. He doesn't like the new Audis, he doesn't like the new BMW's, and he *hates* the new Benzes. He's flip-flopping between an Aston Martin, one of the supercharged Jaguars, a Bentley Continental or a Maserati. We're trying to push him toward either the Maserati Quattroporte or the Aston Rapide."

"Man, you guys must be loaded."

"Between our salaries here and the business our uncle gives us, we do alright."

"So how does that all it work?" Roche had opened up the suspension tuning kit and was rolling under the Oldsmobile to inspect the rear end. "What exactly do you guys do for, uh, your uncle?"

"How much are you allowed to know?"

"Kahlil swore me to secrecy. Anything I see or hear in Iran stays in Iran."

"Dad's the money man," Nima explained, as he helped Roche adjust the rear axle springs. "He directs funds from the US to about twenty different resistance groups here in Iran. He also handles Kujet's money transactions, which are substantial. Keeping his money is a major operation in of itself. Kujet actually lives off of the profits from his front business, selling ancient treasures to Europeans and importing cars and stereos and French wine for rich Persians like us. The money he makes in the arms trade gets divided up into eleven bank accounts in Switzerland, the Cayman Islands, and Belize. He keeps three shares in separate countries as his own retirement fund, the rest are used at our uncle's discretion, which dad directs if it's going anywhere in the Middle East."

"That sounds like a serious deal."

"My brother and I are like well-paid errand runners. We are employed by CBI as security handlers – in the banking business that means we are 'couriers with guns' – and we travel a lot. We go all over the Middle East, Europe, and occasionally the Caribbean. We make deliveries and pickups working for the bank and for our uncle about equally."

374

Roche measured the tension on the leaf springs. Satisfied, he crawled out and lowered the car. "Well, that sounds like a really nice family business you guys have."

Nima changed subjects as they started on the front end of the vehicle. "Now, if you don't mind my asking, what are you doing here? On the ground in Iran running around with Kahlil, I mean. How'd you get mixed up with this?"

"Do you remember hearing a really loud bang up on the Avenue of Victory yesterday, at about noon?" Roche asked.

"I heard many explosions yesterday, but one especially loud one at about twelve o'clock I do recall, yes."

"That was my Super Hornet slamming into an ammo truck, which was sitting in the middle of an artillery battery. They were about to pound Kahlil, Kujet, a few of my Navy friends and about two dozen very nice and innocent Russians into very tiny bits."

"Ah, the embassy rescue fiasco. I should have guessed. You're that heroic fighter pilot that they were talking about on TV."

"What?"

"It was all over the news this morning. CNN and everyone else have the story saying that Navy SEALs were trying to evacuate the Russian ambassador and his staff, but the plane they were using for the rescue was shot down and everyone was stranded at the embassy."

"Well, that MC-130 wasn't for the extraction itself. It was just supposed to get the SEALs to the target area, which it did."

"Then, they're saying, the embassy came under fire from Iranian ground forces, but a lone US Navy fighter fought them off, and got shot down in the process."

"That was me, alright. But all that was over twenty-four hours ago. Are they reporting what's happened since then, that the Russians and SEALs are all safe?"

"I don't know, I haven't seen the news since this morning, but the US military had apparently cut off all the media feeds after your plane crashed. The news channels were just going over their usual twenty-four-hour speculation BS, but your trick with crashing the Hornet was the top story, last I checked."

At three o'clock, Sam came down to check on them. "Nima, your three-hour lunch is officially over. You need to go back up and pretend to work."

"Okay. Nice talking to you, my new friend."

"Likewise," Roche sincerely answered.

"Sharki, I'm leaving the key in the elevator here. If you need anything between now and five, just come up to my office, Okay?"

"Sure thing, Sam."

By a quarter to five, Roche had tuned the custom suspension system to closely approximate the settings on his own car. He had replaced the worn street rubber with brand new Goodyear Eagle F1 max-performance tires at the store, again very similar to what he had equipped on the Battleship. The supercharger was completely different from the one he'd designed for his own car, but it was fairly easy to install without much modification to the engine bay and promised plenty of boost. The nitro system was something he had never used before, because he refused to do anything to his own car that wasn't street-legal. But in this case he needed to squeeze every bit of power that he could out of the stolen muscle car. The bottles of nitrous oxide he placed on the floor of the rear cab, over the driveshaft hump. He could reach back easily from the front seat to switch from one bottle to the next when the first one ran dry. He used a high-pressure valve switch that would allow him to use the nitro in short pulses, and rigged that to a toggle button glued to the steering wheel. With all that done, he decided to get the old car's stereo working. He discovered an old Scorpions album in the eight-track deck, and left it in to play.

Twenty minutes later, with nothing else to do but wait, he was playing air-guitar to "Winds of Change," and watching the elevators, the entrance tunnel, and the main garage. If everything was going according to plan, the rest of the crew was waving guns at the people in the lobby of the bank, and Sam was locked inside the vault, and someone had the sense to trip the silent alarm to get the police to come over.

Roche saw a van pull in to the main garage, but it wasn't a police vehicle. Six people emerged, dressed like stereotypical terrorists and armed with assault rifles.

"You have got to be kidding me," he said aloud to himself. *Bank robberies are extremely common – that's what Sam said – you get these oppressed minority groups, they form gangs, rob from the wealthy ruling class to feed their people...* Two days ago Roche couldn't have told the difference between a Palestinian and a Pakistani, but by now he knew enough to see that these fellows weren't Persians.

They were still unloading their van, removing explosives, ammunition, and several large, empty sacks which were clearly intended for more than just shopping. Roche imagined several scenarios that could play out when these real bank robbers met the three fake ones upstairs. All of them involved a lot of people getting shot. By the time the gang had organized their weapons and pressed the call button for the elevator, Roche decided how to stop them.

The power to the elevators was out. The robbers didn't know that, and they would wait for at least a minute before deciding to take the stairs to the lobby four floors up. Roche took Sam's elevator, which still had its own, independent power, and rode it up to the fourteenth floor. He ran through Sam's outer office – startling his secretary – and kept going down the hall to the main stairwell. He ran down the stairs three at a time, descending to the lobby in about thirty seconds. Here there was a problem he didn't anticipate: the stairwell was not continuous all the way to the garage levels. He would have to step out into the lobby itself, and go through another door to reenter the stairwell that continued down to the basement and parking.

Through the tiny window in the stairwell door, Roche could see Cannon and the two Iraqi agents, now dressed similarly to the real bank robbers he'd just seen, in complete control of the lobby. Roche's concern was that his guys would shoot him instinctively if he surprised them. Roche rattled the door handle to get their attention. As he hoped, Cannon looked right at him. He raised his gun, but he had to look closely before he fired because the window was so small. Then he recognized Roche and lowered the gun. Roche opened the door and stepped out.

"What in God's name are you doing here?" Cannon demanded loudly in Russian.

"No time to explain, stick to the plan," Karl answered in the same language. He drew his Desert Eagle, put his back against the door that led downstairs, and pushed through. As he hoped, the others ignored him and went back to work. Roche ran downstairs with his pistol held in front of him, pointing it around corners before he followed down each flight of stairs.

He had descended two stories when he ran right into the first gangster. He was cradling his Kalashnikov and was running hard, and appeared to be bleeding from the left arm. Roche did not calculate this information before he drew his leg up, planted his foot on the man's chest, kicked him back down the stairs and fired a single, lethal round through the terrorist's torso. The next bank robber was coming up the flight below and saw his partner splatter on the landing. He cautiously peered around the corner with his gun at his shoulder, but again Roche fired first, shooting the bandit through the eye as he aimed. The rest of the gangsters held up when they saw the two bodies on the landing, and shouted amongst themselves, saying something Roche didn't understand.

He wished he had a grenade that he could bounce around the corner, but he didn't, and charging four guys with their AKs ready to fire seemed like a bad idea. He looked back up the flight of stairs he'd just come down. The landing above him was shorter than the landings that had doors, and there was a railing about two feet short of the stairwell wall and only empty space in between. Roche went back up the stairs and grabbed the rail with his right hand, hooked his right leg over the bars, and hung off the other side so only his head and left arm extended below the landing. He could now see two more bank robbers crouched below him with they're rifles ready, but aimed up the stairs away from him. The heavy pistol was now in his left hand, which he held steady despite his extremely awkward firing position. The gangsters turned and looked up just in time to see Roche fire two more huge bullets. Then he swung his leg over and dropped down.

He kept moving downstairs and didn't pause when he heard gunfire further down below. People with noisy automatic weapons were shooting each other in the garage. Roche should have realized that this meant the police had reached the garage and were engaging the last two gangsters, but he was moving to fast to think about the implications. He opened the door on the parking level, and a dead bank robber tumbled back through the doorway. He was clutching an empty AK and had been riddled with bullet holes. The sixth gangster appeared to have melted into the side of their van.

The Tehran Civic Police Department had the doorway covered and started shooting at Roche. He jumped back and tried to close the door, but the dead bandit was in the way. He fired both of his guns into the garage without bothering to aim and the police officers took cover. He fired over their heads until the magazines were empty, then he dragged the dead man through the door and closed it. Roche paused, looked at his empty guns, then at the dead guy. He had a thought about taking the assault rifle, but it wasn't loaded. Roche pulled the weapon free and quickly searched the body for a banana clip. Before he found one he noticed what the gangster held in is other hand. It looked like a coffee can with magnets on the bottom and with flashing numbers on the top. 00:17, 00:16, 00:15...

Roche turned and ran back up the stairs and collided with Cannon on the landing. "What's going on?" the agent demanded.

"RUN!!" Roche shoved past him and Cannon turned and followed. They got passed the four dead guys and halfway up the third flight of stairs before the bomb exploded.

It was a shaped-charge device, intended to blow a hole through the door of the safe. As it turned out, Roche had aimed it directly at the stairwell door when he dropped the body. A police officer whose life Roche had deliberately spared opened the door just as the timer reached zero. He saw only bright light. His fellow officers saw him briefly silhouetted by the flash before being consumed, and then they too were incinerated. The van was thrown across the garage and several other vehicles caught in the blast were also thrown around. Outside, on the street level, the cloud of fire and dust finished its three-story climb and blasted out the security gate.

Dust and smoke was all that reached the two Americans, apart from the terrific noise of the blast. It took a moment for the ringing in their ears to stop, and then Cannon asked with belated surprise "What the hell was all that?"

"Real bank robbers," Roche explained. "I came around to stop them from getting up here and shooting it out with you guys."

"That was good thinking," Cannon admitted.

"The cops caught them before I did, and chased them up to me."

"What was that bomb? A shaped-charge for getting into the vault?"

"I guess so. I think they tried to blow themselves up once the cops found them."

"Okay, this actually works out for us, because now the police think our getaway plan just got blown up along with the rest of our gang. Also, big explosions will make them cautious. So they think we have nowhere to run, but they won't try and make another direct assault."

"That makes sense. What should I do now? Should I go back to the car?"

"No, the hostages have seen you, so you'd better stay with us now. Don't say anything unless you have to, and only speak Russian."

"No English?"

"The rest of us don't speak English; we're uneducated Baluchis from the mountains. But if we worked in the oil fields we'd probably know some Russian. It fits the cover for all of us. We need to keep that straight otherwise someone will figure out we were up to something else."

"Why wouldn't I speak Farsi to you?"

"Different dialects. It would be like a Texan trying to talk to an Irishman after they'd both been drinking. We're speaking a tribal dialect that the people up there have trouble following."

"Got it."

With that settled, Cannon and Roche went back up to the lobby, where the two Iraqis still had things covered. Cannon explained what had happened, and the Iraqis reported they'd finished looting the tellers' counter and the ATMs. Then the police started shouting at them over the bullhorns. Roche didn't understand any of it, but he correctly assumed it was something along the lines of "we have you surrounded, your friends are dead, come out with your hands up." Roche casually checked his watch, noting it was five-twenty. They only had to keep this going for another ten minutes.

Cannon saw Roche's movement and shook his head, then pulled the sleeve of his shirt over his wrist and signaled that Roche should do the same. Roche wondered why, and then he realized that he was wearing an eighteen-hundred-dollar TAG Heuer watch. The stainless steel band and black-faced tachymeter dial were often mistaken for a much more expensive brand. It might make the police suspicious if they saw it being worn by a poor street thug. He discretely removed his watch and put it in his pocket.

The police continued talking over bullhorns, and Cannon shouted back angry retorts. Roche could see more police forces gathering outside, and warily watched the stairwell door in case they tried coming through the garage again. Cannon turned to the small crowd of hostages and asked something in Farsi. Apparently his question was garbled because the bank employees and customers just looked confused. Cannon reworded the question twice but didn't get a different reaction. Then he asked "Does anybody speak Russian?"

Razi timidly raised his hand and said "A little bit, sir."

"What do you do here?" Cannon asked angrily, mostly so the young man could explain to his coworkers why he spoke the language. The conversation was in a mix of Russian and Farsi, so the conspirators could pretend they barely understand each other.

"I-I-I'm a courier, a-a package boy. Sometimes I work in Eastern Europe."

"Okay. Listen, the police have the building surrounded and they sealed the garage. You need to show us another way out."

"I, I don't know another way out."

"Liar! Tell me how we can escape or I shoot someone's brains out!"

380

"Dad's parking space," Nima suggested in Farsi.

"SHUT UP!" Ellirat yelled at him.

"He says there is a parking area for executives," Razi said.

"For *who*?" Cannon pretended not to understand the Russian word. Roche was also having trouble following the dialogue but he thought the actors were putting on an Oscar-worthy foreign-language drama.

"The bosses," Razi said again, using a different term. "They have a separate parking area."

"I told you, the garage was sealed. You heard the explosion, right? We can't go out that way."

"No, listen to me, this garage is separated, protected, it would have been safe from the bomb, okay?"

"Okay..." Cannon acted skeptical. "How do we get to bosses' parking garage?"

"They have elevators in their offices."

"Elevators are out too."

"These ones run on backup power."

"On *what*?"

"Emergency power?" Razi tried. Cannon still looked confused. "Generators. Separate generators, not the main power. Look, they work okay?"

"You'd better be right," Cannon told him. "You come with us. If we can't get out, we shoot you!" he grabbed Razi and shoved him roughly toward the stairwell.

"Okay! Okay! Quit pushing!"

The four bank robbers followed Razi up the stairs, but first Cannon dropped a backpack he was carrying and shouted to the police. "Stay back! This is another bomb and it will kill the hostages if you come in here!"

"Will that fool them?" Ellirat asked once they were all in the stairwell.

"Not likely," Cannon admitted, now speaking in English. "Do we have to go all the way up to Sam's office?" he asked Razi. "Can't we take someone else's elevator?"

"All the executive offices are on floors fourteen and higher, so yes, we do have to go all the way up there."

"Damn, I hate stairs."

"They'll do you good, you soft westerner," Ellirat teased.

They'd gone up three flights when they heard the stairwell door bang open below them.

"Police! Stop where you are!" The cops shouted in Farsi.

"I warned them." Cannon pulled a remote device out of his pocket and hit the switch. The backpack in the lobby blew up. It wasn't a high-explosive bomb, just a smoke grenade and several tear-gas canisters. The policemen coughed and gagged and gave up on the idea of chasing the spies up the stairs.

They finally reached the fourteenth floor, and found Sam's office. The secretary screamed when they came in. Roche pointed his empty Desert Eagle in her face and said "Shut up," imitating the Farsi phrase he'd heard Ellirat use. She stopped screaming. Cannon held Razi at gunpoint while he opened the elevator.

The elevator dropped them off right where Roche had started half an hour ago, in the executive garage. "What the bloody hell happened here?" Razi asked, when the doors opened. The van that had belonged to the real gangsters had hit the big bulletproof window. There was a huge spider web of cracks where the three-ton vehicle had impacted, and the glass was half-melted in places by the explosion, but the luxury cars and their Oldsmobile were all still safe and sound.

Roche had intended to leave the trunk and the doors open for a speedy getaway, but in his haste he'd left the car without any preparation. He ran around the car unlocking the doors and popping the trunk before settling in the driver's seat and starting the engine. The Iraqis loaded the trunk with their bags of cash and then climbed in the back seat. Then finally Cannon put the front seat back and sat down.

"Fasten your seat belts and hold on to your silly hats," Roche ordered. He put the car in reverse and made a tire-smoking, axle-hopping, backward dash up the tunnel. A patrol car sat at the security gate, blocking the exit. Ellirat shouted a warning which Roche ignored. The car was doing fifty-five miles an hour when the tunnel leveled out, and the heavy coupe went airborne. It vaulted over the gate and narrowly cleared the police car. The four wheels slammed down together on the pavement in the middle of the street, and Roche spun the car around to kill the momentum before they hit the other curb. His passengers all shouted some combination of excited profanities but Roche wasn't paying any attention to them at the moment.

The spectacular exit had not gone unnoticed by the police officers surrounding the building. They all began piling into their cars and trucks, anticipating a pursuit. Roche didn't disappoint. He was facing away from the CBI building's main entrance, where the police had concentrated. He dropped the clutch and burned rubber all the way

382

through first gear. He stayed on the same road, which was the wide-open Revolution Boulevard, as he accelerated to over a hundred miles an hour.

"What's the plan here, Sharkey?" Cannon asked. "We obviously didn't make our getaway unnoticed."

"Plan? You're asking me like I've done this before."

"You volunteered to drive, so you must have a plan," Ellirat said.

"I volunteered to drive because I didn't want to have to hold up a bank. And I honestly didn't expect to have anywhere near this many cops coming after us." Roche's voice remained steady but he was as close to panic as he'd ever been. His rearview mirror was filled with flashing lights.

"Video game, Karl," Cannon recognized his distress and tried to calm him down. "You can do this – you've done it a hundred times in games like Need for Speed, or Grand Theft Auto or something. Now you just need to do it for real."

It worked. Cannon could see the panic leave Roche's eyes as he looked away from the mirror. "Step one: clear the datum," he said. "The farther we get from the scene of the crime, the harder it will be for their backup units to find us." He kept the pedal down until they had gone a mile and a half further, at which point Roche made a left turn. "Step two, attempt to evade, immobilize or disable pursuing vehicles." They were now heading straight for the heart of the market district. Traffic was thickening and the sidewalks were crowded with vendors and shoppers. Roche weaved through the traffic at high speed but carefully avoiding the civilians in his way. The police that were following them tried to keep up but quickly found themselves in a traffic accident.

Roche made a right and a left, continuing south but now on a narrower road. He slowed up a little, and held his hand on the horn as he slalomed through the traffic. The road abruptly ended in a pedestrian mall. Roche drove right through, twisting around bazaar stalls and sending the shoppers scrambling for cover. More police cars followed, and were tenaciously keeping up with the heavier Oldsmobile. Roche made another left into a narrow alley. He ploughed through heaps of garbage and old crates, and turned back on to the parallel street he'd used earlier. The first police car that followed him out of the alley got broadsided a by a city bus, and the wreck blocked the alley.

"You lost them!" Elessar cheered. "No, never mind." More cops came out of side streets. Roche made another right turn, and two patrol cars closing from opposite directions got in a head-on behind him. Ahead there was a restaurant with a second-floor patio extending over the sidewalk. Roche put the car in a controlled slide and clipped one of the wooden support beams with his rear quarter panel. The balcony collapsed, dumping tables and dinner patrons into the path of the pursuit vehicles.

By now the police were trying to shoot at the speeding 442. Bullets started zinging off the fenders, and the three passengers ducked. Roche looked back. Two cars were right behind him, and in his mirror he could see guns pointed at his car from the inside windows on each car. He started weaving a little bit, and instinctively the police drivers spread their cars apart. Then Roche abruptly hit the brakes, and the cops rushed past on either side. As they tried to shoot at him they hit each other with crossfire, killing one driver and causing the other to veer into a shop window.

Roche accelerated again, passed the wreck and turned on the next street he crossed. Another cop car pulled up right behind him, and the officer in the passenger seat was leaning out with a shotgun. Roche saw it in the side mirror. "Duck!" he ordered. The passengers went down again as buckshot perforated the trunk lid and rear window. Roche watched the rear-view mirror as the police officer pumped his weapon. Roche swerved sharply to the left as the cop fired again, and the passenger-side window imploded, showering Cannon with glass.

Karl kept his left hand on the wheel and reached into his gear bag with his right, fishing out his Desert Eagle and a full clip. He released the clip in midair and caught it in the gun, and rapped the butt of the pistol against the dash to lock the magazine in place. Then he put the slide in his teeth and loaded a round. As Cannon watched the driver do this, his eyes widened in amazement.

Then Roche abruptly swung the car into a ninety-degree drift, doing a balancing act with the four wheels to slide along with the car facing perpendicular to the course of the road. The cop car rammed into them and pushed the Oldsmobile sideways. "Lean back," Roche instructed. He pointed the gun just past Cannon's nose and fired. The bullet punched through the frame of the Mercedes patrol car and the stomach of the cop hanging from the window. The door and the cop with the shotgun fell from the car and tumbled into the street.

"Left side!" Elessar yelled. Another police car was approaching from the other way at high speed.

"Hold this." Roche dropped the pistol in Cannon's lap. He grabbed the gear knob and downshifted to break out of the wheelspin and straightened the front wheels, and the Olds shot down an alleyway with a fiery trail of nitrous-laden exhaust. The cops slammed into each other and blocked the passage when they tried to follow.

The alley dumped Roche on to another street on the southern edge of the market district. Several more police cars were on this road, racing to set up a road block before the bank robbers could escape onto wider streets. Roche showed up right in the middle of them. "shit, we're surrounded!" Cannon noted.

"Not for long." Roche turned the same way the cops were going and floored the accelerator. There were two cars ahead of him and five more coming up fast behind, now trying to form a solid box around him. On the two-lane road, Roche's options were limited. He took the path of least resistance, and rear-ended the Suzuki in front of him. The police driver lost control as he was pushed hard from behind, and clipped the left rear corner of the car in front of him. This caused that police car to spin out as well, in the opposite direction. The two patrol vehicles slammed into walls on opposite sides of the street as Roche drove on right between them. The wrecked sedans bounced back into the traffic lanes just in time to cause the rest of the police vehicles to slide into an unavoidable pile-up.

"That was cool," Cannon remarked, looking back at the wreck.

Roche said nothing. He skidded around a traffic circle that marked the southeast corner of the market district and kept going on what was now a much wider and busier thoroughfare. Roche slowed down and tried to blend in with the traffic, but only two blocks further a police car found them again. By now the rumpled sheet metal was giving the fugitive vehicle away. Roche switched nitrous bottles and accelerated to try to outrun the police.

"They must be calling all cars," Cannon remarked, as more vehicles rejoined the pursuit. "These guys keep coming out of the woodwork like-"

"Gun," Roche demanded, cutting him off mid-simile.

Cannon stared blankly. "Huh?"

Roche snapped at him. "Give me my gun. Don't make me feel around your crotch for it." Cannon picked it up from his lap and Roche grabbed it out of his hand. He was coming up behind a flatbed semi-trailer loaded with huge concrete pipes. He passed it on the right at ninety miles an hour and fired at the cables holding the pipes in place.

The men in the Oldsmobile didn't see what happened on the other side of the trailer, but one of the heavy steel cables whipped around and struck the windshield of a patrol car trying to pass the truck on the left. That car peeled off. An instant later a nine-ton tube of concrete landed on another patrol car, crushing it to go-kart dimensions. Another police car drove right through another one of the large-diameter pipes as it rolled across the lanes. That vehicle was inverted and launched out the other end on its roof.

The Iraqis twisted in their seats to watch the destruction behind them, and uttered profanities in awestruck tones. Two more pipes skewed around and completely blocked the right side of the road, and another police car managed to drive right into the stopped semi at full speed.

Up ahead the traffic thinned out and after they passed another intersection the whole street was completely deserted. "This road is closed ahead," Ellirat told him. "They're building a new interchange over the highway about three miles up, and there are other construction projects before that."

"Excellent." Roche called maps from his memory, and remembered a four-level overpass system under construction in this part of town. "I know where I'm going," he said – without any reassuring effect – as he drove between two sawhorses marking the end of the road. Five squad cars followed him into the work site, and the all-wheel-drive, turbocharged Suzukis started to catch up on the softer dirt. Roche let one pull alongside, then swerved and slammed it. The cop lost control and ploughed into a parked bulldozer at ninety-five miles an hour. Another officer tried to use a PIT maneuver. Roche slowed abruptly again, causing the patrol car to spin in front of him. Karl used another shot of nitrous to accelerate, and he T-boned the car and pushed it into a mobile crane. The impact sliced the Suzuki and its driver in half. Roche drove on without flinching.

The other three police cars dropped back a little. Roche took out a guy wire, bringing down a huge billboard sign across their path. Up ahead he saw the incomplete overpass. Two branches of the road connected with the south-bound highway lanes, and two others started to cross the highway to join the north side. But these towering bridges ended in mid-air. Roche kept driving, intending to take the unpaved ramp to the southbound highway, but the police beat him two it. Two more patrol cars came off the highway, cutting across Roche's path. Roche clipped one and sent it spinning off into a guard rail. The other forced him to drive up the overpass and rode his tail up the rise.

386

Cannon, Ellirat and Elessar looked at where the road was going to take them. The overpass curved south before ending sixteen feet above the oncoming highway traffic. Roche put the pedal to the floor, punched the nitro and took the flying curve.

Cannon looked at the driver, saw the steely determination on his face, and said "No fucking way."

Roche said nothing. At one hundred and twenty five miles an hour, one hundred feet from the edge, he let the steering wheel move left against the turn. He immediately cut it hard to the right, and hit the clutch, and yanked hard on the hand brake. The rear wheels locked up and the car spun on a dime.

To the four men in the car, everything seemed to move in slow-motion as the 442 sailed off the ramp, backwards, flat parallel to the road below. The cop car followed them over the edge, despite the driver stomping the brake as hard as possible.

In mid-air, Roche straightened the wheel, shifted down to first gear and let out the clutch. He had made a mental calculation in the very brief moment he had to think before launching his car into the air. He knew that after falling eight feet the vehicle would have accelerated downwards due to gravity to a downward impact velocity of sixteen feet per second. He knew the high-performance shock absorbers were designed to handle that kind of force, barely. He also knew he would land on the roof of a city bus and not on the highway another eight feet further down.

The passengers didn't know any of this and they screamed in terror.

The Oldsmobile sailed over a hundred feet through the air before it landed flat on roof of the bus. It bounced hard and sparks flew from the undercarriage, but the shock absorbers did their job and kept the car from punching its springs through the chassis. The rear wheels spun forward but the car continued to slide backward for a moment. Meanwhile the police car had plunged off the overpass and landed on its nose in the middle of the freeway, directly in the bus's path. The police car exploded under the dual impacts. At that moment the fat Goodyear tires on the Olds got purchase and launched the muscle car forwards, off the bus, over the wrecked cop car and on its way down the highway. The bus skidded to a stop, and was promptly rear-ended by a fuel truck resulting in a fiery pileup that blocked all the northbound lanes.

The Mukhabarat brothers felt themselves, clearly amazed to be in one piece. "Praise be to Allah, we're alive!" Elessar muttered.

"We'd better be," his brother replied, "because you are not the sort of virgin I have in mind for when I reach paradise."

Cannon just looked back and watched the disastrous wreck unfold, then he turned to Roche and said with infinite understatement, "You really have to learn to deal with road rage differently."

The CIA agent directed Roche to get off the highway at the next exit. Roche parked behind a gas station and waited while Ellirat made a call on his cell phone.

"What are we doing now?" Karl asked.

"Ellirat's telling one of his friends where to find us," Cannon explained. "This car is too hot to drive anymore, but we planned ahead for this."

Five minutes later a flatbed wrecker and a limousine arrived. The battered 442 was loaded on the flatbed and covered with a tarp, and the four robbers boarded the Mercedes stretch limo. The bags of cash contained over a hundred and fifty thousand dollars in rials and international currency. Chump change compared to what the bank had in its vaults, but a decent haul nonetheless.

"We're billionaires!" Elessar exclaimed. "Before the exchange rate, anyway. How do you want to divide the swag, Kahlil?"

"Don't look at me, I'm leaving town tomorrow. I can't spend rials anywhere."

"There's other currency too. Swiss francs, euros..."

"Help yourselves. It's too much of a bother for me to launder it, and Sam can't touch this money either."

"What about you, Sharki, you want a cut?"

"I have the same problem," Roche said. "How am I going to spend it?"

"I could clean it for you right now." Ellirat pulled out his wallet, fat with US and local bills. "How much do you charge for that little thrill ride?"

"Just give me, uh, thirty million rials, so I can pay back Nima for the parts he bought for me."

"Fair enough. I'll add a couple grand in US too. We owe you that much for the car anyway."

Roche accepted the money. "What are you going to do with it?"

"You mean the car? We're keeping it."

"You should drop it in empty lot and torch it," Cannon said, "or at least take it to a chop shop. It's way to hot for you to hang on to."

388

"WHAT?" Roche was appalled at the thought that such a fate should befall a 1970 Olds 442 W-30.

"Nonsense," Elessar said. "All the cops have on it is the make, model, color and the phony plate number. We have somewhere safe to hide it for now. We just need to do a little body work to fix it up, find another clean set of plates, put a fresh coat of gloss on it... I'm thinking black, Ellirat. What do you say?"

"Yeah, black or maybe dark green. You have excellent taste in automobiles, Sharki. I will enjoy our new ride very much."

"Well thanks. You two had better take care of that car. It's a rare classic."

The limo dropped Cannon and Roche off at a huge house in a very nice part of town. The Iraqis wished the Americans a fond farewell before the Mercedes whisked them off into the night.

Razi opened the gate for the Americans to enter the Samadad estate. Mrs. Samadad had prepared a delicious dinner and Roche and Cannon sat down with their family to eat together.

Cannon recounted the car chase, and Roche only nodded his head in confirmation when the hosts looked at him in disbelief. Sam then told them that the operation was a success on his end; the accounts were erased and the money was liquidated. He'd already set up new clean deposit accounts for the money in Switzerland, which one of the boys could deposit later.

"Thank you both for helping me," Sam said. "Without you guys and the robbery this would have been impossible. Thanks especially to you, Mr. Sharki. You have nothing to do with any of our work, but without you I don't think Kahlil or the Mukhabarat brothers would have been able to escape."

"There's no way we could have evaded the police without his talents behind the wheel," Cannon agreed. "And I probably would have been killed yesterday if it weren't for his skill in the air."

"I'm just glad I could do some good for your cause," Roche said. "I really hope we don't completely screw up trying to put this country back together like we did with Iraq and Afghanistan."

"I wouldn't worry," Mrs. Samadad said. "Our people know you aren't here to invade us, and we all look forward to a future partnership with America."

"To once and future allies," Sam toasted. "Now, Sharki, what can I do to help you get home?"

"I think Kahlil and I are going to leave in the morning," Roche said. "Our military can pick us up once we're clear of the urban center.

389

If we could get another car we'll just go south on the highway until we find a good landing zone for a helicopter."

"So, all you need from us a clean set of wheels."

"And a place to spend the night."

"Well, that's a given, but Sharki, I feel I owe you something more. Not you," Sam pointed at Cannon, "you owed me a favor. But for you, Sharki, to risk so much to help me and my family, well, my honor demands I make some form of compensation."

"I can respect that. What did you have in mind?"

"One of my two accounts that you just helped me salvage was my fund for buying my family a home in America someday. I will split that with you, and put your share in a high-yield annuity account in your own American bank."

"Oh, Sam, please-"

"No, I insist. I shall be left with more than enough to purchase and furnish a very respectable house in the American southwest; your real estate is not so expensive as it once was. And I believe that you should have a rightful portion of the money you were instrumental in securing for us."

"Okay, I'm not going to turn down an offer like that. But just give me a quarter, not a half, okay? That's more money than I'd know what to do with."

Mr. Samadad smiled and shook Roche's hand. "We have a deal. Now we just have to get you out of here so you can enjoy it."

# CHAPTER 19: ESCAPIST ADVENTURE

## *REAGAN* – 0330 LOCAL, JUNE 3RD

Deuce stood on the bridge, watching Hannibal's flight take off into darkness of the small hours of the morning. "He's been out there for forty hours now."

Krause was standing behind him, drinking coffee. "We'll have him on the deck before the morning's over. Hannibal will get him home."

"He still has to get out of Tehran, past that manhunt. The news might have made him a superstar in the US, but he's also Iran's most wanted now."

## TEHRAN

Roche and Cannon were given their own guest accommodations in the Samadad home, and they both slept very well that night, although not nearly long enough. They woke up at 4:30 and were given a hearty breakfast prepared by Mrs. Samadad. Roche radioed the *Reagan* to let them know they were on their way out of town, and then Sam took them outside to see their vehicle. A black and charcoal Buell 1125R motorcycle waited in the driveway, with Razi holding two helmets and the keys.

"Razi, you're giving us your motorbike?"

"My gift to you, my friends. I was going to trade it in before too long anyway. Take it, and have fun on your last drive through Tehran."

Cannon's cell phone rang just then, and he excused himself and stepped aside.

Roche tried to protest to Razi, despite his own desire for the marvelous sportbike. "I can't deprive you of your own daily driver, Razi. How will you get around?"

"Don't worry. I'm not going out that much in the middle of a war. And I'm going to Switzerland with the money as soon as the airport opens. I was going to buy a new Ducati once I got there anyway. Now please stop trying to argue with our culture of generosity and go catch your flight."

Roche and Cannon embraced each of the Samadads in turn and took their leave. "Very nice family," Roche said, as he drove slowly down the driveway. He accelerated and turned hard onto the street, and the Buell responded with minimal effort. Roche eased off the throttle and remarked "And a very nice bike, too."

"This thing is *loud*," Cannon observed unnecessarily. "It sounds like a Harley."

"It does," Roche agreed, "sorta. The engine's a big V-twin, not one of those screaming inline four-cylinders in a Japanese sportbike. It doesn't rev as high and make quite as much peak horsepower as a real top-end liter-class bike, but it makes positively ridiculous amounts of torque, so no matter how fast you're going you can accelerate like you lit a rocket." To demonstrate, Roche twisted the throttle. Suddenly the front wheel was off the ground and the speedometer bounced up from fifty to eighty.

"Stop that!" Cannon yelled.

The tach and speedo needles came down, followed by the front wheel. "I didn't even downshift just then. I can do that in any gear. That's pure torque right there."

"Cool," Cannon said, even though he was more frightened than impressed. "But I'm nervous enough on two wheels. Try to keep them both on the ground, okay?"

"No problem. This thing is really stable, don't worry."

"Yeah?" Cannon didn't think a motorcycle that weighed less than a self-propelled lawnmower and had more power than a small car could be described that way.

"All the weight is right in the lower center of the chassis. The big engine's mounted low, and the muffler's slung under the body instead of under the seat or over the rear swing arms like an ordinary sportbike. Even the fuel is actually in the frame of the motorcycle instead of up here where it is on most bikes." Roche slapped the black body panel in front of him, which housed a small storage compartment instead of a fuel tank. "Everything else is built as light as they can make it, especially the wheels. They even design the brake rotors around the rim of the wheels instead of the hub, to make them as strong and light as possible. As a result, you got a low center of gravity and almost no unsprung weight, so this thing handles better than any other machine in the world."

Cannon was rolling his eyes inside his helmet as his companion gushed over the motorcycle. "Great." He pointed to the next intersection. "Take a right turn here. I need to meet with someone before we go."

"Is that who was on the phone?"

"Yeah, some kid who works for Kujetski," Cannon said.

392

"What's the errand?"

"Don't worry, it's nothing dangerous. He's got a data disk that I need to pick up and take with me, that's all. He's in an old apartment building in the west end."

Roche remembered flying over the western part of the city, and it looked pretty seedy from the air. But he didn't see how they could get in much trouble as long as they didn't linger. "Okay, how do I get there?"

"Just go west on the main street here, until we get to the highway."

"Okay. What does this guy do for Kujet?"

"He's a hacker. Kujetski had him trying to find some schematics for- actually I shouldn't tell you what it's for." Roche was in on a lot of secrets but none as big or important as the actual operation to locate and destroy Rannovich's command bunker. Cannon decided to keep the aviator in the dark on that one. "Anyway, he found something useful and I need to take it with me."

"Can't he just email it to you?"

"No, the Ministry of Information scans people's email much more than our own NSA does, and if its encrypted, they won't let it out of the country. And if this kid tried to hack the national email servers, he'd be arrested in fairly short order."

"So he needs someone to physically carry a flash drive or something out of the country, and since the airport is closed, only you and I are eligible."

"Exactly. But like I said, it's no big deal. This will take half an hour tops, and we could borrow a few things from Kujet once we get to his safe house."

"Like what?"

"Ammo for your sidearms. You're down to your last short clip on the Glock, and you're out of fifty cal for the Desert Eagle, right?"

"Yeah, but we're not expecting to have to shoot anyone today."

"Better safe than sorry."

Kujet owned four apartments on the top floor of a thirty-story complex on Tehran's west side. As Roche expected, it was in a bad part of town, and the building was very poorly maintained. But Kujetski had done a pretty good job of furnishing two apartments as semi-permanent living quarters. The third was a storehouse for small arms, and the fourth was a computer center. This apartment was converted into one giant office, housing a huge supercomputer with a twenty-year-old Indian kid sitting in the middle of it. Indian as in he was from India, not a Native American.

"Good morning, Albie," Cannon said as he let himself into apartment 30-D.

"Not yet, C, it's not a good morning yet." Albie faced away from the door, and was surrounded on three sides by rows of LCD monitors. One showed whatever program Albie was writing right then, another was on a website with probably illegal content, another was connected to satellite TV, and another fifteen showed feeds from closed-circuit security cameras all over the building. Roche noticed his own face was on TV, but the volume was turned down low and he couldn't hear what Fox News was saying about him. A caption under his face read "Top Gun Hero." Roche suddenly did not look forward to going home.

"What do you have for me, buddy?" Cannon asked.

Albie spun his chair around to face them. He held a tiny chip in one hand and a bottle of Mountain Dew in the other. "I only have everything that our defector didn't have with him. It's the whole complex, baby."

"You hacked the mainframe?"

"Well, not really." Albie looked despondent. "I couldn't get in on my own. I had to call Kuj and get that engineer guy to walk me through the main security. But once inside, I was able to hack the rest of the designers' files."

"You called Kujetski?" Cannon asked unhappily.

"Yeah, on his satellite phone. Don't worry, it's untraceable."

"Right." Cannon reached for the thumbnail sized micro SD card Albie held out to him. "You packed all the files on this little chip?"

"That little chip can hold thirty-two gigabytes of data. I only used twenty percent of its capacity. Did you know a soda bottle like this full of cards like that could contain the data equivalent of your Library of Congress, plus every song recorded and every movie filmed in the last decade?"

"Thank you," Cannon sighed. "That's the second most useless piece of information I've learned today. Can you give a package to carry this little thing?"

"You can plug it into your cell phone if you'd like."

"No, I'll need you to get me some sort of casing for this thing that will provide better protection than my phone. It needs to be waterproof, fireproof, bulletproof, shockproof, and EMP and ESD shielded."

"No problem." Albie took the micro SD card back and rummaged through a drawer under the desk.

Roche didn't like the way Cannon described that packaging. "Do you know something I don't?"

"Yes. I mean no. I'm just taking precautionary measures in case something happens. Like if my helicopter somehow gets shot down."

"Uh-huh…" Roche was now feeling very uncomfortable around that card.

"Here, Karl, why don't you go next door and grab some ammo for yourself. Cannon gave him the key for apartment 30-B. "And find an Uzi for me. Oh, and you can probably go ahead and wash off your disguise, too."

"That's Lieutenant Commander Karl Roche, I presume?" Albie asked after the aviator had gone out.

"Why are you asking?"

Albie pointed to the Fox News screen and turned up the audio.

"…Has now been missing in action for thirty-six hours since the SEALs and Russian civilians escaped. Roche's been out of contact but not out of the thoughts and prayers of millions of people. We have many emails of support to share with you, and we will be replaying Mrs. Roche's press conference at the top of the hour…"

"His *mom* held a press conference?" Cannon was stunned.

"About eight hours ago," Albie explained. "I haven't seen it yet, but apparently the local news had her under siege all weekend. This Roche fellow has been leading every single news program ever since the embassy rescue. He's like a national hero now. The American media is just eating him up. Actually, every single news channel I get has the same thing, even al-Jazeera. That guy's a global phenomenon right now."

Cannon watched for another minute as the Fox News anchor discussed details of Roche's brief Special Forces career that had been classified, but were now apparently international news. The events that led to his horrific injury in Iraq were being discussed in exacting detail, with input from former members of his SEAL team. "He's going to be awfully unhappy when he finds out about this," Cannon said.

"Not a fan of the press, is he?"

## SANTEE, CA

Tracy had been practically glued to the TV since early Sunday morning. At first she had only been watching cable news in an attempt to cure her insomnia. That's when they reported that a rescue operation in Tehran had run into major opposition, and that one transport and two Navy fighters flown by a squadron called the *Stingrays* had been hit. Tracy spent the next four hours switching from one news channel to another waiting for updates, before finally dozing off into a fitful sleep.

When she woke up she tore herself away from the TV, cleaned up and went to church for the first time in a month. She found plenty of people willing to pray with her for Karl Roche's safety. When she returned to her apartment she found that the news networks were leading with footage taken on the ground in Iran, showing a dark blue Super Hornet bombing an artillery battery, getting hit by a missile, and crashing into a second cluster of armored vehicle in a massive explosion. The news broadcasters didn't know the name of the heroic pilot, but as Tracy studied the image of the aviator floating over the city in his ejection seat, she got the awful feeling that it was Karl.

Later that afternoon while she was watching NBC, she saw a special news bulletin confirming her fears. Brian Williams read a press release from the flag admiral of the USS *Ronald Reagan* battle group, announcing that the downed aviator was indeed LCdr. Karl "Sharkey" Roche. The announcement was accompanied by video footage taken from Karl's plane as it was hit and crashed. After a while, they replayed the video with recorded radio communications between the aircraft. The last thing Karl said was "Don't worry buddy, just cover that Osprey and I'll be fine." But Tracy *was* worried. There was no report yet of whether or not the Osprey had been able to complete the rescue mission.

That news came at around five PM on the west coast, first reported on CNN but quickly spreading through all the networks. A video shot from the Osprey showed Karl Roche remaining behind on the ground, firing a machine gun at an Iranian soldier armed with an RPG. There was another statement from Admiral Krause, saying that Karl Roche had volunteered to stay behind to cover the Osprey's escape, and that no effort would be spared to mount a second rescue attempt to extract the brave aviator. Tracy wanted to cry herself numb, but she stopped herself when she saw Karl's face on the screen. It was only a stock photo of Karl in uniform, but there was a confidence to his smile – really more of a smug smirk than a smile – that seemed to tell Tracy *it will be alright.*

After that there was no new information about the operation or any rescue effort being made for Roche, but that didn't stop anyone from talking about it. The reporters dug up everything they could about America's newest hero. When the Special Operations Command confirmed that Commander Roche was a former SEAL and that seven of the nine SEALs he'd rescued were from his old platoon, well that just drove them nuts. Then they got into his service record from Iraq, something Tracy didn't know anything about, except somehow he now had a plastic arm.

One day, about four weeks earlier, Tracy had started to give Karl a chair massage. They had spent the day fishing and they were taking a long boat ride back through San Diego harbor. They had just taken the picture that was now displayed in Tracy's locket.

"So, what's the difference between a chair massage and a back rub?" Karl asked.

Tracy started squeezing his neck from behind, firmly and gently loosening the muscles. "A back rub is just rubbing your back. It feels good, and anyone can do it, but a chair massage is a little more intensive. It's a deep-tissue massage I can give you while you're sitting in a chair. I can reach pressure points like this..."

"Ooooooh." Tracy put her thumbs against the base of Karl's skull, and he felt like his head was weightless.

"And release all the tension in your muscles. By the way, you're really tight up here. Have you ever had work like this before?"

"I did do some sort of physical therapy thing after I got hurt, but nothing like this, no. Ow! Mmm, that's a good kind of hurt." Tracy's fingers were realigning his neck. The muscles resisted, then relaxed as they shifted to their natural positions.

"You mean when your shoulder got hit in Iraq?" She'd been trying to get him to talk about it more. So far nothing, except he'd killed some terrorists and got himself wounded. She started working his shoulders and immediately noticed the injury. "Your left shoulder doesn't feel right at all. The muscles are totally off."

"The doctors told me they couldn't attach properly to my new shoulder joint. Something to do with to do with the Teflon, I guess."

"Teflon?"

Roche leaned back to look up at her. "I didn't just get shot in the arm, babe. It was almost blown off. My shoulder blade, upper arm, collarbone and three ribs on that side were all completely shattered.

My shoulder is now made of plastic, and the ball joint is lubricated with Teflon."

"Oh my God." Tracy stopped rubbing the muscles for a second, then resumed even more gently.

"Squeeze as hard as you want. I can't feel a thing right there."

"How did that happen?"

"I don't remember the explosion," he answered honestly. "I just remember waking up a couple days later in the hospital ward of an aircraft carrier. Anyway, you know more about muscles and bones than I do. You can figure out why I can't rotate it over my head and swim anymore."

"Yeah, that's, uh… I can see why that's not going to work for you." She could feel what should be his rotator cuff muscle adding rounded mass to his shoulder but it wasn't properly connected in a way that would give him full range of motion. "So this muscle here is why you couldn't go back to Special Forces."

"I don't look at it that way. It eventually brought me to meet you." That was all he would say.

Now the story behind that injury was public knowledge. Bowers, Williams, Yao, Ramirez, Morris, Coles and Sherman all got interviewed by reporters and all referred to that incident in the warehouse when Karl saved all their lives. Tracy watched them all describe that day, and felt their emotion as the toughest men in the world started to tear up at the memories. Tracy understood immediately why Karl wouldn't talk to her about it. He couldn't talk about anything like that. He would never be comfortable with the knowledge that these men owed him their lives now three times over, and worshiped him as a legendary hero. Karl didn't like to be worshiped.

## YORBA LINDA, CA

A reporter from one of the LA affiliate stations had tracked down Karl's parents by Sunday evening. Soon, like a colony of ants finding fresh food, there were reporters with cameras and microphones and fake hairpieces swarming all over the Roche's front yard in Yorba Linda. Sharon Roche did her best to hide indoors and wait them out, but was unable to sleep with all the TV lights illuminating her bedroom window. She decided to arrange a press conference and get all the cameras out of the street. It was really becoming a hassle for the neighbors. She called Karl's friend Ricky Jordan and asked for his help, and he quickly set her up for a proper media circus.

He drove in to rescue her at 3AM on Monday morning, and invited everyone to the ESPN studio in Anaheim for the conference. They had her set up five hours later. Dr. Larry Roche wanted to be at his wife's side, but unfortunately he had to perform a heart transplant surgery and apparently would be unavailable for comment for the next several days. Sharon and Rick sat at the ESPN sports desk, now almost buried by microphones representing every television and radio news network imaginable. They went live at noon Eastern, nine Pacific, on every news channel in the country.

"My son will not appreciate me going on TV like this, but since you all found me I might as well answer a few of your questions. As you of course know, I am Sharon Roche, the mother of Commander Karl Roche. His father, Lawrence, is performing a surgery at Children's Hospital and cannot join us this morning. This is our friend Richard Jordan, from ESPN and ABC Sports, and he will try to protect me from your barrage of personal questions." The reporters laughed nervously. Having grown up in Washington DC on Embassy Row, Sharon was fairly comfortable with handling the media. "Well, I've got all day and you obviously don't have anything more important to do, so let's take your questions one at a time alright?"

Rick pointed to an Associated Press journalist to ask the first question. "Ma'am, what was your reaction when you heard that your son was missing in action?"

Sharon answered with unflappable grace, as if it never occurred to her that her oldest child could ever be in any real danger. "Well, I received the news about an hour before you did. Karl's Air Group Commander and the Admiral of his Battle Group called Larry and I personally from the *Ronald Reagan*, and they said his plane had been hit and he had bailed out over Tehran. They explained that he was fairly safe on the ground, and he'd already linked up with the rescue team, so I was not immediately fearful for his safety. You may have noticed I'm still not afraid that he could be hurt. He's got Special Forces and survival training and he's been in dangerous places before. I am worried about him, of course, and I will be very relieved when he gets back to his ship safely, but I don't imagine he would let himself get killed over there.

"Anyway, at first I was surprised. He's a very good pilot, and he'd told me his plane is almost immune to missiles, so at first I didn't understand why he'd been shot down. Then his commander explained he'd let the missile hit him and let the plane crash in the city so he could destroy some artillery in order to save the rescue team, and I thought, that is just like Karl. He's always been diving in to help people first and looking for his own needs second, that's just the way he is. Ricky here is living proof, right?"

Jordan wished she hadn't brought that up, but now everyone was looking at him. *If Karl ever gets home he's going to kill me for this*, he thought. "That's right. When he and I were sixteen we were on a camping trip in Yosemite, and uh, well I'd gone out to gather wood in the dark and I tripped and fell in the river. I got knocked out and just sat there for half an hour before Karl found me and jumped in to save me. Now that water was freezing; it was about this time of year so the water was all just snow melt, and he was suffering from the effects of hypothermia just as much as I was after the three or four minutes it took for him to wade across and get me out. Well, he got me out, and he kept me warm all night while another friend went and got help. I would have been dead if it wasn't for him. Anyway, that's just what Karl does, you know? You put him in any situation like that and you'll see him charging in to save people."

Tracy frowned at her TV as she heard Rick Jordan's story. She hadn't heard that one either. But she knew enough from her medical classes to know that Rick wasn't exaggerating. Three minutes in thirty-five degree water could easily kill you. It was a wonder that either Karl or Rick were alive. She shook her head in amazement and wondered how much there still was to learn about the man she had fallen in love with.

Talking about Roche's childhood prompted the next questions. "What was your son like as a little boy? Did he always want to join the military? Did he ever do anything dangerous when he was a kid?"

Sharon smiled. "Karl was a very good kid. He never got in any trouble with us or at school. His little sister was born when he was nine, and he was a great older brother. He was very protective of her. When she would play in the neighborhood Karl would hang around outside and keep an eye on her. He would wash his car or something but he would make sure none of the older kids bothered her.

"He never talked about the military until he got to college. His first career aspiration was to be an auto mechanic. Then he realized that it didn't make very much money, and he decided he wanted to design custom cars. My husband gave him our old car for his fourteenth birthday, and since then he's built it into an award-winning super-street hot rod. He also wanted to play football. He didn't ever look into the military until he was a sophomore in college. He started taking just one ROTC class, and moved sideways into the Navy program, and next thing I know he's a fully commissioned Navy officer. I was happy for him. My husband was in the Navy, and my father was in the British Royal Navy, and so I guess it was a family thing.

"The first time Karl did something really dangerous and scared me, he was about two-and-a-half years old. He'd made a pile of pillows behind a couch, climbed up on the back of it, and jumped down to the floor, right over the pillows. I grabbed him, made sure he was okay, and said, 'Karl, don't do that, you might hurt yourself.' He said 'sorry mommy, I won't jump like that any more,' and five minutes later he'd repositioned the pillows and started jumping again, and this time landing on his safety pad."

The reporters all chuckled at that, imagining Karl as a toddler introducing himself to skydiving.

"Karl grew up with the notion that nothing was dangerous if you knew what you were doing," Mrs. Roche continued. "He learned to ride a bike without training wheels when he was four, and soon he was doing BMX jumps. A friend of ours is a police officer, and he taught Karl about guns and gun safety when he was twelve, and he would spend hours at the police shooting range shooting paper targets. We started teaching him about driving when he was thirteen; once he got his license he started doing drag races at the local race track. He's raced motorcycles, he's gone skydiving, he used to compete in martial arts; all sorts of things that normal people think are dangerous, to him they're just hobbies. Now he has one of the most dangerous jobs in the world, but it's perfectly safe for him because he knows exactly what he's doing. And God has always protected him. That's why I never have to worry about him."

The press conference lasted almost ninety minutes. Tracy called Mrs. Roche a short time later and they talked for several hours, giving each other much-needed emotional support. Tracy remained close by the TV, and at five-thirty in the afternoon they announced that Roche had made contact with the *Reagan* again and would be attempting another extraction in the next two hours. Tracy couldn't remember the last time she'd prayed so hard.

Roche found the armory apartment divided by different types of guns. First he found the bathroom, which had been converted into a room for cleaning weapons. He soaked a wad of paper towels in warm water, and scrubbed the putty and coloring off his face and arms. Next he found one room full of various submachine guns, and picked out an Uzi 9mm for Agent Caspian to carry. He took a nylon shoulder strap for the gun and three extra clips and set it all by the door. Another room was full of ammo for all types of guns. There were boxes of alloy-jacket 124-grain 9mm Parabellum ammunition, and Karl took enough to load his Glock and Cannon's Uzi and all the extra clips. But he couldn't find any .50AE ammo for his Desert Eagle.

Cannon came in after a minute and picked up his Uzi off the floor. "Thanks for finding this," he said. "Does he have what you need in there?"

"I got your Uzi and my Glock squared away, but I don't see any fifty cal in here."

"Huh. He might not have that. He's got metric and imperial calibers separate."

"Yeah I see that, but he doesn't have anything bigger than .45 ACP."

"Do you want to just trade it for another gun in his inventory? I'll bet he's got a nice Colt to go with that forty-five ammo."

"No," Roche said. "I really like this thing. I've put a lot of work into it to get it balanced just right."

"I guess you're out of luck then."

Roche stared at the ammo racks for a second, and noticed the .44 Magnum rounds next to the .45 section. "Not quite." He went into the room full of pistols looking for something to match the magnum and found a Desert Eagle .44, as he suspected. Roche sat down at a work bench and dismantled both of the big handguns. "The Action Express cartridge has the same diameter rebated rim as a .44 Magnum," he explained nebulously.

"Meaning…?"

"Meaning that either cartridge will fit in the same receiver, so just by swapping barrels I can turn my fifty into a forty-four." He took the bigger barrel out and secured it carefully in his bag. Then he reassembled his gun with the cannibalized .44 barrel and packed each of his magazines with eight rounds of the smaller Magnum ammunition.

Cannon didn't bother to conceal how impressed he was by Roche's resourcefulness. "That's amazing, especially if it works. Let me grab that card and we can get out of here." An alarm went off before they got through the door. "This could be bad news." They hurried to the other apartment and found Albie preparing for war.

"The IRG has set up a perimeter around the building," he said. He was trying to buckle a body armor vest around his pudgy waist while holding an unwieldy Spectre 9mm submachine gun.

"They traced your call," Roche said.

"Impossible."

"It was either that or they found out that you're stealing satellite TV service," Cannon suggested. "Or that you're accessing illegal web pages."

"I think they're here about something more serious." Albie pointed to one of the security camera screens, which showed a Fennek Mk. 2 armored car surrounded by a dozen fully-armed soldiers. "They're after Kuj, not me. I haven't done anything to get this kind of heat on me."

"You found those plans," Cannon reminded him.

"Yeah, I know, but I've been toying around with their computer network for a long time and they haven't caught on to me yet. Besides, there's no way they can physically trace my hack to my real-world location. Rannovich's people must have found this address some other way."

"Who?" Roche asked.

"Forget that name," Cannon told him. "Albie, have they found our motorcycle yet? How close are they to us?"

"They're just establishing a perimeter around the block right now. Your bike is safe in the garage for the time being." He tapped a button and one of the screens shifted from a view of an empty hallway to a camera in the garage that was looking right at the Buell. Suddenly the overhead lights in the room went out, and several of the screens went dark before changing to a night-vision view. "They just cut the building's power. But my computers and cameras have their own power supply."

Roche watched the screens as the soldiers outside prepared to storm the building. "Don't you think we should leave now?" he asked.

"Yes," Cannon said. "I don't know if we're what they're looking for but I'm sure they'd know what to do if they found us."

Roche grunted. "Yeah, especially after CNN has made every TV in the country my wanted poster."

"I'll go down with you," Albie said.

"No, they can't find your computer either," Cannon said, "you need to rig the explosives and take your rooftop exit. Our bike can only take the two of us anyway."

"Okay. Here's the SD card." Albie picked up a carbon-fiber case about the size of a paperback novel, and gave it to Cannon along with a radio earpiece. "And take this. I'll talk you guys down by radio."

"Nothing to it," Cannon said, while fitting the earpiece and slipping the case into a back pocket. "We'll use the elevator."

"But the power's out," Roche observed, "And they'll have it covered anyway."

"I said nothing about *riding* the elevator. Albie?"

The Indian kid nodded and typed a command into the computer. With a loud snap a small explosive charge cut the cable and dropped the elevator car from the thirtieth floor to the sub-basement. The elevator doors in the lobby were blown off by the energy of the impact. Roche looked at the motorcycle apprehensively. Dust filled the garage level but the bike wasn't harmed.

"Now they think we're dead," Cannon explained, "And we can take the bad stairs down to the garage."

"What do you mean, 'bad stairs'? I'm not going down thirty flights of bad stairs."

Cannon was already out the door. "There's nothing wrong with them, Karl. Kujetski sealed them off except for at the roof and top floor here." Roche followed Cannon into the stairwell, ignoring the Farsi warning signs which read *Danger: Bad Stairs.* Cannon continued, "There are four stairwells in the building. Kujetski got the building management to close this one. Because the building is such a dung pile, no one even bothers to find out why the stairs are out. We should make it to the garage without the IRG knowing we were here."

"Okay. How's Albie going to get out?"

"He's got a hang-glider on the roof. He'll just float down to a parking lot a few blocks away where he keeps his car. He'll be fine, as long as he doesn't wait too long. You hear me, kid?" Cannon spoke into his earpiece, "don't wait for them to knock down the door before you get out of there."

"I'm already on the roof," Albie answered. Kujetski had ensured that Albie would be well prepared for emergencies, and the hacker closed up his shop quickly and efficiently. He'd pulled the

404

computer's hard drives out off their quick-access trays and packed them away in another water-and-bomb-proof case – similar to Cannon's case but much larger. He loaded that in a backpack that already contained emergency supplies, and finally set the computer on its automatic self-destruct sequence. "I can watch the cameras on my handheld," he said. "The garage is still clear, but the IRG is starting to sweep the floors one by one, and they're using your stairwell."

"Karl, do you have silencers for your guns?" Cannon asked.

"No."

"Okay, let me do the shooting unless we get swarmed." Cannon drew his silenced FN Five-Seven, which is the quietest gun in the world.

They were halfway down when Albie gave Cannon an update. "Two soldiers have gone down to the garage, and they're checking the cars one at a time. They're on the other side from where you left the bike."

"Okay."

"The IRG are kicking down every door in the building. They obviously don't know which apartments to look for."

"Good. We have plenty of time before they get to the top."

"Ask him about helicopters," Roche said.

Albie heard him over the tiny condenser microphone. "No air cover that I can see. The US Air Force has been flying fighter sorties around the outskirts since midnight and Iranian birds are staying away."

"No aircraft," Cannon repeated to Roche.

They were able to time their descent to avoid the squads of IRG soldiers searching the building. They reached a landing on the stairs one flight above the garage level when Albie stopped them. "I can't see those two soldiers on the cameras anymore, but they're between the door and the bike. You'll have to kill them."

"Do they have their weapons ready?"

"When I saw them last they had their AKs on their backs and no sidearms."

"Okay. Roche, break the door down, I'll cover you."

"I thought we wanted to keep it quiet," Karl said.

"There are only two of them between us and the motorcycle, so that's not an issue now. Albie, we're signing off."

"Good luck, guys."

"You too." Cannon removed the earpiece and nodded to Roche.

Karl ran down the stairs and was at his top speed when he hit the bottom. He jumped and drew his legs up, hit the door with both feet, and kicked through it as his kinetic energy was transferred to the stationary door. This was quite a bit more force than was necessary to get the job done. The door exploded off of its frame and smashed against the side of an old pickup truck. Roche landed on his feet and continued running, right toward an astonished IRG soldier. Roche swung his fist overhand, stepping into an incredibly powerful punch. His knuckles caught the hapless man right between the eyes, cracking his cranium apart on impact like it was an eggshell. He was knocked head over heels and landed on the back of his skull, dying instantly from massive head trauma.

Cannon followed Roche, only slightly less surprised than the Iranians. He shot the remaining guard twice in the head and put a bullet in the broken skull of the man Roche had killed to make sure he wasn't getting up. "Where'd you learn to do *that*?"

"Do what?"

"Never mind." Cannon jumped on the Buell behind Roche, pausing only long enough to secure his helmet as Karl had already done. Roche squeezed the throttle and brake together, and made a rubber-burning one-eighty. He accelerated out toward the street exit and started to make a right turn but Cannon stopped him. "No, not that way!"

Roche swerved and went left. "Why not?"

"That's where Albie's going. We should lead them the other way."

"Oh no, don't go that way," Albie said, even though no one could hear him. Roche was now driving straight toward the intersection where the IRG had parked their armored car. Albie checked his other cameras and saw that the soldiers had finally reached the top floor. "Time to go." He activated a timer on his smartphone and put it in his pocket, then strapped on his hang-glider and ran for the south ledge. Just as he jumped he saw two fast-moving angular shapes coming in his direction. "Damnation. Perfect timing, you stupid fighter jockeys."

The dark gray F-22 Raptors crossed the sky directly over the building, about five thousand feet above the ground. The soldiers on the perimeter looked up to watch and saw something else in the sky: Albie's hang-glider. Albie suddenly had a dozen AK-47s trying to shoot him down, and they succeeded. He was only hit twice and his body armor stopped the rounds, but the wide sheet of nylon fabric that kept him aloft was perforated. The glider collapsed and Albie made his two hundred-and-fifty-foot descent screaming in terror. The screaming stopped when he landed on his face in, of all places, a very dirty and fairly deep public swimming pool.

As soon as he realized he was not dead, Albie wrestled himself free of his glider and swam to the edge. He was only half a block from his old Toyota Sprinter Trueno and presumably written off by the IRG. He would be able to get clear without further incident. As he stood there dripping, the top floor of the old building blew up with spectacular force. Chunks of concrete and metal rained down around the block. Albie said a quick Muslim prayer for the Americans on the motorbike.

Roche crossed an intersection at sixty miles an hour, and looked both ways out of habit. On the right there was nothing. On the left... there was a five-ton German-made Fennek Mk. 2 armored car. An IRG officer stood up in the roof hatch behind a FN MAG 7.62mm machine gun. Cannon saw it too. "I hope you haven't gotten tired of leading dangerous car chases," he said.

"Not even remotely." The Fennek was after them in a flash, and the machine gun spat bullets at their tail. "I don't think they're giving us a choice anyway." Roche turned on the next street and ran flat out, but the Fennek followed closely. The top of the building blew up behind them, scattering wreckage in all directions including a burning mattress that landed right in their path. Roche had to swerve around it and the powerful Fennek began to gain on them.

"Can't this bike outrun that thing?" Cannon asked.

Roche explained what they were up against as he took evasive action. "That thing is the Ferrari of armored vehicles. It's got a modified Audi V-12 TDI diesel making almost seven hundred horsepower. It has a top speed of over a hundred and twenty miles an hour, and does zero-to-sixty quicker than a Ford Mustang."

Cannon wasn't in the mood for car talk. "Can we outrun it or not?"

"Yeah, we can outrun it, but only if we get to an open road, and we can't outrun the machine gun." Roche made another hard turn into a narrow alley. The driver of the armored car expertly drift-steered into the gap and the machine gun was chewing up the pavement again.

"This is very, very bad," Cannon noted. They were in a long alley with no exits, and the Fennek was again catching up to the high-performance bike. Roche had to weave around laundry lines and trash cans, but the armored car just ploughed through and the incredibly powerful six-liter Audi turbo-diesel engine pushed the big vehicle ever faster.

Roche saw a gap between buildings ahead screened by a flimsy wooden fence. He turned sharply, crashed through and cut across an empty lot and found himself on a busy street. The Fennek followed and the IRG gunner didn't let up, and took out several civilian cars unlucky enough to get between him and the evasive target. Karl watched in horror as they passed a minivan – one second it was full of women and children, and then it was filled with bullets, blood and gore. "We need to do something about that MAG," Roche said. "You need to shoot back with your Uzi and take out that gunner!"

"There's no way I can hit him!"

"You might get lucky." A bullet whizzed past them both and punched out the right-side mirror. "Hopefully you'll get lucky before he does."

Cannon grabbed Roche's vest with his left hand and twisted in his seat, lining up his shoulders with the bike for maximum control. He fired the Uzi in short bursts, but his normally excellent aim was thrown off by the motorcycle bouncing on the bad road and weaving through the traffic. He saw sparks when the bullets ricocheted off the armor, and the IRG officer ducked a couple of times, but he emptied the clip without hitting the gunner. "It's no use!"

"Reload!"

"I need two hands. I can't load a gun with my teeth like you can."

"Take my Glock!"

Cannon pulled the automatic pistol out of Karl's vest but couldn't do any damage with the smaller gun either. He considered using his Five-Seven in desperation, but they'd moved out of range of the smaller gun.

Roche had put a little distance between them and the Fennek, but up ahead of them traffic was thinning out and there would be no cover on the open road. An alley on the left was his only hope. He cut across the opposing lanes and roared through what turned out to be a half-paved ditch. The Fennek rammed a taxi out of its way and continued to pursue.

"Oh, shit, look out!" Cannon saw something ahead while Roche was looking over his shoulder at the Fennek. Roche's eyes came forward and he saw the brick wall eighty feet away. He also saw a metal staircase on the side of it. Roche twisted the throttle and popped a wheelie and the roaring Buell went up the stairs and over the wall. The Fennek just smashed through, right into a schoolyard playground.

Roche thought he'd had quite enough of life's cruel surprises at this point. The bike landed in a sandbox, bounced once, took out a seesaw, and went straight for a slide. Roche pulled the front wheel up just enough and the bike took it like another jump. A little kid at the top ducked right before the bike launched past his head. The motorcycle sailed over a jungle gym and crashed down on a picnic table.

The Fennek cruised through with reckless abandon, sideswiping a swing set and running down two little girls in the sandbox. At least the gunner let up on the machine gun until they got past the playground.

"It had to be recess," Cannon said, "of all the times to run through a schoolyard, we pick the early recess period. Kids everywhere, man."

Roche went around the schoolhouse and on to another empty, narrow road that offered no cover. He looked for a side road, and saw one just as he passed it. It was another tiny alley that was fenced off and hidden from view. Roche shot past it at seventy miles an hour but he saw something interesting at the other end. Roche passed two more alleys, watching something on the next street over.

"You need to make a move here," Cannon said, "or he's going to kill us." Bullets were getting awfully close to hitting them again.

"He's right where I want him." Roche made a left turn down the next alley, this one slightly wider than the others they'd seen. The Fennek was about a hundred feet behind them. Roche accelerated, but he didn't open it all the way up. Rather, he let the Fennek close to within about twenty feet. The gunner couldn't shoot them, though, because the alley was crisscrossed with clotheslines that were just over the bikers' heads and just under the machine gun mount. The gunner kept losing sight, and the driver couldn't see further ahead than the next line of laundry.

Roche had timed it perfectly. He'd seen a tanker truck several blocks back, moving parallel to the last road at fifty miles an hour. The alley connected the two roads, and Roche had put all three vehicles on a collision course. He and Cannon saw the end of the alley and suddenly the tanker loomed in their path. Cannon shouted something that Karl didn't pay attention to. Roche kicked the bike into a slide, moving sideways and skidding right under the rig. The two men were dragged under the trailer and clear across the street by the irresistible momentum of the bike. Roche's right hand came free, holding the huge Desert Eagle, aimed at the rear tires of the tanker.

Two bullets penetrated the four tires supporting the left side of the trailer, and a millisecond later the Fennek crashed straight into the other side. The tanker rolled and the Fennek was vaulted up, and it scraped over the filling valve on the side. Cannon was watching the same thing Roche was, but he saw only moving metal and gushing gasoline. Roche saw a target: the emergency brake light on the side of the trailer, now right under the armored car and in the middle of a powerful stream of fuel.

Roche fired another bullet, and by the time he heard the sound of thunderous gunshot it had done its job. The driver of the tanker truck was standing on the brake pedal, sending hydraulic fluid through the brake lines and electricity through the red lights all over the truck. The brake light shattered and sparked, igniting the torrent of petroleum and ending the chase with a massive ball of flame and wreckage.

The Fennek was blown fifty feet straight up in the air, engulfed by the fireball. The flames found its own fuel tank and a second explosion gutted the car. The blazing hulk slammed down on the street next to pyre of the tanker.

Roche slowly stood and watched the flames dance on the wreckage with grim satisfaction.

Cannon did not enjoy the show so much, because his jacket had caught on fire and he had to beat it out.

They soon heard sirens in the distance. Roche stood the bike back up and put the gun away. "We need to keep moving. Every emergency vehicle we didn't knock out yesterday will be here in a minute."

Cannon was unable to put out the patch of burning gasoline that had landed on his windbreaker so he just threw it off and got back on behind Roche. "The highway is south of here. I think we can get on from this street."

Roche went south. "I have *got* to get me one of these bikes," he said. "First thing I do when I get back home; I'm going out to that dealership in Old Town and buying one of these babies. I wonder if they come in blue."

"First thing, Karl?"

Roche smiled as he reconsidered. "Well, second, after I make out with Tracy on the North Island tarmac."

## USS *RONALD REAGAN* AIR OPS CENTER – 0730 LOCAL

Deuce paced the deck impatiently, checking his watch every two minutes and staring the clock on the wall the rest of the time. Roche was supposed to make contact with the extraction team half an hour ago. Anytime Roche wasn't reliable was time to be worried, as far as Thompson was concerned.

"Captain, relay on the SAR frequency," a comm officer reported. "It's Sharkey."

"Oh, thank God." Deuce took the headset from the officer. "Talk to me, kid."

"Hey, sorry I'm late checking in. We got a little sidetracked down here."

"Are you guys ok?"

"Secret Agent Man is afraid to ride with me again, and we got a few bruises, but nothing serious."

"The guys watching the Global Hawk feeds said they saw a building blow up and some serious IRG movement. Was that you?"

"Uh, yeah. They sent a lot of firepower after us, but we got away from them."

"Where are you now?"

"A gas station on the western edge of downtown, just off the highway. We'll be out of the city in twenty minutes."

"Okay, your callsign is 'Nike' and the pickup team is 'Swoop,' got that?"

"Copy, Nike and Swoop. I'll give them a ring as soon as we see a spot they can land on the highway."

"We already got it picked out. Your dust-off is half a click past the last exit on the southbound highway."

## TEHRAN

"Okay, Captain, we'll look for it." Roche clipped the radio to his vest and stuffed the gear bag back into the trunk in front of his seat.

"We need to get out of town," Cannon said as he came out of the gas station after using the restroom. "I just heard on the news radio that the IRG is still looking for us and they're stopping every black or gray motorcycle on the highways. We need to get on the highway without using an onramp checkpoint."

"No problem. I'll go to the construction site we used yesterday."

"Right, but this time, please don't go off the fifteen-foot jump."

411

Roche got them back to the unfinished interchange without incident and used the unpaved onramp to get on the southbound highway undetected. But about five miles further south, halfway to the proposed dust-off site, they were spotted. Three large SUVs with IRG markings passed them going north. They all hit their brakes, turned around, bounced across the ditch separating the lanes, and pursued the Buell. "These guys we can definitely outrun," Roche said. He twisted the throttle and the bike accelerated eagerly from the posted limit speed to a hundred and thirty miles an hour. Roche hugged the left shoulder and zipped past traffic. The IRG Land Cruisers soon lost sight of them.

"They're going to be looking for us down the road," Cannon said.

"I'll give our choppers the heads up." Roche clicked the SAR radio and plugged it into the earpiece in his helmet. "Swoop, this is Nike, do you read."

"Roger Nike, we are standing by over dust-off."

Roche recognized the voice. "Hannibal? What are you doing here? I thought they were sending us a pair of Cobras."

"Too dangerous, Nike. We're going to land a pair of Fish on the highway and put you guys in the back seats. Two Eels are covering."

Roche smiled. *Deuce, you're a genius.* He instantly realized the advantage of using a division of Super Hornets instead of relatively slow and vulnerable helicopters. "Okay, well, we've been spotted by IRG again and it's a sure bet they're gonna come after us, so be ready to use your guns."

"Roger. We see a roadblock at exit two, and a few trucks between here and there. Someone's trying to catch you, alright."

"Okay, I'll call back once we get past them."

"What's the matter?" Cannon asked. He only heard Roche's side of the conversation, but he heard it clearly through the helmet intercom.

"Roadblock two exits ahead," he answered. They had just passed exit four, counting down to the last exit in the Tehran metropolitan area. Traffic started to get thick, but Roche stayed on the edge of the shoulder and went right past the civilian cars. Soon he saw flashing lights ahead. It was police vehicles, not the IRG. Roche picked a gap between two cop cars and ran through it, surprising the police who apparently anticipated an easy arrest.

Sharkey radioed Hannibal again. "We're clear of the road block."

412

"Roger that. The Army is setting something up down the road. We'll take care of them before you reach them, though."

"Copy that."

The road ahead was clear, so Karl moved to the middle lane and pushed the bike to its top speed. He passed an army truck at over a hundred and fifty miles an hour and heard gunfire, but they were out of range in a matter of seconds. Exit one came up fast, and with it, another roadblock. This time it was manned by heavy trucks and APCs and stretched across the center median and both sides of the highway. Roche slowed down, and looked up, thinking he should be able to see the Hornets. He couldn't, and there was no way around the road block. "We could be in trouble," he said.

"DUCK!" Cannon had heard a noise that got louder as the bike slowed down, and looked back to see a pair of Super Hornets bearing down on them. They passed only twenty feet over their heads, sprayed the road with cannon fire, pulled up sharply and dropped CBUs right on top of the roadblock. The perfectly-placed series of explosives sent the trucks and armored vehicles bouncing in all directions, and the road was suddenly clear, apart from a large amount of wreckage.

Roche went through at forty-five miles an hour, carefully avoiding running over sharp pieces of shrapnel. As he passed the exit, two Fenneks came up the onramp behind them. "Aw, not those things again." Roche opened the throttle wide and ran for it, but it would take a while to get far enough away that Hannibal could safely land. He looked at the sky ahead, and saw the two Super-Fs making their approach. Roche clicked the radio. "Swoop Lead, we have two armored cars behind us, landing is not safe."

"Yeah, I see 'em Sharkey. Keep your head down." The Hornet on the right, above the south lanes, fired a pair of Maverick missiles over the motorcycle and into the armored cars. The wickedly accurate anti-tank weapons blew the Fenneks to scrap. "Problem solved, now pull over so I don't hit you."

Roche brought the bike to a near-stop and rolled into the ditch. The Fish touched down side-by-side on the highway a quarter-mile ahead and stopped right on top of them.

"What happened to helicopters?" Cannon asked.

"These are faster and have bigger guns," Roche said. He led the spy over to the Hornet on northbound lanes, being flown by Hardcase. He lowered the ladder and helped Cannon climb up. The large man in the pilot seat reached down to assist. "This is your pilot, Hardcase Wilkes. Hardcase, Mr. C."

"A pleasure," Cannon said.

"I'll help him buckle up," Wilkes told Roche.

"Alright. I'll see you guys on the Gipper." Roche started to climb down.

Hardcase stopped him. "Hey Sharkey."

"Yeah?"

"I'm glad to see you made it out."

Sharkey was so surprised he almost fell off the ladder. "Thanks, man."

"Go get in the skipper's plane."

Roche dropped to the ground and put the ladder back in its well under the port strake, then looked to the other plane. Hannibal was standing up in his seat and waved him over. Roche stopped to get his bag off of the bike and ran to the other Hornet. He pulled himself onto the starboard wing and walked carefully up to the cockpit, avoiding stepping on the airframe where it said *Do Not Step*. Roche reached the strake next to the cockpit and shook Hannibal's hand. "Glad to see you, Sharkey," the CO said.

"Not nearly as glad as I am to-

Roche was interrupted by gunfire for what must have been the fourth time in the last forty-eight hours, which he thought was very rude. The pilots ducked into the armored cockpit to take shelter, but Hannibal got hit before he could make all the way down. Roche peeked out and saw the road ahead – north toward Tehran – was swarming with soldiers. "Swoop Two and Four, this is Nike with Swoop One; we're taking ground fire," Roche called on the SAR radio.

"Where the hell is my forty-five?" Hannibal fumbled for the bag at his feet.

Roche stood up behind him and fired his Desert Eagle at the Iranian Army troops. *Behold, the definition of irony,* he thought. *I've eluded capture in the enemy's capital for this whole time, and now just when I thought I'd been rescued I find myself defending the world's most powerful attack jet with a handgun.* But the Hornet's missiles couldn't be fired from only five feet off the ground, and the Vulcan cannon in the nose was aimed over the soldiers' heads.

Shredder and Hitman responded quickly, coming in from the southeast. Shredder fired a line of 20mm shells from a spot a hundred feet from Bulldog's nose diagonally through the mass of infantry. Hitman followed up with another stick of CBUs that decimated most of the survivors. The concentrated gunfire became very sporadic. Hardcase took the opportunity to turn around and take off.

414

"Sharkey, you'd better fly. I took one in the right arm."

"Okay, switch seats." There were no flight controls in the rear cockpit – it was configured for a WSO, not a trainer pilot. Roche stepped out on the port strake and Hannibal went on the starboard side. Then more shots rang out from the side of the road – another squad of Iranians had snuck up on them through the trees off the highway. Hannibal yelled as more bullets hit him. Roche straddled the front cockpit, with a foot on each strake, half-shielding the skipper. He drew his Glock and emptied the gun into the Iranians, hitting most of them with the 9mm rounds. The Iranian survivors ran, and Roche turned around. "Are you okay?"

Commander Burke dragged himself into the rear seat and looked up. "I'll live. Just get us out of here. Hey, you're hit too."

Roche looked where the skipper pointed. There was a bloody hole in his shirt over his left shoulder. He couldn't feel it. "It's nothing." He dropped into the front seat and throttled up the port engine, and then released the brake on that side. Roche quickly checked the instruments and lowered the canopy while the plane spun in a tight 180. He heard more shots ricochet off the bullet-proof alloy-composite skin of the fighter, and when he checked the rear-view camera and saw more soldiers running up right behind them. With a malicious grin Roche pushed both engines to full thrust with his thumb holding down the afterburner switch, frying the infantrymen in their tracks and leaving them far behind. "Swoop One is airborne," he reported, after swapping his motorcycle helmet for a spare flight helmet that Hannibal handed up to him.

"Swoop elements, return to Shoebox," Deuce ordered. "Glad to hear you on this channel again, Sharkey."

"How's it look, skip?" Roche engaged the autopilot and turned around in his seat to help the CO. "I have a full medkit in my bag down there." Hannibal had already found it. He had his shirt off and was soaking gauze pads in iodine and taping them over his bullet wounds. Roche counted four holes in the skipper's arms and torso. "Wow, you look a lot like one of those paper targets I practice on."

"That's pretty funny, because I *feel* a lot like a gunshot victim. Could you fix up the holes on my back please?" Burke handed Roche the medkit and turned around.

Roche winced when he saw the three additional wounds. "Huh, so much for seven being a lucky number."

The CO was highly superstitious and appreciated the irony. "Yeah, well so much for karma too, right? I volunteer to come down and rescue a guy who nearly got killed to save another rescue op, and now I'm almost killed."

"Nah, they'll fix you up. The bullets were almost stopped by all this hair on your back, anyway. Just flesh wounds." Roche slapped the last gauze pad down. He was lying. The bullets in his back had been fired from close range and gone deep.

"Now could you jab me with this?" Hannibal handed up a morphine syringe.

"You got it." Roche injected the narcotic into his lower lumbar.

"Thanks. I feel better already." Hannibal sat back down in the rear seat and closed his eyes. "If you don't mind, XO, I'm going to pass out now."

Roche resumed control of the plane and called the *Reagan*. "Shoebox, this is Swoop One, please prepare medical for the skipper. He's been shot up pretty bad."

Deuce answered right away. "Roger that, Swoop One, we've been watching you on your cameras. The medical staff is standing by for both of you."

"Captain, do you think I can make a phone call from here?"

"We thought you might ask for that. We're setting it up now."

### SANTEE, CA – SAME TIME, 2125 PDT

NBC cut the local news show's weatherman off in mid-forecast and showed a Super Hornet taking off from a highway. Brian Williams from Nightly News was put on live coast-to-coast to tell the viewers what was happening. *"This is live footage being fed to us by the Navy, I don't know how they're doing this but these planes all have onboard cameras and they are giving us a live picture. Karl Roche is on board that plane that just took off right there. He is on board, alive and well."*

Tracy jumped up and cheered. The camera view switched to the Hornet's cockpit and showed Karl, wearing a helmet but without the mask or visor covering his face, sitting inside the plane. It stayed on his face for a moment while the plane climbed, then switched to a rear camera view to show Tehran disappearing behind him.

*"The Navy landed a pair of Super Hornet F-model fighters, which is apparently a two-seat version of what Karl was flying when he went down on Sunday over there. Anyway, they landed them on a highway just south of Tehran."* The TV showed footage from ten minutes before, shot from under the nose of a Super-F as it touched down. *"You can see Roche right there with a Russian civilian who was*

416

left behind, standing next to the motorcycle which I guess they drove out from the city to the rendezvous point. *The fighters came under attack by Iranian infantry a moment later, but two more Hornets cleared the area and everyone's still okay."* The TV showed a view from Shredder's plane, showing infantry on the ground near the parked airplanes. The nose-mounted camera shook as Shredder fired his cannon, and then cleared in time to show the shells cut down the soldiers. *"I repeat, both Commander Roche and the Russian are safely onboard US Navy aircraft and are on their way back to the* Ronald Reagan.*"*

Tracy knelt in front of her TV and touched the screen when it showed a live picture of Karl's plane again.

*"Ah, this is just in,"* Williams said, *"apparently when the Hornet took fire on the ground, the aviator who landed it was hit. Commander Roche himself is flying that plane now, with the wounded pilot in the back seat. You can see here, Roche is assisting the other aviator and administering first aid."* The back seat camera came up, showing Roche's arms reaching around to help Burke, who was applying bandages to his chest.

*"Our liaison on the carrier is telling me that the other man you see is Commander William Burke, the commanding officer of Roche's squadron. Lieutenant Commander Roche is the executive officer, or second-in-command, for his squadron,"* the anchor elaborated unnecessarily, as almost everyone in America already knew all about Roche's rank and position. On the screen, Burke was turning around so Roche could apply the bandages to his back. *"Oh, my, he looks bad,"* Williams continued. *"Although he's obviously conscious, so he must not be hurt too much. Again, ladies and gentlemen, you are watching Karl Roche administering first aid to the pilot that landed to rescue him, and now it is once again Karl Roche to the rescue, as he has assumed control of the plane which is now presumably on autopilot, and he's dressing the gunshot wounds Commander Burke received on the ground."*

The camera shifted to the front cockpit view, showing Roche twisted in his seat, with his left shoulder to the camera. *"Roche appears to be injured himself, ah, you can see blood on his arm and his side there, but he's apparently doing much better than Burke. If Commander Burke's family is watching, I'm sorry you had to see that just now, but he appears to be stable and he's obviously in good hands. Yes, Karl just gave him a shot of something and he's now resting comfortably.*" Burke came on screen again, sitting back with his eyes closed.

Tracy's phone rang a moment later. She barely noticed it. Whoever called hung up when her outgoing message started. It rang again a few seconds later, and Tracy ignored it again. The caller tried a third time and let her greeting play through, and Tracy turned up the TV. Williams was saying: "*Karl is now being put in touch with his family – his parents Larry and Sharon in Orange County, his sister Dannae in Colorado Springs, and his girlfriend Tracy in San Diego...*"

"Oh, holy cow, that's Karl calling me," Tracy said to herself. The caller had just started leaving a message, but it wasn't Karl; it was a female voice. Tracy paused with her hand hovering over the phone.

"Ms. Davis, if you can hear me please pick up. This is Ensign Hammil, I'm a communications officer on the USS *Ronald Reagan* and Commander Roche is trying to-"

Tracy grabbed the phone. "I'm here," she said.

"Oh, good. Please stay on the line. Commander Roche wants to speak with you in a moment."

"Is he okay? I saw blood on TV."

"I don't know. I only work phones around here. I can't see the TV monitors from where I'm sitting, but we are all very excited that he's safe."

"Me too."

"He did want to talk to you first, ma'am, but we couldn't get through to you right away so we put him through to the immediate family members."

"I understand; they must be just as anxious to talk to him as I am."

"As soon as we connect you, this will be a totally private line. No one will be able to hear you but him."

"Okay, thank you." Tracy took the cordless phone to the couch and waited for Karl to speak to her from across the world.

"*...The Navy can't reach Tracy at the moment.*" Williams was still narrating in exacting detail. "*But I'm told he's talking to his parents and sister right now; one can only imagine how much of an emotional lift this must be for all of them. If you saw Mrs. Roche's conference earlier today, you must know she is no less of a hero than her son for her handling of this ordeal. She had said she was never afraid for her son's life, and she is certainly rewarded for her faith now.*

418

*"He's still in Iranian airspace, ladies and gentleman, about halfway between the capital city and the coast, but he's surrounded by three more Hornets and flying through what the military calls the safety corridor. Air Force fighters keep this hundred-mile-wide stretch of airspace clear of ground defenses and hostile aircraft, and so Roche is as safe as he would be flying over the TOPGUN training ground in Nevada."*

"He's on the line now, Ms. Davis," Ensign Hammil said over the phone.

There was a click, and slight change in the background static, and Karl's voice reached across ten thousand miles to Tracy's phone. "How are you doing, babe?"

"Oh, Karl." Tracy started crying. "I love you so much."

"I love you too. Are you okay? Do you have anyone there with you?"

"No, I don't want anyone here with me but you. But I'm fine, now that you're safe. Hey, forget about me being okay! What about you? You got shot!"

"You're watching me on TV too?"

"Of course I am! So is everyone else in the world. Now tell me you're okay!"

"Relax, babe, you can't hurt that shoulder." She watched Karl poke the bullet hole on the TV. "See? It's just a flesh wound anyways."

"Why did it take so long to get you out of there?"

Roche hated lying to Tracy but now he was discussing national security matters. Cannon had explained in no unclear terms the penalties for discussing what had really happened since lunchtime the day before. "Uh, well thanks to our friends at CNN and everywhere else, the Iranians decided that I'd make a nice trophy if they could kill me or an even better bargaining chip if they could take me alive. So I had to lay low while they all went on a manhunt."

"Oh, man, that explains it. I didn't even think about that. What if they caught you and put you al-Jazeera TV or something?"

The Arabic network doesn't broadcast in or from Iran but Karl didn't bother to correct her. "I don't know what they would have done to me, but fortunately I didn't have to find out. That Russian I found lived in the city, so he helped me hide out at night and blend in during the day while the heat died down."

"Where'd you get the motorcycle you were driving?"

"The Russian got that; a friend of his imports cars and stuff from Europe."

"Oh."

"That bike saved my life. I told him I'm going to go buy one, right after I get home and kiss you."

"Okay," Tracy giggled. "You just get home and kiss me then. No more crashing in to artillery trucks and shooting it out with the whole Iranian army, got it?"

"You got it. That sort of thing is definitely not in my job description. I'll be home before you know it."

"In one piece, right?"

"Fully intact and ready for lovin'. Don't get too lonely now, I love you and I can't wait to see you."

"I love you too," she said, staring into his eyes through the TV screen.

# CHAPTER 20: A WAYS TO GO

**USS *RONALD REAGAN***
**TWO HOURS LATER, 1030 LOCAL, JUNE 3<sup>RD</sup>**

"Thanks for the lift, Hardcase," Cannon said as he awkwardly removed himself from the Hornet's back seat.

"Sure thing, Mr. C." LCdr. Daniel Wilkes swung his muscular body out of the cockpit with surprising ease and grace.

Cannon moved carefully, lowering his right foot under the strake where somewhere, he trusted, there was a ladder waiting for him. He kicked it once, felt for the rung, tested his weight and then slowly lowered himself to the flight deck. A short distance away he saw the other two-seat Hornet that had just rolled to a stop. Roche pulled himself from the front seat and simply hopped to the deck, not waiting for the ladder.

"Take him out carefully," Sharkey said to the medics who were trying to get up the ladder themselves. "He's shot up pretty bad." He helped them get Burke out and on to a stretcher, and then argued when they tried to get him on a stretcher as well. "I flew all the way here; I can walk myself to sick bay, thank you."

Cannon watched from a short distance away, quietly amused. Three men approached from the carrier's island. Two were in naval uniforms and they went straight to Roche. The aviator saluted the officers. "Admiral, Captain."

Deuce Thompson grabbed Roche's good shoulder and pulled him into a half-hug. "I'm glad to have you back, son."

"So am I," Krause added, offering a handshake. "Great work out there, Commander. Let's get those wounds checked out before you gotta be debriefed."

Cannon looked at the third man who'd followed the officers. He was wearing a blue windbreaker with the CVN-76 logo that he'd obviously just bought from the ship's store, and was lighting a cigarette as he ambled over to the agent. "Mr. C," he said.

"Mr. K," Cannon replied, shaking Kujetski's hand.

"To quote my mentor, Sallah, 'I am so *pleased* you are not *dead!*'" Kujetski comically imitated John Rhys-Davies' character from Raiders of the Lost Ark.

"Imagine my relief." Cannon looked at Roche, who had finally submitted to being loaded onto a litter to be carried to sick bay. "I

421

probably *would* be dead if it wasn't for that guy. That kid got me in and out of some tough scrapes."

"What happened to our dirty laundry?"

"It's been sorted out. How's our package?"

"Mr. Sabonis is quite safe, if not exactly comfortable, locked in a cabin downstairs. Did you get that other package from Albie?"

"Yes." Cannon held up the carbon-fiber hardcase. "You and your pet hacker will need to be finding a new penthouse though."

"I thought they might eventually trace me back there. I trust Albie handled the situation well."

"He blew the top of the building off, at least. I didn't see if he got away safely."

"He practices with that hang glider of his every night. I'm sure he's okay. I'd like to give him a call though. The Admiral found out about my satellite phone and confiscated it. I don't think he really believes that I work for your government. He seems to think I'm some sort of international weapons dealer or something."

"Whatever gave him that impression?" Cannon asked sarcastically.

The Admiral returned to the deck, looked around and spotted the spies, and walked up to join them. "Welcome aboard, Mr. C."

"Thank you, Admiral."

"Your boss at Langley is expecting a phone call. I'll take you up to our secure comms booth."

"Thanks."

"Now that Mr. C is here," Kujetski spoke up, "when can we get outta here?"

"Mr.- uh, Sabonis needs to be taken to Langley as soon as possible," Cannon added.

"We'll put you on the next COD to Bahrain at 1800 hours," Krause said. "From there you'll take an Air Force VIP jet direct to the government terminal at Reagan National Airport."

"From *Reagan* to Reagan." Kujetski seemed amused. "What's a cod, anyway?"

"Carrier Onboard Delivery. A cargo plane that shuttles people, mail, spare parts and fresh fruit between us and the nearest base."

"And the next one doesn't leave for eight hours?"

"Normally I'd put you on a chopper, but they're all out looking for more rogue subs. We don't think there are any more out there but after the *Roosevelt* we're not going to take chances."

"Can't you put us on one of those Ospreys?" Kujetski asked.

"Sorry. The Marines are using all of them at the moment."

"That's okay," Cannon said with a yawn. "I could use a nap."

"And a shower," Kujetski noted without jest.


"I'm telling you, I feel fine, and that's perfectly normal. It's normal for me to have no feeling in that area." Roche was locked in sick bay, with a significant percentage of *Reagan*'s medical staff attending to his left side. "I have no nerve endings between my neck and elbow on that arm, okay? I can't tell you how much my shoulder hurts, because it doesn't hurt at all, now or ever."

LCdr. Dr. Tobias sighed. "Okay, Commander, if you don't want us to put you under for the operation, you'll have to sign a waiver."

"What operation? Just dig the bullet out, disinfect the hole and slap a gauze pad over it. I would have done it already with my multi-tool if it was clean."

"Look, Karl, the shoulder wound isn't what we're concerned about. You were shot three times. In addition to that nice little hole in your shoulder, you have two bullets in the side of your chest, here and here." The doctor prodded the wounds with a gloved finger, hard.

Sharkey suddenly became aware of a stabbing pain in his ribs. "Oh, ooh, I feel that one."

"Are you telling me you didn't notice these two gunshot wounds?"

"Not until you poked me just now."

"We're going to have get at least one of those bullets out," Tobias informed him. "It very nearly hit your lung. The other one is lodged under your pectoral muscle, just below your armpit. Are you sure you want to refuse anesthesia?"

"Now that you mention it, it would be nice to sleep through that. Okay, knock me out and do your thing. By the way, how's Hannibal?"

"Commander Burke is in OR One right now. The surgeons are having some trouble stopping his internal bleeding, but if they can do that and patch up his pancreas he should be okay."

"His what?"

"We'll know more in a few hours. It's your turn now. Let's bring the anesthesiologist in here."


"Sam briefed me on what you were doing yesterday," Casey said as soon as Cannon closed himself in the secure Telepresence booth. "Let's hear it from you. I want to know how you involved the pilot."

"What did Sam tell you?"

"Never mind what he told me. You tell me what you were doing, and how much Roche was in on."

"Okay. Nice to see you too." Sarcasm dripped through Cannon's tired smile.

"Spare me the damned pleasantries. It's the small hours of the morning over here and I'm running low on coffee."

Cannon started talking about his activities. "Sam called me on Saturday night and said he was going to be audited by SAVAK. Somehow they were tracing Special K's money and it led back to Laundry Pile. He needed to move the funds to renumbered accounts and the best way he figured to do that was for us to stage a bank robbery and lock the computers while he worked."

"So you and the Mukhabarat brothers and Roche did that on Monday."

"I had Roche wait in the car. He didn't know what was going on. All I told him was that I had to bury a trail with a contact in the bank."

"He bought it?"

"He didn't have a choice. He wasn't going to make it out of the city without my help, and he knew it. He couldn't speak Farsi. He's pretty good with Russian, though."

"It sounded like you needed some help too."

"Yeah, the bank situation got a little out-of-control when some real bank robbers showed up and blew up a bomb in the garage. After that we had the whole police force coming down on us. Roche did a great job as a getaway driver."

"Did Roche have any contact with Sam?"

"No," Cannon lied. "I only spoke with Sam alone."

"What about the brothers?"

"We had them in the car with us but they didn't talk. I didn't tell Roche who they were, and he didn't ask. He was a little busy driving fast."

"You stayed in the safe house at the end of the embassy tunnel?"

"The first night. We went to Albie's tower last night."

"And that was compromised."

"Not by us. Rannovich's people were tracing Special K."

"Well the important thing is that you got the packages."

424

"Yes. As soon as Krause can arrange to fly us off, we'll be on our way to Langley to deliver them."

"Okay." Casey yawned. "I gotta wait for Roche to get out of sick bay so I can debrief him too."

"Please go easy on him, J," Cannon pleaded. "K, Red and I would all be dead if it wasn't for him."

"Don't worry," Jarrod Casey assured his operative. "I'll be nice."

Roche woke up an hour post-op. They had given him a shot of something to snap him out of it, which he would have preferred to forgo. He could have slept for days, but now he was forced to endure being grilled by the Deputy Director of Operations of the Central Intelligence Agency. He was dragged up to the secure Telepresence booth.

Casey looked him over. "You look pretty much the same as the last time I saw you, Commander."

"What are you talking about, sir?" Roche yawned. He was much more tired than he remembered being before the surgery.

"Never mind. First of all, let me thank you personally for salvaging the rescue mission and helping my agent get out alive," Casey said, with an expression of frank insincerity. Roche was not aware that Jarrod Casey's face always looked like that, even in his wedding photos.

"You're welcome," Roche replied curtly.

"Now unfortunately, in the last two days you've been exposed to some highly classified CIA operations in the area. I need to find out how much you know in order to determine how your knowledge may compromise those operations."

"I can promise you I'm not going to compromise anything. I'm not going back to Tehran again, and I don't have any interest in your spy games over there."

"I'll spare you from telling me anything I can find out by watching TV," Casey said in a brusque tone, which was just the way he usually spoke but to Roche it just sounded rude. "Why don't we start with what happened after the SEALs left you?"

"Okay. I was shooting the IRG troops with the squad's machine gun to keep them from going for the Osprey with a rocket launcher or something…"

"You were covering the line of retreat. I already got that on my TiVo."

"Anyway," Roche realized he was going to lose his temper very soon. "Your agent snuck up behind me and started shooting at the enemy also. I was very surprised, and asked what he was doing. Up until then he was undercover, and I thought he was one of the Russian civilians."

"You knew there was an American agent in the embassy, right?"

"I had thought that was the whole point. The briefing I was given by Admiral Krause stated that we'd be extracting at least one CIA asset along with the ambassador and anyone else in the embassy. I had assumed the agent would have left in the Osprey."

"Did you have any contact with the agent before the gunfight?"

"I talked with him at the embassy. He was pushing some guy in a wheelchair and I asked if he needed help."

"Did he speak to you in English?"

"Not at that point. Like I said I thought he was a Russian civilian so I used that language. I know it well enough to get by in casual conversation."

"Yes," Casey said, "my agent mentioned that you spoke nearly fluent Russian."

"It would probably save some time here if you told me what he already told you."

"I don't think so. I need to make sure your report matches his. He's not going to tell me if he gave away any classified info to you. Did he give you a name?"

Roche figured that he shouldn't admit to knowing Cannon's real name, or his agency codename. Cannon would definitely keep that a secret as well. "He told me to call him Mr. C in private. The Russians called him Kalinov, and the Iranians called him Kahlil." The aliases would have come up in conversation, so Roche figured it would be okay for him to admit to knowing those.

"No first names?"

"No."

"Okay. Tell me about the other people you met in Iran."

*I didn't actually meet that Kujetski character, and that's good because he is one dude I am definitely not supposed to know about.* "I briefly met two guys that I think were Iraqi special agents. Mr. C called them the Mukhabarat brothers, which I think is a reference the old Iraqi intelligence service. They were calling targets for my air strike team on Sunday and I saw them in person on Monday. I didn't speak to them. They spoke to Mr. C in Arabic or Farsi or something. I

426

think I remember one of their names was Eli-something. I also saw this Indian guy that worked on computers for Mr. C. That was this morning. His name's Albie."

"Casino Indian or Kwik-E-Mart Indian?"

*That's kinda racist.* "He was from India. I think he was either Muslim or Sikh – I'm pretty sure he's not Hindu, just guessing by the way he dressed and spoke. He was sitting in an apartment with a lot of computer equipment, and Mr. C had to retrieve a data card from him. That's all I know about him."

"Let's go back to what happened yesterday."

"You mean the incident at the Central Bank of Iran?"

"Yes. Tell me why you were involved in that."

"I was involved because your James Bond wannabe dragged me in to it. He told me that he and those two Iraqis had to take care of something at the bank, but I didn't know they were robbing the place until it happened. He and I stole a car that morning, and they made me the getaway driver. I sat in the parking garage for an hour while they did all the work."

"Did they tell you why you were robbing a bank?"

Cannon had told Roche that when this came up he should lie like a rug. Roche hadn't thought of a plausible cover story so he played dumb but offered a few bits of truth so he sounded cooperative. "No, I've got no idea what was up with that. They said something about 'salvage of funds' and 'cleaning the record,' and they mentioned some guy named Sam who works undercover in that bank. Why that was more important than getting Mr. C and me out of the country, I don't know."

"Okay." Casey didn't sound convinced but he didn't press the issue either. "Now after they robbed the bank, you were involved in a high-speed pursuit, right?"

"Right. The police were understandably upset about us having robbed the nation's largest financial institution. I was in the getaway car, so I lost the police and took Mr. C and the surviving bank robbers to a safe house."

"How many police officers did you kill?" Casey asked offhand.

Roche actually hadn't thought about that at all. "Several policemen were killed in an explosion at the bank that I had nothing to do with. I know for sure least four officers were killed in the pursuit. I shot one, another got shot by another cop, and I put at least two cars in wrecks that definitely weren't survivable. The car chase wrecked or disabled about twenty other patrol cars which might have injured or

427

killed several more policemen, but I tried to avoid causing civilian casualties whenever possible."

As he thought about, Roche realized that what he'd just said was simply untrue. As the chase progressed he had become less and less concerned with who got hurt in the escapade. He thought for a second about the one car he had T-boned and deliberately pushed sideways into parked crane. The car had been sliced in half on impact, and he remembered watching the police officer getting turned into red spray as he came apart with his vehicle...

"What about IRG?"

"Since I got shot down? I have no idea. Between Mr. C and me we killed about fifty IRG in the gunfight on Sunday, the SEALs took out a few dozen more, and a whole bunch got toasted by the Air Force. We killed a total of four IRG troops this morning. More got killed I'm sure when Albie blew up the top of his building. Then we were attacked by regular army soldiers at the extraction point. I'd estimate there were a hundred casualties there, mostly caused by Navy aircraft."

"Let me ask you about the vehicles you were using. What did you do with the car you had on Monday?"

"The Iraqis took it after we split up."

"And where'd you get the motorcycle you had this morning?"

"It was delivered to our safe house last night."

"You don't know who it belonged too?"

Roche had to suppress a smile when remembering the young Samadad brothers. "Some affluent and youthful member of the local resistance, I'd guess. Mr. C kept me in the dark as much as possible when it came to his network."

"Did anyone mention the name 'Kujet' or 'Kujetski' to you?"

"Um," Roche pretended to think for a minute. He knew the arms dealer and the spy worked together on their semi-legitimate cover, so he figured it would be safe to let that slip. "Mr. C and the Russian Ambassador did talk to one of the Russian civilians a lot. His name might have been Kujetski, or something a lot like that anyway. I think he owned the safehouses we used."

"Describe the safehouse."

"There were two, actually. The first night we were in a warehouse at the end of a tunnel leading from the embassy. Last night we went to rundown apartment building."

"What do you know about his involvement with my agent?"

"I'm guessing he had something to do with Mr. C's cover. From what I gathered they have some business together exporting

Persian rugs and antiquities. The warehouse was full of rugs and ancient artifacts." Roche thought he saw a hint of a smile play at the corners of Casey's mouth. That was the only hint he got that the CIA man had bought one of his lies.

Next Casey asked about the next-most-important man in the network. "Do you know anything about Sam?"

"Surface-to-air missiles?"

"No, the guy you said worked at the bank."

"Oh." *That nice old guy is the center of the CIA's entire operation over there. I'd better keep quiet about him too.* "No, I never met him. I only heard Mr. C use his name once, but I don't remember the context." Roche yawned pointedly.

Casey decided to hurry it up a little. "I'll just throw out some words and phrases and you tell me if they mean anything to you ok? Let me know if you heard Mr. C or one of the Iraqis mention it, or if you saw it written down somewhere ok? 'Caspian.'"

Roche knew it was the spy's codename but instead he answered "As in the Caspian Sea? Nothing else comes to mind."

"What about 'Caspian Monster'?"

Roche didn't know that one, and responded with genuine puzzlement. "Huh, no. I can recall that was a Russian experimental seaplane of some sort, back in the eighties..."

"Okay. What about 'Special K'?"

Roche correctly guessed that was Kujetski's agency codename. "Besides the cereal brand, no, that doesn't mean anything."

"Laundry Pile, Laundry List, Dry Clean, Steam Clean, or Clothesline?"

Roche again correctly guessed that those codenames referred to various aspects of Sam's operations. "No, nothing."

"Are there any details you might have left out?"

"Yeah, try this on for size. Those cots in the safehouses were very uncomfortable and I haven't had a decent sleep in several days. I'm very tired, and I think we're done with this debriefing."

Casey glared impassively. "In the interests of national security, I have to be sure you're not holding any secrets, Commander."

"Oh, I keep plenty of secrets, Mr. Casey. But I don't know anything about what you're doing in Iran, and I don't want to know. I don't want to know why there's a tunnel between a warehouse full of rugs and the Russian Embassy. I don't want to know why your agent brought me along to rob the Central Bank of Iran. I don't want to know why a college drop-out from India was running a miniature Fort Meade out of a dumpy apartment building in West Tehran, or why he blew it sky high when the IRG closed in on it this morning. If you're concerned about anything else I don't want to know but might have found out anyway, you can drug up your spy when he gets home and grill him at your leisure. By the way, if you're interested in national security breaches, why don't you look in to how the Iranians knew we were going to attempt a rescue at the embassy before we even got there? Now, I'm late for my phone call to be debriefed by SPECWARCOM. Have a nice day, Mr. Casey." With that, Roche disconnected the feed from Langley and opened the channel from Coronado.

Captain Ames, Roche's old battalion commander, was now the Pacific Fleet Operations Director of the Navy's Special Warfare Command, overseeing all SEAL ops out of Coronado. "Nathan says you saved our team, Commander," Ames said.

Roche shrugged wearily. "Yeah I know, CNN said the same thing."

Ames smiled benevolently, a welcome change from Casey's grim face. "I know you don't want me to praise you or kiss your ass, so let's just stick with the debriefing. Someone will pin you with all the medals you deserve later. So let's just stick to what happened down there. At what point did you assume command of Nathan's squad?"

"Basically, as soon as I got to the command post, I became the de facto team leader. They had no comms, Commander Clark was dead, the extraction plan was not an option because of the enemy artillery, and Nathan was just overwhelmed. He asked me to help them get out of there."

"Where had he established the CP?"

Roche paused for a second, trying to remember. The embassy seemed like the distant past at this point. "In the main dining room, on the second floor of the embassy."

"What is your tactical assessment of Nathan's actions prior to your arrival?"

"The only mistake he made was putting Morris behind the sniper rifle. Williams had been hurt, but Nathan should have assigned the sniper duties to someone who could actually perform as a sniper, like Ramirez. Morris can shoot a big rifle well enough, but he was up there without a spotter and he wasn't cutting it as a sniper. He actually shot at me when I approached the embassy grounds."

"Okay, we've noted that the sniper assignment was a poor call. What about the location of the CP?"

430

"Setting up the command post in the dining room was fine for the original plan. It was a central point in the building that all the Russians knew how to get to, it was a large room where everyone could wait comfortably and it was right next to the stairs that went to the helipad on the roof."

"Okay, but shouldn't he have moved downstairs when the artillery hit?"

"The lowest point in the building was the wine cellar, but if the embassy took a direct hit it wouldn't make a difference."

"What about the bomb shelter?"

"I don't know anything about a bomb shelter. If Nathan was aware of a bomb shelter he should have gone there."

"He says he didn't know about it. The Russian ambassador was the one who said he should have used it when we debriefed him later."

"That was the other thing that messed the mission up," Roche told him. "There was nobody on the team that spoke either Russian or Farsi. I speak some Russian and so I was able to figure out the escape tunnel, but before I got there they were talking through some accountant on the embassy staff."

"The operation was hastily assembled," Ames explained. "We couldn't get anyone with the necessary language skills to send to the METO on short notice. Believe me, we tried."

"Also, the SEALs didn't know about the CIA agent."

"Langley instructed us not to contact the agent personally. They wanted to maintain his cover. So on the team itself only Commander Clark was given that info."

"Overall, I'd give a B-plus to Nathan and a C-minus to whoever planned this thing," Roche summarized. "But I guess it would have worked out fine if it wasn't for the leak. By the way, that could have come from your area."

"We're looking into that, but I don't think that was us."

"Who else knew the Op details?"

"Just Langley, your superiors on the *Reagan*, a few people at the Marine base in Bahrain where we got the Osprey and the Talon from, and of course the Fleet HQ guys there in Bahrain."

"What about the media contingent?"

"I don't know anything about them."

"I was told they had real-time coverage of the rescue attempt."

"Well, that's where I'd start looking for a leak then. It wouldn't be the first time. Back to the operation: when the Osprey arrived, how did Nathan handle the extraction?"

"Like a professional. He didn't want to leave me, but he figured out that he didn't have a choice."

"He said you had to give him your trident before he would leave you behind."

"That reminds me, I'll have to get that back from him. But yes, I had to remind him that the mission was a higher priority than getting every SEAL and former SEAL home together. Once I gave the order to clear out, he had his men aboard the Osprey in a matter of seconds."

"Okay. I don't have any more questions, Karl. I'll let you get the sleep you obviously need. Thank you again for saving Nathan and the other guys."

"Yeah, no problem."

When that was over, Roche still had to be debriefed by Captain Thompson and Admiral Krause. They tried to keep it short, but Karl was already yawning uncontrollably. They let him know he was unofficially promoted to full three-stripe Commander and would be the provisional CO of the *Stingrays* until either Burke recovered or they got back to North Island. Roche was too tired to care. Finally, at 1700, Roche was allowed to go to bed. He was exhausted, but he was still floating on too much adrenaline to close his eyes. He let CNN talk him to sleep. Nothing was less interesting to him than himself, and that's all anyone was talking about on TV.

## SHEIK ISA AIR BASE, BAHRAIN – 1945 LOCAL

"Now this is nice," Antonov said, examining the interior of the Air Force plane. The aircraft was a C-37A, a slightly militarized version of a Gulfstream V business jet. The appointments were toned down slightly but it was still clearly intended for VIP transportation. Quite an improvement over the canvas-and-aluminum seats in the rattling C-2 Greyhound COD they had just left.

"Finally someone springs a first-class ticket for us," Kujetski agreed. "Come on, you, up the stairs," he goaded Rannovich's agent Number Five.

"I'm moving, I'm moving," he protested. "Why don't try to climb stairs wearing these leg irons?"

Cannon didn't say anything. He just picked a chair and immediately went back to sleep. As soon as they landed in the States he was going to be grilled all over again by Casey; he'd need all the rest he could get.

## REAGAN – 0500 LOCAL, JUNE 4<sup>TH</sup>

Roche woke up about eleven hours after the news put him to sleep, and CNN and was still talking about him. In was half-past nine PM in Atlanta, he'd been feet-wet and safe for nineteen hours, surely there were other things going on in the world, but despite all this Karl Roche was still the hot item.

He channel-surfed for a few minutes to see if it was only CNN that was crazy. The major networks had gone back to regular programming. Roche watched a medical drama on Fox for a few minutes, happily trading his own troubles for some doctor character. But a commercial break told him to stay tuned for the ten o'clock local news and they would have the latest on Karl Roche. "He is out of Iran, but is he still in danger? He had been shot before the rescue, now Navy doctors update us on his condition."

"Give me a break." Roche flicked through the stations again and it just got worse. Fox News and MSNBC had their programming packed with Karl Roche Trivia. He watched long enough to find out that everyone in America now knew more about his SEAL service in Iraq than his mother had. He moved to ESPN; surely the NBA Conference Finals would be leading Sports Center's coverage. No, they were discussing Roche's brief college football career.

Roche wondered why this was happening. The military never let the media have this much personal information on servicemen, and certainly not those engaged in active operations. He changed channels again. The Discovery Channel was airing a program on the development of the F/A-18 Super Hornet. The Speed network reran an amateur racing show that had featured the Battleship tearing up Laguna Seca, which was the only time Roche had ever enjoyed being on TV. Finally Roche found something on TV that had nothing to do with him: Comedy Central and an old South Park episode. But that ended five minutes later and Jon Stewart started The Daily Show with – what else? – more news about Karl Roche.

Roche turned off the TV in utter disgust. He got dressed and opened the door, and was stopped by an armed Marine.

"Good morning, sir!" The Marine snapped to attention.

"At ease, Corporal." Roche started to exit his room, but the Marine stepped forward to block him. "What the-"

"Sir, I have orders that you are not to be disturbed under any circumstances, sir."

Roche stared. "But I'm not being disturbed. I'm just going to the gym."

433

"I'm sorry sir, but that activity would inhibit your much-needed rest."

"You have to be kidding. Who put you up to this?"

"This is an instruction from the chief medical officer, sir."

"So I'm not allowed to leave my room?"

"You are confined to quarters, sir, as a medical precaution."

"Confined to quarters?" Roche was incredulous. "But what if I want breakfast?"

"You may call the wardroom staff and they will bring you your meals, sir."

"When do you orders expire?"

"When I am relieved at 0800 hours, sir."

"Can I leave my room then?"

"No sir, you are not disturbed until 0600 hours tomorrow, sir."

"You mean I can't leave my room until tomorrow morning?"

"Yes sir."

"I don't believe this." Roche went back into his room and dialed the number for sick bay. Tobias told him he could not engage in any strenuous activity or exercise at all until his sutures healed. Given his habits, the only way to enforce that was to keep him in his room. No sit-ups, pushups, or pull-ups either, the doctor warned. Roche grumbled for a minute but gave up. He asked about Hannibal, and was told that the CO was resting comfortably and recovering from a successful surgery. Roche thanked the physician and hung up. Then the Marine knocked on the door.

"Sir, I'd almost forgot. There was a civilian who came down yesterday around 1740 looking for you. He said he wanted to talk with you, but he was going to be flown back to the States and couldn't wait for you to become available. Anyway, he left this with me to give to you, sir." The Marine handed him a dog-eared paperback book of poems and essays by Ralph Waldo Emerson.

"You've been standing here all night?"

"No sir. Two other Marines and I take four-hour shifts."

"I see. Did he tell you his name?"

"Not as such, but he said you would know who Mr. C is, sir."

Roche thanked him and went back inside. Cannon had left a bookmark and highlighted a passage of Emerson's short essay on Heroism. Roche read the selection.

*"The characteristic of a genuine heroism is its persistency. All men have wandering impulses, fits and starts of generous courage. But when you have resolved to be great, abide by yourself and do not*

434

*weakly try to reconcile yourself with the world.   The heroic cannot become common, nor the common heroic."*

Roche smiled.  "Whatever you say, Mr. C."

# CHAPTER 21: FIRE IN THE SKY

## SHEIK ISA AIR BASE, BAHRAIN – 0800 HOURS, JUNE 4$^{TH}$

Worm couldn't figure out how it could be twenty degrees hotter here on this little island than it had been out on the *Reagan* just sixty miles off shore about twenty minutes earlier. This early in the morning, it shouldn't be over a hundred degrees *anywhere* in the world. Sitting on the black tarmac with the engines off, the poly-plexi-canopied un-air-conditioned cockpit was a torture chamber. At least the thermagel flight suit was keeping his legs cool, but his bald head was simmering inside his helmet.

"'Ey Worm, mate, what's the name of that Boeing boffin?"

"Silverman," Commander Bellbrook answered Nelson "Bonzer" McGee's query.

"Righto. We're gonna have to grill him up on a barbie for this."

"For what?"

"For the bloody A/C blower not running on battery power."

Worm laughed. "I thought you grew up in the Outback. This should be a taste of home for you."

"I lied, mate. I grew up in Brisbane – that's a nice temperate clime. I ain't never been more than twenty miles from the sea at any point in my life."

One of the techs rapped on the side of Bellbrook's plane and flashed a thumbs-up. Worm gratefully restarted his engines, and was soon rewarded by an arctic blast of air from his air vents. He lifted his helmet and leaned forward, letting the cold artificial breeze evaporate the moisture from his scalp. He looked back and saw that the rest of his squadron was powered up again as well, except for Bonzer. One of the ordnance jacks had gotten stuck, and it took the techs a moment to yank it free from the bomb under his left wing. Once they finally got clear McGee quit swearing at them and turned on his own engines and air conditioning.

"Isa Tower, this is Badger Lead," Worm reported. "Ready for north departure on active, over."

"Roger that, Badger. Your flight is clear to depart on runway three."

"Copy, clear on three." The Warhawks took off from the wealthy little Arabian island and settled into a high-speed run across the gulf. The new bombs they had just picked up from the Air Base in

Bahrain were Paveway III bunker-busters fitted with experimental BLU-118/B thermobaric warheads. Theoretically, they should be highly effective against deeply-buried targets, such as the Iranian oil pipeline tunnels that Rannovich was using as underground superhighways.

## RHUD-E DEZ VALLEY NORTH OF DEZFUL, IRAN
## TWO HOURS EARLIER

It took a while for US Army Captain Rayford Pondsmith to realize that he had led his company of tanks into a trap. The twelve M1A2 Abrams tanks of Tango Company had pursued a battered battalion of mixed Iranian armor twenty miles up a dry river bed, and then the enemy vehicles simply disappeared. Then, just as suddenly, Pondsmith's company was caught in a brutal artillery barrage. He dropped down into his turret and secured the hatch over his head. "Turn around and get us out of here!" he yelled over the intercom to his driver.

As the tank spun around, Ray Pondsmith watched the fireworks through his periscope. He recognized immediately that the Iranian gunners were using a mix of munitions. Some of the shells exploded violently above the ground – these were high-explosive shells with proximity fuses. They shouldn't be too dangerous to a heavily-armored tank as long as nothing vital was exposed to the blast. Some of the shells exploded on the ground – impact fuses. More dangerous, but not exactly a knockout blow. But some shells plunged beneath the surface and went off with a muffled thud. These were anti-tank penetration rounds – very effective against their intended targets.

Ray spotted one of his lance commanders – Lt. Jacobs of Snapshot Lance – still standing upright in his hatch. An instant later he was gone, vaporized by a proximity shell that went off right over his head. "SEAL YOUR HATCHES!" He yelled over the team frequency. When the smoke cleared, Snapshot-1 appeared to be undamaged except for the burn mark where the commander and his gun and hatch had been.

Another tank almost ran over an impact shell just as it exploded. It flipped the tank on its side and ripped the right tread off. The commander was able to roll it back over by pushing the turret against the ground, but with a thrown tread it wasn't going anywhere fast. "Ricochet Lance, this is Rick Two," the commander of the crippled tank called. "We just lost a tread. Can someone push us out?"

"Ricochet One," Pondsmith called to the other lance commander, "he just needs you or Rick Three to push on the rear right corner so he can limp out of here."

"No problem, Ray-Ray," Lt. Vialpando answered. "I-AAAAAUUUGGHH!!" Ricochet-1 was hit in the weakest point by an anti-tank round. It stabbed through the cooling vents over the engine and the 1500hp Lycoming turbine became a grenade, blowing the massive vehicle apart from the inside.

"Dammit!" Pondsmith realized his men would be slaughtered if they all slowed down. "Rick Three, see if you can help Two. The rest of you, keep your speed up and don't stop for anything!"

"I can't see you, sir," Tracer-2, Pondsmith's wingman said. "I can't see through the smoke!"

Pondsmith looked back again. He could hardly see any of his tanks through the flame, smoke and dust. "Fix your heading to one-niner-five," he ordered. He watched a series of explosions engulf the rest of Ricochet Lance. "Let's get the hell out of here!"

Another tank took a direct hit from a ground-burst shell, right on the front of the turret. It didn't penetrate the armor, but it almost ripped the main gun out of its mount. Another received a glancing blow from an armor-piercing round which ripped off a tread. Then another anti-tank round found its mark, this time on Pondsmith's tank. It went straight through the driver's compartment, killing Corporal Blythe outright and wrecking the driver's controls.

"Are you guys okay?" Pondsmith called to the other two men in the turret.

"We're fine, but Blythe is toast," his gunner called back.

Pondsmith yelled a string of curses at nothing in particular, but he stayed in control of his vehicle. He noticed the tank slowing, the engine winding down. With the driver's station destroyed the tank automatically started to grind to a halt. Pondsmith overrode the controls and pushed the tank forward at full power to both treads.

"Are you okay Captain?" someone asked over the radio.

"Yeah. Keep moving," he said.

Abruptly, the shelling stopped. Then after a moment, more rounds came flying toward the American tanks. But these shells weren't coming from an artillery battery miles away, they were coming from an enemy tank company dead ahead. A round exploded square on the nose of Pondsmith's tank, but caused no damage, being unable to penetrate the thick ceramic-alloy composite armor on the front end of the hull. After a moment the dust and smoke cleared enough that he could see the line of T-80s charging toward him, only a few hundred yards away.

Pondsmith swore and fired the main gun himself from his override, seeing a T-80 right in his sights. The uranium slug had scarcely slipped free of its sabot casing when it slammed through the front armor of the T-80. The heavy metal round carved through the armor like a chainsaw through a birthday cake. The kinetic energy of the slug was spent in a spray of white-hot molten metal which ignited everything it touched. The tank blew up from the inside, launching its turret high in the air.

Pondsmith had no time to celebrate though. His company was badly outnumbered and wouldn't last long in a close range fight. "It's an ambush! Turn around!" he ordered his men. "But shoot back!" The Captain reversed the gears on his left tread but held the turret steady on his next target while the hull pulled a 180. His gunner fired back as fast as the loader could ram fresh M829A2 rounds into the gun.

The other Abrams tanks joined fire, but Pondsmith saw some of the rounds explode violently but harmlessly before actually hitting the enemy tanks. That was because the T-80s had reactive armor, designed specifically to defeat NATO standard High Explosive Anti-Tank rounds. "Use the DU sabot rounds only," he told the other tank crews. "HEAT shells are useless against that armor."

"I'm out of silver bullets," Tracer-2 answered, using the tankers' nickname for the depleted uranium slugs.

"Me too," added the commander of Ricochet-4. After running and gunning all night in pursuit of the light battalion, Tango Company was very low on ammo and fuel. Now they were being chased deeper into enemy territory, half their tanks were destroyed and disabled, and two of the lance commanders were dead. Just when Pondsmith thought the situation couldn't get worse, a report came from the other end of his column.

"Captain! Enemy armor in front!" called the tank commander at the rear of the column, now leading the retreat.

"Where exactly, Snap Three?"

"Right where those BMPs disappeared. I make a company of T-72s. They have defilade, and they-" Snapshot-3's transmission was abruptly terminated when his tank received a concentrated volley from the enemy T-72s. The combined force of the 125mm shells tore its turret from the hull and incinerated the interior.

Pondsmith was beside himself. He rattled off a string of curses.

"We can't get through these guys," Snapshot-4 called back, after taking cover behind Snapshot-3's wrecked hull. "They've got the ground and they can defend it. We should take our chances with that other company."

"I don't-" in the moment Pondsmith hesitated, Snapshot-4 and what was left of his wingman were annihilated in another salvo. "Fuck it, let's go." Pondsmith kicked both treads into reverse and let the tank accelerate to its full speed going backwards, then he put the right side in neutral and let the tank slide into a turn, then jammed the right lever to full forward, then put the left in forward as the hull whipped through a very hard 180 J-turn at forty miles an hour. High-powered shells were still flying in all directions as two companies of tanks closed like medieval knights jousting on a tournament field.

The T-80s' commander tried to physically impede the American's escape, directing his tanks to turn sharply and line up nose-to-tail across the riverbed. Pondsmith steered his tank toward a narrow gap between two of the Russian machines. He aimed for the one on the right, but as the gun fired, the Abrams took a glancing blow that spun their turret and the shot was thrown wide.

"Last sabot," the loader called on the intercom. Pondsmith wrestled with the turret controls, but the damaged motor responded sluggishly. Meanwhile the T-80s he was charging were bringing their guns to bear on him. Pondsmith lined the turret up with the tank on the left, and the gunner fired a split-second late. The round slammed the enemy turret hard, destroying everything inside. The off-center impact slewed the turret around, and its main gun went off, hitting its neighbor at point-blank range. Pondsmith pushed through the two burning tanks at full speed.

He looked back in time to see Snapshot-1, formerly commanded by Lt. Jacobs, ram a T-80 broadside. The Russian rolled over, and the Abrams vaulted itself over the wreck. Pondsmith watched the other T-80s explode one by one, but none of the other Americans followed him past the line. "Jesus, they're all dead," he said to himself. There had been twelve tanks carrying a total of forty-eight men. Now all but six of those men were dead or captured. He slid the Abrams to a halt and stared at the burning metal, and waited for something – anything – to pass through the flames. But there was nothing.

Snapshot-1 ground to a stop beside him. "Are we clear Captain?" the driver called through his open hatch.

"We're clear" the Captain said, "but we're the only ones."

"Ferret Lead to Mongoose Lead, copy that target." Lt. Sergei "Deadeye" Unther double-checked that the radar signal he had locked on to matched the GPS coordinates that Palerider had given him. Then he released one of the AGM-88 HARM missiles from his left wing. The supersonic anti-radiation weapon took off, homing in on the enemy radar. Somewhere forty miles ahead, a mobile SA-6 station was about to be toast.

"Mongoose Two, is there anything in your sector?" Commander Scott "Palerider" Tachini called to Fozzy Bear.

"Negative, Lead," Lt. Foster answered. "The only radio signal I'm picking up is civilian-band broadcast of some sort of religious news service."

Palerider stifled a yawn and a laugh. "Roger that. Shift your track ten degrees to the north, and we'll head due west."

"Copy, new heading three two zero. I'll wake you up if we see anything interesting."

Palerider let himself yawn again. Other than that one SA-6 site, this Wild Weasel mission had been about as wild as a trip to the cleaners. His two Growlers and Deadeye's Hornet-C division carried a total of twenty-four HARMs. Palerider had been planning on using most of those. Something had been ambushing friendly aircraft in this area, and it was certainly a little more formidable than one SAM battery.

A white-haired Russian man in a black flight suit watched as the decrepit radar van on the top of the hill was struck by the $300,000 American missile. The van exploded into a shower of flaming wreckage that tumbled down the hill. Colonel Victor Lenonov snickered as he walked back to the shack a few feet up the slope. "Did you intercept the jamming signal?" He asked the young technician, who sat at an old table working on two notebook computers at once.

"Da, comrade Colonel. Triple-source ALQ-99 system. Signal-strength derivation indicates fast-mover. Too fast for a Prowler."

"Prowlers move pretty fast," Lenonov said.

"Not over a thousand kilometers sustained ground speed," the technician countered. "And they don't carry their own missiles if they have three ALQ-99 pods."

"So it must be a Growler."

"At least one. The Americans don't like to work alone."

"Good. Activate the next decoy once I take off." The white-haired Russian opened a door in the back of the shack, which led down a flight of stairs into a large man-made cavern. It was actually a hangar, hidden under the hill. He looked around, letting his eyes adjust to the dim light. One thing Rannovich had failed to supply to Lenonov's wing of mercenary pilots was adequate lighting. But the planes themselves lacked for nothing; especially Victor "The Black Cobra" Lenonov's command division. The four Sukhoi-37 Super Flankers in the hangar were fully armed and fueled, and tuned to a state of mechanical perfection by Lenonov's technicians.

Lenonov called to the other three pilots, who were in the corner of the hangar near the living quarters playing cards. "We have a good target in the area. Get to your planes." They dropped their cards and chips and ran to their mottled gray and black-banded fighters, while he turned to his own all-charcoal-black machine. He gave the powerful aircraft a quick once-over, inspecting the clamps securing the missiles under the wings, checking for heat fractures in the vectored-thrust nozzles, looking for scratches in the radar-absorbent paint, anything the mechanics may have missed. Meanwhile the Iranian Air Force conscripts that served as his ground crew were opening the camouflaged door in the hillside. Satisfied, Lenonov climbed the padded ladder leading up to the cockpit. One of the attentive ground crew pulled it away as soon as his boot left the top rung. He settled in to the hard contoured seat and started the engines.

A steady gust of hot exhaust and dust rebounded off the far wall and rolled past the planes out to daylight. Lenonov eased his plane forward onto the narrow dirt runway, letting his eyes readjust to the harsh desert sun. Under daylight, the Black Cobra's plane looked a little different. The matte-black radar-absorbing paint was somewhat mottled with slightly lighter shades, in a pattern similar to snake scales. A darker band traced a serpentine pattern across the Flanker's back ending in swirls on the top of the canard wings, imitating the back of a cobra's hood. There was an evil face painted on the nose: green snake eyes, white fangs and a red forked tongue. The Black Cobra clearly didn't mind being identified once in the air. He didn't intend to let any enemy live long after seeing his plane.

Lenonov rammed the throttles forward and unleashed the massive Saturn AL-31 engines. He only needed half of the unpaved runway's 2600-foot length to lift off and climb out of the gully at a steep angle. His wingmen followed closely, settling into a diamond wing pattern. "Ivan, any update?" he called on the radio to his electronic warfare technician.

"I'm uploading my vector estimate for your Growler. I'm tracking him on my passive radar receivers, and two Hornets also."

"Super Hornets?"

"No, the older models. I can tell, they have different radar. Also, the Iranians visually identified a second group of three aircraft flying north-northwest toward Red Division One's hangar."

"Okay, deploy them as well."

"They're already rolling. Good hunting, comrade Colonel."

"Another radar trace, right band for an SA-6 but it's pretty low-power." Palerider sounded bored as he processed the threat radar signal. "I suppose it's strong enough to steer a missile. You guys might as well take it out."

"Right, uh, where is it?" Deadeye asked.

"Oh yeah, I keep forgetting you don't have SHOCLink." Palerider resolved the contact and gave Ferret Flight the GPS coordinates.

"Okay, I see it on my scope. You want to get this one, Chef?" Unther asked his wingman.

"Yeah sure, why not." Lt. Elroy "Chef" Jameson rolled away from the trident formation and headed toward the target. Soon his HARMs acquired the signal, and Chef released one from his right wing. Forty miles ahead, it successfully vaporized a 1971 Ford Transit with a salvaged radar transmitter duct-taped to the roof. "Target... destroyed," Chef yawned. "Hey, Commander, I'm getting kinda close to my no-return fuel point. When are we heading back?"

"We have to make sure this airspace is clear when the bomber groups come back. There's got to be something down there, but they're keeping quiet. We need to hang around and hit anything that tries to go after the bombers."

"Right. When are the bombers coming back?" Deadeye asked.

"The first squadron should be approaching their targets now, so, I'd say another two hours before the last one shows up over here."

"Damn. My ass is gonna be numb before we see the deck."

"Let's move down to the coast," Tachini decided. "There's a tanker out there. You guys can get a drink while I keep sniffing."

"Alright." Unther reset his heading bug and let the autopilot steer south. He groaned and stretched, brushing his arms against the canopy over his head. "It's gonna be a long day."

*　　*　　*

According to the data being uploaded to Lenonov by Ivan's receivers, the Growler and its escorts were directly in front of him. At his speed the Black Squadron would catch them in fifteen minutes. "Comrade Colonel," the technician called. "General Mikhail wants to speak to you."

"Very well. Put him through."

The radio clicked. "Colonel Lenonov?"

"I'm here, comrade General."

"Where is 'here?' Are you in the air?"

"Yes sir. I'm about to intercept one of those American Navy Growlers."

"Send one of your other squadrons after it. Our agents in Bahrain reported a large force of fighter-bombers that are heading up to attack our pipeline tunnels. I need you to lead at least two squadrons north to engage them."

"You can send my other squadron from your base," Lenonov suggested.

"We are six hundred miles from the ends of the tunnels. You are much closer."

"Fine. I'll send Blue and White Squadrons to intercept them now, and I'll join them with Red Squadron as soon as we-"

"No, lead them yourself," Rannovich himself cut in. "Those tunnels are vital to my operation. You must stop the attackers yourself. You have no higher priority."

Lenonov swallowed his pride hard. The Black Cobra was known to be fearless, but even he feared the wrath of the man called Rannovich. "Understood, comrade."

"Don't ever call me 'comrade,'" Rannovich snapped, and he terminated the conversation.

The Russian mercenary took a long drink of water from his pouch before calling back down to Ivan. "The situation has changed. Direct one of the White Divisions to intercept my Growler, deploy Blue Squadron and the rest of Black Squadron and send them and my group headings to the pipelines. Tell Red and White to join us once they have killed their targets."

"Okay, Colonel."

Lenonov took another look at the computer screen Ivan had rigged into the cockpit, which allowed him to access by satellite the technician's computer system and see his targets without using his own radar. The Growler's estimated position was now only six miles beyond missile range. He swore. "We go north," he told his wingmen.

## 120 MILES NORTHEAST

Fozzy Bear was rummaging through the gear bag at his feet looking for one of his Clif Bars when he got the feeling he was being watched. He checked his displays and saw no threats. His pilot, Lt. jg. Seth "Scooter" Jones didn't seem worried about anything. Then he turned around in his seat and looked behind him. "Holy hell!" Four gray Super Flankers sporting blood-red stripes and tons of missiles were bearing down on them fast. "Bandits on our six! Take evasive!"

"*What!?*" Scooter looked back as three of the Flankers accelerated forward and fired two AA-11 Archer heat-seekers apiece. "Whoa, shit!"

The IDECM's proximity warning unit detected the incoming missiles and the SHOC, aware of the two friendly Hornets lacking sophisticated defenses, formulated a coordinated evasion maneuver. A more experienced pilot would have probably reacted instinctively, ignored the computer's input and pulled a quick turn-and-burn, which would leave the Hornets exposed to the deadly accurate missiles and probably not save the Growler either. But Scooter was a rookie, and like most of his generation of Super Hornet and Growler aviators, he had learned to rely on the SHOC. In this case, the computer's suggestions saved his life.

He cut his throttle, slowing down in front of the missiles and letting them home in. Then he pulled the stick back and to the right, and tapped the afterburners with the throttle still set to low power. Doing this made the engines belch a long tongue of fiery exhaust which stole the missiles attention from the engines themselves while accelerating the plane in another direction. Scooter steered behind the Hornet on the right while the Hornets rolled down to the left. The IDECM automatically dumped a string of flare shells to cover the Hornets' escape. Then Scooter abruptly nosed over into a full-throttle dive. Between the clouds of white-hot aluminum and the crisscrossing exhaust trails, the Archers were thoroughly confused. They lost track of the Navy planes and zeroed in suicidally on the razor-sharp fragments of hot metal.

The mercenary pilots weren't fooled though. The three that had fired jumped to full afterburner in pursuit of the Hornets. Their leader held back and watched the Growler. Colonel Lenonov had promised a bonus for killing a Growler. Red One intended to collect that bonus.

"Jam them!" Scooter yelled back to the Electronic Warfare Officer.

"There's nothing to jam!" Fozzy said. "They aren't using their- oh wait, now they are." The Flankers had switched to radar-guided weapons to try to catch the fleeing Hornets. Fozzy Bear was able to force them to abandon that tactic, and pursue the Americans at supersonic speed.

Red One wasn't affected. He had slipped into a dive behind the Growler and was gaining. Fozzy noticed. "There's one on our tail!"

Scooter pulled up and to the left, corkscrewing out of the Flanker's line of fire. He slowed down, and the Flanker flew right around them. Scooter dropped inside Red One's turn, and found himself in the perfect position for a Fox-two kill. The Sidewinder's target was only three thousand yards away, committed to an eight-G turn. Red One hadn't even realized the Growler was capable of shooting back. The missile that exploded between his engines caught him completely by surprise.

"Nice shot!" Foster cheered. "Now let's get those other guys."

"Okay." Scooter turned the plane around. "What's the range?"

"Forty-six miles."

"Going to afterburners."

The Hornets were in trouble. They were low on fuel, and the Super Flankers were closing in on them. With no better options, the aviators decided to split up. They didn't get far. The faster, more agile Super Flankers quickly ran them down and killed them at close range.

Fozzy resolved his radar scope just in time to see the Hornets get knocked out of the sky. "We're too late to help them," he told Scooter. "Take out the leader and get us out of here."

"Got it." Scooter fired both their AMRAAMs on a pincer spread with passive guidance. The target wouldn't detect the incoming missiles until they went active, and by then they'd be closing in from two different directions. Count that as a probable kill.

Meanwhile the mercenaries had realized that the Growler was still out there jamming them. They fired a salvo of missiles in the general direction of the blinding energy source. Fozzy had been tracking their own weapons and didn't notice the incoming AA-12s

446

until they were almost on top of them. "We got missiles inbound! Take evasive!"

"They're firing blind," Scooter said. "We're fine."

The missiles went active and locked on. "No, we're screwed," Fozzy said. "I don't have time to jam them!"

"Hang on!" Scooter knew the IDECM wouldn't be able to help him with six missiles closing head-on. He followed the SHOC's guidance for a desperate move, pulling up sharply and releasing his disposable stores, tossing the drop tanks, HARM missiles, and jamming pods in the path of the Russian weapons. Flying metal and explosives collided in a massive fireball, which blew the Growler into an inverted dive and snuffed out the engines.

The mercenaries now had use of their radar, and could see the Growler plummeting toward the earth out of control. It certainly looked like they got him. Red Two and Four watched the Growler fall on their radar scopes until it converged with the ground return. They turned west to meet the rest of Red Squadron and Colonel Lenonov's forces, arguing on the way over who would collect the bonus.

Lt. Foster was terrified. The plane was dropping like a rock, and there was nothing he could do from the back seat. Scooter muttered curses as he tried to coax the Growler back under control. He didn't fight the controls – he knew the computer knew what it was doing – but it didn't seem either he or the computer had any influence on which way the plane tumbled. Worse, the sustained G-load was overpowering the resistance of the thermagel flight suit and draining the blood from his head. His vision stared to collapse into a tunnel, and he knew soon he and Foster would black out. Probably right before the plane crashed.

Scooter forced himself to relax, and looked at his instruments. He noted the plane was tumbling with a positive pitch rate – meaning it was doing a series of back flips, and the engine intakes under the wings couldn't catch any air. Scooter moved the stick to roll with the plane, and pushed forward with a hard rudder twist. The plane snapped itself into negative pitch and the spinning intensified. But Scooter saw that the recovery move had worked. The intake pressure spiked; the engines could breathe again. He restarted the powerful turbofans used the fresh thrust to straighten the descent.

Fozzy was on the edge of blacking out when he felt the engines rumble to life. His tunnel vision was locked on the altimeter, and unless his oxygen-deprived mind was playing tricks on him, they were descending even *faster* now. "We're still going down!" he yelled.

"It's okay, I got the plane," Scooter answered. "I'm going to take us down to the deck and let those Russians up there think we crashed." As Scooter steadied the descent, the G-forces normalized and blood returned to their skulls. Scooter leveled off a hundred feet above the Rud-e Mahat River, which he could follow back to the Gulf.

## TEN MILES SOUTH OF THE IRANIAN GULF COAST
## SAME TIME

"Okay, I'm full. Backing off now," Unther reported.

"Copy that," confirmed the boom operator on the Air Force KC-10. "Go ahead and separate, Ferret One."

Deadeye throttled back and let the Hornet fall behind the tanker. The refueling probe gently pulled free of the drogue at the end of the hose snaking behind the KC-10. Deadeye retracted the probe and rolled away. "All done. Your turn, Ferret Two."

Chef had been waiting a few hundred feet off the KC-10's right wingtip. He drifted sideways behind the fuselage and extended his refueling probe from the side of his nose. The drogue – a stabilizing device shaped like an oversized badminton birdie – guided the one-way valve at the end of the probe to the one at the end of the hose. The connection transferred thousands of gallons of fuel from the giant tanker to the nearly empty fuel cells on-board the Hornet.

"Mongoose Lead, this is Mongoose Two!" Foster called over the team frequency.

"What's up, Fozzy?" Palerider was cruising a few miles north of the tanker, just over the shoreline.

"We got bushwhacked, sir. A flight of Super Flankers; they came out of nowhere! We got away, and took a couple of them out, but our Ferrets got iced."

"Damn," Deadeye muttered.

"What's your status?" Commander Tachini asked.

"We are at zero-percent op-cap. We're hugging the deck, running for feet wet. I'm sending coordinates on satcom."

"Got it." The TacOps computer received the satcom burst transmission from the other Growler and updated Palerider's screen. Commander Tachini frowned in concern. Fozzy had said 0% operational capacity, meaning his plane was useless. "Any damage?"

"Nothing serious to the airframe. But we had to ditch our disposables to get away, including the EW pods."

448

"Alright. You'd better return to Sea World," Tachini used the codename of the day for the USS *Ronald Reagan*.

"Okay, but, it looks like it's out of our range. Can you send us a tanker?"

"Sure. I have an Extender up here. I'll tell them to turn around and meet you at feet wet."

"Thanks. And you'd better watch out for those Flankers, Commander. They knew right where we were, and got a firing angle without using radar. They could be coming after you now."

"We'll keep our eyes out for them. Lead out." Palerider tapped his pilot, Darius "Crush" Crenshaw on the shoulder. "Do a slow three-sixty and put the radar in search mode. I'll do a full band check with the 99s. Let's make sure we're alone up here."

But White Division One was already attacking. The flight crew of the KC-10 saw them first, diving down from high altitude and closing in at high speed. They spread their formation, and White-1 and White-2 opened fire with their guns.

"Holy crap!" The tanker pilot hit the radio. "We're taking fire! Ferret Two, get the hell out of here!"

"Oh, boy." Chef couldn't see the Flankers because the KC-10's tail filled his field of vision. But he saw 30mm tracer shells zipping past the wide-body fuselage. Soon they would find their mark. Chef cut his throttle and pulled back on the stick, letting the big plane yank the hose away, and tried to climb out of the blast radius.

The Super Flankers bored in, and their fire became more accurate as they closed the range. Their shells ripped into the cockpit and forward fuselage of the Extender. One found the main tank, and the effect was immediate and spectacular. The entire fuselage disintegrated from nose to tail – the thin aluminum simply vaporized by a 4500-degree fireball. The fuel tanks in the wings followed, and the blaze filled the sky as fifty thousand gallons of jet fuel reacted with the thin oxygen of the stratosphere. A wall of flame slammed Ferret-2, still trying to pull away. The engines sucked in the hot combusted gasses and blew up, gutting the fighter and ending Chef's futile effort to save his life. He fell with his plane, burning alive, into the sea four miles below.

Unther swore. He had been following a thousand yards off the tanker's right rear quarter and still had to turn sharply to avoid the mile-wide fireball. He almost ran into two Super Flankers going the other way. "Get back here, you motherfuckers!" Deadeye ditched his heavy

449

HARMs and sped after the Flankers. They were ignoring him, looking for the Growler. Deadeye lit them up with his radar and locked his AMRAAMs on to the leader. Just as he fired, he picked up two more AMRAAMs coming the other way. White One tried to turn away from the Growler's missiles and found two more behind him. They converged together and vaporized the mercenary squadron leader. His wingman pulled out of the line of fire. "That's *my* kill!" Unther yelled.

"Fine, but I get an assist," Crush answered.

"Tally up the score later, you idiots," Palerider admonished. "There're three more Flankers out there, and you just threw all our AMRAAMs at one bad guy."

"Now what do we do?" Deadeye wondered.

"Stick close to me so my IDECM can protect you," the Commander said. "I'll call for help." Palerider switched frequencies. "This is Mongoose One calling all friendlies. I'm in grid R-4, engaging three Sukhoi Flankers. I need immediate repeat *immediate* backup. Any friendly fighters, please respond!"

## 60 MILES SOUTH, OVER THE PERSIAN GULF

Hardcase had seen the northern horizon light up with a massive explosion. Rightly fearing it was the demise of an Air Force tanker, he was leading his patrol flight to investigate. He had just picked up five contacts on his radar when he heard Palerider's distress call. "Mongoose, Sea Lion Flight has you. We'll be in missile range in fifty seconds." He switched to his team channel. "Let's burn rubber." The four *Stingrays* went to afterburner, accelerating into the dogfight.

The other two Flankers had come up behind Deadeye. White-3 fired a pair of AA-11 heat-seekers at his tail. "Oh, fuck." Deadeye rolled and dove away, shooting off a series of flares in an attempt to evade. He fooled the Russian missiles, but not the Russian pilots. They lined up for a second shot. "Mongoose, give me a hand here!"

"We're still too far away to cover you," Palerider said.

"And I'm not about to take those guys head-on," Crush added.

"Dammit sir, I need some *help*!" Deadeye called desperately.

Palerider watched his radar screen. "Here it comes."

Two AMRAAMs went active only a hundred yards from their targets. The Flankers were shot out of the sky, taken completely unawares by Hitman's trick shooting. "You're in the clear, baby," Hardcase called on open channel.

"Oh thank God."

450

"You can call me Hitman," Lt. Armani said.

"That last one is bugging out," Palerider reported.

"I guess we know what's been causing all the commotion around here then," Unther declared. "I don't think we need HARMs anymore."

"There's got to be more of those Super Flankers lurking out there," Commander Tachini figured. "I think we'll need Sharkey to flush 'em out."

## THE *REAGAN* – 20 MINUTES LATER, 1010 LOCAL

Captain Joshua "Deuce" Thompson sprinted down the corridor and skidded to a halt in front of Karl Roche's stateroom door. He heard screams and gunfire coming from the other side. "What the hell is going on in there?" he asked the Marine Corporal standing guard.

"I believe, sir, that Commander Roche is playing a video game, sir."

"I need to see him."

"The commander is not to be disturbed, sir."

"Dammit, I'm the Commander of the Air Group. I'm his boss."

"Yes sir, but he is under medical convalescence and I am under orders from-"

"From me." LCdr. Dr. Tobias had finally caught up with the CAG, breathing hard. "Let us in his room, please," he ordered. "*I* need to see Commander Roche, and I authorize Captain Thompson to be present."

"Yessir." The Corporal tapped the security override code into the electronic keypad lock and held a card against a sensor. The lock beeped and clicked, and Deuce opened the door.

Roche was leaning well back in his desk chair and seemed quite relaxed as alien bodies exploded all over his laptop screen. He turned quickly to greet the visitors. "Hi. Just a second." His on-screen character ran down a hall firing a shotgun at everything that moved, clearing a path through the alien bodies. He opened a door, and found the next room occupied by a towering boss alien. He could only squeeze off a couple of shots before being gruesomely killed by what looked like tentacles covered in teeth. "Yeesh. I shoulda switched to my rocket launcher before going in there." He saved his last checkpoint and exited the game. "What's up doc?"

"Like I haven't heard that one before," the air wing medical officer groaned.

"Sharkey, do you think you can convince the doc here you're ready for flight ops?" Thompson asked the aviator / alien-hunter.

"I'd certainly like to try. What do I have to do?"

"First I need to inspect your wounds," the doctor said. "Have a seat on your bed and let me have that chair." Roche complied, and removed his t-shirt. The doctor turned on the lights before sitting down and peeling the bandages off Roche's chest.

"So how did you talk him into this, Captain?" Karl asked. "What do you need me out of bed for?"

"I really need you and your squadron on an intercept and escort sortie," Deuce told him. "A few Super Flankers just ambushed a wild weasel team I sent out looking for camouflaged defenses. We lost three Bugs and an Air Force tanker. Now I've got a bomber group going through that same airspace."

"Was Santos in that wild weasel group?" Roche was concerned for his friend.

"No. And we didn't lose a Grizzly anyway. But we're almost certain that they have more of those Super Flankers are out there. Our guys say they approach without radar and hit in groups of four. You're the best when it comes to ambush and evasion, so I need you to pick off those bandits and escort our bomber group to feet wet."

"Can't you just circle the bombers back through Iraqi airspace?"

"Well, that's how they got in, but they won't have enough fuel to get out that way. And the Air Force just lost a tanker to these guys so they're not putting another one in hostile airspace until we're sure it's clear."

"So without me…"

"Without you and your freaky super skills, I think a lot of our guys are about to be killed," Deuce concluded. "We need you fighting your way across southwestern Iran as soon as possible."

"Okay, I get it," Dr. Tobias said. "Roche, this guy is going to hold me personally responsible if I don't put you in a plane in the next fifteen minutes. But I can't let you out of here if you will cause severe injury to yourself. Does your left arm hurt at all?"

"It never does." Roche poked the bullet wound in his shoulder. "No feeling, remember? You can shoot me again if you want."

"Right, maybe later. How's your range of motion?"

"Same as ever." Roche twisted his arm around. He couldn't reach over his head, but everything else worked. "It didn't make my old injury any worse."

"Okay, that's nothing to worry about then. And the two wounds in your chest are healing much faster than I expected. You'll be okay as long as you still avoid demanding exercise for a couple days. But I don't suppose flying will put too much strain on it."

Roche and Thompson looked at each other. It occurred to both of them that the doctor must not have ever experienced a sustained nine-G turn. But neither of them wanted to point that out. "So I can go?"

"Yeah, you can go. I'll leave a bed open for you in sick bay though. I sense you may be about to hurt yourself again."

## 12 MINUTES LATER

The cat shot hurt; a little. Just enough to remind him that he had twenty-six fresh stitches in his left side and two cracked ribs.

"There wasn't time to brief you on the ship, so I'll show you what's going on," Hunter told him. "Watch your MFD."

"Okay." Sharkey looked down at his TacOps screen, which Hunter was now manipulating from the back seat.

"Palerider was leading the original Wild Weasel group. He's up here working with Sea Lion Flight. That's Hardcase and his division. They're doing a preliminary search at low level, looking for hidden airbases or another group of Flankers."

"Airbases? There aren't any Iranian airbases left in that area. We bombed them all last weekend."

"That's why I said 'hidden' airbases. It's either that or the bandits are coming in from about five hundred miles away. Anyway, Blackjack has his division about a hundred and fifty miles north of us. They answer to Whale Flight. They just finished refueling Fozzy Bear, who apparently had a pretty close call. They're going to catch up with Sea Lion and top those guys off, then ditch their external tanks. Right about then, we should catch up with them and we'll all have roughly the same fuel load."

"Do we have any more Grizzly support?"

"Yeah, Toymaker has three more Lightning Bugs to link up with Palerider. That's Bottlenose Flight."

"I see. And what predatory marine mammal are we?"

"Orca. The rest of our division is twenty miles ahead."

"So we have twelve Rhinos and four Grizzlies to take on an unknown number of Super Flankers with a penchant for ambush," Roche summed up.

"Plus the bombers once they finish their job."

"Deuce said that's three squadrons, right?"

"Yeah, it's two squads from the *Lincoln* – Mole and Groundhog flights – and then Worm's squadron answers to Badger."

"Well that ought to be enough to even the fight."

## SOMEWHERE OVER THE IRANIAN DESERT – 0950 LOCAL

Lenonov was furious when what was left of the lead divisions from Red and White Squadrons reported in. He had not anticipated losses – certainly not the loss of two of his squadron leaders. He directed the survivors to deploy the rest of their squadrons and catch up with him. There was still much work to do. General Mikhail had just informed him that the first bomber squadron had already reached the pipelines. As soon as they finished dropping their bombs, the Super Hornets would be transformed from vulnerable heavy bombers to sleek and deadly fighters. Lenonov was glad he'd brought so many of his own planes.

## AT THE PIPELINES

Worm's first target was an easy one. It was right in plain sight, and there was a column of tanks marking a trail right to the open doors of the tunnel. Worm ignored his computer's attack profile suggestion and flew low over the road. He released his Paveway fifty yards short of the opening and pulled away. The bomb sailed a hundred yards deeper into the tunnel before landing on the front of a tank. The experimental thermobaric warhead worked just fine, sending a powerful shockwave up and down the tunnel, frying the armor column in its tracks. Tons of flaming wreckage blasted out the front door, and an equal force of devastation was unleashed in the opposite direction.

"That would be a hit," reported Worm's wingman, Lt. "Money" Emmanuel.

"Good. On to the next one." Worm's second one wasn't easy to spot. It had only been identified by a high-flying Global Hawk with a thermal camera, and the ventilation shaft was only visible to Worm as a GPS tag on his TacOps map. Worm let the computer tell him where and how to drop this one; he pulled up sharply and released the weapon at a sixty-degree angle from horizontal, and rolled away. The bomb followed a parabolic arc before dropping right into the six-foot wide hole. The small puff of smoke and dust that emerged from the vent belied the untold carnage wrought in the depths of the earth.

Meanwhile "Bonzer" McGee was locked on to his first target – another tunnel entrance, this one sealed up. He flew right toward it at low altitude, and released the weapon only eighty feet short. The bomb sliced right through the heavy steel doors and exploded somewhere on the other side. The doors bulged out but held, directing the full force of the blast down the pipeline.

"On to my second target," McGee reported. He pulled through an immelmann turn to get a good drop angle and hit the pickle at the correct release point, but nothing happened. "What the bloody hell?" Bonzer asked his control panel. The WepCon screen dutifully informed him that some mechanical fault had prevented the bomb from releasing. "I got no drop," he told the commander.

"What's the matter?" Worm asked.

"I think those Air Force buggers busted up my hardpoint clamps."

"It did seem they were having some trouble under your left wing," Worm acknowledged.

"Now's a bloody swell time to find that out."

"No worries, mate," Cmdr. Bellbrook said cheerfully. "Mole flight is carrying spares. I'll call them and let them know we missed a target." Worm switched to the team frequency. "Mole Lead, this is Badger Lead, do you-"

"Where the hell have you been?" demanded the *Lincoln*'s squadron leader. "We've got a couple squads of Russians chewing up our asses back here! I can't-" Mole Lead was lost in a burst of static.

"Lead is down!" another aviator called. "Mole Five assuming command. We're completely surrounded! These Flankers are killing everyone! God help us!"

"Jesus! Okay guys," Worm switched back to the squadron channel. "The other bombers are getting torn apart. Drop everything you don't need and get ready to fight." Worm led the way, ditching two of his three external tanks. He soon had what was left of the other two squadrons on his radar screen, but he couldn't see the attackers. "Groundhog lead, are you there?" he called the other surviving squadron leader.

"Yeah, I'm here."

"Where did those Russians go?"

"I don't know! As soon as you turned around they stopped shooting and disappeared. It's the damnedest thing I've ever seen."

"We should have Echo-threes up here," Money remarked.

"The Sentries keep getting shot down," Worm reminded his wingman. "Those Air Force pussies won't even leave one up across the border for us. But these Flankers can't hide from us for long."

"Somehow I don't think they plan to hide for long."

No sooner had Money said those words than the two Warhawks trailing the formation found they had missiles locked on to them. A moment later, one of the six sections of Worm's squadron was blown out of the sky. He swore at no one in particular. "Bandits on our six! They got around behind us!" Two more missiles came from nowhere and took out Bonzer's wingman. Worm was on the verge of hysteria. "Somebody please just shoot something!"

### REAGAN AIR OPS

"How in the hell did they get behind them?" Admiral Krause wondered. "There was nobody there a minute ago."

"It's the same bunch that hit Groundhog and Mole," Deuce figured. "They just cut their radar, dropped to the deck, and let Worm fly right over them."

"That's impossible."

"Not if you're really good." Deuce Thompson was speaking slowly, amazed by his own thoughts. "Whoever's in charge of those Flankers isn't just good, he's phenomenal. He's an ambush fighter, an airborne guerilla, like he's using The Art of War as a flight manual."

"I've never heard of anyone operating like that."

"Yes you have," Deuce said. "This guy fights like Sharkey."

### ORCA FLIGHT

Roche could see the four survivors from Mole Flight heading toward him. The other bombers were still out of radar range, but the TacOps gave him an idea of what was happening to Worm's Badger Flight.

"Sharkey, you'd better hurry," Deuce said on the command channel. "We're losing rodents fast."

"Roger that."

"And be careful, buddy. Their leader is painted up like a black cobra, and this guy is extremely good."

"How good?" Roche wondered.

"I just told Krause he reminds me of you."

Roche didn't know how to respond to that, so he just said "Okay" and switched to the squadron frequency. "Sea Lion and Whale flights, you get to save our friends. I need you to split up into sections and engage from opposing vectors. Hunter will upload waypoints in a second."

"Okay sir." Blackjack and Harcase split their divisions and flew on ahead.

Roche turned his seat and looked back at Hunter. "Give them approach to Worm's current position with thirty degrees of separation, but centered around our track."

"I got it." Hunter tapped the waypoints into his computer. Hawk and Mystique – from the back seats of the two division leaders – confirmed the commands. Hunter stopped for a second to examine the tracks he had laid out. "Why?"

"If the enemy commander is as good as Deuce thinks he is, he's going to push back against the inbound vector and-"

"And come right toward us and the Grizzlies."

"That's what I'm hoping."

The American Super Hornets were disorganized, and weren't putting up much of a fight. Colonel Lenonov was disappointed. He let his wingmates pick away at the bomber group and waited for an American pilot to emerge who was worthy to challenge the Black Cobra.

"Bloody 'ell!" Bonzer had just watched his wingman's plane disintegrate and knew he was going to be next. His radar warning told him he had a missile on his tail. Bonzer banked hard and manually fired a flare shell in the path of the AA-12 missile. He held the sharp left turn until he was facing the Flankers. He counted over twenty of them. "Blow me over, that's a lot of targets." He picked out two and fired his AMRAAMs at fairly close range. He hit one Flanker, and the other dropped out of formation to shake the American missile. Bonzer rolled into an intercept vector. "C'mon ya rat bugger." He launched a Sidewinder into the Flanker's engine for another kill.

A shadow crossed his canopy, and Bonzer looked up and saw an all-black Flanker swooping toward him. "Oh, crikey!" He pulled up hard on the stick and cut his throttles, and the Black Cobra flew by beneath him. Bonzer cranked into a hard left turn, releasing his right drop tank to lighten that wing so he could tighten his curve. But when he brought the plane around he saw the Black Cobra was already facing him, flying *backwards*. "What the-?" McGee didn't have time to figure that one out. The Black Cobra had just fired two missiles at him.

"Bollocks." Bonzer pushed his turn into a dive and fired two more flare shells to deal with the missiles. But the shells were a fraction of a second late. They exploded just as the first missile passed them, destroying its control surfaces but leaving the engine, warhead and infrared seeker intact. It could sense the Hornet ahead and pulling away, and when the tiny computer realized that the missile wasn't getting closer, it triggered the warhead forty feet short. Still close enough to do some damage. Nelson McGee felt the jolt of the near-hit and frowned at his display as the EWOC screen went dark.

"Electronic warfare system failure," Bitchin' Betty told him. "ECM offline."

"Thanks, Sheila," Bonzer groaned. "That's just what I need." He looked back and saw another missile closing in; a bigger, radar-guided AA-12. Bonzer made a hard left and cut the throttles back, then pushed his stick hard to the right, snapping the plane into a zero-airspeed roll. As the left wing snapped up past horizontal, Bonzer released his other drop tank, tossing it in the path of the missile. It was a clever move, but he cut it too close. He was only a hundred feet away when the missile punched through the half-empty fuel tank and detonated. Bonzer's Hornet was rocked by the fireball but it was still flying for the moment. He pushed the throttles to the stops and leveled out, hoping to get some more distance between him and the Black Cobra.

Lenonov glared at his elusive target. He was being led far away from the fight and had already wasted three missiles, and this was a Hornet that still had a heavy bomb clipped to his wing. This aviator was too worthy, he decided. He hit the afterburners and held down his trigger as he closed in.

Bonzer felt the cannon shells hitting his tail and instinctively made a snap roll. As he turned he looked and saw the Black Cobra on his left, coming straight toward him with guns blazing. The 30mm cannons stitched a line across the Hornet's wings. Bonzer swore at his displays. He was losing fuel and airspeed and altitude in a hurry. He held the throttles at the stops and punched the afterburners, and his damaged engines screamed in protest. Despite the noise he was gaining precious velocity, but his perforated wings weren't gaining any lift. He was getting engine fire warnings and now the fuel streaming from his ruptured wing tanks had ignited, blazing a trail across the air. The plane was in a supersonic stall and the rear end was fully engulfed in flame.

Bonzer wrestled with the controls but at this point he was trying to control a meteor screaming toward an inevitable earthly impact.

Bonzer tore his eyes from the alarms on his panel and looked up to see a rocky outcropping looming ahead. "Well fuck a duck-billed platypus." He fumbled for the ejection straps and blasted clear of the cockpit the instant before the flaming wreck of his plane slammed into the rocks at a thousand miles an hour. He might have made it if not for the live thermobaric bomb still attached to his left wing. The massive blast overtook the rocket-propelled ejection seat, and Bonzer McGee died with another colorful curse on his lips.

# CHAPTER 22: SUPERFIGHTER SHOWDOWN

## USS *RONALD REAGAN* AIR OPS – 1122 LOCAL TIME

Deuce glared at the huge map board that showed every air contact and surface-to-air threat that the *Reagan*'s computers presently knew about. It was currently zoomed in on the activity in the small corner of western Iran, where his Super Hornets and those belonging to his counterpart on the *Lincoln* were fighting for their lives. They appeared to be dying much more quickly than the red triangles representing the Super Flankers. Deuce followed with his eyes as one of the blue triangles separated from its squadron, took out two red triangles, then went one-on-one with a third Flanker and lost. Deuce checked the readout to see who that was. Badger-9, Lt. Nelson "Bonzer" McGee, VFA-97 Warhawks. *That's a damn shame,* Deuce thought. *I like Bonzer.*

## 30 MILES EAST OF THE IRAN-IRAQ BORDER, 13,000 FEET

"I think we just lost Bonzer," Money reported.

Commander Bellbrook risked a glance at his TacOps screen. Badger-9's IFF tag was indeed missing. Worm had seen the Australian break formation and charge the Russians. He thought at the time it was a stupidly brave move. He hoped the Aussie at least had the sense to eject. "That's four we've lost now."

"Yeah, it's like we-" Money's transmission was lost in a fireball. A pair of AA-11 Archer missiles suddenly materialized and blew the rear of his Super Hornet apart.

Worm swore and wheeled away from whoever had fired the missiles. He looked back over his shoulder and sighed with relief when he saw a parachute unfurling above the falling wreck of his wingman's aircraft. Then he saw a line of tracers cut through the white canopy, and the life-saving envelope of air collapsed, dropping Lt. jg. Emmanuel screaming to the desert floor two miles below. Worm swore at the blue-striped Flanker he saw following the arc of 30mm shells.

Worm pulled up into a half-corkscrew and dropped in behind Blue-1. The Russian mercenary squadron leader noticed, and tried to roll away. "Nuh-uh," Worm muttered. "You're not getting away with that one, you asshole." The Top Gunner kept accelerating through the curve, matching the Flanker's tight turn and closing the range. He was pushing nine Gs, as much as anyone could sustain for any measurable length of time. "C'mon, you gotta break soon," Worm said, as he clenched his legs to slow the blood rushing to his feet. The Flanker abruptly rolled the other way, both to relieve the brutal G-load and try to shake the Super Hornet on his tail. Worm anticipated the move and snapped a hard negative-G turn, pushing the stick forward and rocking the throttle back and forth to push the Hornet against its own inertia into a horizontal somersault. His timing was impeccable – his crosshairs were immediately centered on the target. He squeezed his trigger and unleashed a stream of 20mm rounds into the enemy fighter's cockpit. "See how *you* like it, Ivan."

After Lenonov watched Bonzer's plane crash he turned back to the fight. On his radar he could see his Flankers spread out widely, chasing down the scattered Super Hornet squadrons. The bombers were fighting back now but so far they had only shot down three of his fighters and winged another. His well-trained mercenary pilots were pressing the advantage. Then as he watched his screen he saw eight more targets emerge at the extreme range of his radar coverage. They were moving at supersonic speed on a converging attack approach. "Enemy reinforcements inbound!" he warned his men.
"Where?" one of the pilots asked.
"All around you!"

Worm rolled level and took another glance at his screen. While he'd been engaged with Money's killer, three of the Groundhogs had been taken out, including the squadron leader. Now the Flankers were pairing up on targets of opportunity, including him. Worm spotted the two Flankers closing in on him. He took a snapshot with an AMRAAM, turned and ran. The Flankers dodged the missile easily and chased the Warhawks' CO.
"Fly nice and steady, Worm," someone said on the command frequency. "Me'n Gator are comin' up on yer four o'clock; you set 'em up, I'll knock 'em down."
Worm recognized the southern Appalachian drawl. He felt much better with the knowledge that Rooster had his back.
One of the Flankers was slammed from the side with a pair of well-placed Sidewinders. The other one broke off to lose a pair of AMRAAMs.
"Hot dog! He blew up good!"

461

"Thanks, man. How many of your friends do you have, Rooster?" Worm asked.

"There's eight of us right here, and there's a Shark lurking out there somewhere to the southeast."

"There's too many now! Break off and regroup," Lenonov ordered. The tables had been turned quickly. The new Hornets were loaded for bear and weren't looking to make friends. Lenonov lost half a squadron in a matter of seconds. He knew when to pull back. He had to separate his remaining Flankers from the now numerically superior American fighters. They were fighters now, he had to remind himself. The surviving bombers were switching to offense and were now just as lethal as the fresh fighters that had joined the fight.

"Head up against their line of retreat. I'll rejoin and we'll rendezvous with Red and White Squadrons before we reengage." If he could position all his forces between the American aircraft squadrons and their carriers, he could draw them in to fight again on his terms. Once his other two squadrons found him he would again have all the advantage.

"This is Sea Lion One. Let them go," Hardcase ordered. The Flankers were getting out of the airspace in a hurry. "Sharkey's waiting for this. We are to regroup and pursue but don't use afterburners. Wait for Sharkey to engage."

"You heard the man, Badgers." Worm didn't know what the plan was but if Sharkey was behind it he knew it must be a good one. "Mole and Groundhog, you're joining us."

"Roger that," Groundhog-5 answered. Lt. Cmdr. Mike "Steel" Pondsmith had assumed command of the remains of the two squads from the *Lincoln* after both squad COs had been shot down. He had made a kill himself, but he was very disappointed that he had been forced to abandon his bombing target. His older brother had nearly been killed that morning by enemy armor using those tunnels. That measure of payback had to be served later. Now he had to deal with the scumbags who'd slaughtered half his squadron. "Don't they know we're gonna be going home this way?"

"That's what Sharkey's counting on." Hawk explained.

"I don't understand."

"That's why it's going to work."

*     *     *

"They're coming your way now," Hawk reported to Sharkey on a secure channel a moment later. "You were right."

"He's good, no doubt about it," Roche answered. "Just as good as Deuce thinks."

"Here's hoping you're better."

"Wouldn't be the first time he's underestimated me."

Orca Flight was flying low and hugging the hills, waiting out of sight along the track between the pipelines and the Gulf coast. According to the information on Hawk's radar, the mercenaries were going straight along that track.

"Where are they?" Hunter wondered.

Roche pointed up into the sky at a single white contrail coming in from the north. "There's the Black Cobra, the one that ran down Bonzer." He then pointed to the northwest horizon, where over a dozen more trails were coming into view. "There's the rest of them. They'll be in position in just a couple of minutes. We'll need to shift our track a little, but I'll wait until they meet up with each other."

"Okay." Hunter was still not clear on how exactly they would be able to take on a squadron and change with only his one division, but the new CO seemed confident enough in his plan.

"Bottlenose Lead, this Orca Lead. Are you guys ready to play?" Sharkey called to Palerider, leading the Growler division in the clouds.

"Aff."

Roche watched the Russians carefully. "Orcas, turn to track prime now. Bottlenose, showtime on my mark."

As the Black Cobra joined the head of the Flankers' formation they slowed to subsonic speed. Lenonov was calling to his other squadrons to try to figure out where they would all meet up. He did a quick count. Including him there were fourteen survivors from Black and Blue Squadrons. Adding nine from White and ten from Red gave him thirty-three Super Flankers. Enough to take out the twenty-four Super Hornets he had counted, but it would be quite a fight. His only disadvantage that he could see was that all three of his other squadron leaders had gotten themselves shot down. It would be imperative that he maintain close control over his pilots and their tactics. But between his superior numbers and equipment and stronger position and his own skills as a leader and a pilot, how could he lose? And just as he had this thought his radar scope was filled with static. And his next thought was *uh-oh*.

*     *     *

"Alright, Bottlenose," Roche called. "Showtime."

"Copy that, jamming all Scarab bands," Commander Tachini confirmed in response to the younger officer's order.

Sharkey kept watching the sky, tracking his targets visually to time his attack just right. "Orcas, initiate missile attack Sierra-Two-Alpha on my mark; three, two, one, mark!" Like Roche, the other three aviators already had the attack sequence called up on their computers. The SHOC-WepCon interface programmed and launched four AMRAAMs from each aircraft, sending them to climb to the target's altitude in a wide half-loop before going active and engaging the Russians head-on.

Roche waited another eight seconds after the sixteen missiles had been launched. "Our turn. Let's go ballistic!" The four aviators acted again in unison. They pulled back their sticks until they reached a sixty-degree angle of attack, then pushed the throttles to the stops and held their thumbs down on the afterburner switches. The Hornets were now no longer airplanes in the aerodynamic sense – that is to say they did not require the lift of their wings to climb into the air. For the moment, Bernoulli and his theorems could take a hike. This was all about Newton's Second Law of Motion. The Super Hornets rocketed up behind and above the Flankers and dropped in to a perfectly-orchestrated scene of airborne carnage.

"Where the hell did these things come from?" Lenonov asked when his threat receiver alerted him that an AMRAAM was trying to lock on to him. He could see the missiles ahead of his formation, but he couldn't see where they came from. Before he lost the use of his radar a few seconds ago there was nothing in range in front of him. These missiles had come from nowhere. They weren't a serious threat – he and his men were very good at dodging American radar-guided weapons. He had trained his mercenary pilots with the less sophisticated but more maneuverable AA-12 Adder, sometimes using live warheads. But despite the low threat the weapons posed, their sudden appearance was disconcerting. "Take evasive action," he instructed unnecessarily. His men were already zig-zagging this way and that to avoid or break radar locks from the incoming American missiles.

Lenonov climbed and turned to shake his own assailant and then saw where the missiles had originated. Four bright blue Super Hornets were diving toward him and his disjointed formation. In the brief instant of rational thought before fear kicked in, he noted that each of these planes had four empty spots on their missile racks but still carried enough weapons to destroy a whole squadron apiece. "WHAT THE FUCK!?" was suddenly all he could think to say. "Where did *they* come from!?" No time to look for an answer. The Hornets were launching Sidewinders at very close range, and those weren't so easy to dodge.

He knew he was spiked. He rolled hard and showed his cold side to the incoming weapons and dove toward the ground. He deliberately put one of his other men between him and the missiles that were locked on to him, and succeeded in getting himself clear. Three more members of Black Squadron had the good sense to follow him toward the deck. The others were very efficiently butchered by the blue *Stingrays*.

"And that, comrade, is what we Americans call an ambush," a voice said in Russian on the open channel.

"Who the hell are you?" Lenonov yelled at the radio in English.

The American answered in the same language. "My name is Sharkey and I'll be serving you today. Our specialty is speared Black Cobra, flame-broiled to order."

The Black Cobra hit his afterburners and put some distance between him and Sharkey, and dropped down to the deck, hoping to lose the Hornets in the ground clutter. "Well done, Sharkey," Lenonov answered, unaware of the double meaning his words took in English. "That was very good, but this isn't over."

"Yes, I gather you have some more friends out there. I'd be happy to serve them all a round of Sidewinders on the house."

"You seem pretty cocky for someone who just showed up," the Russian mercenary sneered. "You think you can take me man-to-man, ship-to-ship? Bring it on."

## CIA HEADQUARTERS, LANGLEY – SAME TIME

Evan Decker hesitated outside the Deputy Director's office. He could hear the operations chief arguing loudly with Agent Caspian. But the Russian bureau needed their input on a developing situation, and it couldn't wait until the boss was in a better mood. Evan pushed the door open.

Both men inside had dark circles under their eyes. Evan knew neither of them had probably slept for longer than a couple of hours at a time in the last five days. Casey hadn't left his office since Friday when the fighting started, and Caspian had suffered through God-knows-what in Tehran and had just spent the last half-day jetting back home.

Cannon ignored his former partner and stared at the DDO's desk, wondering in which drawer the boss might have hid a bottle of whiskey. Decker wasn't aware of it, but Robert Cannon hadn't actually been inside CIA headquarters since 1991. He had clearance of course – one of the beyond-top-secret level badges with no name that gave him access to any part of the massive building. But the field agent hadn't ever used it until today. He hated Langley. It wasn't that he hated the Company; just that he hated the faceless bureaucrats that populated the headquarters of any government agency. Being here reminded Cannon of the Agency's gross inefficiency and the political quagmire it had been trapped in. That's why he never came here to debrief. He had always met the DDO at his home in Chesterbrook when he needed a face-to-face with the man who had been his case officer since early nineties. Unfortunately, the DDO wasn't leaving his office, so Cannon had to come to him here to be mercilessly debriefed.

"What is it, Ivan?" Casey asked.

Evan had been born Ivan Dyakir in a suburb of Moscow before his parents had defected to the United States in the sixties. The CIA had recruited him as a teenager slightly disillusioned with his new country and sent him to operate in his homeland. Primarily he acted as a contact for Casey, who was deep undercover in the highest levels of the GRU. Later he had been Cannon's protector within the FSB, when the young agent went in deep with the Russian Mafia. Both had been suspicious of the other; Cannon was sure that Dyakir and long since severed his loyalties to America, and Dyakir was convinced that Cannon had gone crooked. They had compromised each other's covers and almost got each other killed. It had taken an extraordinary act of resourcefulness on Cannon's part to get them both out of the country alive, and quite a bit of string-pulling from Casey to keep Dyakir in the CIA's employ after the resulting fiasco. Cannon and Dyakir hadn't spoken since, though Ivan knew he owed the younger agent his life. Cannon never forgave Dyakir for imploding his cover with the *Mafya*.

Evan Decker had more than redeemed himself in his new life, at least as far as Casey was concerned. And since Decker only answered to Casey and Casey only answered to the Director of Central Intelligence, that was all that mattered. He put up with Jarrod Casey calling him "Ivan" sometimes. It was good to remember the past, to remember his mistakes and to remember what he had learned. Especially since his past life had become relevant again.

466

"I just got a priority flash from Admiral Krause on the USS *Ronald Reagan*," he announced. "He bypassed the channeling protocols and routed it directly to my desk."

"How did he-" Casey started to ask, but stopped as the name clicked. Admiral Krause – Wally Krause – had been in his counterpart at the NSA for many years. The former Deputy Director of National Security would certainly know his way around the spaghetti logic of the intelligence community's communication system. "What does Wally need?"

"It looks like his pilots encountered an old friend of ours. He wants to know if we know anything about a Russian pilot known as the Black Cobra."

Casey and Cannon looked at each other. "Lenonov," they both said.

"Exactly."

Casey went to his filing cabinet to look for Lenonov's dossier. But he couldn't find it under "L" for some reason. He tried to remember if he filed it under "B" for "Black Cobra," but he was sure he had just recently seen it in this drawer. Than he remembered he'd removed it three days ago to add to the file. He found it on his desk, half-buried in a stack that contained processed and analyzed reports on all the information Kujetski had sent him recently.

"Colonel Victor Visilyich 'Black Cobra' Lenonov," Casey read the summary page. "First entry, April 1987, demonstration of Sukhoi-27 Flanker fighter at the Paris Air Show. Last entry, just last Saturday, mercenary air units key element of Rannovich's air force." The DDO thumbed through the documents for a minute, then buzzed in his secretary. "Carol, I need you to make a complete copy of this dossier on the classified-only Xerox."

"Give me three minutes." Carol took the folder and disappeared.

"So the Black Cobra and his boys are bothering our guys in Iran," Decker said. "Kind of weird, after all these years, he's back to working for Rannovich."

Cannon nodded. He remembered Victor well. They had been both been working for the *Mafya* back in the early nineties. The out-of-work ex-Soviet fighter pilot had found a job analyzing and reverse-engineering western defense systems that the Russian Mafia managed to steal. It was an old game in Russia, one the engineers at the old Soviet military design bureaus had come to rely on. Without the KGB to supply them with stolen hardware, they had turned to the mob. But after Cannon shut down that racket, Lenonov had found better money doing what he did best, flying Flankers for anyone who could afford him and his mercenaries.

Carol came back after three minutes with two identical folders. "This one's the original," she said, holding out the dossier in her right hand.

Casey replaced that one back in the filing cabinet, and opened the other dossier on his desk. He took a broad-tip felt pen and blacked out lines of text, removed entire pages and fed them into his crosscutting shredder, and highlighted other lines and pages for the Admiral's attention. Then he quickly filled out a form authorizing the release of materials and added it to the folder and handed the folder back to Carol. "Stamp all those pages as classified – eyes only and fax them to... did Wally leave you a number?" Casey turned to Decker. The Russian bureau chief handed Carol a page torn from his *Dilbert* desk calendar with a number scrawled on the back. "Fax them to that number. Then destroy those copies once Krause confirms the receipt."

"Got it."

Casey sighed wearily. "That dossier's been on my desk since Saturday and it didn't even occur to me that the Navy and Air Force ought to know about him. God knows how many of our pilots he's killed already."

"Does it make a difference?" Decker asked. "None of our pilots are any match for Lenonov."

"I think one of them is," Cannon said.

## IRANIAN AIRSPACE

Roche reorganized his air assets as the other Super Hornets caught up to his position. His twelve *Stingrays* were all now included in Orca flight. The survivors from the bomber team – seven from Badger, six from Groundhog, and three from Mole – were all grouped together as Otter flight. Roche kept them separate because they were low on fuel and ammo. None of them had more than four missiles to start with, and they had been forced to lose their drop tanks when they turned to fight off the Flankers. They would be useless in an extended dogfight. Roche planned to let them fire one salvo of missiles and then send them running home while the *Stingrays* finished off the Black Cobra's mercenaries. He kept the Hornets flying along the track back to the Gulf while waiting for the Cobra to strike back.

**90 MILES EAST**

After he caught up with Red Squadron Lenonov reassessed his options. The other three survivors from Black Squadron were practically useless. They had expended most of their weapons when they engaged the bombers and now had burned up most of their fuel running from Sharkey. When he reengaged the Americans, Black Squadron – now just Black Division – would only be able to fire their remaining AA-12 missiles and then try to make it to the nearest camouflaged airfield. Lenonov's own aircraft had been modified with a huge extra fuel tank between his engine intakes, and he'd only used three of his missiles so far. He could still fly and fight for hours. He would still be able to command from the front lines. That left the matter of joining White Squadron, which was on the other side of Sharkey's airspace.

*Sharkey's airspace,* he thought in disgust. The arrogant American had beaten him soundly at his own game. Even if his radar hadn't been jammed, he never would have seen the attack coming. Sharkey had appeared out of thin air and fired from two directions at once. He realized that Sharkey had used basically the same tactics he himself employed, hugging the terrain and letting the unsuspecting prey fly overhead into the trap. But Sharkey was better at it than at least Lenonov's squadron leaders had been. Red One and White One had failed miserably, ambushing an inferior force and allowing themselves to be killed by the obsolete Hornet-Cs or the heavy, lightly-armed Growlers. Sharkey on the other hand had routed an entire squadron and he and his three wingmen weren't even touched. There may have been some luck to that, but the talent of the American Navy squadron leader was undeniable.

So Sharkey controlled the airspace between him and White Squadron. Sharkey had superior numbers of Super Hornets, plus an unknown number of Growlers which gave him a clear advantage with radar. But Lenonov wasn't completely blind. He still had Ivan. The technician and his array of passive radar sensors could track the Americans across the desert. Lenonov could see them now on his computer, twelve of them anyway, spread out across the same track and blasting the airspace in front of them with their APG-79 AESA radars. *They must be leading the others*, Lenonov thought. *All I have to do is get in behind them.* He could do it, he decided. He picked a rendezvous point that should put all twenty-three of his fighters behind the Americans in easy AA-12 range in just a few minutes. He turned toward the intercept, and relayed the coordinates to White-5, now in command of that squadron.  Soon it would Sharkey's turn to feel the Black Cobra's bite.

## *REAGAN* COMMS CENTER

"This guy's had quite a run," Admiral Krause said to Deuce, reading the pages of Lenonov's CIA dossier as they were printed out of the fax machine. "Here's his Russian military career.  He flew Su-24 Fencer attack planes in Afghanistan in the early eighties, worked as a Sukhoi test pilot in the mid and late eighties, then trained the Republican Guard Air Force in Iraq from '88 to '90. He flew three combat sorties against us in the Gulf War despite orders that he was only to participate as an observer.  He's credited with four kills – two of ours, one Brit and one Saudi.  When he came back to Russia they canned him for that.  Then he worked for the Russian Mafia doing some sort of industrial espionage... Casey didn't let us have any more details on that.  We're missing a few pages, and half of this page is redacted.  I guess there's a lot of background material that we're not supposed to see.

"Mercenary career: uh, in 1993 he started recruiting out-of-work fighter pilots from all over the old Soviet Bloc.  He used a Ukrainian scrap company as a front and bought three dozen Su-27 Flanker-As.  In 1994 he was hired by the Chinese to participate in an extended aggressor-training exercise program – kinda like the red flag exercises we run with the Air Force – released in '96 when two Chinese pilots were killed.  1997, the Malaysian government hires him to hunt pirates around Borneo and Singapore.  Singapore and Indonesia protest loudly.  Oh, wow, in 1998 he accepted a contract from the Luzon Liberation Army to attack Philippine and US Navy ships near Morro Bay.  He attacked and sank one Philippine Navy Frigate but cancelled the contract when the terrorists were unable to pay the full bounty. Holy crap – 1999, discusses terms with Iranian government to provide air cover for their planned Naval offensive in the Gulf of Oman, but no agreement was reached.  'Operation Jonah' was cancelled soon after that, when the admiral in charge of their submarine program decided their ships weren't capable enough to perform the proposed mission without air support."

"What was the plan?" Deuce asked.

"Don't know.  The rest of that article and its reference links are redacted.  Next, 1999 to 2002, resumed training operations in China with the People's Liberation Army/Air Force and Navy.  2002, discussions with al-Qaeda leadership to conduct air strikes in the southwestern United States from bases in northern Mexico-"

"What the *hell!?*" Deuce had to look over the Admiral's shoulder and read that one for himself.

"Obviously nothing ever came of that," Krause commented.

"Obviously, but *Jesus Christ!* Air strikes against America? Did you know about that?"

"Of course." In 2002 Krause had been in charge of all signal intelligence that passed through Fort Meade. His people had intercepted some of the al-Qaeda communications that exposed the plot. The CIA had convinced the Mexican Army to conduct joint drug interdiction exercises with the DEA at the same time and place that al-Qaeda had planned the mercenary attack. They also arrested six known terrorists in Veracruz along with a shipping container full of air-to-ground missiles. Like most thwarted terrorist attacks in the last decade, none of it was ever made public. "I didn't know about Lenonov, or at least I didn't know his name, but I was aware of the plan and I played a small role in directing our response."

Thompson shook it off and Krause continued. "2002 and 2003, repeatedly approached by Saddam Hussein to help build and train a modern Iraqi Air Force to protect Iraq from imminent attack by US and Allies. Lenonov refused to be involved. 2004 to present, covertly trained Iranian Air Force pilots on modern Russian-built aircraft. 2005 to 2009, consulted with Dassault Aviation Industrie at their independent facility in Sidon, Lebanon. Believed to be involved with design and integration of avionics and control systems for the Defiant fighter. 2008, Sukhoi liquidates a build overrun of sixty brand-new Su-37 Super Flankers. Somebody – the names are redacted again here – somebody consulted with somebody else and brokered the purchase through metal recycling plant in Kazakhstan that doesn't really exist. Lenonov took delivery in May, 2008 and has been training newly recruited pilots on the new aircraft ever since."

"And now he's here in Iran, conducting aerial guerrilla warfare," Deuce added.

"Not anymore. I'd say Sharkey wrapped him up quite nicely."

"Not completely. He said the Black Cobra got away. And by my count if he started with five dozen planes he's still got three whole squadrons out there somewhere. But I think Roche can handle him."

"We'd better let him know just who he's dealing with," Krause decided.

## ON THE TRACK, 200 MILES NW OF THE GULF – 1105

The three squadrons rendezvoused right on time. Lenonov checked the position of the Hornets on his screen and looked up at the skies above him. He made out twelve distinct contrails marking the targets about twenty-five miles ahead and twenty thousand feet above him. He used the high-resolution camera built into his Flanker's nose to inspect the targets from afar. They were all the same bright blue he had seen before. Suddenly the Hornets turned darker, then lighter again. He wondered if the camera was malfunctioning, then he realized the Hornets were just crossing shadows made by the cirri-stratus clouds that were forming at a higher altitude. He couldn't see any other Hornets, and wondered if they were following behind him somewhere. He decided it didn't make much difference. Once Sharkey's heavily-armed squadron was dealt with, the Growlers and the remains of the bomber group would be easy pickings.

"Fire Adder missiles on passive guidance, target heading, set altitude at twenty-five thousand feet," Lenonov ordered.

"How many of our missiles, Colonel?" Red-5 asked.

The Black Cobra glared at his video screen, at the two-seat F/A-18f leading the formation. "All of them."

## 50,000 FEET UP

Commander Tachini's lone Growler was invisible in the cloud cover, transmitting nothing, tracking the Black Cobra's squadrons on infrared. "Contacts are flaring," Palerider reported as we watched his ATFLIR display. Tiny bright white spots surrounded the fuzzy white blobs that represented the twenty-three Flankers on his screen. The bright dots accelerated away. "Contact separation. They're launching missiles. Count..." There were too many to count. "Lots of missiles."

Lenonov flew through a curtain of smoke left by nearly a hundred missiles as they climbed away. Once they reached their target altitude they would automatically switch to active search mode and look for targets. Sharkey's squadron would be right where they were looking. Meanwhile Lenonov's Flankers would accelerate to intercept the Hornets, coming in below the Americans, and complete the ambush attack. It would be a textbook lesson Sharkey wouldn't live to learn.

"Contacts are now accelerating," Palerider announced. "Aspect change; they're increasing altitude." The fuzzy blobs became more distinct as they climbed away from the warm floor of the desert. "Time to intercept, four zero seconds."

## ORCA FLIGHT, 20,000 FEET

"Roger that," Sharkey answered. "Otters, you are minus thirty to engage. Orcas, weapons check. Hot warheads and free-fire enabled."

The other *Stingrays* confirmed that their missiles were armed and ready to fire with or without weapons lock.

"Bottlenose, come around and commence jamming on Adder band."

"You got it," Santos answered. His Growler and two others were twenty miles ahead and also at fifty thousand feet, concealed in the clouds. They flipped around and powered up the ALQ-99 EW pods, transmitting an overwhelming wave of radiation energy that completely wiped out the AA-12 missiles' radar. They had just reached their target altitude and the instant they went active they exploded. The overwhelmed radar processors translated the massive radar signal as a very close return and set off the proximity warheads. They hit nothing.

"What do you mean, 'weapon failure'?" Lenonov asked his control panel. His other pilots were wondering the same thing. All of their AA-12 Adders had blown up without hitting anything.

"Comrade Colonel!" Ivan called desperately on the radio. "Massive radar spike! It's a jamming signal! The Growlers are ahead of you somewhere!"

There was nothing Lenonov could do about that now. He was committed to the attack. The blue Super Hornets were almost in range of his Archer missiles, and those couldn't be jammed.

"Here they come," Roche said. His TacOps screen showed the contacts Palerider had on infrared and Toymaker now had on radar. "Bottlenose, engage! Otters, engage! Orcas, bunt on my mark! Uh, you all know how to do a bunt, right?"

Santos had the targets lined up nicely on his radar. The tandem-transceiver radar had no problem distinguishing the Super Flankers from the similarly-sized Super Hornets in the same immediate area. His pilot locked their two AMRAAMs on the leader. "Fox-three, fox-three!"

Worm had to marvel at his friend Karl Roche's ability to anticipate the ambush and set up an even better ambush in response. This was exactly why he didn't like to play chess with Sharkey Roche. When he had given Otter Flight "minus thirty" Worm and the other fifteen former bombers slowed down to a hundred knots – a crawl for a jet fighter. They had been in position directly below Orca Flight, hugging the terrain and safely out of sight. They saw the mercenaries climb right over them, obliviously focused on the bright blue *Stingrays*.

When Sharkey said "Otters, engage!" Worm and the other Otters switched on their radar and blind-fired every AMRAAM they had. As the AESA radar systems warmed up, the aviators picked their targets and guided in their missiles.

Roche watched the radar feed Santos provided, watched the Black Cobra make his approach from below. "Three, two, one, mark!" Roche and the other Orcas pitched forward hard and cut their throttles. A bunt is the opposite of a tailslide but it achieves basically the same thing. It is a brutal, high-G maneuver for rapid vector change. Their wings absorbed the air resistance and brought the squadron to abrupt mid-air halt. The Flankers flew by right in front of them. "Lunch is served! Fire at will!"

Lenonov was just about to fire a burst of 30mm shells at what he guessed was Sharkey's Hornet when it suddenly jerked backwards like a puppet on a string. Now it pointed down, straight at him. He swore. One part of his brain realized that he had been outwitted again. Another part of his brain realized that there was a 20mm Vulcan cannon aimed right at it. That part of the brain took over and Lenonov executed a sharp tailslide, pitching up through and over Sharkey's field of fire.

Roche could actually see Lenonov's gloved hand haul back hard on the sidestick inside the Super Flanker's cockpit. He reacted off that, pitching up as well before the Hornet could plunge into a dive. For an instant he had the Black Cobra in his crosshairs, but he held his fire. At that range he would create a lethal field of flaming wreckage right in his path. It would be a suicide kill. The Flanker had much more momentum than the Hornet did and the Black Cobra flipped into a very tight loop. He and Sharkey stared at each other, appearing inverted to one another, for the brief instant their superfighters stood nose-to-nose.

474

Lenonov held the loop until he was pointing straight down and then dropped behind *Stingray* Fish-2.

Claymore was following Sharkey closely and to swerve hard to avoid a mid-air collision with the Black Cobra. "Hoooly smokes," he yelled. "That was *close!*"

"Are we going after him?" Hunter asked.

Sharkey had locks on two red-striped Flankers that pulled up in front of him. "I'll catch up with him later. Fox-two, fox-two!"

In the next twenty seconds VFC-233 *Stingrays* fired more than fifty missiles. After a brief instant of panic, the well-trained mercenaries filled the air with chaff and flares and expertly maneuvered around the weapons trying to kill them. They weren't all successful; with that many tons of ordnance flying through the air; it was impossible for all of them to avoid being hit. But twelve members of White and Red Squadrons were able to cheat death for those twenty seconds and break away from the furball of the dogfight, to the frustration of the *Stingrays*.

Otter flight got out of there. They had nothing to add to the fight and not enough fuel to hang around anyway. "Good luck, guys," Worm said. And he led the retreat to the carriers waiting just offshore.

The Growlers likewise were out of AMRAAMs. They had their Sidewinders but those were only to be used as last-ditch self defense. And since the Flankers were in a close-range dogfight, they didn't really have anything to do with their jammers. Palerider and one of the other Growlers headed home. Santos and his wingman stuck around at high altitude so they could observe and assist if needed.

It was all up to the *Stingrays* now, and since even odds really meant odds in their favor, Sharkey didn't mind at all. "Single up on your targets and watch each other's backs," he said.

"Sharkey, either we miscounted or some of them escaped," Toymaker said.

"Yeah, the Black Cobra bugged out," Sharkey confirmed.

"I see him. He's looping around to the west. But three more are missing."

"I saw where they went," Palerider said. "They split right after they all fired the AA-12s. Three of them went south. It didn't look like they were coming back. Also, Deuce says the Black Cobra has another squadron somewhere that we haven't met yet."

"We'll worry about that later," Roche decided. He had something more pressing to attend to. He had a Flanker in front of him and another one behind him. The one in front was easy to take care of. Roche accelerated forward, then turned sharply, anticipating the Flanker's evasive roll to the right. Sharkey fired a Sidewinder into his back. The one behind him was now closing in though. "Hacksaw, I've got one on my tail," he called.

"Me too. Where are you?"

Hunter checked the MFD and answered. "Four miles off your ten o'clock."

Roche could see Hacksaw and turned toward him. "You know what to do."

Lt. "Hacksaw" Miller, former Blue Angels tryout, smiled as he responded. "Yeah, I sure do. Opposing solos, knife-edge pass."

"What is he talking about?" Hunter asked.

"You'll see," Sharkey answered. He and Hacksaw flew right at each other, then when only a thousand yards separated them, they each rolled ninety degrees to the left and pushed down a little on the stick to give them just a couple feet of separation. They shot past each other at over 1400 miles an hour closing speed, and had each others' pursuers dead in their sights. Sharkey's target was stunned. He did nothing but watch a spray of cannon fire rip his Flanker wide open. The fighter behind Sharkey tried to pull away, but Hacksaw had a Sidewinder ready for him.

"That was cool," Hunter said. "Scary as hell, but cool."

"Nice work, number two," Roche called.

"Thanks. There's another one on your five o'clock high. I've got him."

Roche looked back over his right shoulder and saw a Flanker rolling away from a pair of Sidewinders.

"Shit!" Hacksaw yelled. "I *thought* I had that guy!"

Roche pulled up and to the left to intercept. "I'll take care of it." He got an infrared lock almost immediately. But at the moment he fired, Red Six dropped a flare and rolled away. The Sidewinder decided to chase the flare instead of the Flanker. "Oh, come *on!*" Roche stayed behind the target, and uncaged his last two Sidewinders on the wingtips. He waited until he was close enough that they couldn't be fooled, and fired. The mercenary hit the afterburners and barrel-rolled at supersonic speed, creating a weird effect that spread his exhaust trail in the cone of the sonic shockwave. Then he cut the throttle and dropped away. The bewildered missiles lost track.

"That's a nice trick," Sharkey said, as he dove after the Russian. "I'll have to remember that one." The more-agile Super Hornet brought Roche in gun range, and he frowned in concentration as he tried to close his sights on the target. He fired a burst that chipped away pieces of the Flanker's right wing. It rolled hard to the left, then harder to the right, momentarily out of control. Roche took advantage and fired a killing burst of 20mm rounds into the Sukhoi's engines. He watched it break up and fall, and kept watching until he saw the pilot bail out. "That guy was good."

"Eyes front!" Hunter snapped.

Roche looked up and saw a Flanker and two Archer missiles coming toward him. "Whoops." He rolled up and around the missiles, which didn't have a solid lock on his nose. When they turned to follow they ran right into a flare shell. The Flanker stayed right in front of him and started firing with his gun. Roche fired his own gun a little wide as he rolled out of the Flankers crosshairs. He zeroed in again squeezed the trigger. Nothing happened. Then he saw his ammo counter was on zero. He'd gone through all two hundred rounds already. "Oh boy." Roche held his course though, flying right at the enemy fighter.

"Sharkey…" Hunter warned.

"Hang on." Roche rolled and pitched just slightly, and used his right wingtip camera to keep him on target. The razor-sharp wingtip pylon crashed through the Flanker's plexiglass canopy, punching through the pilot's head and his headrest. Once free of the canopy the wingtip passed between the Flanker's vertical stabilizers. The out-of-control Russian fighter plummeted to the ground.

"Did you just fox-zero that guy?" Hunter asked.

"Yep. I think I might've damaged something though. Or there's something stuck to my wingtip." The camera view had gone dark.

Hunter looked back at their right wing. "Uh yeah, you have someone's flight helmet stuck out there."

Roche looked back as well. "Oh." He shook it free. "That's better."

*Sharkey must die!* Lenonov was screaming inside his head. The humiliation he had suffered at the American's hands was tearing at him. But outwardly he remained calm. As he circled back toward the fray he used the long-range camera to asses the situation. His Super Flankers were losing. He counted seven remaining, and all twelve of the blue Super Hornets were still in the fight. Lenonov was no longer interested in saving his men. *Sharkey must die.* He identified the three tandem-seat Hornet-Fs flown by the division leaders. One was being chased by a Flanker and was having trouble shaking it. Another two-seat Hornet was hot on the tail of another Flanker but was struggling to make the kill. Neither of those could be Sharkey. He found the third one, and as he watched the Hornet's pilot smashed his wingtip into the cockpit of a Flanker, brutally killing the mercenary. *That* has *to be Sharkey. Sharkey must die.* The Black Cobra accelerated toward his target.

"Yo, Sharkey," Santos called. "Your friend is coming back around. Check your two o'clock low."

"Roger." Roche banked until he was facing the threat vector. He found the black Flanker with his eyes before the radar could resolve the contact. He fired his last missiles – the fuselage-mounted AMRAAMs – as soon as he had radar lock.

As Lenonov watched, the Hornet turned toward him and fired missiles. A second later his radar warning informed him that those weapons were in fact looking for him. "Damn you Sharkey, you know I'm coming." He accelerated toward the missiles, rolling around them at the last instant. He continued flying toward Sharkey.

"Here he comes," Sharkey said, watching the big Russian fighter coming in dead ahead. The Black Cobra slipped around the missiles easily. Roche knew he was in a dangerous position – he was now unarmed, after all – but he also knew the AA-11 Archer missile was weakest in head-on engagements. He stayed on the collision course waiting for the Cobra to strike. He saw flashes under the black wings, and spotted the two small missiles accelerating toward him. "Hacksaw, I'm going to need you to get behind this guy in a minute," Roche ordered. "The rest of you, pair up on the remaining targets."

The Archers were on their way, but Lenonov suspected that the American ace would be able to evade them as easily as Lenonov himself had dodged the AMRAAMs. Sure enough, Sharkey waited until the last minute and then killed his engines and pulled a tailslide. The Archers lost their lock on the cold side of the plane and sailed past harmlessly. Sharkey's Hornet dropped upside-down and backwards. Lenonov nosed over to intercept it. The Hornet's engines came back to life, spitting a trail of hot exhaust. Lenonov locked two more missiles and fired. The Hornet began to climb back the way it came, then it suddenly flipped around and accelerated toward the earth, leaving a

478

cluster of flare shells between it and the heat-seeking missiles. The missiles were confounded. The Black Cobra swore and pitched into a vertical dive.

Hunter shuddered as the missiles exploded in their wake, only a few hundred feet behind his head. Sharkey keyed the mike and taunted the Black Cobra again. "Is that all you've got, comrade?"

"Not quite, Sharkey," the mercenary called back. "I have two more missiles and about a hundred cannon shells with your name on them."

"Let's see 'em." Roche accelerated sharply as he leveled out at two hundred feet. He went right past the Cobra's nose.

It took Lenonov a split second to switch from his missiles to his gun, and by the time he squeezed the trigger the Hornet was out of his sights. He had to slow down and pull up sharply to avoid slamming into the ground. Sharkey was already out of range by the time he leveled out. He swore profusely in Russian and hit his afterburners.

"Do you have him, Hacksaw?" Sharkey called on the secure channel.

"Can't miss him." Even against the background of the hot desert floor, the redlined Saturn AL-31 engines stood out like signal flares; especially to the super-sensitive seeker heads of the AIM-9x Sidewinders. Hacksaw fired two at the Super Flanker's back.

The "stinger" radar mounted between the Flanker's tailpipes picked up the inbound Sidewinders and alerted the pilot. Lenonov swore and hesitated for almost a second. Sharkey was almost in missile range again, but those Sidewinders were closer. He spat out a pair of flares, pulled the throttles back and let the plane drift down to the deck. The missiles noticed the hot engines starting to cool down, and now had to pick between those, and the warm sand, and the red-hot flares. They went for the flares.

"Sweet Jesus." Hacksaw had followed the Black Cobra closely, but now his digital radar altimeter flickered between *0* and *100*, unable to tell if he was a hundred feet above the deck or right on it. His airspeed indicator read 620kts. Hacksaw was as good as anyone at flying low and fast, but he had never heard of anyone flying *this* low and *this* fast, and certainly not while shooting at each other.

Somewhere up ahead, Sharkey was leading the chase. The terrain was opening up into a series of low hills and shallow valleys. He found a small stream and tracked it northeast, using the valley it followed as natural cover. The Black Cobra stayed in pursuit, now about six miles behind, with Hacksaw hot on his tail.

Now that he and the Cobra were at the same altitude, Hacksaw's Sidewinders weren't confused by the thermal background of the earth. He locked on to the Flanker's engines again and fired his last two missiles.

Lenonov was waiting for that. He pulled up sharply and hit his afterburners, leading the missiles into a vertical climb. Then he cut the engines and rolled away. The Sidewinders were staring straight into the sun, and immediately lost their lock when the Flanker went cold.

Hacksaw swore as he tried to get back behind the Black Cobra.
"Orca Two, what's happening back there?" The CO asked.
"I'm out of missiles," Lt. Miller answered. "I'll have to finish this the old-fashioned way."

"Roger that." Roche clicked off the mike and frowned at the tactical display. The chase had drawn them away from the main fight; there weren't any other friendlies within fifty miles of Hacksaw. He was on his own. "We need to reengage," he said.
"With what?" Hunter asked. "We're unarmed, remember?"
"We need to get the Black Cobra to chase us again and set him up for Hacksaw. If we leave them in a one-vee-one, he's going to get killed." Roche pulled out of the valley and turned west toward Hacksaw's position.

Lenonov looked back at the Super Hornet. Its wings were empty. It was no threat as long as he could stay away from that 20mm gun. He brought his radar back online and looked for Sharkey. He spotted a target off to the east. Lenonov quickly shut off the radar again and dropped into a wadi to set up another ambush.

Hacksaw warily followed the Super Flanker into the dry riverbed. The low-flying Russian was kicking up a cloud of dust and small rocks. Lt. Miller didn't want any of that in his engines. He rolled upside down to keep the intakes out of the dust trail. Bits of debris rattled off the canopy but that was no concern. The polycarbonate-plexiglass composite was supposed to be impervious to fifty-caliber bullets. A pebble shouldn't be able to hurt it.

But his exposed gun port was a different story. Hacksaw got the target in his sights for an instant, but nothing happened when he pulled the trigger. He safe-locked the gun and unloaded it to try to clear the jam. He got his crosshairs on the Black Cobra's left wing and fired again. This time the six-barrel Gatling mechanism spun freely, and the ammo feed loaded links of 20mm rounds into the rotary chamber. The gun brought a fresh shell to the very top of the assembly where the trip-hammer was ready to slam the firing pin forward. The cartridge exploded, propelling the shell through the barrel at nearly 3000 feet per second. Exactly ten milliseconds later, the next barrel swung into line and fired, launching a second projectile into the wild blue yonder where it would hopefully intercept some Russian sheet metal. A third round was fired but it didn't get far. This barrel was clogged with pulverized rock dust. The shell wedged tight and ground to a halt just before it reached the muzzle of the cannon. The hot exhaust gasses back-blew through the firing chamber and vented into the receiver assembly, setting off the next shell in line. The contained explosion ripped the Vulcan cannon clean out of its mount, shattered the radar transceiver and cracked open the Super Hornet's nose cone. The SHOC detected a disastrous malfunction and ejected the Vulcan's magazine before any more rounds could cook off.

Hacksaw swore. He could see the smoke pouring out of a newly-formed crack over his gun bay, and Bitchin' Betty read off a string of warnings and alarms. "No weapons sir," he told Roche. "I'm done."

"Great." Roche's computer received the status message from Hacksaw's SHOC to inform him about the weapon malfunction. "Get on out of here, Orca Two." He looked back at Hunter. "I guess that one got aw-" as he was looking back he saw twin trails of fire spiraling toward their engines. "Whoa, hang on!" He fired flare shells and twisted away. One of the AA-11s was fooled, the other wasn't. Sharkey juked the other way and turned his belly to the missile, then yanked a hard horizontal tailslide. The missile lost them.

Roche held the turn and looked down to his right. There was the Black Cobra, lining up for a gun kill. Sharkey snap-rolled the other way just before a stream of cannon shells zipped past his right wing.

He pulled hard to the left and cut the throttle, hoping to pull out of the mercenary's line of fire. He watched as the black Super Flanker bored in. "This is gonna be close!"

Lenonov pressed the attack. He had ignored the bullet hole in his left wing – it hadn't hit anything important and the Hornet that had fired at him had abruptly stopped shooting for some reason now. He was out of missiles and low on gun ammo, but he would use every shot it took to bring Sharkey down. He turned left and pulled up. The Hornet was above him now, banked hard toward him, way out of his sights. Lenonov tried to pull up harder to cut inside the turn, but the Hornet was hanging almost motionless and there was no way he could possibly bring the gun to bear. Lenonov howled in frustration and continued to charge, slamming the top of Sharkey's left wingtip with the leading edge of his own left wing.

The impact flipped the Super Hornet around and spun the Super Flanker into a sideways skid. The Black Cobra recovered and transferred the wild momentum into a left-hand turn, bringing the momentarily disoriented blue *Stingray* back in his line of fire.

Roche pushed through the roll as more shells narrowly missed the airframe. He pulled out of the spin and turned right to get out of the Flanker's sights. The Black Cobra came back, so Sharkey went left, again forcing the Flanker to miss. They were in a scissors engagement, cutting into and away from each other. After a couple more failed passes the Black Cobra stopped shooting. Roche leveled out and slowed down.

"What's going on?" Hunter asked.

Roche looked back at the Super Flanker. "I think he's out of ammo."

Lenonov stared blankly at the steady target in his crosshairs. He was holding the trigger down, but no shells were being fired into other plane. He looked down at his weapons display. The digital counter read "0" and flashed the number mockingly. He pounded the panel with his left fist, cracking the screen. Sharkey slowed down until the Flanker had pulled even with him.

The two pilots stared at each other. Lenonov looked at the stenciling under the front seat. It read L̶t̶. *Cmdr. Karl "Sharkey" Roche* – with the "Lt." crossed out with a marker. "Commander Karl Roche," he called on open channel, "you realize you and I have unfinished business."

"I'll catch you later, Colonel Victor Lenonov," Roche answered.

Lenonov nodded slowly and yanked back hard on his stick.

Roche turned to follow and hit the afterburners.

"Sharkey, stop! Let him go!" Hunter yelled.

Roche released the afterburner trigger but remained on course, following the Black Cobra to the southwest. "He's right there. If I can just-"

"Give it up! You'll catch him later, like you said."

"I can catch him now."

"No, you can't. He's faster than us, and we're almost out of fuel. And now you're bleeding through your flightsuit, on top everything." Hunter was looking at his pilot with the cockpit cameras.

Roche glanced at the sticky red patch on his left side. "It's not too bad."

"And we're *still* out of weapons," Hunter reminded him. "What would you do if you caught him? Pop off the canopy and shoot at him with that giant pistol of yours?"

Sharkey looked down and prodded the Desert Eagle in the gear bag at his feet. "The thought did cross my mind."

"Well, forget it. We'll be back. He'll be waiting for you. Let's get home while we still can."

"You're right," Roche admitted grudgingly, and he turned back toward the USS *Ronald Reagan*.

# CHAPTER 23: THIEF IN THE NIGHT

## THE BUNKER – 1600 LOCAL, JUNE 4$^{\text{TH}}$

Rannovich glowered at the face on his screen. "Your failure, Colonel, is entirely unacceptable."

Lenonov made an incredible effort to remain expressionless. "Sir, I succeeded in my mission to disrupt the American bomber attack on the tunnel network."

"Not enough. I lost enough tanks and tunnels to terminally cripple my offensive on the Iraqi border. All you succeeded in was losing forty-four of your fantastically expensive aircraft to the US Navy. The very bombers you were supposed to destroy turned around and made your pilots look like flaming idiots. Emphasis on *flaming*. As in 'going down *flaming*.' I can go on if you like."

"I fully appreciate the severity of my losses, sir. And I assure you my humiliation could not be more complete. But I did not expect a US Navy fighter squadron to counter-attack so swiftly. I certainly did not expect a squadron led with such extraordinary skill and daring as displayed by Commander Karl Roche."

"Roche- *he* is the one who beat you?" For once Rannovich was taken aback.

"That was the name I saw stenciled on the side of the cockpit of the squadron leader's Super Hornet. I tried my best to kill him, but he evaded every missile and cannon shell I had."

"This is the same pilot who eluded capture in Tehran – the one who thwarted my ambush on the Embassy rescue team and allowed their spies to escape with a traitor I wanted dead. This Karl Roche has made himself quite a nuisance."

"So you understand the measure of the challenge I faced today."

Rannovich removed the sunglasses he always wore and aimed the full force of his glare through his webcam. Lenonov thought his computer would explode. "Colonel," the gangster said after a long moment, "I will give you one chance only to redeem yourself. If you fail me again, I suggest you find another country to land your plane in because you will not be allowed to live in this one."

Lenonov swallowed hard, and could feel the color draining from his face.

"The Americans continue to make our lives miserable with their B-2 stealth bombers," Rannovich went on. "They attack any target they can find – our supply depots, our airfields, our missile installations, our communications facilities, our power plants – you name it, they bomb it."

"With impunity, I note."

"That's where you come in. Tonight, you will patrol the air corridor they use to make their bombing runs. You will wait for a B-2 and you will shoot it down. Ignore any other targets. Do not reveal your presence. You must wait for an unsuspecting B-2 to pass through, and then you must bring it down."

"Sir-"

"I'm not finished," Rannovich interrupted. "It will not be sufficient for you to merely blow a B-2 out of the sky. It must come down relatively intact, so I can film the wreck and put its highly recognizable shape on television and show what you have done to the world. I wish to prove to the world that I have the power to defeat the most advanced tools of the American war machine. That is why I have risked entire divisions of armored units to destroy a few companies of Abrams tanks and handful of Apache helicopters. That is why I sacrificed dozens of ships to sink one *Nimitz*-class aircraft carrier. And I will use you to bring down the B-2 stealth. Your survival is of secondary concern to the success of your mission."

Lenonov could not help expressing his excitement. He could not have asked for a greater challenge with which to redeem himself. "It will be done, sir. I will depart immediately with the surviving members of Black Squadron, and I shall bring down a so-called 'stealth bomber' for you. You honor me with this opportun-"

"Honor has nothing to do with it," Rannovich interrupted again. "Just prove to me that you are still useful." And with that, the crime lord signed off.

Lenonov stared at the blank screen for a full minute. Despite the harsh words of his employer, he was grinning widely.

## DIEGO GARCIA – SAME TIME

Lt. Colonel Patrick Mundy studied the photographs of his target while his pilot powered up their plane. Major Will Escher, in the left seat of the B-2 Spirit's cockpit, mumbled along with the lyrics to "Kryptonite" by Three Doors Down, which was blasting through his headphones. *"I watched the world float to the dark side of the moon... After all I knew it had to be somethin' to do with you..."* With its engines turning at a fast idle, the flying wing crept out of its armored bunker-hangar onto the moonlit runway. The pilot did not need to address the tower for takeoff clearance.

In fact, he was not allowed to communicate with anyone except in case of emergency. Their callsign – Overlord 3 – was only to be used in one-way Flash messages to Strategic Command. Stealth meant radio silence. Null signature was as important as the radar-absorbing black-hole paint or the computer-generated shape of the airframe itself. From above or below, the B-2 was one of the most recognizable shapes in the world. From the side, it looked like a black trout that had lost all its fins. From the front, it looked like nothing at all on radar. After twenty years in operation it was still the pinnacle of stealth technology.

Escher gently nudged the throttles forward and the bomber hurled itself into the air. He set the autopilot to follow the prescribed course he had programmed remotely while still in the briefing room. The route zigzagged an untraceable path generally north across the Indian Ocean until reaching the shore of Iran, then it followed the safety corridor across the country, and took a left-hand turn just northwest of Tehran toward the bomber's target in the Alborz mountains.

Mundy continued studying his target while the plane climbed to sixty thousand feet. A valley shaped like a tea saucer contained hastily-erected buildings around a long-abandoned mine. Intel suggested that it was a loading zone for mobile missile launchers, possibly to be armed with chemical or biological weapons. What was visible in the photographs was presumably the tip of the iceberg – like other high-value Iranian targets, the core of the facility was apparently underground.

That is why this B-2 bomber carried the hideously powerful 33,000 pound GBU-57b Massive Ordnance Penetrator. Essentially a hardened bunker-buster derivative of the MOAB, the MOP is capable of slamming through up to two hundred feet of concrete and more or less vaporizing anything under that hardened shell. Like its air-burst-effect cousin, the explosive power of the MOP is only exceeded by a low-yield nuclear weapon. Mundy had already programmed the GPS coordinates of his target into both the weapon and the bomber. He had also selected the attack profile and release point from several options that were generated by the B-2's onboard attack computer.

The B-2's flight computer flew the prescribed course. The attack computer waited for the drop point. The humans were just along for the ride. Or to intervene in case something went totally wrong. Since their arrival at Diego Garcia two weeks before, Mundy and

Escher had flown over twenty sorties, including "Operation Mouse Hunt." So far every mission had gone just like the simulator runs they performed every week back at their home base at Whiteman AFB, Missouri. They'd flown right past enemy patrols and SAM sites unnoticed and wiped out dozens of high-value targets. The B-2 just made bombing too easy.

## THE BUNKER – 2000 LOCAL

"We are ready for the next stage," Rannovich told the President of Iran.

"Are we now?" Ahmadinejad asked dejectedly. "My army has been destroyed. My navy clogs the bottom of Bandar Abbas Harbor. Even the air force is in tatters, including your celebrated mercenaries."

"Their losses were to be expected and accepted. Victory against the Americans using conventional weapons is simply impossible. We gave them some nasty surprises, to be sure, but I've known all along that their military would dominate ours. That was essential to the plan. Now that the Americans are committed to the fight, our total victory is assured."

"I'm afraid I do not follow your logic."

"We are ready now to reintroduce the world to the concept of nuclear war."

"I thought our weapons were not ready."

"Come with me." Rannovich led Ahmadinejad down a corridor to a door marked with a radiation symbol. Inside the room was a table with three steel cases. "These weapons, Mr. President, will be your tools of victory." Rannovich opened the three heavy cases. Inside each was a device that was about the size and shape of a soccer ball, connected by hardened cables to a small computer processor.

"Those aren't nearly as large as the bomb you dumped back in Iraq," Ahmadinejad noted.

"Their size belies their power. These were developed by the Americans, and are in fact the most efficient nuclear fission detonators ever created. The Americans call them B82 mod 3 warheads. They were designed to be dropped from B-2 bombers to destroy bunkers like this one." That was all true. "They are much more powerful than that atomic pipe bomb I placed in Lake Tharthar." That part was a lie. The bunker-buster warheads only had a blast yield of ten kilotons. Nevertheless, in Rannovich's scheme they would be far deadlier than he would ever let his Iranian pawns believe.

"Can they be fitted to my missiles?"

"Yes. My engineers have made a casing that will allow you launch these with your Shahab-III missile. The warhead only weighs a few hundred kilograms, so your missile will have an effective range of well over two thousand kilometers. You will be able to hit the Israeli Defense Forces High Command in Tel Aviv, as well as the American Central Command headquarters in Kuwait City, and their Fifth Fleet headquarters in Bahrain."

"Perfect." Mahmoud Ahmadinejad reached out and touched the soccer-ball shaped weapon core, surprised to find it cool to the touch. He realized there must be quite a lot of metal shielding and HMX explosive between his fingertips and the plutonium inside. "Why didn't Saddam ever use these?"

"They can only be activated by a special computer. That computer is only found in a B-2 stealth bomber."

"You can obtain this computer?"

"I will do so tonight."

"And how long will it take to make my nuclear arsenal ready to fire?"

"Not very long at all. My engineers must program the warheads before they are fitted to the missiles, but that entire process will only take two days. They will be ready by dawn on June seventh, Mr. President. The world will awake to find a new atomic superpower in control of the Middle East. The Americans will flee in terror. Iraq, Afghanistan, Saudi Arabia and especially the crippled Israel will cower before you. This part of the world will be yours."

"And all the oil in it will be yours," the President of Iran added with a wry grin. Then he frowned. "But what happens if the Americans choose to respond by nuking my country into utter oblivion?"

"China will not let that slide. Without your oil, they will form an alliance with Russia to secure their energy needs. While the Middle East burns, Russia's supply would be the *only* supply large enough for anyone. A desperate US will be forced to challenge them for dominance. Global nuclear war will be inevitable. If Iran is destroyed, the rest of the world will not be far behind. You and your countrymen will die holy martyrs, the agents of the apocalypse."

Ahamdinejad's grin returned. "I can live with that."

## USS *RONALD REAGAN* FLAG CONFERENCE ROOM - 2200

Karl Roche put down the redacted CIA dossier on Colonel Victor Lenonov. "Colorful character," he remarked.

Admiral Krause took the dossier away and locked it in his briefcase. "You beat the best aerial terrorist in the world at his own game."

Roche shrugged. "It's easy to take advantage of your opponent's over-confidence."

Deuce raised his eyebrows at that.

"I'm putting you in for the highest possible commendation," Krause announced. "Taking your squadron into that battle against that kind of opponent, rescuing the strike package and coming out with no further losses; that's one for the books. Incredible."

"We lost a few very good men before you showed up though," Deuce said.

Worm nodded somberly.

"Did SAR find Bonzer?" Sharkey wondered.

"Not a trace of him," Thompson said. "There's just a huge hole in the ground where his plane went down. It looks like that thermobaric bomb he was carrying detonated on impact. The Hornet was completely vaporized. Bonzer might have been too close to the blast."

"We'll keep looking for him," Krause said. "A couple of the guys from the *Lincoln's* wing are still MIA as well. But it could have been a lot worse, Sharkey. It would have been a hell of a lot worse, if it wasn't for you."

Deuce passed a folder to Worm Bellbrook. "I still need you to maintain a twelve-plane combat squadron, so I'm bringing in some Super Hornets from the *Roosevelt* Air Wing to replace the ones you lost. I'm also transferring two of the survivors from the Fists' division we lost to your squadron to replace Money and Bonzer. Deadeye Unther and Red Rove are both rated on the Super."

Bellbrook skimmed over his orders and the files on the two new pilots. "Alright. I'll give Deadeye command of Bonzer's division with Red as his wingman, and I'll move Bonzer's wingman to my section."

"We don't have any feet-dry sorties on our plate at the moment," Krause announced. "The Air Force is suspending tanker ops until they're sure the southern airspace is clear. You two get some time to cool off."

Deuce nodded. "The Renegades will stay on CAP. Everyone else has twenty-four hours to reorganize and recover. Except you." He pointed to Sharkey. "Medical says you're grounded for a forty-eight hour period, starting at your last landing."

"As long as I'm not locked in my room, I'll be happy to comply with the doctor's orders," Roche said. He had been in the infirmary for the last six hours. After he'd landed and jumped out of his plane, he had taken three steps and passed out. Hunter had called for help and pulled the pressurized flight suit off of his pilot. It was full of blood. Sharkey had torn his sutures and reopened his gunshot wounds. Dr. Tobias had only released him from the infirmary a few minutes before the flag debriefing.

"See him in the morning, and he'll decide if he should make your bed rest compulsory," Deuce instructed. "But I don't think you need anyone to tell you that you need to get some sleep now."

"You got that right." Roche stood, saluted the Admiral, and went out the door.

Krause turned to Thompson. "We need to take good care of that kid. I'll bet we'll need him to pull off another miracle before we see the endgame."

## BLACK SQUADRON, 100' OVER THE IRANIAN DESERT

The Sukhoi Flanker was not built for stealth. The towering twin vertical tails, air intakes that could swallow Volkswagens, racks of big missiles – all-in-all the Super Flanker is about as stealthy as a flying barn on fire. The Black Cobra and his wingmates, however, were invisible. They flew so close to the terrain that any radar trying to track them would have better chances following the dust trails they kicked up. They transmitted no signals – no radar, no radio. They kept the engines set to run light and lean, and so even on infrared they barely left a trail in the warm wind. The black-skinned fighters even disappeared from the naked eye.

Colonel Victor Lenonov lurked under the very noses of the United States Air Force fighters and AWACS planes patrolling the so-called safety corridor. Patiently he waited for the opportune target.

## OVERLORD 3, 60,000' OVER THE ALBORZ MOUNTAINS
## 0021

"Turning to three-one-five," Major Escher announced as the B-2 Spirit gently banked to the right. "On the target leg now. Two minutes, forty seconds to drop point."

Lt. Colonel Mundy closed his Dale Brown paperback and activated his bombsight. An ultra-advanced night-vision camera showed the terrain eleven miles below and seven miles ahead, where the bomb would land if it were dropped at that instant. Mundy uncaged

490

the camera and tracked it northwest to the target coordinates. The attack computer made its own calculations for time and distance to target release, and the numbers matched what Escher had on his navigation screen. "Two minutes. Arming weapon."

Ten feet behind him, a guidance processor built in to the GBU-57 clicked on and ascertained its whereabouts from the GPS telemetry. Mundy double-checked that the weapon and the bomber each saw themselves in the same position. The attack computer updated its proposed drop point based on weather variables and moved it up a few hundred yards. Mundy watched the numbers tick away. "Thirty seconds. Opening bomb bay doors."

## IRAN DESERT

Ivan was intently monitoring the Iranian air defense radio channels, waiting for the magic words. *"Anomalous transient contact – just appeared out of nowhere... altitude nineteen thousand meters, heading three one five, bearing two nine two and range one seven oh kilometers relative Tehran... contact separation. Larger contact descending rapidly..."*

Ivan pressed the transmit switch on his direct UHF channel to Colonel Lenonov. "I have a target for you."

## OVERLORD

"Weapon is released," Mundy announced. "Closing doors."

"Commencing return flight." Escher instructed the computer to revert to nav route beta. The bomber turned around and set itself on an indirect heading back to Diego Garcia. "Countermeasures ready for enemy pursuit."

"Not likely," Mundy muttered, and he went back to his book about a much more exciting bomber mission. "Any radar traces?"

"Couple seconds while the doors were open. Nothing anyone could track."

The bomb fell, reaching its terminal velocity at twenty thousand feet. The GPS guidance chip directed the grid fins on the bomb's body to adjust slightly to compensate for changes in wind speed and air density to keep the weapon aimed square at its target. It dropped into the valley and slammed into the earth between a canvas tent and a parked Czech-built TATA transport. The bomb kept going down, through dirt, rock and concrete. The accelerometer in the nose sensed when it finally came to rest halfway through the concrete ceiling of a bunker, and the computer turned this signal into another directed at the electric detonator.

The Australian chemical engineers who developed composition H6 created an explosive with an interesting property. Its explosive velocity exceeds its burn rate, meaning that when a large quantity of H6 detonates, the material is launching itself out of the point of impact to ignite and explode in an expanding radius around ground zero. This greatly increases the magnitude of the blast in a manner disproportionate to its base explosive force factor relative to TNT. The more H6, the more this effect increases. In other words, bigger bombs made with H6 become exponentially more powerful. One pound of H6 equals 1.6 pounds of TNT, but ten pounds of H6 will equal the force of over twenty pounds of TNT, not sixteen. And a hundred pounds of H6 will match nearly four hundred pounds of TNT. The GBU-57b's warhead, the BLU-120, is the same as used in the MOAB. It contains 18,700 pounds of H6. The blast is *sixty* times greater than an equivalent weight of TNT. Nine and a half tons of H6 equals *hundreds* of tons of TNT.

Those within a thousand yards of the MOP's point of impact could not appreciate the difference between this and a nuclear weapon. The TATA transport and the tent on either side of the hole moved about twenty feet apart in the instant before they were obliterated by what could only be described as a volcanic force that came from below. Fire and fury filled the valley, destroying dozens of missiles and transport/launch vehicles and a great quantity of lethal chemicals. When the cataclysmic reaction was complete, the debris settled to fill a crater the size and shape of the Rose Bowl Stadium. The fullest force of the titanic blast, however, went underground in a violent shockwave that shook the buried bunkers apart from their armored ceilings to their foundations. Nothing within a half-mile of the MOP in any direction survived.

*"Lost contact with a missile loading facility right where that second transient contact disappeared. Looks to me like it was hit by a really big bomb from a stealth bomber... Somebody better break the news to the General..."*

Ivan was immediately passing the news to the Colonel.

## BLACK SQUADRON

Lenonov flashed his wingtip lights on and off twice, signaling his wingmates that he had received their target. He turned northwest, into the escape route of the American stealth bomber. He took a risk and let his plane fly on autopilot at five hundred feet for a moment while he checked his target location on his GPS map. Once he had a fix on his heading, he went back down to ground level.

## ORION FLIGHT, 60 MILES BEHIND BLACK SQUADRON

Major Dave "Screwball" Duvall frowned at his MFD screen. Something popped up – briefly – on his radar, and disappeared. "Stargazer, this is Orion Lead. I just had a transient contact. Low altitude, high speed. Were you tracking?"

"Ah, roger, Orion. We saw your skimmer," the E-3 replied. "We've been seeing something moving around down there, didn't have a good fix or ID on it. This looked like a Flanker, came up to five hundred feet for a few seconds. It's moving fast on a northwest vector."

"Copy, Stargazer. Log my division on a pursuit. Advise if you regain contact." Screwball banked his F-22 Raptor to the left and accelerated out of the safety corridor. "Division with me. Orions Five and Nine, stay on your patrol tracks."

"Roger, Lead."

## BLACK SQUADRON

"Colonel," Ivan called through the radio, "the Americans might have spotted you. A flight of Raptors just broke their patrol pattern about a hundred kilometers behind you. They're on an intercept heading."

Lenonov swore. He knew he should have waited until he was over level terrain to check his bearings without coming out of the grass. He changed course to throw off the pursuers.

## OVERLORD

Pat Mundy reached the end of a chapter, and took a moment to look at the ECM screen. Minor threat traces. The B-2 was skirting the fringe of what was left of the Iranian defense coverage in that sector. There had been something about that in the briefing. There was still this one zone of overlapping air defenses that was basically impenetrable, even to a stealth bomber. It was the one piece of Iranian airspace that they had to avoid. Mundy leaned over and looked at the nav screen. Escher pointed out their route, a big sweeping curve around the edge of the radar mushroom and back toward the safety corridor. Mundy nodded and went back to his book.

## BLACK SQUADRON

*The bomber will have to go around the defense zone around the command bunker network,* Lenonov reasoned. *He'll stay closer to the Iraqi border – the 'safe side' – and come straight toward me on this side of the mountains.* Lenonov used his powerful night-vision camera to watch the sky above, waiting for the bomber to appear on the track he predicted. After a moment he found himself humming one of the old American folk tunes he had learned as a boy. *"Oh, she'll be comin' round the mountain when she comes..."*

## ORION FLIGHT

"Stargazer, do you have anything yet?"

"Sorry, Orion. He's out there, but he's still using ground cover."

"Copy. I'm going down into the canyons to see if I can flush him out."

"Be careful. This might be the same guy that bushwhacked the Navy this afternoon."

"I can handle it." Screwball Duvall went low, looking for terrain that the Russian fighters might be using to hide from the E-3's radar. He spotted a deep canyon and running around one side of a ridge, and rolled toward that. "Stay close to me, guys. Activate TERCOM for COLA flight." Using radar to image the terrain ahead and compare it to maps stored in its memory, the onboard computers could navigate the terrain-following flight and also actively manage the Raptors' altitude to fly as low to the ground as safely possible. "Keep an eye out, guys. We won't have much time to engage after we pick them up on radar."

## BLACK SQUADRON

Looking through his night-vision scope, Lenonov watched a shadow as it appeared on the horizon and grow as it moved across the sky. As he got closer, he saw it form the unmistakable shape of the Northrop B-2 Spirit. The B-2 would not use radar. It would be operating alone, using no radio callsign. It would not be able to see the Black Cobra and his wingmen when they emerged from hiding to strike.

The time for stealth was over. Lenonov pulled back on the stick and hit the afterburners. He was far enough away now from the safety corridor that he didn't have to worry about the Americans intercepting him. Even if they could see him, it was already too late for them to stop him or warn the stealth bomber.

## ORION FLIGHT

"Pop-up!" the call from Stargazer came in. "Orion, I have four contacts that just broke cover. They're climbing – climbing fast!"

"Where are they?"

"Check your MFD."

Duvall looked at the screen which showed the E-3's tacops feed. The new contacts were about seventy miles north of him. "Dammit! He shifted tracks on me." Duvall climbed out of his canyon, and turned north.

## BLACK SQUADRON

The threat radar receiver squawked loudly as it processed the incoming energy. Lenonov expected that an E-3 would lock on to him sooner or later. He didn't expect four fighters to be on him as well. But they were still too far away for missiles, and unless the Americans were still flying their old F-15 Eagles instead of the newer but slower Raptors, they had no chance of catching up with the powerful Super Flanker in a Mach 2 climb.

He could see the big, blind 'stealth' dead ahead of him now. It wouldn't be visible to his radar- or infrared-guided missiles. No matter. The Black Cobra preferred to use guns. He broke radio silence to address his squadron. "I shall make the kill using cannons. Do not join fire without my order. Save your weapons to deal with the American fighters." He stroked the trigger as he closed the range.

## OVERLORD

Mundy had just glanced at the ECM screen and noted some new contacts. "Hmm, computer says there's some F-22s down there. They're way outside the safety corridor."

"Maybe they're chasing someone."

"Could be. Looks like they're really moving, and-" Mundy broke off abruptly. He saw something flashing ahead of him – not on the display panels but out through the windscreen. And the flashes were sending white projectiles through the air. And they were going to hit the plane. "Holy-!"

The first round to hit was a tracer that scored a burning mark square on the Spirit's nose. The next five rounds were high-explosive shells. They punched hard into the thin composite skin of the bomber,

495

gouging a diagonal dotted line across the blended fuselage from the nose across the port engines. Another tracer struck home in the middle of a stream of leaking hydraulic fluid. The engines caught fire.

Escher yelled curses as four dark fighters rushed over his head, one after the other. "We're under attack!"

"No frikking duh!" Mundy replied. He broke radio silence to call for assistance. The enemy had found them – there was no longer any point in hiding. "Any US fighters, this is B-2 Spirit Overlord Three, under fire from multiple bandits. We are hit and require immediate repeat *immediate* assistance!"

The radio crackled back on open channel. "Overlord, this is Orion Flight. We have your bandits and are closing to engage."

Mundy had powered up the radar – an integrated omni-directional antennae that saw the sky all around him like a compact version of the E-3's eyes. He immediately spotted the four bandits coming back around. "Make it fast, Orion!"

## BLACK SQUADRON

Lenonov heard the exchange and guessed he'd have time for one more pass before the American Raptors were in range to fire. He wasn't particularly worried about them. He knew almost exactly where they were. He could dodge their missiles all night, and he suspected that the heavy and complex Air Force superfighters weren't as capable in a dogfight as the Navy Super Hornets, let alone his Flankers. He addressed his pilots again on his coded channel. "Mishka, break your section off and fall in behind me. When the Americans fire, allow the missiles to lock on to you and descend to ground level. Then we will deal with the Raptors the way we do things best."

"Da, comrade Colonel."

Lenonov was able to reacquire the B-2 on infrared. Its hydraulic lines had ignited on the port wing, setting fire to at least one of the engines on that side. The trail of flame was easy to see on infrared, and even easier to spot visually once he got above the plane again. "Fire on his starboard wing," he ordered his wingman. "I will shoot at the port side again."

## OVERLORD

The entire plane shuddered as more shells struck home. The shooting stopped, and two big Russian fighters blew by on either side. "Not good," Escher said. "Control surfaces are shot to hell. We're gonna lose port engines and I can't maintain altitude."

496

"Shit. What are our options?"

"Nearest divert field that can land us is Inkirlik, Turkey. We'd never make it. We can try to put down in Iraq but they do not have secure facilities. I doubt we'll make it over the border anyway."

"So we bail."

"I'll try and get us back over flat terrain."

Mundy hit the radio again, this time to the secure satellite channel that was relayed to the US Strategic Command at Offutt Air Force Base in Omaha, Nebraska. "STRATCOM, STRATCOM, this is asset bravo-two-alpha, callsign Overlord Three, authenticating: Romeo-uniform-sierra-hotel-two-one-one-two. Report aircraft in distress, probable loss over hostile terrain. Engaging emergency locator beacon." Mundy hit a blue button under a plastic shield. The ELB was not designed to guide rescue teams to the crash, but rather to guide a salvo of cluster-munitions-dispensing cruise missiles that would obliterate the wreck of the bomber before it could be recovered.

### ORION FLIGHT

"Dammit, they're all over that B-2!" Duvall exclaimed. The crippled bomber was now clearly visible to radar. The amorphous contact was surrounded by the four enemy fighters. "We'll need to use active guidance-to-target; keep your radar on those bandits until the missiles get terminal lock."

"Roger that, lead."

"Single up the bandits, and fire at max range. Let's get this done by the numbers, people." Tearing across the sky at the Raptor's supercruise speed of Mach 1.2, Major Duvall was in range to fire a second later. "Weapons hot. Fox three!"

### BLACK SQUADRON

"Incoming. Black Three and Four, split off, hang back and let the missiles chase you down. Be in position when I drive the Raptors into the terrain."

"Da, comrade Colonel."

"Black Two, stay with me, and stick close to the B-2. We're going to ride her down and use her as a screen."

"Da, comrade Colonel."

### OVERLORD

"What the hell are they doing?" Mundy and Escher looked out their side windows as the fighters that had fired on them tucked into

497

tight formation on their wings. "It looks like they're using us as a shield!"

## ORION FLIGHT

"Damn. Check fire on the lead bandits! Contacts have merged with the stealth!" Duvall ordered his missile to self-destruct. His wingman did the same. The other bandits were heading for the deck and looked like they were going to be out of the picture. "We need to close within visual to take care of those other bandits."

"Visual?" The stealthy Raptor was built to engage and win from beyond visual range. Close-quarters combat was not its forte.

"Visual, as in right on their asses. We *have* to get them off that stealth!"

## THE PENTAGON – 1652 EDT

The Chief of Staff of the Air Force had not slept through more than ten of the last seventy-two hours. He looked at his chirping cell phone – which he had come to consider his personal tormentor – as though he were deciding whether or not to fastball it into the concrete wall. Fortunately he saw the caller ID tag on the screen just before he reached his decision. He answered the phone. "Speak."

"Sir, this is General Rovelli, at STRATCOM."

"What is it, Ryan?" General Caleb did not say that he had only answered the phone because of who was calling him.

"We just got an emergency channel Flash message from a B-2 over Iran. It's come under fighter attack and is on its way down."

Caleb did not need this kind of news. He pushed his glasses onto his forehead and massaged his eyes. "Follow protocol and bomb the hell out of the wreckage. You already have full authorization."

"Sir, if the B-2 comes down on its current course it's going to be right in the middle of Hamadan." The city is one of the oldest and most densely populated in the country. "We're trying to establish two-way contact with them but it looks like they're in the middle of a running dogfight with the Sukhois that attacked them and some Raptors trying to protect them."

"Get in contact with those Raptors. If the B-2 can't recover control, they'll need to knock that bomber down before it crashes in a populated area!"

"Understood sir."

"Keep me informed." Caleb hung up and sagged in his seat.

# THE BATTLE FOR THE OVERLORD

"Holy Mother of God!" Duvall exclaimed. The B-2 loomed ahead, wreathed in flames, looking like some sort of other-worldly flying aberration. Somewhere behind it there were two Super Flankers. "Look for those bandits. We'll loop over the stealth and come in behind them."

The bandits were waiting for them. The Black Cobra pulled up and caught Screwball's wingman square in his crosshairs. He pulled the trigger and the two-hundred-and-eighty-million-dollar Raptor disintegrated into about two hundred and eighty million pieces.

Orion Four swore as he flew threw the field of debris that had been Orion Two. A moment later, cannon shells tore through his tailplanes and vertical stabilizers.

"Take evasive!" Duvall ordered. "Nose in and beat them into a dive!"

The Raptors came over the top of the loop pulled into a steep dive. The Black Cobra was waiting for that. He completed the cobra maneuver, snapping his nose forward and pushing through negative Gs, and into a shallow dive directly above and behind the Americans. "How disappointing," he said in English on open channel. "I had hoped you would have made this interesting." He fired two AA-11 missiles.

"He's locked on to you guys!" Duvall yelled. "Three, four, peel off!" Three was able to twist into a ten-G turn and get some distance from the missile. Orion Four had lost most of his maneuverability with his damaged tail surfaces. He managed to roll inverted and pull a split-S with his thrust-vectoring, but the missile was far enough behind that it stayed locked on to the hot side of the fighter all the way through the turn. The rear end of the Raptor disappeared in a fireball. The front end porpoised wildly as it broke up. The pilot ejected seconds before the fuel cells gave way and exploded.

"I don't believe this shit!" Orion-3 – Captain Brian "BB" Bradley shook the missile free in time to see his wingman's plane explode. "We're actually *losing* to these goddamn sand monkeys!"

"These guys aren't Iranian," Duvall observed. "They're Russian. And they're very, very good."

*     *     *

The Black Cobra watched the Raptors pull away. He could catch them easily if he used his afterburner, but there was no need to waste fuel. He could be patient; he was driving the Americans down, and soon the rest of his squadron would catch up. The outnumbered Raptors would be forced into a low-speed, close-range dogfight – the type of fight they were not meant for.

"Orion, this is Stargazer. Come back on secure channel Theta One."

"I'm a little busy right now, Stargazer," Duvall replied.

"You must respond on Theta One. Priority comms."

Duvall swore as he switched channels. "Stargazer, Orion Lead on Theta One."

"Orion, stand by for orders from STRATCOM."

*STRATCOM?* Duvall never got orders from the Strategic Command. They controlled bombers and ballistic missiles, not fighters. *What the hell do they want with me?* he wondered.

"Orion Lead, this is General Rovelli of STRATCOM"

"Orion reads, General."

"Orion, I've got some difficult orders for you. That stealth bomber is heading for a crash-landing in a populated area. You will need to prevent that."

"How?"

"Use your imagination. Failing that, use your AMRAAMs."

"Sir, you're asking me to *shoot down* our *own bomber?*"

"Unless the pilot can recover enough to change course, yes."

"Holy shit."

"I know what you're thinking. Don't think about it. You have your orders."

"Understood sir. Now if you'll excuse me, I'm in the middle of a dogfight."

"STRATCOM out."

Major Escher honestly wondered if his controls were even connected to anything else in the plane. The engines were not responding to his throttle inputs. And the elevons seemed completely dead. "I can't steer this thing, Colonel."

"Um, we have a problem," Mundy said.

"You mean besides being on fire and out of control?"

Lt. Col. Mundy pointed to the nav screen. "At our descent rate we are going to crash right about here." He tapped the screen right in the middle of Hamadan. "That's a pretty major city. We'll kill some people, and command won't be able to fry the wreck."

Escher swore and glared at his heads-up display. Twenty-one thousand feet and four hundred knots, still in a shallow dive. "That is a big problem."

Black-3 spotted the light gray Raptors leveling off five miles ahead. He and his wingman pulled up to take them head-on. "Got the targets," he reported to Lenonov.

"Excellent." Lenonov was twelve miles behind, waiting to see how the Americans would react to this.

"Bogeys, twelve o' clock!" Duvall yelled. The Flankers were already firing their guns. Duvall pulled back on the stick and throttle and rolled inverted, taking himself out of the line of fire. Black-3 tried to follow with his crosshairs but immediately overshot the rapidly maneuvering target.

Orion-3 was not so quick on the draw. He turned right, and Black-4 followed him into a scissors engagement. BB Bradley tried to shake the Flanker with a series of sharp turns, but the tighter-turning Flanker closed the gap until the Raptor crossed his nose. A burst of 30mm shells cut into one of the engines, creating an inviting infrared target that an AA-11 missile could not miss.

"I'm hit!" BB yelled into the radio. Duvall heard a second blast over the channel. "Hit *again!!* I can't hold her. Engines gone. I'm bailing out..." And then Screwball Duvall was all alone in the midst of a pack of lethal enemy fighters. And he still had an impossible mission to complete.

Lenonov was impressed with the lead Raptor who had managed to juke Black-3 out of a firing line. The other Raptor had been taken out but had drawn Black-4 out of the fight. For the moment, it was up to the Black Cobra to deal with the last Raptor. But now the Raptor did something completely unexpected. Using afterburner, it went into a fast climbing turn, putting itself far out of range of Black Squadron's guns and missiles and chasing after the crippled B-2 Spirit. "*Promudobliadskaja pizdoprojebina,*" Lenonov cursed the American. "Stay and fight, you cowardly bitch!"

\*　　　\*　　　\*

501

"She's coming up," Escher said. "Starboard engines are cooperating a little, and I'm getting just enough of a push to balance this sucker out and get some control back."

"Enough to level off?"

"Maybe. Enough to get us away from the city, anyway."

The crippled Spirit showed up plainly on radar. Duvall checked its heading again. It was still on a glide slope to crash land in downtown Hamadan. "God forgive me," he said, as he locked an AMRAAM at maximum range and fired it off.

"Missile! We got a missile tracking us!" Mundy stared in horror at the ECM panel. "Mother of God, it's an AMRAAM! The Raptors are trying to knock us down!"

"They're trying to keep us from landing in the city," Escher said calmly. "Tell them I have the plane, and they should disengage."

"Orion! Orion! This is Overlord Three! Disengage! We have control of the plane and are steering away from the city! Check fire!"

"Roger, Overlord," Duvall radioed back. "Sorry. I was ordered to make sure…"

"Understood, Orion, just call the dogs off."

"Wilco." Duvall tapped his wepcon screen and was about to self-destruct the missile when he died in a fireball.

The Black Cobra watched the blossoming explosion with profound disappointment. By firing the AA-11 missile he had only wished to provoke the American flight leader into reengaging. But the Raptor pilot, plainly distracted, had just sat there obliviously while the Russian missile bored in to his redlined engines. The afterburners back-blew through the turbines, gutting them and splitting the fighter apart. The main fuel cell ruptured and the spray of fuel immediately ignited. A spectacular kill, to be sure, but not very satisfying.

Lenonov turned his attention to the B-2 bomber. It was leveling off and banking left. As he wondered how he should force it down, he noticed the American AMRAAM missile closing on it. He watched the result with great interest.

"Orion? *Orion, come in!*" Mundy was frantic. "Dammit, we lost him."

"Did we lose his missile?" Escher wondered.

502

Mundy looked back at the ECM screen. "No. Ten miles and closing fast. Fifteen seconds to impact."

Escher released his controls and grabbed the ejection handles. "I guess I'll see you on the ground then." And without further ado the pilot blasted off into the night.

Mundy sighed, leaned back and braced himself in his seat, and followed the Major out.

Moments after the crew ejected, the AMRAAM connected with Overlord 3's right wing. That side of the plane immediately lost lift and the bomber slewed sideways before dropping into a right-hand bank. The pilot-less bomber turned itself back toward the city of Hamadan. The stub of the right wing clipped the top of an apartment building and sent the bomber into a cartwheel. The trailing edge of the left wing crashed through the side of an ancient mosque. The wing sheered off, and the fuselage bounced off the dome and tumbled on, like a Frisbee rolling on its edge. The bomber skipped across the roof of a department store and into the parking lot, losing momentum as its tough reinforced composite airframe took out everything in its path. It finally came to rest, burying its knife-edge nose in the ornate wall of an ancient library.

Lenonov flew low and slow over the trail of the downed bomber until he came across the wreck itself. He flew in tight circles, documenting the crash site with his onboard camera. He opened the secure command channel on his radio. "Black Cobra calling Molehill Actual."

Rannovich himself responded almost immediately. "You are calling to report success." This was not a question.

"Of course. I am sending you video of the fully-intact fuselage section of a B-2 that I brought down over Hamadan."

Rannovich took one look at the images. "It came down in the city itself?"

Lenonov sighed. "Yes sir. The civilian deaths-"

"This is excellent. The Americans won't dare shoot a missile at the wreck if it's in the middle of a dense civilian population." He paused for a moment. "But just in case I am wrong about their resolve, continue to orbit the crash site and deal with any bomber or cruise missile they may send after it. I'll send another squadron of fighters to support you in a moment. I need the wreckage to survive until my camera crew can get there and get out."

"Very well sir."

"Congratulations, Colonel. You have shown me that you may still be of use."

## THE PENTAGON

General Caleb answered his phone by asking "You have an update?"

General Rovelli sighed at the other end of the line. "The B-2 came down in the city. I just got word from an E-3 that saw the whole thing."

"How did this happen?"

"Apparently the Raptors got taken out in a scrape with the Flankers that attacked the bomber. The flight leader managed to get off a shot at the B-2 to take it down, but right then the bomber pilot was recovering and turning away from Hamadan. The missile knocked it back over the city."

"Crap."

"I'm sorry sir, but I'm afraid I must recommend we follow protocol. The last telemetry we got from the B-2 makes it look to us like the fuselage may be relatively intact, and we can't allow any material to be recovered."

Rovelli didn't know the half of it. Caleb's mind flashed back to that Situation Room meeting when all this started – had it only been two weeks ago? – when the CIA announced that the Iranians were in all probability holding three American prototype low-yield nukes. Those nukes could only be armed with the onboard computer of a B-2 Spirit, such as the one that was now down in enemy territory. "That decision will have to be made by the President, but I'll pass along your recommendation, Ryan."

"Good luck, sir. It's your problem now."

*Not for long.* Caleb ended the call and sent another to the White House. "This is General Caleb. I need to speak to the President."

He was put through to Lane Bender. "This is the President's Chief of Staff. The President is taking a nap."

"Then you need to wake him up."

"Is it really that important?"

Caleb's mind by now was racing through a long list of targets that could be hit by those three nukes. He thought of the proud carrier USS *Ronald Reagan* vaporized in a ten kiloton blast. He thought of the CENTCOM headquarters going up in a mushroom cloud with half of

Kuwait City. He thought of Baghdad burning and millions dying under lethal fallout. "Yes, Ms. Bender, it really is."

## HAMADAN – 20 MINUTES LATER

The man called Boris chuckled as he watched out of the helicopter's small side window. "I think it was Stalin who said 'Nothing controls a crowd like a tank.'"

Valentina, the woman sitting next to him, said nothing but she looked out as well. Two huge T-80s were rolling down the street below, dispersing the crowd of Iranians who had been jolted awake by the crash. The Mi-24d Hind gunship they were riding landed roughly once a space had been cleared in the street near the crash site.

"Oh boy, oh boy." Boris could barely contain himself as he unfastened his seatbelt and clawed at the door handle. Once free of the helicopter he ran to the wreck, climbing up the pile of rubble against the top side of the bomber's fuselage. Valentina jogged after him, while behind her the camera crew set up their equipment. Boris and Valentina were Russian Mafia – like many in their organization they were known only on a first-name basis or by epithets. In most circles they were called Valentina and Boris, the *Teknikiri*.

The Technicians climbed up over the rubble of the library wall into the open cockpit escape hatch over the bombardier's seat. "First thing we do is find and disable the ELB," Valentina said in English. Speaking English helped her to concentrate on the language of the stolen maintenance manuals she had memorized.

"Da. Should be here in bulkhead, behind cockpit." Boris pulled a folded up schematic from his back pocket and unfurled it to pinpoint where he needed to cut. He opened his backpack and produced a cordless 18-volt power drill and a two-inch hole saw, and began to cut into the composite airframe just above the center console. "Find the arming computer module," he shouted over the drill.

Valentina unscrewed the bombardier's display panels and cut through the cables with a Spetsnaz-issue fighting dagger. She crawled into the avionics bay up to her waist holding a small flashlight in her mouth until she found the weapons module of the computer. She double-checked the serial number prefix against a list she had written on her left arm before disconnecting the computer and pulling it out with her. "I have it!" she exclaimed.

"Excellent." Boris had just put the drill away and was inspecting what was behind the bulkhead. "Here is the ELB." The small component was epoxied to the interior of the bulkhead. Its indicator LEDs were flashing. "How do I disconnect it?"

"Just shoot the thing."

"Good idea." Boris reached into his shoulder holster and produced a 12.3mm UDAR revolver and noisily fired an armor-piercing slug through the ELB unit. Its indicator lights went dark.

They left the cockpit and found the Iranian camera crew at work outside. One of them was excitedly and inaccurately recounting the battle that produced the wreck, pointing out the holes in the left engine nacelle produced by Lenonov's 30mm shells.

Valentina swore as she ran past the cameras. "Those idiots," she told Boris. "We aren't supposed to be seen on the news."

"The boss will edit the video before it is sent out. He knows what he's doing."

Valentina stopped next to the Hind gunship and looked up at the fighters circling overhead. "I hope so," she said.

## THE PENTAGON – SAME TIME, 1816 EDT

The President looked through the big screen, bleary-eyed. He was wearing a robe, his hair was tussled, and he was yawning uncontrollably. Caleb didn't feel sorry for him. At least the Commander-in-Chief had been able to grab a few hours' sleep. "What's the mini-yuhaah..." President McNeil yawned mid-question. "Sorry; minimum blast yield you'd need to destroy that plane?"

"I'll differ to General Rainier on that one," Caleb said. "He's the weapons expert on my staff."

Major General Paul Rainier had just been dragged out of bed himself. In the back of a staff car on his way to the Pentagon he'd managed to put on the top half of a clean Air Force uniform and he hid his bed head under a cap. He had also shaved with an electric razor while walking through the E-ring to the Air Force Chief of Staff's conference room. At least he looked professional to the Telepresence cameras. Under the table he was wearing track pants. "Mr. President, we're pretty sure that the fuselage is largely intact. That is, that the engines, the avionics and the weapons systems are all within a few yards of each other in a concentrated debris field. That being the case, we can wipe out the wreck with nothing more than a five-hundred-pound warhead."

"And what kind of effect would that have on nearby civilians and structures?"

"Well, it would make the hole in the library a lot bigger..."

"What library?"

"Sorry sir," Caleb spoke again. "We hadn't briefed you on that. The point where the Emergency Locator Beacon is transmitting from is against the wall of this building." He pointed to a slide displayed on the opposite wall. "This is a thousand-year-old library containing mostly historic records and religious texts."

"Dammit. The bomber crashed into *that?*"

"Into the wall, anyway."

"The bomb blast we're talking about will damage the building further," Rainier went on. "But it won't destroy it. As far as civilian casualties, we're hoping local authorities will have cordoned off the site and evacuated the library. Further casualties should be very minimal."

"Leaving the crash site intact is not a viable option, I assume."

"No sir," Caleb said. "Normal protocol aside, it is absolutely imperative that we destroy the weapons control module. That's what Rannovich needs to deploy the stolen low-yield nukes."

"Those three from-" the President broke off. He glanced at Rainier.

"General Rainier is fully briefed, sir," Caleb guessed why the President hesitated. "He's my go-to guy for planning the command bunker strike. He has total clearance."

"Did I authorize his clearance?"

"Yes sir. Three days ago."

"If you say so."

"Anyway sir, if Rannovich gets ahold of that control module he could conceivably use it to arm those three nukes."

"And those are small enough to be fitted into a Shahab-III intermediate-range ballistic missile," Rainier added.

"I understand those missiles are hopelessly inaccurate."

"They're good enough to drop a nuke on a major city or airbase. They also have enough range to land in Israel."

The President frowned deeply. "If Iran nukes Israel, Israel will nuke Iran back and there will be nothing we can do to stop them."

"Correct sir," Caleb said. He knew what the President was thinking. The National Security Council had determined after repeated calculation and simulation that of all the possible paths that could develop from that scenario, there was a ninety-percent chance that it would lead to World War III.

"Take it out. Do not let anyone recover that computer."

Rainer opened a folder. "We have several options for a tactical strike that-"

McNeil waved Rainier off. "I don't care about the details. Do it whichever way you think is best."

"Yes sir," Caleb nodded. "We'll take care of it."

"Good night," the President signed off.

"What's the best option?" Caleb asked his expert. "Cruise missile?"

"They'd expect that, and they'll be ready to shoot it down."

"Is that possible?"

"They've got Sukhoi-35 or -37 Flankers with the best look-down/shoot-down radar in the world. You bet they can nail a cruise missile if they know where it's going. No, I recommend sending in a pair of Raptors to launch a JSOW. Quick and clean and a lot harder to stop."

"It had better be quick."

"We already have the planes in the air," Rainier told him. "We just have to give them the target."

## F-22 FLIGHT, 16 MILES NORTH OF HAMADAN
## 25 MINUTES LATER

"Confirming target coordinates, GPS guidance activated, weapon armed." Captain Ryan "Race" Bannon said as he poked at his weapons display.

"Roger lead," his wingman replied. "I got my eyes on the hostiles." The two Raptors were inside Lenenov's patrol zone but so far the stealthy superfighters had not been noticed.

"Bomb's away." The weapons hatch on the Raptor's belly opened for only five seconds and released the glide bomb.

## BLACK SQUADRON

"Contact, forty-one miles ahead!" Black-4 called.

"What kind of contact?" Lenonov asked.

"Brief trace, separating, first contact is gone, small contact tracking southwards and descending…"

"A stealth fighter just tossed a bomb or missile at the crash site," Lenonov figured. "Shoot down the missile!"

Black-4 tried, but by the time his AA-12 caught up with the glide bomb it was locked in to its glide slope. The missile blew up short of its target, having almost no effect on the trajectory of the JSOW. The bomb slammed into the underside of the wrecked B-2 and detonated, gutting the derelict airframe.

Lenonov muttered a curse when he saw the explosion on the ground. He radioed the command center. "Molehill, this is Black Cobra. The Americans snuck in with a stealth fighter and destroyed the crash site."

"No matter," Rannovich calmly replied. "I have what I need."

## THE BUNKER, ONE HOUR LATER

The helicopter flew slowly through the cavernous underground hanger, directed to its landing space. Rannovich, Ahmadinejad and a few technicians waited nearby. The two *mafya teknikiri* stepped out of the chopper; Boris proudly held out the captured computer component.

"This is it?" Ahmadinejad asked.

One of the bomb techs took the control module. "This is it," he confirmed.

"How long until the weapons will be ready?"

"Forty-eight hours at the most."

"Excellent."

Rannovich looked to his camera crew. "Prep that footage and release it to the Iranian news service."

## ALEXANDRIA, VA – 2108 EDT

General Caleb was glaring at his television. Now that the crisis with the B-2 had apparently been neutralized, he had gone home and was trying to get some rest. Turning on the news was a mistake. The news annoyed him. But just before he turned it off he saw something that arrested his attention.

*"We received this footage from the Iranian news services,"* Brian Williams announced.

Caleb sat up straight when he saw the first frame.

The screen showed a night-vision picture of the crashed B-2 fuselage. A narrator speaking in Farsi was translated by a female voice with a light accent. *"This American stealth bomber was marauding innocent villagers in the mountains northwest of Tehran, when it was engaged by elements of the Iranian Air Forces. They tracked it visually, defeating its sophisticated stealth. They damaged it with cannon fire and finished it off with a short range missile. The American bomber pilots, knowing they were about to crash, deliberately steered their crippled warplane into the historic city of Hamadan. The bomber damaged several buildings, including an apartment building and a mosque, before coming to rest buried in the side of this library. After this footage was taken, the Americans bombed the crash site, killing dozens of civilians and destroying the library which had preserved our nation's history since the Eleventh Century..."*

Caleb ignored the embellished report. He was focused on two people crawling out of the bomber cockpit. Even on the night vision view, he could tell they were not Iranian civilians. They were carrying something the size of a small briefcase. He knew exactly what it was. He picked up the phone. "Paul, sorry to wake you again."

"I was just about to call you, sir," General Rainier said. "You have the news on?"

"Yeah."

"You see what I see?"

"That's the weapons module, isn't it?"

"That's it."

"How long before they will be able to launch the weapons?"

"If they know what they are doing, and I suspect they do, I'd say thirty-six hours to reprogram the nukes, twelve to fit them to missiles, and then they just have to position them for launch."

"We have two days to figure out how to hit that bunker."

"That's our deadline now, yessir."

"I'm calling the President. You call Casey and ask him how soon we can debrief his Russian friend."

Rainier sighed. "I hate talking to Casey."

## CHAPTER 24: NO WAY OUT BUT DOWN

## THE PENTAGON E-RING – 0540 HOURS, JUNE 5<sup>TH</sup>

"No way," General Rainier said. "That's absolutely impossible." He was looking at a schematic on a large computer screen in a Pentagon conference room. Casey, Antonov, General Chappelle, and General Caleb were with him. The schematics showed a network of bunkers, deep underground. "We don't have any weapon that can reach that deep," Rainier went on, "And even if we *could* hit them, you built this place to be immune to any kind of conventional bomb."

Antonov said something in Russian and Casey translated. "He wasn't exactly sure what our new weapons were capable of, so he kind of planned for everything."

"Even a nuke would be useless," Rainier continued. "The whole structure is cushioned on giant shock absorbers. They could be hit by a magnitude-9 earthquake and barely feel it. And the command unit is EMP shielded, heat shielded, ceramic armor... we'd have to hit them with a megaton warhead right on top of the bunker, and it's a thousand feet underground." He switched to another view; a 3-D wireframe drawing. "Even these ventilation shafts are bomb-proof. The shortest one is over four hundred feet long, and there's no possible way to get a bomb through that machinery on top."

"What about a double-tap?" Casey asked.

"A what?"

"Use two bombs. Hit the top of the shaft to clear it, and then drop another one down the hole."

"There's too much stuff at the bottom too. You'd have to drop three or four bombs in there to clean out machinery and wreckage before you would hit the bunker itself. And dropping even one bomb straight down a thousand-foot shaft is close enough to impossible."

"Even then it wouldn't work," Chappelle noted. "The shafts dogleg half way down. We wouldn't get a straight shot."

"Wait a second," Caleb pointed at the screen. "Why is that shaft so shallow? It's only four hundred feet long; all the others are at least a thousand. Does it just end in the middle of the mountain?"

The Russian spoke, and Casey again translated the explanation. "That shaft meets an old borehole. There are several of them in the mountain. Apparently they were looking for uranium up there a few years ago, and never found any."

Rainier looked at the shaft thoughtfully. "Maybe we could drop a bomb down that shaft. It doesn't seem as well-protected as the others."

The Russian shook his head and said "It is offset. Six meters."

"That won't work then. We'd have to penetrate six or seven hundred feet to reach it from the top, or if we went down the borehole we'd still have another four hundred to go." The generals had stared at the image for a long while. They could see the entire bunker complex, and the mountain that protected it. Apart from ventilation shafts it had no weakness.

"Is four hundred feet close enough for a nuke?" Chappelle asked.

Rainier pulled a calculator and a sheet of tables out of his briefcase. "About five megatons, at that range, would vaporize the whole bunker. But we haven't had bombs that big in our stockpile since the seventies, and they wouldn't fit down that hole anyways. The biggest thing we have is the B83 mod 2 high-yield strategic bomb, which packs two and a half megatons. If you want guaranteed total destruction of that bunker, we'd need to detonate it within no more than two hundred feet. Thing is though, that sucker's over five feet in diameter, and there's no way it's going to squeeze through a ventilation shaft. Our most realistic option is the variable-yield B61 mod 12, which is a lot slimmer and goes up to one-point-six megatons. If we set that for maximum yield, we'd have to get it in around a hundred and fifty feet from the ceiling of this bunker. The trick of course, is going to be getting any of our bombs that deep."

Chappelle was silent for a moment. Then he looked at Antonov. "What diameter were those boreholes?"

"Sixty centimeters," Antonov answered.

"Two feet," Caleb said. "We couldn't even fit a normal BLU bunker-buster down there anyway."

"But we widened that shaft to, uh, make way for air exchanger machineries. Now it is a meter and a half. And the borehole goes lower, another forty meters I think, below air exchanger."

Rainier looked hopeful for a second, but then frowned. "Five feet is still an awfully small target. And three hundred feet is still too far to punch through with one of our bombs. In order to slam a nuke through all that rock..." Rainier trailed off when he glanced at Casey, who had an odd expression on his face. "You look like a man with a crazy idea."

Casey smiled. "Antonov, wait outside a moment, please."

When the Russian had left the veteran CIA man spoke again. "Generals, have you ever heard of the Nuclear Hornet papers?"

## THE WHITE HOUSE SITUATION ROOM, ONE HOUR LATER

President McNeil and Vice President Bowman dropped everything they had for the emergency meeting with Casey, Rainier and the Joint Chiefs. "Where's McLeary?" the VP asked.

"In a meeting with the NSA and the DCI at the NRO," General Chappelle said, double-checking his notes on his smartphone. "I think I got those acronyms straight. Anyway, I briefed all of them on the phone and we have their support."

"For what?" the President asked.

Chappelle sat down and opened his briefcase. "Sirs, we may have a way to end this war before Rannovich can bring his nukes online."

The President looked at each his military commanders. They all displayed the same conviction that the CJC did. "Well, that would be just terrific. What's your plan?"

"We take out Rannovich's command bunker."

"I thought we had no way to do that except pounding it repeatedly with ICBMs until you melted it of the mountain. That's what you said yesterday."

"We found an alternative. But time is of the essence sir; we need to get the ball rolling on every aspect of this operation as soon as possible and we need your authorization for some preliminary actions," Chappelle told him.

"Shoot."

"We need an Aurora to make a low-level pass over the target area."

"Absolutely not," McNeil said curtly. Then after a split-second's hesitation he asked "Why?"

"We need high resolution ground-penetrating radar scans of the mountain, and also better ImInt and SigInt data for the air defenses in the immediate area."

"Risk to the Aurora is minimal, sir," General Caleb added. He had his cell phone on the desk with his thumb on the *send* button. "We only need one pass, at Mach six, and it will be gone before the Iranians know what buzzed them."

"We can't make the strike without better data," Chappelle continued. "And only the Aurora can provide it."

513

The President nodded. "Alright, fine. But if it gets shot down I want a cruise missile right up its ass to vaporize the wreckage and prevent the crew from being captured." He paused and frowned. "I know that sounds cold but-"

"It's done," Chappelle promised. "We already scrambled a B-1 loaded with ALCMs."

"Go," Caleb said into his phone.

"Next we need to build a bomb," the CJC said. "We need a Robust Nuclear Earth Penetrator with a modified and hardened casing and refitted with a B61 warhead."

General Rainier had his phone out now. "We already have the components at Los Alamos, we just need to assemble the device and fly it to the METO."

"A B61? Wait a second." After winning the election, McNeil had studied up on his country's nuclear arsenal. He had memorized the list of all in-service warhead types and their maximum yields. "Are we talking about using a megaton-range nuclear bunker-buster?" The President asked.

"Yes," the Joint Chiefs all said.

Rainier explained. "The man we brought out of Tehran, the guy who designed the facility, confirmed that only a bomb of this size will have the desired effect. The underground blast should completely destroy the bunker network and vaporize the command center. But anything less than this would be a futile effort. The bunker is shielded to be immune to anything up to and including a nuclear blast any smaller than this magnitude."

The President stood up and started pacing behind his chair. "I can't believe what I just heard. I have the top military men in the country and the CIA in here telling me they want to use nuclear weapons on Iran."

"Not *weapons, plural*," Chappelle hastened to clarify. "Just one weapon, and it would be very far underground, so-"

"You're talking about starting nuclear war!"

"No, I'm talking about-"

"Using nuclear weapons, in anger, in wartime," McNeil interrupted again. "What do you want to call it?"

"Sir, we're looking at nuclear war starting already," Casey said. "About forty hours from now, Rannovich will have nuclear missiles in his hands, most likely aimed at Israel. If those missiles are launched at Israel, they will respond in kind. From there we're looking at least a mere thirty million civilian deaths between just those two countries, then potentially total warfare blowing the entire Middle East apart, and finally the very real possibility of us and the Russians and the Chinese all getting pulled into World War Three. Someone is going to drop the bomb sooner or later, Mr. President. But if we're the ones to do it, we can make sure it's the last one."

President McNeil sat down, shaking his head. "You're saying we *need* to use the bomb to *prevent* a full-scale nuclear war."

"Yes sir."

"This sounds like dialog out of 'Dr. Strangelove' except you're totally serious."

"Yes sir," Casey said again, after swallowing hard. "The situation can only be contained if we take out the guys with their finger on the button. If we exercise our nuclear arsenal in a very tactical measure, we can eliminate those people, their button, and probably the bombs themselves in an instant. Game over, we win. Or we can keep playing Rannovich's game until he escalates the conflict on his own timetable. We know you don't want that."

"Mr. President," Rainier said, still holding his phone with his thumb on the *send* button, "this might not be our last option, but it's the best one we have right now and it is imperative that we make preparations immediately in case we do need resort to this plan. We're not asking you for an irreversible decision yet; we're just getting ready so we can act promptly if it comes to that."

The President scowled. He looked over at Bowman, who always wore a scowl anyway. He made a small nod. "Okay, build it," McNeil said.

"Do it," Rainier told whoever was on his phone.

"Lastly," Chapelle said, as the CNO also brought his phone out, "We need your permission to share some of our data with a civilian contractor. We'll need to use computer modeling to determine exactly how to deliver the bomb."

"What contractor?"

"A Boeing program rep, currently on board the *Ronald Reagan*," Admiral Marsh answered. "He can use flight simulation software to model the target profile for a Super Hornet to deliver the weapon."

"Now I see where this is going." The VP leaned back in his seat, as if trying to physically distance himself from the people planning the operation. "Mr. President, I strongly advise against this whole scheme."

McNeil was surprised by Bowman's reaction. "What are you talking about?"

Bowman, who had long ago been one of President Ronald Reagan's principal advisors, felt like he was having déjà vu. "Let them tell you. You'll see what I mean."

Paul Chappelle looked across the table at Jarrod Casey. "You might as well lay it out. It was your idea."

Casey knew he was already being disavowed by the military but he didn't care. "Mr. President, during the latter days of the Cold War a Pentagon think tank devised a zero-strike option contingency plan, calling for the Navy to use F/A-18s to deliver nuclear bunker-busters to destroy hardened Soviet missile silos. The Nuclear Hornet papers detailed a bombing maneuver that would greatly improve the effective penetration of any weapon – a tactic called slam-bombing. This is when a fighter-bomber dives from its maximum altitude at its maximum speed and releases the weapon from a vertical angle of attack at beyond terminal velocity."

"As I recall," the Vice President added, "the Navy rejected that proposal out of hand, because, A, there's no way they could have deployed enough Hornets to pull it off, B, there's no way they could have made it past the air defenses, and C, the maneuver itself wouldn't work."

The military commanders looked away. Admiral Marsh nodded assent.

Casey persisted. "The first two points won't apply to this case, and the maneuver itself *does* work. The Navy and Air Force conducted a test on the seventh of June, 1985, at Burdick Air Force Base in North Dakota. An F/A-18 Hornet assigned to the Naval Air Warfare Center successfully dropped a dummy bunker-buster at an altitude of less than a thousand feet and pulled out of a supersonic dive safely. The bomb casing over-penetrated a hundred-and-twenty-foot-thick concrete silo door, impacted an Atlas missile, and inadvertently caused the fuel residue inside its rockets to ignite and destroy the weapon, but not before the test bomb transmitted its data. Simultaneously, scientists from Sandia and Los Alamos detonated a low-yield nuclear bomb similar in design to a B61 primer underground at the Nevada test range after subjecting it to an impact with similar G-forces to a supersonic weapon drop. Both tests were successful and confirmed that at least that aspect of the Nuclear Hornet plan was viable."

"How in the *hell* do *you* know about *any* of that?" Hal Bowman demanded. He already knew what Casey had said about the test, and

516

more.  There had been no separate nuclear test in Nevada.  President Reagan had been so enthusiastic about the potential of Nuclear Hornet he had authorized a live drop of a nuclear weapon in North Dakota.  The weapon had built-in safeties in case it failed to penetrate the silo, but nonetheless it was an unbelievably reckless act.  Although, compared to some of the things the last few administrations had allowed to happen…

Casey was smiling.  He had never told anyone about this.  Even the DCI didn't know about his role with the Nuclear Hornet papers.  "After the Navy rejected the proposal, President Reagan gave the papers to the CIA to be leaked as disinformation to the Kremlin.  I was part of that operation, undercover in Moscow, twenty-five years ago."

Vice President Bowman's jaw dropped.  The military commanders turned and stared at the DDO.  McNeil did not change his expression.  "Did it work?" he asked.

Casey shrugged.  "It's hard to say what effect it actually had.  But we do know that the same day Mikhail Gorbachev saw the Nuclear Hornet papers, he initiated the arrangements for the Reykjavik summit."

The Reykjavik summit was where Gorbachev presented Reagan with his grave concerns about the Americans' Strategic Defense Initiative, and began to discuss disarmament.  It was the official beginning of the end of the Cold War.  President Brett McNeil asked again "You think he was convinced it would work?"

Casey let himself think back a few years.  He had been undercover as the top military analyst in the GRU – Soviet Military Intelligence.  He had actually handed the papers to the Soviet Premier himself.  He had stood there and watched as Gorbachev read the summaries of the reports, and the color drained from the Premier's face.  "It must have seemed feasible to him, sir."

"So we do it again," the President summed up, "for real this time, and have a Super Hornet dive-bomb a nuke into the Alborz Mountains and take out the bunker?"

"Basically, yes."

The President was silent for several seconds.  Then he said "Well, the more I think about it, that doesn't sound like such a terrible idea.  Why don't you guys tell me how you think we're going to make this happen?"

The Joint Chiefs breathed a collective sigh of relief.

Brett McNeil made a small smile. "Oh, and Terry, go ahead and make your phone call. I'm not giving this operation my approval yet, but you may as well get prepared."

## 120,000 FT. ABOVE THE CASPIAN SEA
## SAME TIME, 2000 LOCAL JUNE 5$^{TH}$

"Copy that, Northern Light, we are beginning our descent." Major Curtis put his Aurora into a gentle, banking dive, leaving the assigned orbit pattern and heading toward the Alborz Mountains beyond the Iranian north coast.

"What's going on?" the other pilot asked from the back of the plane. The Air Force had their six Auroras remaining aloft for up to forty-eight hours at a time, so the planes carried two separate crews to alternate the duties. Crew 2 was manning the controls now while the three members of crew 1 were lounging in the berths behind them.

"We're goin' in for a GPR scan," Captain Wright, the crew 2 systems officer said.

"How does the radar screen look?" Curtis asked Lt. Martin, the navigator, who was sitting at the controls behind his right shoulder.

"All clear."

"Emissions?"

"None. We're a ghost."

The navigator's title was a misnomer. The computer did all the calculations and gave the flight path data directly to the pilot. The navigator's real job was to find threats and make the plane invisible to those threats. The systems officer, seated on the left side of the cockpit, had the opposite task. He used the Aurora's collection of sophisticated instruments to find things that were designed to be hidden – like underground bunkers. The pilot sat in front of them, in the center of the wide cockpit. Curtis delicately finessed the incredibly powerful engines to direct the big plane toward its target.

The Aurora is possibly the worst-kept secret in military aviation. Although the government denies the existence of any operational aircraft and insists that the program was cancelled in the early nineties, hundreds of substantiated rumors and credible sightings make it clear that the mysterious Aurora is flying today. It has been spotted in several places from Scotland to Scottsdale, Arizona. Its sonic booms rattled windows in Orange County, California and Orange County, Florida. Radio hobbyists in the San Fernando Valley have heard air traffic controllers at Edwards Air Force Base talking down an airplane that covers twenty miles in thirty seconds on its landing approach. From the archives of the reports, aviation experts have been able to piece together what the Aurora looks like and guess at its unique hypersonic propulsion system.

It is painted black, with an anti-reflective coating, which makes it so dark you could shine a flashlight right at it and the beam would simply disappear. Its wings are a broad delta shape, down-turned at the tips, blended with a curved fuselage and rounded engine nacelles, much like a B-2 stealth bomber but stretched out longer. The engines are the most unusual part of the aircraft. They are believed to be some sort of pulse-detonation / scramjet hybrid, capable of attaining hypersonic speeds possibly exceeding Mach six. No funding has ever actually been allocated for the Aurora, according to Pentagon audit reports, but the various technologies that would make it possible are openly funded under research and development contracts to Boeing, General Electric and Northrop-Grumman.

"Radar threat warning," Martin said. "Just a sweep from the coast."

The plane is virtually invisible on radar but an attentive operator might have picked out its ghostly return. It only looks to be about the size of a bat on a radar screen but someone would still notice a bat flying at supersonic speeds. For this reason Curtis was descending to low altitude to fly in literally under the radar.

"Leveling off at five hundred feet," Curtis announced.

"We're in the grass," the navigator confirmed. "Hit it."

The pilot looked over his shoulder at crew 1. "Hold on back there."

Two massive air scoops extended from beneath the wings, which would make the plane a little more visible on radar but not when flying this low. Curtis punched the throttles forward, and the huge scoops force-fed tons of air into the white-hot engines, mixing with cold fuel and exploding, pulsing enormous thrust out the exhaust diffusers and into the night. In only thirteen seconds the plane accelerated from Mach two to Mach six, screaming across the sky at over four thousand miles an hour. The plane crossed the coastline a few seconds later.

An elderly fisherman casting a line off a dock looked up as a black shape blotted out the stars above him, and then he was thrown on his back by a concussion of air and deafened by the sonic boom.

The computer had plotted a course into the mountains that would avoid known military installations and populated areas, but the shockwave of noise did not go unnoticed by a handful of locals. The Aurora climbed, banked and dipped, following the contours of the hills, curving around mountains and hugging the floors of the valleys. The computer worked out a COLA flight path for the pilot to follow, allowing enough time for the human to react to mountains rushing toward him at six times the speed of sound. They covered two hundred miles in only three minutes.

"Approaching target area," the navigator said.

"Bringing cameras and GPR online," the systems officer reported.

Something on the navigator's screen chirped. "Threat radar sweep," he informed the pilot. "Recording the signature."

The Aurora had three objectives to complete on one single pass over the target. They would scan the mountain with ground-penetrating radar, photograph the entire area, and allow themselves to be searched by as many different radar systems as possible and analyze the signals.

"Slowing down for the pass," Curtis said.

The other five people in the plane braced themselves as the pilot chopped their speed in half. The plane was still moving at the incredible velocity of three times the speed of sound when it cleared a ridge and came in sight of the mountain.

"We're lit up like a Christmas tree," Martin reported. "Three sources have locks."

"Commencing GPR and photo scans," Wright said.

Three digital cameras mounted under the plane's nose whirred busily, snapping photographs at lightning speed. The systems officer manually aimed the radar system at the rocky south face of the mountain, sweeping the area directly above the command bunker the Russian named Andre Antonov had built.

"Missiles," Martin calmly announced, "two contacts, on our four and nine o'clocks, ranges three miles. Eight seconds to impact."

"I need six seconds," Wright said, with not quite as much calm in his voice. He concentrated on the complex displays in front of him.

Major Curtis remained cool. Two radar-guided missiles had been fired at essentially point-blank range. They would reach them only a second after the systems officer could finish his job. But the Aurora had a few tricks to deal with enemy missiles. "Deploy the FOTD," he ordered.

The navigator punched a button, and a decoy device about the size and shape of a traffic pylon was jettisoned from the Aurora's tail. It trailed five hundred feet behind them on a fiber-optic cable. As the Aurora received the radar pulses from the ground stations, it retransmitted false echoes from the towed decoy and tricked the missiles into locking onto the strong artificial radar return. The missiles collided and exploded, vaporizing the FOTD device but not harming the airplane. The fiber optic cable was automatically discarded.

"Got it!" Captain Wright shouted. "Scans complete; get us outta here!"

Curtis pushed the throttles back to full power and the plane jumped back to full speed. The enemy air defense grid launched more missiles but the weapons hit the wall at Mach four and the Aurora was safely out of range.

## THE SITUATION ROOM – SAME TIME.

The Vice President was still not pleased with the Nuclear Hornet plan. "If I have this straight, you identified a weak point in the mountain where you can drop an RNEP to the necessary depth, but you need a Super Hornet to dive into the ground to do it?"

"Yes, sir," General Chappelle answered.

"Why can't a B-2 drop it from 60,000 feet?"

"For one thing, sir, despite its stealth characteristics it will very likely be spotted and shot down. We learned last night that our B-2s are not as invincible as we thought. We'll need to penetrate a cordon of overlapping radar defenses, which could track even a stealth bomber. A squadron of Super Hornets supported by Growlers would have a much better chance against the defenses, especially if they made a low-level approach. Also, the shaft is too small to hit with a guided bomb from that altitude. We need to drop a weapon that is two feet wide down a shaft that is only five feet wide. That's an 18-inch margin of error. Only one of our best Navy aviators can pull that off, and only with a Super Hornet and its precision strike package. It's the only plane in the world that is fast enough, stealthy enough, smart enough, and also has enough payload capacity to put this bomb where we need it." General Chappelle showed the President and Vice President a photo of the underside of an F/A-18e. "See this fuel tank here? That's mounted on a centerline universal hardpoint capable of supporting any munitions in our arsenal that weigh less than fifteen thousand pounds.

No other strike fighter in the world has that capacity. And our bomb is too heavy for a Raptor or Strike Eagle to carry."

"Besides that, even at terminal velocity an RNEP can't punch through more than a hundred and fifty feet of rock," Rainier added. "But by slam-bombing, a Super Hornet can accelerate the weapon far beyond its terminal velocity. If it impacts at over Mach two, it will easily reach the target."

"But a Super Hornet can't go that fast," McNeil said. "Its top speed is only one point eight Mach."

"That's not quite true, sir," Admiral Marsh said. "That was the design specification that the Navy laid out in 1993. But the actual capabilities of an aircraft are always different from the design specs. Defense engineers always try to over-build. In the case of the Super Hornet, the Navy got a hell of a lot more than it bargained for. It's been tested to exceed every performance category in the design spec by up to fifty percent. And we still haven't found the physical limits of the aircraft. Just a few months ago, Commander Roche put a Hornet through a maneuver at TOPGUN that nobody knew was possible. Now his squadron is routinely using similar maneuvers in combat."

"So you're sure the Super Hornet can hit well over Mach two?"

Admiral Marsh didn't look sure. "No one has ever actually tried a supersonic dive from maximum altitude sir, but we're reasonably certain it can reach sufficient speed to punch the modified RNEP deep enough."

"What about that new Massive Ordnance Penetrator we have?" President McNeil asked. "It can punch through two hundred feet of concrete, and it can be fitted with a nuclear device. We spent millions on it to do jobs like this. Why can't we use that?"

"Same reason," Rainier answered. "Only a heavy bomber can carry a MOP; it weighs thirty-three thousand pounds, which is more than a Super Hornet can carry on all of its hardpoints combined. That's almost the dry weight of a Hornet. Plus, the MOP is four feet across in diameter, not counting the grid fins so now you're talking about a six-inch clearance. No bomb is that accurate, no matter what delivery system we use."

The White House Chief of Staff entered the room just then. She was one of the few people permitted to interrupt a meeting within the Situation Room. With the President behind closed doors, all news and information went to Lane Bender. "General Chappelle, your office at the Pentagon just faxed this over."

The CJC took the printouts and put them on the table so the Air Force Generals and Admiral Marsh could see them too. "Tell my office to forward all the data from the Aurora to the CNO's office," he instructed.

"Yes, sir." Bender left quickly.

"There's a solid plug of concrete right under the air exchanger at the bottom of the shaft," General Rainier observed, pointing to a lightly shaded region on the GPR density scan. "There's no way the RNEP can get through that and another hundred feet of solid rock. Hell, I guess its back to the drawing board."

"We always can do what Casey suggested earlier," General Caleb said, "a double-tap. We can drop a GBU-37 bunker-buster down the shaft to clear the plug and then follow up with the nuke."

Rainier thought about it for a few seconds. "Yeah, that could work. Another Hornet could drop it vertically from a split-S at any altitude; no need to do a super-terminal dive like with the nuke. It should punch right through that plug and blast it to dust. And the air coming out of that shaft will clear the light debris."

"I still have a concern about the nuclear warhead itself," Bowman said. "Suppose you miss, and the bomb just goes off somewhere near the surface. Rannovich will know we tried to nuke him, and he could retaliate with nuclear weapons of his own."

"That thought occurred to us," Casey admitted.

"That would have the exact opposite effect of what we're aiming for," the President declared. "If we hit them with a nuke on the surface without killing Rannovich, he'll just get mad and he'll definitely use the nukes on anyone they can reach. And then we'd be looking at World War Three all over again."

"The bomb can be rigged with a safety switch between the GPS unit and the primer," General Rainier told them. "If the bomb fails to reach the target depth, it will stagger the detonation of the primer so that the core materials are annihilated without achieving critical mass."

"So the bomb would self-destruct without going nuclear," Bowman clarified.

"Correct."

McNeil looked at Bowman. "I'm out of objections. I say we give this a shot."

The VP shrugged. "I can think of a dozen worst-case scenarios if it fails, but there's nothing worse than what we're already looking at."

"I approve Operation Nuclear Hornet as discussed on one condition," President McNeil announced, "I want Commander Karl Roche to be the one who drops the bomb."

## 0900 HOURS LOCAL TIME, JUNE 6TH

Beyond Roche's windscreen the ground was rushing toward him – 50,000 feet away and coming a thousand feet closer every second – but he looked no further than his heads-up display. His left hand held the throttles at their stops. His right made minute adjustments to his angle of descent, which was almost perfectly vertical.

Lt. Cmdr. Hidelmann sat behind him, directing the tiny variations to the angle of the insane dive. "Two right, one down… steady… one left, half up… half right… okay, we're in the pipe. Burn at forty thousand feet."

"Forty-three… two… one…"

"Hit it."

Roche depressed the red button on the side of the throttle, sending raw fuel to flood the tailpipes. At that point the Super-F became an upside-down rocket. The jet accelerated violently, and shook hard as minute cavitations in the engines became massive turbulence in the fiery exhaust flow. The vibrations blurred Roche's vision, compounded by the incredible G-forces that tried to suck the blood from his eyeballs. After a moment the HUD's auto-stabilizer caught up with the pilot's eyes and allowed him to focus on the instrument data. "Thirty thousand feet, one point eight Mach." The Hornet had just hit its design top speed and kept accelerating.

"We're drifting up, Sharkey," Hunter warned. "Down a point."

Roche gently nudged the stick forward, lining up the target bug on his display in the middle of the screen.

"Okay, we're on the marker. Keep her steady…"

"Mach two at twenty-one thousand."

"Jesus, this is insane. Arming the weapon."

Roche's controls beeped as the nuclear bomb he was sitting on armed and set its trigger mechanism. He didn't look down to check his MFD, but he knew the Super Hornet Onboard Computer had automatically selected the weapons control screen and had the RNEP primed for release. He put his right thumb on the "pickle" – the large button on the sidestick that would release his selected ground-attack munitions. "Ten thousand feet, two point three Mach, approaching release point."

"At one thousand feet," Hunter reminded him, looking up from his controls. He stared forward, which actually meant straight down, and saw the craggy mountainside rushing toward them at a fantastic rate. "Oh, holy shit!"

"Five thousand… three, two, RELEASE!"

"PULL UP, FOR THE LOVE OF GOD!!"

Roche pulled back hard on the throttle and the sidestick, and grunted as the enormous G-forces shifted. As the nose pitched back to horizontal he rammed the throttle back to max power. With the full wing area of the plane resisting the their descent and the full might of the engines pushing them away from the mountain, the stresses on man and machine were beyond comprehension. Roche watched the radar altimeter as it measured how far they were above the rocky slope. Their descent had slowed, but they were still getting closer to the ground. "It's… not… pulling… hard enough… Three hundred feet… two hundred feet… one hund-"

Hunter yelled something, and everything went black.

The instruments blanked out, the world outside the cockpit disappeared. The roar of the engines and the wind also vanished, replaced by the whirring of electric motors and hissing of hydraulic pistons. The two aviators were momentarily disoriented by the loss of sensation and the sudden return to normal gravity.

"Aw, nuts," Roche muttered, as a door opened in the side of the opaque screen surrounding the simulator. The replica F/A-18f nose section settled on its cradle and the plastic canopy opened to release the crew.

"Okay kids, come on out of there," Deuce called from outside the door.

"You killed me again, Sharkey," Hunter grumbled.

"I really don't think so," Roche answered. He went straight to the control booth and grabbed a printout. "Reason for test termination: Minimum safe ceiling violation. I went down below a hundred feet, that's all. My decent rate at that point was, uh," he flipped through a few the pages of dense data. "Less than twenty feet per second, on a downward slope. I had at least six seconds to level off. We would have been fine."

"You might not have hit the mountain, but you definitely would have died when the bomb went off," Deuce said. "You weren't going fast enough to get away from ground zero, Roche. You would be riding a mushroom cloud right now if that had been the real deal."

Roche stared at the printout. Deuce stared at Roche. Hunter and the technicians stared at Deuce. "Reset the simulators," the captain told the technicians.

"I'm going to have Silverman look at these numbers and see if we can't work something out," Roche said. "I'll be right back."

After he went out the door Hunter spoke. "I'm telling you, Captain, this isn't going to work. I just know that maniac is going to get me killed."

"Jules, we went over this. I need the best fighter jockey and the best wizzo working together on this op. That means the two of you. You need to work together whether you like him or not."

"It's not that I don't like him, I just don't trust him. I think he has a death wish or something. I just know he's going to cut it too close."

"Do you trust me?"

"Of course," Hidelmann answered without hesitation.

"Well, I trust Commander Roche with my life, and yours. You couldn't be in better hands."

"What about your hands?"

"He's better even than me," Thompson said. "Besides, the President ordered him to be the one to make the drop."

That had been a major issue for Roche to deal with personally. When first presented with the order he flatly refused. Being the first man to drop a nuclear bomb in anger since WWII was not a distinction he wanted.

"I've killed enough people," Roche said, "without using a nuke. There's no way I'm going through with this."

When Admiral Krause told him it was on the President's order, Roche was furious. He and Krause and Thompson argued for an hour, during which Roche vented his infuriation with being plastered all over the news for the last five days as America's poster-boy war hero. Then Krause told him that was also the President's order.

Deuce thought he knew the younger pilot well but he had never imagined Roche being so angry. He'd also never, even once, heard Roche swear. That was unusual in a profession where the f-word was used as a punctuation mark; Roche kept his language church-group clean. Or at least he did before this conversation.

"I really don't mind getting my ass shot out of the sky or having my damned arm blown off to protect my fellow soldiers. I don't even really mind being used by the CIA for that batshit crazy op that agent got me in to. But making my mother go on national TV while I'm trapped in hostile territory, having my girlfriend sitting at home watching my war record on the news and learning classified details I swore I'd forget, having the entire country watching Commander Burke almost get killed trying to save me; that seriously pisses me off. And now you tell me all of this was the President's idea of putting a 'good news' spin on the war effort?"

"Karl, it worked," Admiral Krause said. "Your story was compelling enough to shield the public from the awful reality of this situation. The truth is that World War Three could still start any day now, but you kept that fact from being public knowledge."

"It *should* be public knowledge," Roche growled. "And so should the fact that we've lost more troops in six days than we did in six freaking *years* in Iraq. Not to mention the thousands of Chinese and Russian sailors we drowned last week, or at least ninety thousand Iranians that have died, and a good number of those at my hands. But nobody cares, because every freaking news network has me and my life's story to talk about. I'm being used to con America."

"Look, the confidence of our country is hanging by a thread. You're not a distraction from the war, you're a symbol of the war – a symbol America can support. You represent the honor and courage of our country in the middle of a bloody struggle. Can you really fault President McNeil for exploiting that image?"

Roche was silent. He could see the point, but his frown indicated that he still didn't like it.

Krause continued. "At midnight Greenwich Mean Time, tomorrow night, we will destroy that bunker with a nuclear device and end the war. The President will go on live TV, right on the East Coast primetime slot, and announce it. Imagine the reaction of the public if he just said, 'we used a nuclear weapon against Iran.' There would be shock and outrage. For God's sakes, America's now going around nuking people. We haven't done that since 1945. But what if he could use your image? 'American hero Karl Roche once again answered above and beyond the call of duty in this nation's greatest time of need. He volunteered to lead a highly dangerous mission to swift put an end to this conflict with a single bomb.' What will people think then?"

"That would look better on the news." Roche admitted grudgingly. "Until they figure out that makes me a mass murderer."

"Knock that off, son," Krause ordered. "You just knock it off with that shit, ok? You know better. You know there's a difference between war and murder."

Deuce leaned away from the table, shaking his head, bewildered by the change that had come over his protégé. "You're upset because what, you took out a few pilots? Bombed a few soldiers? Shot some IRG?"

"No, I'm upset because I'm *not* upset."

"That doesn't make any sense at all," Thompson said.

"Look, Blackjack blew up a hotel full of soldiers and he's been moping ever since. Worm can't stop thinking about those men on the destroyers and the carrier he took out. Shredder's freaked out after shooting guys on the ground even though he knows he saved me, Hannibal, Hardcase, and that agent... But what's bothering me? I lead the whole fleet in kills in the air and on the ground. I shot people at point blank range. Not just soldiers either – I killed Iranian civilians, police officers even, guys just trying to do their jobs. I drove through the city and saw the aftermath of the bombing. And I saw little kids dying while I was being chased by the IRG... But I have no trouble sleeping at night. I don't see their faces in my cereal. I don't care at all. What does that make me? Am I some sort of monster?"

"Just a good soldier," Krause said. "You were doing what you had to in order to save our men. There're twenty-five Russian civilians, nine SEALs, a CIA agent and a bunch of guys on this boat now who'd be dead now if it wasn't for you. Would you rather have those men dead instead of those Chinese and Iranians and Russians who were perfectly happy to die for their countries? Some civilians who were in the wrong place at the wrong time, just like in any war?

"You've gone over this before, haven't you?" Krause leaned closer to the young aviator. "You were thinking the same thing after you were in Iraq."

Roche just stared at him.

Krause went on. "It's in your file, a classified addendum. You were bordering on clinical depression while your injuries were healing, but you got that sorted out and your dad got someone to clear the records and we put you back to work. You seemed to be okay until now. I don't know if you need to pray to Jesus or whatever to get your conscience clear, but you need to do whatever it is that worked last time to get you ready to kill again. A week ago you were cold and ruthless, not this confused and disillusioned sorry son of a bitch I see now. We need the real Sharkey to come back."

Roche glared at the Admiral. "If I have orders from the President I guess I have no choice."

"We'll only get one shot at this Karl, so we need to do everything we can to make this work. That means we need our best plane and our best pilot. That's you and your Super Hornet." Krause patted him on the shoulder. "We'd make you do it anyway."

Deuce couldn't tell if the real Sharkey was back or not. Roche seemed confident though as he returned to the simulator room with Marty Silverman and Greg Sander close behind. Silverman carried half of the printout pages that Roche had left with. Sander carried his Dell XPS laptop and a bundle of cables under his arm.

"Captain, I need to reprogram the simulator again," Silverman announced. "We need to change the limits for the Hornet's physics processor."

"What's wrong with it?"

"Wrong numbers," Roche said. He showed Deuce a few circled lines among the pages of data. "My positive Gs peaked at 8.5 coming out of that dive."

"That's the original design limit for the airframe," Silverman explained. "But it's tested to exceed 12 Gs. That's not all. The drag coefficient is a couple of points too high, the weight's too high, the center of gravity is a few inches too far forward... tiny differences in the numbers, but it makes a good bit of a difference in performance. Greg's going to upload new constants so the program matches the test specs instead of the design specs."

"I thought we already *were* using the test limits," Hunter said. "We just hit two-point-four Mach at the release point."

"We removed the top speed constraint," Silverman told him, "but that's it. I thought that would be enough to get us an attack profile, but Commander Roche has showed me convincing data to the contrary. We need to get this simulator as close to the real thing as possible in order to find a viable approach-and-escape solution."

One of the technicians opened an access panel on the side of the computer console. Greg's wires got tangled with his earphones from his mp3 player and he accidentally pulled out his left earpiece. Roche started involuntarily bobbing along with the Led Zeppelin tune he heard over the tiny speaker.

After a minute Sander had everything plugged in where it belonged and he sat down at the console. "Okay, I installed the program patch," Sander reported. He'd actually written it himself in the last ten minutes. "I'm going to run the replay of your last attempt with the new numbers to check for bugs."

The motion simulator behind the curved screen suddenly sprang to life. Roche and Hidelmann watched through the door as it ran through their suicidal dive. It ended the same way.

Hunter sighed, "We're still dead."

"What happened, Greg?" Silverman called to the booth. "Do you have to debug the patch?"

"No, the numbers transferred just fine, but the plane was going so fast, the extra maneuvering envelope still didn't give them room to pull out."

"Well, if we're going faster, couldn't we release at a higher altitude?" Hunter asked. "Say, around two thousand feet?"

"Yeah, it hit two-and-a-half Mach at twenty-five hundred feet," Sander answered. "You could probably release up there. The problem is there's another mountain peak right on your line of departure. With this target profile, you're going to hit it anyway. Either that or you'll have to slow down way too much, in which case you won't get out of the valley before the blast."

"Can they put a timer delay on the warhead?" Roche wondered.

"Nope," Deuce responded. "Well, I suppose they could, but they won't. Every electronic component they add to the trigger increases the chance of it not working. At this point it only has a GPS chip. Adding a timer means adding a clock and a processor and more wires. Remember, this thing's going to be going from two and a half times the speed of sound to a dead stop in about the same span of time and distance that my Corvette brakes from a hundred miles an hour. That kind of impact will probably break loose anything they jury-rig at this point."

"We'll have to figure out a new escape plan then." Roche stared at the mockup fighter nose as if it could speak to him.

"You're the bombing expert here, Jules," Captain Thompson said. "Any ideas?"

"Considering I haven't actually *flown* a bomber in eighteen years, no I have no ideas. No one has ever done anything like this before."

"Someone has. Marty," Deuce turned to the engineer. "You told me they tested this maneuver twenty-some years ago, and bombed a missile site in North Dakota. We need to see the actual Nuclear Hornet report. Maybe it describes exactly how the pilot broke out of a super-terminal dive."

"The copy Casey gave me was censored, and it didn't have the logs of the actual bombing run itself. He said he couldn't give me a full copy electronically, but he's flying one out with General Rainier and the bomb."

"That won't be here until late tomorrow. That's not enough time to work out a simulation."

"Casey?" Roche asked. "You mean that royal jerk from the CIA?"

"Yes, I mean Deputy Director of Operations Jarrod Casey."

Silverman was unaware of Roche's past encounter, but Thompson wasn't. He could sense that Sharkey's simmering cauldron of rage was about to boil over again. Thankfully Sander interrupted.

"I think I got it!"

"Got what?"

"Sharkey, can you do a tailslide in a vertical dive?"

"No," Roche answered.

"Sure you can," Deuce said. "I saw you do it at TOPGUN. That's how you beat me, remember?"

"That was at four hundred knots, not sixteen hundred and my dive angle wasn't approaching anything like vertical."

"I don't know what a tailslide is," Hidelmann said, "but I really don't like the way it sounds."

"We pulled a couple the other day," Roche told him. "It's just a rapid vector change. You deploy the airbrakes, chop the throttles, vent the strakes and pull back hard on the stick. The tail slides forward and your momentum carries you in the same direction, meanwhile your wings catch air and slow you down to stall speed. If you do that and snap the nose forward again, it's called a 'cobra.' If you hit the throttle at the right moment you go back in the exact opposite direction, and that's called a 'flatliner.' Or you could try doing it to pull out of a supersonic dive and that's called a 'kamikaze.'"

"Not if you're diving into a column of hot air," Sander said. "The ventilation shaft is releasing five hundred cubic yards a minute, and you'll be right in the middle of that. The profile we have now shows you pulling away from the vent, but if you tailslide you'll catch a cushion of hot air under you and you'll bounce right out. You'll be in free-fall for about a thousand feet and you might stall the engines if you screw up with the throttles, but if it works you'll be out in open space and you can get clear of the blast area without any trouble."

"What about tearing the wings off when I put supersonic wind resistance on them? I already did some math on this, Greg. The wing loads can only go up to four hundred and fifty thousand psi."

"Was that with full fuel tanks? Any weapons on? Flaps and slats?"

Roche frowned. "I didn't consider any of that."

"Well, I did. And you applied the operating limits of stress, right?"

"Yeah."

"Those have a factor of safety of up to five. That means the airframe fails at five times the operating stress limits."

"I didn't realize that."

Sander typed into his computer. "I figured as much. It's called a factor of safety because exceeding the limit is simply not safe. But we're not concerned with what's safe so much as what's possible. I'm pretty sure the wings can handle this much stress."

Roche came over and looked at Sander's computer. He'd pulled up software to simulate all the forces that would be acting on the plane's wings. The stresses were extremely high – far higher than the operating limits, but well below the predicted point of failure of the airframe's design. "You're right, that doesn't look safe. But it does look possible. Alright, let's give it a shot in the simulator then."

"It'll work," Sander promised.

"It had better," Roche said, "because apparently there's no other way out of this stupid war."

## SICK BAY – TWO HOURS LATER

"I know why you're here," Dr. Tobias said as Thompson opened the door to his office, "and the answer is an emphatic 'no.'"

Deuce sat down heavily in a chair in front of the doctor's desk. "If you don't clear me you'll have to clear Hannibal."

Tobias reached over his desk and pulled one of the cigars from the CAG's shirt pocket. "What do they put in these things? You have to be high on something. You're not flying combat, and Hannibal's not flying anywhere. Period."

"He's that bad?"

"The surgeons pulled a bullet out of his pancreas. That's not something you recover from in a few days like your miracle boy. And by the way, I'm still leery of clearing *him* to fly again after what happened last time."

Deuce Thompson frowned at his old friend. "You know what the mission is."

"I've been briefed."

"We need someone up there to lead a hundred planes fighting their way across Iran. Hannibal and I are the only ones qualified to do that."

"The CAG on the *Stennis* can lead. You're staying on the deck."

Deuce shook his head. "That guy just got his fourth stripe a couple months ago. He sounds like he's fifteen years old. I don't trust him with my boy."

"Boys. Plural."

"I'm talking about Sharkey," Deuce said. "He'll need me up there. I'm worried about him, Doc."

"I know what you're talking about. But I'm worried about your cardiomyopathy and the very real possibility that if you go out there you will die before you land."

"With the defenses we're facing, that's a very real possibility for everyone." Deuce pulled a tube of pills from his pocket. "This should keep me alive if I feel chest pains, correct?"

"You know, it's strange, but that's never been tested in the cockpit of a high-performance jet under fire." Dr. Tobias stretched his neck. "Allow me to be perfectly clear, Deuce. Any measurable level of adrenaline could make your heart explode."

"So give me something that will suppress my adrenal gland."

Tobias sighed. "Even if you do survive this, you will definitely worsen your condition to the point where you'll never be cleared to fly again."

"After this mission I won't care."

Tobias stared at his friend. He knew Deuce was going to get what he wanted, one way or another. "Alright, I'll prescribe you Nefazodone as an adrenal suppressant and clear you for back-seat duty."

"If you keep me in the back seat I might as well be stuck back here."

"Well, that's still my preferred option."

Deuce leaned over the desk, and growled in the doctor's face. "If you don't clear me to fly this mission, and Roche goes out there and doesn't make it back, I'm going to have to shoot us both."

Tobias leaned back in his seat. "I know when you're not kidding." He opened Thompson's folder. "But if *you* don't come back, I'm never gonna forgive you."

## CHAPTER 25: RIDE OF THE *STINGRAYS*

**THE DECK OF THE *RONALD REAGAN***
**0035 LOCAL, JUNE 7<sup>TH</sup>**

"What in the hell are we waiting for?"

Karl Roche was wondering the same thing. Hunter had asked the same question three times – to Roche, to the Air Boss, and to his own control panel. The highly advanced electronics had no answer; neither did the pilot in the front seat or the flight ops commander up in the island. They had been told to stand by, and so they had, just sitting on catapult one for the last twenty minutes after the other thirty-five Hornets in the Chesspiece group had been launched. Even the catapult crew was just standing around looking confused. "This is completely ridiculous," Roche needlessly remarked.

"The other guys are going to run out of fuel waiting for us."

Finally Roche keyed his radio. "This is Checkmate Lead. How much longer are we going to be delayed, Castle?" He was calling on the mission command channel instead of the flight control frequency. All the aircraft in the operation – Hornets from two carriers and several Air Force assets – could hear Sharkey's impatient query.

"Checkmate One, this is Castle King, go to secure line one."

Roche smiled as he switched the radio channels. He'd prompted a response from Admiral Krause himself, and he sounded annoyed. "Checkmate One responds."

"Sharkey, don't do that again," the Admiral ordered wearily.

"Sorry. I thought that channel was for general mission chatter."

"Not until you're off the deck and actually part of the mission."

"Okay, so what's the holdup? Is Washington backing out?" Hidelmann asked hopefully.

"No, it's technical. The steam crew can't figure out how much juice to put on your catapult."

"You're kidding," Roche said.

"Unfortunately, I'm not. We don't have an accurate load weight."

"What's wrong with the load weight I filled out?" Roche asked. The pilot's last task before suiting up for a mission is working out the exact weight of the plane so the number can be passed on to the launch crew.

"What did you use to for the weight of the bomb?" Krause asked Roche.

Karl hesitated. He had guessed this might have been what the delay was about. "The 2009 ordnance manual listed a weight for the RNEP. I used that."

Krause sighed. "That's what we thought. Unfortunately this bomb has a hardened casing and a different warhead so that figure isn't accurate. It's not your fault. Nobody actually knows how much it weighs."

"Not even General Rainier?" The Air Force Major General had personally accompanied the weapon to the *Ronald Reagan* and personally oversaw it being loaded on to Fish-2. Roche assumed he would know some of the technical specifications for the device, like how heavy it was.

"He knows the exact weight of the new warhead, but not of the old one or the modified casing. The best he can give us is an educated guess."

"What about the guys who made it?" Hunter wondered.

"We're trying to get Los Alamos on the line now, but its taking forever to get these scientists to get a secured line. Someone from Army Intel is trying to hook them up, but their IT architecture doesn't meet the crypto standard..."

Krause went on for another minute speaking in incomprehensible jargon. Roche had almost forgotten that the Admiral had used to work at the NSA. "Slow down, sir. You're telling us this whole mission is SNAFU'd because Los Alamos doesn't have the right telephones?"

Hunter was a high-strung individual to begin with, and the situation made him especially edgy. "Why can't-" his voice cracked and he cleared his throat. "Why don't we just use Rainier's ballpark figure?"

"We don't like to do that," Krause answered. "You know as well as anyone what can happen if the catapult is not calibrated to the exact mass of the aircraft."

"Can a couple hundred pounds really hurt a Rhino, though?"

"Yes, it could," Roche said. A hundred pounds of an aircraft's load weight equated to several thousand pounds of steam pressure. If that force wasn't correctly balanced by the momentum of the mass of the plane at takeoff speed, it could severely damage the nose landing gear, where all that energy was concentrated. Or if not enough pressure was applied, the plane could stall at takeoff and drop right into the ocean and get run over by the carrier. Roche had once seen a Hornet get its nose wheels completely ripped off, forcing the pilot to ditch in the middle of the Pacific.

Hunter had also seen it happen several times in his career. He remembered one fatal incident and suddenly felt a lot more cautious.

"Just a second guys. We're looking at Rainier's figures." Krause had put down the microphone, but Sharkey and Hunter could hear the Admiral and the General discussing bomb parts and numbers. "Okay, we've settled on an approximation if you guys are willing to risk it."

"How close do you think you are?" Hunter asked.

"Within a hundred pounds," Krause said, even though he was sure the margin of error was a bit wider than that.

"Well, that won't cause a *spectacular* failure," Roche said. "What do you think, Hidelmann?"

"Couldn't we just take it off and put it on a scale?" He was grasping for any solution now; suddenly the thought of uncontrolled steam energy ripping the front end off the airplane made his own ballpark suggestion seem very distasteful to him.

"The techs say that would take an hour at least, which would completely destroy our timetable. We've already blown through half the time that Deuce had factored for SNAFU recovery." Krause did not mention that they had a very strict deadline – by Rainier's own estimation, the Iranian nukes would be armed and ready by midnight UTC. They had less than three hours to make the strike.

"What the hell," Hunter said, again ignoring his better judgment. "Let's do it."

"What he said," Roche added.

"Two minutes," Krause told them.

A minute and fifty seconds later, they were launched off cat 1. It turned out that Rainier was off by a hundred and fifty-one pounds. This resulted in several tons of excess force impacting the nosegear assembly. Roche felt the extra-heavy jolt as the shuttle released them at the edge of the deck. "Too hard," he muttered.

"What?"

"Nothing, Hunter." Roche throttled back a little and pitched up, and raised the landing gear. "Uh-oh."

"What?" Hunter asked again with an entirely different tone.

*"Sensors disagree, nosegear not aligned in wheelwell,"* Bitchin' Betty 2 explained in her stern but slightly seductive voice.

"Oh shit," Hunter moaned.

Roche remained calm. "I'll re-extend the gear and see if that clears it." When he put the wheels back down, the warning light went out briefly but came back on with a new message from Betty.

*"Sensors disagree, nosegear not extended."*

"Is this from the cat launch?" Hunter wondered. "You think they over-shot us?"

"No, I'm pretty sure this is just a completely unrelated coincidence," Roche said sarcastically. He leveled out at five thousand feet and retracted the gear again. The sensors still didn't see the gear properly stowed. "Checkmate Two, where are you?" Roche called to Hacksaw.

"Coming up behind you, boss."

"Our nosegear got tweaked on the launch. You'd better take a look."

"Okay, fix your altitude, I'm coming in under you now."

Roche let the autopilot hold the fighter at exactly five thousand feet.

Hunter looked back to see Hacksaw's Eel-4 maneuver around their invisible jetwash and slide under Fish-2's belly.

"Okay, your hatch is flush with the skin and the locking dogs are in place. It's secure from the outside, at least."

"You're sure?" Roche checked.

"I'm as sure as I can be with my face only nine inches away from it."

Hunter's eyes widened with alarm when he realized how close the other Hornet was. Roche was completely unconcerned. He knew his wingman was a master of precision piloting, having once been a candidate for the Blue Angels. Hunter looked at the camera views. He could see the Super-E's vertical stabilizers sticking up between the wings and tail of their own plane. He took Hacksaw's video feed and saw the huge RNEP bomb almost kissing the back of Hacksaw's canopy.

"Okay," Roche called, "I'm extending the gear. Better drop down a little."

"Roger that," Hacksaw answered. "I'll match your speed."

Hunter sighed audibly as the other aviator put another forty inches between them.

The Super-F slowed a little as the wheels came down again, but the auto-stabilizer kept the altitude constant. "What do you see?" Roche asked.

"Nothing. The hatch is open, your main gear is down, but the nosewheel is still stuck up there somewhere."

"I'll try again." Roche cycled the landing gear one more time.

"Nothing. I can't see the assembly very well."

"I'll turn on my taxi lights," Roche said, and reached for the switch.

"No, don't, you're leaking hydraulic fluid, and you might have a lot more damage on the assembly. If there's an electrical short on the light you could set yourself on fire."

"I don't see a hydraulic warning light."

"It might be from the brakes, which are isolated from the mains, but trust me, you're leaking something. I've got a flashlight; I'm coming up for a closer look." Roche and Hunter felt a tiny bump as their main wheels touched Hacksaw's wings. "Oh yeah, it's mangled up pretty bad. The wheels are kinda twisted and wedged up in the well."

"Can you see where the leak is coming from?"

"No. Hit your brakes."

Roche tried, but the computer intervened and reminded him he was a mile above any runway. "Uh, Castle, can you get a hold of Silverman?" he called. "I need to override the computer."

## REAGAN

Hannibal went to the flag conference room where Sander was alone with his laptop. "Where's Silverman?"

"Downstairs getting chow," the intern replied. "What do you need?"

"Roche says he needs to override the computer to do a diagnostic in mid-air. Is there some sort of code he needs to-"

"Yeah," Sander nodded. "Tell him to type nineteen-sixty-eight into his keypad. That's the universal SHOC override."

## CHECKMATE FLIGHT

"One, nine, six, eight…" The computer cleared the warning and let Roche engage the brakes. The rear wheels had been rotating free in the slipstream and now locked up.

Hacksaw could see the pistons move and calipers closing on the nose wheel. "It's not the brakes. Hunter, do a hydraulic static pressure diagnostic, but be ready to close the nosegear assembly if anything pops."

538

"Just a second." Hunter complied, overriding the computer which again tried to tell them that this procedure is supposed to be done safely on the ground, not at five thousand feet. The system raised its pressure by five psi, and abruptly the leaky seal on the nosegear piston popped open.

Hacksaw swore loudly as a shower of pink fluid smeared his canopy. Hunter quickly isolated the nose gear before it dropped the pressure in the rest of the system.

"Okay," Roche said, "I guess we figured out what's wrong. I'm closing it up. Hacksaw, can you make sure it's sealed again?"

"I can't see a damn thing, sir. There's fluid all over my windscreen."

"Use your wingtip camera."

"Just a sec." Hacksaw maneuvered and put his wingtip directly behind the hatch. "Yeah, you're good. But now I have to go back and get this pink shit cleaned off. I'm flying half-blind."

"No problem. Follow me to sea level. I'll clean it up for you."

"What are we going to do about our landing gear?" Hunter asked.

"Nothing," Roche answered after a moment. "It doesn't affect our mission. We'll worry about landing when we're ready to land."

"What about me?" Hacksaw asked.

"Flip on your back and hold steady at fifty feet," Roche instructed. "I'll give you a quick steam-cleaning."

Roche skimmed the surface of the Gulf twenty yards ahead of Hacksaw, kicking up a rooster tail of steam and hot salty spray. Eel-4 was cleaned off in seconds.

"Checkmate One, Checkmate Two, this is Knight One, what's your status?" Deuce called.

"We're ready op," Roche answered. "We'll be at the rendezvous in five."

Hunter wasn't so sure about being "ready op." Ten minutes into the operation and it was already a one-way ticket.

Eighty miles north of Sharkey's current position, another seventy Hornets and Growlers clustered around the rendezvous point. Chesspiece Group – the *Reagan*'s strike package – consisted of three whole squadrons. All eight Growlers from the Yellow Jackets squadron were now designated Bishop flight. The Warhawks were called out as Rook flight, and they would support the Growlers with the suppression of enemy air defenses. The *Stingrays* were divided into two flights.  Sharkey and Hunter of course carried the nuclear bomb, and Hardcase and Hawk were carrying the GBU-37 bunker buster with Fish-3.  Their Super-Fs were mission critical.  Along with their wingmen they were referred to as Checkmate flight.  The rest of the of the *Stingrays* were assigned to provide air superiority under the tag Knight flight.  They were led by Deuce, who had taken Hannibal's Fish-1 with Buzz in the back seat.

The *Stennis* had launched Bartender Group in support – an equal number of Hornets, each carrying three external fuel tanks to top off the Chesspiece Hornets before going feet dry.  The Bartender Hornets would then fan out, launching diversionary strikes on multiple military targets and hopefully drawing Rannovich's air force away from the mission critical.  The Bartenders were divided into four flights to correspond to the Chesspiece elements they would refuel.  They were named after San Diego-area bars and clubs for easy reference: Side Bar, Kansas City, Stingaree, and Blind Lady.

Somewhere over Kurdistan in Iraq, two squadrons of F-22 Raptors were forming up for their part of the operation.  Like the Bartenders they would be a diversion, drawing off defenders to the northwest.  They reported as Checkers and Domino Flights.  The Air Force was also providing several E-3s which would report collectively as Moderator.  Altogether over a hundred aircraft were participating in the largest coordinated air strike since World War Two.

"I know you have enough to worry about," Hunter said, "so I'll keep an eye on the hydraulic pressure for you."

"Worried?" Roche asked in mock surprise.  "I'm never worried."

"Yeah, I noticed, and that has *me* worried.  It's spooky the way you just ignore this kind of stuff."

"Relax," Roche tried to reassure him.  "It's just a little mental condition I have."

"Oh, God help me; now you're just trying to scare me right?"

"No, really; the amyglada – that's the fear center of the brain – isn't hooked up right for some reason.  Technically I'm brain-damaged but the only symptom is that I never feel normal levels of anxiety or preoccupation.  It's actually very beneficial."

"I see.  So you're not suicidal, just-"

"Quite the opposite.  I simply feel no fear or worry whatsoever."

540

"But you do still realize there's a million more things that can go wrong tonight."

"Not quite that many, but yes I'm aware that we still have to tank up in the dark, fight our way across hostile airspace, attempt a bombing maneuver that I'm quite sure is impossible, escape a nuclear explosion, and land on two wheels. All that while trying to reassure an incurable pessimist and hoping our entire hydraulic system doesn't fail."

"Well, as long as we're more or less on the same page..."

Their tanker broke in on the radio just then. "Checkmate One, this is Kansas City One, do you have a fix on me?"

"Copy K.C. One," Roche answered, "Checkmate One has you on screen; I'm coming up on your six, angels minus point five, over."

"Aff, Checkmate, I see your transponder. Steady on your approach."

Aerial refueling is a fairly difficult process for a Navy fighter in normal circumstances, but doing it in the dark is so dangerous it's normally only done in dire emergencies. It's especially dangerous when the tanker aircraft is just another fighter.

"Remind me why we're even doing this?" Hunter asked.

"We need as much fuel in our wings as possible to keep them stiff when I try to flatline this thing at Mach two-and-a-half, and once we go feet dry we're not going to be able to refuel safely. By safely I mean without getting shot at, because this is obviously not safe either."

"I don't even see him."

"K.C. One, landing lights please," Roche requested.

Dead ahead and slightly above their Hornet, about two hundred feet away, a Hornet-E suddenly lit up.

"I see you in my rear camera, Checkmate One, your approach looks good. I'm deploying the drogue now." A red light appeared on the other Hornet's underside, and slowly extended out on a long, snaking hose.

Roche extended the probe from the side of Fish-2's nose, and tried to align the blue light on the probe with the red one on the drogue.

"I'm fully extended, sir," the tanker pilot reported. "Go ahead and gas up."

Roche disabled the auto-leveling system and manually adjusted to keep up with the drogue, which fluttered in the 350kt slipstream. After a minute of precise maneuvering he got the one-way valves connected, pumping just over nineteen hundred pounds of JP-8 military-grade jet fuel between the planes in just under eight seconds.

"We're clear, K.C. One."

"Roger." The other pilot turned off his landing lights and retracted the drogue. "That's a lot of work for less than two thousand pounds, Commander."

"It'll be worth it later," Roche told him.

With the refueling complete, Roche's computer directed him into a pre-programmed formation, leading the rest of Checkmate flight in a staggered diamond, surrounded by the Knights. The tactical display showed the other seventy-one Hornets and Growlers spreading out as they approached the coastline. Checkmate One was among the last to cross the beach, 20,000 feet below. "Checkmate Lead is feet dry," he reported. He allowed himself to relax a little. They would be flying in the safety corridor for the next twenty minutes, crossing the hundred-mile-wide lane of controlled airspace at an angle before making a beeline for the bunker, flying over a hostile landscape of mobile air defenses and hidden airfields.

Apparently the safety of the corridor was an illusion, however. Already Side Bar Flight, some eighty miles north of the *Stingrays*, was in contact with bogeys.

"I thought the corridor was supposed to be clear of hostiles," Hunter said.

"Yeah, as long as it's being enforced," Roche explained. "Right now, Side Bar is doing the enforcing."

"Side Bar has made kills," Deuce reported on the *Stingrays*' private channel. "We're officially in hostile skies."

The *Stingrays* were unmolested for several minutes. Sharkey and Hardcase flew side-by-side, with Hacksaw and Hitman trailing their wingmen closely. Deuce, Blackjack, Bulldog, Blaze, Beowulf and Rooster kept the other six sections in a protective ring around Checkmate Flight.

"Action rear," Blackjack said suddenly. They had been feet-dry for twenty minutes. "There's something behind me, trying to sweep us with radar."

"Division, break," Deuce commanded.

He dropped out of formation, followed by Shredder, Bulldog, and Doc. They turned around sharply to see what was coming up behind the group.

"That's Fulcrums," Buzz announced, once the compound radar image resolved. "Four of them. I don't see where they could have come from."

"The Iranians have been busy redeploying while we were grounded the last couple of days," Deuce explained. "Lock AMRAAMs; one missile each – we need to conserve ammo." They fired once they'd closed to maximum range and scored three hits. The one that Bulldog missed ran off. Deuce didn't bother chasing the survivor.

Meanwhile, Bishop and Rook Flights kept busy destroying radar and missile sites on the ground. Hunter monitored their progress, and noticed the Growlers were spreading out over an increasingly wide area as they engaged the defenses. "Close up, Bishop," he advised. "You only need to clear us fifty miles of airspace."

Commander "Palerider" Tachini saw that he was right. "Let's tighten it up guys. We only need to bother going after any contacts that can reach Checkmate's flight path."

"I got contact with bandits," Toymaker reported. His radar had picked up four blips as he turned back toward the rest of the group. "Looks like four MiG-23s."

"Do you want to bring someone up to deal with them?"

"Negative. We can handle this. Engaging at range." Santos and his pilot and their wingman each fired both their AMRAAMs and took down the older Russian fighters with ease.

"So far, so good," Hunter noted to Roche, but he spoke too soon.

"Chesspiece elements, this is Checkers Lead, we're engaging a huge pack of Flankers and Defiants, at least four squadrons. We're trying to slow them down, but a bunch broke off and they're headed your way. Oh, hell, more Defiants now, stand by."

"Moderator, this is Knight Lead," Deuce called. "Are you tracking?"

"It's a real furball, Knight," one of the comm officers in the E-3's answered. "It looks like thirty or so bandits are tangling with Checkers Flight, and an equal number are heading southeast."

"That's right across our track," Deuce said.

"I'll divert Domino to help them out," Moderator said.

"No, don't," Roche cut in. "We need cover in place to the north. Divert Stingaree and Blind Lady to engage."

"Stingaree Flight is just a squad of Hornet-Cs," Deuce noted. "Whatever's tearing through those Raptors will wipe them out."

"Well, then maybe you should back them up," Roche suggested.

A panicked female Air Force pilot called out over the command channel. "This is Checkers Three, we're being massacred by these little French fighters. They closed in too fast and they're stuck to our asses. We just lost Cappy- I mean Lead. Repeat, Checkers Lead is down. We're at fifty-percent strength and, oh shit, fuck, shit! Make that thirty-three. We're finished, guys!"

Deuce took over. "Stingaree and Blind Lady Flights, this is Knight Lead. Form on me, we're going after those guys. Bishop, I could use your help too."

"Five, take your division." Palerider ordered.

"Copy." Lt. Santos took half the Growlers and joined the *Stingrays* and the two squadrons form the *Stennis*.

"He's taking our cover," Hunter noted, as Knight flight shot away from them at high speed. "There's no one guarding us here."

"No problem," Roche said. "Kansas City, what's your status?"

"Pretty quiet in our sector, Checkmate," answered the same pilot who'd refueled them earlier. "We hit our ground targets and nobody's trying to shoot us yet."

"Okay, we could use some cover over here. Let's have you guys split your sections and form up on my four and eight o'clock."

"Copy, Checkmate. K.C. One and Two are coming over to cover low at your eight; look for Three and Four at your four o'clock high, over." Four more Super Hornets came around behind them and settled into the new formation.

"Is that better Jules?" Karl asked.

"A little bit, yes."

## CHESSPIECE GROUP

"Whiteout," Toymaker ordered. His Growlers began jamming the squadron of Flankers that led the group of bandits, leaving them helpless before an AMRAAM onslaught. Within two minutes, Deuce's mixed team effortlessly destroyed the group that had broken away, bringing down two and a half squadrons unanswered. The Growlers gave the other Hornets total radar immunity.

"It's like hittin' tin cans on a fence!" Rooster crowed. His missiles had downed three of the enemy fighters.

"Checkers Three," Deuce called, "are you still there?"

"Yeah, but Gopher and I are the only ones left. We're trying to get clear."

"Hit the gas and run toward us, we'll take care of those Defiants for you."

"Those guys are going to be a lot harder for me to jam," Toymaker said. "We don't have their radar bands programmed."

"Okay, just do what you can." Deuce said. "Watch the friendlies people."

The two surviving Raptors were closing fast, followed by a pair of Defiants. The Iranian pilots noticed the huge formation of Hornets and broke off.

"Get them!" Blaze called, "they're crossing left!"

Bulldog and Doc rolled away and chased them down. One shot away at nearly Mach 3, the other didn't run fast enough and took a hit from one of Bulldog's AMRAAMs. "That's a kill."

"Bandits closing," Toymaker said. "We have multiple threat radar traces."

"Okay team, this is what we came for. Engage shadows," Deuce ordered, activating his own RFCM system. "Stingaree Flight, mix yourselves in with the Rhinos. We'll hide you in our false contacts."

"Fifty miles," Toymaker announced.

Deuce continued calling out orders as he made up a plan on the spot. "I want an AMRAAM barrage at BMR once they close to forty."

"They're firing blind, missile traces closing fast."

"We hold this line, people," Deuce declared. "I don't want so much a shred of shrapnel to get past us."

"Forty miles."

"Now this is a right proper fight," Beowulf said. "Tally-ho!"

## CHECKMATE FLIGHT

"I'm spiked!"

"Who is this?" Roche asked.

"K.C. Four! Someone's behind me!"

"Dammit, I'm marked too," Kansas City Lead said.

"Quick, engage your RFCM and split up," Roche instructed. "Monitor, do see what's attacking them?"

"Transient contacts at your altitude; they must be Defiants. At least four, no more then eight."

Roche glanced at his MFD. Kansas City flight was now spread out over thirty miles. "K.C., converge on my current vector. Checkmates, when I say, turn around and start shooting."

"Does that include you and me?" Hardcase asked.

"Yes."

"What?" Hunter didn't like that idea. *"They're* supposed to be covering *us*, not the other way around."

"If you want them to be around to cover us later, we'd better help them out here," Roche declared.

"He's right," Hardcase said. "We're both sitting on four good missiles; it would be a shame to let them go to waste."

"They got a missile lock on me," K.C.-1 said as he roared past. The other three followed.

"Hacksaw, Hitman, one-eighty now."

The two escorts flipped around, presenting their missile loads. The Defiants noticed and slowed. Sharkey and Hardcase followed their wingmen, doing tight Immelman turns to get the Defiants in their sights. The overlapping radar picture form the four Supers picked out eight pursuers just as they closed into AMRAAM range.

"Gotcha. Fox-three!"

## KNIGHT FLIGHT

Two hundred miles away, forty Hornets and thirty Defiants were shooting hundreds of missiles at each other. The advantage was all on the Americans side – they only had thirty targets to shoot at, the Iranians had over two hundred, most of which were not real. Unfortunately, the Defiants were extremely good at dodging missiles. So after each side had fired their massive salvos of radar-guided medium-range missiles, they'd only scored a few hits. Four Defiants went down in flames, and two Stingarees and a Blind Lady also took near-hits or close misses and had to drop out of the firefight.

The warplanes continued flying straight toward each other. Soon they were in visual range, and the Americans lost their ECM advantage. That's when things turned nasty. "Switch to Sidewinders," Deuce ordered as he swallowed one of his pills. "Pair up and confirm your targets." For Deuce, the rest of the team faded into the background. He and Shredder were the only Navy aviators in the sky. He picked out a pair of Defiants that were coming right toward him. He fired two Sidewinders at the leader, and dropped away before the fighters could shoot back. The leader was destroyed, and his wingman broke away from the formation to pursue Deuce.

"He's gonna come up on our left," Shredder said.

"Roger. Breaking left." Deuce cut his throttles, rolled to the side and yanked back on his stick. Shredder matched the sharp turn. The Defiant didn't compensate in time and went right by. It turned right, trying to gain distance from the Super Hornets. Deuce and

546

Shredder whipped around and fired one Sidewinder apiece. The Dassault's pilot found himself caught between the missiles and ejected a moment before his plane was hit from both sides.

"We got two more coming up behind us," Shredder observed.

"Yeah, they're locking on to us," Buzz confirmed.

"Nobody gets a radar lock on me. Not even Sharkey can get a radar lock on me." Deuce rolled two-and-a-half times and dove straight down. The Defiants moved closer to try to use their heat-seekers. "Are you covering me, Knight Two?"

"Oh, I have this," Shredder answered. "Dropping in to cover." He held a right-hand bank and let the Super Hornet drift downwards, matching Thompson's descent rate but also cutting inside the turns of the Defiant interceptors. The Dassaults went around him to chase Deuce, and he rolled left to come in above and behind them. "Game, set and match." Shredder had them lined up perfectly, just a mile in front of his nose. His famously accurate cannon fire ripped the smaller jets apart.

"Good shooting Two," Deuce lauded, "as usual."

But Shredder had left himself open to the rear. Four more Defiants saw him and dropped in to chase him. "Aw, hell. More bandits, coming in on my six, now."

Deuce had moved too far off to assist. "I can't do a thing about it. Can anyone up there give him some cover?"

Blackjack had just scored his second kill and his sector was clear. "Knight Five dropping in. Hang in there, buddy."

Shredder wasn't used to being outmaneuvered. The smaller, lighter, faster Defiants had spread out and were surrounding him. He swore. "I can't get off their radar! IDECM is having minimal effect."

"We're about to cut your problems in half," Blackjack said. He and Creep got radar locks on the two bandits closest to Shredder's six-o'clock. This forced the pilots to pull away and take evasive action.

"Thank you very much." With his tail clear, Shredder was able to hit the brakes and flip his plane back the other way. The Defiants trying to flank him had to turn around to reacquire him on radar. Shredder had bought a little time, but before long the Defiants had him locked again, and started launching missiles. Shredder took evasive action, but as he twisted in the air the Defiants kept getting closer until they'd approached within heat-seeker range.

"This isn't looking good," he called. A near-hit from a radar guided missile punched a hole in his starboard engine, venting hot exhaust gases and making him a wide-open target for the heat seekers.

A short-range Matra Magic hit his damaged engine and almost tore it clean out of the airframe. "I'm hit bad! I gotta drop out."

Deuce had turned back in time to see Knight-2 plummet toward the ground, trailing smoke and debris as wrecked pieces of the plane peeled off in the slipstream. "Can you make it to one of the safety corridors?"

"I'd be lucky to even hold her upright. Maybe I- oh, wait, no. My right wing just tore off. I'm bailing out..." Shredder's transmission ended as his seat rocketed him out of the cockpit.

"Buzz, give SAR his coordinates."

"I'm on it."

"What's going on with our matchup?"

"We lost another Stingaree, and Blaze has minor damage from cannon fire. We've destroyed fifteen Defiants. The others seem to be regrouping and crossing west, like they're trying to go around us. Oh yeah, they're running alright. Lead elements just went to afterburner."

"Chase them down, team," the Captain called on the command channel. "They'll try to go south again and we can't allow that. Don't let them get away!"

"Those guys can do Mach three," Rooster said, "We're lucky to make Mach two."

"They can't keep up that pace long. Just don't lose them!"

## CHECKMATE FLIGHT

"Six down, two to go," Hawk said. Checkmate and Kansas City Flights were having no trouble at all with their own smaller dogfight. The last Defiants tried to run, heading north up Checkmate's original track.

"I got another group of contacts headed your way," Moderator told them. "Looks like a mixed group of MiGs."

"This is K.C. Lead. My flight will handle it."

"There's twelve of them."

"On second thought," K.C.-1 came back, "could Checkmate Two and Four back us up again?"

"You guys go ahead," Roche said. "Hardcase and I can take care of ourselves and these last two Defiants. Are you up for a little chase, Three?"

"As long as they're heading for our objective anyway. Only thing is, I'm out of AMRAAMs."

"Me too. That'll just make it more fun."

The Defiants had gone past them at top speed, but with their limited fuel load they soon had to relax their pace. Sharkey and Hardcase cruised along at 600 knots and closed the gap quickly. The Defiants couldn't get away, but they weren't giving up either. They kept dancing around on the edge of Sidewinder range, and they constantly tried to turn around but the Hornets kept herding them north. After a few minutes, Sharkey almost got a lock on one of the smaller fighters. It made a hard turn to the left, and crossed right in front of Hardcase, who put a Sidewinder through its back. The two Supers closed in on the last Defiant. The pilot had no escape, and so he tried something radical.

The four American aviators watched in amazement as the Defiant suddenly pitched forward, rolled hard to the left, and continued twisting until it was facing backwards, upside down, flying tail-first. The pilot fired his twin 30mm cannons wildly as the Dassault continued to spin away, but something else happened. Roche thought he could see the airframe warp – it looked like the cockpit of the Defiant had twisted out of line with the tail. It wasn't an illusion. The extreme maneuver had overloaded the plane with G-forces and strained it beyond its limits. Rivets began to pop, the wings flexed, the nose of the plane tore free from the fuselage, fuel tanks ruptured, engines shattered, and the French fighter just blew itself apart.

"What the hell happened?" Hunter gasped.

"We didn't even hit him," Hardcase said. "The little fucker just disintegrated in mid-air!"

"It looked like he rolled around his stick," Hawk observed.

"That's impossible," Wilkes countered. "No one can do that."

"Obviously not," Roche said, looking down at the shower of flaming debris, "but I think that's what he was trying to do."

The act of "rolling around the stick" means the pilot pushes his control stick as far forward as it can go, pitching the plane straight down. Then he moves the stick around the edge of its mount, rolling it in a counter-clockwise motion. This rolls the plane left, pitches it upward, and rolls to the right, and finally pitches forward again, should the pilot make it all the way around. But halfway through the attempted maneuver the enormous g-forces spell doom for any plane at any speed. The plane would just tear itself apart under its own inertia, like what just happened to the Dassault.

"And that, kids, is exactly why we don't try that at home," Roche concluded.

Wilkes shook his head in amazement. "Crazy Frenchie."

## THE DESERT, 10 MILES NORTH OF CHECKMATE FLIGHT

An Iranian Air Force sergeant observed the distant explosions, and peered through night-vision binoculars to glimpse the two dark American fighters heading his way. He guessed they'd be overhead in just under a minute. He relayed the information into his walkie-talkie. The hillside below him opened up, revealing a camouflaged aircraft hanger. A straight dirt road leading north from the doors made a suitable runway for the four Su-37 Super Flankers parked inside. Colonel Lenonov and his three surviving mercenary pilots from Black Squadron scrambled to their jets and started the engines. The Hornets might be the *Stingrays* that defeated them the day before yesterday. The promise of revenge made them hungry with anticipation.

"Is anybody covering us?" Hawk asked a moment later.

"Um, no," Hunter answered.

"Feeling exposed again fellas?" Roche ribbed the wizzos. "Yo, Hacksaw, let me have a sitrep."

"We brought down half a dozen Fulcrums and Floggers. The rest of them are trying to figure out how to get around us."

"Okay, sounds like K.C. and take it from there. You and Hitman better get back on station. You're about a hundred and twenty miles away now."

"Yikes, I didn't realize how far we'd drifted."

"No worries, just come back to formation as soon as you can."

Hacksaw worked out the speed differential as his computer plotted the course. "We'll be on your wing in twenty minutes."

"We're going to be sitting ducks for the next twenty minutes?" Hunter's worried voice came back.

"Relax, buddy," Roche tried to reassure him. "K.C. has the bandits bottled up to the southeast, Side Bar has our southwestern flank, Rook can guard us to the north and northeast, and Knight and the others are tying up every bandit in the northwest corner of the country. Plus we have the Echo-threes watching the airspace all around. How could anyone get to us?"

"Checkmate Lead," Moderator called. "I have four new contacts coming up right behind and below you. I have no idea where they came from!"

"Perfect timing," Hunter muttered. "Just when you had me feeling all warm and fuzzy again."

"Shut up," Roche growled. "How'd they get so close, Mod? Are they stealths?"

"No sir. These things are *huge*. Flankers for sure."

"It's the Black Cobra again," Roche realized. The intel they had been given pre-op told them that the mercenary's forces were decimated and he was no threat. But unless there was another group of Flankers hiding out in camouflaged bases out here, that intel was dead wrong. He knew the Black Cobra himself must be leading what was left of his mercenary air force. He called up to the Sentry. "Moderator, you said he was right behind us. By right behind us do you mean-" Roche broke off when his threat radar warning arrested his attention. "Never mind. Hunter, jam them."

"I can't! They've already locked on to us!"

"Well then overpower them!"

"I can't do it with this gear. To overpower a Scarab radar lock I'd need a mark-seventy-seven pod, and you didn't let me put one on the loadout, because *you* said-"

"Shut up!" Roche yanked back on the stick, chopped the throttles, hung on the edge of a stall, and rolled into a dive, slammed the throttles to the stops, dropped two thousand feet in four seconds and leveled out. The Russians lost their radar lock. "Okay, *now* jam them. Hardcase, what's your status?"

"I got two of them on my tail. They haven't locked me yet, IDECM's doing its job, but Hawk says we can only hold them off that way for a couple minutes."

"Okay, Danny, lets split up and hit the dirt. There're some canyons a few miles ahead. We'll try to lose them in there."

"Whoa, whoa, whoa," Hunter protested. "Flying through a canyon in the dark with a seven-ton nuke on our belly? I'd rather take my chances with a Flanker."

Roche pointed back over his shoulder with his thumb. "Are you sure about that?"

Hunter looked back. Two huge interceptors were coming straight for them, including the Black Cobra. With their radar thwarted they were trying to close into visual range, and their landing lights were glaring into Hunter's eyes. "Oh, fuck, take us down!"

Roche pushed the plane into another steep dive.

Hunter kept watching the Russians gaining on them, and then they each fired a missile. "Down, down, down!" Hunter looked forward, and saw that Roche was taking them straight into an impossibly narrow ravine. "Not *that* far down!" The Hornet

551

disappeared below the rim of the canyon and the missiles exploded on the jagged rocks. Hunter held on for dear life, while Sharkey hugged the rocky walls. Then Jules Hidelmann briefly wondered why he was holding on so tightly to something he was sure was about to crash and kill him.

Lenonov pursued his target into the canyon. It shined brightly under his landing lights. He recognized this plane. The shimmering blue paint on this Super Hornet's wing tips had been scratched in familiar strips. "Sharkey," Lenonov said to himself. "I had hoped to meet you again."

Lt. Dave Richards watched from his E-3 Sentry as the two Super Hornets and four Super Flankers disappeared from his radar, losing themselves among the ground clutter. He could still track the Navy planes with their GPS tags, however. The two identifiers on his screen labeled CKMT1 and CKMT3 were zigging and zagging this way and that, and the altitude numbers next to each were bouncing all over but never more than two hundred feet above the terrain level. "Checkmate Two and Four," he called, "your guys need help. They've shifted tracks for evasive and are following the terrain. You'd better get up here now. And where the hell is Knight Flight?"

## KNIGHT FLIGHT

Deuce took slow, deep breaths, trying to slow his heart rate. The dogfight was taking a lot out of him.

"Looks like Sharkey's in trouble, Cap," Buzz said.

Deuce checked the situation on his MFD. "Where the hell did those Flankers come from? And who left Checkmate all alone like that?"

"Knight Lead, this is Checkmate Two. You read?"

"Yeah, I'm here Hacksaw. What in God's name happened to you?"

"Hitman and I were backing up Kansas City. We didn't mean to move off so far. Then Sharkey and Hardcase got ambushed."

"They're safe for the moment," Buzz updated. "They're playing keep-away now, but they can't run too long. Sharkey can't use much more fuel because-"

"I know – he needs to keep his wings heavy." Deuce didn't like the situation, but he kept his cool. Too many things had gone wrong too quickly; he had no specific target for his anger. Buzz picked up on

552

his tone. It was so calm it was scary. "Hacksaw, how far are you from intercept?"

"We'll be in missile range in fifteen minutes."

"Running flat out?"

"No, just FMT. Their course is taking them away from us. If we use afterburners we'll be out of fuel before we reach them."

"Okay. We're falling back and hopefully we can reach them in time to save their lives. Knight Flight," Deuce switched channels, "break off to intercept aggressors at prime track. Bartender, there's only eight Defiants now. Can you guys wrap up here?"

"Yeah, we got this under control," Blind Lady Lead answered.

The eleven remaining *Stingrays* broke away from the group and turned southeast, heading toward an intercept point. "I don't think we're going to make it," Buzz said. "We're eight minutes away and Sharkey and Hardcase will be lucky to last half that long."

"They're very lucky," Deuce said, "but you're right. Knights, you all know the situation. I need four of you to hit the afterburners and make the intercept. That means you'll run out of fuel very soon and have to ditch in the desert. I can't order anyone to-"

"Hey, I'm game," Bulldog cut in cheerfully. "I've always wanted to test the weight rating on this seat."

"I'm with you," his wingman, Doc Holliday chimed in.

"Great, put yourselves on Checkmate Three's heading."

The two Hornets shot away from the formation, and Deuce continued. "I need two more to cover Sharkey."

"What do you say, sub?" Beowulf asked.

"I say let's do it!" Sub-Lt. "Claymore" Bruce hit the afterburners and jumped away with Beowulf close behind.

**CHECKMATE FLIGHT**

"They've almost got a lock," Hawk warned. "They're killing our jammers."

"And I'm running out of canyon," Hardcase said grimly. "I'm gonna have to try something crazy here…"

"Hold it; I think something's interfering with their radar. It looks like-"

"Look out, cowboys!" A familiar voice called on open channel. Doc's Super Hornet appeared over the ridge directly in front of them. Hawk cringed as Doc fired a pair of missiles right over their heads. "Yeeeehaaw!!"

The big Russians forgot about their quarry and tried to escape form the confines of the canyon. But Bulldog appeared above and behind them and pinned them down. "You punks are goin' nowhere."

Hawk looked over his shoulder and watched the Super Flankers get vaporized in a series of intense explosions that filled the canyon with fire and wreckage. "Checkmate One, this is Three. Help has finally arrived."

It couldn't come soon enough for Checkmate One. The winding canyon Roche had been flying through straightened out into a long, narrow trench. The Flankers had them pinned with nowhere to go but straight up and right into their sights, or straight forward until they were run down. Running was futile against the faster Sukhois, but it was their only choice. Roche tried rolling and weaving but the gorge squeezed tighter until all he could do was run in a straight line, an easy target.

"I'm sorry it ends like this, Sharkey," Lenonov said in English on open channel. "You were a worthy opponent."

"You won't live to enjoy this," Roche answered in Russian.

"They've got us locked again, top-down," Hunter said. The Flankers were in the best possible position to make a missile kill. "We're screwed."

"Not yet." Roche looked back. The Black Cobra fired a single AA-12 missile. "Have you ever used an FOTD before?"

"No. You?"

"Nope, but now looks like a good time to try."

Hunter selected the device from the EWOC panel. The high-tech decoy deployed on its five-hundred-foot fiber-optic cable, luring the missile in.

"What in the hell?" The Black Cobra watched his missile fall behind the Super Hornet and home in on a small device dangling on a string in Sharkey's jetwash. It intercepted the decoy and exploded, leaving the Hornet unscathed. Lenonov frowned. He'd heard of the FOTD. He'd also heard that the IDECM system only came with one of the sophisticated lures. "Let's try that again."

"I guess that worked," Hunter remarked as he watched the Adder explode far behind them.

"Unfortunately that only works once," Roche said.

Hunter kept watching the Black Cobra. "Okay, then I guess *now* we're screwed."

Roche didn't disagree. He could maybe outmaneuver the Super Flanker on his tail, but even if he somehow managed to slip behind him, the other mercenary would be on his back in seconds. Roche considered trying it anyway, but then the Black Cobra fired a missile right at them. He just shook his head in resignation.

"This is Checkmate One," Hunter called on the command channel. "We're about to be killed."

"Not today!" someone answered, just as a screaming blue shape split the sky and dove on top of them, and then exploded.

"We're hit!" Hunter yelled.

"No we're not," Roche answered, as he pulled the plane out of the canyon. "Someone just took the missile for us."

Hunter twisted in his seat and saw their plane was indeed still intact, and not lost in the cloud of smoke that marked the missile's deadly impact. "Who was that?"

Roche didn't look back, but he knew who it was. The accent was unmistakable. "It sounded like Claymore."

"Ian old boy, that was a damn foolish thing to do," Claymore said to himself, as he felt the missile smash into his plane.

He had slowed to subsonic speed just as he came within visual range of the Flankers. He saw the missile streaking toward the mission critical, and hit the afterburners again. He'd once heard Roche talk about how time slows down around you when pure adrenaline takes control of your mind. Now he'd felt that himself, allowing him to maneuver his fighter into the sixty-foot gap between the missile and the other plane. He watched the AA-12 missile come down over his head, and felt it punch into his Hornet right between his tail fins.

The whole rear of his plane was engulfed in flames, and every warning alarm was blaring in the cockpit, but the engines were still providing thrust, the wings were still generating lift, and the tail surfaces still gave him a degree of control. He saw the Flanker roar by over his head. He pulled up and flipped upside down, above the big black Russian fighter that had just hit him and tried to kill Sharkey and Hunter. Claymore figured that they must still be alive, because the Russian appeared to be trying to line up another shot.

Claymore's computer wouldn't let him use a missile, because it had to devote every bit of processing power it had to keep the splintered fighter in the air. Instead, he let the Hornet fall directly on top of the Flanker. The astonished Russian pilot looked up just in time to see Claymore slam in to him. "Hello there," the Scotsman said on open channel as the superfighters collided. "Fox-zero, you commie bastard." The jets locked together, back-to-back. Sub-Lt. Ian Bruce and Col. Victor Lenonov glared at each other through their canopies. The Black Cobra tried to shake his plane free, but Claymore rolled to the right and pegged the throttles, pushing the heavier Sukhoi to the ground. Lenonov kept trying to roll out from under the Hornet and Claymore rolled with him, pushing them into an irrecoverable dive. Claymore bailed out at the last minute, rocketing passed the Flanker, flat parallel to the ground and only two hundred feet above the desert floor. The superfighters ploughed into the terrain at 500 knots in a cataclysm of fire, rock and metal.

"Holy shit!" was all Hunter could think to say.

"Way to go, Claymore," Roche said. "Did Beowulf get the other one?"

"Yeah, we're clear. How's the plane doing?"

"Not good. The computer's fighting with me, throwing the trim all off... I'm turning on all of our external lights. Take another look back there and make sure we're really not missing our tail."

Hunter took a long look. The visual identification strobe shed a little light on the damage. "Now that I look closely, it seems like we're missing the tips of our fins, and our right rudder is almost completely gone. And the elevators looked like they've been chewed on by a giant rottweiler."

"Well, that would explain why the autopilot keeps trying to make me crash. Okay, I need you to run a complete SHOC diagnostic from your terminal."

"Can you still fly it?"

"I think so. The SHOC should adapt to the new handling characteristics once you reboot the flight assist computer. I'm actually more concerned with our EW and comm systems. The diagnostic will tell us what's missing."

"Missing?"

"From the tips of our vertical stabilizers. That's where we keep all the little antennas, you know. ECM, VHF radio, satcom, GPS, threat radar receiver..."

"Oh, great. Yeah, IDECM is definitely history," Hunter reported. He checked the other systems. "Radar warning... I'm getting null signature, so that's toast. Satcom... out. GPS... okay. Radio... should be intact."

"I'll give it a try." Roche tuned the radio to the command frequency. "This is Checkmate One. Radio check." No answer. "Checkmate One calling all friendlies, can anyone hear me?" Silence. "I seem to be experiencing radio difficulties. If anyone can hear me, I'm not receiving your copy."

"I'll try the SHOClink once the computer boots up," Hunter said. "That antenna is on a separate dorsal mount."

"Good idea."

Beowulf pulled alongside just then and waved to get Roche's attention. Roche waved back, and Beowulf tapped the side of his helmet over his ear.

"Beowulf," Roche called, "can you hear me?"

The Englishman nodded.

"We took some damage. The radio seems to be working on transmit only. Use the SHOClink SMS to respond."

The Short Message System allowed Super Hornet aviators transmit flight data and coordinates between their computers without tying up their radio channels. It worked almost exactly like a cell phone's text messenger.

Hunter read Beowulf's reply. *"Copy your last, I'll tell the others, and one of us will relay pertinent team chatter. You look pretty shook up."*

"We're okay," Roche answered. "Is Claymore alright?"

*"I thought I saw him punch out. I don't know if he made it after that, though."*

"What about Hardcase?"

*"Checkmate Three is clear. Bulldog and Doc took care of that. The three of us are low on fuel, though. We'll have to ditch before we reach the target."*

"Understood. Thanks for the backup, you guys. We woulda been toast if you hadn't charged in to our rescue."

## SOUTH EDGE OF THE TARGET ZONE

"Rook flight, this is Bishop Lead, I've selected your targets. Confirm and make your approach," Palerider instructed.

"This is Rook Lead," Worm answered. "I have my target profiles." The rest of his squadron echoed the report. "Rook Flight, break formation and begin roll-on." The twelve Hornets still carried plenty of bombs and missiles to assault the air defenses in the target area.

"Don't get lazy with your self-protection jammers," Palerider advised. "We have their radar locked down now but they could always pull up something else."

As if to illustrate, an SA-10 radar site suddenly activated right behind Worm's division. "Deadeye" Unther turned around and shot a HARM down its throat before it could lock on. Worm led his division right up to the mountain, firing missiles at the targets the Aurora had scanned two nights before.

## CHECKMATE FLIGHT

Within a few minutes, the rest of the *Stingrays* had reformed their protective ring around the mission criticals. Somewhere ahead of them, Stingaree and Blind Lady had finished clearing the airspace of Defiants, and Bishop and Rook were dismantling the wall of defenses around the bunker complex.

*"We're coming up on the target area,"* Deuce told Sharkey and Hunter via SMS. *"Are you still okay to do this? Castle has been advised of your condition and wants a go-no-go confirmation."*

"What do we tell him?" Hunter asked the pilot.

Roche thought it over for a moment. The flight-assist computer was now compensating for the damaged control surfaces, and the plane was flying almost normally. The engines were running strong, and everything related to dropping the bomb seemed to be in working order. "We can do it," he told Hunter.

"Are you sure? With all the damage we took back there-"

"We're battered, not broken," Roche declared. "The Rhino won't let us down."

Hunter keyed his radio. "Checkmate One is go."

"Castle, this is Knight Lead," Deuce called back to the *Reagan*. "Checkmate elements confirm go."

"Do it," Krause said.

"Checkmate Three, this is Knight Lead. You are 'Sandhog,' repeat, you are 'Sandhog.' You may begin your target approach."

"Copy that," Hardcase answered. "Sandhog has the target." He accelerated away from the pack, followed by Hitman.

Hunter read the SMS from Deuce. *"Checkmate One, you are 'Nuclear Hornet.' Stand by to make your target approach."*

558

"Nuclear Hornet confirms," Roche radioed. He flexed in his seat and looked back at Hunter. "Don't worry, buddy. I have a feeling we'll make it, somehow."

# CHAPTER 26: MIDNIGHT

## THE BUNKER – 0255 LOCAL

"The bombs have been programmed and are fitted to the missiles," Boris the *Teknikir* announced.

Rannovich acknowledged him with a nod and looked to President Ahmadinejad. "Your weapons will be ready to launch as soon as we move the missiles to the surface."

"Excellent!" The Iranian president exclaimed. "I will give the order to launch as soon as they are in place."

"They will be ready within the hour," Boris assured him.

## USS *RONALD REAGAN* – SAME TIME (1125 UTC)

"Admiral, we have a serious problem," General Rainier said as he stepped into the AirOps Center.

"What kind of problem?"

Admiral Krause guessed it was something to do with the nuclear bomb, because that was as far as the Air Force General's responsibilities extended.

Rainier was holding a small plastic bag. He handed it to the Admiral and told him what was inside. "That's the GPS switch that was supposed to be installed into the RNEP. Apparently the bomb technicians overlooked it. Don't touch it, please!"

Krause had opened the bag to peer at the circuit array inside. The plastic material of the bag was heavy and nearly opaque, impregnated with a thin layer of lead foil to protect the sensitive device from electrostatic discharge. A static spark strong enough for him to feel would be ten times more intense than necessary to destroy the tiny circuits.

Krause glanced around. Everyone in the room was looking at him, not at their screens. "Let's take a walk," he said, leaving the AirOps Center and walking toward his conference room. "Remind me, what does this thing do again?"

Rainier followed as he explained. "This interferes with the timing circuit if the bomb is triggered outside of the specified GPS coordinates. Basically it's a safety backup so in case Commander Roche misses, the bomb won't detonate on the surface."

"Okay, well what am I supposed to do about it? Roche is less than twenty minutes away from the target right now."

"Washington was adamant. We can't risk a surface blast. You need to recall Commander Roche immediately."

Krause stopped mid-stride. "Impossible. The whole air wing just fought through hell to get this far. Besides, Sandhog is going to make their strike in about three minutes. Then the Iranians will know we've found the bunker and that we have the ability to hit it. They'll evacuate before we can rearm for another crack at it."

"Then recall Wilkes also," Rainier said.

"Only the President can recall the strike package at this phase," Krause told him. He turned and went to the Combat Information Center and spoke to one of the comm officers. "Lieutenant Page, get the Pentagon on the line and tell them I need a conference with President and Joint Chiefs immediately, if not sooner. Ensign Hammil," Krause called to another officer. "You get the White House; ask for the same thing. Get us all connected via Telepresence."

"I got the damage report from Hunter, sir," Hannibal announced from the doorway to AirOps. "Nuclear Hornet is still operational within parameters."

"Roche's plane was damaged?" the General asked.

"Only slightly," Commander Burke said. "He had a near-miss with a missile. But the Rhino is a very robust platform, designed to survive this kind of damage. They're still mission-ready."

"Pentagon says they'll be online in just a minute, sir," the comm lieutenant told Admiral Krause.

"Good."

"I'm telling the President that the plane was damaged," Rainier declared.

"Fine," Krause said, "but I'm still telling him that this is still our only shot."

"No, its not. If we pull Sandhog back also-"

"Sandhog is on final roll-on approach," Hannibal interrupted, "thirty seconds to release. We will definitely be scrubbing the mission if we recall Nuclear Hornet now."

## THE TARGET ZONE

Hardcase and Hawk were upside-down at thirty thousand feet. Hardcase pulled back on the stick gently, putting the plane in an inverted dive. He adjusted their angle until they were in a vertical descent, directly over the ventilation shaft. At ten thousand feet, Hardcase released the bomb and pulled back on the stick again. The Hornet leveled off and headed south, back to the *Reagan*.

561

The GBU-37b stabilized its fall with small fins on its nose and tail, checked its coordinates with the GPS and wobbled itself into line above the shaft. It plunged through the opening only inches off the center of the circle. After falling another six hundred feet it punched through a machine assembly – a particle filter and cooling unit designed to hide telltale radiation traces and heat from American satellites. The smashed machinery followed the bomb another hundred feet to the bottom of the shaft. The bomb went fifty feet further into solid concrete, before finally detonating and vaporizing the wreckage on top of it. The current of air sucked dust and small bits of debris back up the shaft, leaving a clear shot and only two hundred feet of rock between the next bomb and the bunker.

"Direct hit," Hawk announced as the bomb's telemetry went dead.

"That was easy," Hardcase said.

Sandhog had done its part.

## THE BUNKER

"What the hell was that?" Rannovich looked up, puzzled, while everyone else in the command center dove for cover.

He glared at General Mikhail until the Russian came out from under a desk. "I asked 'what the hell was that?' So? What was that?"

Mikhail grabbed his keyboard and started looking for an answer. "A bomb of some sort, sir. With our radar all knocked out I can't say for sure."

"Yes, obviously it was a bomb, and we could feel it way down here, which means it was either way too big or way too close. Check our ventilation shafts. That's the only way it could have come that close to us."

Mikhail complied. "Uh, the air exchanger units on shaft seven appear to have gone off-line, and that's right over our heads so I imagine that's where they hit us."

"What are they doing?" Ahmadinejad asked. "Are they carpet-bombing the mountain and just happened to drop one right down that hole?"

Rannovich looked up again. "That would have to be an unbelievably lucky shot. I'm going to go check our armor units and see if we can get some mobile radar out there to give us a look. I'll be right back. In the meantime, send that last mercenary squadron out to stop them."

"We need your decision, Mr. President," Rainier said. "Roche needs an order either way." The video conference was patched directly into the *Reagan*'s op center.

McNeil nodded. "Explain to me again what the problem is with this safety chip."

"Yes, sir." Rainier started to describe the system again.

Krause looked away as he rolled his eyes. Apparently the President didn't realize that this was not the time to stall a decision. Then he saw Hannibal waving him over to the mission comm station.

"We can't wait any longer, sir." Burke told him. "Right now Roche is holding position fifteen minutes from the target, and every minute he waits gives the enemy a better chance of finding him. He's in very hostile airspace."

"I know, I know." Krause checked his watch. "With his radio out, we can't recall him after he moves out of the Knights' formation though."

"No, we can; Hacksaw is going to stick with him until he starts his dive. He can relay an abort order by SMS up until that point."

"Wally," Brett McNeil called, "what's your take?"

Krause turned and walked back toward the other station. "It's pretty simple from where I'm standing, sir. Either we take our chances with Roche, or we scrub the mission entirely. He could pull it off and we can all go home, or he could miss by two feet and the whole world will start blowing itself up. I'd put my money on Sharkey though."

"Okay, give me a couple minutes."

"Sir, you don't have much time to play with." But the audio feed had already been shut off.

Krause looked at his watch again, then at the video. He waited until he caught the eye of the CNO, and then he nodded to Burke. "Alright, tell them to go."

Burke relayed the instruction, and Krause saw Admiral Marsh nod in tacit approval.

"Admiral," Rainier stepped in, "we need to wait for the President's orders."

"No we don't. My original orders stand unless the POTUS says otherwise. So far he hasn't, and he's got just under fifteen minutes to change his mind."

"He doesn't know that. Dammit Wally, you're gambling with one point six megatons of energy here. This kind of decision is way beyond your pay grade."

"Yours too," Krause reminded him sharply. "And on my ship yours counts for nothing. If you step out of bounds again, I'll kick you over the rail myself, got that?"

"Uh, sirs?" Burke spoke up. "Did you just say 'one point six megatons'? As in the size of the bomb?"

Krause bit his lip.

Rainier said "Yes. A B61 warhead, variable yield from ten to sixteen hundred kilotons. It's set for the max. It has to be in order to make sure we get the bunker. The way it's hardened, anything less than a megaton might not do the job."

"Okay," Hannibal said, "but that's not what they simulated. Sharkey, Hunter, Deuce and those guys from Boeing were working on the escape profile based on a bomb in the low kiloton range. Does that mean…"

"Yes," Krause answered the question that Burke couldn't finish. "I knowingly sent Roche and Hidelmann to almost certain death. There's almost no possibility that they can escape the blast. But look," he pointed to the map display, which was now swarming with red triangles between the target area and the coast. "The Iranians have committed practically their entire air force to stopping our guys on the way back. Our Hornets are just about out of missiles. They'll get creamed. The only chance any of them have at getting back now is if we take out that command bunker."

"But there's a very good possibility they'll put that blast on the surface instead of a thousand feet underground," Rainier said.

"Roche can do it," the Admiral stated. "He *will* do it."

"…And probably die trying," Burke muttered.

"Maybe," Rainier said with an indifferent shrug.

Krause glared at him, then raised his eyes heavenward. "God forgive us."

## FIVE MILES SOUTH OF TARGET ZONE – 0314 LOCAL

Roche had been flying in a tight circle for the last fifteen minutes since Hardcase had gone in. Hunter was getting impatient again, as could be expected. "Deuce," Roche called, "what's the word?"

Hunter read the response. "*Stand by, Castle hit a snag.* Oh, damn it all, they're actually gonna scrub us."

"I thought that was what you wanted all along," Roche said.

"Well, that was before we put all the effort into getting here."

"I see."

564

*"Nuclear Hornet:"* Hunter's screen flashed, *"you may begin target approach."*

Hunter read the message and told Roche, "Never mind, it's on."

"Nuclear Hornet copies," Roche said over the radio. "Climbing to angels sixty for final target approach." Roche pulled back on the stick and pushed the throttles forward to begin his long climb.

Hacksaw followed closely.

## DOMINO FLIGHT, 50 MILES NORTH OF TARGET ZONE

Three Raptors exploded from the sky for no apparent reason.

"Domino flight under attack!" the squadron leader called on the command frequency. "It's an ambush – someone's in the grass behind us shooting heatseekers!"

Lt. Dave Richards on board his E-3 saw the enemy fighters emerge just behind Domino's position.

"Twelve bandits just popped up on radar. Big contacts. Identifying Super Flankers attacking Domino flight."

"I thought we were finished with these idiots," Deuce sighed. "Domino, hit the gas and head southeast to draw them up. We'll join you on a northeast vector."

"Assuming there's any of us left," Domino-1 replied. "We can't outrun Flankers. They're keeping in infrared range and- oh, fuck, we've lost another one."

"This is Moderator. Contacts are splitting up. Four bandits broke away and are heading southwest. They're intercepting Nuclear Hornet!"

With his nose pointed to the sky, Roche's radar wasn't picking up the contacts coming up below him. Hacksaw was monitoring the command channel and let him know what was going on.

"Okay," Roche said "we've only got three Sidewinders between the two of us, Hacksaw. We're basically defenseless here. Knight, you're going to have to pull them off of us somehow."

Knight Flight was reduced to seven Hornets and very few missiles. And they were heading the wrong way, trying to save Domino somewhere east of the target zone. They'd have to use afterburner to rejoin Checkmate. Deuce didn't spend a lot of time thinking about the situation. "I'm going after them. The rest of you, stay on this heading." Deuce turned the plane around sharply and punched the throttle.

"Good luck, Captain," Blackjack called after him. "Knight Five, taking command. Bandits coming in range."

"Domino just lost two more Raptors," Mystique noted, assessing the TacOps from Knight-5's back seat.

"Let's get their attention." Blackjack fired a pair of AMRAAMs at maximum range. The other Knights joined in with the remainder of their medium-range weapons. "Domino, we're gonna drive in to close range. You circle behind us once we've tied them up and reengage at a more comfortable distance."

"You got it, Knight."


Roche leveled off at 60,000 feet. As his nose dropped toward the horizon, his radar detected the enemy aircraft on intercept. "Not again. Hacksaw..."

"I'm on it," Hacksaw said, forgetting for a moment that his wingman couldn't hear him. He accelerated in front of Roche and jammed their radar. The Russians split their attention, pairing up on each Hornet.

"I can jam them up," Hunter said, "so they can't get a radar lock, but once they get close to us we're doomed."

"Hacksaw," Roche called, "it probably won't work, but you need to get all four of them to chase you."

"You're right," Miller said to himself, "it won't work, but what the hell."

He abruptly accelerated toward the Flankers going after Sharkey and fired both of his Sidewinders. The Sukhois he'd targeted rolled away and dropped flares to dodge the missiles, giving Roche the opportunity to accelerate past them. The other two Super Flankers shot at Checkmate-2. Hacksaw rolled and dove out of the line of fire.

"He bought us some time," Hunter said, "but he wasn't able to take anyone out."

Roche nodded grimly, thinking for the second time in an hour that they were about to be killed, and then he saw something else on the radar. "Deuce?"


Two Sidewinders destroyed the Flanker closest to the mission critical. Deuce went right through the enemy formation and the mercenaries chased after him.

"That's right," he said. "Come and get me."

"Holy crap!" In the back seat, Buzz was on the edge of panic.

"Just hold on back there, buddy. I'm not going to let them kill you." Deuce said that with no real assurance. In his position, there was no way to keep the Flankers from closing in and getting a missile lock. He could dance around with the more agile Hornet, but not for long.

"Deuce," Mystique called, "two more Flankers broke off from us. They're out of our range already and they're heading straight toward you at max speed."

"They're cutting us off to the east," Buzz noted, checking the MFD. "They're going to push us right over the blast area."

"Brace yourself!" Deuce realized just in time that a Super Flanker had got a lock on him and it took a snap shot with a short-range Archer. The most accurate missile in the world streaked right toward the side of the plane. Deuce rolled away and the missile exploded short, but shrapnel from the fragmentation warhead perforated his right wing. The plane spun wildly.

Deuce clutched his chest, grunting at the pain. He held his breath, and seized the controls, trying to wrestle the Hornet into submission. Finally he got some air under the good wing and leveled out. He checked where the Flankers had gone. The mercenary fighter that shot them moved in behind Knight-1, and the other two broke off.

Deuce swore. "They're going after Sharkey again!"

"He's right on our tail, Skipper!"

"Not for long."

With his damaged wing, Deuce couldn't roll or turn fast enough anymore. So he pushed the plane over sharply and dove toward the ground. The Russian followed closely. "Here's a little trick I learned from Sharkey." Deuce pulled back hard on the stick and throttle, coming to a near stop directly in front of the Flanker. The enemy pilot pulled up to avoid a collision, and Deuce followed with his crosshairs, firing a stream of 20mm shells between the Russian's engines. The Sukhoi split apart in mid-air. Deuce punched the throttle and flipped the Hornet back the way it came.

The pain hit again. Deuce pulled his pills out of his vest pocket and popped the lid off, but while fumbling for his facemask he dropped the pills. He cursed again.

"They're almost in range," Buzz told him.

The Russians saw him, and turned to face him. "I'll teach you not to ignore me." Deuce fired his last two Sidewinders at maximum range and took out the leader. Two more Super Flankers were closing in from the southeast, and Deuce was now out of missiles. "We're in serious trouble, now," Buzz said

Buzz didn't know the half of it. Deuce could feel his heart pounding – the pain was immense. He knew he didn't have long before he went into cardiac arrest. One way or another, he'd be dead very soon. "We've got their attention now," he said. "We just need to lead them away from Roche."

"That means going right over the fallout area. If they shoot us down…"

"I told you I won't let them kill you," Deuce said. He reached down on his console and hit the master arm switch for the ejection seats.

"What are you doing?"

"Punching you out here where it's safe. Watch your arms and legs." Without further ado he yanked a handle on the floor and the canopy disappeared. Lt. jg Bobby Edwards screamed as his seat rocketed him away from the Hornet.

"Knight One squawking on SAR and command channels," Deuce shouted into the radio over the roaring wind. "One chute at my current position."

Deuce could hear nothing but the white noise of wind rushing around the plane at 400 knots. The alarms fell on deaf ears as enemy missiles came screaming toward him. He suddenly yanked the stick and twirled the plane in the air. Flare shells shot off in all directions, luring the missiles away. Deuce leveled the Hornet on a collision course with the Super Flankers. He held the trigger down and shot a steam of cannon fire right through the nose and cockpit of the lead fighter. The other two pulled away in alarm but Deuce came right after them. "None of us is going anywhere."

He flew straight under them and pulled up into their path. His wings sliced into the Flankers and the impact tore all three planes apart in mid-air. The Hornet's nose peeled away from the wreckage, and tumbled away toward the ground as all three superfighters blew apart in an explosion that filled the sky. Deuce tried to eject, but he had disarmed his seat and had no electrical power to reset the master switch. The spinning motion applied enormous G-forces to his body.

*It's almost over,* he thought. *Loraine, boys, I'm sorry.*

The pounding in his chest stopped abruptly. He felt nothing when the armored cockpit of the Hornet slammed into the desert floor.

*     *     *

"We're clear," Hunter said. "The bandits are out of the picture." He wasn't sure what was happening with Deuce but he saw all the contacts vanish from his MFD.

Roche could see the same thing. He felt no need to comment further. "We're at roll-on point in thirty seconds."

## REAGAN

Krause watched the blue triangle marking Knight One disappear from the map display, along with the two red triangles that had converged with it.

Rainier diverted his attention back to the telepresence video screen just as the Commander-in-Chief came back.

"Okay," the President said. "Admiral, I want you to go ahead and call him off. Confirmation code N-H-X triple-zero."

"Yes, sir," Krause said. His voice betrayed no emotion but as he turned from the camera his face filled with anger and sadness. "Commander Burke, relay the order."

## DEEP INTO THE TARGET ZONE, THREE MILES FROM GROUND ZERO

"Hacksaw," Roche called, "When we roll in, you should turn east and maintain altitude and don't slow down for anything until you put a good ten miles between you and the target. Then rejoin with Knight once you're clear of the target zone."

Hacksaw keyed *ok* into the SMS to acknowledge.

"Checkmate Two, this is Castle," Hannibal called on a private frequency. "The President orders Nuclear Hornet to break off the target and cancel the strike. Relay order and confirmation code November hotel x-ray zero zero zero by SMS."

Hacksaw looked out the windscreen and saw Sharkey Roche roll the damaged Hornet away, beginning his eleven-mile supersonic dive toward the end of the war. He looked at the radar, and saw the empty airspace to the west where Captain Thompson had met his end. "Negative, Castle," Lt. Miller answered and lied. "Nuclear Hornet is on his dive, and I am out of SHOClink range, over."

## REAGAN

Burke wore a thin smile as he looked up from the comm station. "Too late, sir."

Krause turned back to the President. "It appears Commander Roche is out of communications range, sir. He's begun his dive. We can't reach him now."

Several of the Joint Chiefs sighed heavily, and General Rainier groaned out loud.

The President just nodded. "Very well."

Krause saw Admiral Marsh flash the thumbs-up sign. He had been in private counsel with the President a few minutes before. Krause realized they'd planned it this way. Marsh had told McNeil that Krause had ordered Roche in, and the President deliberately delayed his decision until it was too late to stop the strike, ensuring that Roche got his chance but simultaneously diverting responsibility if it all went wrong.

"Clever, for a politician," Krause muttered.

## DIRECTLY ABOVE THE TARGET

"We're in the pipe," Hunter announced.

Roche had to fight hard to get the injured Super Hornet to reach its perfectly vertical angle of descent over the target, but he got it and held it.

"Afterburner on my mark, eleven seconds," Hunter told him

"Did you adjust for the added drag caused by all the missile damage?"

"Uh, no."

"I did." Roche hit the afterburner. "I actually changed the plan quite a bit," Roche yelled over the roaring engines. "Like slowing down is going to be a little more difficult too. I'm going to have to deploy the landing gear, so get ready to lock out the hydraulics."

"When were you going to tell me that?"

"Just now. You had enough to worry about. I didn't want you to die of a heart attack before I could slam you into the mountain."

"I don't really give a damn anymore," Hunter groaned. "Take this thing into the rocks and make it count. I don't wanna walk away from this wreck."

"Whatever you say. How's my track?"

"Go down a little."

Roche pushed the nose down. With the added thrust the Hornet was trying to angle upward. Roche compensated for the resistance and held steady pressure on the stick. "Forty thousand feet, one point five Mach."

"Too slow."

"Too much drag."

The Hornet abruptly rolled to the left. Roche corrected quickly and put them back on target. "What the hell was that?" Hunter demanded.

"I think we just lost a little piece of our left wing. That's nothing to worry about. Thirty thousand feet, Mach two." They were descending now at nearly a thousand feet per second.

Hunter looked over his shoulder and saw that large panel was indeed missing from the upper surface of the wing. "Huh. How about that."

"Trim is all messed up on that side," Roche announced calmly. "I'm going to jettison our last Sidewinder to compensate." The missile on the left wingtip fell away and tumbled in the slipstream behind them. "Coming into the clouds now." He tried to hold the plane steady as turbulence bounced them around. They broke through and Roche steered back on course. "Twenty thousand feet, begin countdown."

"Arming weapon and beginning countdown to release at twenty-four hundred. We are now at sixteen thousand... Fifteen thousand."

"Mach two-point-four." The engines burned hotter in thicker air – something the simulators didn't account for.

"Thirteen thousand... Twelve thousand."

"Two-point-five."

"Ten thousand. Weapon is armed, GPS tracking and telemetry is five-by-five. Seven thousand feet."

"Two-point-six Mach!" The Hornet was going faster than any American fighter had ever gone before.

"Release in five, four, three, two-"

"Now!" Roche's right thumb depressed the pickle and the Hornet lurched as the seven-ton bomb dropped away. He yanked the throttle back to idle and jerked the stick back as far as it could go. His fingers flew around the controls and hit the airbrakes, flaps, slats, and landing gear. The plane groaned as the wings absorbed the air resistance. The nose came up from the ground, passed the horizon and reached for the sky. Roche jammed the throttles open and punched the afterburners again. The Hornet drifted downwards for only a moment, floated on the cushion of air exhausted from the ventilation shaft, then jumped forward as if had been kicked. Roche leveled off and willed the screaming machine to go faster. He had only a moment to escape from the imminent blast, and his windscreen was filled with mountains.

The bomb rattled off the sides of the shaft as it dropped seven hundred and fifty feet in a heartbeat. The reinforced nose bit the rock and ripped it open, tearing the bottom out of the pit. It took all two-hundred-and-fifty-two feet of solid rock to slow the bomb from Mach 2.65 to a more earthly velocity of eighty feet per second. The Bunker was nestled in a cavity, separated from the rock by a layer of oil and springy foam. The bomb fell through that and broke through the twenty feet of copper and lead-lined, reinforced ceramic protecting the bunker itself.

President Ahmadinejad was at his desk, preparing a speech that would follow the launch of his nuclear missiles. He looked up and then fell back in his chair as the battered titanium-carbide nosecone crashed through the ceiling of his office and ground to a halt halfway through. He brushed the plaster and dust off his jacket as he stood up to examine the weapon suspended inches above his desk. "A dud!" he laughed to himself. "All that trouble and the Americans drop a dud on my desk!" He walked around the desk and saw that an access panel had torn away from the casing. He peered inside and saw LCD numbers flashing away, counting down from some infinite sum and rapidly approaching zero. "Oh, hell."

A column of brilliant white light reached from the depths of the earth to the heavens. The ground shook, then leapt for the sky, forming a mile-wide dome of displaced rock. The dome collapsed as the fireball reached the surface, splitting rock asunder with an almighty thunderclap. A solid wall of dust marked the shockwave which raced in all directions at the speed of sound and obliterated anything that stood before it. The cloud of fire and radioactive debris seemed to climb from the crater in slow motion. Miles away, hidden doors were blown open from the inside by tongues of flame reaching out from the underground blast. Wreckage of man and machine tumbled from the dark tunnels out into the desert. Rannovich's war machine was annihilated in seconds.

### REAGAN
The *Reagan*'s command staff, the Joint Chiefs and the President watched an infrared camera feed from an Aurora fifty miles north of the target. Nuclear Hornet was a tiny hot spot on the screen. They watched as it separated from the bomb, and a moment later the smaller

speck of heat suddenly expanded into a mile-wide white-hot ball of fire and destruction.

"What's the time?" President asked.

"Double-ought-oh-three UTC, sir," Krause answered.

"Look, it's blasting through the tunnels." Rainier pointed at the screen, and everyone could see a surge of heat spreading through the spiderweb network under the mountain. "We definitely got them."

"Admiral," the President spoke again. "Is there any chance at all that Commander Roche could have survived that?"

"There's always a chance, sir, but I don't see how he could've gotten clear."

"I'll address the nation at the next hour. If there is any word on him, make sure I know about it, okay?"

"Understood, Mr. President."

## KNIGHT FLIGHT, 30 MILES NNW OF GROUND ZERO

Lt. jg. Palmer was the first *Stingray* to say something. He just blurted an expletive in a tone of awe.

"That's what we came for, Gator," Blaze said. "What did you expect, the Disney World fireworks show?"

"I know, but…" he ran out of words and just stared.

"Are we safe here?" someone asked.

"Yeah, we're okay," Mystique answered. "The wind should blow all the fallout to the northwest. Whatever gets out of the mountains will dissipate over the Caspian Sea."

"Any sign of Sharkey?" Blackjack was the first to ask.

"There's not going to be much left of him," Ronin said.

"You don't know that," Blackjack countered. "He made it out in the simulator."

"He wasn't shot up in the simulator," Ronin said. "And I'm pretty sure the bomb wasn't that big either. That was no low-yield device, I can tell you."

"He'd radio us if he was clear, wouldn't he?" Hacksaw wondered.

"Maybe his radio got knocked out the rest of the way," Blaze suggested.

"Does anyone have anything on radar?" Rooster asked

"Nothing," Mystique reported. As the last wizzo in the squadron she'd taken the responsibility of monitoring all radar. "The background radiation screws everything up."

"I'm going down there to take a look," Blackjack decided.

"I'm coming with you," Hacksaw replied.

The two Hornets turned on their landing lights as they cautiously approached the giant mushroom cloud. The entire desert seemed to be alive, now moving *toward* the crater as wind tried to fill the vacuum under the pillar of fire.

"I can't see anything in that dust storm," Blackjack said.

Hacksaw watched a river of dust flow down a canyon and saw lights moving against the current. "Two o'clock low. It's him!"

The bright blue Hornet with the flashing strobe on its back stood out against the background. Blackjack and Hacksaw closed in and formed up on either side. Inside, Sharkey and Hunter had taken off their masks and appeared to be laughing hysterically.

The command channel crackled with static for a second, and then Karl Roche's voice broke through. "Are you looking for us?"

Hacksaw started to type an answer, but Roche spoke again. "Just use the radio. I can hear you guys now."

"Sharkey, you freaking lunatic. I can't believe you made it."

"Neither can Hunter. I'm trying to convince him he's not dead. I dropped into this canyon and the blast went right over our heads!"

"Are you guys alright?" Blackjack asked

"I'm reading minimal radiation, well within safe exposure. And the plane is still holding up. Hey, I think I even got the nose gear down!"

"I don't believe it," Hacksaw said again.

"Believe it, baby. *We did it!*"

Blackjack looked back at the mushroom cloud, now ten miles high. "Yeah, you sure did. Okay, Sharkey, let's get you guys home."

### REAGAN

"I don't believe it," Hannibal muttered. He looked through the door into the CIC and called to Admiral Krause. "Sir, it's Sharkey! He's alive!"

General Rainier entered Air Ops first. "No way," he said.

Admiral Krause followed, and he did not look surprised. "How is he?"

"You can ask him yourself, sir. His radio appears to be working again."

Krause plugged his headset in. "Nuclear Hornet, this is Castle King. How are you doing, son?"

"Not bad, Castle," Roche replied, "considering I just outran a nuclear shockwave."

Wally Krause smiled, and a tear started to form in his left eye. "Good work, Commander. I'll talk to you when you get back."

"I look forward to it, Admiral."

## SIX MILES NORTHEAST OF GROUND ZERO

Somewhere amidst the swirling dust and ashes there was a titanium shell crumpled into an impact crater. Still cocooned in the protective armored cockpit, the body of Joshua Thompson serenely rode out the nuclear maelstrom.

# CHAPTER 27: NOT AS STRONG

## THE WHITE HOUSE – 2058 EDT

White House Press Secretary Evan Schwab stood at the lectern embossed with the Presidential Seal and scanned the eyes of the Washington press corps. Some of them were watching him impatiently, expecting an announcement. Some of the TV news reporters were trying to rearrange their camera crews. Several people were talking on cell phones or doing something with their laptop computers. One or two were idly watching the sound engineers make their final adjustments. But Schwab spotted a handful of observant veteran reporters who were looking at the Seal on the lectern, at the eagle facing to his left, toward the olive branch of peace.

The engineers waved at Schwab to get his attention. They pointed to his camera and one counted down with his fingers. Five, four, three, two, one… Evan Schwab looked into his camera and waited half a beat before speaking. He was looking through nearly every television set in the country, and much of the world right at this moment. He was on every network and cable news station in the US, plus BBC in the UK, and CNN broadcasting everywhere else. Evan felt a smile playing at the corner of his mouth. The announcement that President McNeil was about to make would rewrite history. The mistakes the previous administrations had made in the Middle East and the criticisms they had received – deserved or not – all would soon be forgotten. And this President's legacy would be set forever. This moment would change the world.

"Ladies and gentlemen, the President's address will be followed by a short press conference, at which time he will address any questions you may have. Please hold your questions until that time. Ladies and gentlemen, I give you the President of the United States." He stepped aside to quiet applause, and the President himself came on stage and approached the lectern.

"Thank you, Evan." President McNeil looked down at the podium for a moment, and picked up a small stack of blue index cards. "My staff and I prepared this address earlier this afternoon, but what I'd wanted to say then has been rendered moot by events of the last two hours." He dramatically dropped the cards on the floor behind him and went on, appearing to go off-script. The press corps looked on with rapt attention.

"My fellow Americans, this country and much of the world has fallen victim to a great deception, a conspiracy decades in the making; a plot that drew the great nations of the world to the very brink of a nuclear war. Iran was of course at the center of this plot, but control went far beyond the Iranian government or that of any other country on earth. Terrorists and crime lords on several continents conspired to manipulate Iraq, Iran, Russia, China, and the United States into an increasingly hostile encounter.

"Our involvement began on March 16th, 2003, when the United States invaded Iraq under false pretenses. Despite the Bush administration's justifications, the public has always felt there was something wrong about our motivations. They were right. The WMDs we were looking for had been removed from the country long before, by a group that fed us false intelligence. Our presence in Iraq gave Iran the excuse to build up its own military and nuclear program, under the direction of this shadowy cabal. They drew their resources from Russia and China, committing acts of piracy and theft to seize the military hardware that was used against us in recent weeks.

"When they were ready they launched their offensive against our friends in Iraq, prompting a response from us. Russia and China felt compelled to protect their national interests, and sent their navies to the Gulf, unaware that the cabal had corrupted key military leaders in these countries. After the first shots were fired it seemed nothing could stop the war from escalating out of control. The plan, we now see, was for Iran to wait until the crisis reached the boiling point, and then they would use nuclear weapons on Israel, Iraq, and our forces in the region.

"Our intelligence community began to uncover pieces of this plot a few months ago. To the best of our understanding, Russian and Chinese oil interests were at the heart of the cabal. They have been brewing this crisis for the last decade to create a fear-driven inflation in the oil market. Oil that they pump out of Iran, the Caspian Sea, and Siberia was sold on the market at vast profits. All they needed was for a nuclear war to consume the Middle East and they would sell their vast stockpiles at outrageous prices. Were it not for the resourcefulness of our intelligence agents, this plan would have succeeded.

"When I saw how grave the situation had become, I instructed our military commanders to find some way to bring a speedy end to the fighting. Two days ago they presented me with the only possible solution. A bunker, buried deep in the mountains of Northern Iran, housing the leaders of this cabal and the Iranian military commanders, needed to be destroyed. The only way to do that, we learned, was to

577

deliver a nuclear weapon directly on top of the facility. A nuclear bunker-buster delivered by one of our strike fighters, deep in enemy territory and fighting through all of their defenses. As horrifying a notion as that was to consider, my advisors and I determined that this was what held our only hope. A long shot, to be sure, but it would completely wipe out the enemy command structure with minimum hazard to innocent life.

"The assignment was given to a US Navy aviator who has repeatedly proven himself to be extraordinarily skilled and willing to go far above and beyond the call of duty for his country. Earlier this evening, Commander Karl Roche and his Super Hornet fighter-bomber launched from the carrier *Ronald Reagan* and, with the support of over a hundred Navy and Air Force assets, fought through the defenses to the target. At 8:03 PM eastern time, he dropped the bomb down into a deep ventilation shaft over the bunker, where it detonated and completely destroyed the bunker and tunnel network. We confirmed the hit by satellite. The blast was a thousand feet underground and the fallout was largely contained by the mountain.

"While there's no way to know who exactly was in the bunker at the time, it would seem we got all the bad guys. Iran's surviving leaders contacted me twenty minutes ago to offer to unconditionally surrender their remaining military forces and to dissolve the corrupt government that allowed this terrible scheme to develop in the first place. And so now I stand before you to announce the end of this appalling war in the Middle East. We have achieved complete victory more quickly and cleanly than we could have hoped for, thanks to our intelligence community and our military presence and especially to our young hero, Karl Roche.

"I've been informed that his plane has been severely damaged, but he did survive the blast and every missile the Iranian Air Force could throw at him. He is now being escorted by his squadron back to their aircraft carrier, where he will attempt to land the wounded fighter. My fellow Americans, I ask you to join me in prayer for the safety of this brave man."

McNeil bowed his head and listened to the room. The White Hose correspondents had been stunned into utter silence.

*Father God, thank you for Karl Roche.*

## CHESTERBROOK, VA

Casey muted the TV when the President walked off the podium and the Fox News analysts started their comments. "So, that's that."

"Yep." Robert Cannon poured more scotch into the tumbler half-full of half-melted ice cubes. Casey's den was his home away from... wherever else he could call "home." He could help himself to the DDO's liquor.

"So," Casey looked at his agent. "What do you think? Mission Accomplished?"

Cannon answered with a derisive snort and took a long swallow of Johnnie Walker Black Label.

Casey continued. "Sam seems optimistic, anyway. Did you see his preliminary?"

"I skimmed it before the speech started," Cannon said. "I respect his opinion, but to be honest, he really isn't that well in-touch with the realities of Iranian politics."

"The Iranian political structure just got vaporized though."

"Only the guys at the top. There's still that foundation of religious insanity that the new guys will have to break up. Assuming they'd even want to. And even then, it's not likely that mushroom cloud Roche just bloomed will melt any hearts."

"So, *meet the new boss, same as the old boss* is basically what you're saying."

"*And the party on the left is now the party on the right* or some crap like that. If I was sober I would probably have a better metaphor than The Who lyrics, but, ah, forget it." Cannon drained the glass and refilled it. "They're not gonna be sending us a thank you note, that's for sure. If we're lucky they'll at least cancel their oil deals with KUPEC and the NPE companies and toss a couple bones to BP and Mobil. And yeah, there'll be talks of social reforms and economic revival and new partnership with the West and stuff. Maybe they'll actually make friends with Iraq and stop funding Hezb'allah the Shiite terrorists, and they'll definitely stop talking about blowing up Israel. That'll be nice."

"But they're not going to cozy up to us."

"I don't think so. Not in any sincere way, at least. We dropped the bomb on them for crying out loud. They're not gonna pretend to like it. And you can bet your last red cent Hezb'allah and al-Qaeda and the rest are gonna make hay out of that."

Casey poured himself some of his whisky. He threw back a shot, sighed, and looked at Cannon. "Did we have a choice?"

"No. We did the only thing we could do. And we saved that whole corner of the world from a literal meltdown. And they're gonna hate us even more for it. I guess that's what we get for trying to make the world a better place."

Casey had his smug little smile forming at the corners of his mouth. "Yeah, well, that's why we're here; to make sure the monkeys across the river in D.C. – or down at the Pentagon for that matter – don't screw it all up too badly. I just wish someone would explain that to the allegedly educated populace."

Cannon looked thoughtfully at the bottom of his glass. "I think it's for the best if the public never figures out what we're really up to."

"Maybe you're right," Casey shrugged. "You usually are."

## THE PENTAGON

"If there is one thing we should take away from all this," Mike McLeary said as he clicked off the TV, "it's that we are not as strong as we think we are."

The Joint Chiefs didn't know how to respond to that. "How do you mean, sir?" General Caleb asked the Secretary of Defense.

"The M1 Abrams. The *Nimitz*-class. The Keyhole satellites. The B-2 and F-22. All our most advanced systems were defeated in ways we never anticipated. Our belief has been that we can dominate all dimensions of warfare, on land and sea, in air and space. We were just proven dead wrong on all fronts."

"We've been adapting our arsenal to move away from big wars," Chappelle added. "I don't think we can justify that anymore. I mean, just think of how close we were to getting caught up in a big, messy, old-fashioned conventional war with both Russia and China. Think about how much damage Rannovich was able to deal us with just a tiny fraction of the firepower those two countries posses. And then look at them continuing with major military gear-ups, while we're downshifting our defense industries in order to focus on quick responses to limited-scale conflicts. I think we need to find a way to be prepared to confront any conflict, from a terrorist insurrection to a conventional World War Three fighting Russia, China, or both, because this whole thing could easily happen again."

"I think we have a new frontier now in the militarization of space," Caleb said. "The first shots have been fired. I think that opens a door for us."

"You're talking about Project KRISHNA?" McLeary asked.

"There's that, but also laser defenses. With the technological advances we've made in the last twenty-five years, I think it's time we took another look at Star Wars."

580

"I think we should examine our failures before we can look further," Marsh said. "We need to change our strategies with respect to existing systems before we come up with anything else."

"The biggest failure in my mind," McLeary said slowly, not looking at the Chief of the Air Force, "is the failure of the F-22."

Chappelle nodded. "I agree. An air-supremacy fighter that loses one plane for every three kills is simply not providing air supremacy. It puts our entire concept of battlespace dominance in jeopardy."

"I'm not going to argue with that," Caleb conceded. "The cold hard fact is that the Raptor can't really dogfight. It's like the sixties all over again: we made a big, mean, fast, high-tech superfighter that's beat by more maneuverable, less sophisticated planes."

"It was supposed to be able to dogfight, though," McLeary pointed out. "It has the speed and the turning rate. But not like the prototype had. It lost a lot of performance in the development process."

"It gained a lot of weight," Caleb admitted. "That hurt the performance, especially the acceleration. It's crippled by its sheer mass."

"The Air Force needs to change the way it handles development," McLeary said emphatically. "The path from drawing board to service took twice as long as it was supposed to, and cost five times as much as it should have. And the F-35 is well along the same track."

Marsh and Schilling nodded in agreement. Their branches were being held waiting for the new Joint Strike Fighter as well.

"I can't tell," McLeary continued, "if the fault is with the Air Force or with Lockheed. So I'm going to order the program to be audited from both ends. Because that program was grossly mismanaged, and not only did it waste billions of taxpayer dollars, it gave us an inferior product that got a lot of our people killed. Heads will have to roll for that."

"I can't help but contrast that to the Super Hornet program," Chappelle added. "I mean, that went from first flight of the prototype to dropping bombs in Afghanistan in just six years."

"That's different," Caleb argued. "It wasn't an all-new airplane."

"Actually, it was," Marsh countered. "I know it looks similar to the Legacy Hornet, but the Super was completely redesigned as an all-new aircraft. It has fewer parts in common with the Legacy than the F-35 has with the F-22."

"And the Navy got a hell of a lot more plane for their money," Chappelle went on. "We can see which fighter handled itself better in combat."

"We lost almost as many Super Hornets as Raptors," Caleb pointed out.

"But we had a hundred and twenty-two Supers deployed, and we only lost twenty-six of those," Marsh said. "You lost fully half of the sixty Raptors you had in the theater. Of the Supers we did lose, two thirds of those were in the bomber group that got ambushed by the mercenary Super Flankers. Then there was Sharkey's plane which he deliberately crashed into a target in Tehran, and there were three that just ran out of fuel on the Nuclear Hornet run, and a couple of fox-zeroes. We really only lost three Rhinos in fighter-versus-fighter dogfights. You lost *thirty* Raptors; you went oh-for-ten against the Super Flankers and lost twenty to the Defiants."

"A large part of that may be due to the training," McLeary suggested. "Just look at what Sharkey did – what did he have, thirteen, fourteen kills?"

"Fourteen and seven assists."

"That's not a bad stat for the NBA all-star game. Anyway, that's definitely more man than machine on his part. And that's something we need to see more of. I'm not suggesting all our pilots go to TOPGUN, but some of that training should filter down to all of our fighter programs. All our guys should know how to track targets visually, when to take BMR shots, when to hold fire to the last second, how to fly at terrain level, how to dodge missiles with tailslide maneuvers; all these things that Roche made routine. If all our pilots were half as good as Sharkey Roche, we wouldn't have lost nearly so many men and planes."

Marsh nodded. "It's a thought."

"Now, what about the carrier, Terry? What do you think went wrong there?"

"The *Roosevelt* was sunk by a diesel-electric sub that we didn't think to look for. The next day, we were looking, and we found another one waiting to ambush the *Reagan*. We took that out, and I ordered close-in ASW operations to be standard operating procedure in shallow waters where those subs operate best. I think we self-corrected on that one, if we just stick to what we've implemented."

"Expensive lesson," McLeary said, "but I agree. They just happened to find the one chink in the CVBG's armor, and we can patch that easily. Chappelle, the tanks we lost. What's your idea for dealing with that?"

The Chief of Staff of the Army had been thinking hard about this one. "We can't let our armored units behave like cavalry any more, charging into enemy territory unprotected. That's what happened to the tanks we lost – our helicopters too. They went in to unknown territory alone and got ambushed. We've had almost zero losses when we kept in large composite groups, with armor, infantry and air assets providing mutual support. We need to be able to use mixed units as strike teams. There's no reason why tanks, IFVs and attack helicopters can't stick together. And we need to keep up close interaction with Air Force UAV assets."

"There's a few more things the Air Force needs," McLeary turned back to Caleb. "Better fighter protection for AWACS and tankers is one of them."

"Yeah, those and the B-2s. It might be time to discuss unmanning all of our long-range airborne assets going into hostile territory."

"Now hold on just a second," Marsh said. "Unmanning an E-3 or KC-10 isn't going to make it any less vulnerable to attack, and our strategic bomber assets are one area where we absolutely must not lose man-in-the-loop. You can't risk sending a robot after a set of GPS coordinates when it's dropping nine tons of comp H6, or God forbid, a nuclear weapon."

Chappelle sighed. "Manned versus unmanned may be too big of a topic for this discussion. We can save that for another night."

McLeary looked at the stacks of unopened reports on the table. "We're discussing anything and everything. We're starting a major reevaluation of our strategy and doctrine – a very long process that's going to keep us up for many nights to come. It all comes down to how we reestablish our battlespace dominance and confront all threats – conceivable and inconceivable, large and small. Whether we use the tools we have a little differently or build all-new ones; I'm sure Congress will loosen the purse strings now that we've all seen first-hand the sort of threats we will be facing in the future.

"And this will be a pivotal boom for our country. We've all seen it before; there's no better economic stimulus plan than defense spending. Give money to American companies building products in American factories and by legal requirement employing only tax-paying American citizens. They subcontract out to other American companies, the technology they develop moves downstream to the consumer market... you spend in this decade, reap exponential rewards in the next." He took a sip of water. "But I may be getting ahead of myself a little."

The CJC nodded. "I think we need to back up and confront all of our assumptions with what you said earlier, and go from there."

"What did I say earlier?"

Chappelle crossed his arms. "We are not as strong as we think we are."

## THE WHITE HOUSE

The President sat in a recliner in his study, drinking a Crown Royal and soda, and watching the media try to make heads or tails from his speech. Lane Bender sat on a sofa nearby. "They seem to think you set the record straight," she said. "On Iran, Iraq, and everything."

"But I didn't, really. I just fed them a new lie that's a lot more plausible than what Bush fed them years ago."

"Well, what else would you tell them? The truth? They can't handle the truth."

Brett McNeil let himself chuckle at that. "It's true. Unfortunately, there's only so much the American public can handle, and the real story behind all this just won't wash."

"Maybe someday it will be different."

"I doubt it. I think they will always fear the truth. There's this thought that's been growing in my mind ever since September Eleven. It's that we, the people of the United States, are not as strong as we think we are."

McNeil took a long sip. "That day, four planes crashed and two thousand, nine hundred and seventy-five innocent people died as a result. This temporarily ground the country to a screeching halt and the economic aftershocks are still felt today. In our outrage we brought our hammer down on a sandcastle and got it stuck in the quicksand. After all the years that passed, we have made nearly no progress improving the security of our ports and border crossings. And we have still not caught all of the terrorists responsible for the attack.

"Yet at the same time, we resent the efforts our own intelligence agencies are making to track and neutralize agents of terrorism, saying our own government agents are violating our human rights and civil liberties. We even complain on behalf of the terrorists we captured and locked up at Guantanamo Bay, saying they are being treated inhumanely. This is coming from the American Civil Liberties Union, an organization which last I checked is supposed to protect the civil liberties of Americans, like the whole concept of Life, Liberty and the Pursuit of Happiness, all of which those guys in the orange jumpsuits at Gitmo would cheerfully die to deny us.

"We lack the strength to absorb such blows and not be wounded. We lack the strength to stop it from happening again. And mostly we lack the strength of will to face reality and to fight to change it. Are we not at war? Have we not been at war since that day? But we are a people who have no stomach for war. We can't even stomach paying four bucks a gallon for gasoline, paying for our own healthcare, or putting a decent down payment on a home. Now we've lost almost nine thousand men and women in the last two weeks. Once the shock wears off, there's going to be outrage that will not be blunted by anything I can say.

"The American people of this day and age just can't understand the concept of sacrifice. Never mind that it's the entire purpose of our military, never mind the honor of those who serve and sacrifice for freedom. These people think the best way to support the troops is to keep them warm and safe in their own beds away from the scary world around us. We don't want to be told that we're in a fight for our very lives. We just want to be told it's all over."

McNeil glared at Anderson Cooper, who was wondering aloud when the troops sent back to Iraq would be brought home. "It won't ever be over. There will always be someone out there who wants to hurt us. And so," McNeil finished his drink before concluding "we will always need to be ready to hurt them back."

### *REAGAN* – 0217 UTC, 0717 LOCAL, JUNE 7<sup>TH</sup>

"We have the crash barrier out, Sharkey," Hannibal said, "Go ahead and dump your remaining fuel."

"That won't be necessary, Castle," Roche answered. "The needle's been on 'empty' for a couple minutes now."

With the added drag the Hornet had burned up all its remaining fuel on the flight back, and Karl could no longer hold it steady enough to tank up.

"Okay, then just bring her in easy."

"Roger that, Castle. I'll make a nose-up approach so I don't trip over my nose gear."

The front wheel was still twisted sideways. Landing like that is only slightly less dangerous then landing with no nosewheel at all.

Roche kept the crippled fighter level, drifting in at just above stall speed, pulling up at the last possible instant as his shadow crossed the *Reagan*'s fantail. He pulled back on the stick and cut the throttle – forcing himself not to obey the rote procedure and gun the engines. The tail crossed the deck, and the hook caught the three-wire and held it. The tension on the cable slammed the wheels to the deck. Roche winced as the front wheels skidded across the non-skid coating on the steel plates, and then finally the plane came to rest with the nose just inches from the crash net webbing.

Greg Sander watched from the bridge. He was amazed at the level of damage the Super Hornet had withstood. He was reminded of WWII photos of Boeing B-17 Flying Fortress bombers returning full of holes and missing half their engines and control surfaces, but somehow still landing in one piece and saving their crews. Now he looked at this plane on the deck below him – scorched and mauled almost beyond recognition – that still landed safely and brought two aviators home. Clearly the Rhino had inherited that legendary Boeing toughness.

The plane was already surrounded by cheering sailors and aviators when Roche lifted the canopy and stood up. He jumped to the deck and Hardcase caught him in a bear hug. Krause grabbed him to shake his hand. Roche took it, and followed the Admiral a short distance away from the crowd. "Did it work?" Roche asked.

"The President just announced it on television worldwide an hour ago," Krause answered. "It's all over. You got a direct hit and blew that command bunker into the ionosphere, and the Iranians surrendered what's left of their army."

"Great. What about our guys?"

"I just got the call from SAR command. All our pilots have been picked up. Bulldog broke his legs, and Claymore was a mess, but everyone's alive except-"

"Deuce," Roche finished.

Krause nodded.

Roche said nothing. He just stared to the northern horizon.

"How are you feeling?" Krause asked.

"About Deuce?"

"About you."

Roche kept staring in the general direction of the glowing crater he'd left in the Alborz mountains. "I don't feel a thing."

"Are you okay with that?"

He thought of one of the sentences that Emerson had written, and that Cannon had highlighted. It made a lot more sense to him now. *But when you have resolved to be great, abide by yourself and do not weakly try to reconcile yourself with the world.*

"Yeah," he said. "I think I'm okay."

"Good. I'm glad you're back, Sharkey."

Roche looked right at him. "I wasn't supposed to make it back, was I?"

"What do you mean?" Krause asked, knowing full well what he meant.

"The bomb. The blast, I mean. It was at least ten times bigger than it was on the simulator."

"Try a hundred. You're right; we didn't expect you to make it. There was a chance, obviously, but not a good one. We decided to let you guys think your odds were better. I'm sorry I did that to you," the Admiral concluded with the utmost sincerity.

"No need to be sorry," Roche said, and he turned to watch Hunter, who was surrounded by other aviators and animatedly recounting the nearly-lethal dive. "You did the right thing."

"I don't think I would have been able to tell myself that if you hadn't come back."

After a moment, Roche asked "So what do we do now?"

Admiral Krause let himself smile a little. "Now we get to head back home."

## NAS NORTH ISLAND – 1400 PDT, JULY 3$^{RD}$

It had taken almost the whole four weeks to repair Fish-2, but it was finally put back together in time for the air wing to fly back home. Roche led the formation of the depleted *Stingrays*. Hannibal, Claymore and Bulldog wouldn't be able to fly for months to come. Several members of the remaining squadron were flying borrowed aircraft, to replace the eight *Stingray* Hornets that had gone down over Iran. The brilliant blue paint on Fish-2 had burned off the rear end in streaks, and the replacement parts were painted with gray primer. The plane that had narrowly escaped a nuclear blast certainly looked the part.

Roche eased the plane down onto the runway, and let it bounce once on the main wheels before putting the nose down. The nosegear assembly, which Terry Newman and Hector Domingo had reassembled from spare parts, held up just fine. Roche coasted to a stop as close to the squadron hangar as he could get, without rolling too close to the roped-off area around Air Force One and the huge crowed of people that had gathered to see him. The Secret Service and a platoon of Marines kept the excited mob back while Roche slowly went through his checklist.

"You know," Hunter said, "I was with that bomb the whole time you were, but those guys aren't here to put *my* picture all over the place. I'm not getting any ink at all."

Roche grunted. "Would you rather be in my shoes? Because I would love it if all these people just forgot all about me."

"No thanks buddy. You made your own bed with that whole Tehran thing. Hey, look, there's the President!"

Roche glanced down at Brett McNeil, standing at the rope, surrounded by Secret Service agents, patiently waiting for Roche to come down and shake his hand. "I've already met him."

"It looks like someone else wants to say hi." Hunter pointed to the President's left, where Tracy was standing inside his Secret Service bubble. She clutched the rope and gazed at the cockpit with an expression of love and longing.

Roche hurried through the rest of the list and powered the plane down. Dozens of cameras followed his every move as he pushed the canopy away, swung his legs out of the cockpit and dropped to the tarmac on the right side of the plane, forgoing as always the ladder that someone had already pulled out on the other side.

Tracy came over the ropes and ran into his arms. Karl heard only her voice among the cheering and shouting of the crowd and the whining jets. "I love you so much. I'm completely in love with you, Karl Roche. I missed you so much."

He said nothing; he just held her and kissed her deeply, right in front of the President and everybody else. He closed his eyes and held her close, wishing he could say something.

He looked up through watery eyes and saw more figures standing nearby. He nodded toward them.

A man put his hand on Karl's shoulder and said "Good job, son."

Karl blinked his tears away and saw his father. "Thanks, dad." He hugged him, and his mother, sister, grandparents, his closest friends… he was surrounded by people he never knew he loved so much.

When he could take it no more he pulled himself away and swallowed back his emotions. He walked toward the ropes to greet President McNeil. "Sir, it is an honor to meet you again."

The men shook hands firmly.

"No, Commander," the Commander-in-Chief answered, as microphone booms came from nowhere and appeared over their heads, "The honor is once again all mine. This country owes you a profound debt of gratitude that can never be fully repaid. Your service to your country reached far beyond your direct actions."

Roche glanced to the cameras jockeying for angles on either side of him. "I think I understand, sir."

One of the Secret Service agents discreetly handed the President a black leather case, which he opened in plain view of several cameras.

"Commander Karl Larson Roche, on behalf of the people of the United States, I present you the Congressional Medal of Honor, as a tangible measure of our appreciation for your heroic deeds."

"Thank you Mr. President, but I wasn't the only hero over there."

"I'm aware of that. Commander Hidelmann! If you please."

Hunter was leaning against the Hornet and he looked up in surprise. Roche and his family stepped aside as the veteran wizzo approached.

The President shook his hand. "I had asked Admiral Marsh to let me give this to you myself." The agent produced another case, which McNeil opened and handed to Hunter. "Lieutenant Commander Jules Frederick Hidelmann, it is my honor to present you with the Navy Cross, for your courageous level of service only slightly less conspicuous than Commander Roche's."

Hunter's nervous demeanor returned. "Wha-, why, I, uh, thank you, v-very much, Mr. President, sir."

Two blue Navy staff cars rolled to a stop a few yards away. Mrs. Hidelmann and their kids climbed out of one of the cars and surrounded Hunter. Roche stood close to the President for a moment. Unsure of what to do, he waved dumbly for the cameras. One of the warrant officers driving the cars approached him and said "Whenever you and Ms. Davis are ready sir, I'll take you back to your house."

"Okay, let's go." He turned and shook the Commander-in-Chief's hand again. "Mr. President."

Brett McNeil flashed his infectious smile and let him go.

Karl's mother nodded to Tracy. "You're a lucky girl."

She smiled. "I know."

Roche looked at his mother. "I-"

"Go with her now. We'll meet up with you later."

"Okay. Goodbye, I guess..."

The warrant opened the back door of a Buick Lucerne for them. They had their arms around each other as soon as they sat down. "Tracy," Karl said, "there's so much I want to tell you about. I don't know where to start."

"Shh, it's okay." She kissed his lips again. "There will be time to talk later."

## 1200 PDT – JULY 4TH

The F/A-18e Super Hornet was fresh out of the paint shop and looked just as Captain Thompson had left it at Fallon – matte silver with wide black stripes, and an opposed pair of black spades on each tail fin. The stenciling on the side of the cockpit said Capt. Josh "Deuce" Thompson flew this plane, but it was his protégé, Karl "Sharkey" Roche at the controls. He flew behind once and future Top Gunners Worm, Shredder, and Doc in a perfect diamond formation over San Diego Bay. Directly ahead was Ft. Rosecrans National Cemetery, where Captain Joshua Thompson was being laid to rest as the cemetery's twenty-third Medal of Honor recipient. Roche and the others flew low over Point Loma, toward the manicured lawns on the top of the hill.

The Navy band had just finished playing "Amazing Grace," and a lone bugler started playing "Taps."

The guard detail lifted the flag off the casket as it was lowered. They folded the Stars and Stripes and passed the triangular package to Admiral Krause. The President of the United States placed the Medal of Honor on top, and the Admiral presented it to Loraine Thompson.

She held her younger boy close with her free arm as both wept silently, and the President placed his hand on the older son's shoulder.

Tracy stood nearby, overwhelmed by the solemn and respectful ceremony.

As the bugler sounded the last note, seven Marines in full dress uniform raised their M-16s to their shoulders and fired single shots in unison. They lowered their weapons, raised them and fired again, then lowered and fired once more.

The roar of jet engines rose over the fading echoes of the last gunshots, and four Super Hornets came into view. The first three went straight overhead, thunderous in their passing. The fourth pulled up and climbed directly over the grave, flying straight toward heaven at full throttle.

590

All in attendance were moved to tears by the perfectly-executed "missing man" formation fly-by, carrying Thompson's spirit to eternity on the gleaming wings of the metal angel.

Roche was blinded by the sun and the tears filling his eyes. He felt the plane slow as the engines lost power in the thinning air. He whispered a prayer, commending the soul of his friend and mentor to God, before he eased back the throttle and drifted back towards the earth.

*So this is what it feels like,* he thought, *to have someone die for you. This how my SEALs felt when they saw me jump on a grenade; why they cried when I came out of that coma. This is how a hero weeps.*

He looked down at Coronado, at the beach where he'd trained to die for his country, to kill for his country. But he was never prepared to deal with this. *Now I know. We are not as strong as we think we are.*

# PHOTOGRAPHIC GLOSSARY

## U.S. MILITARY AIRCRAFT

**Boeing F/A-18e/f Super Hornet aka "Rhino" – multirole strike fighter**

Super-f goes supersonic without afterburner.

2x General Electric F-414-GE-400; 22000lb thrust each, 38500 with afterburner
Max speed at 30000 feet: 620 knots; 1470 with afterburner
Max operational ceiling: 62000 feet
Max range: 1400 mi on internal fuel, +400 mi per drop tank
60.3 feet long, 44.7 foot wingspan, 16 foot height with landing gear; 35800lb dry, 67200lb max take-off weight

1x M61A2 Vulcan 20mm rotary cannon with 200 rounds; 19100lb max total weapon load; two wingtip hardpoints mount AIM-9 Sidewinder or mk77 ECM pod only; six underwing hardpoints ea. 2300lb max load; fuselage outboard hardpoints mount AIM-120 AMRAAM or AIM-7 Sparrow; Center fuselage universal hardpoint 15200lb max load

**the Super Hornet and it's vast array of supported weapon systems.**

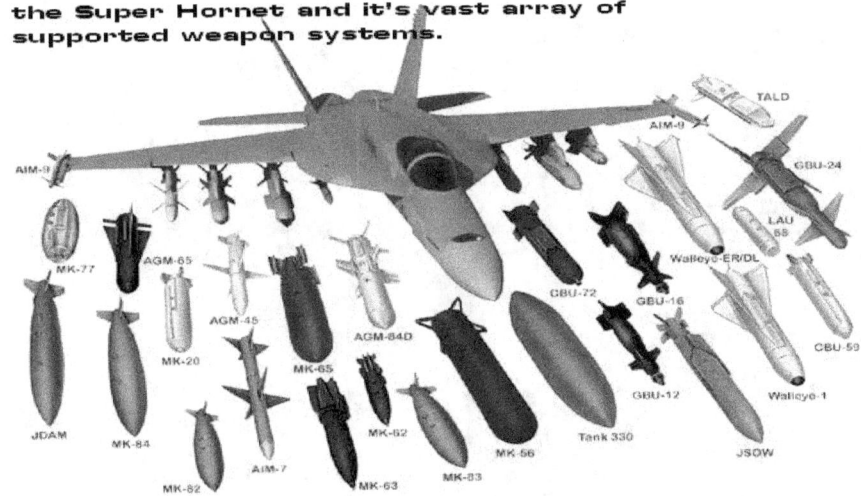

The Super Hornet possesses many unique features that make it the most powerful, agile and versatile fighter-attack aircraft in the world.

The prominent curved extensions leading from the wing edge to the cockpit are called "strakes." At low speeds these strakes dramatically increase lift, giving the Hornet the lowest stall speed of any fixed-engine jet aircraft. Computer-controlled servomotors adjust vents in the strakes in high speed maneuvers, altering airflow through the engines and over the inside portion of the wing, dramatically improving agility at high speeds. For instance, creating a "dead zone" of minimal airflow over the inner wing allows the Hornet to roll faster than any other jet fighter.

Least visible but most important is SHOC, the Super Hornet Onboard Computer. Actually a parallel network of seventeen powerful supercomputer processors, SHOC takes the pilot's flight control input and translates it for more control surfaces than a human can simultaneously manipulate. It also processes radar and runs the Hornet's advanced Integrated Defense Electronic Countermeasure (IDECM) system, and interacts with other Hornets in the area through SHOClink, which works like an airborne wireless computer network and allows Super Hornets to share tactical data. Super Hornets can also use satellite communications to transmit data to the aircraft carrier.

The IDECM itself allows the Super Hornet to disguise its own radar signature and hide itself from the enemy, and to confuse and distract incoming missiles. The latest iteration of the IDECM makes the newest Super Hornets nearly immune to enemy radar-guided weapons, without compromising performance for stealth. Operating in a group, Super Hornets are just about unbeatable. Thanks to SHOClink, they can provide overlapping radar and ECM coverage to each other and outsmart the enemy as well as out-fight it.

US Marine Corps Hornet-D

**Boeing (formerly McDonnell-Douglas) F/A-18c/d Hornet aka "Bug" – multirole fighter / attack**

2x F404-GE-402 engines; 16700-22000lb thrust
Max speed at altitude: 570 knots, 1190 with afterburner; max operational ceiling: 50,000 feet
Max range: 600 miles + 320 mi per external tank
56 feet long, 37.5 foot wingspan, 15.3 ft height, 23,000lb dry weight, 56,900 lb max takeoff weight

1x M61A1 Vulcan 20mm cannon, 16700lb weapons load; AIM-9 on wingtips, AIM-7 or AIM-120 on fuselage hardpoints, four underwing hardpoints and centerline fuselage universal hardpoint.

The first-generation 'Legacy' Hornet has served the US Navy and Marines admirably for over twenty-five years, and has been successfully exported to several other nations including Canada, Australia, Poland and Switzerland. The Hornet has been combat-proven as one of the most effective and versatile strike platforms in the world. The key to its success is its ability to carry a fighter weapon load in addition to a complete load of strike weapons, so it can perform close air support missions and fill the fighter role in the same sortie.

The Hornet has its shortcomings, however, mostly stemming from its low internal fuel capacity. For this reason it is finally being replaced by the more-capable Super Hornet and the new F-35 Lightning II Joint Strike Fighter.

By 2016 the Hornet will be retired from frontline service in both the Navy and Marines.

The Super Hornet inherited the best traits of the original and improved on its deficiencies. It is 25% larger, considerably faster, carries more fuel and weapons, and features more advanced avionics than the Legacy Hornet. Visually they can be distinguished by two external design differences. The air intakes on the early Hornets are rounded, but on the Super they're parallelogram-shaped for better airflow. Also the strakes on the Legacy Hornet are double-curved, as opposed to the broader single-curve form on the Super.

**Northrop-Grumman F-14d Tomcat – carrier-based interceptor / light bomber**

2x General Electric F-110-GE-400a; 18000-27000lb thrust
Max speed at 30000 feet: 580 knots, 1520 with afterburner
Max operational ceiling: 53000 feet
Max range: 1600 mi on internal fuel, +400 mi per drop tank
61.8 feet long, 64 foot wingspan, 38 ft swept, 16 ft height
43600lb dry weight, 72900lb max takeoff weight

1x M61A1 Vulcan 20mm cannon, 13000lb max weapon load; two wing hardpoints mount AIM-9 Sidewinder, AIM-7 Sparrow or AIM-54 Phoenix. Four fuselage hardpoints mount AIM-9, AIM-7, AIM-54 or AIM-120 AMRAAM, or guided/unguided air-ground weapons up to 2000lbs ea.

The legendary Tomcat, immortalized by the movie "Top Gun" remains one of the top fighters in the world after over thirty years of service. Its swing-

595

wings provide a degree of flexibility rivaled by few other machines; it has extraordinary maneuverability or blinding speed available on tap.

The Tomcat was originally designed as a fleet defense interceptor, to keep long-range Soviet bombers at bay. But with the end of the Cold War the 'Cat's role was modified to include long-range high-speed strike. This was a crucial gap in the Navy's ability during the nineties, since the first-generation Hornets were limited by inadequate range and the Navy's other bombers - A-6 Intruders - were simply to slow. The Tomcat performs surprisingly well as a bomber, although its ability is restricted by its modest weapon load and limited number of hardpoints.

The Tomcat positively shines as an interceptor, however. The huge nose houses the Hughes APG-7 pulse-phased-doppler radar system, the most powerful system carried by any fighter. When combined with the long-range Phoenix missile, the Tomcat becomes the most effective stand-off air-to-air weapons system in the world.

The Tomcat was scheduled to be phased out in 2006 and replaced by Super Hornets, but delays in the F-35 program have forced the Navy to adjust the deployment schedule of the new Hornets and keep a few Tomcat squadrons in service until at least 2013. It remains a top performer at the end of its life cycle.

the raptor carries its weapons internally to reduce its radar cross-section

**Lockheed-Martin / Boeing F-22a Raptor – multirole stealth fighter**

2x Pratt & Whitney F-119-PW-100; 24000-35000lb thrust ea.
Max speed at 30000 feet: 750 knots, 1320 with afterburner
Max operational ceiling: 70000 feet+
Max range: 2500 mi on internal fuel
62 feet long, 44.5 foot wingspan, 16.7 ft height
51000lb dry weight, approx 74000lb max takeoff weight

1x M61A2 Vulcan 20mm cannon; 16500lb max weapon load; eight internal weapon bays mount AIM-9 Sidewinder, AIM-120 AMRAAM, or guided/unguided air-ground weapons up to 2000lbs; 2x optional wing pylons mount two AIM-9 or one AIM-120 ea, or air-ground weapons up to 2500lbs.

The sleek and angular shape of the Raptor defines the triumph of form-follows-function. Every angled surface lines up exactly 44 degrees from horizontal, creating an exquisite, jewel-like appearance and also nearly eliminating its radar cross-section. The Raptor's impressive weapon load is carried internally, like on a heavy bomber, in order to eliminate any external radar signature. In addition, the skin of the superfighter is radar-absorbing carbon-ceramic composite. The result of these anti-radar efforts is the stealthiest airplane ever built. By comparison, the fabled F-117 "Stealth Fighter" appears 100 times larger than the Raptor on radar.

In addition to its cloak of invisibility, the Raptor's pride is in its performance. A first for aviation, the Raptor is capable of super-cruise; that is, the ability to fly at sustained supersonic speeds without using afterburners. This gives the Raptor a combination of range and speed to envy. The Raptor is also highly maneuverable, thanks principally to its large fins and advanced thrust vectoring system, which adjusts the flow of exhaust from the engines to maneuver through tight turns. Test pilots report however that the maneuverability of the Raptor does not meet design expectations. Changes made to the program added nearly ten thousand pounds to the dry weight of the plane between prototype and production, and the added mass has a detrimental effect on acceleration and turn rate. Even so, it is able to perform maneuvers that are impossible for any of its enemies to match.

Originally the Raptor was intended to only be an air-superiority fighter, but its design was modified to fill the attack role as well. It can carry two JDAM bombs internally and up to four more air-ground weapons on its wings, but with a wing load it forgoes much of its stealth capability. This new multi-mission versatility should somewhat justify the high price tag of the new Raptor when it hits the front lines. The first Raptor squadron entered service in mid-2006, seven years behind the original schedule and at a per-plane cost over five times the original budget. It remains to be seen whether or not the Raptor is truly worth the long wait and high price.

**General Dynamics / Lockheed-Martin F-16 Fighting Falcon aka "Viper" – multirole fighter**

1x Pratt & Whitney F100-P-229; 19000-27000lb thrust
Max speed at 30000 feet: 500 knots, 1350 with afterburner
Max operational ceiling: 50000 feet
Max range: 1300 mi on internal fuel + 400mi per drop tank
49.5 feet long, 32.7 foot wingspan, 16 ft height
19200lb dry weight, 37500lb max t.o. weight

1x M61A1 Vulcan 20mm cannon; 11200lb max weapon load; two fuselage hardpoints mount AIM-120 AMRAAM or AIM-7 Sparrow; 4x wing pylons mount drop tanks, AIM-120, AIM-7, AIM-9 sidewinder or most air-ground up to 2800 lbs; wingtip mounts AIM-9 or ECM

       Light and deadly, the F-16 has been the foundation of the USAF fighter force for twenty-five years. The original design by General Dynamics beat out the Northrop YF-17 Cobra – a design which eventually evolved into the F/A-18 Hornet - for the Air Force contract. The F-16's merit was its small size and high maneuverability. It was hailed as a pocket superfighter that could out-gun the bigger Russians and outmaneuver anything or anyone. And until the appearance of the MiG-29 in 1988, the Falcon was indeed the most maneuverable fighter in the world.

       The Falcon shined bright in the spotlight during the Gulf War; not only as the agile fighter, but as the extraordinarily accurate light-strike fighter-bomber. By the time the air strike phase had merged into the ground campaign, the Air Force had actually run out of smart bombs. Smart bomb close air support was demanded by the Army, regardless of the shortage.

598

The solution the Air Force found was combining dumb bombs and smart planes. F-16s began dropping unguided iron bombs at low altitude with precision and lethal effect.

The Falcon is slated to be completely replaced by the F-35 Joint Strike Fighter by 2018, after forty years of brilliant service.

**Northrop-Grumman EA-6b Prowler – electronic warfare / attack aircraft**

2x Pratt & Whitney J52-P408; 11200 lbs thrust ea.
Max speed at 30000 feet: 605 knots
Max operational ceiling: 40000 feet
Max Range: 850 mi internal, +380 mi per drop tank
59 feet long, 53 feet span, 15 feet height
33600lbs dry weight, 61500 max takeoff;
14500 lb max load, ALQ-99 Tactical Jamming System, AGM-88 HARM (high-speed anti-radiation missile.) 4 man crew

The role of electronic warfare evolved toward the end of the Vietnam War, when the technology became available to jam and deceive enemy radar. The ALQ-99 pods carried by the Prowler represent the very cutting edge of this technology. Each pod is a self-powered, electronic beehive of instruments and computers that reacts to radar from multiple contacts. Typically a Prowler carries three pods, which are programmed to work in concert. One is dedicated to tracking, logging, and triangulating the source of every radar signal. A second breaks down the incoming signals and isolates the carrier frequencies, and the third retransmits false signals on those frequencies. Each individual pod can perform all three functions simultaneously, but dividing the process among three units maximizes the Prowler's effectiveness.

The Prowler can also be armed with HARM missiles to kill enemy radar. These weapons home on the actual radar transmitter and destroy it with a fragmentation warhead designed specially to tear up transceiver dishes.

The Prowler is based on the reliable A-6 Intruder, and is set to continue service through 2020 as it is gradually superseded by the new Hornet-based Growler.

Like the Prowler, the new E/A-18g Growler typically carries three ALQ-99 pods.

**Boeing EA-18g Growler aka "Grizzly" – electronic warfare / strike fighter**

2x General Electric F414-GE-200; 19800-31500 lb thrust
Max speed at 30000 feet: 620 knots, 1470 with afterburner
Max operational ceiling: 62000 feet
Max range: 1950 mi on internal fuel +400 mi per drop tank
53.8 ft long, 42 ft span, 16.5 height
35800lb dry weight, 67200lb max t.o. weight

17200lb max load; two wingtip hardpoints mount AIM-9 or mk77 ECM pod. Six underwing hardpoints 2300lb max load. Fuselage outboard hardpoints mount AIM-120; Center fuselage hardpoint 14800lb max load. Typical load: 3x ALQ-99, 4x AGM-88, 1x mk77, 1x AIM-9, 2x AIM 120 and 2 drop tanks. 2-man crew.

If the Prowler has a weakness, it is its relatively slow speed and limited strike capacity. The Prowler can only carry HARM missiles if it forgoes drop tanks and thereby limits its range. The new Growler, however, which is based on the Super Hornet, has much greater capacity for weapons as well as being capable of supersonic speeds. Also it shares and expands the airborne communications abilities of the Super Hornet.

The Growler looks much like the two-seat F/A-18f, and is in fact built on the same assembly line in St. Louis, but it is distinguished by a longer nose without the 20mm Vulcan cannon. The extended snout houses the Raytheon APG-79 AESA-Tandem radar package, which surpasses all other systems with unprecedented clarity and image quality. The Super Hornet uses the same AESA radar, but by using dual transceivers, the AESA-

Tandem creates a more detailed radar picture that can even see stealth aircraft in most conditions.

SHOC (the Super Hornet Onboard Computer) also dramatically improves the effectiveness of the ALQ-99 jamming pods, which are otherwise identical to the Prowler's system. SHOC also connects with the mk77 ECM pod, which is designed confuse enemy missiles, and links its software with the ALQ-99 to jam enemy missiles in flight. With SHOC's ability to link the tactical displays of multiple Hornets, any nearby Hornet pilot has access to the same data gleaned from the Growler's systems. This allows pilots to more effectively attack enemy air defenses. For instance, one Growler running point and three Hornets loaded with HARMs would form a lethal "wild weasel" pack to hunt down and eliminate any and all surface-to-air defenses.

This ability to keep up with the strike fighters is in of itself perhaps the greatest improvement over the Prowler. On several occasions during Operation Desert Storm, groups of Navy strike aircraft including Hornets and Tomcats were forced to loiter in hostile airspace waiting for the Prowlers to catch up. In other instances the Navy simply couldn't reach targets in time. The Growler will provide the Navy with much greater flexibility in mission planning simply on account of its speed.

One other improvement the Growler has over the Prowler is its ability to defend itself with air-to-air missiles. The Super Hornet is of course one of the most exceptional fighters ever built, so obviously a properly armed Growler would have no trouble engaging enemy aircraft either. Its usefulness as a fighter is limited, since it has no gun and only three or four air-to-air missiles at most, but at least it has the good option of shooting back.

This self-protection capability allows the Growler to take on solo strike missions, something the Prowler could rarely if ever do. Carrying up to four air-to-air weapons in addition to its jammer systems and air-to-ground anti-radiation missiles, the Growler is a formidable strike weapon in its own right.

When operating in concert, Growlers and Super Hornets form an incredibly powerful strike team. With the Growlers able to deny enemy radar and communications and share their tactical data with the Hornets, the strike fighters can hit their targets with near-total impunity.

**Boeing B-52h Stratofortress aka "BUFF" – heavy bomber**

8x Pratt & Whitney TF33-P-3/10; 17,000 lbs thrust ea
Max speed at 30000 feet: 560 knots
Max operational ceiling: 50000 feet
Max range: 8800 mi unrefueled
159.3 ft long, 185 ft wingspan, 40.7ft height
185000lb dry weight, 488000lb max t.o. weight;

72000lb max weapon load in two bomb bays and two inboard wing pylons. Capable of carrying virtually any air-ground weapon ever deployed by the USAF in flexible loadout.

One of the most iconic images of the Cold War was the B-52 flying toward Soviet airspace, trailing smoke from its eight engines, off to deliver nuclear death to the Russians should World War Three break out. The B-52 is still a heavy lifter in the USAF Strategic Command, but its main role is now to carry a massive payload of smart bombs. Armed with cruise missiles, GPS and laser guided bombs, and even massive weapons like the MOAB and MOP, the B-52 still leaves spectators trembling in fear and awe.

**Northrop-Grumman B-2 Spirit – heavy stealth bomber**

4x General Electric F118-GE-100; 17300lbs thrust ea.
Max speed: 510 knots
Max operating ceiling: 60000 feet
Max range: 6000mi unrefueled
69ft long, 171ft wingspan, 17ft height
140000lbs dry weight, 345000 lbs max t/o weight

58000lb max weapon load in two internal bomb bays. Capable of carrying up to 16 nuclear gravity bombs, two MOPs or any combination of conventional gravity bombs.

Probably the most recognizable of any military aircraft, the B-2 Spirit stealth bomber is the ultimate display of American military supremacy. A single B-2 costs nearly as much as an entire *Nimitz*-class aircraft carrier, but no price can be put on its capabilities. Crossing the world with aerial refueling and delivering a punishing payload deep behind enemy lines with little regard to radar defenses, the B-2 can reach virtually any target on earth and destroy it utterly.

**"Aurora" (Contractor unknown) – strategic reconnaissance aircraft**

2x or 4x Pulse-detonation / scramjet / hybrid ?  Thrust unknown
Max speed at altitude: Mach 6+ (4000+ knots)
Max operational ceiling: 100000+ feet
Max range: 10000+ miles unrefueled
Approx 150ft long, 100ft wing; weight unknown

Unarmed, carries advanced sensors and ECM

The Aurora is the so-called mystery plane that has allegedly replaced the SR-71 Blackbird both as the fastest and highest-flying plane on earth, and also as the spy plane of choice for the USAF and the National Reconnaissance Office. Although its existence is officially denied by the military and intelligence community, credible sightings have been reported worldwide and especially near Edwards and Nellis AFBs. Few observers claim to have seen the shape of the plane itself but rather identified the tell-tale "donuts on a rope" contrail left by the pulse-detonation engines.

Many aviation experts consider the Aurora a poorly-kept secret at best, and have reached something of a consensus on the appearance, propulsion and performance of the dark project. The shape of the plane is considered to be something of a cross between the blended wing-body of the

SR-71 and the long, finned, delta wing and underslung engines of the XB-70 Valkyrie prototype.  Some experts believe that this popular rendering is inaccurate, and that for stealth reasons the Aurora has internal engines and no tail surfaces, and appears more like stretched-out B-2.  Other experts on propulsion systems believe that the engines are a two-stage system, utilizing conventional turbofans for subsonic or low supersonic speeds, and engaging the pulse-detonation scramjets for non-stealthy high-speed runs.

For the purposes of this fictional account, the author assumes the existence of the Aurora as an operational platform, and depicts its description and performance in a manner most in-line with current military doctrine.  That is, the Aurora is described along theoretical lines combining the best characteristics for stealth and speed.  And it should be noted that while the Aurora itself may merely be an over-analyzed myth, the technologies of the aircraft described are quite real.

KC-10 refuels B-2 stealth bomber using boom

**Boeing (McDonnell-Douglas) KC-10 Extender – tanker transport**

3x General Electric CF-6-50C2, 52500lbs thrust ea.
Max speed at 30000 feet: 530 knots
Max operational ceiling: 50000 feet
Max range: 4400 mi w/ cargo; 11500 mi w/o;
181.5 ft long, 161.4 ft wingspan, 58.1 ft height;
223200lb dry weight, 590000lb t.o. weight;

310000lb refueling load, via boom for Air Force aircraft (shown above with B-2) or drogue and probe for Navy aircraft (F/A-18 below)

Navy F/A-18c refuels with probe-and-drogue

The strength of the United States Armed Forces is not the size of the armies or the number of ships at sea, but the ability to rapidly deploy that force anywhere in the world. To that regard, the heart of the US Air Force is the KC-10. This is of course a modified DC-10 airliner, with nearly all passenger capacity eliminated and replaced by a huge fuel tank. The KC-10 can literally fly to the other side of the world without refueling, and it lends this ability to any fixed-wing American military aircraft.

Air Force planes use a "boom" to refuel – this is a long rigid hose with tiny wings for stability that reaches from the KC-10 directly to the fuel intake valve on the receiving aircraft. The Navy uses a method called "drogue and probe" which consists of a flexible hose with a drogue device on the tanker and a retractable or fixed probe on the receiver. The drogue is shaped like a badminton birdie and both stabilizes the hose and houses the valve and seal for the fuel transfer. This method is much more cumbersome than the boom method, but the Navy also uses carrier-based tankers (modified A-6 and S-3 aircraft, and unmodified F/A-18s with drogue-equipped drop tanks) which are all too small to be equipped with booms. Also, though the KC-10 is too fast to refuel helicopters, many transport choppers use aerial refueling. Because of the way the rotors extend in front of the fuselage they can only use the drogue and probe configuration.

The Air Force has also used the KC-135 – a modified Boeing 707 which is long overdue to be phased out and replaced with a new tanker called the KC-46 to be based on the 767. Contract disputes between Boeing and Northrop-Grumman have delayed this new program, shifting even more of the burden to the KC-10. For refueling helicopters or strike aircraft operating from forward bases, many variants of the C-130 Hercules can be deployed for aerial refueling. But thanks to its ultra-long range and its vast capacity, and its ability to completely fill the tanks of a C-17 or a B-52, it is the KC-10 that remains the true lifeline of the Air Force.

**Lockheed-Martin MC-130h Combat Talon – tactical transport**

4x Allison T56-A-15 turboprop; 5910 shaft horsepower ea.
Max speed at 30000 feet: 340 knots
Max operational ceiling: 36000 feet
Max range: 3100 mi on internal fuel + 800mi per external tank
100.9 ft long, 132.7 ft wingspan, 38.5 ft height
79200lb dry weight, 155000lb max t.o. weight

4x external fuel tanks for aerial refueling (drogue and probe, used for Navy / Marine fixed wing and all equipped rotary wing); carries up to 75 special forces troops or 52 paratroopers (HALO/LALO-capable); LALO combat drop capacity for HMMWV "Humvee" –based weapon systems or Stryker Medium Armored Vehicle; also precision drop capacity for BLU-82 "Daisy Cutter" heavy demolition bomb and GBU-43b MOAB.

MC-130 combat-drops a Sheridan tank

The Combat Talon is the Federal Express service of the US Military – "when it absolutely, positively has to be there on time." The C-130 has been on point for the military since Vietnam as the premier close-support cargo transport. The C-130's strength is in its flexibility. The Hercules, as the basic cargo version is called, is usually equipped with JATO rockets for assisted-short takeoff, which allows the C-130 to operate out of fields only 1200 feet long. That's no longer than it takes a Ford Mustang to accelerate to 100 mph, and the 78-ton Hercules reaches *takeoff speed* in that distance.

The MC-130 Combat Talon package incorporates these short-field capabilities with highly advanced air-drop equipment designed to allow the MC-130 to deliver troops and/or light vehicles right on top of the enemy. The JPADS-HALO system (Joint Precision Airdrop System – High Altitude, Low Opening) operates much like a guided bomb, except it drops cargo palates or canisters or even live paratroopers, aimed at a target no more than thirty feet in diameter, with parachutes that open only 600 feet above the ground. Cargos and Special Forces troops can be released up to 30000 feet above the combat zone and land right where they are needed.

As impressive as that ability sounds, the most spectacular drop is the LALO (Low Altitude, Low Opening) system. The MC-130 flies at between 500 and 2000 feet and drops paratroopers right over the target, minimizing their exposure to ground fire although maximizing danger to the plane. Using this approach, the Combat Talon can also drop vehicles like Humvees, M2 Bradleys or even 35-ton Stryker light tanks. For these drops the parachute actually opens inside the plane, and the vehicle is violently yanked out the back door. Despite the danger of these drops, the spectacle provided is actually the best defense. The sight of the big plane diving out of the sky and dropping a fully crewed *tank* only 500 feet above the ground is so shocking, the Combat Talon often meets no resistance despite heavy enemy presence.

As a more practical form of protection, Combat Talon aircraft are also fitted with highly advanced ECM systems to ensure that they get to where they are needed safely.

**Boeing E-3 Sentry – AWACS special electronic aircraft**

4x Pratt & Whitney TF33-PW-100a; 21000lb thrust ea
Max speed at 30000 feet: 460 knots
Max operational ceiling: 39000 feet
Max range: 4300 mi, 8 hr endurance unrefueled
145.5 ft long, 130.9 ft wingspan, 41.3 ft height
21200lb dry weight, 34700lb max t.o weight

AN/APY-2 rotating radar system, 200 mile detection range for low-flying or ground targets 320+mile range for aircraft at medium to high altitude. 17-man crew

The E-3 appears to be a 707 airliner being terrorized by a UFO. It is indeed a modified 707, but the flying saucer is actually the most advanced airborne radar system in the world. The E-3 is an AWACS platform, for Airborne Warning and Control System. The million-watt AN/APY transpulse multi-false-aperture Doppler radar operates on multiple simultaneous frequencies in all directions, behaving like a network of concentrated radar rather than a single system. This unique and highly evolved system can see even stealth aircraft, if told where to look. It can't pick up a stealth aircraft in "search" mode, but once found it can track even the super-stealthy F-22. More impressive is the onboard computer control system's ability to filter out ground clutter, by comparing the radar picture with the normal TERCOM terrain-mapping radar image. Low-flying aircraft that would normally be almost invisible show up in high resolution under the E-3's all-seeing electronic eye.

  The E-3 formed a critical link in the NORAD radar chain during the Cold War, flying over the oceans and the North Pole to watch for soviet missiles launched from Siberia or submarines at sea. Today the AWACS mission is to provide oversight and guidance for allied aircraft and watch enemy movements from a safe distance.

**Northrop Grumman E-2D Hawkeye – carrier-based AWACS special electronics aircraft**

2x Allison T56-A-427, 5100 shaft horsepower ea
Max speed at 30000 feet: 350 knots
Max operational ceiling: 36000 feet
Max range: 2500 mi on internal fuel + 400mi per drop tank
57.8 ft long, 80.6 ft wingspan, 18.3 ft height
40484lb dry weight, 74500lb max t.o. weight

AN/APS-145 radar system, two drop tanks.
9 man crew

The Navy's AWACS counterpart is the E-2 – the "eye of the fleet." Every aircraft carrier since 1961 has carried at least two of these, considered by many experts to be the most essential component of the carrier arsenal. The new AN/APS-145 is a slightly scaled-down version of the Sentry's AN/APY system with similar capabilities. With a Hawkeye in the air over the carrier group, every moving object on or above the surface in a 250 mile radius becomes a target. The Hawkeye's ungainly appearance belies its effectiveness. By the time the latest version is replaced it will have been in service for well over half a century.

The replacement aircraft is slated to arrive in 2022. It will be a dedicated variant of the Navy's Common Support Aircraft that will also replace the C-2 Carrier Onboard Delivery cargo plane, the S-3 Viking sub-hunter, and the KS-3 and KA-6 tankers. The as-yet unnamed CSA AWACS will use the same AN/APY radar system as the E-3 Sentry. But for the next decade or so, the dedicated guard dog of the carrier battle group remains this classic old prop-driven freakish-looking plane, the beloved E-2 Hawkeye.

**Boeing / Bell Textron MV-22 Osprey – VTOL tactical transport**

2x Allison / Rolls Royce AE1107C turboprops, 6150 shaft hp ea
Max speed at 15000 feet: 375 knots
Max operational ceiling: 25000 feet
Max range: 600 mi on internal fuel + 200mi per drop tank
57.3 feet long, 84.6 foot rotor span, 22 ft height
33100lb dry weight, 57500lb max vertical takeoff weight

Load capacity of up to 24 combat troops, 35 passengers, 12000lb cargo load

MV-22 takes off and lands vertically

Perhaps the most unique aircraft ever conceived; the tilt-rotor MV-22 offers dozens of exciting possibilities to the military. The MV-22 can take off and land vertically like a helicopter, but it flies level like a fixed-wing: far faster with a much greater load than any helicopter transport. This capability makes it ideal for rapid insertion and extraction of Special Forces, or amphibious assault, or combat search-and-rescue, or any medium-duty transport odd job that military commanders can come up with. The MV-22 will replace the Vietnam-era cargo choppers in all services, including the Air Force HH-3 Jolly Giant, and the Navy and Marine CH-46 Sea Knight and SH-3 Sea King. The Osprey will supplement, but not completely replace, the venerable heavy-lift CH-47 Chinook and CH-53 Stallion or the Pave Low series MH-53 variants, and mostly take over the long-range loads that are now put upon the flexible but over-worked H-60 Blackhawk series.

The MV-22 is just now entering service in the critical Special Forces role. It should have been in full service by the turn of the century, but the program has been fraught with major setbacks. Several high-profile crashes in the pre-production phase, including one that killed 7 marines in 1992, and another in 2000 that killed 19 men, sent Bell engineers back to the drawing board twice with the rotor design. And miscalculations at Rolls Royce, who co-developed the engines, caused the original transmission system to be scrapped and a new one built from scratch, which turned out to be overweight and forced Boeing to redesign the wings. Then just as everything was getting settled, the Department of Defense asked for the whole thing to be eighteen inches shorter so it could fit inside a new cargo plane that was going to replace the C-130. That program was cancelled, but not before Boeing wasted a year on the unnecessary changes.

By 2002, the whole project was six years behind schedule and $12 billion over budget. A senate committee hearing came within a handful of votes of killing the whole project, but Vice President Cheney and Secretary of Defense Rumsfeld pushed the Osprey's case. (They had been pushing the project through since 1989.) Between their persuasion and several Marine

611

Corps generals practically begging on their knees for the aircraft, the project was given the green light for production, at a cost of $80.9 million per aircraft. The Marines' desperation is understandable. Perhaps no service relies more on rotary support aircraft, and presently their reliance is on the dangerously obsolete and unreliable CH-46 Sea Knight. In the first eight years of the Marines operations in Afghanistan and Iraq, over a dozen CH-46s have simply fallen out of the sky, not counting several others that have been hit by ground fire. These crashes have claimed the lives of over a hundred Marines to date.

The MV-22 is too late to fill the US Marine Corps' needs in Iraq, but the Osprey is now finally on hand for use in Afghanistan and any future conflicts.

**Sikorsky SH-60f Seahawk (LAMPS III) – SAR / ASW / tactical transport helicopter**

2x T700-GE-401C turboshafts 1662hp ea
Max Speed: 130kts sea level
Max op ceiling: 20000ft
Max Endurance: 4:20 hours w/ two external tanks
64.9ft length, 17.2ft height, 53.7ft rotor dia.
14600lb dry weight, 21800lb max t/o

LAMPS III (Light Airborne Multi-Purpose System) equipment for combat search-and-rescue (SAR) and anti-submarine warfare (ASW), includes 6000lb winch, Doppler radar, FLIR (forward-looking infrared,) dipping sonar – 1500ft depth capability, 120-capacity sonobuoy launcher, 99-channel sonar receiver w/ advanced digital processing, advanced autopilot with automatic approach, hover and departure modes. 2x weapons hardpoints for Mk50 torpedo, ASM-84 Harpoon, 2x AGM-114k Hellfire II. 4-man crew

As a part of the most flexible line of aircraft ever produced – the H-60 series – the SH-60 is naturally a superb multi-role helicopter. In addition to impressive anti-submarine warfare capabilities, it excels at maritime search and rescue, and to date has saved no fewer than 2700 lives. All USN surface warships carry at least one of these helicopters – most carry two.

The SH-60 is supplemented at sea by the HH-60 Jayhawk – a dedicated SAR variant used primarily by the Coast Guard – and the MH-60r/s Strikehawk – a slightly larger model that retains SAR and ASW capabilities but adds longer range and load-carrying capacity for missions inland. The Strikehawk is better equipped for Special Forces insertion and extraction, as well as combat search-and-rescue, and is often armed with machine guns on the doors in a configuration similar to the Army Blackhawk and Air Force Pavehawk variants.

The Seahawk/Strikehawk is an essential component of the carrier battle group's defenses. It has the ability to acquire, track and neutralize enemy submarines unassisted, but is normally used as an investigator to check out contacts acquired by the surface ships and aircraft. This role is invaluable because it allows the battle group to evaluate a target and deal with a potential threat without shifting one of the warships and disrupting the escort perimeter.

The Navy depends on Seahawks to fill all these missions and for almost twenty years they have stepped up to the call.

CH-53 is capable of in-flight refueling

**Sikorsky CH-53e Super Stallion – heavy-lift transport helicopter**

3x T64-GE-416A Turboshafts 4380hp ea
Max Speed: 150kts sea level
Ferry Range: 990 miles
Unrefueled Endurance: 5.1 hrs
99ft length, 24.3ft height, 79ft rotor diameter
33226lb dry weight, 73500 max gross t.o. weight

Up to 6x M2HB .50 machine gun emplacements
34000lb external cargo lift capacity
Up to 55 passengers or 32 combat troops
Or 24 medevac litters; 3-man crew

The Marines' iconic Super Stallion is one of the most celebrated helicopters in the world. Variants of the Stallion have been in service since Vietnam, and congress recently authorized development of a new variant that will be serving until at least 2025.

The Super Stallion has similar capabilities to the Air Force MH-53 Pave Low, including in-flight refueling, external fuel tanks, and heavy defensive armament in the form of fifty-caliber machine guns. This gives the Super Stallion the range and flexibility to serve in amphibious assaults, Special Forces insertion and extraction, combat search and rescue, and also heavy lift. Its three engines give it the lift power to hoist armored vehicles, and even another Super Stallion.

Two weeks after commissioning in Newport News, Virginia, USS *Ronald Reagan* CVN-76 transits the Strait of Magellan en route to its new homeport of San Diego

USS *George Washington* CVN-73 in Chesapeake Bay

An F/A-18 Hornet launches from the USS *Nimitz* CVN-68

The hangar deck of the *Washington*

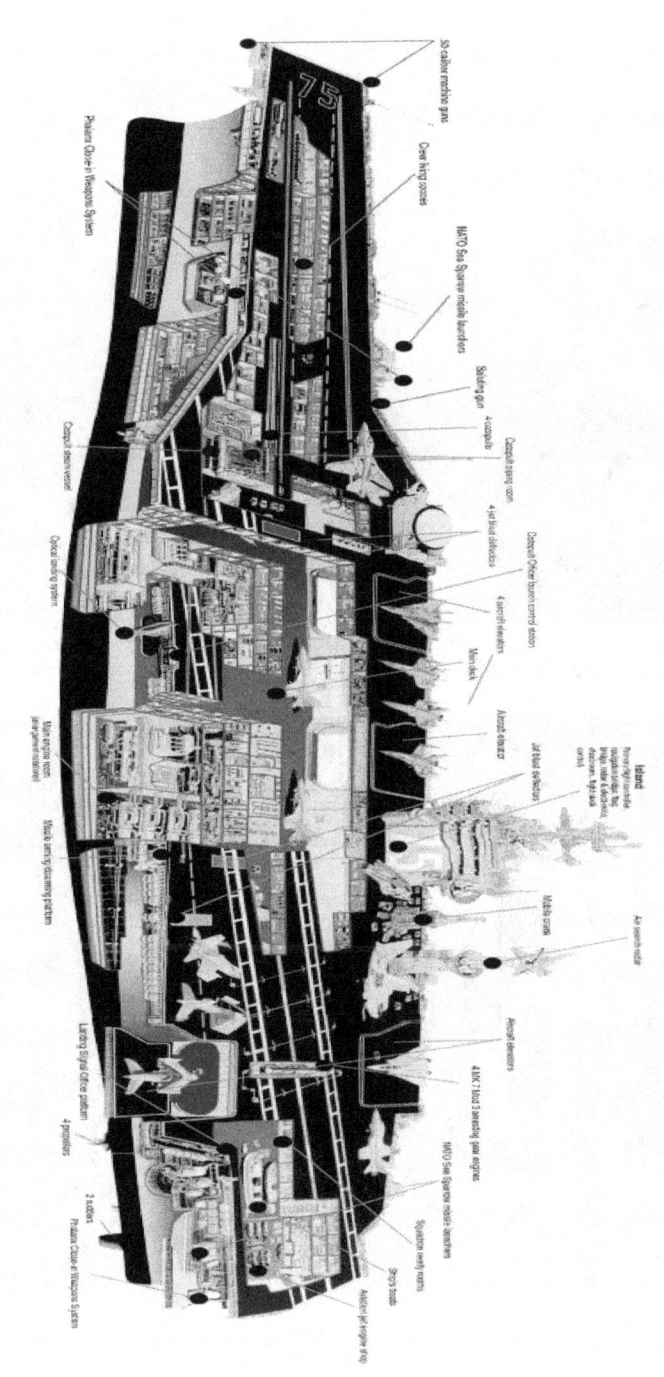

**USS *HARRY S TRUMAN* CVN-75:**
cutaway view of a Nimitz-class aircraft carrier

Aircraft Operations Center on the USS *Abraham Lincoln* CVN-72, commissioned in 1989

Air-Ops on the *Reagan*, commissioned in 2003 (note the dramatic equipment upgrade)

# *Island*

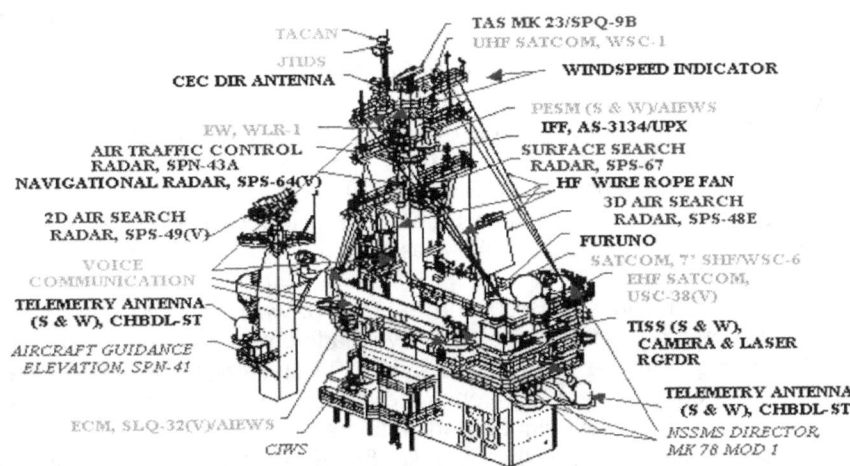

TACAN
JTIDS
**CEC DIR ANTENNA**

EW, WLR-1
**AIR TRAFFIC CONTROL
RADAR, SPN-43A
NAVIGATIONAL RADAR, SPS-64(V)**

**2D AIR SEARCH
RADAR, SPS-49(V)**

VOICE
COMMUNICATION

**TELEMETRY ANTENNA
(S & W), CHBDL-ST**

*AIRCRAFT GUIDANCE
ELEVATION, SPN-41*

ECM, SLQ-32(V)/AIEWS

*CIWS*

**TAS MK 23/SPQ-9B**
UHF SATCOM, WSC-1

**WINDSPEED INDICATOR**

PESM (S & W)/AIEWS
**IFF, AS-3134/UPX
SURFACE SEARCH
RADAR, SPS-67
HF WIRE ROPE FAN
3D AIR SEARCH
RADAR, SPS-48E
FURUNO**
SATCOM, 7' SHF/WSC-6
EHF SATCOM,
USC-38(V)

**TISS (S & W),
CAMERA & LASER
RGFDR**

**TELEMETRY ANTENNA
(S & W), CHBDL-ST**
*NSSMS DIRECTOR
MK 78 MOD 1*

The baffling array of radars and antennae on the "island"

The *Reagan*'s Combat Information Center (CIC)

## CVN-68 *Nimitz*-class nuclear-powered aircraft carrier

-68 USS *Nimitz* (commissioned 1975), Homeport: San Diego, CA; -69 *Dwight D. Eisenhower* (1977), Norfolk, VA; -70 *Carl Vinson* (1982), Currently in refit; -71 *Theodore Roosevelt* (1986), Bremerton, WA; -72 *Abraham Lincoln* (1989), Everett, WA; -73 *George Washington* (1992), Yokosuka, Japan; -74 *John C. Stennis* (1995), San Diego; -75 *Harry S Truman* (1998), Norfolk; -76 *Ronald Reagan* (2003), San Diego; -77 *George H. W. Bush* (2009) Norfolk

Northrop Grumman Newport News Shipbuilders, Newport News, VA

Propulsion: 2x Westinghouse A4W pressurized water reactor nuclear power plants

8x steam turbines 61000shp ea (*Nimitz-Vinson*), 62000shp (*Teddy R.-Truman*), 72000 *Reagan*; 4x five-blade propellers.

1092 feet long; 134 feet beam at waterline, 144 on *Reagan*; 252 feet widest point on flight deck, 264 on *Reagan*, 250 on *Nimitz* and *Ike*; 39 feet draught; 212 feet height waterline to masthead, 196 *Reagan*

92000 tons displacement, (*Nimitz* and *Ike*) 88000 (*Vinson*) 97000 (*Teddy R. – Truman*) 108000 (*Reagan*)

*(Bush* specs classified but believed to be similar to *Reagan.)*

35 knots max speed, 42 *Reagan*, 36 *Vinson*; Range unlimited

Defensive systems: SPS-48E and -49V5 multifunction multimode air search-scan radar, mk91 fire control suite; AN/SLQ-32V4 ECM; 4x RIM-7 SeaSparrow SAM launchers, or 3x RIM-7 and 1x RIM-166 SM3 LEAP ABMM for *Reagan*; 4x Phalanx CWIS 20mm mounts, or 3x *Nimitz* and *Ike*; 6x .50 M2hb machine gun "sweeper" mounts

Air wing (74 Aircraft): 14x F-14d, 38x F/A-18c/d/e/f, 4x EA-6b, 4x E-2c, 8x S-3b, 6x SH/HH-60f/h; (*Reagan* 86 aircraft): 14x F-14d, 44x F/A-18c/d/e/f, 8x EA-18g, 4x E-2c, 8x S-3b, 4x MH-60r, 4x MV-22

3500 ship's company, 2720 *Reagan*; 2480 Air Wing, 2560 *Reagan*; total crew: 5980, 5280 *Reagan*

Unit cost: $2billion initial+$2.4billion refueling/modernization overhaul *Nimitz* and *Ike*, $2.6billion *Vinson*, $3.2billion *Teddy – Truman*, $4.2billion *Reagan*; $4.8billion *Bush* $298million per annum operating cost; estimated service life 50 years with modernization @ 25 years; total life cycle cost $22.2billion, $444million average annual. (All figures 2008 dollars)

The US military strategy is all about deploying force – bringing enormous firepower to the enemy's doorstep – and nothing embodies this philosophy better than the nuclear aircraft carrier. At around one hundred thousand tons, the *Nimitz*-class supercarriers are huge, but hardly the largest ships in the world. VLCC oil tankers have been built up to three-and-a-half times the size of a *Nimitz*. What makes these ships so impressive is what they carry – obviously the aircraft carrier carries navy aircraft, and they carry a lot.

The concept of a self-deploying airbase has only been around since the late 1970's. During WWII, the role of the carrier was set more as a warship armed with airplanes and not guns. But today, a single Super Hornet can carry the same raw firepower as a battleship firing broadside, and the modern US supercarrier holds dozens of these. The role of the aircraft carrier was expanded to best utilize the massive firepower it handles. It is impossible to overstate just how much force the *Nimitz*-class wields.  74 aircraft, including at least 50 strike fighters, make up the air wing.  The newest supercarrier, USS *Ronald Reagan*, and USS *George H.W. Bush*, have expanded capacity for twelve additional strike fighters. In the hold of a *Nimitz* there is a huge stockpile of bombs, missiles and even nuclear devices, and tons of jet fuel. This supply can be topped off indefinitely by the Navy's fleet of ammunition and fuel carriers.

Basically, it is the carrier's job to loiter around international trouble spots and terrify everyone into behaving.  Ongoing crises or potential crises have been contained for decades by the mere company of a *Nimitz*-class aircraft carrier.  In the Persian Gulf, the Straight of Formosa, and the Sea of Japan, potentially hostile situations are mitigated by the presence of three-and-a-half acres of sovereign United States property, dozens of lethal warplanes, and one unmistakable message.  Tomcat pilots sum that message up with the words on their flight patch: "Anytime, pal."

# ESCORTS AND SUPPORT SHIPS

The supercarrier never operates alone. They operate in carrier battle groups (CVBGs) with about a dozen escorts and support vessels, including frigates, cruisers, destroyers, submarines, fuel tankers and ammunition carriers. The escorts form a defensive perimeter with radar and missiles that makes the carrier battle group nearly impregnable.

**USS *Arleigh Burke* DDG-51 – guided missile destroyer**
***Arleigh Burke*-Class**

**USS *Cowpens* CG-63 – guided missile cruiser**
***Ticonderoga*-Class (CG-47)**

624

**USS *Vandegrift* FFG-48 – guided missile frigate**
*Oliver Hazard Perry*-Class (FFG-8)

**USS *Hayler* DDG-997 – guided missile destroyer**
*Spruance*-Class (DDG-963)

These four classes of warships constitute the bulk of the escort fleet. They are organized into Destroyer Squadrons and cyclically assigned to CVBGs. Their main weapons are guided missiles. All carry the deadly Harpoon anti-shipping missile, and a variety of surface-to-air missiles. The *Burke*-class destroyers and *Ticonderoga*-class cruisers also carry Tomahawk cruise missiles. In addition to missiles, the cruisers and destroyers are armed with the classic five-inch gun to engage surface targets at close range. The *Burke*s and *Tike*s are also equipped with the Aegis system, which is built around the SPY-1 radar (note octagonal panels). This is the most advanced surface radar system in the world.

**USS *Toledo* SSN-769 – nuclear-powered attack submarine**
**Improved *Los Angeles*-Class (SSN-688i)**

**USS *Jimmy Carter* SSN-23 – nuclear-powered attack submarine, Special**
**Operations-capable**
***Seawolf*-Class (SSN-21)**

Whether working alone or screening a CVBG, the nuclear attack submarine is one of the Navy's most dangerous weapons. Fast, silent, and invisible, the SSN hunts with passive sonar, listening to the telltale sounds of nearby warships, and strikes with torpedoes and missiles.

The *Los Angeles* was the first of 55 boats in its class, the last 23 of which (751-773) are improved versions (called 688i-type in Navy shorthand) with increased missile capacity, advanced electronics and sonar systems and a newly designed, quieter hull.

The *Seawolf* class was initially intended to replace the early-model *L.A.*s, but drastic budget reductions that were made during the Clinton administration limited the production run to only three boats. The third and final sub, the ironically-named USS *Jimmy Carter*, was lengthened by inserting 105 feet of hull from an unfinished fourth vessel. This new space was crammed with advanced and mostly classified gear for underwater reconnaissance, as well as to provide extra space for SEAL teams. All 688i and *Seawolf*-class subs are capable of deploying SEALs, but the crowded space onboard limits the SEALs to teams of 12 or so. The *Carter* can embark 52 SEALs at a time.

688is can be distinguished from older *L.A.*s by the location of the foreplanes – the small wings that adjust the submarine's trim underwater. They are mounted on the sail of first-generation *L.A.*-class boats, but are mounted on the hull of the newer subs. *Seawolf*s are distinguished from *L.A.*-class subs by a curved fillet at the base of the sail, and by relative size.

**USS *Essex* LHD-2 – amphibious dock landing assault ship**
***Wasp*-Class (LHD-1)**

844 feet long;
40500 tons displacement;
28 knots max speed
9500 mi range;

Carries 3 LCAC (landing craft, air cushion) or 40 amphibious assault vehicles; up to 42 aircraft including some combination of MV-22, AV-8b, CH-46, CH-53, UH-1n, AH-1w, SH/MH-60; 1 Marine Expeditionary Unit (1600-1800 embarked troops).

Although it resembles an aircraft carrier, the Wasp class fills a very different role. An LHD is a jump-off point for a Marine Expeditionary Unit and a forward helicopter base for amphibious assaults. A single LHD, its aircraft and MEU can single-handedly invade a small country.

## MISSILE SYSTEMS:

(f/f) = fire and forget; refers to missile's ability to engage a target without further input from the launch platform

IR = infrared; homes on heat signatures

Radar; uses active (on-board) or passive (input from launch platform) to track target

Internal; onboard computer guidance

A-R = anti-radiation; homes on emitted enemy radar signal

Laser; guided by laser beam reflected off target

GPS = Global Positioning System; uses satellite data as guidance

TERCOM = terrain-comparison; uses radar to scan terrain and compare to pre-loaded target and approach profile

Range values: effective-max

### US missiles:

AIM-9x Sidewinder, air-air, IR (f/f), 6-10 mile range, 21lb fragmentation warhead

AIM-120 AMRAAM, air-air, active radar (f/f), 20-32 mi, 27lb shaped-charge warhead

AIM-54 Phoenix, air-air, passive guidance / active terminal radar, 93-115 mi, 65lb frag

AGM-88 HARM, air-ground, A-R (f/f), 57-80 mi, 144lb frag

RGM-84 Harpoon, surface-surface, passive-active radar, 67 mi, 488lb penetration

ASM-84 Harpoon, air-surface, passive-active radar, 92 mi, 488lb penetration

AGM-65f Maverick, air-surface / air-ground, IR/laser (f/f), 17 mi, 80lb heavy penetration

BGM-109 Tomahawk, surface-surface / surface-ground, GPS/Tercom (f/f) 900 mi

TLAM-C/E, 1000lb penetration warhead

TLAM-D, cluster submunition dispenser

TLAM-N, W80 5-or-150 kiloton-yield nuclear warhead

### Russian missiles:

AA-11 "Archer" air-air, IR (f/f), 9 mi, 24lb fragmentation

AA-12 "Adder" air-air, active radar (f/f), 42 mi, 32lb fragmentation

### French missiles:

Matra Magic IV, air-air, IR (f/f), 20 mi, 25lb fragmentation

Matra Mystic, air-air, passive guidance / active terminal radar, 50 mi, 21lb shaped charge

## BOMB SYSTEMS:

D = dumb, unguided

L = laser guided.

S = GPS/Satellite

AGM-154 JSOW (Joint Stand-Off Weapon,) S/internal, 30 ft precision radius
  BLU-97b warhead – 145x frag/incendiary submunitions
  BLU-108 warhead – 24x armor piercing submunitions
  BLU-111 warhead – 1x 500lb penetration bomb
GBU-31/32 JDAM (Joint Direct Attack Munition,) S/internal, 20 ft
  BLU-109 warhead – 2000lb bomb
  BLU-110 warhead – 1000lb bomb
GBU-37b, S, 18 ft
  BLU-113 warhead – 4000lb penetration bomb
GBU-27/28 Paveway III, L, 3ft
  Mk82 warhead - 500lb bomb
  BLU-109b warhead – 2000lb penetration bomb
GBU-43b MOAB (Massive Ordnance Airburst,) S, 30ft
  BLU-120a warhead – 18,700 airburst bomb
GBU-57b MOP (Massive Ordnance Penetrator,) S/Internal, 20ft
  BLU-120b warhead – 18,700 deeply-buried target penetration bomb
CBU-59 Rockeye-2, D
  AMAP warhead, 717 BLU-77 anti-material / anti-personnel bomblets
  BLU-97b warhead – 145x frag/incendiary submunitions
  BLU-108 warhead – 24x armor piercing submunitions
CBU-97 Sensor-fused weapon, D/S 15ft precision radius, 4,800 square yard
  dispersal area
  BLU-108b warhead – 10x submunitions with 4x armor piercing skeet
  charges each
Mk82, D, 500lb bomb
Mk83, D, 1000lb bomb
Mk84, D, 2000lb bomb
RNEP (Robust Nuclear Earth Penetrator), GPS/Internal, 16 ft
  Low-Yield-Penetrator warhead, 3 kiloton nuclear
  B61/7 variable-yield warhead – 10-1600 kiloton nuclear

**AIRCRAFT GUN SYSTEMS:**

**US Aircraft:**
M61A2 Vulcan 20mm 6-barrel gatling-type rotary cannon;
  6000 rounds per minute, 1.2 mi effective range, 3 mile max range

**Russian Aircraft:**
GSh-301 30mm autocannon
  1800 rounds per minute, 1.2 km effective range, 1.8 km max range

**French Aircraft:**
Giat 30/791b 30mm revolver autocannon
  2500 rounds per minute, 1.5km effective range, 2 km max range

**Russian Aircraft Corporation MiG-29k Fulcrum – fighter-attack, land or carrier-based**

Max speed: 560/1420 knots
12000 lb weapon load

Once the pride of the Soviet Air Force, the Fulcrum now serves under many flags as an elite multi-role fighter. Its capabilities are similar to the American F-16 or F/A-18c; the MiG has a slight advantage in performance, but American avionics are far superior. The MiG-29 has been a huge export success and is used by many countries including China.

**Sukhoi SU-27/30/35/37 Flanker – multirole / fighter-attack, land based**

Max speed: 490-570/1310-1520 knots
15000-18000 lb weapon load

The Flanker family of heavy fighters would have dominated the sky had the Cold War ever came to blows. At least equal and in many ways superior to the US F-15, the big Russian jet now appears in the arsenals of many nations. Its latest variant – the SU-37 Super Flanker, has only been produced in limited numbers but it is a true fourth-and-a-half-generation superfighter, much like the USN F/A-18e/f Super Hornet. Other variants include the SU-35 Flanker-M, which features the same high-powered "Scarab" radar as the SU-37 and also packs an ultra-long-range missile designed especially for bringing down AWACS aircraft.

**Kilo-class (type 636k) – diesel-electric submarine**
2400 tons; 20kts surfaced, 16 submerged, 5 silent running; 4400 mi max range

The Kilo-class submarine is an ambush predator, specialized in lurking in shallow, littoral waterways and waiting for its prey to cruise by. On battery power it is almost undetectable to all but the most sophisticated passive sonar systems.

*Admiral Kuznetzov* **– aircraft carrier**
67000 tons; capacity for 36+ aircraft

Built at the end of the Cold War as the USSR was running low on cash, the *Admiral Kuznetsov* and its unfinished sister ship never entered regular service. The second ship was purchased by China for unclear reasons.

**T-80 – main battle tank**
125mm smoothbore cannon

The T-80 was the most common tank produced in the Soviet Union during the latter years of the cold war. It remained in production well into the 21$^{st}$ century and remains the most numerous tank type in the Russian Army's inventory.

**NS219 – self-propelled artillery**
157mm howitzer

Standard artillery of the Cold War; the NS219 (also known by the NATO code M1973) was widely distributed around soviet bloc nations and the Middle East, where it was used in the Yom Kippur, Iran-Iraq, and both gulf wars.

**SA-10 / SA-N-6 Grumble – surface-air missile**
Radar-guided; 34 mile max range

Widely used both on warships and on dry land, the extensively exported SA-10 is perhaps the most versatile and effective anti-aircraft weapon ever produced outside the US.

634

**Dassault Defiant – interceptor**
550-1900 kts max speed
7200 lb weapon load

A secret project by the French aerospace and defense contractor Dassault to build and export an inexpensive, stealthy, compact fighter, based on the Rafale superfighter. It is allegedly in pre-production phase. No known photos exist.

**Fennek-2 – armored scout car**
120 mph max land speed
1x machine gun or light automatic cannon or automatic grenade launcher

The Fennek was designed for rapid deployment and urban recon in hostile settings. To that end, it is fast, agile, and well-armed. It was built jointly for the Armed Forces of Germany and the Netherlands, but since its introduction in 2000 it has received many export orders. It has been deployed by the Iranian Army, among others.

# ABREVIATED RANKS (US NAVY)
listed in order of pay grade

Enlisted
SM – Seaman; SMr – Seaman Recruit; SM1, SM2, SM3 – 1st, 2nd, 3rd class.
Sp – specialist, 1st-3rd class. Called "radioman" or "machinist" or "SEAL" or
      other depending on actual specialty.
NCO – non-commissioned officer, applies to PO's and Warrants
PO – petty officer; PO1, PO2, PO3 – 1st-3rd class; CPO – Chief PO.
      Senior and Master CPO called "Senior Chief," or "Master Chief"
CW – Chief Warrant Officer. (Warrants are senior to POs but not to CPOs)

Commissioned Officers – uniform rank indicated by stripes on sleeve
En. – Ensign, lowest commissioned rank (1 stripe)
Lt. jg. – Lieutenant, junior grade (1½ stripes)
Lt. – Lieutenant (2 stripes); Lt. pronounced "L-T" by enlisted
Lt. Cmdr. or LCdr. – Lieutenant Commander (2½ stripes)
Cmdr. or Cdr. – Commander (3 stripes)
Capt. or Cpt. – Captain (4 stripes)
      Commanders and Captains are considered senior officers; usually
      one must obtain the rank of at least Commander in order to be
      considered eligible to be named commanding officer of a ship, aircraft
      squadron or SEAL Team.

Flag rank – uniform indicated by stars
L.R. Adm – Lower Rear Admiral (1 star)
U.R.Adm – Upper Rear Admiral (2 stars)
V. Adm – Vice Admiral (3 stars)
Adm – full Admiral (4 stars)

Other armed services:
Army, Marines: Private is the lowest rank. Air Force: Airman is the lowest
rank.
NCOs: Corporal (not in AF), followed by Staff Sergeants, Gunnery Sgts, 1st
Sgts, Master Sgts.
Commissioned: 2nd Lt,(Gold bar) Lt,(silver bar) Cpt, (two silver) Major,(gold
oak leaf) Lt. Colonel, (silver leaf) Cnl, (eagle) Brigadier General, (1 star) Mjr.
Gen, (2) Lt. Gen, (3) Gen. (4)

# LIST OF TERMS AND ANCRONYMS

A (aircraft designation): attack aircraft – i.e. A-6 Intruder.

Aegis: sophisticated radar targeting, tracking and fire-control system on some US warships.

AESA: Active Electronically Scanned Array (APG-79) – the Super Hornet and Growler's advanced, multi-band, highly adaptive radar system.

AFB: Air Force Base.

Aileron: a control surface on an airplane's wing that directs roll.

Airfoil: A curved surface such as a wing that generates lift by Bernoulli's Principle.

Air Boss: Officer in charge of carrier flight deck operations.

Angle of attack: angle of an aircraft's long axis relative to its direction of travel.

ASW:  Anti-Submarine Warfare.

ATFLIR: Advanced Tactical FLIR (Forward-Looking Infrared.)

Aviator: Navy calls pilots and flight officers "aviators."

Avionics: electronic systems (radar, computers, etc.) onboard an aircraft.

AWACS or AEWACS: Airborne Warning (or Early Warning) And Command System.

B (aircraft designation): bomber, i.e. B-52 Stratofortress.

Barrel roll: a maneuver that rolls an aircraft 360 degrees.

Bernoulli's Principle: fast-moving air has lower pressure than slow moving air, and the slower-moving higher-pressure air tends to push objects toward lower-pressure regions.

BGOO: Battle Group Operations Officer – directs the actions of surface escorts in a carrier battle group from aboard carrier.

B/N: Bombardier/Navigator – the co-pilot position in an A-6 Intruder.

Brigade: Army unit consisting of three or more regiments.

BMR: Beyond maximum range – sometimes if two aircraft are closing on each other they will fire missiles at beyond the weapon's maximum range hoping the other target will continue to close on the missile.

Bunt: in this maneuver, a pilot pitches forward sharply while reducing throttle; the opposite of a tailslide, but the result is similar (the aircraft slides to a halt in mid-air.)

BVR: Beyond visual range – engagement beyond the range of the naked eye.

C (aircraft designation): cargo transport, i.e. C-5 Galaxy.

Callsign: military pilots and aviators have a permanent callsign, usually a nickname concocted by their peers; mission callsigns are assigned for specific missions – usually each flight will have a shared callsign and individual aircraft will be differentiated by numbers.

CAG: Commander, Air Group – officer in command of a Carrier Air Wing.

CAW: Carrier Air Wing - all aircraft and assigned aviators and personnel on board a carrier; includes several squadrons that fill various roles – typically 1x VF, 2 or 3x VA or VFA, 1x VAQ, 1x VAW, 1x VAS and 1x HS; totaling 7 or 8 squadrons and 70 to 88 aircraft, depending on the carrier.

CG (warship designation): guided-missile cruiser, i.e. USS *Ticonderoga* CG-47.

CIA: Central Intelligence Agency – America's foreign intelligence service.

CinC: Commander-in-Chief, typically used in USN parlance to identify fleet commanders, i.e. CinCPAC (Commander-in-Chief, Pacific Fleet.)

CIWS: Close-In Weapon System, also known as Phalanx – anti-missile defensive cannon.

Click: common military abbreviation for kilometers or km per hour.  1 km = 0.62 miles.

CO: Commanding officer of a warship or any military unit.

COLA: Computer-Ordained Lowest Altitude – a system for guiding an aircraft or missile to follow the terrain using TERCOM and fly under enemy radar coverage.

Composite materials: by combining two or more materials with very different physical properties, engineers can apply composite materials that are both lighter and stronger than metal alone; used extensively in modern military aircraft – such as the carbon fiber alloy matrix composite skin of a Super Hornet.

CVBG: Carrier Battle Group – a carrier and its escorts and support ships.

CVN (warship designation): nuclear aircraft carrier – i.e. USS *Nimitz* CVN-68.

DCI: Director of Central Intelligence, administrative head of the CIA.

DDO: Deputy Director of Operations, second-in-command and operational head of the CIA.

DDG (warship designation): guided-missile destroyer, i.e. USS *Arleigh Burke* DDG-51.

Division: Army unit consisting of three or more brigades, or a unit in an aircraft squadron consisting of two sections, and a total of four aircraft.

DNR: Director of National Reconnaissance, administrative head of the NRO.

DNS: Director of National Security, administrative head of the NSA.

Drag: force of fluid (air or water) resistance on a moving body; counters thrust.

E (aircraft designation): electronic specialty aircraft – i.e. E-3 Sentry.

ECM: electronic countermeasures – devices to interfere with radar, typically in self-defense.

ESO: Electronic Systems Officer – back-seat command position on a Prowler or Growler EW aircraft, also called "EWO" – Electronic Warfare Officer.

EW: Electronic Warfare – use of countermeasures or jammers to interfere with enemy radar and communications systems.

EWOC: EW Operations Control – ECM and EW systems control screen on an MFD.

F (aircraft designation): fighter – i.e. F-14 Tomcat.

FFG (warship designation): guided-missile frigate, i.e. USS *Oliver Hazard Perry* FFG-8.

Flaps: control surface on an airplane's wing – when extended it increases the wing area, increasing both drag and lift.

Flight: when referring to a group of aircraft, usually consisting of elements from a single squadron, organized for a specific mission and assigned to a specific series of objectives.

Flight Display: attitude, altitude, airspeed and direction indicators – the information a pilot needs to fly his plane; in a modern military aircraft, this is a digital display.

Fly-by-wire: flight control systems that use analog electronic input signals to control motors and hydraulics to manipulate control surfaces instead of mechanical linkage systems.

Fox-#: military aviation shorthand for an air-to-air weapons attack. The higher the number, the greater the range of the attack; fox-1 refers to guns, fox-2 is short-range missile (i.e. Sidewinder,) fox-3 is medium-range missile (AMRAAM,) and fox-4 is a long-range missile (Phoenix;) rarely-used fox-0 refers to a deliberate mid-air collision.

Geiger counter: device used to measure the concentration of radioactive particles.

H (aircraft designation): helicopter – i.e. HH-60 Jayhawk.

HS: designates a Navy helicopter ASW/SAR squadron (i.e. HS-14 Chargers.)

HUD: Heads-up display – a pilot's flight display projected in his field of vision through the canopy.

ICBM: Intercontinental Ballistic Missile – strategic nuclear weapons delivery systems.

IDECM: Integrated Defense ECM (AN/ALQ-214) Super Hornet and Growler's ECM suite.

ImInt: Image intelligence – photographic or video data from satellites or aircraft.

Immelmann: a maneuver where an aircraft makes a half-loop followed by a half-barrel-roll, gaining altitude, losing airspeed and reversing direction of flight.

Infrared: heat energy appears in this electromagnetic spectrum range – abbreviated "IR."

Infrared or Thermal Imaging: hot objects (bodies, engines) contrast against cold surroundings.

Infrared guidance: heat-seeking – this system is used for most short range air-to-air missiles.

Intel: Intelligence, processed data relevant to a mission or discussion.

Jamming: interfering with enemy radar or communications by use of a powerful transmitter.

Jammer: transmitter system designed for jamming.

K (aircraft designation): tanker – i.e. KC-10 Extender.

Kiloton: a measure of the blast yield of a nuclear device, equal to 1000 tons of TNT.

Knots: nautical miles per hour; 1 knot = 1.15 mph or 1.85 km/h; abbreviated kts.

Lift: force by which an aircraft overcomes gravity, by Bernoulli's Principle over an airfoil.

Long-Range weapons: typically any weapon with an effective range greater than 50 miles.

Low-yield nuclear device: a nuclear weapon with a blast yield of less than ten kilotons.

M (aircraft designation): special military operations – i.e. MC-130 Combat Talon.

Mach: unit to measure the speed of an aircraft relative to the speed of sound; Mach 1 = 661.5 kts = 761 mph = 1225 km/h at sea level; the speed of sound decreases at higher altitudes.

Medium-Range weapons: typically any weapon with an effective range of between 10 and 50 miles.

Megaton: a measure of the blast yield of a nuclear device, equal to 1000 kilotons or 1,000,000 tons of TNT.

MFD: Multifunction display – a computer screen that can show several different system displays.

MiG (aircraft designation): any aircraft built by Mikoyan-Gurevich Design Bureau, now known as Russian Aircraft Corporation – i.e. MiG-29 Fulcrum.

NAS: Naval Air Station

Nav: Navigation.

NRO: National Reconnaissance Office – America's image intelligence agency.

NSA: National Security Agency – America's electronic intelligence and security agency; also an acronym for the National Security Advisor to the President of the United States.

P (aircraft designation): patrol – i.e. P-3 Orion; formerly pursuit, prior to 1948 – i.e. P-51 Mustang.

Pitch: angle of an aircraft's long axis relative to horizontal; also, a maneuver to change this angle.

POTUS: military and intelligence shorthand for President of the United States.

Production block: military systems are produced in blocks differentiating upgrades.

Radar: radio or microwave energy transmitted through air to locate and track targets.

Radar Cross-section: how large a target appears on radar.

RAM: Radar-absorbing material – composite material that absorbs radar energy instead of reflecting it.

RFCM: Radio Frequency Countermeasures – a component of the IDECM that retransmits incoming enemy radar signals to create false target contacts; RFCM and similar systems are often referred to as "shadow" gear or systems.

RIO: Radar Intercept Officer – back-seat position in an F-14 Tomcat.

Roll: angle of an aircraft's wings or rotor relative to level; also, maneuver to change this angle.

S (aircraft designation): anti-submarine warfare – i.e. S-3 Viking.

SAR: Search-and-Rescue; operational role or mission intended to retrieve missing personnel.

SatCom: satellite communications.

Scope: in context of a weapon, refers to a telescopic sight; could also refer to radar screen.

SDI: Strategic Defense Initiative, Reagan-era proposal for a missile defense network aka "Star Wars."

SEALs: US Navy Sea, Air, Land teams; the most elite Special Forces in the world.

Section: two aircraft within a squadron, consisting of a section leader and a wingman.

SHOC: Super Hornet Onboard Computer – the sophisticated parallel-processor system built into Super Hornets and Growlers to greatly enhance flight control and electronic capabilities.

SHOClink: wireless network allowing SHOC-equipped aircraft to share computer data in flight.

Short-Range weapons: typically any weapon with an effective range of 10 miles or less.

SigInt: signals intelligence – data acquired by intercepting enemy transmissions.

Silencer (or Suppressor): a metal sleeve attached to the barrel of a firearm to reduce gunshot noise.

Skipper: Navy slang for CO (Commanding Officer) of a ship or aircraft squadron.

SLBM: Submarine-Launched Ballistic Missile – a strategic nuclear weapons delivery system.

SMS: short-message system, like the text message capability of a cell phone.

SOCOM: Special Operations Command; joint armed forces command structure for Special Forces, including Navy SEALs, Marine Force Recon, Air Force Special Ops, Army Green Berets and Delta Force.

Sonar: Sound Navigation and Ranging – acoustic energy transmitted underwater to locate objects.

SPECWARCOM: US Navy Special Warfare Command – Coronado, CA headquarters for SEALs.

Split-S: an aerial maneuver consisting of a half-barrel roll followed by a half-loop, reducing altitude, gaining airspeed and reversing direction of flight; the opposite of an Immelmann turn.

Squadron: four to sixteen aircraft organized as a single unit; divided into divisions and sections.

SSBN (warship designation): nuclear ballistic missile submarine, i.e. USS *Ohio* SSBN-726.

SSN (warship designation): nuclear submarine, i.e. USS *Los Angeles* SSN-688.

Standard Issue: equipment that a military unit issues to most if not all of its servicemen, aka GI or Government Issue.

Stick: control device to manipulate aircraft control surfaces. Usually located between pilot's knees, or in some modern aircraft, on right armrest, in which case it's called a sidestick.

Strake: an extension from the edge of a wing along the fuselage; feature on modern fighter jets.

Su (aircraft designation): aircraft built by Sukhoi Aviation – i.e. Su-27 Flanker.

T (aircraft designation): trainer - i.e. T-38 Talon.

TacOps: Tactical Operations – any activity relating to a mission in the area of operations; also in the context of an aircraft system, an MFD screen that shows such activity to the pilot.

Tailslide: a high-performance aircraft maneuver where a pilot pitches up and reduces throttle, causing the plane to slide forward tail-first while flipping backward; failure to counter the maneuver with pitch or thrust will stall and crash the plane, but when executed properly the maneuver allows a fighter to change direction very quickly or shoot at a pursuer.

TERCOM: terrain-comparison – aircraft and some missiles use radar to scan terrain ahead and compare it to pre-loaded target and approach profiles.

Throttle: control device to adjust engine thrust in an aircraft.

Thrust: directed force to move an object in an opposite direction, by a jet engine or propeller.

Thrust vectoring: ability in some aircraft to alter the exhaust flow to direct thrust in other vectors besides straight backwards.

Toss-bomb: attack maneuver to release a bomb while flying at an upward angle, causing the bomb to continue upward and then fall on a parabolic arc.

Turbofan: jet engine type using both exhaust and a turbine-driven fan to produce thrust.

Turboprop: propeller engine type using a turbine-driven prop to produce thrust.

Turboshaft: engine type using a turbine to drive a shaft – used in helicopters and some tanks.

U (aircraft designation): utility – i.e. UH-60 Blackhawk.

V (aircraft designation): vertical – i.e. MV-22 Osprey; also VIP i.e. VC-25 (Air Force One.)

VA: designates a carrier-based attack squadron (i.e. VA-23 Rays.)

VAQ: designates a carrier-based EW squadron (i.e. VAQ-118 Yellow Jackets.)

VAS: designates a carrier-based ASW squadron.

VAW: designates a carrier-based radar-early warning squadron (i.e. VAW-117 Wallbangers.)

VF: carrier-based fighter squadron (i.e. VF-24 Renegades.)

VFA: carrier-based fighter attack squadron (i.e. VFA-97 Warhawks.)

VFC: carrier-based fighter composite squadron (i.e. VFC-233 *Stingrays*.)

WepCon: weapons control – weapons systems display and control screen on an MFD.

WSO: Weapon Systems Officer or Wizzo – co-pilot position in a two-seat F/A-18 Hornet variant.

XO: executive officer, 2nd-in-command of a military unit such as a warship or aircraft squadron.

Yaw: lateral turning angle or maneuver along that axis.

# AUTHOR'S NOTE

I would like to gratefully acknowledge the support of my friends and family during the process of writing and editing this book. My parents, my sister, my brothers, aunts, uncles and cousins have all instilled in me confidence in my writing and encouraged me to publish my work. They were also very helpful as sounding boards for me to bounce ideas off of and were instrumental in revising my early manuscripts. I also thank my friends and colleagues for their encouragement and support, in particular Ari, Charlie, Jamie, Jon, Pete, Raza and Tom. Thank you all; I could not have finished this without you.

This is a work of fiction, and although it centers around real current events it is not intended to depict reality. This is not intended to be political in nature; I do not endorse any political party, past presidents or candidates or any policy positions or ideologies with this book. The opinions expressed in these pages belong to my characters and are not necessarily shared by me. That said, I do encourage my readers to take a closer look at the world around them before forming opinions on current events and geopolitics. One cannot turn on a cable news program without being bombarded with malformed opinions – I encourage the reader to research the background information and use source reporting material when forming their own ideas.

I have made a conscious effort to realistically portray modern aerial combat and other highly intense situations, and the dialogue in some particularly stressful moments produces some foul language. I apologize to anyone offended by this or any other content in my book.

Most characters in this book are fictitious, and any resemblance they bear to any actual persons, living or dead, is unintentional and purely coincidental. The exception being the character Greg Sander, who does bear resemblance to the author. Real-world political figures are also referenced and depicted in a manner most resembling their real-world actions and behaviors. In particular, Iranian President Mahmoud Ahmadinejad is presented here as a willing agent of the apocalypse. This is not an exaggeration – he is portrayed realistically based upon his past statements and actions. It is quite obvious to any astute observer that given the chance, this man would cheerfully end the world as we know it.

Finally I wish to acknowledge the efforts of GlobalSecurity.org, a non-profit online research tool, news resource and think tank. If you wish to learn more about the military forces, weapon systems and geopolitical environments described in this novel, all of this information and more can be found at GlobalSecurity.org for a nominal membership fee.

Thank you for reading my first novel. I hope you enjoyed it. Please recommend my work to your friends and family, write and post a review on Amazon.com, and visit Facebook.com/NuclearHornet for news, photos and updates. Karl Roche, Robert Cannon, Greg Sander and I will return soon.

*Greg Hodgson*

## ABOUT THE AUTHOR

Greg Hodgson is a recent graduate of Stevens Institute of Technology with a degree in Mechanical Engineering, with which he has engaged a career as a test engineer with experience in multiple industries including aerospace, defense, automotive and medical devices. He is also an associate with a financial planning firm.

He grew up in Orange County, California, where he now resides.

From an early age he cultivated a strong interest in military history and weapons technology, which he now channels with his writing. Additionally he serves a senior docent at the Lyon Air Museum in Santa Ana, CA where he uses his knowledge of the WWII-era aircraft and vehicles on display to inform and entertain visitors.

*Nuclear Hornet* is his first novel. He is developing follow-up novels featuring many of the characters from *Nuclear Hornet*. The immediate sequel will be *Cobalt Blue*, in which Karl "Sharkey" Roche will be called upon to defend the United States against terrorists armed with highly radioactive dirty bombs

www.ingramcontent.com/pod-product-compliance
Lightning Source LLC
Chambersburg PA
CBHW071329020726
47502CB00001B/27